The ACADEMY

POSTED
NO TRESPASSING
KEEP OUT

CJ DALY

BRANDYLIGHT INK

For my eternally beautiful sister, Susie, the person for whom nothing really happens to me until I share it with you.

PROLOGUE

FIRST ORDERS

We are all the walking wounded. Some scars are just more visible than others. Mine are the inside kind: unhealed, pink, festering. Outwardly, I'm still a perfect specimen. That's why I was chosen for Missions.

"Cadet Davenport . . . it's time." The voice came from the generically pretty assistant, standing in the doorway to my future. The clichéd metaphor that sprang to mind was subpar, unworthy of a cadet. Something a civilian girl would write in her ACT essay and think herself clever. Maybe something *she* would write. I glanced at the photo peeking at me from the folder—my mark. I let out a sigh. *Six-freakin'-teen.* I clung to the knowledge she had a birthday coming up.

Seventeen is the age of consent in New Mexico . . . not that I had to worry about staying within the confines of civilian laws.

She must be subpar because The Academy wasn't looking at her, just her brother, the Potentially Gifted Civilian. He was the ripe old age of eight. The same age as—I mentally snapped a rubber band. I couldn't even look at his picture without a twisted gut. I was the wrong guy for the job. That's likely why I was here—dismissed so Ranger could take over. Take-over. That should be his motto: *Taking over the world, one mission at a time.*

The assistant said something to get me moving. She spoke using the clipped tone I'd been accustomed to my whole life. The softest nuance of accent marked her for what she was—a former cadet. If sympathy was what I was looking for today, I wouldn't find it here.

The reflexive, knee-jerk reaction I'd been fighting for weeks hit me—fight or flight. Neither option was possible. I ran a finger along the nape of my neck, feeling the small, precise scar that was a permanent reminder of what I was . . . what I would always be.

Unfolding myself as slowly as a six-foot, one-inch frame would allow, I finally stood. The assistant narrowed her eyes at me—no one kept the General waiting. I was sure she had preconceived notions about me. *Oh Well.* Like the uniform at the end of a scheduled day, I shrugged it off then flicked back my hair, grown out indulgently in the interim. I was surer than sure General Weston wouldn't be a fan (not that he was anyway). I could claim it was for *her,* the civilian girl. My eyes wandered to her picture again: dark hair, forlorn eyes, a little unkempt around the edges. The only thing missing from the wholesome face was dimples.

She didn't look so tough . . . I could break her.

May as well get on with it. Trudging forward, I caught the assistant looking from her doorway and shot her one of my "special" smiles. It did its job—a little color brought the puppet's face to life.

"Right this way," she said, her professional tone giving nothing away. Textbook manners, inbred.

A lot of inbreeding went on here.

I followed her neat bun and long legs through the unmarked door, where my throat immediately closed with the same metal resonance as the door behind us. Deep breath in, I put one foot in front of the other down a long, gray corridor that seemed to wrap around us like a tunnel. Our footsteps automatically fell into the marching rhythm of our youth. I concentrated on the clacking sound of her heels against granite, anything to take my mind off where I was headed.

Like a prisoner walking toward my execution.

I snorted at the second bad metaphor. She slid me a disapproving glance that had me slowing to a swagger in order to needle Little Miss Efficient. And thumb my nose at The Establishment.

Secret, defiant games were a go-to defense mechanism I'd used to keep my sanity over the years.

But she didn't really appear bothered, peeking coyly over her shoulder at notorious Peter Davenport. I rewarded her with a grin and checked out the nametag pinned to her chest.

"So . . . Blair. What say you lace that third cup of coffee Weston's gonna have with a relaxer we both know he's in dire need of?" I dropped an arm around her shoulders. "It's a beautiful day for sailing with a beautiful girl."

Flirting: my next go-to defense mechanism.

"The Commander limits his coffee to two cups a day," she said as though the answer were just as programmed in. And just when I thought she was a lost cause, she let out a girlish giggle but fought it like an unwanted advance.

"What'd ya say?" I waggled my eyebrows at her.

"I would never!" She tried for outraged, but I knew she'd only set the record straight for the benefit of the cameras, eyeing us discreetly from the corner.

"Never's a long time," I said, giving her the eyes. She pressed her lips together but couldn't hide her smile.

My own smile died. We had arrived at our destination, and the plaque said it all: **Commander General Richard Weston**—*Commander Dick.* I paused to belly sigh, but literally could not put this off another minute. The powers-that-be had decided today was the day to put all that training to good use, so I guess it was.

She did the discreet throat-clearing thing. "Aren't you going to go in? It's two minutes after." A tragedy worth being written up for here.

"Why don't you wait two minutes then pull the fire alarm?" I countered. "Then we'll make our getaway." I guess this was said too close to the mouth of the lion's den, because she sucked in her breath like I'd said *Wait two minutes then throw the pipe bomb.* Did I really have to state the obvious? I raked back some hair. "That's what one refers to as a joke."

"Well, not very mature behavior for an *elite* cadet." She took the jab poorly, spinning on her heel to continue going about her duties diligently— another cog in the ruthless machine known as The Academy.

"*Future* elite cadet. I don't graduate till next week!" I called after her departing back. "And, apparently, I'm only *seventeen* anyway . . . so I have a ways to go." I thwacked the paperwork against my jeans. *Should've worn my blues.* This oversight would likely cost me. I just hated to dress like a reproduced soldier boy on my brief furlough. Sucking down a last lungful of freedom, I rapped on the door.

"Come in." Even muted behind solid oak, dude sounded like a douche.

I stepped in, as reverently as one would, when meeting the figure of authority that could put your balls in a sling and fling 'em to the canines.

"Cadet Davenport reporting for duty, sir." My fingertips tapped my forehead a beat too late to be believable.

Not rising for the occasion of my arrival, Weston stared me down (an intimidation technique used liberally around here). His eyes tightened when he took in the sight before him: floppy hair, black T-shirt fading to gray, torn jeans, scuffed sneakers. A smirk, that didn't go unnoticed by Weston, snuck to my mouth for a nanosecond. He took his silver pen, and a moment of his valuable time, to tap out some Morse code on top of a closed folder. With my name on it. I took the same moment to take in his man-cave.

The ebony desk he was presiding over came equipped with an embedded touch screen and was located dead center of the room. Flanked across from him were two tanned-hide chairs, the likes of which once belonged to animals you might see on a safari. The floor was the polished naked of a woman's skin, adorned by a single black rug, sliding beneath the sideboard like a discarded robe. A nod to the arts, our corner of the world was renowned for, broke up the wall of windows—gray squiggles framed in black. The kind that was light on the art and heavy on the prestige.

Rows of gold-star awards ate up all other wall space. And all other frames were taken over by staged photographs: Weston and a couple of ex-presidents, Weston with the governor of California, Weston with the mayor of Tiburon, cutting some bullshit charity ribbon. I looked at Mr. Glad-Hander, commanding from his leather chair and masked my derision. A lot of training went into that.

"At ease," Weston finally growled, and I relaxed my stance. "Peter Anthony Davenport the Third . . ." Just the way he said it sounded like an insult.

While that lingered in the air, Weston deliberated over a selection of identical cigars, wedged together in a glossy humidor; their bands of gold flashed like rings. A worthy candidate was brought up to inspect with a critical eye before being run along the tip of his nose. It passed inspection, but I suspected I wouldn't get off so easily.

"I've spent—*wasted*," he clarified, "my morning reading the saga that is your file." He snipped the end of the cigar while eyeing me like it was a euphemism for something else.

I kept my well-trained face smooth.

Weston abruptly stood—iron hard and pushing sixty—to stalk over and open a window. The vista beyond the seawall revealed sailboats, bobbing like bright bathtub toys, in the San Francisco Bay. Back at command post, he ignited his stogie with an ornate lighter before dropping it into a bowl. A loud *ping!* infiltrated the silence.

Then he scooped up the slick navy folder emblazoned with the Academy logo—a lion in mid-roar—and fixed his steel-blue eyes on me.

"I don't recall," Weston began again, puffing around to face me squarely, "in all my years, ever seeing a cadet get through The Elite Program while being such a screw-up."

I had nothing to say and couldn't speak out-of-turn anyway.

"Or be so goddamn stubborn. Or stupid depending on which way you want to look at it. Attempts to mitigate such behavior . . . have only been moderately successful."

A chimney's worth of smoke blew my way. This almost brought back my delinquent smirk because smoking, or tobacco use of any kind, was strictly banned for cadets. Junk food, too. Hell, sometimes, I even thought *fun* was banned here. Weston regarded me through the smoke, one eye at half-mast like he could figure me out better that way.

"You *trying* to get kicked out, Davenport?"

"No, sir." Who did he think he was fooling? There was no escape (that didn't require embalming or a lobotomy).

Weston poked his tongue around his mouth, deliberating. "Good to hear it. But in my experience, *actions* speak louder than words. Doesn't appear like your heart's in the program, son . . . worries me." His eyes bored into mine while I tried not to look bored. "However, your training profile indicates that you *are,* indeed, a match for Missions. Despite your shenanigans, you seem to pass everything with flying colors. No easy feat." A grudging admission.

"So you up for your first solo one?"

"Yes, sir." I was on autopilot.

He nodded thoughtfully, surveying me as though he were sizing me up for a new suit, he wasn't sure I would fit. I stared at his mustache, noting it was groomed with an artist's precision, and that it was the exact grizzled color and bristled texture of his crew cut.

"You've been handpicked for this job, Davenport," Weston reminded me. "Tailor made for you, if you will. Should be a cake walk, but I don't want you sleep-walking your way through."

"No, sir."

"Because I'm not taking any chances with this particular PGC—I have high hopes for him." Weston picked up the photo of golden-boy, and my stomach seized, yet you'd never know it by looking at me. My face remained impassive as the Queen's Guard. Next up for inspection: the photo of the girl. After assessing it for a long, drawn-out moment, he set it aside and rearranged some phlegm. "Should be a fun, quick one."

I could've taken that a couple of different ways.

"But no screwing up. Whatsoever. Period. The end." A fat, finger-wrapped cigar punch punctuated each sentence.

I breathed in through my nose, nodded my compliance. Didn't think I could force out another *yes sir*.

The General must've taken this for subtle insubordination because he said, "You may not give a deviled dog about furthering your own career, but I'd hate to see Cadet Caruthers be painted with the same yellow paint brush when she doesn't deserve it. She's been hard at work on this mission for the last couple of months while you've been growing out your hair at the beach."

"I was just recently called to duty, sir," I reminded him while telltale heat crept up my neck. *Bastard.* That wasn't even a veiled threat.

Yellow paint referred to a dishonorable discharge—very few and very conspicuous. The unchosen were plucked-out, their navy lockers painted over in yellow, a black DD slashed across the front for all to see. The reminders remained up till December 31, when sledgehammers were passed—baton like—into cadets' hands to take turns beating down their lockers. Locker-bashing to ring in the New Year . . . funny how that good ole Academy tradition never made it into the brochure.

Weston considered me another moment. He'd already found a soft spot with Reese, now he was probing for more. "You should thank your lucky stars for your *parents'* longstanding dedication to this organization or you'd have been out on your ass in Civilian Land a long time ago . . . after a brief pit stop through Siberia!"

I waited for the chill that was supposed to follow this threat.

"Need I remind you of the long arms and far-reaching powers The Academy has in this country?" Weston prompted. "In the *world?*

"No, sir." He didn't. I was all too aware.

"Then we understand each other?"

"Yes, sir." Not a lot was needed here: some boot licking, a pair of ears, a dash of contrition.

"Because if you fail, I'll personally bash in your locker and stamp your file with double D myself."

"I won't let you down, sir," I capitulated, as we both knew I would. *The Academy will always win . . . no matter who gets hurt in the process.* The innocent civilian girl and her brother flashed in my mind. Bitter bile clogged my throat. I wanted to hock it out like a loogie—he gave me an impatient hand gesture—right on his boots. I relinquished the mission file to Weston, and he added it to the briefcase holding my first orders.

"Cadet Davenport, you are to report directly to the Ops Building at o-nine-hundred hours where Ranger will finish briefing you, give you your civilian ID, and any additional accoutrements needed for the success of this mission," Weston finalized, clicking shut the briefcase and handing it over. "I highly suggest you *finally* live up to the potential bred and nurtured in you these past two decades." He patted my shoulder. "I do hate wasting the valuable resources of the institution I've dedicated my life to."

I wanted to shrug his filthy hand off but held myself tightly in check.

Weston was good at reading minds. And mind games. He leaned in to hiss in my ear: "However, if you do *not* succeed in bringing this PGC into our ranks forthwith, I will see to it that you are worse than ousted. You will be deployed . . . *elsewhere*, your parents will be demoted, and this blight will haunt you for the rest of your *short* life."

The chill I was waiting for came, and it penetrated my whole being like an iceberg up my ass. I'd heard enough rumors to know what "deplored elsewhere" was code for; it would make Siberia look like a day at the beach.

Weston smiled benevolently at me. "Please give my regards to *both* Doctors Davenport. I understand your mother isn't doing so well these days. Do be careful, Cadet Davenport . . . another loss, like your brother's, would be catastrophic to your mother's well-being."

With one final warning pat, Weston strode from the room and closed the door with a resounding thud.

A paranoid is someone who knows a little of what's going on.

1

ALARM BELLS

Ah. Home sweet home, I thought as I scraped off the remaining traces of mac-and-cheese into the plastic bucket under the sink. I was getting ready to wash the dishes, me being the only dishwasher our house had. And by "house," I mean the trailer kind, without it even having the excuse of being a doublewide. It could be worse though—we didn't live in an actual trailer park. Although living in a trailer park certainly had its advantages: they generally had community pools and were within a stone's throw of civilization.

Nope. We lived an official eleven point five miles out of town limits, on almost two hundred acres of dry pasture, located on the wrong side of New Mexico—the one *without* enchantment. This barren land, in the plains of Eastern New Mexico, was what my father was bound and determined to cultivate (without the benefit of an irrigation system, I might add). I mentally rolled my eyes at the number of hair-brained schemes our father endeavored to make his living at since leaving the military, ranching being the latest and greatest, and the one that seemed to have stuck, unfortunately. I thought ruefully of all the chores involved and shuddered.

Things didn't used to be quite so awful. When Mama was alive. She would've given us breaks from the monotonous chores we set our clocks by, taken us to an afternoon movie in a cool theatre, put some clothes on layaway before school started.

My throat started to feel tight. *I will not cry, I will not cry,* I repeated this mantra over and over, willing the tears away.

"Katie-girl!" my father bellowed from the living room. "Time for bible readin'!"

I pictured his sunburnt face in my mind, the exact way he would be kicked back in his king's recliner with a popcorn bowl balanced on his belly, and a sweating sody-pop, set carefully on a coaster next to him.

"Aw, come on!" Andrew protested. "Let's finish till the end tonight—it's still summer-time."

Andrew was the only Connelly kid who could get away with "back talking" Daddy. But just a little. Sprawled across the sunken-in couch, he was dividing his time between perusing his library book for more information on his growing bug collection and listening to sound bites of World War II.

Last (and least) would be Mikey, lying on the linoleum floor. He was tossing puffs of sweet cereal into his mouth while inspecting their latest acquisition: a buzzing cicada. It was trapped in a jelly jar with punched-in holes in the lid—tonight's honored guest.

Daddy started to lecture about "yearnin' for learnin' more than pearls." And nobody could conjure, nor butcher, a bible lesson like my father, so I intervened before he really got going.

"Daddy," I called from the sink, up to my elbows in dirty dishwater. "I ain't done with the dishes yet."

"You can finish afterwards. The boys gotta get on to bed . . . Mornin' comes early."

"Yes, sir," I auto-answered. "But there's a little bit of that strawberry ice cream leftover . . ." I knew his sweet tooth would be our best bet at getting our way.

During the pause that Daddy habitually used to make us sweat it out, I dried my hands, Mikey grumbled that strawberry was the worst flavor in the world, and Andrew began asserting his opinion that Rocky Road was the best.

"It'll give me time to finish dishes and take out the trash while y'all finish your program and eat your ice cream," I said, plunking frozen chunks of pink into bowls.

"Well alrighty then, Katie-girl. Just this once . . . Bring it on out to us."

"Yes, sir."

I was on my best behavior since returning from summer camp. I wanted to reward Daddy for rewarding me with that unprecedented slice of freedom. A smile curled my lips at the thought of my first real kiss. *Right in the piney woods. Right after campfire. It was a doozy. Well, at least a doozy of a guy,*

I amended. *Abercrombie and Fitch* material all the way. If my old friends could've seen him, they would've swallowed their tongues.

A crisp whack from a rolled-up *Farmers' Almanac,* followed by an outraged protest from Daddy's usual scapegoat, Mikey, interrupted my thoughts.

"You can't sit on the couch and eat at the same time." My father had a strict no-drip policy where it came to food and furniture. Even though our couch cost less than most girls' handbags.

"Yes, I can!" Mikey insisted.

"Whatdi'jasay?" My father released the lever that dropped his boots to the floor.

"You have the ability, but not the permission." Andrew cleared up the confusion.

"All I wanna hear from you boys is yessir." This was my father's standard reply in a situation like this, being of the "Children Should Be Seen and Not Heard" school of thought when it came to parenting. Andrew was the only exception seeing as how he was *exceptional.*

"Yes, sir" was immediately forthcoming from the exception-to-the-rule, a boy who knew which side his bread was buttered on.

Daddy threw Mikey a dark look when he didn't respond as prompted—a dark look reserved for his dark boy. Mikey retaliated by folding his arms into an X, his lips pulling in to form a tight seam.

Uh-oh. I knew the end to both these beginnings.

Daddy pushed pause on the remote (never a good sign). Andrew and I exchanged glances. He immediately went to peel Mikey off the floor, moving him to the other side of the couch . . . and farther away from Daddy's boots.

"Three bowls of scrumptious ice cream comin' up!" I barreled in, practically throwing a bowl into Daddy's lap and another into Mikey's.

Andrew said, "Hey Daddy, didja know radar was first developed to use as a death ray weapon to destroy enemy airplanes?"

Keeping Daddy's mouth and hands occupied was essential to Mikey's health and wellbeing.

"Huh? Yup. Think I might've heard somethin' along those lines." Daddy pushed play, popped his footrest back into position, and commenced to eating.

I handed the last bowl over to Andrew, and now we exchanged smiles of relief. I was struck again by his intelligence and little-boy beauty. His skin shone lustrous with good health, his blue eyes marbleized with green and framed by lashes a shade darker than his cornhusk hair.

Daddy always liked to claim Andrew like a winning lotto ticket, using him like a badge you flash to cut in line. "This here's my boy!" was almost always the first thing out of his mouth. Good manners allowed me next: "Katie's my girl. Don't let the purty face fool you . . ."—*wait for it*—"she's meaner'na Rottweiler!" This, his go-to public joke.

If Mikey was introduced at all, he was last, as an afterthought, like a shadow of a real child. Shadow: the nickname Daddy stuck on him since he could walk and follow his brother around.

I brushed my hand over the Shadow's bristled buzz cut, a "daddy special" shorn with rusty clippers in our kitchen the first Sunday morning of each month. He lived up to his name in a few key ways: wherever Andrew went, Mikey was sure to follow (not sure Andrew was always deserving of this devotion), and he was dark, at least compared to his daddy, whose eyes, hair, and brows were an unfortunate bleaching of color that lent him a washed-out look. Like the denim overalls he wore for no good reason I could think of but to embarrass me.

Mikey had inherited Mama's bronze skin tone as well as her wise hazel eyes. And, like a shadow, he was easy to miss against the golden light cast by his big brother.

I looked at my two brothers sitting side by side and had to admit: they looked nothing alike. Peas and carrots. Milkman comments were routine from the good citizens of Clovis—said with a smile but with an undercurrent of something I didn't understand until a year after Mama's passing. I didn't believe it. Not of her. It was the "disappearance" coupled with the yin and yang looks of the back-to-back boys that set tongues wagging.

When all I heard was rhythmic scraping of spoon against plastic, I decided it was safe to head out with the garbage. I was spent and wanted to finish "my responsibilities" so I could read. I wouldn't be able to message my new camp friend, Reese Caruthers, until school started—no Wi-Fi access on the Connelly compound. *Sigh.* And no Internet allowed. *Double sigh.*

Trash bags and ten-gallon slop-bucket in hand, I backed out the door then watched it bang shut, automatically lock, and snuff out the light. *Dang it!* I forgot to grab the flashlight. Not wanting to pound on the door and disturb the peace, I whistled for Blue. A few seconds later, the wet muzzle of our blue heeler nudged my leg. I was happy to have company on my nightly trek.

I faced the lonely mounds of shape that formed our pasture. A gusty breeze picked up in a sudden-like fashion, rolling a skeletal tumbleweed across our dirt backyard. Branches waved around, animating the old elm tree into a night creature. I eyed the sphere of light glowing neon in the darkness.

Something creep-crawled up my spine. That feeling—the same kind Mama suffered from.

Shaking off the icy sensation (something I'd been doing a lot lately), my thoughts turned to the "Andrew problem." Skipping up another grade wasn't an option on account of his age. But he didn't belong here and everybody and their brother knew it. "Like a gold coin in a bucket full of pennies," Daddy always liked to say. Now there was talk of an afterschool tutor. Felt like an invasion. And more homework for him meant more outdoor work for me. My shoulders sagged at the very thought.

"Come on, boy." Blue and I trudged down the dirt trail, feeling our way along in the dark. We lived too far out for garbage trucks to come, so we burned most of our trash. The bigger pieces my father periodically hauled out to the city dump in a trailer dragged behind his old Bronco. Until then, it was all piled up in a volcano-trash-heap out in the middle of our pasture.

Sometimes, I was *glad* we lived so far out in the country.

Just then a sharp rustle cut through the tranquil white-noise of our pasture. The cattle quit lowing. Crickets ceased chirping. It startled me so badly I nearly dropped the slop bucket. My heart always beat just a little faster on these nightly treks, but tonight I had the heebie-jeebies crawling all over me.

Gah, Katie! Get a grip! Nobody's out here, in the middle of nowhere at night, but you and your pathetic life . . . and we've got nothing worth taking anyway. A pit formed in my stomach nonetheless.

Needing to pinpoint my fear, I set down my load and rubbed at my shoulder while I scanned the brushy horizon for something out of place. *Maybe the coyotes are out foraging in our trash?* Doubtful—they usually liked to keep a respectful distance on account of Daddy's shotgun. A sharp *crackle* froze my body. *Snap.* My head jerked up.

A foot on a dead tree branch?

I dismissed it—just hungry pigs grunting in anticipation of their dinner. *May as well get this over with before I lose my nerve.* Yanking off the lid, I turned my nose away from the sickly-sweet stench of our rotting leftovers, and poured it over the fence into their trough. The greedy slurping noises of the pigs masticating their meal made it impossible to hear anything else.

We were stumbling determinedly onward to the trash heap, when Blue stiffened by my side like he was suddenly struck by rigor mortis. He let out a low growl. "Shhhh, Blue! There's no one out here but some cows." *Right?*

Another twig snapped. Followed by . . . ominous silence.

"W-who's out there?" I decided *not* to wait for an answer. My fear of coyotes, or *whatever* was out there, had me backing up in double time. Blue barked sharply and lunged forward. I made to grab his collar, but he was already furiously charging into the pasture. Goosebumps raised on my arms like poor man's armor.

"Bluesy, come on boy!" I tried adding a coaxing whistle, but my mouth couldn't hold the proper form.

The mechanical roar of a motorcycle growled to life—so close it reverberated throughout my whole body. My heart plunged to my stomach, overflowing trash bags fell from my hands. I started running back to the house like starving zombies were after my brain. Daring a glance over my shoulder, I tripped over an exposed root and flew forward. *Shoot!* I threw my hands out to break my fall, and a particularly unforgiving cactus stabbed my palm. That's when I saw a figure toss something like a computer— with antennae sticking out of it—into a bag before peeling off into the night, spewing chewed-up pasture behind them. It wasn't a motorcycle, but some kind of souped-up four-wheeler I'd never seen before. But I didn't linger long enough to take mental notes. Scrabbling back to my feet, I took off again.

My heart thudded wildly, gushing blood into muscles. Scraggly bushes and cobbled-together animal pens flew by in my crazed, adrenaline-rush back to the house. I made it back, panting and shaking, but in one piece. Sagging against our trailer, I listened as the last echoes of the buzzing mechanized vehicle disappeared into the distance.

"Ouch!" I swore under my breath as I yanked the needle from my palm. *That's gonna leave a sore and bother me relentlessly tomorrow.* About that time Blue came bounding back from his guard dog prowess, shaking with excitement and pride.

"You could've been killed, boy!" I scolded, then exhaled and bent down to stroke his neck, trying to sort out what the heck just happened.

What was that thing doing out here in the middle of nowhere? I looked up at the face of the moon as if it had the answer. Got nothing but more chills so decided to head in. But the industrial strength locks—Mama insisted on installing—kept me in the dark.

Some kind of intuition flickered around in my brain, grabbing hold of flashes of memories from when she was alive. I remembered how, after her disappearance, she became so suspicious of outsiders. She refused to leave home, even for church or the grocery store, claiming she was a homebody and preferred growing our own produce anyway. But instead of alleviating our fears, we steadily grew more worried for her. After Mikey was born, she became even worse, refusing to let *us* leave the ranch. Then her neurosis began to include things like government conspiracies and body snatchers— things that never happened in real life. Especially not out here in Nowhere, New Mexico.

By the time she died, Daddy and I had become armchair psychologists. We'd diagnosed her with everything from paranoid personality disorder to agoraphobia. Seemed like reasonable explanations for her bizarre behavior. But since she flatly refused to see doctors (and we didn't have health insurance to pay for them anyway), we never really knew *what* was wrong with her.

Now I wasn't so sure there wasn't something more to her behavior than just run-of-the-mill paranoia. *Maybe there really is something sinister out there, just waiting to snatch one of us up?* Andrew instantly came to mind. *Who wouldn't want my beautiful, gifted brother?*

A pang of remorse hit me as I thought of a dozen ways, I'd stopped doing what I *thought* were the silly precautions Mama took to protect us from the external world. Things like going back to public school and allowing us to be photographed for the yearbook. I also enrolled Mikey in preschool, even though she made me swear not to. What could I do? Drop out of high school to raise my brothers? *Pathetic.*

The tinny voices of the boys calling my name echoed from inside the metal box. So I pushed all thoughts of body snatchers and four-wheelers out of my mind for now, retrieved the key from under a cactus pot, and headed in. I wouldn't inform Daddy about the trespassers just yet . . . in case he decided we needed extra precautions that would involve a shotgun. I was afraid he would shoot first and ask questions next! And I didn't need the blood of innocent joy riders on expensive recreational vehicles on my head. I had quite enough bad luck in my life as it was.

Besides . . . keeping secrets was in my DNA.

But I couldn't quite stop the weird feeling in my stomach when I went to tuck the boys in. So I added Mama's prayer to deliver us from evil—it suddenly seemed relevant tonight.

2

QUEEN-B ASHLEY-LEIGH

When I finally closed the door to my room, I had myself convinced I was spooked for no reason—it was just some idiot out for a good time, paying no heed to the multiple No Trespassing signs posted around the fence. But then, what was with all the weird equipment? Maybe he was out surveying our land for oil? Maybe underneath the acres of infertile land, there was actually a fountain of oil about to spew forth, and we were gonna strike it rich.

I snorted. *With our luck it would most likely be buried plutonium!*

Anyhow, I had other problems to worry about, like where in the H-E-double-hockey-sticks was I gonna find money for new school clothes for us kids? I had about seventy dollars saved up from my job at the diner, enough to buy the boys a couple of new pairs of jeans and T-shirts. *Sigh* . . . We all needed new sneakers, too.

I threw my closet door wide open, hoping to find some inspiration inside. *Arg!*—shapeless floral dresses, bell skirts, boxy Oxfords—the hangers clanged, one-by-one, as I shoved the offending garments aside. This was all I had to work with. All Daddy would allow me to wear. "Sister-wife" clothes my former best friend, Ashley-Leigh, always called them. I heaved a great sigh. Too bad I never took Mama up on those sewing lessons when I had the chance.

I fell back onto my bed ready to finally allow myself to wallow in it. Lord knew I had a crap load of stuff to choose from. A couple of sobs broke loose. *Why?* I looked up at the rivers of cracks and water stain lakes, slowly turning my ceiling into a disaster map. *Why can't I catch just one little break?*

I flipped over, dragging my furry pillow over my head, ready for a good, long cry when I heard the shrill ringing of the phone from the kitchen.

Well shoot! No time to even wallow in my own self-pity. I quickly blinked away a couple of fat tears before Daddy could see them and count them against me: two strikes. His heavy footsteps came tromping down the hall. It would be Ashley-Leigh no doubt, calling to bring me her exciting day from the Clovis Country Club pool. *Where she is the prettiest social butterfly in the bunch*, I thought meanly.

Daddy spoke through the door, heedless of sleeping boys. "Katie-girl, Ashley-Leigh's on the phone for ya."

"Comin', Daddy." I wiped my nose on my sleeve and followed Daddy's broad back as far as the kitchen.

"Five minutes," he warned, before returning to his recliner and favorite pastime. "I can't hear what they're sayin' with all that gabbin' girl talk goin' on . . . and I deserve some peace and quiet after the day I've had!"

I snorted but said the requisite "yes, sir." Then: "Hello." My voice sounded a little thick, but she wouldn't notice.

"Katie!" A too bright voice boomed from the receiver. "You'll never, *ever* guess who was at the CCC today!"

"You're right . . . so why don'tja just tell me."

"Aw, Katie. You're no fun sometimes," she pouted. "Go ahead . . . three good guesses." While she waited for me to amuse her, she was probably posing for her next selfie or checking her smooth platinum hair for split ends in the mirror. It was Ashley-Leigh's custom to talk and admire at the same time.

"Hmmmmm," I pretended to deliberate. "Kevin, Joe, and Nick?"

"*Jonas Brothers*, right?" She laughed merrily. "Nope. Keep guessin'!"

I audibly sighed, bored already.

"Never mind," she huffed. "I'm just gonna tell ya, since you're obviously in one of your moods again tonight."

Gee wonder why? She never asked how I was doing, usually just calling to inform me how truly "fab" her life was. I really wasn't much for envying Ashley-Leigh's shallow existence, but I had to admit: juxtaposed next to my life, it sounded pretty dang great.

"Remember that hot guy we saw at Chapa's when me and my mom took you out to dinner for your birthday last year?" she asked.

"Uh-huh," I said noncommittally. I did vaguely remember her going on about something, but she usually found something or someone to go on about. I was still in too much of a stupor at the time to remember much of anything clearly. Mama's death had still been so raw and painful.

"Well . . . he's *baaaaaaaack!*"

"Wow. That's uh, really . . . cool, Ash." I tried and failed to infuse my tone with the right amount of enthusiasm.

"Yeah. He, like, works as a lifeguard now! Swoon!"

That was enough to have her off and running for a while. As Ashley-Leigh droned on enthusiastically about the hot college guy, her accent became more exaggerated. She thought southern accents "drove men wild" and never failed to add that to her repertoire of feminine wiles. You had to give it to her—she was a force to be reckoned with. I pitied the poor guy she set her sights on.

When it came to me and boys . . . well, it felt like I was mostly blind these days. It wasn't always like that. I used to at least be slightly interested. I recalled the wild feeling of being chased by boys at recess, my ribbons unraveling in the wind as I nearly outran them. There had never been a shortage of admirers, both girls and boys, surrounding us. All that came screeching to a halt the day Mikey was born. Mama yanked me out of middle school, in the middle of seventh grade.

I thought of the phrase I learned in last year's Spanish class. "*Como cambio el mundo,*" I muttered under my breath.

"Say what?" her bright voice broke into my dark thoughts.

"Uh . . . just seems like everything's changed so much."

She let out a great heave of a sigh to convey how my wet-blanket mood was smothering her girl-crush high. "Yeah, I guess things have changed a lot," she allowed, "but mostly for the good, right?"

I guffawed into the phone.

"Except for your mom dyin'," she stuttered quickly. "That, like, totally sucked!"

"Like, *totally*," I said.

"Oh, you know what I mean, Katie. You can't always dwell on the negative. You gotta focus on all the *good* changes in your life instead." She sounded like a life coach I didn't want.

I bit anyway, grasping for straws. "Like . . . ?"

"Like bein' sixteen and able to car date—finally!"

"You must be thinkin' of someone else. Like, I'm not allowed to car date till I'm old enough to vote."

"*Really?*"

"Do you count ridin' to church functions in mixed company datin'?"

She laughed like I was making a joke. "Okay then . . . how 'bout bein' just two years away from graduation and freedom from the iron shackles of your tyrantical father!"

I laughed despite myself. "I don't think tyrantical is a word," I said, too embarrassed to cop to not leaving this place when I graduated. It was all we ever used to talk about—how we were gonna move to L.A. the day after we graduated. While she was out living the California dream, I would still be here, in a town that barely made a dot on the map, raising my little brothers. Leaving them alone with Daddy was tantamount to throwing them to the wolves. So my life was effectively over for the next . . . oh, decade or so. I shuttered while Ashley-Leigh continued her quest for positivity.

"Okay, let's see more good changes . . . *hmmmmmm* . . ."

I hoped she wouldn't short circuit on my account.

"I already came up with one for ya," she self-affirmed. "I bet I can think of at least two more." Andrew and Mikey were just coming to mind when "Boobs!" blasted in my ear. "You finally got some boobs! Ha! I win! Toldja I could come up with two more!"

I could practically see her readjusting hers so they sat up higher in her bra, like they were such miraculous things they needed to constantly be on display.

"Aren't they so much fun?"

I looked down doubtfully at my own breasts, gently swelling out from my chest. "Well, just because your cup runneth over, doesn't mean we all wanna get up and celebrate."

"I think the Wildcat football, basketball, and baseball teams would all beg to differ!" she positively crowed.

She had me there, and the entire male population of Clovis High. *No wonder she'd moved on to greener pastures*—she'd already chewed up and spit out all the "worthy" boys at school.

I'd suddenly hit my limit of Ashley-Leigh and her "feel good" perspective on life for the time being. "Um, Ash, thanks for the . . . er, pep talk, but I'm bushed. Think I'm gonna call it a day."

"Yeah, me too. I'm exhausted."

I let that one pass, inwardly rolling my eyes at what constituted exhaustive behavior for her. *Sucking in her stomach all day at the pool?*

"*What?*" Ashley cut off the sniggle I'd accidentally let slip into the phone. "I am. Mom made me babysit Benny all afternoon, and it totally sucked!"

I failed to remind her that I also babysat my brothers every single day on top of everything else I had going on. Playing Who's-The-Most-Exhausted? was the one contest I would definitely win hands down. And Ashley-Leigh was a sore loser. And I wanted to leave on a positive note. So I just went with the course of action that always worked best with her—I agreed.

"Yeah. It's pretty sucky to spend your summer babysittin'. Speakin' of which . . . I gotta do that exact thing tomorrow, and then I'm workin' the late-shift at the diner, so I really gotta go. Good news about the hot lifeguard though," I finished, determined to be a good sport.

"Yeah! Totally!" she said, mollified.

I yawned into the phone. "Okay . . . let's talk soon."

"Wait!" she screeched before I could hang up. "I totally forgot why I called."

"There's more?" Usually it was just a litany of admirers, boy crushes, and petty rivalries she wanted to regale me with.

"Yeah. So my mom wanted to . . ." she stalled, "I mean *me* and my mom wanted to take you out for your birthday next Saturday, like we did last year . . . Yunno, kinda make it a tradition."

I hesitated. It really burned me up when Ashley-Leigh acted like she was doing me a favor by hanging out with me. Actually, she really would be doing me a favor because I could use another life-break. But I worked every weekend now, and the fact was we really, truly needed the extra money (not that I would admit that to her).

"Um . . ."

"Are you, like, checkin' your busy calendar or somethin'?" Obviously, she thought I should jump at the chance.

"It's not that. It's just . . . I work Saturdays now," I explained, which she'd know all about if we were actually still friends. "And I have to see—"

"Perfect! You get a night off from work, get to go out with me, and a birthday dinner all rolled into one!" she trilled as if the matter had all been cleared up.

She was clearly missing the point. "I actually have to ask *not* to work. It's not like I can get off any ole time I want. And I just started last month so hate to ask off so soon. They pretty much hired me because I said I could work weekends."

Ashley-Leigh snorted rudely into the phone. "I seriously doubt that dinky dive has enough customers to keep *one* waitress busy, much less two. You should just quit so you can have a life again."

"Okay."

"You're quittin'?" She seemed only mildly surprised I would instantly follow her suggestions.

"Okay, I'll ask Ms. Norma for the night off," I elaborated.

"Well don't do me any favors."

I was growing weary of this conversation. "No, Ash. I totally want to, of course I do. Thanks so much for askin'. *Really.*"

"Okay then . . . it's a date!" she exclaimed, back to her sunny self in two-point-two seconds flat. "I'll tell mom. Meet at our house at seven thirty cause we have a little *surprisey* for you before we leave!"

"That's alright, Ash. You don't have to do that. Just a girls' night is plenty for me."

I was secretly dreading the big reveal outfit I got every year on my birthday. It was always something wildly inappropriate, like the shimmering gold cocktail dress last year. *Where was I gonna wear that to? Church?*

She laughed at my pitiful protests. "See ya next Saturday!"

"Okay. Sounds good. Tell your mom—" The buzzing of the dial tone in my ear interrupted me.

I exhaled. *Maybe I really do need some girl time?* It would certainly be a nice change of pace, and Mrs. Montgomery was certainly gracious. I just couldn't help feeling like Ashley was sometimes positively gleeful about my dive from the social stratosphere, not that she would ever come right out and show it. I was puzzled why. I certainly posed no threat to her and was happy to let her have the lion's share of the spotlight she reveled in.

And Mama made me anyway.

"Katie!" Daddy bellowed from his recliner. "Time for bed. We gotta lotta work to do tomorrow," he added, unnecessarily. I knew the drill.

"Yes, sir." I hopped off my stool and headed obediently to the sanctuary that was my bed.

Yup. I could bear a girls' night with Ashley-Leigh if it would mean a couple of hours break from the monotony that threatened to choke me daily. And maybe I'd be able to sneak five minutes on her laptop to email Reese. That thought perked me up, and I fell asleep feeling like the morning light might actually bring with it the possibility of something *good.*

3

AT FIRST SIGHT

I pulled off the long, flat stretch of Highway 70 and into the back alley of Norma's Diner where I sputtered to a stop. Despite pulling down my visor and wearing sunglasses, I arrived nearly blind. Facing the beat down rays of the afternoon sun was becoming an occupational hazard. I blamed my Dollar Store glasses. And the lack of hills, trees, or buildings to help buffer the blaring sun along the way.

It's funny how much the heat can wear you out (but not in a ha-ha kind of way). I expelled some tired air from the same-ole, same-ole that was my life, arriving in no mood for more work but needing the *dinero*. Mama's old Subaru Hatchback was due for a new transmission. Luck had been getting me to and from work for the last couple of weeks, but I was pretty sure it was getting ready to run out on me. And Daddy wasn't likely gonna part ways with his precious Bronco any time soon. It wasn't much newer, however, it was much cooler.

Cooler. Sigh. I readjusted the icepack around my neck. Air conditioning was another thing I would have to pay for—a luxury I couldn't afford.

Oh well. I had a few me-minutes before I had to go clock in and didn't want to waste them dwelling on the negative. *Maybe Ashley-Leigh's pep talk worked?* I parked in the shade of a dumpster and rolled down the window, but the stench of overflowing garbage cans immediately molested my nose. *What did I expect? A meadow in spring?*

The back alley of Norma's was a shantytown of cardboard boxes and graffiti-decorated walls. Shattered beer bottles and discarded cigarette butts littered the cracked pavement. Rolling the window back up, I closed my eyes against the mosaic of broken dreams to recreate some of my most memorable moments from Camp Pinewood, the best week of my life . . . since Mama died. But arriving on time for once, Beatrice beeped in beside me, waving madly

So much for my R&R.

I sighed and readjusted the rearview mirror to get ready—a twenty-second job—then dug around in my bag for the brown tie that no longer matched my hair and the forgotten glasses I promised Mama I would wear. While scraping my hair back into a ponytail, I noticed quite a bit of the "golden" streaks from my summer dye-job remained. Even though I knew it was an epic fail, it was fun to be someone different for a while. I'd been channeling Reese, but the bottle-blonde had turned my chestnut hair a burnt, brassy orange.

So much for my foray into hairdressing.

Most of the color had washed out, thank goodness, because I looked like a total imposter as a blonde. I thought I'd never hear the end of it from Daddy, who claimed I looked like a "dime-store hustler" . . . *Whatever that is.*

He would have grounded me for it, too, if there were actually something to ground me from. It's not like I really missed the half hour of Disney Channel I was no longer allowed to watch, so Daddy moved to banning books. Well, I'm ordinarily pretty obedient, but I couldn't abide that. So I'd been sneaking around to read behind bushes and in the bathroom all summer like a crack addict. Daddy must've caught on, because my romance novels kept disappearing on me. Eventually he caved on the TV saying "looking like poor man's Barbie" was punishment enough. And I wasn't allowed to dye it back to brown, hence the three inches of dark roots I was sporting.

Recalling Daddy's horrified expression, I smiled broadly in the mirror until my eyes lit upon my teeth and I automatically closed to the Mona Lisa smile I'd perfected. I made a face. *Could've been worse.* My teeth were actually pretty straight—not braces straight like most of the popular kids, but not crooked either. Just my front teeth protruded out slightly, forming an overbite I was acutely self-conscious of.

Mama disagreed with me, of course, saying my natural pouty expression was actually an enhancement. *Yeah right.* I looked like a hick, and the way my lips stuck out only made me look hicker. She just always knew how to make lemonade out of lemons—one of her many talents.

A lump formed in my throat, so I quickly patted lip balm onto my chapped lips and threw my pink and red trucker-hat and stupid glasses on before the golf ball threatened to choke me. I took a final glance in the mirror to see if I looked as hideous as I thought—*yep*. Growling out loud, I shouldered my way out the door and stomped up the stairs to go clock in. The bright ponytail swinging cheerfully behind me felt completely incongruent with my dark mood.

"Hey, Hon!" Beatrice greeted from the walk-in, where she was putting on her apron.

"Hey, Bee," I acknowledged her with a smile while reaching into my cubby for my own apron.

"Ya think it's gonna get busy tonight?" she asked.

I shrugged my shoulders. "I dunno, but I hope so . . . school's about to start."

"I know, sweetie." A sympathetic smile erased five years from her face. Beatrice was a single mom working nights to make extra money, which pretty much made us comrades-in-arms. "It's just the two us tonight, Carlos in the kitchen, and Norma of course." Bee rolled her eyes exaggeratedly.

She and Ms. Norma went at it on several occasions, and I diligently played my role of peacemaker when either Bee threatened to quit, or Norma threatened to fire her. "Maybe we'll get some of the truckers passin' through from the dairies," she added hopefully.

"Yeah, maybe," I said noncommittally. Remembering some of the awkward encounters with truckers in the past, I was instantly grateful I'd decided to wear my dorky glasses tonight.

As if telepathically, Ms. Norma came bustling in and frowned when she zeroed in on them perched on my nose. "Lose your contacts, Katie?"

I ducked my head. "Um . . . yes ma'am."

Norma preferred me glasses free. She seemed to think it helped with repeat customers. *As if.* The only thing that would help this place would be a complete menu overhaul. "Greasy Spoon" was a very apt expression when describing Norma's.

"Okay, listen up." Ms. Norma was all business now. "There's an early bird two-top in your section, Beatrice." Bee automatically got the first table since she had seniority. "Well, what are ya waitin' for? Go on and get out there!"

"I'll finish settin' up for you," I volunteered, relieving Bee of the ketchup funnel.

She gave me a grateful smile. "Thanks, hon!"

"City slickers from the looks of 'em. Probably be a good tip, so be on your best behavior." Beatrice grabbed her tray, and eagerly pushed through the double doors leading to the dining room. "And no flirtin' neither!" Ms. Norma warned to doors still swinging on their hinges.

That left just the two of us standing there, a perfect time to make my request. I grabbed the two-gallon ketchup jugs, began refilling the table bottles. "Hmm-hmm," I awkwardly cleared my throat.

"Got somethin' on your mind, Katie?" Ms. Norma took the hint.

"Um, I wanted to see if maybe it's okay . . ." I fumbled before setting the funnel down, determined now. "I wanted to ask for next Saturday off." Ms. Norma was unblinking and silent as a horned toad, so I continued on in a rush, "I know I said I could work every weekend, no exceptions, but . . . it's my birthday and—"

"Stop!" She threw an extravagantly jeweled hand up in my face. "Course you can, Katie Connelly." Relief was just flooding me when she said, "If *anyone* ever deserved a night off, hon, it's you."

And then my face flooded with color. *Oh.* "Thank you." *So* hated getting unnecessary sympathy for my pathetic life.

"Don't mention it," she said, "cause I need you to work next Thursday to cover for Doreen. Now get your cute behind out there and make some money for both of us!"

"Yes, ma'am." I snorted to myself. The uniforms came in two sizes here: large and extra-large—a potato sack would've been more flattering.

Just then Bee came barreling back through the swinging doors like someone had lit her fuse. "What the hell?" Ms. Norma exclaimed as Bee smacked into her bosom, causing a Jell-O-mold-like quiver.

"You took the words right outta my mouth!" Beatrice said hotly. "What the hell is an Arnold Palmuh?"

I shrugged. *No clue.*

"Did ya list the specials for 'em?" Ms. Norma said as if that was the solution to all our problems here.

"Not yet. I was just takin' their drink order to start with, like I always do," Bee said defensively.

"Then go on back out there and list *all* the drink options we offer."

"Yeah. Maybe it's some fancy sports drink or somethin' . . . Them boys sure do look real athletic-like," Bee mused, a droopy smile softening her face.

Uh-oh. This was just the sort of thing that usually got Bee into trouble. Not that she did anything more than flirting, but Ms. Norma frowned upon a mother "carrying on like that." She preferred it if *I* would do that particular task.

Unfortunately, my flirting skills were nonexistent.

"Get on back out there and offer 'em some cola. We ain't got no Gatorade, but I never met a youngster who turned down a cold Co' Cola on a hot day," Ms. Norma offered sagely.

"Okay." Bee smoothed down her hair. "I'm headed out." *Strange.* She was usually so unflappable even during our busiest of times.

"And don't forget to push the meatloaf tonight," Ms. Norma hissed after her.

I rolled my eyes. *So it's gonna be one of those nights.* I was busy pairing squeezy ketchup and squat hotsauce bottles together on my tray when the office phone interrupted my concentration. I looked up to see that Ms. Norma appeared to be too busy adding another layer of frosty lipstick to bother picking up. It continued to ring, and I continued to consider answering it when it finally stopped. Me and my condiment couples were just heading out when the ringing started up again. Sighing, I clattered the tray back down and ran to the office to grab it.

"Good evenin', Norma's Diner. How may I help you?" I mechanically answered, then listened while a panicked pre-teen voice asked to speak with Beatrice Howard right away. One of her kids was apparently throwing up. *Ew.* "Hang on a minute," I said calmly. I'll just go get her."

On my way out the swinging doors, they swung back open to reveal Bee muttering something about "This ain't no cloth napkin joint."

"Hey, Bee," I intercepted her before she could rush on. "I'm real sorry, but I think one of your kiddos is sick. Your cousin's on the phone."

She instantly came down from her tizzy, chagrin and concern fighting it out for control over her face. "Oh, Good Lord! I tol' Shawntel she had no business eatin' two hot dogs on top of all that ice cream!" Concern won out.

"Well, I can take over for you—" I stuttered to a halt when I saw her face fall. "I'll split the tip with ya," I said, easily reading her.

After a beat, she heaved a resigned sigh and shoved her tray and order pad into my hands. "Alrighty, Miss Katie. They's all yours, and hoity-toity as all get out, but I 'spect you'll get a fine tip if you're willin' to put up with their strange demands and sneerin' attitude." After that bit of advice,

Bee scurried to the office already in mom-mode, shouting their drink order over her shoulder, "Them Arnold Palm-things is really just half-tea, half-lemonade!"

Huh? That's a new one. I pondered what kind of people ordered such an exotic drink, and if it was any good, while I pushed through the double doors. My feet stopped dead in their tracks two paces in.

Whoa!

A set of ice-chip eyes, belonging to a very large male, looked up at me expectantly for a hard beat, then just as quickly looked away before blithely continuing his conversation. Well, *obviously* I wasn't their waitress returning with their drinks. But somehow, I felt stung by his frosty stare. I was still frozen, mid-step, like an ice sculpture when he looked up again. His mouth curled into a sneer to say something to his friend, who very briefly glanced in my direction and then away as though annoyed.

Double whoa! I felt color begin its creepy appearance up my neckline.

They were sitting nonchalantly, in the booth that sat up to six well-fed customers, and were doing a nice job of taking up the ample space. The one wearing a tattered baseball cap was facing the opposing side, which was standard seating practice. The one with dark hair, pronounced muscles, and cold, staring eyes was sprawled out across from him with his back against the wall. He was facing outward, with one long arm draped across the backrest, his feet crossed at the ankles on top of the seat I was gonna have to wipe down as soon as they left.

Make yourself at home, why don't you? I thought before realizing that Beatrice had been holding out on me. She had failed to mention the two "hoity-toity" guys sitting in her booth could easily pass for movie stars. Not sure why, but I would've liked to have been prepared for that. Hoity-toity I could deal with. But when you added looks that could slay Aphrodite . . . well, I wasn't sure I could even speak to them without stuttering. They simply exuded self-confidence, money, and class. *Two seconds.* That's all it took for me to see exactly who they were. Which meant they'd used the exact same two seconds to see exactly who I was—a waitress in a dumpy uniform, working in a dive, at a dead-end job.

Feelings of inadequacy instantly flooded me.

Furiously, I yanked down the back of my skirt, where it rode up in the back, then whirled around to get their drinks going. If I waited any longer, they would think I was dumb on top of dumpy. So I hustled to the prep area where the drink dispenser was hiding, and after expertly filling red plastic cups halfway with lemonade from the fountain, I hesitated over the tea options. *Should I go for the sweet or unsweet tea? Probably sweet.* Like Ms. Norma said, most teenagers preferred their drinks on the sugary side. Not that those guys looked remotely like teenagers . . . more like college-age superheroes.

After topping off each drink smartly with a lemon wedge, I retied my drooping apron and pulled back my shoulders. *Go time.* I could do this. I mean . . . just because those guys more resembled male models than frat guys didn't mean they were better than me. Besides, I reasoned, they were probably perfectly nice. Winding my way around tables towards their booth, I plastered a smile in their general direction trying to convey how efficient I was. The one facing me didn't acknowledge my entrance in any way. Just talked right along, staring right through me with flinty eyes like I was made out of glass.

Self-consciousness flew my eyes from his haughty face to the window behind his talking head, where I saw what clearly must be their vehicle. Parked up front and center, was a shiny-black, ultra-flashy SUV. The kind with thick, knobby tires that could flatten entire buildings. The kind that made girls in short skirts cringe and teenage boys drool with envy.

Figures—rich boys. Totally had them pegged.

Upon arrival, I paused courteously, waiting for the dark-haired one to finish his monologue. Drinks balanced on my tray, I stood there dumbly until the one in the baseball cap finger-halted him to acknowledge me with a brief smile. But the talking only stopped long enough to switch to some kind of cheap insult like: "What took so long? Was I in the back squeezing the lemons myself?" But I couldn't pay much attention because it felt like I'd just been flipped upside down on a rollercoaster.

Baseball Cap was far and away the best-looking guy I'd ever laid eyes on. My heart skipped a couple of beats and everything. Oddly enough though, his eyes looked flat, and he had a defeated look upon his face. He was also slumped over, almost as though he'd been getting a lecture from a parent instead of having a conversation with a buddy. *Could that be right?* It was hard for me to reconcile how someone who obviously had so much could look so miserable.

While I was musing, the dark-haired one—with the bluest eyes I'd ever seen—hurled another flimsy insult at me. Another unoriginal. Apparently, good looks and a highly developed wit didn't necessarily go hand-in-hand.

"Cut it out, Ranger!" Baseball Cap glanced up at me apologetically. "You'll have to excuse my buddy here. See, we've been on the road for the past eight hours, and he gets a little cranky when he's hungry. He'll straighten out his attitude when he gets some grub down him," he explained in a smooth voice.

"And something to drink might help prevent dehydration." The big one, with the bigger attitude (whose name I now knew was Ranger), looked pointedly at the drinks still perched on my tray. He seemed to have a lot of heat coming off him, but his eyes remained chips of blue ice. His gaze held me captive.

I blinked a couple of times, feeling slightly like a bunny cornered by a ravenous wolf. "Here's your, um . . . " I hesitated, feeling silly, "Arnold Palmades?"

Laughter erupted from the massive chest of Ranger. I was miffed to see the one on my left in the baseball cap, aka the-man-of-my-dreams, was also chortling quietly, too. *What exactly is so dang funny?* Stiffly, I plunked drinks in front of each one.

"I told you." Baseball Cap held out his palm to Ranger. "Pay up." After some crisp bills were reluctantly slapped into his hand, he shot me a killer, crooked smile that nearly knocked me out. "Arnold *Palmers*," he corrected as embarrassment crawled all over me like sand fleas.

"Good to know." I took out my order pad, fuming.

Baseball Cap had the good grace to look contrite, but it was too late. He'd shown his true colors and they were as spotty as his friend, Ranger's. "Sorry," he began, "it's just . . . we had a bet that no one here"—he gestured around, indicating anything from me, to the diner, to the whole town— "would know what that was." He finished by shrugging his shoulders in a gesture I took to be more arrogant than apologetic.

He probably thought I'd fall all over myself to forgive him. *Hmmmph.* He'd made me the butt of their joke, something I couldn't abide. *How could I have been so easily fooled by the pretty face? Birds of a feather . . .*

"I'll be back in a minute to take your order. I hope you enjoy your Arnold *Palmers*," I enunciated through clenched teeth before stalking away.

"Nice outfit!" called after me, in the voice I recognized as Ranger's.

The immediate effect of this compliment was a self-conscious tug on the back of my skirt midway to the kitchen followed by deep laughter. Upon my return, I was bound and determined to keep my cool. But my good intentions were beginning to drip from me like condensation from an iced tea sweating in the sun—drip, drip, drip—because when I approached the table, Baseball Cap's lips began twitching, and Ranger shook his big block head at me. Still, I managed to take out my pad and pencil while remaining aloof and professional.

"May I take your order?" I said.

A rude finger snap whipped my eyes back to glacier ice. "I don't know. Can you? Doesn't seem like you can take a simple drink order without flubbing it."

It took all I had in me to look Ranger in the eyes; felt like I might melt from the hate emanating from them like twin beams of radiation.

"We've been sitting in this hell-hole for fifteen freakin' minutes, and we're choking on"—his face contorted into a grimace—"something that tastes worse than . . ." He seemed to struggle for words.

"Buzzard puss?" Baseball Cap offered up humorously.

Well he seemed to be in a better mood

"Buzzard puss," Ranger conceded before continuing on. "And there are clearly no other customers dumb enough to be here, so I can't imagine what the excuse for such subpar service could be." His voice was succinct and polished, and coupled with his incredible physical stature, turned his little tirade from scathing to *scary*.

But I was too heated to feel the chill, my temper flaring right along with the patches of pink skin along my neckline. "Oh, I'm sorrrrry," I drawled out, sweet and thick as molasses. "There must've been some kinda misunderstandin' earlier"—sparks shot from my own blue eyes—"you see, we don't speak asshole here."

Dead quiet.

. . . Until Baseball Cap snorted. Then he threw back his head, laughing out loud like my little outburst was the funniest thing he'd ever heard. I couldn't help marveling at the way it transformed his face. For once, Ranger seemed momentarily speechless. Meanwhile, regret slowly settled over me like a thick blanket of snow. *Shoot! I'm likely gonna get fired for popping off, all because of these two jerks.*

Suddenly Ranger came back to life, shoving the offending drink at me. It went shooting across the Formica like a whiskey in a bad western. A split-second before it slipped over the edge, I righted it with my hand so that only a fraction of liquid sloshed out.

"Nice save," Baseball Cap commented with a smile. He also seemed to have come to life all of a sudden.

Ranger seemed unimpressed. In fact, he looked unequivocally madder that I'd foiled his plan. He probably wasn't used to being spoken to like that, and it was highly likely he didn't enjoy being laughed at either. He slid closer, anger coloring his handsome face a less appealing shade. I instictually slid away, prey retreating from predator.

"Get your ass back there and dump this garbage down the drain!" he snarled, flashing teeth the same brilliant white of his shirt. "When you return, you better have plain, unsweetened iced tea and a plate of lemons in your hands. And bring some real sugar, too." He flicked a couple of pink and blue artificial sweeteners at me. "Think you can manage that, Glasses?"

"Yes, sir," I ground out.

I'd just spun on one heel when I heard Ranger stage-whisper, "I wonder what she's got hiding beneath that get-up?"

"You're such an ass," Baseball Cap replied wearily, sounding like he'd like nothing better than to escape out that window he'd been staring out of.

Not sure why, but I felt a mysterious pang shoot through me when Baseball Cap didn't even give me a cursory glance. To my absolute horror, tears started smearing my eyesight as I headed back to the galley. I absolutely must get this under control before I returned to the battlefield. Could *not* let my enemies see me cry. *Show no weakness.* Daddy's motto played in a continuous loop in my mind as I plowed into the ice with their cups.

Norma came bustling around the corner then, always surprising me by moving so quickly for such a large woman. "Katie, what in Sam hell is takin' so long with their order?" She stopped to size up my face. Tears trickled down my cheeks, traitors in my war against losing control. "Oh, honey! What's the matter?" she instantly cooed.

I knew I didn't deserve her sympathy, and the knowledge that I let her down made me cry. While she burped me over her shoulder, I choked out a mini version of the story.

"Hmmmph! We'll just see what those two . . . two . . . high-falootin' boys have to say for themselves!" With that, she snatched the drinks from my hands and marched to their booth.

I couldn't help but peek around the corner to see what would transpire. Both guys sat up in anticipation of the freight train headed their way. Loaded glances were exchanged as she set their drinks down purposefully before confronting them. *Oh man. What had I got Ms. Norma into?* They would surely make mincemeat out of her. I could practically hear the jokes before they were told, and closed my eyes against the slaughter I was about to witness.

Before I could step from behind my lookout post to rescue her, I saw Ms. Norma's chins wobbling with the force of her words. *Maybe she can hold her own better than me?* I felt irritated because I couldn't hear what was going on. Baseball Cap and Ranger seemed to be murmuring politely back to Ms. Norma and turning the full force of their abundant male charms on her.

Ugh. I could see she was going to buy whatever they were selling her by the way she leaned over, offering up a view of her mountainous peaks. *Oh brother.*

"Why thank you, boys!" Her coarse voice suddenly went up a few obvious octaves. She patted Baseball Cap on the arm matronly before rubbing it like a fine cashmere sweater she longed to buy.

Felt like throwing up in my mouth.

Then she turned her attention back to Ranger and declared the drinks were on her. He smiled broadly, all brilliant teeth and charm, and thanked her for her southern hospitality. My eyes blinked at the sudden transformation. A real life *Dr. Jekyll and Mr. Hyde* was sitting in that booth. And just like magic, he'd hoodwinked her into a free dinner.

Are you kiddin' me? I felt totally betrayed, by both parties really. Them, for not being the arrogant asses they were two minutes ago, and her for not seeing through their little act. Although I had to admit, they were very convincing. *Maybe they really are movie stars?*

That's just like life, I thought bitterly. *The rich just kept on gettin' richer.*

Ms. Norma was heading back all pink-cheeked and perky now that she'd basked in the glow of the royal highn-*asses*. I ducked back around the corner and began wiping down clean counters.

"Katie!" I braced for it. "Now I just talked to those two nice young men out there."

Oh, so now it's "two nice young men."

"And I want you to know the type of behavior you displayed today is completely unacceptable."

That's what I call a one-eighty.

"Those two gentlemen informed me they nicely explained their dietary restrictions to both you girls. That *Beatrice* . . ."—she arched one penciled-in eyebrow—"was more willin' to accommodate them than you were! And the one with dark hair said you were just plain rude when they requested that you remake their drinks to their satisfaction."

"B-but that's not—"

"But nothin'. Now I don't care that you felt ruffled cause you messed up their drinks. That's your problem." I tried protesting again, but she sealed my lips with a bedazzled fingertip and leaned in so close I could smell the stale cigarette and peppermint gum on her breath. "What I *do* care about, however, is the way you treated them. They're payin' customers. If they weren't just passin' through, I would likely fire you!"

She wilted me with a look. "That is never, *ever* gonna happen again. Do you understand?"

I ducked my head in defeat. "Yes, ma'am."

"Now get back out there and show those two hunky visitors the kind of hospitality that Norma's is known for!" And she said the words without one iota of irony, too.

My stomach felt queasy at the thought of facing them again. To tell you the truth, I'd rather wait on a couple of rattlesnakes. *If she likes them so much, why doesn't she do the honors?*

As if reading my mind, she said, "And the dark one, with killer-blue eyes, specifically asked for you to be given a second chance. Pretty damn big of 'im, if you ask me."

Dark. Killer. Big. I wondered how inadvertently perceptive her Ranger adjectives were, and my feet stood in protest.

She double-fisted her wide hips. "You're testin' my patience, Katie."

After a booty-scoot from Ms. Norma, I slunk back out there, dreading it like a soldier returning to the battlefield. *Maybe I just need thicker skin? They're just a couple of regular customers hassling me and nothing more*, I tried convincing myself. I dared a quick peek at them. Yeah right—Batman and Superman couldn't be more conspicuous sitting in that booth.

Okay, fine. So they weren't exactly *regular* customers, but maybe they'd just ignore me now that they'd accomplished getting me into trouble and received a free meal to boot. No such luck. For as soon as I approached their table, they both vied for my attention. It was weird and confusing, kind of like trying to focus on a split screen TV.

Ranger was definitely gloating now, twirling his fingers and smirking. Baseball Cap gave me an apologetic smile, sympathy softening his dark eyes before he returned them to his phone, leaving me nowhere to face but enemy number one. *Gah!* . . . Baseball Cap was dangerously good-looking. I had to remind myself he was dining with the enemy.

"Good to see you back again, Glasses!" Ranger greeted me gleefully. "Hope we didn't get you in too much trouble." His tone indicated the opposite.

I shrugged through the place where words should've been. Ranger was extremely good-looking, too, I had to concede. And dangerous. It positively oozed from his pores. I would have to tread carefully and turn the other cheek—no matter what.

"I was afraid we'd be stuck with good ole Norma," Ranger continued, aiming his sarcasm at Baseball Cap now. "Kind of like going from bad to worse, if you know what I mean. And I definitely don't like getting the short straw. Or in this case—the fat one." He paused to grimace. "Looking at all those rolls would've probably killed my appetite. And we can't have that, right, Glasses?" He swung back my way. ". . . Seeing as how dinner's on the house."

I looked blankly at him, waiting for him to finish.

"Oh, geez. I see I've confused you now. I don't literally mean dinner is *on* the house. What I mean is, thanks to you, it's *gratis.*"

I just continued to take it, my face turning different shades of pink the only evidence I was listening.

"You know *gratis?*"

I quietly seethed, allowing his insults free reign.

"Maybe I should try Spanish seeing as how we're in New *Mexico?*" Ranger tried getting Baseball Cap into the game again, but as far as I could see, the only game he was playing was the one on his phone.

"*No comprende? Gratis,* as in *libre?*" Ranger enunciated loudly.

I was sure my face was a primary shade by now. But I remained silent, except for my foot, which began an angry staccato tap.

". . . Or *free* in English. You outta know all about the free—I bet you've been the beneficiary of *many* free lunches in your lifetime. Am I right, Glasses?"

My eyes blazed, but I resolutely kept my lips sealed.

"I think she may be slightly retarded," Ranger slid across the booth to Baseball Cap, who finally registered he was listening by shaking his head. (The same staccato tap was happening on his phone.) This elicited a smirk from Ranger before he returned to tormenting me. "I mean—we weren't *actually* going to order any food in this dump. However, now that I know it's all *free,* I just might have a change of heart."

Instead of rising to the bait, I turned the other cheek so that I was facing the very quiet guy in the baseball cap. "What would you like to order?"

He glanced up with an impenetrable look upon his gorgeous face. "I'll just have some whole wheat toast."

Oh gah! Baseball Cap's eyes were so dark they were almost black, and staring into their fathomless depths made me catch my breath. I couldn't even manage to look at him for two seconds without blushing all over.

"W-would you care for some eggs with that?" There was a beat of silence, so I hurriedly explained, "We serve breakfast all day long."

"No thanks. Just the toast."

"How 'bout some butter or jelly?" I pressed, cringing as I asked. He obviously dismissed me, but I didn't want to get a single solitary thing wrong. Plus, I had to admit my eyes wanted an excuse to see him again.

But he didn't even bother looking up from his phone. "Nope. Just the toast."

Ranger barked out a laugh. "Told you she might be mentally handicapped."

Sheesh! What's with these guys? They could be competing for world's biggest asses and both would medal in it—gold and silver, respectively.

After a distinct throat clearing, Ranger startled me by throwing some bills on the table. I flinched back like he'd thrown battery acid. "Here's what I'm going to do, Glasses." He stopped and prefaced by saying, "I'm basically a decent guy—"

I raised my eyebrows. His words matched his actions about as well as black socks and brown shoes.

"—and I'm into second chances, so you can earn this ten bucks, *if* you do a good job." He indicated the pile of ones on the table. "I think all you need is a little training; let's start at the beginning, shall we? Restaurant 101. The first rule in business is . . ." Ranger arched one black brow at me, waiting.

I folded my arms, unwilling to play his game.

"Come on, Glasses, I know even *you* know this one . . . and I'm not ordering until you answer." Ranger began drumming his fingers on the table while I debated how much I wanted that money. "Times up!" he declared before removing a dollar from the stack with a *whungh, whungh, whungh* like I'd just lost round one.

I'd already lost the moment he walked through the door.

"The customer is always . . . ?" he prompted again. We both knew I knew the answer. He just wanted to make me say it, force me into his humiliating game. But I was feeling more stubborn than smart at the moment so refused to indulge him.

"Oh, come on, Glasses! You can do it." He spoke using the same cadence one would when trying to coax a kid into crossing the monkey bars. This made me think of my two little brothers sitting at home in their tattered T-shirts and worn sneakers, and the fact that they were very much counting on their big sister. I would not let them down to spite this worthless blowhard. I really needed those nine bucks, and he knew it.

What would it cost me?—just my pride.

"Right," I finally coughed up.

He cupped a hand to his ear. "Sorry, can't hear you. Speak up. The customer's always . . ."

A shot of fear coursed through my veins, causing my intuition to kick in. This guy really had it in for me. Surely it wasn't just because I'd stood up to him earlier. *Aren't I way too over-classed for him to be pushing me down to take my lunch money?*

Although it was obvious Ranger was a Type-A, macho-guy, I couldn't help feel that something more was going on. Two things I was pretty sure of: There was something sinister about him, and there was something about *me* that was drawing this from him. I just couldn't fathom what it was.

And then something else hit me—déjà vu.

It took a few seconds for the vertigo feeling to desist, and when it did, I hissed, "Right!"

"Uh-uh, uh-uh." Ranger waggled his finger back and forth. "Temper, temper . . . That's going to cost you *another* dollar!"

In a flash, Baseball Cap's hand shot out and caught Ranger's before he could remove another one. We both whipped our heads to stare at him in shock.

"What the hell, dude!" Ranger tried to wrench free. I could hardly believe Baseball Cap was able to keep his grip on him—Ranger definitely looked like the steroid type. "Drop that hand if you want to keep it!" Ranger hissed.

Baseball Cap clenched his jaw before letting go as reluctantly as Ranger had paid his bet earlier. "Why don't you grow up, man?"

Ranger snorted and gave him a condescending look. "You're one to talk."

Baseball Cap shook his head, muttered something unintelligible, and returned to tapping on his phone with a vengeance.

Guess I'm on my own again. Aren't I always?

"Alrighty then. Ready to take my order?" Ranger tried capturing my gaze, but I was too afraid I'd spit at him to speak at the moment, so I eyed my pad meaningfully.

"Oh, no-no-no-no." He shook his head at me. "That's cheating, Glasses. You'll need to build up those memory skills if you're going to become a decent waitress. I mean—I don't really see many options for you out here in the sticks, except for this gig, so I'd concentrate on rising above just being able to walk and chew gum at the same time. With a little training, you might actually be *good* at this serving thing. Who knows . . . " he continued his mocking horoscope for my future, "one day, you might even make manager of this dump, seeing as how Norma's clearly going into a diabetic coma in a couple of years . . . just in time for you to graduate!"

I felt like I'd been punched in the gut—this was the exact scenario I feared most.

Baseball Cap shot Ranger a strange look, then quickly returned to his all-absorbing phone. And here I thought he wasn't paying attention. And speaking of attention, I was going to pay the strictest of to get this order right, even if it killed me! I put down my pad and met his hateful eyes. *No way is a scumbag like Ranger gonna win.*

"Ready whenever you are," I said, all traces of tremor gone from my voice.

Ranger lifted half a lip. "That a girl." After this brief flash of approval, he was off and running: "I'll begin with the Cobb salad, no iceberg lettuce just romaine, hold the tomatoes, oil and vinegar on the side. Serve it with a quarter lemon wedge on each side, followed by the chicken fried steak . . ."

At this, Baseball Cap slanted him a look.

"When in Rome . . ." Ranger explained before continuing his rapid-fire order: "No mashed potatoes, unless it's made with real butter, which I highly doubt, so then baked potato, plain, hold the mushy green beans. And for desert I'll have some peach pie, no whipped cream, vanilla ice cream, instead, on the side, in an ice-cold serving bowl."

Ranger smirk-smiled. "I have a feeling Ms. Norma will want me to indulge in one of her 'famous pies,'" he air-quoted, sliding a sly look across to Baseball Cap. "Unfortunately, I think Glasses here is impervious to my charms. However, she may be"—he winked at me—"a bit *sweet* on you, pardon the pun."

To my complete horror, my cheeks began burning to the degree in which I could feel actual heat emanating from them.

Ranger jeered, "It looks like her face is about to burst into flames!"

Baseball Cap rolled his eyes but otherwise made no indication that he'd heard the embarrassing comment.

Is it that obvious? I waited for the pagan god of pride to take pity on me and open up a hole in the floor to swallow me up. "Will that be all?"

"Will that be all, *sir*?" Ranger corrected before removing another one from the dwindling supply.

"Will that be all, *sir*," I ground out before spinning away.

"Oh, one more thing, Glasses . . ." Ranger's tone stiffened my back like a sharp pebble pelted it. "I like cherries . . . add one on top, will you?"

I nodded before continuing on to the kitchen, a defiant spring in my step. What Mr. Superior didn't know was that I actually had a Herculean memory. The notepad and pen were mere props, one of Ms. Norma's requirements for the wait staff, but I didn't really need it. After turning in their order and giving Carlos the heads-up on the rush job, I grabbed the pitcher of tea to refill their cups. I was going to prove what a model waitress I actually was. *Not that it matters what those two think*, I sniffed to myself. I was just going for the tip—I *deserved* that tip.

On my way back out, a familiar face popped up and comically grinned at me through the glass door. I mentally cringed. *Aw man! Not now.* Half-heartedly, I returned Mr. Tatum's smile and picked up the pace when I saw him start my way. Mr. Tatum was a "regular" and often made a nuisance of himself. Not only was he a shoddy tipper, but his unwanted attention was becoming a big problem.

As soon as I hit table, Ranger rattled his ice at me. "About time," he said. "I was running on empty, so that's gonna cost you." He waved a dollar at me, a grin splitting his face, which created two slight indentions in his cheeks that would've been immensely endearing on anybody else.

Did he, like, guzzle the whole thing down? I glanced at Baseball Cap's glass—still half full. I topped his off before refilling the guzzler with an eye-roll. *You know what?* This was just *so* not worth the six, seven bucks left, especially when you factored in splitting it with Bee.

"Did you just roll your eyes at me?" Ranger called me out. "That's gonna cost you two more dollars—one for each eye," he explained cheerily.

"Your order will be up in a minute," I bit out.

"You giving me attitude again, Glasses?"

Before I could respond, Baseball Cap slid out of the booth and stood, towering over me and my pitcher. He penetrated me with a look that caused my mouth to come unhinged. "Where's the restroom?" he inquired in a low voice.

I was so taken aback it took me a moment to find my voice. "Umm . . . right over there." I gestured vaguely to the back of the dining room, where the restrooms were clearly marked, then started to turn back to the taskmaster. But Baseball Cap body-blocked me, thereby moving me a little farther away from Ranger and his hostility.

"Excuse me," I said to his blue shirt. It was about the same color as Daddy's overalls but didn't seem to have the same fading effect on him or his hair, which was the same color as honey. I got a sudden, preposterous urge to lean in . . . and *smell* him.

"Can I get another lemon wedge for my tea?" he asked.

I tipped my head up to see if he was actually serious. "Ah—sure?"

"*Now.*" Baseball Cap left me with another meaningful look before heading off in the direction I pointed.

I just nodded after him while I watched him walk away in those khaki shorts. *Sheesh! Am I staring at his butt?* I patted my heated cheeks and headed to the kitchen for their order and *more* lemons. *What is with these guys and lemons?*

I could feel Ranger's eyes boring a hole into my back but focused my attention on his intriguing friend, pondering what he might have been trying to convey to me. But I couldn't ruminate long because their order was up. After grabbing the plates and the required lemons, I took a moment to arrange them on a cold plate. Then added a few more, just for good measure, and was making good time, until Mr. Tatum accosted me in the aisle with an aggressive hug.

"Katie!" he thundered, breathing all over the tray of food in my hand.

"Hi, Mr. Tatum." I gave him the stiff arm, sure there was some kind of food code violation going on. Undoubtedly, Ranger would dock me another couple of dollars. "Excuse me while I drop off their food. Then I'll be right with you," I dismissed.

He slid his flannel arm around my shoulders, arresting my escape. "Now how many times do I gotta tell ya to call me Frank?—Mr. Tatum's my daddy's name," he said, releasing me the same time I yanked away. The sudden, jerky movement upended the tray holding their food and artfully arranged lemons so that it all fell to the floor with a clatter and a fat splat.

Dag friggin'nabit!—I'd end up *owing* Ranger by the end of this.

"Oh, honey! Golly. I'm real sorry 'bout that." Clumsy hands reached to help.

Laughter (meant to convey what a pathetic loser I was) blasted from the granddaddy booth. I didn't even look, just let out an exasperated sigh. "Please wait for Ms. Norma to seat you, Mr. Tatum." My cold tone must've finally registered, because Mr. Tatum slunk off like a weasel.

Humiliation clung to me, along with a thin film of sweat that just broke out. I removed my glasses, swiped my hand across my chin, and bent down, awkwardly, in my skirt to pick up the mess. Was busy scooping handfuls of vomity-looking splatters when navy sneakers appeared in my line of vision. I actually had a wad of the stuff in my hands when the owners of the sneakers said, "Need a hand?"

Could I not just die now? Too embarrassed to actually look him in the eye, I concentrated on having a conversation with his shoes instead. They were ones I'd never seen before, and I realized they were identical to his cohort's.

"No thanks, I got it!" I said way more chipper than the situation required, then proceeded to scoop more goop. I was living proof that one *could not*, in fact, die from embarrassment.

Another cringe-worthy moment later, and my glasses dangled in front of me. "Looking for these?"

Since he was speaking directly to me, social graces dictated I had no choice but to meet his eyes, which were all lit up with humor to match his tone. "Thanks." I reached for them, realizing, too late, my hand was covered in gloppy gravy. The thermostat that was my face grew hotter. His lips twitched around a bit before he commandeered them.

Is he laughing at me again?

I hauled myself up, with as much dignity as I could muster under the circumstances, only to find Baseball Cap staring at me—intimately—as if we'd known each other for a long time. Instead of glaring, I found myself staring back.

"Waitress!" Ranger boomed, wrecking the magic moment for us.

We both blinked our eyes, but it was only me who stepped away. I was unsure how to proceed because Baseball Cap was still holding my glasses. "I, uh, need those," I informed him artlessly.

He stepped forward, closing the gap between us. Butterflies swirled around in my midsection. We were standing so close now we could've been slow dancing to the country song playing in the background. Long hands slowly lifting, he slid the glasses back over my eyes. My breath hitched in my throat. And as his gaze lingered over my face, a soft, fluttery movement of another kind was going on *outside* of my stomach this time.

I jumped back like I was bit. *Whoa*! *What was that?* The feeling of warmth spreading through me was too much somehow. Moisture amassed in my eyes. Baseball Cap took a step back from me now, like I was crazy. No doubt most girls wouldn't tear up at such a minor thing. Maybe I really *was* losing it? I should've allowed myself a good cry the other night, gotten it all out before it could bubble up at inappropriate times.

A hot guy touches you, and you fall apart. Great, Kate! Very cool.

After my fits of temper, dropping dinner on the floor, and now uncontrollable tears, he probably thought I needed to be fitted for a straightjacket. Actually, my sack-like uniform, cinched in by apron strings, *looked* a lot like a straightjacket. A giggle bubbled up in my throat.

Ranger yelled around a hand megaphone, "I'm not getting any younger over here!"

Somehow, I found the dumbest line in the book funny, so I laughed again. Hysterically. Baseball Cap looked bemused. Ranger bellowed again, and I rolled my eyes. Baseball Cap shocked me with a grin, but I came to when Ranger beckoned to me—a small movement made violent looking by the obvious effort it took to restrain himself.

Leaving me with a warning look, Baseball Cap went and slid back into his booth. Me and my mealy hands followed to see what the tyrant wanted. Unfortunately, another giggle threatened to escape despite my best attempt to stifle it. But the look Ranger seared me with caused the giggle to choke off like he'd reached across the table and squeezed my neck.

"We're ready to leave now," Baseball Cap informed me coldly, "so please bring the check when you come back."

Hot and cold—these two were mercurial quick in their moods.

"More than ready," Ranger seconded.

Stung, I did a reversal, skulking slowly back to my floor tray so I could eavesdrop on the dynamic duo. Ranger was grilling Baseball Cap about our "little mid-restaurant meet-and-greet." My ears strained, but I could still hear Baseball Cap laugh it off, saying he felt *sorry* for me. This was by far the most hurtful thing—like a butter knife to my gut.

Blinded by tears, I scurried back to the kitchen. It seemed the madder I got, the stronger my urge to cry. Made it hard to read the numbers because they were all blurring together. *Oh well.* What did it matter anyway? The whole dinner was comped, or more likely deducted from my paltry pay.

I was also suffering from a hollow emptiness in my stomach that couldn't be filled with food. It was a yearning for *something*. Like when I would go to the mall with Ashley-Leigh and see all the cool clothes I would never be able to afford. Look but don't touch. *What did I expect?* Baseball Cap was someone both out of my league and out of my town. We may as well have been from different planets.

I was also angry at myself for allowing them to get to me. Angry for the insecurities my station in life manifested in me. Angry that I cried in front of them. And mostly just angry, that for a few seconds, I thought I felt something amazing happen between Baseball Cap and me.

Pathetic! I ripped off the receipt and swiped at my tears. Here I thought Ranger was the ass. Turned out—*I* was the biggest ass of all! And that was completely intolerable to me. *Kate Connelly is nobody's fool!* I thought of one of Daddy's sayings: Fool me once, shame on you; fool me twice shame on me. I was a quick learner. Would *not* make that mistake again.

Ignoring Carlos's disapproving look, I blew my nose on a napkin, wiped my eyes, and dried my foggy glasses. I would not shed another tear for them. Armed with my reloaded tray, I inhaled a steadying breath and stalked back out there, no longer a mouse for the predators to play with. I had their check—and my emotions—in hand. At the table I avoided their eyes, staring instead at their shiny boy-toy in the parking lot.

Ranger *tsk-tsked* me. "Do I even need to explain this?" He ceremoniously removed all but one of the remaining bills on the table. "I thought you might be trainable, but clearly, even *I* can be wrong sometimes."

Wordlessly, I slid the appropriate plates to the appropriate jackasses and saw they were almost out of tea again. "I'll be right back with more tea and some fresh lemons."

"No need," said Baseball Cap. "We're leaving."

"Would you care for anything else?" I heard the catch in my voice and hoped they wouldn't.

"I don't know . . . What *else* you offering?" Ranger's eyebrow lifted devilishly.

"I brought you a receipt in case you need it for your records, but there's no charge for the meal," I said tonelessly.

I thought I saw Baseball Cap start to protest then change his mind. Whether it was to object about the bill or Ranger's inappropriate comment, I couldn't tell because words never formed on his lips.

"You not even going to say goodbye then, Glasses?" It was Ranger's question, but Baseball Cap leaned in imperceptibly, poised for something, some kind of reaction maybe, but I gave them nothing but professional courtesy.

"If that's it then, have a nice evenin'." I dropped the receipt on the table, noticing neither one touched a single bite of their meals. Probably thought that if the food didn't poison them here then *I* would. Grateful to finally be free of them, I turned to go when a human handcuff closed around my wrist.

"Did you think your lesson was over just because you failed?"

Ranger. I gave him stony silence.

"Looks like she's playing the silent game," he observed to Baseball Cap, who looked like he was tired of games. Or just tired. "Aren't you wondering about that last dollar?" More baiting, but I wasn't biting. "I see you're done with me, Glasses . . ."—he gripped my wrist tighter, preempting any attempt to pull away—"but what if I'm not done with *you* yet?"

Baseball Cap cupped two hands over his visor as if he were about to make a move but thought better of it at the last second. *Probably just wishful thinking on my part.* I stared out the same window as Baseball Cap now, wishing, like him, I was any other place.

"Well?" Ranger squeezed tighter in an attempt to make me bend to his will.

I gasped quietly, unwilling to give in. After a few more seconds of our impasse, I tried pulling away. Useless. He continued the iron shackle routine even with Ms. Norma staring at us, confused. An unconcerned Ranger gave her a jovial wave with his unoccupied hand. A throb pulsed inside my wrist, but I flatly refused to speak. Didn't even care if my hand withered up from lack of circulation and fell to the floor.

"You're just gonna quit on me then, huh?" He laughed sharply. "Didn't take you for a quitter, Glasses. But I guess I was wrong about you— again. You have absolutely zero potential."

I still refused to meet his eye.

"Pathetic!" Ranger flung my hand away and abruptly stood, threatening as a skyscraper in a sandbox. He scooped up the last remaining bill and slipped it into his back pocket. "I was going to leave a dollar—not that you deserve it, but I do like to give back . . . And you definitely strike me as a charity case," he sneered.

I tried hard not to flinch when he leaned over to whisper, "So here's your tip instead: Get yourself a tailor. Your ill-fitting uniform's gonna cost you more tips than you can make here."

With that parting shot, Ranger plucked the cherry from the ice cream and popped it into his mouth. Something about the way he looked at me made me catch my breath. But he didn't say anything more, just pushed passed me to leave. He started to bypass an oncoming, smiling Norma and changed his mind midstride.

"Thanks for the free meal," Ranger grinned. "It was e-Normas-ly kind of you." A follow up wink and he barreled through the door, the abused bell shrieking after him.

Ms. Norma got caught out in the aisle, turning two shades of pink and quivering with the eleventh-hour realization that she might've been had. She one-eightied, once again, and bustled away at the same time Baseball Cap took his stand. I took back full plates to pass the awkward moment. A cleared throat indicated some sort of apology was to take place.

"Save it," I said, halting him palm up. I stared at him through foggy glasses, with tear-stained cheeks, and grease-stained clothing, but with all the pride bred into me as a Connelly. "I don't want or need your pity."

Before he could say anything, I escaped and fled through the same swinging doors as Ms. Norma.

4

DON'T BITE THE HAND THAT FEEDS YOU

Shoulders slumped and sniffling, I sped home with a tinfoil-covered dish full of Norma's meatloaf for the boys rolling around the back— her idea of an apology. I wondered if actually feeding it to them could be considered child abuse. I feared I was failing them and sniffed again, letting it all out before facing my father. Daddy would have zero sympathy for me crying over a couple of guys hassling me. This would only conjure another lecture. And I didn't think I could take another lecture tonight. Plus, he didn't really want me working outside the home, even though the money sure was useful. I'd barely talked him into letting me work there weekends so didn't want to give him an excuse to make me quit.

I auto-drove down the packed dirt road, stopping at our mailbox, which was cemented into a bald tire by the side of the road. This was the only marker that let people know where we lived. You couldn't see our house from the road, not just because it was a long, low thing, but also because it was too far away. You'd have to drive past the Keep Out! sign nailed to the fence post and follow the tractor tracks two miles, snaking your way through rotting pasture to find it.

I remembered riding my bike determinedly down that bumpy road to retrieve our mail, Blue following closely at my heels as a frisky puppy. A happier time for our family, to be sure.

I sniffed again, noticing I was too stopped up to really appreciate the aroma wafting over from the backseat—a bright light in an otherwise dark night. I quickly sorted through the junk mail, bills, and requisite weekly church bulletin to what I was saving for last. When my fingers registered what it was, my heart sank at once. I glared at the thick, expensive envelope embossed with a roaring lion symbol.

Another one. Can't these people take a hint?

A flicker of anger at Andrew's well-meaning teachers flared in my chest. For once, Daddy was completely justified in the raucous he threw at the school when he found out. "Busy bodies that had no business interfering," Daddy had said, and I agreed. Last year they had sent some of his creative writing samples and standardized test scores to a few exalted boarding schools without our knowledge. Each had accepted him promptly. All were firmly and impolitely rejected by Daddy, who was furious at the intimation that Andrew would be better off at a boarding school than home with us. Andrew was his pride and joy; there was no way he was going to part with him. And he promised Mama he would never send any of us away to special schools, which sounded plain crazy at the time.

Where would we possibly go?

I guess she had more than an inkling of his academic giftedness early on. Actually, we were all pretty good at school stuff (I filed the understatement under inbred modesty). Andrew just happened to be exceptional . . . at everything, really. *Is that why she yanked him out of kindergarten overnight?* That made a lot of sense, because overprotectiveness was the one parenting ideal both my parents could get behind.

I pondered our family situation further as I bumped my way to our house, slowing to a crawl over the more serious potholes. I guess it was a big deal to be so sought after that schools were willing to throw in free room-and-board, in addition to tuition. That was just it though—it was *too* generous. I mean I knew Drewy was gifted, but surely there were plenty of other academically-abled-fish-in-the-sea who were more willing to bite? Well no matter mind, this elite academy would eventually give up when they continued to get no response from us. *Maybe I should just tell them we already accepted another offer?*

Lying was never a good option for me though. I was terrible at it and made all the rooky mistakes: stuttering, looking away, adding random, unnecessary details to avoid actually having to say the lie out right. Mama always busted me right away the few times I tried to get away with deceiving her. She told me to scratch attorney or spy off my list of future occupations.

A picture of her flashed unbidden in my mind. I usually tried to repress the memories because they were still too painful to think about. Since I'd already broken down a few times tonight, I figured one more time would just be an encore. Closing my eyes, I allowed myself to really see her, as she was when she was healthy, smiling at me like I was the best thing she'd seen all day. She was half Cherokee and beautiful in a way that was unique—like an exotic flower blooming amongst a bed of drooping roses.

I remembered how proud I was that she was my mother, how everyone seemed to be especially nice to her. She was light personified. Love radiated from her like heat from a flickering fireplace on a cold day. That feeling a child has, and takes for granted, of being cared for vanished right along with her. Her light snuffed out forever. Ashes all that was left. I shivered as the lonely feeling I'd grown accustomed to permeated my whole being.

I cut off the overheated engine and sat for a while in the dark, listening to the engine tick down. The buzzing insects in my ear were a comfort, almost like friends, or at least friends' watered-down cousins—acquaintances. Blue's shrill bark echoed in the dark, welcoming me home and alerting Daddy to my arrival.

I'd better hurry then. My meager earnings needed to be counted before I entered the house. You see, Daddy always wanted to "borrey" a few bucks from me when I got home. Mostly I didn't mind because if it was a Sunday, he'd up and run off, leaving us kids in peace for a while usually with a litany of extra chores to keep us occupied and "out of trouble." While he was on sabbatical, we'd skim our way through the work and enjoy a little extra TV. When Daddy came home, he'd slyly feel the "idiot-box" for warmth. But we stayed two steps ahead of him by setting an ice tray on top of the TV while we were watching it. When he drove up, we'd put it back in the freezer and change the channel back.

And I didn't feel more than just a twinge of guilt for deceiving him, because it was something we learned from Mama . . . and she was the best person in the world. A smile curved my lips as I thought of all the ways she helped us get one over on Daddy. She knew he wasn't the easiest person to live with, and managed him, much like our money problems and fledgling ranch. I suspected she always felt guilty about the way we lived so smothered us in compensation love.

I dumped the heavy contents of my apron onto my lap—heavy was a bad sign for a waitress. Generally I made one to two dollars off of every table (no matter what the bill said), and one of the two dollars was usually left in change. Folks here thought that was a good tip and felt really good leaving it, walking away smiling benevolently at me like they'd just made my day. Truckers were usually a little better. And you could tell when they got paid, because you might even find yourself with a fiver in your hands (usually folded carefully with a phone number).

I quickly tallied tonight's haul: one five, fourteen ones, twelve quarters, five dimes, and two nickels. I breathed in deeply through my nose, inhaling all the way down into my diaphragm. Not enough. After Daddy's "tip-out" and buying necessary groceries, I wouldn't have anything left over at all to go towards new school clothes. I thought remorsefully of the ten bucks I'd let slip through my fingers tonight. *How could I have been so stupid?* Tears pricked my eyes again, but I couldn't succumb to them now; I had to get inside.

Grabbing my apron, I was fixing to cram all the contents back in when I felt some kind of lump stuck inside. *Huh?* Probably just an old wadded up receipt or someone's business card I politely tucked into my apron and forgot to discard later. I haphazardly dug it out, feeling a definite shape to it. Intrigued, I turned on the interior light and opened my palm to reveal an origami heart-shaped bill.

That's a new one. After running through the night's customers in my mind, I came up blank. I couldn't remember anyone leaving that on the table. The only one I thought it could possibly be was Mr. Tatum, although I doubted he was capable of folding a dollar bill into such an intricate work of art.

And how did it get into my apron?

A diagonal flash of yellow infiltrated the darkness—Daddy pulling the curtain back, a clear signal. I stuffed the origami heart into the bottom of my bag, along with two more dollars I didn't think he'd miss to add to my puny stockpile. I would claim it was a slow night, which was true enough every night for Norma's. After slamming my shoulder against the door, I grabbed the steaming dish from the back, holding it away from my face as I trudged into the house to face Daddy. *Like my night hadn't been bad enough.*

Jumping for joy, yelping, and announcers talking sports like it was world-changing news greeted me with the standard cacophony of welcome-home noise. "Hi, Daddy," I greeted, dropping my bag to receive enthusiastic licks from Blue. *At least someone's happy to see me.*

Daddy acknowledged my presence with a vague grunting noise.

"Did the boys get down alright?" I tried again.

A few seconds of popcorn crunching ensued. "I'd say so," he replied laconically, clearly too immersed in baseball highlights to bother turning around.

"Okay, great. Thanks." *What am I thanking him for? Answering me?*

I paused to see if I could just go on to bed. I was whipped and ready to settle in for the night so I could commence to licking my wounds. All I could hear were the sounds of a double play recap. Couldn't believe I got off that easy.

I cleared my throat. "I'm really tired so . . . think I'm just gonna call it a night." I began tiptoeing away, lamely holding my breath.

"Katie," Daddy's gruff voice halted my progress, "them dishes need to be done before you head in."

Of course. That was one of the conditions to my employment outside the home: that it wouldn't interfere with my chores. God forbid he should lift a finger to do "women's work" while I was slaving away to help put food on the table.

"Okay, Daddy. I was goin' in there anyway to put this meatloaf in the fridge." I held my breath again.

"*Whatdidyasay?*" Daddy rubbernecked out of his comfort zone, missing a great catch by a burly fan in the stands wearing head-to-toe red. I watched long enough to see him hand it over to his mini-me kid and then hold *her* up for the cameras like she was the real prize.

I cleared my throat again; this time a frog was jammed in there. "I said that Ms. Norma pressed leftover meatloaf into everyone's hands tonight."

"She gave it to *everyone?*" he emphasized.

"Yes, sir, we were all accosted on the way out on account of it bein' a real slow night."

His eyes narrowed. "How slow?"

Charity meatloaf forgotten.

"Real." Daddy's face began to contort, so I hurriedly explained, "Ms. Norma says it's on account of folks not spendin' money goin' out to eat because school's comin' up and they have to pay for new school supplies and clothes and what not."

Daddy *harrumphed.* "Don't know why people pay all that money for supplies. I thought we attended public school, and that's what all them tax dollars we pay out is for."

A silence stretched out. I decided I'd better agree with him, because once he got started, he'd go all night before dropping the mike. "Yes, sir," I said, shrugging my bag back on and headed to the kitchen with my re-loaded apron.

Daddy trailed behind me. "You still manage to make anything?"

Opening the fridge, I hid my face inside with the meatloaf. "Um," I hesitated. If I said no, then he was going to point out that my time would be better spent at home working. On the other hand, if I said yes, then he would help himself to the lion's share of my earnings. *Lose-lose.* "About fair," I came up with.

Daddy shuffled forward to add his glass and bowl to my burgeoning load. While I ran water over the dried-on glue that was their former dinner, he hovered over me, humming under his breath. I tried willing him away, but he only hesitated briefly before proceeding on with what we both knew he was going to do.

He coughed into his hand. "Well Katie, since you had a good night tonight, I think I'll just borrey a few bucks to tide us over till my check comes in."

How did my night suddenly go from fair to good? There was an awkward pause while I inwardly seethed, and Daddy waited for me to capitulate gracefully.

"I haven't had time to go to the bank," he added, which wasn't true because he was in town just this morning, picking up feed from Tillman Mills. He managed to stay gone all day, not that I was complaining.

"Okay, Daddy." I tried keeping my voice steady. "You know that any money I earn goes towards helping the family."

That seemed to perk him up some. "Yer right . . . we are a family, and what's yours is mine."

So clearly missed the point. He plucked up my apron and dumped it out on the table. My back stiffened as he sifted through looking for the bigger bills. He seemed to tally up pretty quickly, even turning my apron upside down and shaking it.

"That it?" he demanded.

I squirted a long stream of dishwashing liquid over the dishes, biding for time. I was hoping this was a rhetorical question.

"Is this all you made tonight, Katherine?"

"Um," I hedged again, "I also made my hourly wage of two-thirteen."

"Yer meanin' to tell me you was gone from 3:30 this afternoon till 11:00 tonight and all you made—after Uncle Sam takes his share—is a measly *twenty bucks!*"

"Uhhh . . . more, less." I swallowed.

Daddy's face contorted around a bit before settling into a sneer this time.

"Remember, it was a real slow night tonight," I interjected quickly. "Ms. Norma said it's gonna pick up again after school starts."

He looked at me for a couple of seconds, I guess weighing the worth of the few dollars he pilfered with the smug satisfaction of being right about my employment being a waste of time.

I pressed on during the pause: "I could look for a better job, but you said I could only work Friday and Saturday nights and Sunday afternoons on account of my chores at home and worship."

"If yer dumb enough to waste your time waitressin' for a few dollars down at that crummy café, then I guess that's up to you," he said, while simultaneously slipping the bills into his back pocket.

I flashbacked to earlier when another domineering male did the exact same thing (only that one was much better looking). And I was core hurt. Here I was wasting my glory days slaving away to help our little family survive, and I was being chastised for it. I clamped my jaw shut. No way was I gonna get sucked into a pointless argument with my father. I would never win, and as he liked to point out on numerous occasions: he was the head of the house. I was supposed to just suck it up and fall into line like a good girl. My hands began furiously scrubbing dishes.

"Goodnight, Katie-girl." Daddy's voice softened a bit. "Get some rest . . . we got church in the mornin'," he added unnecessarily. I knew the drill.

After finishing the dishes, I made for the door with my dwindled earningsand paused. Even though I was beat-down tired, the answering machine's light caught my attention. It was blinking at me. Relentlessly.

Blink. Blink. Blink . . .

I was so tired and already mentally checked out. *So why am I so drawn to it?*

Blink. Blink. Blink . . .

It could wait. I would just check it tomorrow then. I shuffled on past and turned out the light, saw red blinking at me in the dark. Like a siren. It continued to gnaw away at me like I was going OCD or something—I couldn't *not* listen to it. *Arg!* Dumping my bag on the counter, I lowered the volume and pressed play. The automated voice communicated that we had one saved message, then a sharp *Beep!* and a cheerful voice began speaking like there was a contest for brisk professionalism:

Hello, Mr. Connelly! This is Emma Mathers calling again from the International Elite Academy. We wanted to formally welcome your family to our mentoring program and thank you for giving us the opportunity to work with your son, Andrew. As per our agreement, an elite cadet will meet with him after school every day beginning Monday, August 29.

My heart stopped, but the bad news didn't wait for it to restart before continuing.

. . . A copy of the contract should be forthcoming in the mail. Please sign the highlighted areas and return it in the return envelope— no postage necessary—at your earliest convenience. Should you have any questions regarding the program, please don't hesitate in calling the office. We will be happy to assist you anytime. Thank you and have a very pleasant evening.

What's going on? My ears began a dull buzz. I leaned over and gripped the counter. I thought Daddy was dead set against any of the schools that were after Drewy. *After* being the right word here. *What had happened to change that and when?*

I was seeing red (not the blinking kind). Instinctively, I dove into the bottom of my bag for the glossy, embossed envelope. I wasn't even gonna wait to recycle it now. I was gonna heave it right in the middle of the trash heap to burn! Something was *off* with this organization. I could just *feel* it, right down in my bones.

Like a deflating balloon, all my angry energy seemed to be leaching from me. I slumped against the wall and slithered into a heap of misery on our linoleum floor. *Maybe I'm overreacting?* I mean she didn't say Andrew was going away anywhere, only that someone from *them* was coming here—an elite cadet. But I'd never heard of a mentoring program for a boarding school. Why would an elite private institution dip its beak into public school that way? If they were that interested in Andrew, wouldn't they just request for him to be tested and interviewed there?

Blue's nudges roused me out of my stupor long enough to get me moving. Even though I smelled like a basket of tater-tots, I didn't have enough energy for a shower, so I splashed some water on my face and brushed my teeth, noticing in the harsh bathroom light just how splotchy my face was and how red my eyes were. *How had Daddy missed that?* And then I realized with a jolt—he hadn't. He just hadn't bothered asking me what was wrong.

How many ways could a person be hurt in one night? Is the ceiling going to cave in on me next?

A sob escaped me. Blue gave an anxious whine. "It's okay, Bluesy," I assured him with a hug. "We won't let anyone take Drewy from us."

I also noticed how enlarged my pupils looked tonight. Like huge, black saucers in my eye sockets, making me look positively bewitched. I usually tried to avoid taking photos because, inevitably, I always had the devil red-eye . . . when nobody else did. I had to agree with Andrew—I did look kinda spooky. Especially after a good cry. I didn't mind though. That part of my eye was from my mother; the color was from my father.

Only one Connelly child inherited Mama's warm, hazel eyes . . . and Mikey, too, suffered from a bad case of the red-eye.

I thought with satisfaction about the other bits and pieces of her I had inherited, like the angle of my cheekbones and my thick chestnut hair. My skin was a shade darker than my Irish father's, but unfortunately, I still inherited his furious blush.

After throwing my scratchy uniform over the shower to air out the cloying diner smell, I pulled on Mama's favorite T-shirt, the one with a leafy tree and the word hugger written beneath it. It was getting really late (or early, depending on how you wanted to look at it), so I turned off the light and on the tulip lamp I'd inherited from Ashley-Leigh, then went and stuffed a towel under the door. Just in case.

My feet dragged back to bed, but instead of falling into it, I kneeled down to withdraw my stash-of-cash from where it was hibernating under there (hoping to grow fat) with some of Andrew's brilliant stories and Mikey's extravagantly macaronied art. After fishing around in my bag for tonight's catch, I hauled it out for inspection. The light cast its pink glow on the origami-heart in my palm. I dropped it onto my bed, along with the other bills I'd pilfered from myself, and the envelope that was starting to burn my hand.

Guilt and relief dueled it out for dominance over me as I stared at the hefty envelope, bearing my father's name. It was long embedded in me to do the right thing. But that was just it though—it felt like hiding it *was* the right thing to do. Already it was a hated, sinister thing, and I knew I didn't want it under my bed, tainting the serenity of my bedroom. So, like a thief in the night, I crept back into the kitchen and stuffed it in the flour jar for safekeeping. I exhaled deeply, instantly feeling better with it sealed up like a neurotoxin.

I tumbled back into bed, but before turning out the light, I wanted to add my three bucks to the seventy-two I had saved for school stuff. I hated to undo the origami heart because it was so beautifully done, but I didn't want it to get lost. Plus . . . it might be a fiver. Before I changed my mind, I lifted the little flap, tucked into the single fold holding it all together, and began methodically unfolding the work of art. After straightening it out, I noticed the face of the president was different from the other bills. My breath caught. The man on this bill wasn't a president at all—it was none other than Benjamin Franklin!

A Benjamin? Holy Cow! A real honest-to-God Benjamin! My mind raced, believing and disbelieving in equal measure. *Could this be real? A hundred dollar tip?* I'd heard stories before but had never met anyone who actually received one. It certainly looked authentic enough, not that I was an expert, but Ms. Norma made me learn how to spot counterfeits my first day on the job. With shaking hands, I fingered it again, feeling the tiny ridges running throughout. It felt just like a regular bill. God knows I received enough of those to know the texture well enough by now. *Hmmm.* The details seemed to all be there. It felt right and looked right. My gut was telling me it was the real deal.

So now that I concluded it was authentic: *Who was it from?*

I quickly dismissed Mr. Tatum and Ms. Norma as being way too cheap. Scanning my mind back through the night's events, it only took about two seconds for the a-hah! moment to hit. And when it did, it was like a swift—but soft—punch to the gut. An excruciatingly beautiful face filled my mind. I recalled, with perfect clarity, the fluttering feeling I felt around my stomach that had me recoiling at the time. I'd barely registered what he was doing because I was so engrossed in staring at him.

Holy Smokes! Baseball Cap is my freakin' fairy godmother?

5

GIRLS' NIGHT

The week following my encounter with the haughty-hot guys, as I'd dubbed them, went by in a blur of chores, church, and chastising Daddy about that Elite Academy Mentoring Program that he went ahead and signed Andrew up for.

As I banged around the kitchen getting dinner ready, I went over how I could've handled the situation better. I'd gone off on Daddy the next day without thinking, with the end result being—I had extra chores all week. Fits of temper never seemed to work with him, yet Mama always seemed to get her way. My ears warmed as I conjured up scenarios of how she might have managed that.

So far Daddy was firm in his belief that a little military training and male bonding would do Andrew some good. Plus, the elite part seemed to gratify his manly pride, and the truth of the matter was: he really didn't want to put forth the time and effort to raise sons properly so was using this "opportunity" as a get-out-of-jail-free card for his paternal duties.

I was disgusted yet felt helpless to do anything about it at the moment. So I was busy taking my frustrations out on the cutting board, dicing up onions like a ninja to add to the hamburger meat browning in the pan. It was taco night at the Connelly house, so I was happy to skip out on dinner. We took our own cows to the meat locker to be butchered, which pretty much made me a vegetarian since I'd raised them up from baby calves.

I was looking forward to a little break from Norma's but somehow found myself dreading my girls' night excursion. Probably because of all the awkward questions I would surely get from Ashley-Leigh's mom: *How are you doing? Why don't we ever see you anymore?*

The splat of dirty feet on newly waxed floors was quickly followed by Mikey's sweet face poking under my arm. "Kadee, can I hewlp do the cheese?"

Even though he would make more of a mess for me to clean up, I obliged, as I always did with Mikey, setting the cheese grater and a plate on the counter for him. "Wash your hands first," I said, privy to all the ick-worthy items I routinely dumped from his pockets.

"But I alweady washed when I came in!"

"Do it again, cause if you're gonna be my sous chef, you gotta do more than just give the germs a bath."

He grumbled but began scraping the stepstool over to the sink to wash his hands, spraying water and dripping suds on the floor in the process.

Andrew strolled in blithely crunching an apple. "The best way to kill germs is to wash in warm, soapy water for thirty seconds," he informed us.

"I can count to thuwty," Mikey retorted over his shoulder and began loudly proving himself. "One Mississippi, two Mississippi . . ."

"Yeah, but can you do it in Spanish?"

"Hey," I greeted Andrew while trying to snatch the apple from him. He laughed at my failed attempt, taking a last bite before tossing it into the sink, where it landed with a *ker-plop* in the bowl I had soaking.

"Hey!" protested Mikey, good-naturedly mopping water from his face.

"Okay, Stef Curry, that's enough three pointers. Go wash up for dinner. You two boys are on your own tonight, so *please* be on your best behavior. *Comprende?*"

"Yeah right," Andrew smirked. "When the Katie-kat's away, the mice will play!"

"Seriously, Drews," I warned. "Daddy's already on the warpath, and you know how he gets." I tipped my head toward Mikey, who was still working through his Mississippis.

"Yeah, but he's not mad at *me*."

"Yeah," I grabbed his shoulders to whisper in his ear, "but you know how he gets with Mikey." Mikey had just turned off the faucet and was drying his freshly cleaned hands on a dirty dishtowel. I ignored the health code violation to stare into Andrew's wide blue eyes.

"*Comprende*, alright? Sheesh!" Andrew shrugged out of my grasp and leapt onto the counter, landing firmly on his backside . . . without using hands. The boy was spry. He proceeded to snatch the wiggling strings of cheese as fast as Mikey could grate it.

"Hey! You stop that, Drewy!" Mikey vainly swatted his starfish hand at the quick pincers stealing his hard work.

"Okay boys, enough," I intervened. I needed to get going or I'd be late for sure. "Drews, fill your glasses with the *fresh* lemonade from the fridge." Both boys perked up instantly. I usually made it from a mix but I'd been squeezing lemons and boiling sugar all week, just like Mama used to do.

"Yeah!" The boys celebrated with a high-five, causing fragments of yellow cheese to squish out between clasped hands. Peals of laughter, like merry bells, flooded our shabby little kitchen. I smiled with deep satisfaction, a case of the warm-fuzzies enveloping me. I knew this is what Mama wanted for us, and I wished she could see us like this—happy, healthy, together.

Andrew sunk another sink-goal with the grater while I swung Mikey down, whirling him around in a circle to prolong his infectious giggles. "Okay short stuff, set the table."

"What are you gonna do, Kadee?"

"What am *I* gonna do?" I repeated incredulously. "I'm gonna shower, get dressed up, and go out for a well-deserved night on the town and leave you two monsters to your vittles . . . that's what *I'm* gonna do!"

Mikey wrinkled his nose. "Is viddles wittle veg'tables?"

Andrew interrupted my explanation to say, "Who do ya think's a better shooter? Me or Steph Curry?"

"Scoot!" I pushed Andrew away and patted Mikey on the backside. "Your tacos are gettin' cold." With a fading smile, I padded to the bathroom and hopped in the shower with a determination burning up inside me to protect my little brothers at all costs. It was my responsibility to pick up where Mama left off . . . and her last request before she died.

I would not let her down.

A few minutes later, I was out of the shower debating the most important question of the day: What to wear? *Hmmm.* That was a toughy. I desperately eyed the few new items I'd bought with my waitressing money. A pang reminded me of where most of that money had come from.

Usually, I just threw on one of my bell-skirts and button-downs and headed out the door, too preoccupied by other matters to worry much about my appearance. But tonight was a rare night off from my life; a night to head out to the hippest restaurant Clovis had to offer. It was also a night I would be scoped out by the "cool crowd" when I walked in with Queen-B Ashley-Leigh.

So I didn't want to just blend into the background like I usually did. Not sure why. Vanity? Or maybe it was that hardest of deadly sins for me to overcome—pride? *Nah.* I chalked it up to the innate predisposition of a female to want to dress up and look pretty. Whatever. I was in the mood to look cute so I put on the butter-yellow tank top I'd bought at an end-of-summer sale, and slipped on the long brown prairie skirt I usually reserved for church. My classic cowboy boots (which were requisite on our snake-infested ranch) and one of Mama's turquoise belts completed the outfit. I'd have to conceal my tank with a button-down while I was still home. No way Daddy would let me walk around in nothing but a tank top. Females are supposed to be modest, don'tja know. I mentally rolled my eyes.

After blowing out my hair and adding a dash of vanilla lip balm, I stepped to the closet door for a final look-see before heading out. I smiled my serene closed-mouth smile and twirled from side to side, liking the way the yellow complimented my warm skin tone. And even though my hair was still streaked with brass and lacked style, it was healthy and shiny. *The best I can do.* I quickly buttoned the overshirt up to my cross, grabbed one of Mama's smaller woven bags, and stuffed my wallet, keys, hairbrush, and lip balm inside.

I took a deep breath. Ready. Set. Go . . .

Walking jauntily into the living room, my momentum was immediately squashed when I realized Daddy wasn't home yet. The boys, still glued to the TV, clued me in.

"So . . . how do I look?" I fished.

Mikey looked up to inspect me critically. "You look pwetty, Kadee!"

"Why thank you, kind sir."

Andrew spared a sidelong glance. "Look fine to me."

"You damn me with faint praise, sir."

"Shakespeare?" wondered Andrew, like he was constantly on a quiz show.

"*Ommmbers!* You said a bad word, Kadee!" Mikey scolded.

I sighed dramatically and slumped onto the couch to wait. Definitely needed a night off. *Where is Daddy?* Of course he would be late the one night I go out to celebrate my birthday. What could I do? I would just have to wait. Waity-Katie, that should be my nickname. I was always waiting on something: on tables, my brothers to hurry up, to turn eighteen, or just plain waiting for something *good* to happen in my life for a change.

Ugh! I punched a pillow. Twenty long minutes and a phone call later (to inform Ashley-Leigh I would be late), and Daddy finally arrived to relieve me.

"Be home at eleven," he ordered, no apology attached.

After kissing the tops of the boys' heads and reminding them to brush their teeth, I ran out the door. *Finally, a free woman!* I started up the car—put it and my mind in reverse—rolled down the window, and headed out, bumping along the dirt road enjoying the wind in my hair. I noted that the dust in my mouth didn't taste quite so bad when it was mixed in with a little freedom.

Speeding down the highway, I admired the late summer sunset. The sun was just beginning to meld together its yellows, pinks, and oranges with the wide expanse of blue sky, creating a kaleidoscope of colors more breathtaking than any painting I'd seen. Eastern New Mexico truly had the most beautiful skies around, and it more than helped make up for any deficits in the landscape, I thought loyally.

I found myself really looking forward to tonight for the first time—especially to the company of Mrs. Montgomery. I missed having a mother figure in my life, no matter how shadowy in comparison. I turned on the radio to the local pop station and sang along heartily to Taylor Swift's latest song. In no time, me and my Subaru pulled into Colonial Parkway, the homes that lined the country club.

After shutting off the sputtering engine, I hastily pulled off my over-shirt and re-brushed my tangled hair. Didn't really have time to mentally prepare, because Mrs. M was already bustling down the sidewalk. So I rammed my shoulder against the door, exiting my car with about as much grace as an escaping convict busting out of jail.

"Hallooooo!" Mrs. M came at me, arms flapping and high-heels clacking, a broad smile showing off capped teeth. It was clearly evident where Ashley-Leigh received her bounty from I noted with good grace—Mrs. M was literally busting out of her summer top.

"Hello, Mrs. Montgomery. It's nice to see—"

"Kate Connelly, as I live and breathe!" she gushed, enveloping me in a big, perfumed hug. "What in the wide world have you been doin' with yourself?"

I shrugged my shoulders, managing to formally say, "Thank you so much for invitin' me tonight."

She swept me out before her to really get a good gander at me. "Oh, Katie! You're so grown up all of a sudden . . . and even more beautiful than ever," she declared, then clucked at me and squeezed my hand. "But you're working too hard. I can tell. It's a good thing we called an emergency intervention."

I smiled at this before she was off again, and the next thing I knew, I was standing in her tiled foyer where an equally enthusiastic Ashley-Leigh came bounding down the mahogany staircase to greet me.

"Katie!"

"Hey, Ash," I greeted, warming a little from being hit with such a warm welcome. Their mood was infectious as a sneeze, and I found myself wondering what exactly I'd been dreading about tonight. I was also struck with a weird sense of déjà vu, recalling when I was a little girl how much I coveted her two-story brick home with its long, sweeping staircase to bound down.

Some things never change.

"Katie Connelly, where have you been hidin' all summer?" She almost repeated verbatim her mom's declaration (though I suspected hers was said mostly for the benefit of the one standing in the doorway beaming at us).

"Oh, you know . . . loungin' round the pool gettin' my nails done in between sips of mai-tais . . . basically livin' the dream," I replied airily. No need to lay it all out for them and be the Debbie Downer.

Ashley-Leigh giggled appreciatively and embraced me in another familiar, perfumed hug. "Katie, I've really missed you!" This declaration had a distinct ring of sincerity to it, and I suddenly felt gratified to be here—among the happy normal.

"Yeah, me too." I smiled, really meaning it. We used to be so close before the catastrophe-that-was-my-life struck, leaving a steep chasm between our two worlds.

There was an awkward pause where we surreptitiously checked each other out as all girls do. She was artfully done up, wearing a coral-colored, sleeveless shirt half-tucked into the front of her short-shorts, and chunky heels that brought her up to about my height. An assortment of silver bangles, that tinkled merrily when she fluttered about, completed the outfit. She was the epitome of a cool girl. Pity entered her eyes as she took in what she considered to be my poor choice of outfit. I tried hard not to feel blah standing next to her in my brown skirt.

She broke the ice again. "Okay, birthday girl, come on in. We've got a little somethin' for ya, and I've just been dyin' to give it to you all day!"

I allowed her to tug me into the beige-on-cream living room decorated gaily with Barbie-pink balloons. A store-bought birthday cake, with a number seventeen crushed in the middle, was next to a glossy bag with ribbons curling out like permed hair.

"Happy Birthday, Katie!" They chorused together. I colored, uncomfortable being the center of attention, no matter how small the occasion.

"Thank you," I simply said, blinking back tears. I really was touched. Birthdays were left up to me now. So tomorrow I would cook my own dinner and bake my own birthday cake. A jelly jar with wild flowers the boys picked for me would likely be the only gift I would receive.

"My dear, you are more than welcome," said Mrs. M, handing me a crystal flute filled with what I hoped was sparkling cider.

"Oooh! Champs! Thanks, Mom—you're the best!" Ashley-Leigh turned to me glass up while Mrs. M filled her own glass from a bottle that read *Moet & Chandon*. Okay then . . . *not* sparkling cider.

Even though I knew my father would have a cow (ha-ha), I shrugged my shoulders. *Why not? . . . When in Rome.* A pang shot through me when I recalled the last time I'd last heard that phrase. *Gah!* Why couldn't I just forget them? This was my birthday celebration, and I was bound and determined to enjoy myself, dang it! I would not dwell on a single encounter with a couple of stuck-up jerks I would never see again.

My reluctance toward the champagne had a sudden reversal, so I raised my glass and took a tentative sip. The bubbles tickled the back of my throat going down. *So this is how the other half lives?* I felt a smile playing on my lips as I watched Ashley-Leigh (who'd already downed half hers) refuel with a wink while her mom fussed with the cake.

"Okay . . ." Mrs. M dramatically cleared her throat before raising her glass. "Here's to the *other* Lee in my life, my Katie Lee . . . I only wish your mother was here to celebrate with us," she said, tearing up a bit. I wiped a tear from my own eye, trying to hold it together.

"Mooom!" Ashley-Leigh groaned. "It's s'posed to be a celebration!"

"I'm sorry. You're right, honey." She faced me again, reclearing her throat. "Happy Sweet Seventeen!"

"I think that's sweet sixteen, duh," Ashley-Leigh corrected.

"Not when it pertains to Katie." Mrs. M smiled while I dipped my head. "May you always be as young and beautiful as you are today!" My cheeks were still burning when she finished, "And may you never get crow's feet . . . at least before you bag yourself a rich husband!"

"Yeah! Happy Birthday, baby!" Ashley-Leigh clinked her glass with mine, sloshing out golden fizz all over the coffee table. I immediately mopped it up with my napkin before it dripped onto their new carpet.

"Oopsie!" Ashley-Leigh giggled. "Come on! Let's get you ready!"

I didn't let up from my cleaning detail, so she yanked on my arm. "Just leave it . . . Mom will get it. Let's go try on your new outfit!"

"Yes, yes. You two girls go on. I'll clean this up in a jiffy." Mrs. M clacked back in wearing neon-yellow gloves over her white-tipped nails. "Go on, Katie. Ashley-Leigh's been waitin' all day for this."

I still felt unsure but obediently relinquished my soggy napkin before following Ashley-Leigh up the stairs and into her very spacious, very decorated room. It came complete with a custom window seat for reading I'd also coveted since I was a little girl.

"Heeeey!" Ashley-Lee whirled around, triumphantly wielding the champagne bottle she'd nicked from downstairs. Like her mom wouldn't notice. "Happy Birthday, BFF!" She tried refueling me, but I put a hand over my glass, noticing my nails were all different kinds of short. "Suit yourself—more for me," she sniffed.

It seemed I'd already managed to put a little dent in our happy reunion. It wasn't that I was a goody two-shoes; it was that I simply didn't dare be irresponsible. Driving was a crucial function for me, so I couldn't afford a DWI—in more ways than one.

After a couple of moments of silence and finger taps on her phone, music danced into the room from a box as remarkably small as it was cute. *Cool.* As usual, everything in her room was cool. I wandered over to the bulletin board and was unsurprised to find our old pictures gone and replaced with clumps of smiling new friends engaged in various stages of teenage debauchery Her calendar was equally full, bleeding pink ink with her busy social and cheerleading schedule. Any leftover space was wallpapered with posters of boy bands and sultry men ripped from magazine cologne ads.

She noticed my quiet study, and our eyes locked. A guilty look fled from her face before she chirped brightly, "My favorite picture of us is right here, see?" She pointed toward an old picture of us doing the spider on her swing set. It was still clinging there, half covered by a poster of an underwear model with a suspicious-looking bulge.

Ah—that pretty much exactly covered the status of our friendship.

"Okay!" she trilled, providing an accompanying drum roll. Leave it to Ashley not to allow the awkward silence to linger. "Open it!" She tossed the candy-colored bag into my arms, and I hugged it to me for a moment. A lot of my father's distaste for charity had rubbed off on me. "Go ahead . . . dig in!"

I was actually curious despite myself, although was sure whatever it was would be inappropriate and therefore render itself completely useless in the padding of my thin wardrobe. But I hated to disappoint them when they went to so much trouble for me, so I would try to be a good sport. Puffing out some air, I burrowed inside to find the hidden treasure, my face, I was sure, nearly as neon as the bag. What I pulled out was scarcely enough material to make up half an outfit.

"Do you *like* it?" I could tell Ashley-Leigh's excitement quotient was about ten times greater than mine.

"Um, yeah. Thanks." Her face dropped, so I added, "A lot. It's *really* cool. Thanks again, Ash!" I hugged her and started to place the shorts and the frothy pink thing back.

"Whad'yathink you're doin'?"

"Puttin' them back in the bag for safe keepin'."

"Oh, no you don't!" She snatched them from my hands. "These are for wearin,' not for waitin', so put 'em on, or you're *not* walkin' out that door tonight!"

Holy crap. She actually expected me to *wear* that (and I was being generous here) *outfit* tonight. In *public*? Daddy would skin me alive! I was beginning a protest when she found my weak chink: "Do you want my mom's feelin's to be hurt?"

"No, no, of course not. It's just that my father . . ."

"Won't be there." She arched a waxed brow at me pointedly. "So you are going to look like an actual *seventeen*-year-old tonight, and not a seventy-year-old!"

Ouch! That one hurt. I snatched the clothes back from her hands and stalked to her bathroom to change in private. Ashley-Leigh was one of those people who always got her way, so I may as well get on it, because she wouldn't let up till I did. Before I could change my mind, I dropped my skirt, kicked off my boots, and shimmied the shorts up. I turned around. *Wow!* They were certainly aptly named. I squeezed my eyes shut. How she walked around—and confidently I might add—in these things was beyond me. The shorts barely covered my, own, ahem . . . assets.

A knock interrupted my inspection. "What's takin' so long? Come on." *Pound. Pound.* "Open up. I wanna see," she whined.

I cracked the door to reveal what I had on so far. My intention was to finish behind closed doors, but Ashley-Leigh busted on through like she owned the place, which of course she did.

"OMG!" she squealed. "You look so amazing! Put your shirt on."

Pink-faced, I shrugged out of my yellow tank and attempted to slip on the flowy material. "Um . . . does this come with an instruction manual?" I complained after a bit of fumbling around with it, feeling completely inept.

Exasperated by my total lack of fashion-know-how, she decided to take over, coming at me with what looked like long, silver nails. "Well, first of all, you can *not* wear a bra with this."

I backed up, going from pink to red. "Ah, Ash, I'm not sure . . ."

"Now." She clicked her fingers and beckoned. An exaggerated sigh hissed from her glossy lips when I didn't instantly obey. "Come on . . . off with it!"

I blew the last of my reserve air before complying. Unhooking my bra, I handed it over. (At least I thought to wear my best one.) Quickly and expertly, she wound the pink straps around my neck and tied them into a bow. Then she reached down to do the same thing with two more straps at the bottom of my back. *How many straps does this thing have?*

She stepped back to inspect her work. "Hmmm. What are we gonna do about shoes? . . . I don't even think we wear the same size anymore."

"I can just wear my boots," I offered up, but I think she forgot I was even there.

"Mom!" blasted in my ear. Two seconds of quiet passed. "*Moooom!*" I winced and plugged my ear. She made an impatient sound in the back of her throat. "You!" She froze me with her pointy nail. "Stay put. I'll be right back," she threatened, then flew out the door and bounded down the stairs, hollering again.

Since I had nothing else to do, I went ahead and checked myself out through half-closed eyes—I wasn't used to seeing so much exposed skin. *Hmmmm.* Except for how short the shorts were, I kinda liked what I saw

. . . okay, more than liked what I saw. A little prideful smile lifted my lips. The form fitting shorts showed off my legs, which were toned and tanned from hours of outdoor work. The soft color of the blouse complimented the natural glow in my cheeks. I turned my torso a bit, admiring how the material flowed loosely over my breasts, exposing just enough cleavage to be flattering but not overtly sexy. It was nothing like what spilled out of Ashley-Leigh—she was pouring out of both ends.

Just then she popped her sunny head back in, holding up a pair of nude heels for me to try on. Warmth flooded my face at my unkind thoughts. *At least she owned it and flaunted what she had with pride,* I mentally defended her as she unabashedly bent over to strap me into pleather stumbling blocks.

"Um, Ash. That's really sweet, but I don't think it's gonna work," I said at the same time she growled in frustration.

"God, Katie! How tall are you now? . . . And your foot is huge!" she accused me as if I had something to do with it.

"I only look so much taller now cause I'm wearin' stilts," I said, feeling like an Amazon.

She caught my face. "No, it's not that. You look good . . . nice and skinny with long legs. You're lucky—I have to work out all the time to look like this, and you don't have to do nothin'," she grumbled. "'Snot fair!"

My eyebrows lifted at her skewed perspective, but I remained silent.

"Well, you're just gonna have to wear your boots," she stated the obvious.

I was secretly relieved—at least my ankles would be covered tonight. I stomped back into my old trustees. "All ready."

"Wait!" she screeched. A jingling arm barred my exit. "Don'tja wanna wear some make-up?" I made a face. "Aw, come on! It's your seventeenth birthday for cryin' out loud!"

The correct answer to her question was obviously *heck yeah!* But I wasn't allowed to wear it and really didn't want to anyway. I looked doubtfully at her rendition of a smoky eye—that looked like a lot of work to do and undo.

"Um, maybe just some mascara?" I compromised. She looked on the verge of a hissy, so I quickly explained, "It's just . . . Daddy will notice anything else, and I won't have time to come back and wash it off before curfew."

To my surprise, she handed over a slick black tube without further comment. As I applied a couple of quick coats, eagle eyes appraised my wand technique. I was so busy watching her watching me that I didn't really notice the full effect until I stepped back.

"Wow!" her outlined lips mimicked my thoughts exactly.

Are these really all of my lashes? I blushed and looked down at my familiar boots, secretly both shocked and pleased by my appearance.

"Okay. Now for the *piece de la resistance*," she butchered the French phrase cheerily, coming at my face with a sticky wand of what felt like strawberry glue. "Just a bit of shine, and we're all done."

She took a moment to look me over, admiring her handiwork. That's when I noticed her face fall, almost imperceptibly. Something flickered in her eyes that she tried to hide. Her smile slipped a bit before she could catch it. I smiled warmly at her, trying to re-fan the flames of our fledgling friendship. Fortunately, Ashley-Leigh was a pro so she snapped out of it, curling her lips back into a bright smile.

"You see, Katie," she chirped waspishly. "Now you look like you actually belong in high school instead of a commune!"

My own smile slipped away. Another awkward pause ensued while she tried to laugh off the insult. *Alrighty then . . . female-bonding time over.* Looked like she'd already stepped back into her mean-girl shoes.

"So long as I don't look like I belong on a street corner," I said, going for glib but managing to sound like a goob instead. She shot back with a loud "mee-ow" and mock scratched at me with her metallic claws.

Disgusted with myself for sounding like a prude, I stomped downstairs, feeling like fun evaporated the moment I touched it. I was so occupied with my fuming that I almost ran into Mrs. M waiting for us at the foot of the stairs, camera loaded. She wolf-whistled at me and Ashley-Leigh, who was right on my heels.

"Don't you two girls look gorgeous!" she exclaimed, oblivious to the tension in the air.

"Thank you," I said, not quite meeting her eyes.

"Thanks, mom!" Ashley-Leigh did a little twirl and hip bumped me into the banister. Obviously, she was over our little tiff, or else wouldn't allow her good mood to be hampered by little ole me. She even linked her arm in mine before proceeding to march me out the door. "Let's get goin' while the gettin's still good!"

"Not so fast girls. I wanna take a few pictures first."

"Not now, Mom . . . we're already runnin' late." Ashley shot me a pointed look. "'Sides, we got our phones. Let's just take some there—that way we can post one with everybody."

"Ashley-Leigh, it's not every day a girl turns seventeen. Now you can spare a couple more minutes." Ashley started to protest again, but Mrs. M cut her off. "What's gotten into you? . . . I've never heard you complain about being the subject of a photo before." She winked at me. "Remember when you two girls wanted to move to Paris to be models?" she reminisced as she posed us like mannequins.

We stiffly put an arm around each other, neither of our hearts quite into it. I did vaguely remember that was one of Ashley-Leigh's many grand schemes. I was to go along as her manager, though I didn't bring it up.

"Too bad you didn't keep growin' like Katie here." Mrs. M snapped a couple of pictures still reminiscing about our long-forgotten plans. "You two could've been roomies!"

"Mom! That was like a million years ago . . . 'sides, models' careers are short. I'm in it for the long haul, so I'm gonna be an actress now." Ashley-Leigh said this as matter-of-factly as 'I'm going to be a redhead now,' and it was as easy as a visit to the hairdresser.

The sky had turned dusky with twilight, so Mrs. M turned on the flash and blinded us with a couple of more pictures. My eyes are super-sensitive to light, so I was only able to see stars for a few seconds. Ashley-Leigh took advantage of the break, bounding out the door, cell phone already up to her ear.

Mrs. M sighed at the sight of her daughter's sudden exit stage right and came over to place an arm around my shoulders. "You okay, Katie?"

"Yes, ma'am." I furiously blinked back tears. "The flash seems to have got me."

"Oh, sweetheart!" she clucked. "I know it's been hard for you—no girl should have to go through her teenage years without her mother." She brushed the tears from the corners of my eyes. "I want you to know that I'm here for you anytime you need me."

I appreciated the sentiment, I truly did. It was just that she was as different from my mother as night is from day. And I didn't want some manicured, Victoria Secret-wearing mom who wanted to be my best friend. I wanted my real mother like I wanted to breathe air, after holding my breath for as long as I could. I dubiously eyed the cleavage I was being smooshed into as she rocked me back and forth. I was clearing my throat, unsure how to extricate myself gracefully, when a sharp honk intervened on my behalf.

At least the girl had good timing.

"Mom! Cut the sentimental crap—we're missin' all the fun!" Ashley-Leigh called from a slit in the window.

Mrs. M and I chuckled together gently at her daughter's expense and proceeded to the car. "Just a minute." I broke away. "I just remembered I brought some heirloom tomatoes for y'all. I'll just go get them."

Another sharp honk hit my back as I hustled to the hatchback, followed by the mechanical buzz of a window going down. "Katie, just ride with mom. I'm goin' on to get a table for everyone," she announced, backing out of the driveway before squealing down the street.

"Okay . . ." I trailed off with a half wave.

Mrs. M came up and put her arm around me again, and I didn't mind so much now. "She's just bein' an impatient teenager. Don't pay any attention to her—not every teenager is as mature as you."

"That's alright. I don't mind. I'm sorry I was late. Daddy—" *What could I say?*

"I know, honey. I know." She accepted the grocery sack of tomatoes from me and peered inside. "Thanks, sweetie. These will be just super in our salads. I always did envy Lara her green thumb—looks like she passed the gene onto you."

"Thanks," I said, feeling the kind of pleased that glowed skin.

"You really do remind me so much of her."

I couldn't answer right away because my throat ached with longing. "We'd better get goin' before Ashley-Leigh disowns us both," I finally said, making a stab at humor.

"Yes! And enough of this sentimental crap—let's have fun, party, and get down tonight!" Mrs. M danced off to her suburban with her mini Coach bag and sparkly key chain, and I tromped after her, feeling distinctly like a fish out of water.

6

ALL THE COOL KIDS

Radio blaring, we rolled up into what was considered the hippest restaurant in town, Chapa's Sports Grill. I couldn't help compare it to Norma's crowd. The cars here were . . . well, mostly cars and not semi-trucks for one. The trucks that were here were newish and freshly washed. The lot was packed with the well-heeled citizens of Clovis out in their Saturday-night-best—casual with mall name brands flashing. Recognizing several kids from school, I cringed. I'd been so preoccupied with thoughts of my mother that I totally forgot what I was wearing for half a second. And now it was time to get out.

"We're here!" Mrs. M trilled, waving at familiar faces coming to-and-fro.

"We are," I confirmed, also giving a half-wave to one of Ashley-Leigh's friends. My stomach clenched when I saw her do a double-take.

Mrs. M's door opened, and the *ping, ping, ping* of the car's electrical system signaled it was time for me to get out. *Ready or not here I come . . .* I heaved myself against the door with unnecessary force and almost fell onto the asphalt.

"Oh, honey! Are you all right?" Mrs. M click-clacked over to assist me, but I'd only hurt my pride. I was being uncharacteristically clumsy—a sure sign of nerves. I needed to get a grip. This was perfectly normal attire, I told myself. No one's even going to notice you.

"I'm fine." I gave Mrs. M a weak smile and gave up on my fight against fidgeting to tug on the back of my shorts.

She smiled warmly. "You look beautiful, darling."

"Thanks," I replied doubtfully. "So do you."

She beamed in response, doing a little twirl. "Katie Lee, I fully expect to see more of you from now on."

"Everyone's gonna fully see a *lot* more of me tonight!" I muttered.

Mrs. M laughed and put an arm around my waist. "Katie, you're only seventeen one time. I highly suggest you try to enjoy yourself tonight . . . and if anyone can pull this look off my dear, it's you."

With that, we paraded through the parking lot to a chorus of greetings from the long list of Montgomery friends and acquaintances. I thought I saw a few of the grown-ups look askance at my outfit, and Meagan Banks and Halie Gomez giggled behind my back as I slunk past. Despite my lack of clothes, I felt myself grow hot and was sure even the backs of my legs were turning pink by this point. I just wanted to get in and sit down so I could at least hide them under the table.

As soon as we walked in, Ashley-Leigh waved us over from amongst a gaggle of girls. They all looked up at once and then down as if on cue, tittering loudly together like blackbirds on a wire.

"I got us a table, even though the wait's over forty-five minutes!" Ashley boasted above the din. ". . . 'sall about who ya know." After a zigzag finger snap, she turned back to gossiping with her minions, leaving me standing there, listening to the buzz of excitement surrounding me.

So this is what the gang does on a Friday night? I observed that several girls were dressed similarly, but nonetheless, most were eyeing me and my outfit and elbowing each other. One by one the group gave me the once over, and I soon found myself on the receiving end of several digs masquerading as compliments.

"I know, right?" Ashley-Leigh cut in as a girl she cheered with commented on how "different I looked tonight"—a left-handed compliment, if I'd ever heard one. "I picked it out for her. You shoulda *seen* what she was wearing earlier"—like I wasn't standing right there. "It's her birthday tonight," she announced, as if to some unasked question. A long trail of "Happy Birthdays" enveloped me right on cue, followed by a lot of enthusiastic compliments on the outfit. "Yeah, me and my mom buy her an outfit and take her out for her birthday every year!"

Ashley's bright smile was no match for my face, and I felt every bit the charity case as everyone pitched in a comment about how nice that was for them to do that. I was grateful when the conversation quickly spun back to the main topic—something about a new boy registering for school as a senior, out-of-the-blue, and how unbelievably gorgeous he was. I really couldn't follow much of it through my haze of embarrassment and general disinterest.

A group of senior guys, who were piling up on each other on their way out the door, nudged and nodded my way. I pretended not to notice. Thankfully, Mrs. M returned from her girls' chat with one of the cheer moms, and we were finally ready to sit down.

"You girls go on and enjoy yourselves. Ms. Rachel and I are going back to her house. The menfolk have taken it upon themselves to grill steaks tonight, so we get to sit back and watch *them* work for once." Mrs. M winked at me. "Happy Birthday, sweet Kate. . . . . Remember, you only live once." With that sage advice, and a quick hug, she headed out the door probably thinking she was doing me a favor. But it felt like my one ally just abandoned me.

"That's right! YOLO, baby!" Ashley-Leigh called, high-fiving randomly as she parted the crowd, leading the way through the packed restaurant to our table. With several chairs crowded around it.

What happened to our party of three? I sidled in next to a girl I hadn't spoken to since seventh grade. *Whew*! I was relieved to finally be seated and quickly spread a cloth napkin over my lap. "Do you mind if I sit here?" I inquired politely.

My icebreaker must not have gone over so well, because she looked at me like I was crazy. "It's your birthday—do whatever you want," she replied, then promptly hair-whipped me to talk animatedly to Stephanie Aguilar.

Wow. Way to turn on the charm there, Kate . . . I must be rustier at this socialization thing than I thought.

Actually, I was sort of surprised by the thread of hostility running through the group tonight. Usually everyone was pretty nice to me, despite my anti-social behavior, leftover remnants of friendships past or else feelings of sympathy for my tragic life. Tonight it was like the polite veneer had worn off, and I was fair game all of a sudden. I guessed everyone's attitudes had something to do with me showing up with Ashley-Leigh's mom. They probably thought we were rekindling our friendship and would be back to being besties like we'd been up through middle school. Everyone was acting like I was out to knock her down a notch from the social rung that dominated high school. But I couldn't care less about social status when I had to care about so many other things—like surviving.

A sudden eruption of laughter roused me from my thoughts, and I found myself laughing along, a beat too late. Ashley-Leigh had just ordered up a "Skinny Bitch." Apparently, it was funny enough to warrant hysterics. When it was my turn to order, I surprised myself by saying Arnold Palmer. A few polite giggles began because everyone was in the mood to laugh, but they soon stalled out when I explained that it was just half-tea, half-lemonade.

Ashley-Leigh commented, "Why didn't you just say that in the first place?"

Embarrassed, I wondered why I *did* do that? Thankfully, the focus returned to Ashley-Leigh, who was asking Meagan detailed questions about the new boy. Everyone leaned in, clearly enthralled with the idea of fresh meat to compete over.

"He was *beyond* gorge!" Meagan gushed, happy to have the dish on the newest item on the menu.

"How tall is he?" grilled Ashley-Leigh. She had a strict policy of not dating anyone under 5' 10," no matter how cute.

Meagan turned to Halie for confirmation. "At least six feet tall." They continued on and on about what he looked like and what he was wearing. I was only vaguely paying attention, wondering how I could slip out, when I felt a heavy tap on my shoulder. I looked up into the grinning, beefy face of Ron Tillman, son and heir extraordinaire to the Tillman Mills fortune.

"Helloooo . . . beautiful ladies!" he smoothly greeted the table, then turned to look at me with what could only be described as ogling eyes. "Katie Connelly, where've you been hidin' my whole life?" he boldly flirted, causing the girls' faces to freeze mid-smile.

"Oh, you know . . . around," I said, lamely gesturing with my hand. I tried smiling, but it felt more like a grimace. I was hyper-aware of the looks coming off the other girls.

"Well if you don't mind me sayin'. . . you sure do look fine tonight." This comment preceded a letch-look that began at my eyes and worked its way down.

I cleared my throat. "Thanks."

"You're welcome." He gave me a cheesy smile, and I swear I saw him peek down my shirt. I squirmed in my seat. A bunch of his football buddies joined him, all jostling for chairs and trying to fit two to a seat with the girls to delighted squeals of protest.

"Scoot over, Connelly." This was followed by a rough nudge by an overly confident Ron. I was frozen with indecision—I didn't want him to sit with me, yet didn't know how to refuse gracefully. "Come on, Katie, you don't want me to have to sit in *your* lap, do you?"

Somehow everyone found this hilarious and obnoxious laughter followed, adding fuel to the fire of my discomfort. Grudgingly, I moved over for him while he accidentally-on-purpose bumped me all the way off. I was left seatless and the lone stander of the group, everyone else already having settled or partnered-up.

"Uh-oh, looks like you'll just have to sit on *me* instead," he jeered, accepting an immediate high-five from a running buddy.

And much to my dismay, he was right. It was either standing up and baring my assets to the world, or risk sitting on him. Inwardly cringing, I perched stiffly on his knee, back ramrod straight.

"Now that don't look too comfortable," he stated, jiggling his leg and upsetting my precarious position. When I began to fall, he caught me, setting me a bit farther up his lap than made me comfortable. "Relax . . ." he urged with an accompanying mini-massage that only managed to stiffen me up more.

I tried to relax out of my statue pose, finally leaning on his boulder of a shoulder but remained frozen as some of the looks on the girls' faces. Conversation began flowing again while Ron gradually shifted my booty more deeply into his crotch. The heat and proximity of his nether regions made me feel claustrophobic and nauseated at once. But it was a struggle to move, because two slabs of meaty muscle were hooked tightly around me.

Ashley-Leigh shot me an annoyed look from her throne at the head of the table—a spot traditionally reserved for the birthday girl. She leaned forward enough that a dangerous amount of cleavage spilled out, and provocatively asked if any of the boys had heard about the new guy. This sparked a new buzz about whether or not he would play football.

After a minute more of watching Ron paw on me, followed by my futile attempts to wriggle away, and Ashley-Leigh had finally had enough. "Knock it off Ronnie!" she snapped, quieting the table.

"What? What am I doing?" he challenged.

"Being an *asshole*, as usual," she cooed, making it sound like a compliment. I had to admire her social skills.

I could see the dilemma present itself to her: She wanted him to let me go but she couldn't really be the queen bitch with him since he was just as popular in his own right. Plus, he was from arguably the wealthiest family in town, which made him especially formidable. And they had a history together. So I wasn't sure if she was intervening because she knew how uncomfortable I felt, or because she couldn't stand to have her ex's hands all over me right in front of everyone's noses. I suspected it was a little of both.

The gears seemed to click into place. "Leave the poor baby alone, Ronnie," she purred. "It's her birthday today."

"Really? . . . Happy Birthday, Katie!" he breathed on me, making me aware he'd imbibed on beer earlier in the evening.

"Yeah, it is," Ashley-Leigh continued, a dangerous edge sharpening her voice. "Well, technically, tomorrow's her birthday . . . " She went for the cut: "So this is her last night to be sweet sixteen and never been kissed!"

Humiliation poured out of me.

Never one to miss her mark, Madison Swain, Ashley-Leigh's lackey, jeered, "You *cannot* be serious!"

"What?" dropped Ashley-Leigh, all sugar and spice now. "I think it's sweet." She gave a high-pitched giggle, and predictably, all of her henchmen began cackling like blackbirds again.

"B-but that's not even true!" I spluttered, wrenching away to stand up.

"Oh really? Have you been keepin' secrets from me, Connelly?"

Heads turned from Ashley back to me. My play. "Uhh, sort of. Not really." I shrugged and furiously blushed again. If this was a typical night on the town, then next time I'd take a big fat pass. Getting attacked with unwanted attention, while wearing next to nothing, in the middle of a crowded restaurant, was pretty much the exact *opposite* of how I would spend my birthday. Suddenly, I'd had enough of the shenanigans, as my father would say.

"Excuse me," I said, dodging around chairs.

"Uh-oh," Madison chimed up. "I think you hurt her little feelers."

Before I could escape, Ashley-Leigh nabbed my arm. I yanked away to a loud chorus of "ooohs!" "Shut up, you guys! . . . I think she's really upset." She hugged me to her, the mean-girl facade fading from her face. "I'm really sorry, Katie-Kat. Don't go."

I could tell she really was contrite but I was still prickling with anger. "Please don't be mad," she apologized in my ear while my resolve weakened. "I was just tryin' to help you escape that gorilla, Ron."

I huffed out some hurt. Ashley could feel me relent—as I always did—and turned back to the table triumphantly, frowny face turned upside down in another victory.

"Guys, Katie's not like us—she really is still sweet and innocent. And I, for one, think it's great!" Now she sounded like a Miss America contestant.

"Come back and sit with me, Katie. I'll make it all better!" Ron flirted, oblivious.

"No way! She's all mine. Here . . ."—she kicked the chair out—"share seats with me, like old times."

So I plunked down, once again resigned to my night of torture. At least I was out of the hot seat. *I would never complain again about reading Batman to Mikey for the thousandth time.* The table gradually started up their insipid gossiping again, and it led repeatedly back to the new guy. Tana just described him as definitely athletic.

Ron cut in, "What position does he play?"

"What am I . . . telepathic?" she asked.

"More like tele*pathetic*." Ron received instant gratification from the laughter track table for that one.

Tana protested prettily, shoving his heavy mass and batting her tarantula eyelashes at him. I was happy to see him turn his ADD-attention toward her. The bantering continued for a while, and I yawned out of sheer boredom. I wanted to slide on out, but couldn't find an opening (or a ride home).

Meanwhile, Ashley-Leigh had come up with a master plan. "Don't worry, Katie. We'll find a cute boy for you to kiss tonight."

I literally shuttered at the thought of who she'd pick.

"Hmmm. Maybe my college hottie will have a cute roomie this semester?" She enthusiastically planned our future again, without input from me.

I just continued listening, not needing to add a thing to the conversation but ears. Daddy would never go for it anyway, but it was an intriguing idea. One of the hazards of growing up in such close proximity to the same people is: you remembered each awkward stage.

I looked over at Ron and could exactly picture him sitting there, in his dungarees, picking his nose like he used to when he was in my second-grade reading group. I could see it like it was yesterday. He even wore his hair in the same super-short style. The only differences I could see were a few more muscles and a little too much hair gel. I felt a little disloyal towards my fellow peers for feeling this way, because some of the boys were cute and several were very sweet, but unfortunately, none of them gave me that weak-in-the-knees feeling I'd only read about.

My thoughts flew back to summer camp, my cheeks warming a bit. I *had* already been kissed. A real kiss too, not the truth-or-dare kind you have in seventh-grade where you press your lips together in the closet while your friends giggle on the other side. His name was Ryan and he was super-cute. Cool, too. I'd been friends with his sister, Reese first. We were assigned the same team, "the winning team," as she liked to rub in to her brother. We'd all ended up going to the banquet together as a foursome—Ryan and me and Reese and her date. She could tell I felt as out of place as my father at a country club, so she'd lent me a fashionable dress and teased me that he wasn't nearly as clever or suave as we both thought he was.

I smiled, thinking back to the easy camaraderie I'd felt with them. We'd just clicked. It was a revelation to be surrounded by people who didn't know my tragic past or treat me like I was from the weird family. She'd been like an older sister to me during that week, the happiest I'd been since Mama died. I didn't know whom I liked more, Reese or her brother. I sighed. Reese, unfortunately. Because even though kissing Ryan was a pleasant enough experience, I still didn't go weak-in-the-knees, just weak-in-the-stomach—I got some weird vibes from him.

I sighed again, wishing for the umpteenth time that I had a cell or access to a computer so I could message her.

"What's the matter with you, pouty?" Ashley-Leigh poked me in the ribs. "You're not still mad at me, are you?" Nothing made Ashley-Leigh madder than you being mad at her. She couldn't stand being outside your circle of love for even a minute without falling apart.

I shook my head. "I'm just ready to go home. Can you drop me off at my car before y'all go out?"

"Fine. It's your birthday . . . do what you want."

"I've heard that before," I muttered.

After a few moments of sulking, Ashley-Leigh huffed out some air. "You know, I went to a *lot* of trouble for you tonight," she reminded me, unable to keep her feelings in for all the iced-tea in Texas. "You could at least *pretend* that you're havin' a good time."

"I *am*," I argued feebly.

"You're no fun anymore, Katie," she stated.

I knew that was almost the worst insult she could give someone, second only to "you're not pretty anymore." I didn't protest that which we both knew was true. "I'm sorry, Ash. I'm tryin', really."

"I don't think you are."

"Well, I *am*."

"Then prove it—come out with us. Be *seventeen*. Get kissed . . . for real. It's your birthday! YOLO, baby!" She nudged my shoulder, nearly dumping me into the aisle.

"I *have* been kissed!" I practically growled.

Her eyebrows shot up, mouth gaping open at once. "I knew it! You *have* been keepin' secrets from me!" she accused. "I want details! Who, what, when, where, and . . . forget the why. I *know* why!"

Thankfully our waitress just showed up, balancing a birthday cake lit with a single candle and a fistful of forks. I recognized the look immediately—*scram!* She slid the cake ceremoniously in front of Ashley-Leigh, incorrectly guessing the birthday girl from her general diva attitude. Ashley-Leigh beamed up at her before reluctantly sliding it over halfway to me. She *shhhhhed* the table into quiet obedience.

"Okay, birthday girl, make a wish!" she directed for the second time tonight.

I debated a moment on wishing for the same impossible thing I did earlier. Maybe wishing for it twice would make the impossible possible? In the interest of teen spirit, I decided to go a more predictable route. Closing my eyes, I blew out the candle to a round of applause, trying not to blush scarlet from being the center of attention. And my secret wish.

"I bet I know what she wished for!" sneered Madison.

"What?" Ashley-Leigh asked, either because she hadn't heard, or to give Madison the opportunity to deliver her line.

Like lightning before thunder, I knew what was coming and braced for it.

". . . To finally be kissed!"

As far as I could tell, about half the table laughed like idiots, and the other half looked like they just plain felt sorry for me. Either way, I couldn't stand it so I rose to my feet, shaking.

Ashley-Leigh took one look at my face and the reactions from the majority of the table. Quick as one of her winks, she turned on her friend. "Shut up, Maddy!"

"What? Oh please—I was just joking. God! Don't be so sensitive, Katie."

Ashley-Leigh yanked on my arm, but I didn't budge this time. I'd had more than enough of my girls' night and was ready to get back to my boys. I bit out a farewell over everyone's heads, then turned to Ashley-Leigh. "Thanks for, uh . . . everything." I threw a fiver down before beating a hasty retreat.

I could hear several protests around the table, and Stephanie Aguilar called out, "Come out with us Katie!—we never see you anymore." I threw a half-wave over my shoulder and saw that Ashley-Leigh was giving it to Madison. And I actually felt a little vindicated by my former best friend in that moment.

Putting one foot in front of the other as fast as I could, I headed for the back exit, hoping to slip out unnoticed. But to my dismay, faces popped up like bobble-heads doing the wave as I walked by. . . . *Dang Daisy Dukes!* I silently cursed Ashley-Leigh and her crazy outfit not two seconds after feeling tender towards her.

How do I get myself into these situations? was just what I was thinking when I hit pavement, heat, and lonely darkness on the other side of the door.

7

A CLOSE ENCOUNTER

There were no two ways about it—I was stranded as a one-winged June bug on a windshield. My clothes were sitting in a paper sack, innocently awaiting my return in the backseat of my car. Which was parked at the curb of the Montgomery house. And here I was, standing in the emptying parking lot of Chapas Sports Bar, dressed like a streetwalker. With my car keys winking at me from my handbag.

"Dagnabbit!" I kicked a piece of gravel with my boot, scratching up my industrious polish job. No way was I going back in there now. I mean—you can't just slink back into the same place you just stormed from. *Pathetic.* No way I was gonna be that.

I was busy huffing back and forth about a tailgate's length of sidewalk, debating my options when I heard a deep voice inquire if I needed a ride. I cringed under the scrutiny of an aging cowboy, eyeing me and my sorry situation from the comfort of his pickup truck.

"Um, no thank you," I replied.

"Really . . . it's no trouble." His voice rose up a persuasive octave.

"No thanks. I'm . . . ah, actually waitin' for someone."

Beneath his oily hat, he stared at my poker face a beat longer before starting his truck with an abrupt roar. "Suit yourself, missy." He flicked his cigarette butt out the window and screeched away.

Charming. Relieved, I decided it was time to strike out on my own before *Animal House* let loose and decided I needed more "birthday fun." But first I needed to tone myself down. I dug into my woven bag—past my useless keys—and grabbed my almost as useless glasses. Thought about putting my hair up with the omnipresent ponytail holder I had dangling around my wrist as a substitute bracelet then quickly dismissed the idea—I was already naked enough without exposing my back, too.

My loose plan was to get the heck out of Dodge and then figure out my next move. Bypassing the snake of cars leaving out the only exit, I stepped neatly over an orangey-yellow parking block and into a ditch, cursing my Connelly pride. Any normal person would've turned back and simply asked for a ride, or at the very least to use a phone. But I couldn't call my father in this condition (if I wanted to live to see my eighteenth birthday), didn't know Mrs. M's cell phone number, and didn't want to get Ashley-Leigh into trouble. No, I got myself into this mess by stomping out like a lunatic . . . I'd get myself out.

Suddenly, inspiration struck—my friend Miguel's family restaurant was about eight or nine blocks north of here. Doable on foot. And my best bet. He worked weekends, and I knew he would give me a ride without giving me a hard time about my night. He was good like that. I wouldn't make curfew, but I wouldn't get caught in my hooker uniform either.

Ducking my head down, I began hoofing it down the main drag. Three car horn honks and four wolf whistles later and the clear message was received—I wasn't going unnoticed. What did I expect? My oversize glasses weren't exactly a super-hero disguise.

Cursing under my breath, I decided to take a right at the next street to get off the main drag. It would be a little farther out of the way, but at least I'd avoid the high school crowd out cruising the night away. At the stoplight, flirty shout-outs and the kind of laughter that burned my face wafted out the open window of a flashy Pontiac, so I cut across the waiting cars to a convenience store. Thankfully the light was still red, so it would take a while for them to find me, if they were so inclined.

Aw man! This is total crap! My toes were already starting to pinch in my pointy boots, and I'd only gone a couple of blocks. So absorbed was I in cursing myself and getting on down the road, that I didn't notice the turquoise pickup sidling up next to me until I heard the whir of an automatic window. Reflexively, I looked up to see a familiar, craggy face.

"Thought you were waitin' for a ride," the smug voice reminded me.

Guess my poker face needed some work. "Um . . . they couldn't make it after all."

"That's a shame . . . pretty girl like you gettin' left all alone. I wouldn't have stood you up." He said this, in what he probably thought was an enticing way, while crawling along next to me.

I didn't respond, hoping he'd get the hint. *Gah!* I decided a cell phone was definitely in my future.

"The offer for a ride still stands."

"I prefer to walk."

A humorless chuckle. "Frosty," he announced as though reporting on the weather.

I didn't acknowledge his comment. The only sound was my feet clip-clopping on the pavement as I made a swift right down a side street into a residential area. Hopefully, he'd keep going straight and head on home. Or at least away from me.

A huge gust of relief billowed from my chest when the man tore off down the street. That was close. *What kind of guy paints his truck turquoise?*

I decided to keep on this sleepy street for a while, stay off any main roads and hopefully walk unnoticeable as a shadow in the dark. A couple of quiet blocks later, and I heard the unmistakable thrum of a truck's engine behind me. I shuddered as the first sliver of fear crawled up my spine. The man had doubled back and was trailing me. Again. I looked all around, noticing the forest of low-income housing I was heading deeper into had most of the lights off. *Where are the streetlamps?*

While the cunning night predator stalked me, I kept my head down and my ears open. I could only hear domestic-disturbance yelling in the distance, and a screen door banging, followed closely by sharp dog barking. Another light snuffed out in a house up ahead. The exact time eluded me, but I knew it was heading past bedtime for most folks. My father never failed to remind me that nothing good happens past midnight. I was hoping to make it home before then.

I had to get off this street, because I *had* to get to the restaurant before Miguel left for the night. Enough was enough. I stopped my tromping to face him squarely. I would just reason with the man. And if that didn't work, I'd just lie—better.

Tamping down the voice that said he didn't buy the first lie, I said, "I really appreciate the offer for the ride, but I live just a coupla blocks this way." I jerked my thumb to indicate a dark street, lined with small houses, with big dogs penned behind chain-link fences.

The man's patronizing tone began to form before he even spoke. "Wwwell, why didn'tja just say so, sweetheart? Tell you what—I'll just foller along right beside you and make sure you git home safe and sound."

I hugged my midsection, suddenly feeling cold despite the sweat beading my upper lip. "That's okay, sir. I'm almost home. And I have friends waitin' on me." I was going for firm, but my voice broke on the word *home*—I was so far from home and so alone it wasn't even funny.

Tears pricked my eyes. I turned away and continued determinedly on . . . farther away from my goal, but also farther away from the man in the truck, whom I guessed was *not* a Good Samaritan. I needed to turn back, but I kept thinking there *must* be a closer exit up ahead. My detour had been a bad idea, one of many tonight.

I clopped, and he followed, humming along to a song I couldn't hear. A pit formed in my stomach. He wasn't giving up. The lights went off in the houses now like someone had flipped a switch. I looked down another side street to a matchbox house with a solitary light on behind torn curtains. It shone like a beacon on this gloomy night. Even though it would take me farther into the twisty neighborhood, I decided to take my chances on it and ask for some *dadgum* help.

The only sounds now were his humming, occasional dog barking, and the faster clip of my feet as I started to jog. My glasses bumped up and down in rhythm to my boots, my cross thumping against my chest to the faster beat of my heart. Maybe it was just my imagination, but the farther I got, the darker it seemed to get. I was hyper focused on the solitary light, looking neither right to the vacant-looking houses, nor left to the creeping stalker.

Suddenly, my beacon of hope flicked off, flooding me in pitch black.

I gasped. My head jerked backwards, eyes groping for light. The creeper had killed his headlights. And quit humming. The witching hour, like the darkness, closed in around me. It seemed to come alive now, taking shape like a scary monster. I was paralyzed with fear, but my ears were still in working order. And I could hear the unmistakable chink of chains and the thudding of large paws charging my way. Dogs, I couldn't quite see yet, hurled themselves against the chain-link fence, viciously barking in my face. I jumped back even as my heart leapt to my throat.

The man shined a flashlight in my face, chortled. "I don't think those two dogs—pit bulls by the sound of 'em—are welcomin' you home."

As if to prove his point, claws appeared at the top of the fence with a snappy snarl. I recoiled back only to find the man had angled his truck over the sidewalk, blocking me. That was fine because the lie was as obvious and out in the open now as a bloody wound. Stumbling backwards, I kept one eye trained on the snarling beasts trying to jump the fence.

"Come on, girl. I ain't gonna bite." The man swung the door wide. "Can't say the same for them dogs though."

The interior light blinked on illuminating the six-pack of beer he had riding shotgun. He plucked a can off and offered it to me like candy. "Come on"—he gave me a greasy smile—"let's get outta here and go party." He must have seen the fear and revulsion on my face because he said, "Aw come on now! I just wanna have some fun . . . and you look like a *fun* girl." A lascivious look followed this ridiculous statement. "Whatd'yasay?"

"N-no thank you," I squeaked, oddly polite, as if that would help my cause. Isolation didn't seem to be working so good for me, so I turned myself around, sprinting back to the well-lit convenience store and the main drag.

But the man was quick, throwing the truck in reverse and fishtailing the back around to block my exit. I was now pinned in the alley with the same vicious dogs, still furiously barking like they would like nothing better than to tear me to shreds. I would either have to go down the blind alley or . . .

Oh no! My panicked eyes looked up to see the man grinning victoriously down at me. I was trapped, and we both knew it.

"Come on, sweetheart, let's go," he directed with a sharp nod.

I was just about to dive down the blank alley when my situation turned from bad to worse—one of the dogs finally managed to hook his front legs over the top of the fence. *Crap!* I closed my eyes, preparing to leap into the back of the man's truck, when a sharp whistle pierced the darkness. Momentarily startled, the dog stopped his struggle to heave himself over the fence, lost his momentum, and fell back down.

Almost faint with relief, I looked around for the source of the sound. Headlights from the street penetrated the darkness, haloing another large vehicle that had just pulled up beside the man in the truck.

Oh, thank God! Someone needed to get through the alley. This was my break! Words were being exchanged between open windows, but it was hard to hear because the dogs started up another furious round of barking, their attention now evenly divided between me and the two trucks parked side-by-side.

The proprietary voice of the creeper rose in challenge: "Who the hell do you think you are?"

"Her ride," a deep, calm voice replied.

Something about that voice sent a vibration down my spine. *That can't be right . . . Unfortunately, nobody knows where I am.*

The man in the truck stuttered, turned red, took one last accessing look at me plastered against the fence before reaching over and slamming the door shut. "Good luck with that one!" he spat before roaring off into the night.

Shaking, I ducked down to take a couple of deep breaths while I waited for the big black Jeep to pull through the alley so I could run. But it didn't move.

Holy cow! I just realized I'd seen this Jeep before. Only it wasn't a Jeep; it was a Hummer. A black Hummer, and I'd only seen one of those once before . . . My eyes traveled up the large, knobby tires and into the open window, where a pair of glacier eyes was looking down on me crouched in the weeds. Disbelief momentarily stunned me stupid. *No Way!* I blinked. Sure enough . . .

"Good evenin', Glasses!" A familiar mocking voice greeted me.

It just couldn't be. Could it?

I stumbled upright to get a closer look. What I saw made my face blanch and my feet scrabble backwards like I'd seen a ghost.

What's he doing here?—nothing good.

"Get her in the truck," someone directed from the driver's seat. I thought that voice sounded familiar, too, but couldn't be sure because my ears were ringing, and I was faint with fear and near exhaustion.

I must've been taking too long to process what was going on, because the door sprang open. A very large, very muscular guy stalked my way, with a determined look upon his face. Somewhere in the recesses of my mind I registered the fact that he was also *very* good looking.

Oh man . . . not again! It suddenly occurred to me that I'd just jumped from the frying pan into the fire!

8

RANGER DANGER

He was coming for me, so I finally snapped out of it enough to scramble out of the weeds. I'd fought capture all night from one deranged man. No way was I going down now . . . *Not without a fight.*

"Come on, Glasses. We can do this the easy way or the hard way," Ranger calmly threatened.

Fear choked me. Alarm bells rang in my mind. I shook my head, backed up a couple of more steps, and then—bolted down the alley. I heard him call out and then tear after me. *Oh. My. God!* I tried running faster, but my exhausted body protested. Heavy footsteps thudded behind me.

Crush! Crush! Crush!

Finally, the adrenaline jolt, my body had been waiting for all night, kicked in. I felt a rush of blood surge through my muscles. Barking dogs tore after me as far as their chains permitted. Dumpsters, rickety fences, weeds, all flew by as I ran faster than I had ever run before. An angry oath pelted my back, sending jangled pulses up my spine. Sure footsteps sped up behind me, faster that I thought possible. Heaving bursts of exertion pushed from my lungs. I prayed just to make it to the street and for a stray car to come along. I ran full out, long legs sprinting, heedless of my blistered feet and clunky footwear.

Unfortunately, the long legs sprinting full out behind me were overtaking me quickly—too quickly. My mind raced faster than my legs. *What could I do?* I was outmatched. I saw a cardboard box sticking out of the next dumpster, and a hysterical plot to trip him up flew to my mind. My chest heaved, and my leg muscles burned like acid, not blood was pumping through my veins, but I fought through it like I was running for my life.

Please God! . . . Just let me get to the next dumpster!

I reached down deep for the last vestiges of energy I had and sprang forward like a gazelle, just managing to grab the box and hurl it blindly behind me. It landed gratifyingly with a dull whap on its target. Another curse blasted my back, followed by stumbling sounds as he tripped over the contents spilling from the box.

Yes! I thought triumphantly, not daring to turn around. It probably only bought me a few extra seconds. I just hoped it would be enough to get me to the end of the alley. Because whatever the outcome . . . I was at my end. Running on fumes. Stumbling to the finish line. My lungs burned so badly I wanted to hurl. Instead, I hurled myself into the last few feet of my sprint with every fiber of my being.

My guardian angel must've been with me, because I heard the unmistakable purr of an engine idling in the street. *Thank you, Jesus!*

I bolted out of the alley and into the street—and right smack into the monster truck just waiting for me at the end. *A trap!* I was so concentrated on running toward it that I couldn't think to stop. Skidding crazily on the gravel, I braced for the crash—*Thunk!*—my hip and shoulder made contact with the side panel of their blasted Hummer.

Ow! That's gonna leave a mark, the least of my worries at the moment because the impact bounced me back—into the waiting arms of one Ranger-from-my-nightmares. A loud *"Oomph!"* erupted from his throat as I plowed into his midsection. I had managed to knock us to the ground, the air from our lungs, and my glasses off in one climatic swoop. I was so out of breath I was gasping for air, wheezing like an asthmatic.

"Goddammit!" blasted into my ear.

I was scrambling to get up first (clearly the more panicked of the two) when a steel hand clamped down on me before I could flee.

"Lemme go!" I screamed with no volume, having no air, while jabbing at his eye sockets. Failing this endeavor, I tried getting in a swift, hard kick at his soft parts.

"Settle down!" Ranger expertly dodged another blow to his groin, so I began clawing at him now, cursing my lack of fingernails. "Get your ass out here and help me with this hellcat!" he ordered, way past the point of being put out with me.

Oh no! . . . No way I could fight off two of them at once! I redoubled my efforts to fight, flailing and clawing desperately. He captured both my wrists, hauling me to my feet like a child in the midst of a tantrum. I took advantage of my standing position by hauling off and kicking him in the shin. With the pointy toe of my boot. Used all the might I had left in me to do it.

"Ahhh! You—" He finished with a swift, reflexive backhand, landing me sprawled back on the ground, a tangle of arms and legs. A cry of shocked pain escaped me, my hair flying about my face in a blinding screen. Ranger was busy hopping up and down cursing, so I blindly closed my hand around a fistful of gravel ready to fling it in his face the moment he touched me.

Didn't have to wait long, because he immediately reached over—with less care than a cowboy does a steer he's roped and tethered—and grabbed me. "You're going to regret that, young—"

I hurled the gravel in his face.

"Mother—*ffffoot!*" He furiously spat on the ground.

I didn't hesitate. I ran for it again—four fast steps—into another set of arms. Then started screaming my head off and was instantly rewarded by a couple of lights blinking on. *Why hadn't I thought of this before?* A large muzzle clamped over my mouth. I strained and squirmed and screamed while muscled bands enfolded me tightly.

A low, soothing voice said, "It's okay. We're not going to hurt you."

Sure . . . that's what they all say.

"Speak for yourself," Ranger spat out, along with some gritty dirt. "You got her?" He began furiously rubbing at his eyes.

I tried screaming again, but it was hopelessly muffled by the hand sealing my lips shut.

"I got her," he confirmed. "You drive. We'd better get outta here before someone calls the cops."

I redoubled my efforts to get free again. Mama told me to never *ever* let someone take you off in their car. To fight to the death if you had to, because once they took you away to a secondary location, it was all over for you. The second attacker yelped as the back of my head made contact with his face.

"Son-of-a-bitch!" He loosened his grip enough for me to bite down on his hand. "Ow! Stop biting me!" His curses assaulted my ears while his fingers resealed my lips.

A barking cackle erupted from Ranger, who was sitting back watching the struggle with cold amusement. "I told you she was a hellcat."

"Yeah, well . . . you didn't have to hit her."

"She's lucky that's *all* I did—she kicked the bejeezus out of me with her friggin' cowboy boot!" Ranger whined, rubbing at his shin.

"No wonder she's spooked out of her mind . . . the way you went after her. There's no calming her down now." With that said, my captor used the full force of his strength to carry me, kicking and screaming, into the truck.

To my utter bewilderment, he didn't bind and gag me and throw me in the back. Instead, he somehow managed to hoist us both into the passenger seat, with me fighting him tooth and nail. But since he only had my arms pinned, my legs were still thrashing about like a lobster fighting the pot. I planted my boots on the doorframe, keeping my legs ramrod straight to prevent him from shutting the door.

My captor huffed out a chuckle. "A little help, please."

Ranger barked out another exasperated laugh before removing my boots from the door and shoving them inside. I tried to kick him in the head, but he ducked.

"Unbelievable. We should've left her in the alley for the dogs—that poor bastard never had a chance anyway." Ranger slammed the door and stalked around to the driver's side, shaking his head and cursing. The headlights glinted off his glossy black head, spotlighting the blood on his mouth. Unnaturally blue eyes glared at me through the windshield.

My heart seized in my chest. I'd swear I'd seen those eyes before—*before* the diner.

And then another door closed, shutting off the memory flash. It seemed especially ominous to me under the circumstances—a final nail in my coffin. A sob tore from my throat. The fight was over. They'd won. I'd lost. *Again.* The Hummer gunned down the street, tires squealing in protest, the driver obviously taking his frustrations out on the road. *Where are they taking me?* Once we got there they could do with me as they pleased, as thy surely would. These were two guys who clearly always got what they wanted.

And for some inexplicable reason they wanted *me*.

And then I started crying, inconsolably, washing my abductor's hand in tarry tears as he held me to him. All I could hear for a long while were the sniffling sobs leaving my body and the roaring engine driving us down dark, empty streets of the deserted town. My thoughts flew wildly around in my head: *What do they want with me? What are they doing here? How did they know how to find me?* My heart palpitated in rhythm to the questions. We went a few more empty miles in silence, each of us absorbed in our thoughts.

Suddenly, all the fight drained out of me like milk from an over-turned bucket. I quit struggling and slumped over. My aching muscles relaxed. In turn, his hand relaxed enough to allow a long, shuttering sigh to leak out. Closing my eyes, I leaned into him for support instead of fighting him.

The one holding me captive immediately responded again by readjusting me so that I was tucked up securely under his chin, my head now resting against his chest. I could hear the pounding of his heart and feel his slow, sure breath caress my face. It was calming—too calming. I felt an unexpected shift in my body's responses. Breathing in deeply, I inhaled the masculine scent wafting from his neck. He smelled . . . like *heaven*. Some kind of intoxicating mix of expensive aftershave, healthy sweat, and good old-fashioned pheromones. At this point, I wasn't sure I *wanted* to get away. Strangely, I felt protected by his solid frame, almost as if my nightmare had finally come to an end.

My God! Am I losing my marbles? Already suffering from Stockholm syndrome?

A flare of defiance bloomed in my chest—I refused to be such an easy mark for these two egomaniacs! I stiffened my resolve, and my muscles again, planting my boots against the dashboard to press back hard and crack his face with the back of my head.

"Oh, no you don't!" He anticipated my move as soon as I stiffened back up, quickly wrapping his leg around my shins so that my feet dropped back to the floor. "I thought all the fight finally left you," he said, sounding more amused than angry.

Ranger snorted. "Don't let her loose for one second, Pete. I would say she's completely outmatched here, but I don't believe even Tyson could take her down tonight."

I dared a peek and noticed, with grim satisfaction, that both abductors appeared a little worse for the wear. I wasn't the only one battered and bruised by our encounter—at least I had that. Ranger was busy blotting his lip with a paper napkin, and the one named Pete was bleeding all over my new shirt. I must have busted his nose when I head-butted him. A quake of fear at all the awful things they could do to me in retaliation overcame me.

"She's shaking like a leaf," Pete said, sounding concerned now. He folded me into him and began murmuring in my ear.

The first stirrings of hope began to rise in my chest. *Could they not be meaning to do me harm?* I wasn't sure of anything yet, but my intuition was telling me that the one holding me captive in his arms wasn't going to hurt me . . . Besides, Pete didn't sound like much of a serial-killer name. I snorted at that thought, on the edge of hysteria again.

"What are you doing over there? Choking her?" Amusement from Ranger.

"I'm going to let her go, so she can breathe better," warned Pete.

"The hell you are! . . . She's like a goddamned wolverine!"

A low chuckle vibrated Pete's chest. "Nah . . . more like a frightened filly, 'sall." That said, he actually unpinned my arms for one second to stroke a hand over my mane. Meanwhile, my mouth continued to be muzzled by his other hand like I was gonna gnaw off his arm or something.

"Don't let her go!" Ranger ordered. "I don't want to end up road kill for these yahoos to scrape off the highway." After a few more minutes of what appeared to be random driving, he pulled off the black asphalt and onto one of the dirt roads arming off the long stretch of interstate.

As we hurtled along, I noted that I liked Pete a heck of a lot better than Ranger, despite the fact that he still held me bound-and-gagged. For one thing, Ranger kept using the Lord's Name in vain, a habit that I personally detested. Secondly, he just compared me to a wolverine, and my feminine ire was curiously aroused by this. But most importantly, I had the distinct feeling that Ranger detested me, despite the fact that he didn't know me from Eve.

Unless he *did*.

We continued to drive into the country abyss, and I continued to wonder where they were taking me. I needed some answers. If they were going to drive me out into the middle of nowhere to hack me into pieces, then apparently, I at least wanted the common courtesy of knowing about it in advance.

Ready to talk, I mumbled into Pete's palm, but he was too busy debating about our whereabouts with Ranger to answer. I gathered they were a bit lost on the unmarked country roads.

"Don't blame me if you missed the turnoff—I'm trying to quell a nosebleed over here," Pete said, tossing his head back.

Another spasm of remorse shook me (which was very disconcerting considering the fact that he had virtually kidnapped me against my will). I redoubled my efforts to harden my heart against him. Trouble was I'd just breathed in another lungful of his exposed throat, and it had me feeling more like snuggling in than escaping out.

"Damned backassward roads!" Ranger stomped on the brakes, and we all lurched forward before coming to a halt. Dust flew up around us in clouds of wispy smoke. He leaned over to fiddle with the GPS system, appearing to get more irate by the second.

This made me feel a smidge better due to the simple fact that I knew where we were and they didn't. Inexplicably, we were just a few miles down the road from my house, where that prairie fire had burned down an abandoned farmhouse a few years ago. I wasn't exactly sure how this knowledge helped me, but it kind of made me feel like I had some small weapon in my arsenal of survival.

And then the neon dashboard flashed the time at me: 12:07. *Crap!* It felt like a small cannonball just made contact with my stomach. My curfew was 11:00, and that was after much wheedling and begging. If I didn't walk through my front door pronto, then I would be better off in the hands of my abductors! I must not have been in my right mind, because not making curfew should've been the least of my worries at the moment. But there it was niggling at my brain like a worm.

"Mmmm." I began squirming now, more insistent. "Mmm-mm-mmm."

Ranger shot me a dirty look before setting right back to work with his keypad. Pete simply readjusted me in his arms as if I were merely trying to convey my discomfort. I huffed out a huge, aggravated sigh. If they were *not* going to kill me, then my father surely would.

"Maybe we should throw a blanket over her," Ranger suggested, glancing up from his task. I glared at him.

"I think it's time to cut her loose," Pete said.

"If she kicks the GPS system out of order, you're walking home." The statement was said with levity. However, I had the distinct impression that Ranger would actually follow through with his threat.

A sigh escaped Pete, the puffed out sweet air stirring my hair. "Duly noted." His voice sounded abnormally nasally now. "Hand me a napkin, will you? My nose is *still* bleeding."

Another pang shot through me. I wondered if it was because I felt bad for inflicting the injury, or because I had inflicted it on the wrong abductor.

The abductor, still holding my mouth hostage, removed his hand as warily as if I were a bomb he was detonating. The sudden release of pressure shocked me into silence. I'd already realized, of course, who it was: it was Baseball Cap from the restaurant, and I now knew his name was Pete. He looked at me for what felt like the first time tonight. A slow burn started that was part guilt for mangling his face and part embarrassment from being so exposed—I just realized I'd been draped across his lap half naked. Blood rushed to the surface of my skin. My eyes retreated shyly to my lap; I was suddenly glad for the sheltering darkness.

Ranger handed over a napkin and snapped on the interior light to inspect the damage. A low whistle discharged from his lips. "Damn, man! No doubt about it . . . that eye's gonna be one black beauty." He sounded cheered by this idea.

Gah! I'd done more damage than I thought. I felt kinda queasy that I'd spoiled the most spectacular face I'd ever seen. It was a travesty to destroy such beauty—like taking a knife to a Michelangelo painting. My actions were perhaps a bit hasty, because I wasn't even sure if he was friend or foe.

Pete snorted, then winced. "You're one to talk. You look like you've been in a street fight with a herd of angry cats."

I felt the weight of both their eyes on me, searching for answers. I peeked up from beneath my wet lashes at Pete. But to my dismay, his soft brown eyes were staring down at me with a hard expression. Well, one soft brown eye, because the other was currently swelling shut. I also noticed, with another twinge of remorse, that his patrician nose was still oozing red. *Did I really do all that?* Frightened from the combined heat of their displeasure, I sniffed again as more tears threatened.

Ranger rolled his eyes. "Crying's not going to get you out of this one, little lady."

I shouldn't be the one on the defensive here. *Is it my fault a big brute chased me down a dark alley?* I didn't ask for them to appear out of thin air. (Although a small voice inside was finally allowing that I might be lucky that they did.)

And that I'd landed in Pete's lap. I realized just how gentle he'd actually been with me under the circumstances . . . unlike others. I dared another glare at Ranger before returning my eyes to Pete. We stared intently at each other for a lost moment, and a mad impulse to brush back his golden hair and tenderly tend his bruised and broken skin overtook me. So I guess it was a good thing he still held me bound.

Pete's expression softened. Something flickered in his eyes that prompted him to finally remove the arm-shackle binding me to his chest to snap off the light. "The light's bothering my eye," he stated in way of explanation.

But I knew that was a lie—something about *me* had bothered him.

My hands used their newfound freedom to hastily swipe at mascara smears. Pete swiped at his nose with the napkin Ranger handed him.

"Maybe you could borrow one of her tampons to plug it?" Ranger suggested while I conveyed to him the depth of my loathing through my eyes. "Uh-oh, I think she's plotting my death again," he said to Pete. Then after a beat: "So let's have it, Glasses . . . Why were you running from us tonight?"

"Why were you chasin' me?" I croaked out, my throat dry as a bone.

"Because you ran." Ranger's gaze roved from my face to my breasts, newly exposed from the removal of Pete's arm. He focused on my mother's cross, and something weird flashed behind his eyes.

I squirmed under his frank scrutiny, feeling even more naked than I was. I became acutely aware that I was alone, out in the country, with two very athletic, angry males, who may or may not want to hurt me.

"I have to get home," I said.

Ranger ignored me, continuing to give me the once over until he zeroed in on the gash in my knee. He retrieved another napkin and began dabbing at it. "I gotta say, Glasses—you're a mess again," he sneered, pressing into my bleeding cut with unnecessary force. "However, this outfit is a vast improvement over the previous one."

I winced but ignored *him*.

". . . Glad to see you took my little talk to heart." A wicked grin flashed dimples at me, and a surge of white-hot rage flew my hand to his face. But it was caught by Ranger's quicker hand. "Uh-uh-uh-uh," he tssked, "temper-temper."

To my utter horror, the silky tie at the bottom of my shirt just came undone . . . and the one around my neck was precariously close to slipping off. *Do not need a nip-slip right now!* I tried snatching my hand back to retie it, but Ranger wouldn't release me. His eyes snaked to my slippery shirt.

"That temper's going to get you into a *lot* of trouble, young lady," he cautioned, a smirk curling his lips.

"Easy," Pete intervened, shifting me back farther into his lap. "She's had a hard night."

My thoughts flew back to when Ron Tillman had done the same thing earlier; I'd been so repulsed. Funny . . . I didn't feel that way now. Maybe it was because I was so angry there wasn't room for any other emotion. In fact, I was so mad, I wasn't even afraid anymore. If I was going down, then I was going down in flames!

Straightening my back, I locked eyes with Ranger. "If you don't unhand me and take me home right now, my father's gonna hunt you down and shoot you between the eyes with his shotgun!" He looked more amused than fazed, so I continued with my false bravado threat. "And he's ex-military . . . so his aim's a little better than average."

A blast of laugh erupted all over my front while an amused chuckle tickled my back. This time my glare was evenly divided between the two abductors. "I wouldn't laugh if I were y'all."

"Ooooh!" Ranger pantomimed a shiver of fear. "Did you hear that, Pete? Ex-military! . . . Maybe that's where she learned her hand-to-hand combat skills?"

"Maybe," Pete allowed, looking at me with a cross between humor and respect. "If that's the case, we *should* be afraid . . . very afraid."

I held back a childish urge to stick my tongue out at both of them. Was sure it wouldn't help my case, and I needed to get home sixty-six minutes ago. "Well, if my father doesn't shoot you, he certainly will *me* if I don't get home soon—I'm out way past my curfew. So can you *please* take me back now?"

"What if we're not done with you yet?" The same loaded question Ranger used at the diner came with the same side of ice-chip eyes tonight.

A chill ran down my spine. "Well if it's a ransom you're after, you're barkin' up the wrong tree—we ain't got nothin' to give you!" I delivered this in my sassiest tone.

Ranger appeared to X-ray me with his eyes. "I'm sure we could think of something."

I lowered my eyes back to my lap. "Can I please have my hand back?"

"Ohhh—you're all manners when you want something," he mocked. After a brief, bruising squeeze, he released me.

I went about quickly retying my bows, but between my haste and trembley fingers, it was like I had mittens on.

"Here, allow me . . ." Pete set me between his legs, his capable fingers making short work of both ties. I was very conscious of his feathery touch, running from the nape of my neck to the bottom of my back. Something I'd never felt before shivered through me.

"You alright?" Pete asked.

Gah! Mortifying! Hopefully, he thought I was going into shock.

I nodded and gave a little dry cough to clear my throat. "Just thirsty. Can I please have some water?"

"See what I mean?" Ranger indicated me with his palm. "All manners when she wants something." Pete ignored him to reach behind the seat, but Ranger intervened. "Allow me. You keep a hold on her—don't want her to bash us over the head with a water bottle."

Pete shook his head but moved aside. A moment later, Ranger's hand reemerged with a very solid-looking bottle in it. I could see how it could be used as a weapon because it was made from glass instead of plastic. I also noticed it had weird numbers on the label instead of a name brand.

Should I be worried? I was so thirsty I could've drained the radiator. Besides, if they were going to kill me, I doubted poison would be the way. Eagerly, I held out my hands to accept the mystery liquid.

"Thirsty?" Ranger taunted. "You know what? . . . I am, too. You made me run pretty far and hard tonight." A slow twist on the cap, and a hiss and wisp of steam escaped. Lifting the bottle in a mock toast, he proceeded to greedily gulp it down until there was just a swallow or two left. He offered it to me. "Hope you don't mind a little of my backwash."

Tears stung my eyes again. *Why's he being so mean? What exactly is my crime? Existing?* Not wanting to give Ranger the satisfaction of a breakdown, I averted my face to the window.

Another low hiss escaped, this one from Pete. "You're such an ass!" He flung the door wide, spilling us both out onto the gravel. I would've fallen had he not grabbed me first.

"What'd you call me?" Ranger challenged.

Pete stuck his head back in. "You heard me."

"Are you forgetting protocol already?"

"Are you?" Pete sniped back. "I don't think your behavior tonight could exactly be called protocol."

They continued arguing back-and-forth. I wasn't sure what was going on, but this was usually the part in the movies where the heroine sneaks off while the villains are busy fighting amongst themselves. I thought about it, wondering if I would get away with it since I knew our location. But I quickly dismissed the idea as likely to get me into more trouble—the way my luck was going tonight, I'd be eaten by coyotes the first fifteen minutes.

Finally, it appeared the two alpha males had reached a stalemate. "What?" Ranger threw his arms out. "I knew there was more."

Pete flipped up the backseat, coming away with another bottle. With a little pop and fizz, he unceremoniously twisted off the cap and handed it over to me. I snatched at the bottle and began quenching my raging thirst. Pete stood watching me with unreadable eyes as I gulped, gulped, gulped at the water gracelessly. *Mmmmmm!* Water had never tasted so good. About halfway finished, I noted to myself it was rude not to share.

"Would you like some?" I offered with a wobbly smile. Self-consciousness trembled the bottle in my hand.

Pete regarded me for a drawn-out moment. "I'm fine, but you should continue drinking—you were likely on your way to dehydration."

"I hate to break up this *special* moment," Ranger cut in from the front, "but I'm rather tired of the country life. And we better get Little Annie Oakley home before her father tries to gun us down in the street."

Pete grabbed my purse from the backseat and tossed it to me. "It is time to get you home," he agreed. "But first, call your father and let him know you're all right."

I clutched my mother's purse to my chest, looking up at Pete with grateful eyes. "Thanks for savin' it."

An exaggerated *ahem* sounded from the front seat. "Actually, you have *me* to thank for that one, Glasses." Ranger picked up something from the console and dangled it between his forefinger and thumb. "But your signature glasses didn't fare so well, I'm afraid. Probably for the best . . . I don't think they really did much for you."

Pete looked up from wiping a blood smear off his face with the hem of his shirt. "What the hell's wrong with you, man?"

"What's wrong with me is I'm out here in the middle of Kill-Me-I'm-So-Bored-Nowhere with a cut lip and a throbbing shin, compliments of your country bimbo over there!" Ranger daggered a finger at me.

How dare he! I was mad enough to go toe to toe with him again. I'd surely lose, and brutally so, but if I managed to get in a couple of shots, it'd be well worth it. I lunged forward while "I'm not a bimbo!" shrieked out of me.

Pete grasped me around the waist.

"If it walks like a duck and quacks like a duck . . . then it's a goddamned duck!" Ranger seemed unaccountably angry, capable of anything. I was secretly glad Pete was holding me back, because not only was Ranger huge, he was also deranged.

"Can't you just take me home? . . . I only live a ways down the road," I confessed.

"We will," Pete said evenly, "after you've called home to explain you had car trouble tonight, and that's the reason you're tardy. That will buy us some time to get you cleaned up. If we take you home in this condition, we'll have the Texas Rangers after us."

That actually sounded like a good plan because my father already knew my car wasn't doing well. And two strange guys driving me home, scratched up and disheveled in this outfit, would likely get us all shot. I stiffly nodded my head and waited for an offered phone, but Pete didn't volunteer his. Instead, he busied himself with a metal first-aid kit, rummaging through extracting contents as expertly as a surgical nurse.

At the point he began unrolling medical tape and tearing it smoothly with the edge of his teeth, he looked up, suddenly aware I was staring dumbly at him and *not* in the process of making a phone call. I colored hotly then made an expression as if to convey that I was merely waiting for a proffered phone. In truth, I was momentarily so mesmerized by his deft movements and sensuous mouth that I totally forgot what the plan was for a few seconds.

A look of annoyance crossed his face. He sighed and dropped the kit with a clunk to hand me my woven bag again. "Aren't you going to call?"

"Uhh . . ."

Ranger gave a short, humorless laugh. "Dude, you can be so clueless. She doesn't *have* a cell phone."

"Oh." Pete looked back at my pink face, a little stunned. "I guess that makes sense now," he said more to himself than anyone else.

I was still waiting for one of these goons to whip out one of theirs, when I noticed them exchange loaded glances. "I know . . ." I said, trying to tamp down my sarcasm. "How about I just borrow one of yours?"

This caused two self-assured, well-spoken guys to splutter and mumble out two different excuses simultaneously. It would have been gratifying to see these two falter so spectacularly, but the news they were delivering didn't exactly tickle my funny bone. According to Pete, we couldn't use his phone because it was out of battery power. And from Ranger, well, he'd lost his during the frantic chase down the alley.

I was feeling dubious on both accounts.

First of all, two guys in a Hummer loaded with well-stocked coolers and first-aid kits weren't likely to run out the door without their phone chargers. They were more prepared than Eagle Scouts on steroids. Even Ashley-Leigh managed to keep hers handy, and she was no Girl Scout. Secondly, I highly doubted Ranger's story, because if he bothered to stoop down in the dirt to retrieve my broken glasses and battered handbag, then he sure as heck would go back for his own cell phone.

They were selling it, but I wasn't buying it. Plus, my gut told me they were both lying through their perfect pearly whites. And Mama always told me to trust my gut. And I always trusted my mama. I *harrrrumphed* a little under my breath, crossing my arms. I couldn't exactly call them out on their lies though, could I? I was still miserably at their mercy.

My eyes flicked back and forth between two sets of guilty eyes. "Well that's inconvenient," I said.

Ranger narrowed his eyes at me. "Let's see here: no cell phone, water, Band-Aids, or Mace . . . *You* weren't exactly prepared tonight, were you, Glasses?"

Loathe as I was to admit it, he had a point. Having no comeback, I relegated myself to glaring at him. Pete intervened again before our glaring contest escalated into all out war. He swiftly scooped me up and set me down on the seat facing the open door. His beautiful, battered face was all I could see now as he got to work.

"Actually," he said, applying a thin layer of cream to my knee, "we should drive back to town to call anyway. I need to hit a pharmacy to get some Arnica for the swelling on my face." I suddenly had trouble swallowing. "And you can use the bathroom to clean up. I'm also quite sure you can use the phone there."

"Sounds like a plan." Ranger started up the Hummer with an abrupt roar.

"Fine." I snatched the tape from Pete's hand to finish dressing my own wound.

"See? She's back to being feisty when she doesn't get her way," Ranger said.

Pete just shook his head like he was put out with both of us. While I scrambled into the backseat, he took his rightful place in front. Then, cracking a plastic bag back and forth with quick precise movements, he laid it over his eye. After a jolting plunge into a ditch to turn around, Pete removed the icepack long enough to address me while I went sliding around the backseat. "Better buckle up," he advised.

I felt terrible about his face but stubbornly refused to apologize. Instead, I complied quietly, and we headed back to town, speeding along faster than was healthy on blind country roads. Nobody seemed to be in the mood to talk again. Gravel pinging the bumper and some clanging going on in the back were the only sounds. Ranger turned on the radio, and I half expected to hear an Amber alert put out on me already.

A long, weary sigh escaped me. *I would've been home by now if it hadn't been for these two accosting me and dragging me off against my will.* Then another voice came unbidden to say, *I might not be here at all if it wasn't for these two.*

Confused and exhausted I slumped in the backseat, eyes half closed. A blinking red light coming from the console caught my attention. *Cell phone?* If the light was still on, then surely it had enough battery power to make one little phone call. I had just leaned forward and snatched the phone when a ninja hand clamped down on mine, forcing me to drop it. Stunned, I looked up to see Pete staring me down from behind his icepack.

"I told you—the battery's dead."

I didn't respond because we both knew he was lying.

"She's stubborn and stupid—a deadly combination in a female if I've ever seen one," Ranger commented mildly.

I glared at Ranger and scowled at Pete before sinking back into my seat. I noted the contours of his cell didn't fit with the typical models, and there was a long antenna attached to the end like walkie-talkies had. *Weird. And what's with all that equipment banging around in the back?* I turned around in my seat to poke around. *Metal detectors?*

"Searchin' for treasure?" I probed.

The two cohorts exchanged looks again. Pete turned around long enough to quirk his lips at me. *Fascinating.* His mouth was a marvel.

"You could say that," he replied shortly, facing forward again.

"Well, good luck with that—you're not likely gonna find anything out here but a bunch of cowpatties and some tumbleweeds."

This elicited edgy laughter from the driver's seat. "You just said a mouthful, Glasses."

I leaned forward again. "So, what *are* y'all lookin' for?"

Pete sighed and turned back around. "We're interested in finding Indian arrowheads. Heard there were still a few out here in this area."

"Indian arrowheads?" The boys had a few of those lying around. "Why? Are they valuable?" *And why is he lying?*

Ranger's eyes cut to mine in the rearview mirror. "As a matter of fact, we heard the Indian artifacts out here can be *quite* valuable." He said this in a weird, cryptic way.

"Are y'all like doin' this for a college class or somethin'?"

Crickets.

"Something like that," Pete finally answered.

"Then I'm sure y'all are both aware that Indian arrowheads are made out of stone . . . so therefore, *metal* detectors can't detect them."

Ranger huffed out some kind of weird, aggravated noise.

Pete re-removed the icepack. "But they *can* detect flint."

"Flint *is* stone," I countered.

He pursed his lips at me. Looked like he was about to shovel more bull-hockey down my throat when Ranger intervened.

"Pipe down back there!" He turned the radio up over my next question. "I need to concentrate, so I don't get sucked into one of these potholes you all have littering the roads like landmines."

I huffed out my own aggravation. I still needed answers, but they weren't talking. So I would wait, biding my time and biting my tongue for now.

9

LEFT BEHIND

When we screeched to a halt outside a twenty-four hour pharmacy, I was relieved for a lot of reasons. For one, I was freezing. It felt like the temperature had dramatically dropped by thirty degrees. And not just because the air conditioner was blasting through my non-shirt. *No.* The whole atmosphere in the car had changed. Ranger's previous heat had dissipated. In its place was an icy indifference made plain to me by the way his eyes went glacier cold when he so much as glanced my way in the rearview mirror. And there was a new coolness coming from Pete that wasn't there before.

I returned the Arctic vibe right back at them. Whatever trust I had in Pete before went sayonara during the short ride back. He was lying to me. Whatever sort of trouble Ranger was involved in, Pete was in just as deep . . . even if he was a reluctant participant. Ranger turned off the ignition, and we found ourselves in stone cold silence. I was the first to break it by unclicking my seatbelt. I tried opening the door, but it was child-locked. *Figures.*

Ranger twisted around in his seat. "No tricks, Glasses."

"What do you think I'm gonna do? . . . Disappear in a cloud of smoke?"

Something peculiar flickered in Ranger's eyes before he lifted half a busted lip. "Just remember . . . we'll be watching you," he warned before popping the lock. "And I know it's a stretch, but *try* to be on your best behavior."

"Well, I wasn't plannin' on stickin' a pack of gum in my purse without payin', so I wouldn't worry," I replied hotly.

Pete's lips quirked up, and Ranger gave a throaty chuckle, like despite himself. I hopped down from my perch, fighting the urge to make another mad dash for it. Doubtful they would chase me through the well-lit parking lot in front of the few witnesses still loitering about, but I wasn't a hundred percent positive. Also, if I didn't call my father soon, he really would have the cops out looking for me. And my blistered feet were just begging for a ride home. And since they hadn't killed me yet, they wouldn't for the remainder of the night, I reasoned. I began stalking to the pharmacy when a hard hand gripped my elbow.

"Not so fast," Ranger said, sounding so much like an arresting officer I actually froze in place.

Really? What does he think I'm gonna do? Hold up the pharmacy?

I was about to throw a hissy when Pete ambled up. "I don't think you're quite fit for public display," he observed.

Rage swept through me. *So they're embarrassed to be seen slummin' it with me? Well they could just suck it!* I wrenched my arm from Ranger's iron clasp, nearly yanking it out of the socket in the process. "I'll have you know, I don't care *what* you think!" I hissed, vehemently bypassing them.

Pete nabbed me before I could get two paces away. "It's just . . . you've got blood smeared all over your . . . er, top," he explained. "And neither am I for that matter." He dropped my arm to indicate his shirt; it looked like it was paintball splattered red.

Oh. While I fought to hold on to my righteous indignation, Pete grabbed the hem of his shirt and pulled it over his head. *OMG!* The popular Ashley-Leigh catchphrase immediately sprang to mind. His bare torso did funny things to my insides. I felt the need to swallow, for one thing. For another, my stomach went all woozy. Thankfully, he didn't give me a chance to drool because he strode back to the Hummer to rummage around before coming up with two lightweight jackets, one of which he handed off to me. I stood, stupidly holding it, as he threw an arm into each sleeve and hastily zipped up, adding a pair of mirrored aviators over his purpling eye.

I cleared my throat and squeaked out a "thanks" before zipping up my own jacket. When I looked up, it was to see *them* staring at *me*—funny. I automatically faced Pete. However, he was presently too occupied with keeping his straight to answer, so I turned to Ranger.

"You look like a flasher." He answered my unasked question.

I tossed my hair at him and flounced away, wondering what was worse—his icy indifference or his cruel clevers. *Well, obviously, the jacket is too big for me,* I grumbled.

But the real problem was my shorts—they were way too short; it looked like I was just wearing an oversized jacket and cowboy boots.

Ranger snickered. "You can flash me anytime, Glasses."

"Ha-ha very funny," I retorted, balling up the jacket in my hands.

Pete put a finger to his lips, contemplating. "Here . . ." He reached for me again.

I scowled at him, unaccountably angry for the amused look still upon his face. But my anger receded about the same time my jacket did—by his warm hands sliding it up my stomach. I audibly sucked in a breath. If he noticed, he didn't make any sign of it. Pulling on two strings dangling at the bottom of the zipper (that I had failed to notice), he tied them into a bow. Now the jacket stayed at my waist instead of dropping to my knees.

Pete stepped back to study the effect. "I think that's the best we can do under the circumstances." A pushy hand on my back prodded me forward, and a bunch of orders followed behind. "Go to the restroom and get cleaned up, then grab a bottle of water and a nutrition bar—wouldn't hurt to put some food into your system." He tried handing me a wad of bills, which I refused.

"I'm not so sure we should feed the animal," Ranger quipped.

Pete suppressed another smile at my expense before continuing on in an authoritative tone like he was my boss. "Then ask to use the phone. Explain that you had car trouble tonight and had to walk to a phone. But now you're with a friend from school, who's going to—"

"I think I can handle myself just fine, thank-you-very-much," I snapped.

A rude, sinusy sound erupted from Ranger but wasn't followed up with a sardonic remark. Instead, he climbed on back into the driver's seat and commenced to looking bored.

Head held high, I stalked through the automatic doors. Oppressive florescent lights immediately made me blink, and it was an instant awakening from the dream/nightmare I'd been living for the past couple of hours. After my eyes adjusted, I scanned the aisles for a restroom sign and was about to head to the back when I noticed Pete staring at me. Again.

I felt another flash of anger. *Really?* I narrowed my eyes at him as he scrutinized my face. Unfortunately, I couldn't really tell what he was thinking because the mirrored lens only reflected back my own distorted face. Embarrassed, I swiped at a black smudge beneath my eye then saw myself go wide-eyed as Pete casually threw an arm over my shoulder and walked me to the back of the store.

"What's with the escort service?" I asked in my most acerbic tone while trying to ignore the thrill I felt with his arm wrapped around me. "Afraid I'm gonna get lost?"

Wordlessly, he released me outside the restroom, where I stood facing him like a huffed-up hen. Taking me by surprise, he reached out to cup my face in his palm, his thumb caressing over the tender spot where Ranger backhanded me. My breath hitched in my throat, and my former anger evaporated as suddenly as a fine mist. Whatever caustic remark I was about to make left my brain like it was plucked-out by tweezers.

His other hand joined my face to draw me forward. It felt like we were moving in slow motion, still part of the dream. He leaned down, and my face tilted up, a flower starving for sun. During that infinitesimal space in time, my heart thudded to a halt, and a sly, almost subversive smile curved his lips. It was the last thing I saw before closing my eyes and parting my lips. I felt teasing lips brush over mine, skimming the corner of my mouth before moving up to find my ear instead.

"Don't look directly at Ranger," Pete breathed, light as a feather, before abruptly pivoting to head to the pharmacy.

I just stood there watching him leave, quivering with unmet expectations. Blink-blinked my eyes a couple of times like he was a mirage. Wound myself around to walk robotically through the door. Stared at my shocked face in the mirror and realized my mouth was hanging open. Snapped it shut to turn on the faucet. Splashed water on my face—enough times to wash the dirty streaks off, but not enough to cool my overheated system.

Don't look Ranger directly in the eye, that's what he said; I was sure of it. *But why?* A vicious bully he was to be sure, but was he also some kind of mythical creature that would turn me into stone if I stared too long into his ice-cold eyes? Or, like a cobra, would he strike me dead if I dared look him in the eye? Neither one made sense to me since I'd already glared at him on more than one occasion. I was mystified.

Something occurred to me as I sifted through the events of tonight looking for lost meaning. I distinctly remembered Pete reaching up to snap off the interior light right before Ranger began raking me over with his eyes. He had explained the light bothered his eye, but I felt like that was an excuse. Now I wondered if it wasn't to keep Ranger and I from having eye contact. *Why?*

I dried my face with some paper towels and stared at my reflection. All I could see was red-rimmed, bright eyes and flushed skin—I was more than a little titillated by the idea of Pete kissing me. And mortified that I'd practically begged him to meet my lips . . . when all he wanted to do was whisper in my ear. *Ugh!* And what was worse—he knew it! I hurled the soggy wad into the trash. I mean, I barely knew the guy and here I was ready to snog him right in the middle of the floodlit pharmacy.

No better than the cheap floozy Ranger took me for!

Of course, he didn't want to kiss me! I yanked a brush through my tangled mass of hair. I was well aware of how out of my league he *thought* he was. He was just trying to . . . warn me? *But why?* Weren't he and Ranger friends? No, not friends, I dismissed the idea immediately. There was way too much animosity between them for that. More like cohorts.

A shiver of fear shook me as I recalled how they showed up tonight— *Poof!*—like figments of my imagination. *What's going on?* Whatever it was, it wasn't any good, and they didn't want me to know about it. My thoughts circled back to Pete's warning. Why *not* look at Ranger directly? I thought through more possibilities, focusing on the most plausible one. Maybe he was suffering from some kind of anger disorder? Like if I glared at him one too many times, it would set him off and he would snap and beat me senseless? I could feel the intense physical violence running like a current right below his skin.

So I would heed the advice. My gut was telling me not to ask any questions either, and that was implicit in the way in which Pete delivered the message. There was a reason he whispered it in my ear, and it obviously had *nothing* to do with him feeling physically attracted to me. An odd pain twisted my insides.

My eyes drew to the mirror once more. That's when I noticed one silky tie had escaped and was stained scarlet. I tucked it back in, re-zipped the jacket, and was preparing to head out when I saw a logo on the left side I hadn't noticed earlier. *Hmmm.* I leaned closer to inspect, smoothing out the wrinkles to read what was hidden in the baggy folds. Something about it looked familiar to me. I read the backward letters: *International Elite Academy* encircled a roaring lion.

I gasped as the bottom fell out of the floor. No wonder my gut reaction had been to run tonight. They were associated with that military academy that was after my brother! Something shady was going on that involved them, their organization, and somehow me. Other than that, I was clueless.

Why didn't they just tell me who they were?

I headed out to find Pete and some answers. When I didn't immediately see him at the pharmacy area, I warily scanned the wall mirrors but couldn't find any tall, golden matinee idols standing in the aisles. Instead, I found the eyes of a male employee, following the line of my legs up to my face with a barely veiled look of lust on his face. *Ew.*

"Can I help you?" he eagerly asked.

"Yes, can I please use your phone?"

"Um . . ." He hesitated between wanting to help me and not wanting to get into trouble. "I'm actually not supposed to do that."

Desperate times called for desperate measures, so I began to slink toward him while batting my eyelashes. "It's just that . . . I got in a fight with my boyfriend," I said, hardly having to pretend to blink back tears, "and now I don't have a ride home."

He pinkened and looked up guiltily at the security monitor.

"Please?" I stared at him helplessly. "You'd totally be my hero, and I sure could use one tonight."

"Okay, sure . . . just this once." He quickly led me to a glass partition dividing the store from the pharmacy and unlocked the door with a key hanging around his belt loop.

I gave him my number, and he proceeded to botch it a couple of times before punching in the right number. He seemed so pleased with his effort, that I gave him a reward smile. It was ringing. I swallowed nervously. This was it, the moment of truth or untruth, as it were. My heart was hammering, and my palms were sweaty. Even if I could pull off the story, I knew I'd *still* be in a lot of trouble.

The intervals of buzzing stopped, and the machine clicked on. Was it possible Daddy had fallen asleep and wasn't even aware I was still out? Maybe, I thought bolstered by the idea. I was certainly due for the pendulum to swing back the other way—for something to go *right* for me tonight.

After the beep, I relayed my rehearsed message, explaining my situation just in case he was out looking for me and came back to check if I called.

I sincerely hoped that was not the case. I actually shuttered at the thought of how mad that would make him.

Mr. Helpful was watching how my little drama would play out. "No answer, huh?"

I shook my head and faced the other way only to find Pete watching me. He gave me a wave and pointed to the exit. He still looked like an absurdly hot star trying to go incognito. I don't know what I thought: he'd suddenly sprout horns and a tail? I watched him glide out the door, handed over the receiver with a dismissive "thanks" and turned to leave.

"I could give you a ride home, if you could wait an hour," he offered desperately.

I smiled thinly at him. "As tempting an offer as that is . . ." I didn't finish my sentence, a plan hatching in my mind. Pete didn't know my father didn't pick up. For all he knew, I was still in a heated debate and would be for the next few minutes. There was a door next to me marked For Employees Only that led outside. If I could get employee-of-the-month to break one rule, maybe I could get him to break one more?

Thirty seconds of bad flirting was rewarded, and I slipped through the side door. Stepping into the dark shadows, I instantly felt like a secret spy and suppressed a nervous giggle. *What am I doing?* I must have a death wish tonight, because if I was caught sneaking up on those two, they would probably kill me. Or worse—torture me by leaving me in the parking lot to walk home. (I resolved to buy some new sneakers, even if I had to starve to do it.) But I badly needed some answers, and my gut was telling me I was heading in the right direction to get them.

Things weren't adding up. Or maybe I was adding all wrong. So far I had the sum of two handsome strangers, hanging around a small town, to chase one lone girl, in the middle of the night. Then I added in the fact that they belonged to that Elite Academy that was after my brother. There was an unknown quotient here—an X-factor—that revolved around us Connelly kids. I knew this in a way that I couldn't articulate. Right now it was a mindboggling equation, but one I was determined to solve. I also suspected the two suspects were busy talking things over right now. So I crouched into my fly-on-the-wall position and started crawling along with that icky feeling creeping up my spine.

Bad things happen when secrets are kept from me.

At the edge of where brick wall and parking lot meet, I poked my head around the corner. *Bingo.* They were both sitting in their ridiculous ride, looking like they were in the midst of an argument—again. Pete bit back something he was going to say to peer into the front of the store, obviously waiting for my reemergence. Ranger continued talking heatedly at him, his bicep flexing as he pointed. A cold sweat broke out at the thought of getting busted. These were *not* ones to cross . . . especially Ranger; he really had it in for me.

My stomach lurched as an opportunity presented itself to me—a mini van pulled in two spaces away. It was now or never. When their attention diverted to the couple walking in, I ducked and scooted around to the back of the minivan. Pausing there to regulate my erratic heartbeat, I drew in a deep breath and ended up choking on the exhaust still leaking from the muffler.

Crap! I muffled a cough, trying not to breathe while peeking around the back fender. *Double crap!* Ranger just glanced in his rearview mirror. I whipped my head back around. A heart-pounding beat later, I dared another peek. It looked like the non-natives were getting restless. Ranger was tapping impatiently on the steering wheel with his thumbs, and Pete was leaning out the open window to get a better view.

Pete's window was down! This was my chance. Quickly crossing myself, I leaped from the relative safety of my current position and landed in a puddle of murky car waste behind them, praying their fancy motion detector wouldn't beep. I didn't come this far to get busted now! The low rumbles of male voices could be heard, but I couldn't quite make out their words.

Muscles tightening with apprehension, I slipped around the humongous back right tire, flattening myself against the pebbly asphalt. A whimper almost escaped me as I scraped my already-scraped knee in the process. (I'd lost count of all the scratches, bumps, and bruises I'd accumulated tonight.)

The murmurs began to translate into actual words I could make out here and there. I belly-snaked closer. It was Pete talking.

"I still don't think she knows anything," he insisted.

Uh . . . wrong-o!

"That's because you're still naïve, rookie."

I couldn't quite make out Pete's reply.

"Then why did she take off like she was running for her life?" Ranger burst out.

"Because she's smarter than the average civilian." Pete's words swelled my chest. After a disagreeing snort from Ranger, he continued, "Plus, if a scary monster like you was chasing me, I'd run for my life, too."

Ha! Funny.

"Not funny, dude." Ranger began fiddling with the stereo until he landed on a country station. "You're blind when it comes to that bimbo."

Pete didn't bother arguing on my behalf, and a dart of disappointment jabbed me, leaking out my earlier smug satisfaction. What did I expect? Birds of a feather . . .

A twangy sad song began playing. Ranger impatiently punched it off. "What the hell is taking her so long?"

"She's probably just waiting in line," Pete said serenely. But then he stuck his head out the window, craning to see inside.

I sucked in my breath.

"I hope she's adding some Ms. Clairol to her basket," Ranger sneered.

Ms. Clairol? What did he mean by—? I fingered my hair. *Oh. What an ass!* My face burned with indignation.

Pete returned his head to its original lookout post. "I don't see her."

Ranger guffawed. "She can't be that hard to track down . . . just follow the trail of hillbilly eyes!"

I noted that Pete didn't bother responding again. Another moment ticked by in silence, broken by the hum and scrape of a car exiting the parking lot. My ears strained from their eavesdropping effort.

"I'd better go check." Pete sounded resolved all of a sudden.

Shoot! What should I . . . ?

I was still rolling under the tractor-sized truck when I heard the *bing! bing! bing!* of the door opening. Navy sneakers stepped out followed by the dull *thwunk* of the door closing shut. *Whew! That was close.*

Pete leaned back in the window. "You know, if you hadn't of been such a royal ass this whole time, then this mission would've been like taking candy from a baby . . . and I would've been out of here in a couple of weeks max."

What?!

Ranger maniacally laughed from the driver's seat, a position I was sure he was well acquainted with. "Couldn't make it too easy for you, now could I? Where's the sport in that? We got to see if you can live up to that famous last name."

Pete cursed, then crunched gravel until he hit sidewalk, the sound of mocking laughter trailing him.

Go time! I wormed out from under the truck. *Bloody heck!* How was I gonna get back inside without being seen?

I crawled back around the minivan and scrambled to my feet. The timing was just right again because the couple was returning. So I hopped on over while Ranger's attention was focused on the sliding door, making it back to the shadows clinging to the side of the building. *Now what?* My heart was thrashing against my ribs, my mind tumbling around the disturbing new info I'd learned. It all intermingled with my exit strategy, and the possibility of my father yelling me to death when I finally returned home.

I stopped to take some deep breaths. *Could a seventeen-year-old die of a heart attack?* Must. Calm. Down. Maybe I could just get back in through the same door? Even though I knew it would automatically lock behind me, I yanked on the doorknob, hoping it would just magically open. *Dang it!* I pounded on the door to no success. The beating on my palms would feel like gnat stings compared to what Ranger would do to me if he saw me skulking around in the shadows spying on them.

And then it hit me—I wouldn't sneak around anymore. I would pretend to run away. They'd been expecting me to do that all night, so I would actually fulfill their expectations. So I hustled to the back of the building and started down the back alley, heading for the street that ran in front of the pharmacy. Hopefully, they'd spot me and put another halt to my "escape attempt" and drive me home. Pete had plenty of time to search the store and would probably be headed out any second to report back to Mr. In-Charge.

As I stumbled along the depressing strip of dirt, I thought how bizarre it was to find myself in *another* lonely, bleak alley. It was like my night was on constant repeat: two birthday cakes with corresponding wishes, two guys' laps, and two kidnapping attempts followed by my bungled attempts at escape. Felt like I'd landed in an episode of *The Twilight Zone*.

The thunder of an engine roaring to life followed closely by wheels peeling off pavement let me know I was found out. I ran and made a hard right at the end of the alley, hustling over to the main street so they could see me. *Aw man!* My heart sank to my dusty boots. I got to the street just in time to see the electric-red taillights of their Hummer skim through the yellow light . . . and keep on going, driving way too fast to be able to see me.

And then I realized—with another hard jolt—that they were *not* looking for me. I was stranded again. And just like that, I watched them evaporate into the night . . . like a wisp of smoke from one of my birthday candles.

10

IT WAS ALL A BAD DREAM

When I regained consciousness the next day, I knew it was late because the birds had ceased chirping, and the shadows in my room had rearranged themselves in all the wrong places. I peeked out from under my comforter and immediately retreated, like a turtle back into its shell.

I was battered, bruised, and confused. It felt like I'd just been through an epic war, had a secret midnight encounter with the devil, or quite possibly a tête-à-tête with the man-of-my-dreams. The possibility of all three occurences happening in one night seemed too much for one mere mortal to bear. My mind was reeling.

Had I fallen through the magic rabbit hole only to reemerge a few hours later in my bed?

I could barely lift the covers. If it weren't for an achingly full bladder, I would've succumbed to the exhaustion that held me hostage to my bed. I finally managed to rouse myself into upright position. *Dag nab*! Amid all my various aches and pains, the two stuffed sausages I called feet required my immediate attention. I cautiously drew them out to inspect the damage. They could've passed for nine-months pregnant. And the blisters would've been curling my toes, if I could've moved them.

I threw my legs over the side of the bed and realized I was sore in places I didn't even know existed. With fascinated horror, I inspected the large array of scratches and bruises decorating my arms. They also felt leaden as if I'd been boxing against heavyweights all night. My mind automatically flashed to Ranger's hateful face.

Even though I didn't believe in the power of my sixth sense as strongly as Mama did, I had to admit: he had my internal alarm bells ringing. I could tell he had more than just a passing dislike for me, like when two people meet and their chemistry doesn't mesh. Somehow, it was personal, his hate. I could feel it. He seemed like some kind of sinister, larger-than-life character right up there with Voldemort, Dracula, and Darth Vador. Even his handsome face seemed a grotesque masking of an evil villain.

A tremor shook me as I remembered the brute force he had used to subdue me, the stinging backhand I received as payback. His face exposed a barely veiled pleasure when I cried out in pain. I felt lucky a tattoo of contusions was the only physical reminder left of our encounter. That, and the ongoing reel of bad memories since the day we met, had me feeling like I was living in a nightmare.

But intermingled with the slides depicting horror, were images of a different genre. Pete's otherworldly face filled my vision. Even though I was unaccountably angry with him for leaving me in the lurch, an involuntary smile curved my lips at the memory of his mouth hovering close to mine. My face burned at the memory, but my body heated in a whole different way.

The thought of him *nearly* kissing me nearly took me to my knees. I recalled the smell of his skin, the way I felt with his arms wrapped around me, and a crushing wave of desire overcame me. I'd never felt anything like this. Heady stuff. I could see how desire could strike down the most rational of human beings with bouts of insanity. I gave myself a mental shake; had to keep in mind who he was running with—wolves ran in packs.

As I limped across my child-size bedroom, a glint of sapphire caught my eye. It was the jacket Pete loaned me last night . . . well, gifted me, since I wouldn't see him again to return it. My hand clutched at my chest—it was physically painful to realize that was a likely possibility; my whole being repelled the idea I would never lay eyes on him again. It was an entirely automatic response, like my immune system fighting off a viral invasion.

I had to squash these feelings like a bug. They were unhealthy and unuseful to me. I'd been taught to focus on reality. And my reality was school was tomorrow. And I had a very busy day ahead of me preparing for that and trying to convince Mikey that cowboy boots and a cape did not constitute appropriate school attire.

It required a lot of energy to go against him—energy I didn't have today. Not to mention the fact that I had to celebrate my birthday. Again. It was the last thing I wanted to do (right behind going for a nice long walk), but it would disappoint the boys not to celebrate with me.

It seemed especially off to me in light of last night's bizarre events. It was like I'd woken up an entirely different person, who was sucked back in time to her old life. Maybe it was being in the presenc of their disturbing mix of good looks and charisma. Or knowing something was going on that somehow involved me. *Something* had changed. I wasn't exactly sure what, but I kinda felt as though I'd been sleepwalking for the past couple of years.

. . . And suddenly just woke up.

I was hobbling down the hall when my father's gruff voice accosted me. "Katie-girl, you up?"

"Yeah, Kadee, you up yet?" Mikey echoed.

"'m up," I yawned.

"Oh, yea! Drewy, she's up!" The pitter-patter of bare feet barreling around the corner preceded a towel-caped crusader flying into my arms.

"I'll alert the media," Andrew replied.

No matter how much had changed for *me* overnight, it appeared everyone else had remained the same.

"I need a word with you," Daddy said so quietly it only implied impending doom.

Uh-oh. He'd already read me the riot act last night. Even though I'd told him the car wouldn't start, he'd still delivered his usual line: "Some people find excuses, others find a way." *Yeah,* I'd wanted to say, *find a way home . . . no thanks to you.* Instead, I'd just hung my head while I listened to his tirade until I'd about passed-out on the couch.

I sighed deeply. "Okay, Daddy. Give me a minute." I dove into the bathroom I shared with my brothers to pee and gather my wits about me.

Gah! The reflection that met me was gasp worthy: puffy eyes, puffier lips, hair that resembled a rat's nest. And there was a faint bluish tint on my left cheek that, if measured, would exactly fit Ranger's handprint. Then there was the angry scratch writhing around my neck before disappearing behind my left ear. Short of wearing a turtleneck, there was little I could do to hide this.

Oh well . . . I'd just have to come up with yet another lie to tell Daddy. *Hmmm.* Usually, I felt a twinge of guilt for the lies I deemed necessary to tell. Today that feeling was noticeably absent. Hopefully, his lie detector would be as inoperable this morning as it was last night. He was really out of it, which was probably why I got off so lightly. It wasn't like him to just let things go so quickly. Daddy usually liked to stretch the punishments out for a longer duration of time, then, just when you thought it was finally over, he'd take it out like a cartoon mallet to bop you over the head.

But you know what? I didn't even care anymore. He was just another problem for me to solve. Like an algebraic equation, he was easily solvable once you knew the right numbers to plug in. Nope, I was no longer concerned about my father. I had bigger fish to fry—like two mysterious guys prowling around town in an XXL SUV.

After vigorously rubbing the sleep from my eyes with harsh cold water, I came up dripping to stare at them in the mirror. I recalled the words Pete whispered in my ear, and a delayed shiver ran down my spine.

I peered closer at the miniature of myself reflected in the onyx of my eyes, noticing again how small the ring of blue iris was in relation to my pupils. When asked what color my eyes were people—who'd known me my whole life—often came up blank. It was hard to recognize the color when so little of it was represented. I'd never really thought much about it, since I'd been staring at my own reflection my whole life. It seemed a normal Connelly trait like long limbs or stubborn pride.

Except I'd always noticed how almost painfully blue my father's eyes were compared to mine, a lot like Ranger's. (That was the second comparison I'd made of the domineering males in a week.) But Ranger's eyes were even more conspicuous, almost neon sitting in contrast to his dark skin and hair. An unlikely combination of DNA.

Thinking about odd contrasts pulled Pete's face into my mind yet again. *So much for shaking him off.* Both of them were unequivocally two of the best-looking guys I'd ever seen. Probably that *anyone* had ever seen. They were both one in a million—in more ways than one—which made them more like one in a *billion.* But while Ranger was dark-haired, light-eyed, and dangerous, Pete was almost exactly opposite. His hair was a golden hue, with eyes so dark and shiny they almost appeared wet, like he was on the verge of tears. This seemed contrary to his personality because good humor seemed to be his natural disposition. I thought of his sensual mouth quirking up into a smile and my insides went soft again.

Dang it! I had to stop this obsession. Pete might not be malicious like Ranger, who wore it on his sleeve like a badge of honor, but he was still dangerous. If for no other reason than he belonged to that organization, he was not to be trusted. No matter how appealing I found him, he was on Team IEA, and therefore . . . my natural enemy.

I finished obsessing about the same time I finished dressing (in a buttoned-to-the-top-top). Shuffling out to the living room, I found Andrew and Mikey belly-sprawled across the floor, faces planted in an animal book.

Andrew looked up lazily from turning the page, eyes sparkling mischief. "What took you so long? . . . Don'tja know the early bird gets the worm?" He was, of course, mocking Daddy, who was completely oblivious that Andrew was always doing this. Instead, he took these regurgitated words as signs of his allegiance. This was just one of many things that helped cement Andrew's status as favorite Connelly progeny.

"Long night," I croaked, leaning over to buss the tops of their heads.

"Well, I hope you have a good, long story to go along with it," he said, pointedly.

"Kadee always tells the best stories," Mikey chimed in, ever the president of my fan club.

I rubbed my hand against the dark grain of Mikey's bristle. "Don't I always?"

Heavy tromping down the hall shook the floor. We simultaneously fell silent as Daddy appeared in the doorway. I half expected to hear *Fi-fi-fo-fum!* My father was a big man, and whatever space wasn't swallowed up by his frame was filled in with his anger.

After a measured silence: "Bedroom, *now!*" he ordered before turning around and tromping back from where he came from. Andrew and I exchanged looks. My father was more of the rant and rave type and usually enjoyed a good audience.

"Yes, sir," I croaked, realizing I must be in more trouble than I thought. Mikey patted my arm, and I smiled encouragingly before trudging after Daddy's stiff back to his bedroom.

Upon entering, I saw that his bed was still habitually and tightly made, but other than that, an almost complete makeover (or I guess I should say make-*under)* had occurred since I'd last been in here to clean. Our cheerful finger-painted milestones had been taken down, leaving dark rectangular reminders of their frames instead, and my mother's graying bathrobe was no longer hanging from the back of the bathroom door. My eyes automatically searched the chest-of-drawers for their wedding photo. It was conspicuously missing along with the tarnished silver tray that held his wedding band, and the keepsake box that held mysterious treasures kept locked away. I realized all traces of her were wiped clean as the commemorative rifle Daddy now prominently displayed from its perch above the headboard.

Blinking back tears, I stood facing him and his army-regulation crew cut while he stared me down, not missing the scratch running for my hairline. I fought the impulse to cover it with my hands.

A few more seconds tocked by before he said, "You sure you told me ever'thing 'bout what happened last night?"

Gulp. "Yes, sir."

His eyes held mine in the kind of staring contest that Ashley-Leigh and I used to indulge in when we were kids. I stared back with what I hoped was my most innocent expression.

"This mornin' I drove over to the Montgomery's to tow yer car back for ya, while you was home snug-as-a-bug-in-a-rug. Funny thing . . ."—he let that hang in the air while my heart plummeted—"it started just fine."

I found swallowing hard while still trying to appear innocent was counter-productive. Then there was the heat factor that gave me away—sweat began blistering my upper lip. I started to stammer out a quick explanation when a heavy hand clamped onto my shoulder. This had the dual purpose of shutting me up and sinking me onto the bed.

Now that Daddy had my attention, he leaned over, finger to face. "I don't know, or care, what kind of shenanigans went on last night with Little-Miss-About-Town. However, you are *my* daughter, and therefore, a reflection of *me*. I will *not* have you out gallivantin' around town with that floozy till all hours of the night. If I were her Daddy, I'd've bent'er over my knee a long time ago. 'Spare The Rod And Spoil The Child,' is the motto that family needs to remember from the Good Book. They lost control of that one a long time ago. But *I* am *not* about to lose control of *my* kid!"

I knew just what to do in these situations—cast my eyes down submissively.

"Now I know what it's like to be young. I was young once, too. You can get yerself into a lotta trouble runnin' around late at night . . . 'specially a girl like you. You gotta be careful not to get caught up in harmless fun." He air-quoted now. "'*Harmless fun*' most often leads to harmful consequences. I outta know." He indicated the leg he injured in a motorcycle accident that effectively ended his military career.

"Yes, sir," I said, almost seeing his point after last night's fiasco.

"Discipline the military gave me is the thing that changed my life, and *discipline* is what you kids need, *not* more freedom. And that's one of the things I wanted to talk to you about . . ."

My stomach lurched. When I braved his eyes again, he gave me the kind of look intended to nail me to the wall.

"I can see now that I can't trust you to be a proper mother-figure, nor moral guide for those two boys in there."

I gasped like he'd slapped my face.

"Your lies and lack of good judgment last night made me realize that yer mama over-estimated yer ability to raise them boys. Maybe it ain't fair to rely on you; yer still immature—like havin' a kid raise a kid. So I realized this mornin' at church, while you was home sleepin' in, that I'm on the right track with this here military academy."

I was still fighting the urge to scream when he said, "I wanted to let you know that I've reconsidered my position on that school."

I stood up, horrified. "Daddy, no!"

"Yer brother has a real opp'rtunity to make somethin' of his life with this *Elite* Academy." Daddy actually cracked a prideful smile, which caused a strong urge in me to smash a pie . . . right in his face.

"B-but, Daddy, you can't do that!" He was using last night's one time transgression as leverage for his plot to enroll Drewy in that military academy. It wasn't right and it wasn't fair. And I *had* to stop it! "You said you weren't about to send Andrew off to be raised by any of those fancy boardin' schools!" I reminded him.

"It aint just some fancy boardin' school—it's 'The World's Most Elite Military Academy'," Daddy corrected me.

"But you promised Mama!" My voice wobbled. "Please, Daddy! You just can't send him away—he's only eight-years-old!"

His eyes moved to a spot above my shoulder. "We'll cross that bridge when we get to it," he said, placating me now that I was on the verge of tears. (Tears were my father's kryptonite.) "Right now they just wanna assess him, see if he's a good fit for 'em. From my understandin', they're only lookin' for a partic'lar type of kid."

Of course they're going to accept him, I wanted to spit—Harvard, Yale, and Princeton all would.

"They're not lettin' in just any ol' rift-raft. And I don't blame 'em one bit. Kids today . . ." Daddy continued droning on about what was wrong with kids today, but I wasn't listening anymore. I was thinking back to what I overheard Pete tell Ranger last night. Something about a mission being so easy, it would be like taking candy from a baby.

What was the mission exactly? Stealing a young boy from his family? Was Andrew the candy, and me the baby?

Fear and rage went coursing through my body, forming a potentially hazardous adrenaline bomb. While Daddy went on and on about "the amazing opp'rtunity this was for Andrew," I felt this liquid outrage begin to bubble over. I had to cork it before I exploded all over him.

". . . If he's accepted, they'll offer him a full scholarship, which includes free room and board. Now you tell me how I can just let that ship sail on by with a good conscious?" Daddy reasoned.

A glare was my answer.

"I'm gonna do right by my boy, whether or not you approve, *big sister*."

It sounded like he was trying to convince himself. He knew very well the promises he'd made to Mama regarding schools that were interested in us. And diminishing my role in Andrew's life to mere "big sister" was really a low blow.

My urge to throw pie in his face had grown to wanting to grind it in for good measure. *Stupid, stupid, stupid,* my eyes transmitted this message, hoping it would sink into his skull telepathically. But I had a feeling his skull was too thick to penetrate.

"Now you stop lookin' at me like that, Katherine."

"Like what?" I challenged, my temper getting the best of me. "Like the man we're all supposed to look up to is too weak-willed to keep his word?"

I flinched back as violence flashed from Daddy's eyes. "*Weak-willed!*" he thundered. "You referrin' to the same weak-willed man who allowed you to go back to public school and get a job?"

I looked down, suddenly absorbed by a water stain in the carpet. He was right—I could not dispute the fact that he'd also made those promises to Mama. And I was glad he'd broken them at the time, wanting a more normal life for us. Now I wasn't so sure. If we'd never gone back to public school, then Andrew's teachers would never have sent query letters to all those schools, and we wouldn't be sitting here having this argument right now.

I just realized, again, that Mama might not have died a crazy, delusional woman after all. Maybe she'd known *exactly* what she was doing. Another shiver ran down my spine when I thought of all the ways we'd already gone against her wishes. We were suddenly off on a course she'd intentionally blocked us from. Daddy had already knocked down the barricade, and we were barreling down it now. Was there a steep cliff at the end that we'd run right over, only to plunge to our death? And Daddy was the freight train driving us. Once he'd set his mind to something, he wouldn't veer off course, no matter what. He suffered from what Mama always referred to as a "one-track-mind."

Everything was still cloaked in a hazy gray fog, but one thing was clear: my mission was to stop that academy from sinking its claws into Andrew.

There was no way I could argue with Daddy once his mind was made up. I couldn't out yell him, or physically make him do anything he didn't want to do. So I had no choice but to outsmart him.

"Have you informed Andrew about your big plans for his future?"

"Not yet," he said defensively. "I hadn't made up my mind until after meetin' with their representatives."

"*Representatives?*" I sprang back to my feet like I'd just sat on a live wire. "What representatives?"

The two representatives my father began describing exactly matched the two that sprang to mind. "Oh, Katie! I wish you could've seen the two young men that *Elite* Academy sent. They were both . . . uh, very handsome and well-spoken, and had a lotta confidence about 'em. I could exactly picture Andrew growin' up to be just like that," he positively crowed with enthusiasm.

I swallowed my snarky retort to focus on the facts. "*When* did you meet with them?"

Daddy's complexion turned ruddier. "Yest'rday afternoon. Over at Cannon Air Force Base. That's why I was a little late gettin' home," he admitted. "I gotta tell ya, Katie. I never seen nothin' like it in all my military years—those two were completely given the royal treatment. You'd a thought they were a couple of four-star generals the way they rolled out the red carpet for 'em!"

Daddy trumpeted some more about them and their Elite Academy. How they convinced him it was the best place for a gifted boy like Andrew. About the strict standards and discipline, and how the world would be his oyster after graduating . . . blah, blah, blah. My thoughts whirled around in my head like a tornado, so I could only pick up a phrase here and there intermingled with my thoughts on Ranger's bizarre hatefulness, Pete's possible role in all of this, and Mama's fear about "special" schools.

"Yep," he droned on, "they came all the way out here from California to meet with me. The graduatin' cadets have the recruitin' duties for new members as part of their graduation requirement . . . kind of a neat tradition if you ask me, passin' on the torch that way. Can you believe that Andrew is bein' considered? And at such a young age? It's very excitin' news. You'll see. I'd never forgive myself if I didn't take advantage of this golden opp'rtunity for my son."

I must've looked green around the gills, because Daddy stopped speaking like he was in an infomercial for that stupid school. "You feelin' alright, Katie?"

No. I felt awful. My ears were ringing and my head was spinning. Too much was happening too fast, and way too much was at stake. I started hyperventilating.

"Katie-girl?" His voice seemed to be coming from far away.

I couldn't speak yet and was sure that if I opened my mouth, I would end up either hurling the F-bomb or last night's birthday cake all over Daddy. I'd only had a gut reaction this visceral once before . . . when Mama told us she was sick.

If Andrew was accepted—which he one hundred percent would be— (cause if they weren't looking for Drews, I don't know who they would be looking for) then my brother would be shipped off to that academy forever. I shuddered at the thought of what that would do to our little family. It wasn't fair. We had so little. All we really had was each other. And now Daddy had decided, overnight, to change that.

Hot tears began trickling down my cheeks, the first drops in front of Daddy since Mama's funeral. I knew he wouldn't react right, unadept as he was with dealing with female emotions. Despite that, I was desperate for him to comfort me.

"Now Katie, you stop that nonsense!" He patted my arm in a gesture I took to be more warning than sympathy. "You gotta pull yerself together before we tell the boys. You gettin' hysterical's only gonna make it harder on 'em."

Sometimes I hate being right.

A timid knock on the door wrenched me from my misery. "Kadee?" Mikey said hesitantly, "Are you okay?"

A warm, fuzzy feeling enveloped me like a hug; he'd come to check on me, knowing full well he was risking Daddy's wrath. I suddenly realized it was my four-year-old brother and *not* my forty-four-year-old father who always comforted me.

"Go away, Shadow, this does not concern you!" Daddy ordered.

"But I am co'cerned cause you're makin' Kadee cry."

I knew I had to get him out of here fast, because Daddy was currently teetering along the thin line between boiling over into a rage . . . or just plain boiling over. Mikey's meddling would definitely tip him onto the rage side.

"Actually, Mikey, we're comin' out in a minute to have a family meetin'," I said, trying to stuff a sock in it. A pause. "So go on back and drag Drewy in from wherever he's hidin' and wait for us in the livin' room."

"Okay, Kadee." He hesitated before running off to do my bidding.

I stifled my sobs until they were as intermittent as hiccups, calmed somewhat by the idea that if anyone could change Daddy's mind, it would be his first-born son. When it seemed I'd calmed down to the point I was no longer a "hysterical female," Daddy tried to reason with me again.

"Now, Katie, you know that Andrew's been bored outta his gourd in school for a long time now."

"If that's what that mentor's for, I can do it myself!"

Daddy continued talking as if I hadn't spoken: "This here *Elite* Academy is the best place for a boy like him to be challenged academically and to learn the discipline it takes to make somethin' of himself in this world."

I snorted. "I don't really know how much more discipline an eight-year-old boy needs."

"That's right, young lady. You do not." He pointed between my eyes like I'd just made a valid point for him. "Accordin' to them two cadets, ninety percent of our brain power goes unused. If caught early enough, they can remedy that sit'eation in Andrew 'fore his brain starts, uh . . . atrophyin' on 'im like everybody else. And account of him bein' so smart and all, well . . . that would just be a cryin' shame," he finished, snapping his suspenders proudly after his little spiel.

I ignored the useless data he'd just babbled. "Have you even taken into account how Andrew feels about this? After all, it's *his* life we're talkin' about here."

"'O' course I have!" Daddy became irate immediately. "I tried tellin' him just last night with you gone . . ."

Convenient timing.

"But could only get so far as to let 'im know that a mentor was gonna meet with him ever' day after school for a while." Daddy stopped to clench his jaw. "When I tried speakin' with Andrew 'bout the possibility of attendin' an *elite* military school next semester . . . I couldn't seem to tell 'im."

Next semester? That's only a few months away! I probed his face for underlying meaning. *Is he having second thoughts?*

As if reading my mind he said, "I'm convinced it's the right place for him."

"Then what stopped you? He has a right to know."

A pause stretched out so long I thought Daddy must not have heard me. I was about to repeat the question when he finally unglued his lips to spit out one word: "Mikey" then remained quiet as if that were explanation enough.

"What do you mean? Mikey's gonna find out sooner or later, and it's gonna be so much . . ." My voice quivered when I thought how painful it would be for him. "So much worse for him to wake up one mornin' to find his big brother's bags are packed to leave. For good."

"I mean I am *literally* unable to—" Daddy broke off, seeming to be at a loss for words. He composed himself with great difficulty. "That's what I need you for—I can't seem to tell him."

Oh. I got it. He wanted me to do his dirty work and deliver the bad news. I was about to impolitely decline when he changed gears.

"Never mind. Come on . . . Let's get this show on the road."

Daddy stalked from the room, and I followed like an obedient puppy he'd just kicked.

11

FAMILY MEETING

A couple of minutes later found us gathered around our living room in poses that more resembled an intervention than a family meeting. Only Andrew seemed to be relaxed—one leg dangling over the back of the couch, he was busy tossing popcorn kernels in the air and catching them in his mouth.

"Listen up everybody. I have a big announcement." Daddy's eyes zeroed in on Andrew until he realigned himself into upright position.

"What's up, Pops?" he asked, oblivious to the seriousness of the situation.

"Yeah, what's up Pops?" Mikey echoed.

An aggravated look from Daddy followed, but he decided to let it slide. "I have some very excitin' news for Andrew."

"Yay!" Mikey was immediately enthusiastic.

Before continuing, Daddy glanced furtively at Mikey then turned around so his back was completely against him. I thought that was odd (not to mention rude), because he usually required all eyes on him when he was speaking.

"Now Andrew, I know I told you that a special mentor was comin' here this semester to work with you after school," he began.

"Yes, sir." Andrew appeared more bored than anything else, being well accustomed to special treatment.

"Well, what I didn't tell you was that I also finally decided on a school good enough to consider for you!" Daddy was smiling maniacally now and paused, waiting for some kind of reaction from Drew. What he got was a roomful of silence. He cleared his throat. "You see Andrew, yer a special kid

. . . and by special, I don't mean like in that retarded way people mean when they say "special" these days."

It was funeral parlor quiet, so Daddy went on determinedly: "You are advanced. So advanced, in fact, that the teachers can't keep you occupied with elementary-school work anymore. And since yer too young to send on to junior-high, yer teachers sent letters of recommendation to all the finest private schools across the country."

"Sure, Daddy. That's old news," Andrew said.

"Right. But what's *not* old news is that I've had a change of heart about one of 'em."

"*Which* one of them?" Andrew was finally interested.

"Well now, the very best one o'course!" Daddy began grinning like an idiot again, and I wished fervently for a pie to be lying around nearby.

Andrew looked from Daddy's beaming face to mine, reading my expression. He unconsciously scooted closer, and I placed an arm around his shoulder. *No way I would part with him without a fight.* Mikey drifted over from his chair behind Daddy, and I picked him up, squeezing him to me like a stress ball.

"Katie, did you know about this?" Hurt accusation colored Andrew's voice.

I shook my head. No words could get around the swelling in my throat. Andrew looked from me to Daddy, who'd started pacing.

"What's goin' on Kadee?" Mikey asked plaintively.

Finding it hard to breathe, I sucked in a lungful of his little-boy neck.

A furrow creased Andrew's smooth brow. "Daddy, which school did you decide on?"

Daddy quit pacing to look his son in the eye. "The International Elite Academy; it's the best one in the entire world, son. Actually, it's so elite that hardly anyone even knows about its existence."

That particular bit of news did not make me feel a smidge better. A deep foreboding started in my chest and passed quickly through my whole body. I prayed for a way to stop this from happening.

Daddy plowed on determined to sell it. "I met with two of the school's ambassadors yesterday. They are elite-trained cadets and are exactly the kind of young man you need to become. Discipline and advanced learnin' will really help you make somethin' of yerself, Andrew. Who knows?—you could even be president one day!"

"When would I go?"

Mikey bolted up. "*Go? Whattayamean go!*" I folded him back into me, rocking him back and forth.

Daddy rubbed a knuckle against his nose. "If—*when* they accept you, and if I agree, January second." A new kind of quiet infused with dread seeped into the room.

Mikey twisted around to find my eyes "How many years till Jan'ary, Kadee?" I had to bite my lip to keep from crying.

"International." Andrew sounded stunned. "Daddy, *where* is the school located, exactly?"

Daddy cleared his throat. "It's here." He noted the relieved looks on their faces so clarified, "In the States, I mean."

"Where here?"

"In, ah . . . Northern California."

"San Francisco?" Andrew clarified.

More throat clearing ensued. "Yes," Daddy coughed out. "At least I think so."

Andrew and I exchanged disgusted looks—so he wasn't even sure where the school was that he was planning on shipping his eight-year-old son off to.

Daddy looked almost as embarrassed as he should. "We can look that up on the Internet, son." As if he was smart enough to own a smart phone. Realizing his gaffe, he back-pedaled. "That sounds like a good assignment for you. Better yet . . . just ask yer new mentor tomorrow after school."

"So . . . we're all gonna move to-to Sanfrisco when Drewy gets 'cepted to that new school?" Mikey looked up at me for confirmation.

I moved some phlegm around my throat to accommodate some words getting by. I looked to Daddy, but he appeared to be frozen.

Andrew answered for both of us. "No, you dope. It's just me."

"*What!*" Mikey's whole body went rigid, eyes pleading with mine to set the record straight.

I still couldn't form words so just squeezed him tighter, hiding my face in the back of his neck—I didn't want him to see the terror I felt mirrored back at him. A limp, sick feeling of powerlessness overcame me.

Mikey sprang forward to face off with Daddy. "Daddy, you can't send Drewy away to a school—you and Kadee still have to grow him up!"

Daddy glared down at his youngest child with all the hateful intimidation he could muster. "You do *not* have a say so in this, little mister."

Legs splayed out, hands balled into fists, Mikey stood his ground. "Oh, yes I do! He's my brothuh. 'Sides—you have to be a grownup to leave yer house," he reasoned, " . . . it's the *law!*"

I had to give it to the kid—he had guts. I, on the other hand, felt like a bowl of Jell-O, a real gutless wonder. I began crying softly, feeling like the most useless human being on the planet. Daddy pointed his death rays in my direction now.

"Daddy, yo'wer *not* gonna send Drewy to that school," Mikey commanded.

"*You* ain't gonna tell *me* how to run *my* house!" Daddy pointed his trigger finger at Mikey, but I could see his finger-gun was shaking. "That's like tellin' the cow how to eat the cabbage!"

I held my breath at the standoff happening in our living room. Daddy began stalking to the wooden paddle, hanging from its hook in the corner gathering dust. Andrew and I clutched each other.

"Yo'wer *not* gonna send Drewy to that school!" Mikey screamed with such conviction that I started to believe he might not through the sheer force of his will.

Daddy whipped around. It looked like he was going to let Mikey have it, but then, some kind of violent internal struggle began happening that prevented him from proceeding. I was relieved, figuring it was most likely to keep his hands from wrapping around his youngest child's neck.

"Daddy, say yo'wer not gonna do it!" Mikey hollered.

Daddy began contorting as if he were in pain. One hand crawled along his chest like he was trying to stave off a heart attack. Sweat began pouring down him, almost as if he'd been doing actual real work.

Andrew and I exchanged looks. *What's going on?*

The sweaty contortionist before us finally spoke with great difficulty through clenched teeth: "You aint . . . gonna dictate . . . how I . . . run my house." Daddy looked at Mikey with such loathing I thought it might actually stunt his growth. It looked like the madman was about to lay into the little guy with his bare hands, so I grabbed Mikey by the shoulders to pull him away, but it was like his boots were nailed to the floor. Hands over his clavicles, I stood behind him.

"Daddy, yo'wer *not* gonna send Drewy away!" Mikey repeated with so much heated force I could feel actual vibrations of energy emanating off him.

Daddy's jaw and fists clenched so tightly I thought one or the other might shatter. That was about the time Andrew also stood up, manfully, to defend his little brother. The three of us faced Daddy together.

"*Say it*, Daddy." Mikey took another step forward as though pressing the advantage.

Daddy shook his head like he was trying to shake off the effects of a particularly tight half-Nelson. His complexion turned from burnt to ashy, his whole body trembling like a volcano was erupting from the inside. I wasn't sure whose health I was more worried about at the moment—his or Mikey's.

Finally, Daddy choked out the words we were all waiting to hear. "I ain't"—pant—"gonna"—heave—"send him"—gargle—"away."

Mikey, who'd worked himself into quite a state himself, seemed to relax now. His eyes, which had been solely transfixed upon Daddy, looked up at us with gloating satisfaction. "See! I toldja . . . he ain't gonna do it."

Well that did it—Daddy finally snapped. Palm raised, he lunged for Mikey. "No!" Mikey and I screamed together. As if on command, the blow completely bypassed Mikey to whap Andrew upside the head.

I gasped, "Daddy!"

We all stood stock-still, shocked as if a tornado had just whipped our house away in a torrent of wind. Andrew's eyes were already watering, but he was determinedly blinking them back, his throat working up and down.

Mikey re-balled his hands into fists. "That was a crummy thing to do!"

Daddy seemed as shell-shocked as the rest of us. White-faced, he moved towards his favorite child, remorse shining through his eyes. "Andy, son, I'm—" He broke off when Andrew flinched back from him. Daddy's shoulders slumped in defeat. After a few moments of soaking up unforgiving stares from his children, Daddy cleared his throat. He walked a couple of steps away, jingling some pocket change.

"You know what?" He whirled back around. "Y'all clingin' to each other like a bunch of monkeys ain't gonna change my mind one bit. And I'm no longer gonna discuss my decisions as head-of-the-house with you kids. I can see now this family meetin' was a mistake. I wanted to give you all the courtesy of lettin' you know of my decision in advance." He glared at me and then said, "I will no longer give you that courtesy."

I blanched. Not knowing what was happening would be the worst-case scenario for me.

Daddy turned down his glare and faced Andrew, who was wiping the back of his hand across his eye. Daddy's face softened, but he kept his tone hard. "Tomorrow, you'll meet the mentor who'll be workin' with you this semester. After school, in Mrs. Woodward's class. Remember son—this is top-notch tutorin' you're gettin', so really apply yerself. This will get you on the fast track to bein' accepted to the *Elite* Academy, not that you need help, mind you, they'd be lucky to have you. But you still apply yerself with all your might. Got it?"

Andrew nodded. Satisfied with that, Daddy turned to me. "You will pick him up tomorrow at four sharp. Do not ask any questions except: Where and when do I pick up Andrew tomorrow? Do you understand me, young lady? I do not want you influencin' or inerferin' in *any* way."

I ground my molars together but knew any more defiance would only succeed in Daddy tightening the screws even further. "Yes, sir," I choked out.

"Because if you do . . ."—he looked at Mikey pointedly—"you *will* regret it," he finalized, grabbing his keys and slamming out the door without a backward glance at the birthday girl.

Mikey looked up at me with earnest eyes. "Don't worwy, Kadee . . . I won't let Daddy send Drewy off to that school."

I pumped his plump little hand while Andrew and I locked eyes over his head. Looked like we'd have to continue our own family meeting . . . after Mikey was in bed.

12

FIRST DAY OF SCHOOL

The buzz surrounding the new boy had managed to permeate even the quiet recesses of the library. I was library-aid again this year so was busy recoding some miscellaneous books that had moved locations over the summer. Boring, tedious work, but if I finished the three chin-high stacks, I might have enough time leftover to email Reese before second-hour. This was my goal, that and searching the Internet for more info about Andrew's "elite" school. I was trying hard not to think about it, but it kept popping in and out of my head like a sinister Whack-A-Mole.

So I was busy tap-tapping in barcodes and listening to Mrs. Greer's oldies playlist when a determined face, that would've been even prettier *sans* glimmer, head-tilted into my view.

"Hey, Steph. What's up?" I infused my voice with as much normalcy as possible considering that the last time I'd seen her I'd stormed off, leaving behind a heap of giggles and a weekend's worth of gossip, I'm sure.

"Just escaped Mr. Irving's class to see if the biographies he ordered was in yet." She waved a hall pass in my direction.

"Hold on . . . lemme check." I reluctantly escaped from my current task. "What's the name?"

She giggled in an affected girly way and stage-whispered, "That's what I'd like to know."

"Well, did you write it down? I need somethin' to go on."

"*Not* the *books* . . ." I stared at her, blank-faced. "The hot, new guy absolutely everyone's talkin' about," she clarified.

"Oh." This morning a tunnel of girls was going on about him like a pop star had been snatched from a live stage somewhere only to land in the middle of our high school parking lot. I was too preoccupied with my family drama to pay much attention to what was going on around me. *Like usual.*

"Have you seen him yet?" She positively squealed.

I plugged a finger in my ear. "Nope. Can't say that I have."

"Oh. My. God! Katie, you cannot *believe* how gorgeous he is!"

She obviously needed some kind of response, but I was less than enthusiastic about some newcomer who would most likely weave himself seamlessly into the CHS social tapestry within a week and then be old hat. This event meant nothing to me and my life, unfortunately.

"Wow. Excitin' stuff," I managed, not even remotely sounding like a normal teenager.

"Yeah, I know! All the guys around here are, like, so beyond boring," she complained with a distinctly Ashley-Leigh twang in there.

"Right." I was sure everyone's perspective on the "hot" new guy was most likely completely skewed because they were simply starved for new blood.

"So," she leaned in conspiratorially, "can you find out?"

"Find out?"

"His schedule." She said this like it was the most logical thing in the world. "Don't you, like, have access to all the students' records?"

"Um . . . we're not really supposed to do that," I hedged, sounding like my unlikely hero Saturday night, who ended up giving me a ride home from the pharmacy after all.

"Oh come on, Katie! *Please,*" she wheedled. "Just this once?"

I switched tactics. "Well if you don't even know his name, I'd have to sift through all the students alphabetically, and it could take a while. Mrs. Greer will *kill* me if I don't get these books done."

She seemed to notice the stack of books for the first time and gave me a cartoon-worthy frown. "Okay. I just thought it would be fun if I—I mean *we,* were the first ones to know his name and schedule and stuff." An Ashley-Leigh disciple if I'd ever seen one. *Maybe I could salvage what was left of my time if I could just get her moving.* I picked up another book.

"I heard he's from Roswell—from that military institute there. What's it called? Somethin' with lots of Ns and Ms?"

"New Mexico Military Institute," I provided.

She snapped her fingers and pointed at me. "That's the one."

I started tapping in numbers again, only half listening.

"And that he's living with a relative here now," Steph mused aloud, not budging from her perch. "Maybe he was kicked out of regular school, and his parents sent him to military school to straighten him out, but he was expelled there, too. So his parents sent him to live with his, ah . . . uncle because nobody can deal with him on account of him being such a *badass*!" she finished, eyes shining.

Ugh. She was piercing my fortress of solitude with all this talk about military schools and badasses. Brought back the queasy, sinking feeling in my stomach I'd had since Saturday night.

"Uh, Steph, don't you have to get back to class?" I snatched the forgotten slip from her. "I'll give this to Mrs. Greer. I didn't see any boxes this morning, so I'll have to wait for her to get back from the office before I can ask."

"Don'tja just love a bad boy?" Like I hadn't even spoken.

"Yeah, badass . . . "—I rolled my eyes—"what every girl dreams of."

"Katie!" She guffawed like a mother does the first time her toddler mimics a naughty word. I stood up to shoo her away and her mouth flew open. "Katie Connelly, are you, like, wearing actual *jeans* now?"

I looked down, as if having to check. "Yup."

"Bad ass!" Steph nodded her approval. "You should get contacts next."

"I'll take that under advisement," I replied, straightening my replacement glasses.

She laughed. "I'll catch you up on everything at lunch," she said before sallying away.

"Okay," I agreed, already preoccupied. Actually, I was planning a library lunch to email Reese and get more info on that school, since I didn't have time now. A few minutes later, I was mowing down the second stack of books still ruminating about how to thwart Daddy.

So far, my biggest act of rebellion consisted of wearing jeans to school. But I'd need to arm myself with something more than a new pair of pants. It was information I needed; knowledge was power. Daddy had cut me off from any information about the school, the mentor, what kind of testing Andrew was going to be subjected to. *Everything*. Despite profusely apologizing and promising not to interfere (with fingers crossed behind my back) I was still getting bupkis from Daddy.

All I knew was that I was picking Andrew up from school today, where he was meeting his "mentor" for the first time. Other than that, I was clueless. *Arg*! *Frustrating*. A sick feeling akin to swallowing too many bitter pills overcame me when I thought of a stranger probing around inside my brother's brain to assess his talents and abilities. It seemed downright invasive, especially knowing how Mama took such pains to hide us from the world. Mikey had never even set foot in public, not even to go for an ice cream, before I enrolled him in preschool.

But I didn't have time to stress for long, because the bell rang. I had Pre-Cal next. *Ugh . . . Guess it's better to get it over with early*. I slipped into the sea of students swimming their way to second-hour, trying not to get eaten by sharks. Pre-Cal was in the same building as the library, so I had time to hit the restroom to wash my dusty hands before class. Pushing through the door, I was instantly accosted by piercing squeals from a huddle of girls in front of the mirrors. Ashley-Leigh stood, front and center, smoothing down her flat-ironed hair and prattling around a sparkling wand of lip gloss.

"Katie!" she gushed, clicking shut the tube before turning around to face me. "Tell me you were able to get his schedule!"

Of course she already knows all about it; it was probably her idea. I shrugged my shoulders. "No such luck."

"Aw man!" She spun back around to her minions. "Okay, so what do we know so far . . . other than the fact that he's drool-worthy gorgeous, just moved here, and is a senior?"

"Drea heard he was an army brat," a minion supplied, hoping to be of service.

"Who moves to a new school their senior year?" a hidden voice wondered behind a stall.

"I heard he got kicked out of his former school for fighting."

"No way!" Ashley-Leigh argued. "I saw him in the front office this morning—he's definitely way more of a lover than a fighter type!"

This clever was followed by high-pitched laughter and high-fives. I just backed out the door and headed to class feeling world-weary. It would be nice to get caught up in the excitement of a new boy. I sighed . . . *in another life*.

I managed to be one of the first students in class and sat near the front. Two seconds after the bell, Ashley-Leigh and her groupies came prancing in after spit-shining themselves up for an appearance from Mr. Wonderful. I had to roll my eyes. They clumped together in the back all jostling for position. I remembered when I was right in the middle of all that; it seemed like a lifetime ago.

First day classes rolled by in a predictable pattern of seat jockeying, new procedures that felt very old, and directions for online resources, which I would access via the library's computers. *Obviouly.* I was in AP English, my favorite class, when I heard more tidbits about the famous (or infamous, depending on whose tale you were listening to) new guy.

"So he like rolls up in this fat daddy, Humvee, man, and I was like, 'Dude, nice wheels, bro.'"

Oh great . . . now the guys are talking about him. Good Lord, make it stop! Hands over my ears, I plunked my head on my desk. Soft laughter erupted from the desk next to mine.

"Don't tell me . . . it's gettin' to you, too?"

"Oh, hey, Miguel," I greeted, cheek still plastered against scarred wood.

"You're not goin' all faint on me now like the rest of *las chicas locas?*" he teased.

I snapped my head upright. "As if!"

Miguel laughed, his eyes slitting up, crescent creases appearing in his cheeks. "How ya been, Katie-kat? . . . Long time no see."

"Yeah I know . . . family duty and all that." I smiled to take the edge off.

"Word," he replied with a smile. Miguel could sympathize with my lot in life since he had to work at his family's restaurant to help make ends meet. "So . . . you into this new dude, too, or what?"

I snorted lightly. "Hardly. I don't really see what all the fuss is about."

"That's because you haven't *seen* him yet!" Ashley-Leigh slid imperiously into the desk behind me. "Because when you do see him, you'll totally, 'get what all the fuss is about,'" she mocked me. "God, Katie! Honestly . . . you sound like my grandma sometimes."

"I doubt it." I shrugged my shoulders dismissively. "Oh, and by the way . . ." The bell rang, so I leaned over to whisper, "I like your grandma, usually a little better than you."

Miguel laughed, but Ashley-Leigh was prevented her comeback because Mrs. Jenkins began calling roll. She opted to poke her tongue out at me instead, flipped her hair over her shoulder, and took out her shiny phone. Miguel and I exchanged smirks.

English Lit always flew by too fast. The bell rang again, signaling the end of class and the beginning of lunch for juniors and seniors. Everyone popped up like prairie dogs from their holes, animatedly talking about lunch plans.

I was still sitting, idly perusing the reading list when Miguel tugged at the end of my hair. "You hear the bell or what, Connelly?"

"Um . . . yeah." I rose to my feet to join my fellow juniors for the mass exit out the door.

"So whatcha doin' for lunch?" As if by joint agreement, Miguel and I ignored the new-guy mania sweeping the school like the plague. I didn't have a chance to answer because loud screams erupted behind me. I turned around to see Ashley-Leigh and her crew hovering over her phone.

"Black SUV, south-end of the parking lot! We're hot on the trail now, girls!" Ashley-Leigh grabbed a disciple by the arm, nearly stampeding over us on her way out.

"Excuse you," Miguel said.

"Oh, Katie . . ." Ashley-Leigh called from the doorway. I looked up automatically. "By the way—nice jeans! It's good to see you out of your nun habit every-once-in-a-while." Tittering giggles and her gang followed her out the door before I could gather my wits about me.

Miguel was faster. "It take you all class to think that one up? . . . Poor bastard," he murmured. "I almost feel sorry for him."

But she was long gone. *Figures.* She would spend her entire lunch chasing some hot, new guy in a—*wait a second*! I stopped walking mid-step while students rolled around me like a rock in a river.

Holy crap! Thunder clapped over my head. Black SUV, Humvee, hot, gorgeous, athletic, military—words I hadn't really been paying attention to all morning just clicked together. Realization hit me, like a bolt of lightening. *It couldn't be, could it?* I'd thought that once before . . . and was proven wrong. And then I knew: It could be and probably was. What were the odds of anybody else fitting that description? Everyone was well past the point of being excited about this "new, hot guy." It was practically mass hysteria in here. And I'd only ever met one person (okay *two*) who could incite such idolatry.

Miguel was a few feet ahead still talking right along, oblivious to the fact I was somewhere else. "Katie?" He backtracked a few paces to take my elbow. "Don't let Ashley get to you like that. You're way above that crap, and she knows it."

I looked at Miguel, bewildered for a second because I was on a different page. Heck, I was in an entirely different book! "Oh. It's not that Miguel . . . I'm hardly ever bothered by her."

"Then what is it?"

I just shook my head. Way too weird and involved to go into.

"Wanna grab some lunch and talk about it?"

I peered into Miguel's hopeful eyes and shook my head again. It would've been nice to confide in someone, but it sounded cray-cray even to me. "No thanks. I'm just gonna head to the library. There's somethin' important I need to look up."

"Now?"

"Right now." After throwing a wave at his puzzled face, I raced back into the building everyone else was leaving (which seemed a little symbolic to my life). There were a few straggling students and some wired teachers clustered by the vending machines. I quickly bypassed them, and rounding the corner to the library, I nearly smacked into the vice principal. I forced myself into a brisk walk, but it was hard to slow down, because my body was trying to keep tempo with my racing thoughts.

Maybe I'm wrong? I mean girls get worked up by any new guy. But not like this. Everyone was acting like the latest cover hottie was gonna pop up in class any moment. This was probably just a weird coincidence, like all the bizarre occurrences that had been happening lately. My gut was telling me it was something more. I almost sprinted to the computers until the sour look on Mrs. Greer's puckered face paused me.

"Katie, you know better than that," she scolded.

"Yes, ma'am. I'm sorry. I just wanted to use the computers, if I may?" My voice sounded trembly and far away.

She eyed me suspiciously from behind her jeweled spectacles then let it pass. "Just be sure to log out before you leave."

"Yes, ma'am." I darted to the last computer facing the back wall and a poster that read: When You're at the End of Your Rope, Tie a Knot and Hang On. Someone had already drawn a mustache and devil horns on the hapless monkey hanging upside down.

Hands shaking, I typed in my student ID and clicked the search engine, holding my breath. I really had to get a hold of myself or I'd go into early cardiac arrest. After retyping it twice, I finally found what I was looking for. On the computer screen, right in front of me, making it as real as the hard-backed chair I was sitting on: *The International Elite Academy in Marin County, just over the Golden Gate Bridge from San Francisco.* I read on. The International Elite Academy repeatedly received the highest rankings among private boarding schools. *No surprise there.*

I reflected on the two egotistical IEA cadets I'd met and couldn't picture them at Clovis High. Besides, they're too old for high school. *Right?* An image of Ranger came to mind, and my heartbeat picked up. He had to be somewhere in his mid-twenties. I allowed myself to exhale. The other one . . . my heart fluttered in my chest. *I could definitely deal with the thought of seeing him again.*

I chastised myself for my momentary lapse and concentrated instead on the aggravatingly little amount of information I could find about them. According to the website that rates these schools, not much was known about what goes on behind the walls of "the world's most exclusive boarding school." I continued reading until I found their mission statement: *The International Elite Academy exists to advance the physical, social, and environmental wellbeing of mankind. Blah, blah, blah* . . . "Turning elite and responsible young men and women from around the globe into future world leaders since 1939."

Oh please. I wanted to puke. I scrolled down, looking for the admissions process. There wasn't one. Apparently, you couldn't simply apply to the school. *They* had to pursue *you.* A chill ran up my spine at this revelation. It was rumored that you had to score in the top one percent on several standardized tests before you could even be considered for their testing process, which reportedly included a thorough physical exam and biological history.

Hmmmm . . . that's a new one. I read on, intrigued. Apparently, candidates were put through a rigorous testing regime, the contents of which weren't specified, but was speculated to include intensive mental and physical conditioning designed to weed out anyone except for the very brightest and most physically-abled. Less than one percent of recruits—who were already considered the top one percent—made it beyond the testing portion. And those who did were added to a remarkably exclusive waitlist that allegedly included four-star generals' children, one of the King of Saudi Arabia's daughters, and the Chief Executive of Hong Kong's only son. There was, however, no published documentation to support these claims. Surprise, surprise . . . *everything* about this school seemed to be classified information.

I extrapolated information in a zombie-like trance, learning very l ittle about the school except that it was considered to be the most renowned military academy in the world, and was ultra-exclusive to the point of "almost anonymity." Consequently, rumors swirled about the great lengths to which billionaires, diplomats, and even royalty went to acquire an invitation for their children. Some were known to give endowments in the millions to a school their child was not even admitted to, in the faintest hope they would be added to the waitlist.

Huh. My body froze up like an ice cube while my brain whirred with the information I'd uncovered. So the world's wealthiest and most illustrious families were throwing millions at the school just for the *chance* of going through the admissions process, and yet Andrew Richmond Connelly from Nowhere, New Mexico was having the red carpet rolled out for him. I pictured our humble abode, complete with balding tires holding down the roof. It would almost be comical if there weren't something so sinister about it. *Why not just go back to their elite pool of recruits? Why go after one particular candidate so hard?*

Mama's "irrational" fear of outsiders and special schools was starting to make a whole lot of sense now. Her protectiveness seemed the opposite of irrational in light of current events. *Why didn't we just listen to her? Oh right—because she was "crazy."*

What made Daddy change his mind? I thought of the two handsome and obviously persuasive representatives, and my blood boiled. *Who do they think they are messing with our lives this way? If they think we're easy marks, just ripe for the picking, then they could just think again!*

I only had a few more minutes left, so I zipped off an email to Reese, logged-out, and sat back to digest what I'd learned, instead of the protein bar I didn't get around to eating. I left the library with more questions than answers, determined to have a come-to-Jesus-meeting with Daddy.

13

THE NEW GUY

When I stepped outside, the afternoon sun glinted off my glasses, scattering prisms of light across the patchy grass and uneven sidewalks that made up our school's terrain. First-day-back excitement united everyone in a blanket of holiday like revelry. My backpack wasn't the only thing weighing me down. I longed to lay down my burdens, if only for a moment, and join the land of the normal.

Usually, I hustled to class to avoid any social obligations I'd be uninterested in or unable to fulfill. Now I deliberately stalled so I could peruse the mingling students for a tall, hunky cadet posing as a senior. I was a black and white domino of dismay—equal parts afraid I would see him and that I wouldn't. But there was nothing new to see, aside from a couple of unfortunate haircuts and some dubious couplings.

I huffed out a sigh. *Really, what are the odds of lightening striking twice in Clovis?* Guys like that generally stayed in their own world.

As I ambled to the low basic brick building for my Spanish II class, I played different scenarios out in my mind about who the new boy could possibly be. Suddenly, I was as interested as everybody else. My heart did flip-flops just thinking about the possibility of it being Pete or Ranger (although for way different reasons).

A Bienvenidos Estudiantes sign greeted us outside the open door, and from inside the room, our names written out on cards greeted us from our desks. We would be seated alphabetically. *How very middle school of him.* Everyone complained as they entered, walking around dejectedly looking for their assigned seats.

Mine would be easy to find—I was always in the first row, four or five seats back behind Zoe Bucknore or Sean Castillos. It'd been the same since kindergarten. *No wonder everyone is so excited for a new face.* I backtracked to my seat right next to the door, second from last.

Steph Aguilar passed me on the way to her seat and grimaced. "Ugh. First row, first seat." I gave a sympathetic smile. "Where were you? We spotted the hot, new guy as he was coming back from lunch. Ashley-Leigh parked as close as possible, but everyone was literally all over him. She decided to stay a little longer and wait it out."

The bell rang, ending our one-sided conversation. I sat down, doodling on the inside of my notebook and mulling over everything. I saw my unconscious doodles had morphed into two questions: *Pete? Or Ranger?*

"Bienvenidos!" Mr. Sanchez greeted us with an enthusiastic first-day-of-class voice and a neon-yellow tie. Both seemed especially jarring considering my frayed nerves.

Just then, the door sucked opened behind me and closed with a *Bang!* that caused me and half the class to jump. This was followed by an "oopsie" and an unapologetic giggle.

"Nice of you to join us, Señorita Montgomery," Mr. Sanchez chastised Ashley while she made her way to the center of the room with a lot of fanfare. "Okay, today we're going to go over the syllabus, hand out your new workbooks,"—he briefly held one up: *Dos Mundos*, Two Worlds—"and then go around the room, so you can introduce yourselves and show off what you did this summer by telling us . . . in Spanish."

Predictable groans followed this announcement. *Not very original.* Teachers must all take a class on how to bore students to death on the first day back. I didn't care one way or the other, too preoccupied with speculation about the new guy and my list of questions for the mentor.

"First, I'm going to take role while," he paused, looking around for a suitable candidate, "Señor Lopez passes out the syllabus."

Miguel popped up with an affable smile while Mr. Sanchez began moving through the "B" names. I was mentally preparing for him to call mine next, when the door behind me sucked back open. Someone stepped into the room and closed the door with a soft click. Twenty-plus heads flew to the back of the room simultaneously. I found myself blushing under all the scrutiny until I realized—they weren't staring at me. Tingles ran up my spine.

It was *him*. Another beat and something else clicked. *Of course!* Andrew's new mentor, and the cadet standing behind me, were one and the same. I closed my eyes and paid close attention to that sixth sense. Even though I was deathly curious to see if I was right, I was way too chicken to turn around.

A current of excitement zapped each female student's face as if they were all connected to the same wire. Eyes were met. Shoulders nudged. Boys glowered while girls glowed. One pink-faced girl even took out a tube of lipstick. Most of the hoo-hah was happening in the middle of the room, where Ashley-Leigh sat bolt upright, smiling seductively and tossing her hair as if an invisible director told her it was time to hit her mark. I had to hand it to her: she was ready and set to go.

A low buzzing, which included the bass and tenor whispers of boys, erupted simultaneously. Even Mr. Sanchez stopped to adjust his tie in preparation for our newcomer.

Oh please—get it together, people. I rolled my eyes until I remembered I'd pretty much acted the same way the first time I saw him, too.

Mr. Sanchez cleared his throat to announce the obvious: "It looks like we have a new student." He backtracked to the podium to check his roster. "*Bienvenidos . . .* Señor Davenport."

Mr. Sanchez beckoned him forward with a toothy smile, and my heart began thumping dramatically in my chest. He lingered in the doorway a moment longer, I guess allowing everyone a moment to drink him in. But I still refused to acknowledge his presence. However, I was the only one in the room *not* staring at him.

My body felt like a high voltage magnet was drawing me to him. Still, I resisted the urge to turn my head. When he ambled forward, he casually brushed his hand along the side of my desk. I automatically looked up just in time to see Pete shamelessly wink at me as he sauntered by. I flushed beet red like an insipid schoolgirl before quickly averting my eyes back to my desk. Only to find my favorite clicky-pen missing.

Palpable excitement roused the bored juniors and seniors from their afternoon slump. It became apparent that everyone was showing off in some minor way for our preternaturally famous guest. Jocks puffed themselves up, acting so cool they were anything but. One guy turned around in his seat to fist-bump a buddy over a girl's desk as she surreptitiously powder-puffed away her shine. Even Mr. Sanchez amped up his already exuberant Mexican-accented voice for the benefit of our new arrival.

I noticed how everyone instantly came to the same conclusion I did: Here was someone special, someone to be reckoned with, someone who had the world by the balls . . . and knew it.

Unable to resist any longer, my eyes lifted to where he was standing, in front of a roomful of gawkers, the picture of ease. Brown leather backpack slung casually over his shoulder, gray clingy T-shirt half-tucked into artfully faded jeans, Pete was a walking advertisement for some upscale catalog nobody here could afford.

His eye was still pretty messed-up, and I felt sick with guilt about it, despite myself. It's funny how that black eye only *added* to his rampant sex appeal. It was the only flaw on an otherwise perfect male specimen, adding a delicious element of danger that had all the girls drooling. I could actually see what Steph was talking about now. Our eyes met again, and I felt my face burn with more than just embarrassment.

Gah! *Get it together Kate! He's the enemy.*

I just realized the enemy's last name was Davenport. And there was only one other D-name, and she was sitting in the seat behind me. That meant if Mr. Sanchez stuck to his alphabet plan, Señor Davenport would soon be occupying Molly Donaldson's chair. My stomach did a funny little summersault, and my hand itched to take out my hairbrush and have a go at my hair.

I vaguely heard a chorus of *bienvinedos* (some more enthusiastic than others). It was hard to keep track of the particulars when blood was roaring through my ears. I thought how the cool wood of the desk would feel pretty good against my cheek right about now. The reality of him being here—in the flesh—was too much, my body already warring with opposing emotions.

I wiped my palms on my jeans, then rummaged in my backpack for my metal canteen. I felt rather like choking at the moment, that I'm-gonna-cough-in-church feeling. Miguel shot me a look. I gave him a sheepish smile before returning my hungry eyes back to the main attraction.

Pete was currently being put on the spot by Mr. Sanchez, who asked him to introduce himself to the class. *"Hola,"* he gamely greeted us. Pete's melodious voice instantly quieted the buzzing classroom. *"Me llamo Pete Davenport. Soy un estudiante de intercambio De La Academia Internacional de Elite en California. Me encanta surfing y echare de menos ir a la playa los fines de semana, aunque tengo muchas ganas de aprender nuevos deportes como la monta de toros."*

Of course he spoke perfect Spanish!

Mr. Sanchez laughed appreciatively at something Pete said that no one else seemed to catch. A couple of girls began fanning themselves, the starting tailback made the retching sign with his finger, and the majority of the guys smirked or rolled their eyes. But all the juvenile behavior didn't put a chip in Pete's rock-solid confidence; he held court, in front of a classroom of strangers, without a flicker of self-consciousness.

After finishing his smooth spiel, enthusiastic applause erupted from a trio of girls near the back. They furiously blushed and giggled as he inclined his golden head toward them. One errant lock of hair fell forward, and he casually brushed it back, revealing a little more of the faint bruising around his eye. I swear I heard audible gasps, and the force of Molly Donaldson's sigh stirred my hair.

"*Muy bien*, Señor Davenport," Mr. Sanchez approved before searching his desk for some paperwork.

In the interim our eyes met again. Pete waggled his eyebrows at me, grinning. Several pairs of eyes followed his while I shifted around in my seat. My blushing returned with a vengeance, but I managed to crack a weak smile to acknowledge him because he was still boldly smiling into my eyes.

Mr. Sanchez called the class back to order. While everyone else faced forward again, two sets of eyes remained on mine, puzzled and looking for answers. I refused to look either Miguel or Ashley-Leigh in the eye. Instead, I cleared my throat and reached for my canteen again—my throat suddenly felt like a dusty haystack.

"Okay. Looks like you'll be sitting . . ." Mr. Sanchez paused to access, and the girls leaned forward, scanning the room for empty desks, "behind Señorita Connelly."

While I did more seat squirming, the bulk of the female population stared at me with various shades of green. I heard Molly huff and puff and get out of her seat.

"Not so fast, Señorita Donaldson. Everyone seems to be all settled today, so *mañana*," Mr. Sanchez enunciated dramatically, "everyone from Molly on will move back a seat." Collective groans. "*Ahora,* Señor Davenport can sit in any unoccupied desk."

Girls in every row proffered several enticing invitations. Ashley-Leigh practically yanked Corinne Mahal's arm from its socket to get her to surrender her desk. No such luck, I noted with satisfaction as Corinne clung to her desk. Pete ambled to the last row, where he sat across from a girl with a skater-boy haircut and one too many piercings. She immediately scooted her desk closer to his.

Gah! Could nobody play it cool? I wondered if I would be able to keep it together in his presence. I closed my eyes, my lips parting involuntarily as I remembered him leaning over to whisper in my ear. My eyes popped back open. Apparently, the answer was no, no I could not. My only option then was avoidance. He was obviously up to no good. How could I avoid him when I'd see him every day at school? The more pressing concern was the amount to which I *didn't want* to avoid him.

Class went by in a blur of mangled Spanish introductions and furtive glances at our newest CHS member, who was twirling my pen between his fingers looking bored. When he became aware of his audience, he stopped, clicked it once, and looked over at me. But I was too quick, whipping my head back into forward position.

When it was my turn to introduce myself, I stammered my way through what was usually easy conversational Spanish. Afterward, Mr. Sanchez called me out for it. "Katie, Katie." He shook his head at me. "Looks like you forgot some of your basic Spanish over the summer."

My neck was immediately gripped by an urge stronger than every ounce of my will not to peek. Pete was waiting with an arched brow as if to say: *That's the best you've got?* A burning started in my chest like I'd swallowed a serrano pepper at lunch, and it just came back up. *Why am I letting him rattle me like this?* Mama would be so disappointed in me. The burning turned into determination not to let him get the best of me.

So when the bell rang, I bolted out the door before he could so much as blink in my direction. *Ha! It'll take him till the next bell just to pry Ashley-Leigh's claws off.* My laugh fell flat as our streets as a jolt more jarring than running over one of our potholes hit me:

What if Ashley-Leigh really does sink her claws into him?

I made it back to the main building and up to the second floor for my chemistry class in record time. Dizzy with anticipation, I slumped onto an empty stool at a lab table near the front. The bell rang and Mr. Benson closed the door. About a minute after roll call, the door opened again, and all eyes flew to the door. I kept mine trained on Mr. Benson as he droned on about the importance of safety precautions. Footsteps maneuvered around dumped backpacks, heading my way. Someone sat down on the vacant stool next to mine—closer than was strictly necessary unless two people were well acquainted. I didn't turn to acknowledge him, and after a few more seconds of staring ahead so hard my eyes were beginning to water, I heard a familiar, muffled whisper.

"What the hell was with you back there?"

"Don't know what you're talkin' 'bout."

"Do you *know* that guy?"

"Um . . . not really," I hedged, not meeting Miguel's eyes.

Thankfully, it was impossible to continue the conversation because Mr. Benson was handing out his version of the three P's: procedures, policies, and permission slips. Chemistry ticked by slowly with me not paying attention to anything except my own swirling thoughts. The bell rang, and Miguel picked up right where he left off.

"Katie, you're such a bad liar," he said, following me out the door. "You're tellin' me you've never seen the guy before?"

He had me there. "Actually," I hemmed, "I think I, ah . . . might've waited on him before."

"You think you might've waited on him before?"

"Correctomundo." I always said stupid things like that when I was evading the question.

"Where? At the diner?" he persisted.

"*Duh* . . . obviously."

Miguel stopped walking to give me a wounded expression. "Wow." He stretched his arms up to get the kinks out. "Now you sound like Ashley-Leigh."

"Really, Miguel. There's nothing to tell," I smiled thinly at him. "Sorry . . . I'm just a little tired. I'll be less weird tomorrow, I promise." I smiled more convincingly.

He eyed me sideways before deciding to let it go. "You work too hard. Have you ever heard the one about the girl who was all work and no play?"

I laughed. "It just so happens I have. But not to worry . . . I get to play now—soccer that is. I've got P.E. next, so I'd better get goin'."

"Okay, *chaparita*, I'll see ya there. I've got Athletics—I play football, remember?"

"How could I forget my favorite player?" I smiled, and he grinned and flashed the peace sign.

I trudged across campus to gym, which was easy to spot with the giant purple wildcat painted onto the brick. P.E. was a requirement I'd been hoping to dodge. It wasn't that I didn't like sports. I did. "Too much," according to my mother. Anything I could poke my ponytail through the back of a baseball cap for was my favorite. Even with Mama insisting I sit out half the game, I still had fun. It was just . . . well, I needed to do jumping jacks like I needed a hole in my head. My day was a workout, so I considered P.E. to be a waste of precious energy. And since I wasn't in Athletics, I was stuck taking Phys-Ed with the rest of the nobodies, who either didn't make the team or weren't interested in fitting in.

My palms slapped metal doors, and the familiar odor of our school's gymnasium wafted over me, reminding me of what high school smells like: sharp sweat, cleaning product to mask it, waxed floors, and teen spirit. I hooked a right to the girls' locker room, where I had to endure more ear-splitting chatter about the "amazing, new, hot guy." *The adjectives are getting a little tired* I thought, slamming my locker shut with more force than was required.

I sat on the bench to put on my new sneakers and realized—they were compliments of the man-of-the-hour. After furiously whipping my laces into shape, I glared down at my shiny new shoes as if they were to blame for everything.

The whistle blew, and I followed behind Coach Sams and the ragtag group of girls that made up our P.E. class, marveling at the variety of clothes they considered athletic wear. High, piercing squeaks from new sneakers stopping short on court, and the hollow thump of balls echoing against palms was the background noise as we filed into gym. It was a busy place sixth-hour because volleyball players and cheerleaders shared floor space. We marched through the middle of the mayhem toward the back door leading to the football practice field.

Ashley-Leigh was sprawled out on the floor, stretching and gossiping with some of the other cheerleaders in a circle. I acknowledged her with a little wave. She just narrowed her eyes at me, leisurely pulling her hair into a ponytail as I filed past. I tried a smile, but that only prompted her to lean over and whisper something into Maddy's ear. They both looked up at me, followed quickly by the rest of the squad. I faced forward again, feeling the weight of their stares pushing at my back as I exited through the double doors outside.

We were sitting together in the scratchy grass lining the football field, listening to our first day lecture on the importance of physical fitness. I exchanged eye-rolls with a girl whose dye job was even worse than mine. My eyes squinted in the sun as I lazily scanned the uniform rows of football players behind Coach Sams. They were jumping-jacking in purple unison, counting down with low huffs of air followed by claps.

I was barely paying attention so was caught off guard when Coach Sams began counting us off, "One, two, one, two." She pointed to me and said "two," so I moved over to where the "twos" were clumped together. A mousy sophomore in a boobtube I recognized from my computer class last year came up to slap me five. I raised my hand with a small smile that instantly froze on my face. A tall guy, with blonde hair shading to brown, sauntered past with a crew of boys, who looked very motley next to him. A toothy grin flashed my way the second he spotted me huddled up with Goth-girl, Gangbanger, and Boobtube.

Oh. My. Gosh! What's he doing out here with the rest of us rejects? Shouldn't he be, like, captain of the football team or something? And why do I get the funny feeling him being here isn't an accident?

My hand was still suspended midair, so Boobtube followed my line of vision. "OMG!" she gasped, mimicking my thoughts exactly. "Is that the hot, new guy *everyone's* been talkin' about?"

"Yup," I said, cringing at the well-worn adjectives.

"Oh man! I gotta say—the rumors don't even do him justice!" She started flapping her arm at him like an idiot, a risky move considering her choice of tops. "Oh my God! He's lookin' right over here!"

I was still staring back at him when I was on the receiving end of a mocking salute.

"Did you see that?" Goth-girl gaped.

"No," I lied, dragging my eyes from something that was beginning to mesmerize me. "I didn't see anything."

The whistle blew, and we followed Coach Sams downfield to an unused portion of grass to practice kicking soccer balls between neon orange cones. It wasn't the most athletic bunch, so I kind of dumbed down my skills to match their level. It was so easy that I would've been deathly bored except for the fact that the boys' P.E. class was right across from us doing the exact same thing.

I tried hard not to look over at him, but it was nearly impossible not to. Even Coach Sams stopped yelling at us for one second to stare at Pete. He was bouncing a stray soccer ball from knee-to-knee then foot-to-foot while waiting his turn. *Show off.* He certainly wasn't keeping his athletic prowess under wraps for the benefit of his comrades. Feeling inexplicably piqued, I hurried off to the gym as soon as the whistle blew without so much as a backward glance. But I may have been the only one out there not glancing back at him.

In the locker room, I changed back into my street clothes, adding a bell skirt to my ensemble instead of the jeans I'd worn to school. I figured switching back here was the safest bet in case Daddy was actually home for once when we got there. Almost all of sixth-hour just remained in their athletic attire. Not me. If Daddy found out I was even wearing shorts in the presence of boys, he would most likely force me back into homeschooling myself.

After stuffing my gym clothes and jeans into my backpack, me and my bell skirt swung back out the double doors into the milling bouquets of laughing classmates enjoying their afternoon of freedom in the sun. I parked close to the gym this morning, knowing it would give me a quick getaway. Unfortunately, most of the jocks and cheerleaders also parked there and were gathered together now, socializing before heading back in for after-school practice.

One hand over my eyes, I scanned the crowded parking lot for my car and saw an imperious hand waving me over. *What does she want?* Whatever it was, I wasn't in the mood. I pushed out a sigh before winding my way through the maze of cars to where my former friends were posing against a convertible Mustang in various stages of undress. I eyed Steph's blinged-out belly button ring. *Guess the dress code is rendered null and void after three o'clock.*

She caught me staring. "Do you like it?"

"Um, yeah . . . it's cool," I said.

"I got it over the summer—my cousin did it in her bathroom."

Ashley-Leigh broke in, "Okay, now that everyone's all caught up . . ." She rounded on me. "Do you mind telling us why you acted like you'd never seen Pete Davenport before when you two, like, obviously already know each other somehow?"

"Yeah, Katie, he was totally flirting with you," Steph added jealously.

"I wouldn't exactly go so far as to say he was *flirting* with her, but," Ashley's made-up blue eyes glared at me, "I could totally tell *somethin'* was goin' on."

Several sets of made-up eyes stared at me expectantly.

"Did you, like, check out a book for him or somethin'?" Ashley-Leigh prompted.

I decided to stick to the same micro-version of the truth I told Miguel. "I, uh, waited on him and a friend a couple of weeks ago."

"Hold up." Ashley-Leigh held up one limp hand in front of her. "So you're sayin' he went *voluntarily* into that dumpy dive you work at to, like, actually *eat*?" The hand moved to cover her mouth in mock horror. I noticed that all her nails were painted purple except one, which was metallic silver with a purple wildcat on it. I wondered how much time it took to do that.

"Katie! How could you? You could've, like, killed him feedin' him that poison!" Of course everyone laughed at her little funny. I didn't bother to tell her it was a mute point since he didn't eat anything anyway.

"Hopefully, he has better taste in . . ."—she eyed me over skeptically—"*other* things."

"Yeah, well . . ." I pushed past her, "I guess we'll see"

Ashley-Leigh called after me, "Hey Katie, I noticed you put your nun habit back on—your Daddy know you started wearin' jeans to school?"

My back stiffened. I spun around, stung. *Wow.* She was really playing dirty now. *How could she?* She was the one begging me to start dressing "normally" all these years. The betrayal on my face must have registered in some tiny portion of her heart not yet petrified by getting her own way all the time.

"I'm just kiddin', Katie-Kat . . . your secret's safe with me." She winked then turned back to her friends and began animatedly talking again, seeming to forget about me the second I left her sight.

14

THE MENTOR

Twitchy with impatience, I crawled through the school zone, my mind racing with unanswered questions. Four o' clock this afternoon I would pick Andrew up at his elementary school. Half an hour. And I would be face to face with Pete Davenport, my enemy and the most intriguing guy I'd ever met.

I was dizzy with anticipation.

He's here to tear my family apart I staunchly reminded myself as the spire from the Mission style Catholic Church we attended came into view. I drove around to the back of the stucco structure—that looked like it was built solely upon earth and faith—to where the preschool program was located. All the kids were shrieking and going about the serious business of play— except for Mikey. He was sitting alone, on the top stoop, shoulders slumped. *Uh-oh.*

As I advanced to the playground, I smiled tentatively at his teacher and threw an encouraging wave at him. His face lit up like a Christmas tree when he saw me, then he bolted over, almost knocking me down with the force of his hug.

"Kadee! Mrs. Reyes is mad at me, but it wasn't my fault! He *gave* it to me—I *pwomise* I didn't take it fwum him, but I *still* gotted in trouble!" he frantically explained.

"It's okay, buddy." I squeezed his sturdy body. "We'll get it all straightened out." I was hoping to convey my support without saying too much of anything because Mrs. Reyes began weaving herself our way. She approached with a sad, starter smile on her creased face. *I've seen worse looks before.*

"Hi, Mrs. Reyes," I greeted, warily.

"Good afternoon, Katie. How was your first day back to school?"

"It was fine, thanks for askin'." I decided to cut to the chase. "What happened today?"

"I already tol' you, Kadee!" Mikey exclaimed.

"Yes, well, now I want to hear from Mrs. Reyes." I turned to her expectantly.

"I'm afraid Mikey is up to his old tricks again," she said, her voice drooping weariness. "I know it's the first day back after a long summer break, so I want to nip this in the bud. We don't want a repeat of last year. He's four-years-old now and more than capable of controlling himself when he *chooses* to." Mrs. Reyes subjected Mikey to her sternest look.

"What did he do?" I asked.

"He, ah . . ." she paused as if searching for the right word, "*persuaded* another child to give him his snack when he *knows* everyone just gets one." She held one bony finger up to Mikey, and he scowled at her.

"Okay . . ."

"The thing is, Katie, Mikey can be a little . . . for lack of a better word, I'll use the term bullying." I started at this, so she quickly explained, "I don't mean in the sense of knocking someone off the swing set. It's more of a . . . lording it over the whole class—myself included."

"I don't understand."

"When Michael gets it into his head he wants something, he can be very *determined* to get it."

True dat. Dogmatic might be his most dominant character trait. I nodded.

"I know it sounds like a minor thing, but I cannot convey to you the amount that Mikey tries and *does* run the classroom!" Her words began picking up speed and volume as though to mimic the chaos.

"I'm sorry this is causin' such a problem for you." I immediately dropped an apology and then a hint to slow things down. "Have you tried timeouts or takin' a privilege away?" She was so quiet for so long I thought she didn't hear me. "Mrs. Reyes?"

Something strange flashed behind her eyes. "I-I find it hard to correct Michael to be honest. I think . . ." she faltered and waved her hand as if waving the thought away. "I think it must be because I know he lost his mother," she finished. "But we're not doing him any favors by letting him get away with so much. A smart boy like Mikey needs firm boundaries or he'll likely run over us all!"

I could see she was quite upset by this. Maybe she was getting too old to maintain control? Four-year-olds could be rambunctious as bucking broncos. "We'll definitely take care of it; don't you worry, Mrs. Reyes."

"Katie, you're a good girl, and I don't want to add to your family's burden by leaving you without quality childcare for Mikey. I'm just at my wit's end!"

"We appreciate all you do," I said, alarmed at the thought of trying to find a new preschool.

"I've been doing this for twenty years, and I've never seen such a precocious child. He literally *runs* the class! I can't have that, and I won't tolerate it anymore!" She fisted her hand as though to firm her resolve. "We only put up with it last year because he was only three, and your family has been through so much. But enough is enough—I have eleven more kids to think about!"

"We'll take care of it," I assured her again. "Mikey, you need to apologize to Mrs. Reyes for today."

"But Kadee, I didn't do nothin' wrong!" he insisted, breaking from my grasp.

I nabbed him back by the arm. "Michael Alexander Connelly, you apologize to her right now!" I leaned over with my I-mean-business look. "It's the right thing to do—she's upset and she's your teacher. You have to respect her."

"Fine!" Mikey looked up at her mournfully, his big eyes tearing up. "I 'pologize that youw're mad at me!" he said in an outraged tone.

I sighed. It would have to do. Apparently, Mrs. Reyes decided she would take it, too. "I accept, Michael." She bent down to hug him, and I noticed how pale she was and that her face had a light sheen of sweat.

"Are you okay, Mrs. Reyes? Would you like me to get you a drink of water?"

"I'm fine, Katie," she said, sounding anything but. "Just make sure you take care of this, or I'm going to have to notify your father."

"Yes ma'am. I hope you enjoy the rest of your afternoon . . . and thanks again for bein' so patient with him," I added diplomatically.

In mutual worried silence, we headed to the car. Mikey peered up at me, and there were a couple of fat tears magnifying the love in his eyes. "I'm sowry I gotted into trouble, Kadee."

One look at his contrite face and I melted on the spot. "Just *please* behave yourself from now on! Obey your teacher and quit runnin' the class, boss man—you don't wanna have to stay home with Daddy, do you?"

Mikey vehemently shook his head. "I pwomise I won't get in twouble no more, okay Kadee?"

"Okay." I squeezed him to me. "You know you're the best boy in the world, right?"

He beamed at me. "Wight."

"You know what else? I'm starvin'," I said, curling his sweaty palm into mine. "Come on, Trouble, let's go get some ice cream."

After a quick trip to McDonalds and then to their restroom to clean Mikey's face (and to run a brush through my hair), we arrived at Andrew's school at exactly five till four. I parked by the front office—two spaces away from a certain enormous, black SUV.

"Wowee! Kadee, wook at that!" Mikey whooped. "I cwaim it!"

"Yeah . . . would you look at that." I glanced in the rearview mirror to find eyes that were the kind of bright that usually induced parents into rummaging through drawers. And my cheeks looked like I'd just given them a good pinch.

Gah, Katie! . . . Get a grip.

Deep breath in. I had nothing to worry about. Drews and I were in this together. We had a long discussion last night and decided he was going to dumb himself down and act bratty. I guess we should add trip every time he walks now that I knew a physical test was involved. *Piece of cake.* All he had to do was flub his way through this mentoring program. *Who knows? If all goes well, Pete Davenport could be packing his bags by the end of the week. Who's the sucker now?*

I tried to squeeze some happy from this thought, but kinda felt more like puking up the ice cream I just downed.

"Huwry up, Kadee. Let's go get Drewy!"

I inhaled some more dry air, then dawdled behind Mikey as he pranced up the stairs to push the button. We announced ourselves, and the lock popped open. Tapping our way down the empty third-grade hallway, I tried to focus on the pigeon-sized insects brightening the halls. Normally, I would stop to look for Andrew's carefully crafted masterpiece, but today I had to concentrate on just holding it together; I was more than a little concerned I would lose it when I saw Pete standing there with Andrew.

Mrs. Woodward would probably think "it" runs in the family after already having dealt with my father and hearing rumors about my mother. She'd surely think an exclusive boarding school would be a better atmosphere for her favorite prodigy than an unstable home life.

"Which one is it, Kadee?" Mikey's anxious voice announced our arrival.

There was a door propped open a couple of classrooms down that had voices spilling out into the hallway followed by laughter. My heart did a nosedive to my stomach. "Think we're almost there," I said self-consciously, knowing he could hear us since we could hear them.

A low voice infused with humor was talking with another higher-pitched one that sounded way too girly to be Mrs. Woodward's. I rolled my eyes before entering the open doorway. Everyone quit talking and looked up at once. I very briefly met his eyes before aiming a smile at Mrs. Woodward and Andrew.

"Drewy!" Mikey ran over to tackle big brother.

"Hey, Shadow." Andrew unpeeled Mikey and deposited him on the floor, where he immediately knocked over some metal bins. After the percussional crash, I was greeted by a reprimand: "Hey, Kate—you're late."

"Yeah, but only by one teensy little minute," I replied, ruffling Andrew's hair. I turned to address his teacher, who was all lip-sticked up today. Glowing, that would be the word I would use to describe her. "Good afternoon, Mrs. Woodward. I hope we're not keepin' you."

"Oh, goodness no!" she immediately demurred. "It's fine. We've just been havin' so much fun. Haven't we gentlemen?"

"Oh, good. I'm glad." My smile didn't quite reach my eyes.

"Katherine, have you had a chance to meet Andrew's *mentor* yet?"

I recoiled at the word and had to clear the bitter from my throat before speaking. "I-I don't think so." I faced Pete with a face out-glowing Mrs. Woodward's, I'm sure.

He raised an eyebrow at me, one corner of his mouth quirking up—a particularly cute expression I was growing familiar with.

"Katherine Connelly . . ." Mrs. Woodward enthusiastically made the introductions, "meet Cadet Peter Davenport, the International Elite Academy transfer and mentor extraordinaire!"

"That's kind of a mouthful," he said, reaching for my hand with a self-deprecating smile. I fought the urge to wipe my clammy palm on my skirt before shaking his hand. "Just Pete's fine. It's so very nice to formally meet you, Katherine . . . I've heard *so* much about you." He smoldered down at me shamelessly.

"It's nice to meet you, too," I managed to croak out, wondering what he could've possibly heard . . . and from whom. I immediately withdrew my hand from his. "And just Kate, please."

I was going for one-upmanship, but ended up with passive-aggressive.

"Oh, my! You youngsters sure are polite. Makes me have faith in the world's youth again." Mrs. Woodward cluelessly beamed her approval.

Pete and I exchanged glances. His lips twitched, and I had to work hard not to crack a smile, too. I'm sure he was also remembering our *not* so polite exchanges the other night. *Was it really just the night before last when it all happened?* It seemed like so much had happened in such a short amount of time. Felt like I was suffering from vertigo . . . *Or is that feeling from being in his presence again?*

"How did it go today?" I asked Andrew, changing the subject and the view.

"Fine." Andrew's standard answer.

"Great." I used my own standby. "Well, we better get goin'. Grab your backpack and thank Mrs. Woodward and . . . ah, Cadet Davenport for their time."

"Just Pete's fine," he reminded me with a smile so shining it almost pierced through my armor.

I had to catch my breath like I'd been running on a treadmill this whole time. "Okay then . . . Pete. I, ah, guess we'll see you tomorrow afternoon."

"My pleasure. I look forward to it . . . Andy's a great kid."

"*We* think so." I threw a possessive arm around Andrew's shoulders, glancing down at him to read his reaction. (He usually hated that name, preferring Drew instead.) Andrew was actually staring up at Pete with what could only be interpreted as admiration. My heart sank like a tank. *Oh no! Not you too, Drews!*

Deciding to move it along quickly, I grabbed Mikey's hand from where it had wandered over to a winking computer. "Thanks again, Mrs. Woodward."

"Oh, my pleasure!" She clasped her hands beneath her chin. "I have such a good feelin' about this!"

Well that makes one of us I thought sourly, but simply smiled back, tight-lipped, while using my other hand to steer Andrew out the door—he didn't seem in any great hurry to leave.

"Excuse me, Kate," Pete said, and I glanced over my shoulder. "Tomorrow I thought I would take Andy to the Learning Center, so you can pick him up there at 4:30, if that works for you. If not, I'd be happy to drive him home. I should also have his Mensa scores by then so I'll be able to share them with you."

I physically cringed—*Mensa* was an IQ test for geniuses, not my eight-year-old brother. Everything was becoming all too real. "Guess that works for me," I let slip through grit teeth. Then whipped my brothers out the door, where we began walk-running down the hallway.

"Where's the fire?" said Andrew.

"Can we go pway on the pwayground?" Mikey asked, while banging into lockers as I half dragged him behind me.

"Not today, buddy."

"Kadee! Yo'wer goin' too fast!"

"Hold up, Kate!" Pete called down the hallway, and I tensed up.

Could I pretend I didn't hear? Both boys automatically stopped and turned around. *Dang!* I thought, but my heart skipped a beat or two as I watched him trot our way. A lock of hair flopped over his forehead. He brushed it back, beaming at us like we'd just made his day by stopping to wait for him.

Wow. I had to force my eyes away. *Avoidance would definitely be the way to go here.*

"Hey." Pete gave me an indecipherable look. "I thought I'd walk you out, if that's okay."

"Sure!" Andrew answered for me.

We formed a tight little quartet as we headed into the front office, where we were stopped by Mr. Brooks. A few eager pleasantries from the principal and secretary held us up for a few more minutes. I leaked out a sigh, debating about whether or not to interrupt their conversation so we could make our escape. Pete caught my eye and smiled privately at me as though we were in it together.

After a moment, he interrupted Mr. Brook's story about his Air Force days. "It was very nice to meet you both. Everyone has been very welcoming and helpful, and I really appreciate it. I look forward to seeing you again tomorrow."

"Yeah, yeah sure," Mr. Brooks blustered, his reddening face finding mine. "Katie, this is a wonderful opportunity for Andrew. Please tell your father he made the right decision here."

"Will do." *No such thing*, I thought, moving to push out the door. But Pete was too fast, reaching out to open it for all of us to walk through. "Thanks," I bit out, manners getting the best of me.

As soon as we exited the building, the afternoon sun pelted us, so we all paused under the small patch of shade provided by the faded-green awning. An awkward silence seemed to have followed us out the door. Pete just looked at me, waiting. Andrew followed his lead. Even little Mikey peered up at me expectantly.

"Uh . . . thanks for walkin' us out," I finally said.

Pete just remained silent, staring down at me with a look I decided was a humor-hurt hybrid. "That's it? You're not even going to ask any questions?"

I wasn't sure what that wounded look was all about (and didn't much care I told myself). And I couldn't exactly speak freely in front of my brothers, and wasn't allowed to ask him anything anyway, so wasn't sure what there was to say. I relegated myself to shrugging my shoulders.

"What happened to yer eye?" Mikey piped up.

"Mikey!" I burst out.

Pete gave a hearty chuckle at my expense. "Wild animal attack." He winked at me, and I scowled back at him.

"What kind of animal?" Mikey persisted.

"Feral cat," he said around a wicked grin.

I arched an eyebrow. "I'm sure you provoked it."

Pete just laughed musically in my ear while my brothers' mouths hung open. Enquiring minds wanted to know more, so I quickly intervened. "Mikey, you're not supposed to ask people personal questions—it's rude."

"I'm sowry, Pete."

He gave an easy laugh, offering up his fist for a bump. "'sall good."

"We gotta get goin'," I said, ushering Mikey down the sidewalk and around the corner to where the cars were parked. Andrew lagged behind to pepper his mentor with questions about what they were going to do tomorrow at The Learning Center.

"Can't tell you," Pete answered.

"Why not?"

"Because it's top secret."

"Aw, come on!" Andrew protested.

"Well, I would tell you . . . but then I'd just have to kill you," Pete teased, effortlessly winning over my little brother.

Andrew laughed delightedly at such bold words and jumped at Pete yelling, "Unh-uh!—you'd have to catch me first!" He tore off down the sidewalk practically leaving track marks, bounded over the parking blocks (managing somehow to do both a vertical and horizontal leap), and skidded to a stop in front of the eye-candy feast that awaited his eyes.

So much for tripping when he walks. I felt like all of my plans were imploding on me.

"Oh, man! Is this *your* car?" Andrew exclaimed.

"Nah, man—it's my truck though." Pete removed an electronic key from his pocket and pressed a button. A loud chirping sound issued from the black mammoth; its blinking lights enticing as a video game.

Mikey broke free from my hand, pumping his little legs to get into the shiny boy-toy first. "It's mine, Drewy!—I alweady cwaimed it when we dwove up!"

Pete threw his head back and laughed before meeting my traitor brothers at the driver's-side door. "Here, allow me show you your Hummer then." He opened it with a flourish and hoisted Mikey into the driver's seat.

Mikey immediately grabbed the steering wheel and began shaking it back and forth with feverish eyes. "Can you take us for a dwive pwease?"

"Sure," Pete easily agreed.

"Yeah! Let's take a spin around the block," Andrew seconded, climbing over his brother to get into the passenger seat.

Pete laughed appreciatively at my brothers' enthusiasm. They were practically foaming at the mouth as they inspected all the widgets and whatnots. After watching them for a moment, I had a flashback to the other night when I was hiding underneath that thing, and I distinctly remembered Pete saying how easy the mission would be: "Like taking candy from a baby."

Well done, Cadet Davenport.

I blasted him with a look so filthy it eroded his smile. "Maybe another day, boys. We've gotta get home now."

Pete frowned but didn't say anything, letting the boys get their loud protests out.

"Let's go, guys. *Now.*"

"One mo'wer minute, Kadee-kat, pwease!" Mikey pleaded with his eyes.

I huffed out some aggravation. "Fine. One more minute."

"Yay!" Mikey celebrated his victory with a fist pump.

While we waited, Pete unzipped the light jacket he was wearing over his P.E. clothes. I noticed it was the same navy one with a roaring lion's head. "Nice jacket," I smirked. "I have one at home just like it."

Pete smirked back. "Keeping it as a memento?"

"More like a reminder," I retorted, reaching past him to fish out Mikey, who obviously wasn't leaving any time soon.

"Can we take a wide tomo'wow?" Mikey asked.

"I dunno, maybe," I hedged.

"Aw, come on, Kadee! Pu-wease!"

"Yeah, or else Pete can just drive me home instead of you picking me up. Right Pete?" Andrew added helpfully.

His mentor took his cue: "Right."

Could *not* have that.

"Pwetty pwease with sugar on top?" Mikey clasped his hands together with his "irresistible" face—all pleading eyes and pouty lips.

"Okay, fine . . . *next* time," I acquiesced with poor grace. "Now get out before I change my mind." I could never say no to that face. No wonder Mrs. Reyes had a hard time disciplining him—Mikey *was* irresistible.

Pete threw his head back and laughed. "Wow!" he said to Mikey, who was straddling my hip now. "That's a neat trick. Can you teach me how to do that?"

"What?"

"Get your sister to do what you want." He glanced at me. "You see . . . I'm having a little trouble in that department."

"It's easy!" Mikey bragged. "You just say pwetty pwease and put your hands together like this." He demonstrated for Pete, who played along, placing his palms together to mimic Mikey's irresistible face. I hated to tell him: his face was already irresistible.

I laughed a little, surprising myself. He was slowly chipping away at my armor. And I was . . . having fun. It was also irresistible and felt very much like manna from heaven. Our eyes met, and I tried reading what was behind the sparkling dark orbs. *Friend or foe?* Pete stared back, his cartoonish expression starting to melt. Something was passing between us, so I quickly averted my gaze back to the monkey in my arms.

"Okay, wise guy, you can drop the cute act now that you've got your way." I moved to set Mikey down.

"No carrwy me," he whined, wrapping his arms around my neck.

"Honey, you're gettin' so big now . . . and you're chokin' me." I stumbled towards my car.

"I gotcha," Pete said, reaching over to pry Mikey from my arms. Mikey started a protest that ended in the air as Pete tossed him up and caught him.

Mikey yelped with pleasure, eyes bulging. "Do it again!"

Pete immediately tossed Mikey up again then threw him over his shoulder so that his giggles spilled down his back. He was squealing and laughing so hard I thought he might be choking. That finally prompted Andrew to exit out the passenger side, where he'd been busy inspecting the complex-looking navigational system.

"Hey! My turn next!" he called, hurtling towards Pete, arms wide. Pete exaggeratedly wiped his brow with the back of his hand. I had to laugh—Andrew was getting pretty big.

Something was happening to me inside, a loosening. He was just so, so . . . dang charismatic. And nice. And witty. And drop-dead gorgeous. I found myself almost helpless against his charms.

Why-oh-why does he have to be the bad guy?

I busied myself unnecessarily buckling Mikey into his booster seat with Pete eyeing me with blatant interest. This facilitated the slow burn creeping up my face. When I went to get in, Pete intervened by wrenching the door open for me. "Thanks," I murmured, trying very hard not to feel the sting of embarrassment at my pathetic wheels.

"You're welcome," he said, continuing to look down on me with eyes that were melting me faster than the afternoon sun. I got in and rolled down the windows in the over-heated car. Looked up to find him *still* staring at me.

Maybe if I roll over his foot?

Shaking my head, I started the car and put it in reverse. But he still hadn't moved except to slide a pair of dark aviators on. I cleared my throat. "Excuse me. I don't mean to be rude but I really do have to go."

"Are you sure?"

"Yes, I'm very sure," I said tartly. "I have a lot to do this afternoon."

"No, I mean are you sure you don't mean to be rude?"

"I don't know what you mean," I sniffed, easing the car back.

"So you're not *trying* to be rude then?" Pete persisted, still hanging out in my window.

He was playing a good game. I glanced in the rearview mirror at the two little pitchers with big ears in the backseat. "No!"

Lips quirking up at my little outburst, he tossed his hair back and leaned in, resting his forearms on the windowsill. I noticed some hair sparkling gold against his tan in the sunlight. "Good," he said, "I'm relieved."

"Okay . . . now that that's all settled." Exasperated, I began backing up again, forcing him to move out of the way. Then got the car turned around and had to endure an enthusiastic round of goodbyes from the boys all around. I finally started to drive off when a sharp whistle automatically caused my foot to hit brake. I distinctly recalled hearing that same exact whistle Saturday night.

"Wow!" Andrew rubbernecked out the window. "Did you hear that?"

"How'd he do that?" Mikey asked in an awed voice as though a piercingly loud whistle was akin to flying.

Pete came trotting up to my window and leaned back in. "So . . . since you've established you're *not* trying to be rude, I thought I'd push my luck and ask you to have lunch with me tomorrow." He followed that bit of boldness up with a lopsided grin.

My heart did a little backflip in my chest, and I just stared for a second, debating how I could squirm out of this one (and if I even wanted to).

"It's just, I'm all alone . . . and lonely," he threw unnecessarily to the backseat. I snorted at this bit, but he just continued playing the violin for his rapt audience. "I don't have one single friend yet . . . except for you, Kate."

"Of course, she will, Pete!" Mikey spoke up, unable to take it another second.

"Come on, Katie! You don't want him to have to sit all alone at lunch, do you?" Andrew threw in, despite my strict warnings about his academy.

I remained resolutely quiet, boiling over with anger and heat.

"You can come have lunch with me tomo'wow, Pete!" Mikey happily solved his problem for his new favorite person.

Pete acknowledged him with a high-five. "Thanks, bro. I wish I could, but I'm in high school with your sister, so *she's* the only one in this car I can sit with tomorrow."

"Pwease, Kadee! Tell him you'll sit with him. Wemembuh the golden rule?"

Called out by my little brother. I ground my teeth.

"Show me how it goes again, Mikey." Pete mimicked the "irresistible" face. "Like this? I need to get it just right—I'm not as good at it as you yet."

Mikey seriously demonstrated the technique again while Andrew rolled his eyes at the proceedings. Pete immediately winked at Andrew to let him know he was in on the charade. You had to hand it to the guy—he had people skills.

"Pretty please, Kate?" Pete clasped his hands in prayer again.

"Pwetty pwease with a *chewry* on top," Mikey added helpfully.

Pete laughed again, a sound so natural and pure, it sent little shivers of pleasure running down my spine. "Pretty please with a *cherry* on top," he added with a sexy pout. "I'll even get down on one knee." He'd just folded one knee when I finally caved by reaching out to pull him up.

"Fine," I snapped, reminding myself of Mikey when he agreed to apologize to Mrs. Reyes.

Pete stood back up and leaned in again. Even closer than before, so I had a chance to inhale his healthy male scent. "Fine what?"

"Fine . . . I'll have lunch with you tomorrow," I mumbled out with the requisite eye-roll.

"Promise?"

"I promise, okay." I glared at his smug smile. "Happy now?"

"Elated." He chuckled a little at my expense. "I'll wait for you after class."

"Fine," I said through clenched teeth, then squealed out of the parking lot with mocking laughter trailing after me through the open window.

I left feeling very much like round one went to the elite cadet.

15

LUNCH DATE

The next day I was on pins and needles from the moment I rolled onto campus. Every time I thought about sitting across from the world's most desirable guy for forty-five minutes—alone—a feeling akin to stage fright hit me. Butterflies stirred my stomach (not an entirely unpleasant sensation).

To avoid seeing him just yet, I'd arrived as late as possible so only laid eyes on him briefly across the main hall while I dashed to class. While everyone bustled with their backpacks and banter to first-hour, I caught a glimpse of his golden head gliding along with two senior girls, who were bookending and bombarding him with questions as they headed for class. Looked like he'd already accumulated quite a horde of followers, and they were trailing behind him like paparazzi after a good story.

Furtively, I watched him for a few seconds, feeling vaguely like a stalker myself. I noticed I wasn't the only one scoping him out—Ashley-Leigh and her lackeys were busy strategizing around her locker and looking at him like a particularly juicy piece of meat they'd like to devour.

Pete seemed oblivious to all the attention, sauntering along answering one of the bouncy girl's questions. He spoke down out of one side of his mouth in a manner I found extremely sexy. She laughed out loud at whatever he said, beaming up at him with admiration mingled with lust.

A pang hit my stomach now that was far less pleasant than the butterflies. I heaved a sigh and forced myself to turn the corner to the library. That pang could only mean one thing—jealousy. *Ugh*! I instantly hated the feeling, always believing I was above petty jealousies about boys.

Not that he was even remotely an *ordinary* boy. *Is he really even a boy at all?* I had my suspicions. He just seemed so sophisticated compared to everyone else. Probably due in large part to the elite life he's led. Self-doubt started gnawing at me. *Why would such an extraordinary person find me remotely interesting?*

I mentally shook myself again. Pete wasn't interested in me *personally*. He was here to do a job. I was just part of the mission I'd overheard him talking about. He probably thought he could pull the ole razzle-dazzle on me like everyone else and then just sally on out of here—with my kid brother—while he watched me blow kisses at him in the rearview mirror.

Well I ain't gonna be no easy country bimbo! I stomped around the library in my cowboy boots, stirring up dust and shoving books in a huff. And feeling stupid because I'd dressed in my cute birthday outfit today, the one Ashley-Leigh made me take off to put on those ridiculous shorts.

I was getting sucked into the guy's vortex of charisma. I mean . . . he obviously had some kind of hidden agenda, and my gut told me there was something fishy about this transfer-mentoring program. *And why all the secrecy surrounding the school?* It was downright scary how little we actually knew about the boarding school—all the way out in California—that Andrew might be attending in just four short months.

My stomach clenched; I wasn't even sure I could eat today. *Maybe he wouldn't show up?* I mean, I didn't recall even telling him what class I have third-hour, so how's he gonna find me? Something told me that if Pete Davenport wanted something, he'd get it. An image of Andrew flashed in my mind. *We'll see about that.*

A plan. That's what I needed, "Operation Derail." Phase One: redouble my efforts to avoid Pete. Phase Two: have Andrew recommit to not performing well on his tests (easier said than done for an overachiever like my brother). Also, there was the little problem of him being smitten with his "mentor." Andrew dropped "so cool" about a half-dozen times during the ride home alone, followed by a "I might *want* to go to boarding school" in the brief exchange we had before bed. After I almost went into cardiac arrest, he quickly changed his tune, but you could tell it was only to appease me.

Daddy, of course, was pleased as punch by the glowing report. He shot me a gloating look that made me start itching for a pie. *Arrgh!* It all made me want to punch something—maybe even a very good-looking, smug cadet.

The morning rolled by quickly and predictably. Before I knew it third-hour bell rang, signaling the last class that stood between me and my lunch date. Between the clenching and the butterflies, I could barely even sit upright. Miguel and Ashley-Leigh slid into the same seats as yesterday, both staring expectantly at me while I studiously perused the contents of my notebook. I was actually going over a list of questions I had for Pete regarding his school, in case he miraculously showed up.

Midway through class, Mrs. Jenkins told us to get together in groups of twos or threes to discuss the Walt Whitman poem we'd just read. *Uh-oh.* I was barely paying attention, so probably couldn't contribute much more than a yawn.

Miguel leaned over. "Wanna partner up?"

"Sure." I smiled, and we lifted and turned our desks to face each other the same time Ashley-Leigh bumped hers up against the side of mine.

"*Uh!*" she huffed dramatically, pretending not to see one of her "besties" waving her down in the middle of the room. "What the hell, *Miguel?*"

"You snooze, you lose," he replied calmly.

"You know I always partner up with Katie."

Miguel and I exchanged looks. "Since when?"

"Since, like, forever," she insisted.

"Why don't you go partner up with BFF over there?" Miguel nodded toward Madison, who was still frantically waving like an aircraft was heading in the wrong direction.

"Why don't you?" she replied churlishly. ". . . 'Sides, Katie's my *real* BFF."

Miguel started to argue, but I interrupted quickly, having lots of experience refereeing squabbling children. "We can all partner up," I said diplomatically. "Mrs. Jenkins said groups of two or three."

Ashley-Leigh poked her tongue out at Miguel before plopping into her seat. He glowered back at her. I inwardly smiled. *This is working out great.* They both obviously wanted to ask me something but neither one wanted to do it in the presence of the other . . . *I couldn't have planned this better.*

Unfortunately (or fortunately), the hour had almost run its course. We were all busy cramming the desks back into rows and packing to leave when I caught Ashley-Leigh eyeing my outfit. I did a swift one-eighty to talk to Miguel, who caught me off guard by asking what I was doing for lunch. I stammered my way through some loose interpretation of already having plans.

"Isn't that, like, the outfit you wore Saturday night for your birthday?" Ashley-Leigh interrupted, tact not being her strong suit. I confirmed that it was and caught myself squirming under her scrutiny. She narrowed her eyes at me. "Why are you so dressed up today?"

"Why you always gotta be so nosey?" Miguel answered for me. "Don't listen to her, Katie. I think you look real pretty today."

"Thanks, Miguel." I rummaged around in my backpack, but before I could hide my face in there, Ashley-Leigh peeled it away from my hands.

"So are you gonna hang with us today at lunch?" she demanded.

"She's already got plans." Miguel plucked my backpack from Ashley-Leigh and handed it back to me. "Plans that don't include you. Right, Katie?"

"Uh . . ." Thankfully the bell rang and everyone began pooling to the door. "Saved by the bell" may never have been a more apt expression. My imminent lunch plans flew a fresh migration of butterflies to my stomach. It felt a lot like I was stepping from behind the velvet curtain and into the spotlight—naked. I sank back to my desk to get my bearings.

"You comin'?" Miguel called, wading against the current to wait for me.

"You go ahead, Miguel . . . I want to, ah, ask Mrs. Jenkins somethin'. I'll see you in Spanish."

"Okey-dokey. *Hasta luego!*" With a wave, he allowed himself to be drained out the door with the rest of the school.

I lingered a moment longer, lubing my lips and brushing out my hair. (I hated myself so much then, you don't even know.) Mrs. Jenkins eyed me inquiringly. I gave her an apologetic smile, shrugged my backpack on, and headed the short distance to the door, hoping the crowds had sufficiently thinned because I was feeling sorta like the girl who was about to be stood up . . . and didn't want a crowd of witnesses.

But I needn't have worried because I saw him almost immediately (he was kind of hard to miss). Everyone within a hundred-foot radius was staring at him, for one thing. For another, he was absolutely breathtakingly gorgeous. My heart did an immediate cannonball to my stomach. *Breathe.*

Leaning casually—in vintage T-shirt and jeans—across the hallway, he was occupying his time pecking on his phone. As if sensing I was staring at him, he looked up and broke into a delighted smile so dazzling, it literally stunned me. I hovered in the doorway, watching Pete shrug off the wall and stride toward me. He slipped his phone into his back pocket and politely brushed someone off, who had finally worked up enough nerve to talk to him. He did this while keeping his eyes on mine the whole time. I swallowed, the butterflies swarming like bees. As he walked, he grinned over at me like he was coming to collect a winning lotto ticket. If he was acting (which I believed he was), he could make a fortune selling refrigerators to Eskimos.

It took me a moment to get my feet to moving again, and we finally met somewhere in the middle of the hall, standing face-to-chest, because he was more than a head taller than me. We just stood there for a moment, absorbing each other's chemistry, until I finally tipped my head up to look at him.

He was the first to break the silence: "Whew! You had me worried there for a couple of seconds—thought you were going to stand me up."

I laughed out loud. I doubted that anyone *had* ever or *would* ever stand him up. "Thought about hidin'," I admitted, a little sheepishly.

Pete chuckled at my honesty. "I'm not as scary as I look," he said, taking my elbow and steering me toward the door. A jolt of electricity ran from my arm to my heart, shocking me with joy. "I blame it on the black eye." He slanted a rakish brow my way.

I colored hotly but managed a slip of a smile. "Yeah, well, that might have somethin' to do with it."

As we talked our way to the parking lot, silhouettes of color (I tried to ignore) stared at us. This was a feat way easier to do than I would've thought because I was so caught up in our conversation. It's like we were in our own little world . . . until we reached his Hummer. There, parked boldly beside him, was the same convertible as yesterday, stuffed to the brim with glossy-lipped girls caught gaping at us as we approached. I saw a series of "OMGs" mouthed, followed by an "I don't believe it!" from the one and only Ashley-Leigh.

I hunched in a little on myself as Pete opened the passenger door and helped me in. Then he walked, whistling, to the driver's side door where the girls were parked.

"Afternoon ladies," he greeted, before hopping in and shutting the door in their collective face. Unconcerned with the amount of fanfare next door, Pete continued whistling away as he tossed his wallet and cell phone onto the console. He threw on the same aviators from yesterday, fired up the engine, and turned to me. "How much time do we have for lunch again?"

"Um . . . about forty minutes give or take."

He was staring, so I moved my eyes along to the carload of disgruntled females driving off, furiously gossiping about me no doubt. I raised my hand in a small wave I knew wouldn't be returned. Ashley-Leigh's big ole stink-eye out the passenger window was the last thing I saw before facing him again.

He arched an eyebrow. "Friends of yours?"

I puffed out some air. "More like frenemies."

"I think I have a couple of those," Pete said with a chuckle before throwing the truck into gear and pulling out. "I like this open-campus thing. We don't really get to leave campus at my school."

I realized he opened up about his academy for the first time, but instead of jumping on it, I just kind of nodded absentmindedly, not wanting to spoil the mood with deep questions right now. I just wanted to relax and enjoy his company. A wormy feeling of guilt let me know how much that was working against my cause.

"Do you mind if I roll down the windows?" he asked.

"Not at all." I wanted the same thing—to feel the wind in my hair, the sun on my arms. A deep breath in of fresh air . . . and the pressures began to melt away.

It was a beautiful day, not too hot yet with a bright blue, welcoming sky. He pulled out of the parking lot going left while everyone else went right towards the main drag, where the majority of the fast food restaurants were located. I idly wondered where we were going but didn't bother asking. A part of me (bigger than was healthy) wanted him to just keep on driving forever. Happiness bubbled up inside me like the first day of spring after a long, hard winter.

An unconscious tug must've been curving my lips because he said, "You seem like you're in a good mood today."

I simply smiled back lazily, enjoying the feel of the thrumming engine beneath me and the rich smell of leather seats. I leaned my head on my hand and propped it on the open window, letting the breeze carry away my hair and my cares.

"I'm glad you're enjoying yourself," he said, turning on the stereo to an appropriately upbeat song.

I mumbled something unintelligible and closed my eyes. Sleep had been elusive lately, and I basked in the luxurious, carefree moment.

Is it that obvious I'm happy? Maybe the French only got it half right:

They say one can't cover a cough or love. Might happiness be just as transparent? It was an alluring feeling, one I hadn't felt in a long time. And even though it was encased in an artificial bubble of fantasy with a ticking time bomb attached, I was still determined to enjoy it—if only for the few minutes left of this drive.

I was thoroughly enjoying my peaceful ride with the extremely hand-some boy wonder (whom I still had a hard time believing was really enrolled in our high school) when I heard tires crunch gravel before slowing to a stop. I expected the butterflies to churn, but they mysteriously stayed away. Pete had managed, somehow, to put me at ease—another skill in his arsenal, I noted. I took another deep breath, not quite curious enough about where we were to open my eyes and break the spell. I could feel his eyes on me, but he remained silent. The quiet enveloped us in a warm cocoon of camaraderie that only enhanced the feeling of fantasy.

"Time to wake up, Sleeping Beauty." He broke the silence again, and my eyes popped open just long enough to roll them at him for such a cheesy line, but I couldn't prevent the upward tilt of my lips. He laughed. "Well, it the slipper fits . . . or I guess I should say *boot* in this case."

After getting out and retrieving a cooler from the back, he came around to get my door. I unbuckled my seatbelt to hop down, unassisted. The benign sun from a moment ago now blinded me, so I threw a hand-visor up, taking in the little park area that would be our lunch spot. *Huh. A picnic?*

"Do you need sunglasses?" He offered me his while I pretended not to squint.

"No thanks. I'm fine."

"Are you sure? I have an extra pair in the truck."

"I'm sure," I replied, stomping my way to the graffiti-decorated picnic tables near the playground.

Of course he has an extra pair, Boy Scout that he is. So wished my sunglasses weren't among the casualties that fell out of my purse the other night . . . when I was running from them. My watery eyes cut to the cheerful cadet swinging a cooler and whistling while he strolled blithely along with his fancy aviators on. *Ugh!* I started to plop onto a scarred bench when he caught my arm. I wrenched away, an overreaction that just as quickly embarrassed me, because he immediately held up his free hand, like in surrender.

"Hey—I just wanted to see if you wanted to sit over there instead." He nodded towards a patch of shade between two trees near the basketball court.

"Um . . ." I did a little *hmm-hmm*. "Okay."

Following after him, I found myself noticing how his low-slung jeans fit his body the exact way it should—loosely at the hips and waist but snug in all the right places. Then quickly averted my eyes to a safer place, grateful to the sun for being a reliable alibi for my red face. Instead, I marveled at how his hair shimmered in the light and thought about how much money girls paid to get their hair to look half as good. We arrived at the picnic spot, and Pete spread out a plaid blanket he'd thoughtfully brought along on the sparse dry grass.

"Can I do anything to help?" I offered while fervently hoping fried chicken wasn't on the menu. "I could've brought somethin', if I'd've known we were havin' a picnic."

He gave me another heart-breaking smile. "Nope. Just sit back and take a load off," he commanded while unpacking glass containers of food.

I thought that was mildly weird because I lived in the land of Tupperware. I made no comment—our worlds were sure to collide in more ways than one. I was reminded of our Spanish II book cover, *Dos Mundos*—Two Worlds.

While Pete laid out our lunch in a remarkably efficient way, he talked nonstop about nonsensical things. And as he worked, I noticed every little detail about him, from the deft movements he made, to certain idiosyncrasies I'd already memorized: how he always placed his cell phone and keys together like they were best friends, the way he constantly brushed his hair back as though unused to it being in the way, how one eyebrow would arch when he wanted to make a particular point, and how, when he thought something was really funny, he threw his head back and laughed out loud.

Oh man . . . I'm gettin' it bad.

I snapped out of it because he just said something that needed a response: "Hope you like PB&J."

"Yeah." I was surprised by his choice. "Actually, it's one of my favorites."

"Good," he grinned down at me wolfishly, "I aim to please." He offered up his half of a very large sandwich in a sort of cheers gesture.

"*Buen probecho*," I said, bumping my half against his.

"*Buen probecho*," he echoed before digging in.

After a few moments of chewing our grainy sandwiches in companionable silence, I felt myself go tongue-tied. *Where should I begin?* The questions were sticking in the back of my throat with the peanut butter. Awkwardly, I groped for the silver thermos and tipped it back to drink the ice-cold mystery inside. A laugh gurgled out, as the familiar flavor hit the back of my throat.

He squinted at me through one eye—a new expression. "What's so funny?"

"Milk?"

"Yeah, milk. Can you think of anything else that goes better with a peanut butter sandwich?

I laughed again. "No, not really. It's just . . . not what I expected."

He laughed a little too, reaching for a grape. "What did you expect?"

I watched as he threw it up and caught it in his mouth. The coordinated movement reminded me of Andrew. It was disconcerting to watch the similarities and realize my little brother might actually *belong* to his elite world. I laughed hollowly, trying to shake off the feeling to answer his question.

"I dunno, maybe something a little more conventional, like ham and cheese."

Pete stopped chewing and looked at me for a second. "Did you prefer ham and cheese?"

Maybe it was the way he phrased it, or I was already on the defensive again, but suddenly my intuition was telling me he *knew* going into this I didn't eat meat. Reality crawled back in, unwelcome as an ant at our picnic lunch. *Has he been spying on me?* He watched my face, trying to decipher why the easy smile from a moment ago was having trouble staying put.

"No. It's just . . . I thought a manly-man like you would prefer meat," I said, trying a better facsimile of a smile. I was still hoping to pump him for info and didn't want him to know my antennae were up. Then I remembered at the restaurant he'd only ordered whole-wheat toast. *Could the explanation be as simple as he was a vegetarian, too? Was I making a mountain out of a molehill?*

"Are you trying to imply a real man can't enjoy a good PB&J?"

I forced a laugh. "No. But . . . are you a vegetarian?"

"Not exactly," he said not elaborating.

"It's just . . . well, I could've had a peanut allergy or somethin'," I prodded some more. "You never know these days. Peanut butter can be risky business, and you don't really strike me as the careless type." I searched his face for answers.

His expression remained loose, but his jaw tightened. "Looks like you have me all figured out," he said with an edge to his voice I'd never heard toward me before. It stung. More than I cared to admit.

He put down his half-eaten sandwich. I dropped the carrot stick I was no longer going to eat.

"Likewise . . . it just so happens, PB&J *is* one of my favorite things because I *am* a vegetarian." I leaned forward to meet his gaze head on. "But you already knew that, didn't you?"

Pete laughed what should've been a very persuasive laugh. "Relax, Kate. Don't you think you're being a little paranoid?"

Blood gushed to my face. *Gah*! I really hated that—when guys tell you to relax. That's about the time you *shouldn't* relax, I'd found out. Didn't that ape Ron Tillman just tell me that exact thing Saturday night, after putting his hands all over me? And Pete said it like I was acting hysterical or something. I *heard* him telling Ranger this mission would be as easy as taking candy from a baby, right after they'd abducted me in the middle of the night. And now he just happened to be Andrew's "mentor" and was testing him to have him shipped away to some super-secret boarding school nobody's ever heard of. And he had the nerve to tell me to . . .

"*Relax*?" I guttered the word. "How dare you tell me that when you've been followin' me around spyin' on me! . . . And I demand to know why right now!"

I was seething. *How could I keep falling for his phony charm time and time again?* He was part of the *enemy* that was after my gifted brother! I was reminded, with a harsh pang, why *he* was sitting here with *me*—silly country girl falling for the charming prince. But instead of us riding away into the sunset together, he rides away with the *real* prize—Andrew.

Unable to sit in his deceitful presence any longer, I trembled to my feet. He rose to his knees pleading, but also like if he needed to spring quickly to grab me, he could.

"Whoa! Hold on a minute, Kate. I don't know what's going on here all of a sudden, but I can explain everything. That's one of the reasons I wanted to have lunch with you today."

"Fine. Explain yourself. Startin' with why you were followin' me the night of my birthday."

"That was your birthday?" he said, with what I thought was a little bit too much surprise sprinkled in. "Happy belated birthday!" Pete smiled his most charming smile, and usually it was enough to make my heart go pitter-patter. Now it just stopped cold in my chest like a stone.

"Why were you followin' me, Pete?"

He sighed, stuffed his hands in his pockets, rocked back on his heels. "We actually weren't following you per se," he hedged. "We saw a girl—you," he indicated me with his chin, "walking the drag. We saw you cut across the waiting cars at the stoplight, and . . . I don't know if you know this or not, but a carload of guys made a U-turn when you started down the side street. We believed their intention was to follow you." Pete peeked through his lashes to see how his little story was going down.

I just stood there, a wall of skepticism.

"And concluded they were up to no good—a car load of dudes turning around to follow a girl, wearing . . ."—he looked at me with chastising eyes—"that *outfit*, walking alone down a dark street at night. That was something we could *not* ignore, so we followed you for a while to make sure you were okay, never realizing you were the same girl from the restaurant."

"So, you're sayin' it was just a *coincidence?*"

He laughed a little at my expression. "Yes. That's exactly what I'm saying. It *was* a coincidence—they do happen in real life, you know."

I folded my arms across my chest. "I don't believe you."

He laughed again. "I didn't really expect you to, you stubborn girl. But I'm not sure why not."

I found myself surrendering again to his good looks and charm so closed my eyes against him. "What were y'all even doin' there in the first place? And don't tell me out cruisin' the drag, cause I don't buy it."

He sighed as if debating, eyed my determined face to determine what he could get away with leaving out—nothing.

"We had a meeting with your father earlier," he admitted. I stiffened instantly, so he explained, "We're ambassadors for The Academy, so we met with him to introduce ourselves and go over how the program works."

I turned to face the empty playground. "Kate . . . " Pete stepped behind me and began to rub little circles on my shoulders, melting my resolve to hate him. "Have you ever felt like you were meant to do something?" I shrugged. "Like you were meant to be somewhere at a specific time to do something?"

Silence was my answer, but he had my attention. As if sensing this, he turned me back around. "I think most of the time life is just a series of random occurrences. But every-once-in-a-while, I feel like there *is* a specific purpose to my life . . . like now," he said, eyes blazing. "Maybe that night, on your birthday, I was meant to be in that specific spot, at that exact time, so I . . . or I guess *we* could follow you." I was slightly mesmerized by his gaze and his words. "And it's a good thing we did, or else we might not be standing here having this conversation right now . . ." And now I was on the receiving end of the kind of look that makes you gulp.

"So you're sayin' it was fate?" I meant to say in a cutting tone, but ended up sounding more like a squeaky toy.

"Really, Kate, is it so hard to believe?"

I nodded my head, not trusting myself to speak. *Gah*! He was doing it again. I wanted to wrap my arms around him, press myself into his chest so I could fully enjoy the sensation of him. It was becoming like an addiction, and like most addicts, I didn't want to stop (even though I knew I should). Instead, I stepped out of his embrace, instantly feeling bereft but needing the distance to concentrate.

"How do you explain the peanut butter sandwiches then?"

"Did you really just throw your hands on your hips?" he neatly countered my question with a question.

"Huh?" I demanded, refusing to be thrown off the scent.

Mama always said the devil is in the details . . . It was just a little bit too perfect—right down to the carrot sticks and grapes. He remained quiet, either stalling for time or allowing me to finish my little tirade. So I continued, "I gotta tell you—cuttin' the crust off may have been just a tad overboard, don'tja think? I mean if you didn't want to arouse suspicion, and allowing for the fact that I at least had a marginally average IQ."

Pete spread his palms out. "Okay, you got me."

"Ah-ha! I *knew* it! You were spyin' on me!" I crowed, wondering why my chest was in the process of deflating when I was just proven right.

"You're right—I already knew you were a vegetarian . . . because I asked Andrew yesterday what you like to eat."

"What?"

"Yeah." He shrugged his shoulders. "I confess—I was pumping your little brother for the 411 on you."

Oh. Could the obvious explanation have eluded me because I was too prejudiced against his academy to accept an innocent answer? My angry tirade from a moment ago now seemed like a psychotic episode, and my face burned a little for being so vehemently on the side of wrong.

"*Really?*" My chest began inflating again.

"Really." He nodded and grabbed my hand.

My heart instantly skipped a beat, the butterflies returning with a vengeance. "Why would you do that?"

"For a couple of reasons," he said. "One, you weren't exactly rolling out the red carpet for me, if you know what I mean." He dropped my hand to start packing up, and I followed suit. "I knew I needed to clear the air with you after the other night, but you just continued giving me the worst case of the cold shoulder I've ever had." He stopped packing long enough to frown at me. "So I thought I would invite you to lunch to get some alone time with you."

"Not mentioning the fact that you played on my little brothers' sympathies to get me here."

A sly smile slid my way. "Yeah. I admit that was a dirty trick, but I was desperate." Pete removed the thermos from my hand and held my gaze. "Kate, I couldn't stand the thought of you thinking I was here to hurt you or your family—that's sincerely *not* my intention."

I quietly absorbed his intentions. And even though his eyes turned from earnest to something less benign, it was hard not to buy whatever he was selling when he was looking at me like that.

I cleared my throat a little. "What was the other reason?" His forehead creased, so I prompted, "You said there were a couple of reasons you were askin' about me . . ." I held my breath, my heart hopeful.

"Isn't it obvious?"

"Not really."

"Because I wanted to woo you, you silly girl."

"Really?"

"Really," he reaffirmed, then, re-grabbing my hand, he swung the cooler up with the other. "So I better get you back to school on time, or else your father will never let me court you. My guess is—he's a real hard ass."

I laughed. "What makes you say that?"

"I got the chance to meet former Sergeant Connelly in the flesh, and let's just say . . . he made quite an impression."

"He has that effect on people."

Pete's eyes sparkled. "So does his daughter."

My face flushed. Unable to meet his eye, I squinted instead at the bright sky while sallying along in the breezy afternoon next to the second brightest object on the planet. When I found my voice, it was to tease him back.

"By the way, did you just recently escape from a Renaissance Fair?" Pete tilted his head quizzically. "You just used the terms 'woo' and 'court' back to back," I said, in way of explanation.

He threw his head back, and the sound of his laughter sent a thrill of pleasure through me. "I guess I did." He dropped another heart-stopping smile on me. "You seem to bring it outta me."

I laughed, feeling so lighthearted I could've flown back to school. "Remind me to thank Drews later for being such a sneaky accomplice."

The smile on his face momentarily froze before he quickly reanimated it. "I wouldn't do that if I were you."

"Why not?"

"Well, I sort of swore him to secrecy, and I don't want him to think I was the one to break the bro-code . . . sort of a guy thing," he explained.

"A guy thing, huh?"

"Yeah. It's one of the first and foremost elements of male bonding—keeping the bro-code. Right up there with catching a football and learning how to spit properly." Back at the truck now, Pete opened the door for me.

"I'm sure Andrew's smart enough to figure out how to face downwind all by himself," I said, hopping in.

Pete huffed out some amusement. "Yeah, he sure is a smart little guy. I'm looking forward to working with him."

"Well, the feelin's *entirely* mutual," I replied in a dejected voice.

After giving me another quizzical look, he shut the door. A short moment later he'd replaced the cooler and came around and fired up the engine. The music automatically came on, but he switched it off to level me with a look.

"I'm not sure why that bothers you exactly," he said, sounding hurt. "I would think you'd be happy knowing he likes me . . . since we'll be spending time together every day."

"I am," I said tonelessly.

Pete looked like he was going to say something then thought better of it. Instead he decided to change the sore subject. "Okay, now that I've come clean about everything . . . it's *your* turn now."

"I wouldn't say everything," I disagreed lightly.

"What do you mean?"

"I still have a few more questions for you."

"About The Academy?" he clarified, and when I nodded, annoyance passed over his face. "Didn't you get the brochure? I don't want to waste our time together rehashing material you can read for yourself. It's really pretty straight forward stuff, Kate."

"I wanna talk about what's *not* in the brochure."

"*All* the pertinent info is *in* the brochure," he countered. "And Ranger and I went over all that with your father at the meeting."

"Yeah, but not with *me*," I said.

Some air puffed from his cheeks. "What do you want to know?"

"More about the mentorin' program, about the kinds of tests you'll be administerin' to him, where you're livin' while you're here—"

"I'm glad to see that made the top three," he cut in humorously.

I ignored his flirt intended to divert me from my fact-finding mission. "I could go on. In fact, I have a list." I was bending to retrieve it from my backpack when he caught my shoulder.

"Not so fast," he said. "It's my turn to ask the questions now." I started to protest, but Pete shook his head. "That's not fair. Besides, that list sounds like it's going to take longer than what's left of this drive to answer. So, like I said—my turn."

I huffed out some aggravation.

"It's called getting to know you, Kate."

"Fine—shoot."

Pete fought a smile. "Funny choice of words."

I made an impatient, flappy hand gesture. "Fire away." He arched an eyebrow at me, and I rephrased: "Interrogate away."

He simply smiled at my pout. "Okay, first: What do you like to do for fun on the weekends?"

I was quiet for a few seconds, watching the familiar sights—fast food joints, architecturally bankrupt banks, fledging strip malls—fly by as we drove back to school. I wondered how he knew his way around so skillfully, but let it pass with the scenery to ponder his question.

When was the last time I actually did anything for fun? "Uh . . ."

"Come on, Kate! That's an easy one."

"I have no idea." I shrugged my shoulders, blushing a little at the admission.

He threw me a sharp look. "Katherine Lee Connelly, you're meaning to tell me you have *no idea* what you like to do for fun?" He truly looked incredulous.

My face blistered. *Dagnab.* I should've said something that normal people like to do like surf the Net or cruise the drag. Instead, I ended up sounding like I had no life, which in fact, was true.

"Nothing at all comes to mind?"

"Look!" I practically spat. "I take care of my brothers everyday and waitress on the weekends—my schedule doesn't exactly have a lot of blank space!" Pete looked sideways at me, and I hated the pity I saw reflected in his eyes. ". . . I probably wouldn't recognize fun if it slapped me upside the head, *alright?*"

Who is he to judge me and my life? He wouldn't know a *thing* about hardship and loss and even less about being poor! He with his fancy-shmancy boarding school! He probably spent his weekends surfing the Pacific with his bubbly California beach babe. *Why would he want a workhorse when he was used to Thoroughbreds?* A bitter lump clumped in my throat. I quickly swallowed it down with a large dose of anger. Kinda felt like kicking a dent in his shiny Hummer.

Pete was quiet for a few moments, waiting for my storm of emotions to blow over. The only sound was the hum of the engine. Embarrassed by my outburst, I spoke again to fill up the awkward pause.

"I already know my life is boring and pathetic, okay?"

"I don't think you're boring or pathetic," he said in a velvet voice. He reached for the hand clenched in my lap. "In fact, I find you to be the *opposite* of boring. And taking care of your brothers full-time while working part-time is *noble*, not pathetic."

I dared a peek at his eyes. What I saw there moved things around in my chest. Inexplicably, I felt even lighter than before. I guess it was finally sharing a piece of my burden with someone. It's like I could breathe freer after having oxygen rationed for so long.

He gave my hand a good squeeze and turned the music back on. "But we gotta work on the fun part. Agreed?" He smiled at me, and my heart did its back-flip thing.

"Agreed."

"Okay, back to the questions now," he said, once again changing the sore subject. "What kind of music do you like?"

16

FLIP-FLOP HEART

We arrived back to school with stereo and laughter blasting out the windows like a couple of regulars. Pete seemed to find my "extremely eclectic taste in music" hysterical. The engine cut off, and I watched, fascinated, as his mouth quirked up again.

"I still can't believe your favorite music is rap. Gansta rap, too?"

I laughed. "Among other things. What did you expect? Country?"

"You got me again," he said before getting out and coming around to get my door. "I hate to repeat any of what I'd like to think of as my witty remarks, but if the shoe fits—you are wearing cowboy boots," he pointed out.

"Guess it goes to show you—you really *can't* judge a book by its cover. And I do like country music every now and again." I hopped down with his assistance. "It's just rap is . . ."—I grinned up at him, finding the exact right word—"fun."

He threw his head back and laughed, but we didn't have a chance to continue talking, because we were immediately blitzed by mobs of gossip-starved eyes.

Ugh. Back to reality.

Again, if Pete noticed the undue amount of attention we were receiving, you couldn't tell. He slid his arm around my shoulder as casually as he slipped on his jacket, and we tromped across the parking lot together like we'd been going steady for ages.

I tried not to feel stiff and self-conscious, but it was kinda hard when the world's sexiest guy had his arm around you. As soon as we entered the classroom, the loud buzzing came to an abrupt stop. I pretended not to see the bitter twist Miguel's mouth, twisting around instead to face Pete so we could resume our conversation. But faster than you can say *hola,* we were accosted by Ashley-Leigh. *Seriously?* We hadn't gotten two words out.

"Katie! I'm so glad you're back!" she proclaimed with a silly side-hug, not taking her greedy eyes off Pete. "I haven't had a chance to meet your new . . . *acquaintance* yet. Looks like you've been tryin' to keep him all to yourself," she pouted, eyes still glued to his. "Not that I blame you." She stuck metallic purple nails out to Pete with a practiced smile. "Hi. I'm Ashley-Leigh Montgomery. Me and Katie have been, like, the best of friends since we were knee-high to a grasshopper."

Laying on the fake southern charm pretty thick, I thought.

Pete looked at her with a charming, if distant smile. "Well any friend of Kate's is a friend of mine." He shook her hand. "It's really nice to meet you, Ashley. I'm—"

"Oh. I already know who *you* are, Pete Davenport," she purred in a tone I found to be more revolting than alluring.

I peeked at Pete to gage his reaction, saw his mouth twitch, smiled to myself.

"Well, that makes it easier on me I guess," he said, removing his hand from her grip.

She giggled liked that was the punchline to a very funny joke, that only the two of them got. The bell decided to ring, bringing with it an Ashley-Leigh pouty frown. "Uh! I guess I'll catch up with *you* later . . ." Her tone, coupled with her pointy nail, made it seem like a threat.

"Sure. Nice to meet you again, Ashley," Pete replied.

"Actually . . ."—she tilted back around—"it's Ashley-Leigh . . . kind of a southern thing." Cue signature wink. After which, she flounced off to her seat sure in the knowledge that she'd left him wanting for more.

Swallowing a smile, I faced the front. I swear the girl had no shame. Hadn't she ever heard of playing hard to get?

"Ash*ley*-Leigh?" He chuckled into my ear. "Isn't that a bit redundant?" I turned around to snigger with him, and he said, "Is she for real?"

"You can't make this stuff up," I whispered before turning back around.

Midway through class, I was mentally revising my list of questions for Pete and replaying back the afternoon's highlights in my mind. I was having trouble concentrating on today's Spanish lesson, because I was hyper-aware of Pete occupying the space behind me. Every little move he made registered in my system on some basic level akin to breathing. Each pencil scratch he made on his notebook, every time he brushed back his hair, or shifted in his seat, sent vibrations of awareness through me.

What I could barely register was anything *outside* of Pete's personal space. Mr. Sanchez had to ask me twice to conjugate the same verb. All the stares I was receiving, both the curious and envious, normally would've had me blushing red; today they barely made a blip on my radar. At one point Pete leaned forward to whisper in my ear, and shivers of pleasure ran down my spine. Being in the endorphin-releasing presence of the world's most attractive person seem to blur the lines between fantasy and reality. And I was so enthralled with living the dream that it was almost easy to ignore the little annoying doubts piling up, waiting to be disposed of in that very aptly F-named it-bucket. *Almost.*

I sighed and made myself lean as far away from him as possible so I could concentrate. Then mentally replayed the footage of this afternoon to focus on what was still bothering me, and all the unanswered questions I had. (Because I certainly wasn't increasing the fluency of my Spanish today.) Flipping the page in my notebook, I began composing my thoughts.

1.) *The brochure only mentioned there was a mentoring program but didn't go into any detail or reveal the kinds of tests that would be administered.*

2.) *The "coincidence" of them seeing me walking on the drag.*

3.) *Ranger's unexplained hostility towards me.*

4.) *Why did they come into the diner that afternoon?*

5.) *"The Mission?"*

I was pencil-tapping my notebook, thinking about how I could bring up "the mission" without revealing that I'd overheard his conversation, when the girl sitting across from me gave me an annoyed look. "Sorry," I mouthed, moving the tapping to the side of my leg. There was something that was slowly gnawing at me, and it was getting more pronounced whenever I replayed the incident in my head. It was right after Pete asked what I like to do for fun, and I'd been so angry and embarrassed that I could hardly think straight. The tempo of my tapping increased when I hit upon the thing that set off a warning bell. Before I could continue with my a-ha! moment, Pete leaned forward and removed the pencil from my hand.

"Kate?"

My industrious mind suddenly blanked out when I saw him looking at me *that* way. The possibility I was about to drool all over my desk prompted me to promptly swallow. "Yeah?"

"I gotta know what that pencil did to piss you off," he whispered out one side of his mouth. "That way . . . I can avoid doing the same thing."

Oh man! He was so sexy when he did that. I couldn't even think so I just blurted out the thing that had been niggling me: "How didja know my middle name is Lee?"

Even though Pete was as polished as a pristine diamond, I saw a flash of anger dart in and out of his eyes. Any normal person would've missed it, but I was really good at reading people and was especially tuned in to him. I blinked, and his face was already rearranged back into its mask of serenity.

A glance at Mr. Sanchez and Pete whispered, "That's at the top of your list? A better question is, how am I going to convince your father to let me take you out?" He ended with the type of smile that normally would've knocked me out.

But something had me on my guard again. That, and years of obedience training, had me turning back around. A few moments later, I heard the familiar click of a ballpoint pen, and after a few quick strokes, I felt a little tap on my shoulder. Pete was handing me a note. *How very high school of him* I instantly thought, but accepted the note with no small amount of curiosity.

Andrew. I told you I was pumping him for the 411 on you . . . I'm surprised you had to ask. Hey, wanna hang out after school? ☺

My stomach twisted. *A lie.* I felt it in my gut, and then it spread all over my body, making me feel ill as if I'd been poisoned. And not just a lie—the tone of the note was all wrong. It was dismissive and slightly insulting to my intelligence. And on top of that, he tried to cajole me out of my fact-finding mission by wooing me again—using himself as bait, a maneuver I was sure worked well for him in the past.

Beauty is its own kind of power. I saw that plainly with Mama. His beauty combined with his charisma created a lethal dose of man-nip for females. Plus, there was something more between us—some kind of magnetic chemistry (at least on my part). I'd never felt so drawn to someone before, and it was as scary as it was thrilling.

So I'd been falling for it all day. But I was *onto* him now. Mama was right about my instinct—it always seemed to kick in when something was *off*. And now it was telling me that Pete was scamming me, so I'd get on board the IEA train. . . . *Like taking candy from a baby.* I literally felt sick to my stomach that the dynamic person I'd gotten to know was actually an 'effing fraud. *Maybe he really is an actor? What kind of school bred such monsters?* I thought of his cohort Ranger—his name practically spelled out danger!

A firm hand grasped my shoulder. I jumped.

Pete leaned forward. "Hey," he whispered. "Everything okay?"

His warm breath sent shivers down my spine again . . . shivers of fear. I hadn't gotten around to answering him when the bell rang, and didn't get a chance to utter a word because, quick-as-one-of-her-winks, Ashley-Leigh came bounding over. She took one look at my face and turned to Pete, batting his arm playfully. I marveled that it took her this long to find an excuse to do that.

"Pete! What did you do to upset *poor* Katie?" she scolded.

"I have no idea." His eyes searched mine for answers.

"Well, you have to be careful with her little feelers—she's like a baby."

"She's a babe all right."

Pete's remark visibly rankled Ashley-Leigh, but she quickly recovered, rambling on as Pete collected his things. He zipped up and shrugged his backpack on then turned his back on her, waiting for me to do the same. A look of desperation clung to her face.

"I don't know if Katie has mentioned it," Ashley-Leigh gave me a pitiful look, taking hold of my arm with her cold hand, "but her mama passed away a couple of years ago, and she's been all torn up ever since . . . so you gotta be real careful what you say."

That got his attention. We simultaneously stiffened at her callous remark. I was too fascinated by the way color began creeping along the ridge of Pete's cheekbones to bother replying. I sorta felt a little afraid for my oblivious frenemy still uselessly gabbing away. I needn't have worried though, because he quickly composed himself. Turning a stony face to her he said, "Excuse us, Ashley, we're going to be late for class." Then, removing my arm from her hand, he slung my backpack over his shoulder and steered me out of class.

"Uh!—it's Ashley-*Leigh*!" she called, but we'd walled up on her, neither one turning around.

A bright, cloudless sky greeted us outside the door, and as we tromped across campus, I saw Miguel and some football buddies shoot us dark looks. I heaved a sigh. It appeared I could make no one happy today—not even myself.

Pete finally broke the silence: "With friends like those . . ."

". . . who needs enemies?" I finished for him, but couldn't think of anything else that needed to be said. We continued through the doors of the main building, up the steps to the second floor, and down the long, lockered hallway with a stretched-out silence trailing us. It seemed he already knew the route to my Chemistry class without being told. Just filed that under more proof Cadet Davenport had been spying on me.

Black-topped lab tables set with white microscopes came into view, which meant we'd reached our final destination with only a sentence split between the two of us. Pete handed over my backpack but didn't immediately take off. He leaned a hand on the wall behind my ear, an enigmatic look upon his face. It seemed as though he were going to say or *do* something, but nothing happened except for some jaw-rubbing.

He sighed deeply. "Wait for me after school?"

I also leaked a sigh. "I don't think so."

The look on his face was the kind that matched my tone. "I hope you'll change your mind," he said then strode back down the hallway with me, the QB1, and everyone else, staring at his tight end.

I mulled over his immediate reaction to Ashley-Leigh's digs. Even an Oscar-winning actor couldn't be expected to instantly put that angry burn on his face. A warm feeling engulfed me when I thought of the ways he had come to my aid since we'd met. *Ugh!* I was so completely confused. Ignoring a Safety Precaution sign posted on the door, I headed to class feeling a glimmer of hope that for once my intuition would be wrong.

Chemistry was a blur of meaningless letters and numbers. I was on automation, still trying to sort everything out. Miguel was loudly ignoring me today. I thought it best to just let it go for now. Eventually, he'd come around. Truthfully, he was doing me a favor, because I was too preoccupied to deal with him on top of everything else right now. The bell rang and I headed to gym, alone, still undecided about waiting for Pete after school.

Several girls attacked me the moment I stepped foot in the dressing room, wondering how I knew the "hot, new guy." I was less than vague in my response, and was immensely grateful when Coach Sams blew the whistle for us to line up. We filed through the gym, past the volleyball players, and hit the exit doors and sunshine. The boys were already suited up and outside kicking the ball around. But they weren't the only ones suited up and ready to go . . .

The cheerleaders decided to leave the comforts of their air-conditioned gym for the great outdoors today. They had spread out close to the boys' P.E. *soccer* team and not the varsity *football* team like they usually did when they came outside for practice. Looked like interest in our pathetic gym class was picking up.

That wouldn't sit too well with the jocks. Sure enough, some of the football players nudged each other and nodded at Pete. All eyes focused on the athletic god dribbling the ball across the soccer field with practiced ease and hammering the poor goalie, who gave a half-hearted attempt to stop the bomb that blasted his way. It looked like he was out there playing with peewee leaguers. An immediate great cheer sprang from the ogling cheerleaders. I shook my head then gave the soccer ball a good, swift kick. It flew right past the stringy junior playing goalie to be the first goal of the day.

Coach Sams blew the whistle. "Great job, Connelly!" She came trotting over with her practical, close-cropped hair and interest in me. I braced myself for what was coming. "Hey, Katie. How ya doin' these days?"

"Fine, thanks."

She cleared her throat. "I was wondering . . . are you still babysittin' those brothers of yours after school?"

"Yes ma'am."

She deflated a little. "That's too bad. I would've liked to have seen you play ball this year—you got a lot of potential for sports."

My face warmed. "Thank you."

She regarded me for a thoughtful moment. "Okay . . . get back out there."

Trotting back out to the scraggly field, I saw a bunch of purple helmets—that included Miguel—huddle up and talk amongst one another. They weren't really doing anything out of the ordinary, but I still got the feeling they were up to no good.

A spasm of fear for Pete's safety clenched my stomach. I didn't think they would jump him or anything. Deep down Miguel was a good guy; I didn't think he'd be involved in anything so ugly. Still. I had a sick feeling about it. Pete had done me the courtesy of saving me from a couple of close encounters, so the least I could do was warn him that some football players might be scheming against him.

The signal for the end of school sounded, and I filed back in with the athletically-challenged class, glad to be in the cool air-conditioning for a few moments before heading back outside. I quickly got dressed and headed to the parking lot to wait for Pete by his very flashy vehicle.

After a few minutes of standing around in my blue bell skirt, feeling alternately stupid and worried, I finally saw him emerge from the gym doors. A couple of guys immediately accosted him, and I braced myself for a showdown. But they seemed to have nothing more on their minds than sports talk. I watched them pantomiming athletic moves while admiring the long, lean lines of Pete's body from a distance.

He began striding toward his truck, still carrying on with the two guys when he looked up. Surprise shifted his face when he saw me standing there. He briefly mouthed an excuse to his new fans before trotting off, a grin already forming. As I watched him head my way, it felt like I'd just swallowed a glassful of butterflies. His hair was still wet, and he paused to shake back some glistening strands that had flopped forward during the trek over. (That little move might've been the sexiest thing I'd ever seen.) He sidled up next to me and removed his ever-present aviators to peer down at me with sparkling eyes.

I swear my mouth started watering like I was hungry for an after-school snack or something. Realizing I probably looked simple-minded, I raised my hand in a goofy wave. "Hey."

"Hey yourself!" He raked his hair back again, waiting with a smile playing on his lips. I was rendered mute by his mere presence for a few more seconds—he was quite a bit more dazzling than the sun in all his freshly-showered male glory. "This is a surprise," he tried again, leaning one arm on the Hummer, thereby blocking the sun from my eyes.

I took a moment to modulate my voice. "Yeah. I, uh, just wanted to warn–"

"Listen, Kate," he cut in, "you've got to start trusting me." While he was talking, a gang of football players over his shoulder caught my attention. "I would never do anything . . ."

And then I saw it happen, as if in slow motion: Ron Tillman—hand loaded, with malice shooting from his squinty eyes—danced back three steps and hurled a pig-skin bomb directly at Pete's exposed back.

"Pete! Behind—" I yelled, not getting the words out before he whipped around and caught it—a split second before it flattened his face.

"Whoa!" dropped loudly from someone's mouth.

"That was a lucky catch . . . " a jersey began then trailed off.

Because Pete licked the tips of his fingers, gripped the football, and let it fire off like a professional in the NFL. Everyone stood gaping as it spiraled straight for Ron, who was too busy accepting a palm-slap from a running buddy to see the bullet bound for him. It hit the bulls-eye—the fleshy part of his gut—with a force that brought him to his knees. This all happened in about two-point-two seconds flat, from the time Ron hurled the ball at Pete and Pete caught and hurled it right back.

". . . golden boy," the one who began his taunt finished. Then: "Dude! Did you see that?" The jeering jersey had changed his tune in the same two-point-two seconds.

"Aw, man! You got played, son!" got thrown down at Ron, whose face resembled a puffer fish. Several of the jocks who mocked just a second ago were now marveling at Pete's athletic prowess. People were so easily won over by him . . . I had to continue trying hard *not* to be one of them.

When Pete turned back to me, his eyes were all lit up with humor. "You were saying something about warning me?"

A baller in wife-beater and baggy shorts aimed a low whistle at Pete. "Nice arm, Davenport!"

"Thanks, man." Pete nodded his acknowledgment, eyes never leaving mine.

"That's why I came—to tell you I saw some football players schemin' together, and I was sure it was about you."

"Well thanks for the heads-up." He grinned down at me as if a handful of beefed-up jocks weren't out to get him. "I'm touched you cared enough to come warn me."

"Yeah, well, I can see it was unnecessary . . . you can clearly take care of yourself." I moved to move past him, when he grabbed my arm.

"Does this mean I'm no longer public enemy number one?"

"No." I dislodged my arm from his grip. "You still are." Dejection weighed my footsteps as I walked away. I'd just cracked open my car door when he called out to me. I yelled over my shoulder, "Enjoy your fifteen minutes of fame!" Then got in my car and drove off, leaving him alone to fend off the many admirers coming his way.

Clovis' pathetic excuse for a museum, The Learning Center, was near empty at 4:30, so I parked next to the handicapped space in front of the revolving doors. The reflection staring back from the plate glass window haunted me. Dispirited would be the word to describe me. He was winning. I was losing . . . and falling further behind every day. I had a ton of work waiting for me when I got home. And here I was, baking on black asphalt, while my brother moseyed around in the air conditioning, looking at plastic replicas of ten-ton creatures that had been dead for millions of years. I growled, piqued for yet another reason at this stupid *elite* academy for intervening in our life.

"Let's go in and wook at the animals." For the fifth time from the backseat.

"I'm sorry, hon," I said, erasing the last answer on my Calc homework, sure I'd computed wrong. "We gotta get goin' as soon as Drewy comes out."

"Pwetty pwease, Kadee with a chewry on top?" Mikey tried his cute impersonation, but I didn't even look.

"Not today, Mike."

"Pweeeeeeeeeease!"

"Mikey! Stop it!" This came out more harshly than I intended. A glance in the rearview mirror revealed unpretending pouty lips and pooling tears. I dropped my pencil and turned around to engage with my little brother, who sorely needed my attention. "I'm sorry, honey. I wish we could but we don't have enough time. We'll come another day."

"That's what you ahways say."

"Well, I mean it this time . . . 'sides, you get to go home and see animals *every* day."

"Not cows and pigs," he said disdainfully, "*weal* animals!"

I started a laugh that stopped the instant Pete appeared from the revolving doors with Andrew trailing behind him. Pete's easy smile also faltered a bit when he saw me, though he replaced it with an affable enough expression. He slid something over to Andrew that had him responding with a laugh *before* he waved back at us in the car.

Well those two are obviously still in the throes of a bromance.

Mikey began thrashing around in the back, clambering for his brother. I heaved a sigh, a renewed desperation to keep our family together blooming in me.

"We got the whole place practically to ourselves today!" Andrew announced, getting in carefully with a box of goodies in his hands. It looked like it was chock-full of science books, educational games, and a high-tech microscope Andrew always wanted but we could never afford. This rankled me almost as much as their budding bromance did.

"No fayer!" Mikey wailed out his injustice. "How come Drewy gets to have fun and not me?"

"Hey, buddy." Pete acknowledged him with a fist-bump, then handed over a plastic dinosaur concealed behind his back.

"Triceratops! Thanks, Pete! . . . When's it my turn for mentorin'?"

"Mikey!" I blanched at the very thought.

Pete chuckled a little. "Wanna come in and help feed the turtles?"

"They also have a Pteranodon in there!" Andrew piled on.

"Weawlly?" Mikey immediately unclicked his seatbelt, so I had to get out and head him off.

"I already told you—we gotta go." After re-buckling a mutinous Mikey, I spared the time to glare at Pete. "Thanks," I said acidly, slamming my door and starting the engine.

Mikey started crying, and Pete's face started melting. "How about you come along next time, buddy? . . . If it's alright with your sister."

Immediately cheered somewhat, Mikey scrubbed the sniffles away with the back of his hand. "Can I, Kadee?"

All eyes on me. I shook my head at his audacity. Wasn't taking *one* of my brothers away from me enough? I shot him another filthy look. "Well, if Pete would've bothered to ask, I would've told him that's probably not going to work because we have to get home to feed our own animals."

Pete gave me a wounded look. "I'm sorry, Kate. I was just trying to be nice."

I nodded through a sigh before quickly backing out. A tap on the window had me tapping brakes. Thought about not stopping this time, but social graces and plain ole curiosity insisted I see what he wanted. I shoved the gear in park and rolled down my window, but he went around to Andrew's side.

"Hey man, one more thing . . ."

"What is it Pete?" Eagerness dripped from Andrew's voice.

"In just this one instance, you can break the bro-code, and I won't hold it against you." Pete shifted his eyes to mine.

"But Pete!" Andrew said, outraged. "I thought you said us guys gotta stick together!"

"I know I did, but this one time we can allow Kate to be the exception to the rule." He looked meaningfully at Andrew.

"Okay, Pete," he agreed, more reluctantly than he should.

I was really miffed that my little brother could switch alliances so quickly but told myself not to hold it against him because he was just starving for a good male role model. And you definitely couldn't ask for a better male model than Pete Davenport.

"Okay then. Tomorrow . . . same time, same place," Pete directed at me. I did the nod thing again.

"Right. Same time, same place!" Andrew answered for me.

"See ya later alligator," Pete called, pointing at him as I backed out.

"After while crocodile!" Andrew called back gleefully.

Mikey waved his new dinosaur out the window. "Bye Pete!" he yelled, not wanting to feel left out.

I knew the feeling.

17

FACTS AND PROBABILITIES

Finishing up with chores about the same time the sun sank behind the shed meant our shadows would beat us to the house and hodge-podge was on the menu tonight. I was wiped out and didn't have enough time (or ingredients) to cook anyway. And I needed to powwow with my traitor brother before bed and try to get some answers.

Daddy was MIA again. It was both a blessing and a curse to have him away (the blessing being, of course, the absence of his presence). Unfortunately, we had family business that needed to be taken care of. I wanted to discuss him picking up Andrew in the afternoons. That way I could avoid getting sucked into Pete's magnetic force field and get a jumpstart on my chores. Also, the water tank out in the pasture was way low, and I couldn't get the water to turn on more than a trickle. I left it on for a few minutes, but didn't really have time to wait for it to fill up because it was already heading past supper.

I just hoped it was enough water to get by for now. The herd always headed in for the evening to drink, and I was worried about some of the smaller calves reaching the water. *Ugh*! *Where is Daddy anyway?* Going out there at night definitely fell into man-duty. I hollered for Andrew to bring me the dirty clothes, so I could get a wash in while I prepared dinner.

"Can't," he hollered back. "I'm workin' on my homework."

I looked over to where he had some of the new books Pete had given him spread out on the floor. *Arg!* "Thanks a *lot*, Andrew."

"What? I *have* to do my homework. Daddy even said it's the *priority* around here."

"Oh, he did, did he?" My blood began to boil.

"I'll do it, Kadee," Mikey volunteered, running off before I could stop him—his help usually entailed more work for me.

I sighed as I spread peanut butter onto celery stalks and poured milk. Snorted to myself. *Who needs thirty-minute meals when you can get the job done in five?* I mentally went down the food groups to fill in the holes. Snapped my fingers—whole grains. Dropping some bread in the toaster, I called the boys in to eat.

"Not done yet." Andrew, not even looking up.

"Well then, you can just multi-task by readin' and eatin' at the same time." I snatched the book out from under his nose and slammed it onto the table.

"Boy! You're in a bad mood today," he huffed, but got up and came in.

I blew some air. "Sorry. It's just been a long couple of days. Here," I finished buttering the toast and set the plates on the table, "sit down and eat. I'd better go rustle up Mikey."

"Where's supper?"

"On the table."

"That's not supper . . . that's a snack," he corrected, picking up a bendy celery stalk doubtfully.

Silent prayer. "Andrew Richmond Connelly, you can either eat what's on the table, or you can pour yourself some cereal."

"But that's for breakfast!"

"Well, that's what's on the menu tonight." I made a Herculean effort to lower the volume on my voice. "Look Drews, give me a break, huh? . . . I can't do *everything* 'round here!" I vented out before stomping down the hall to the bathroom. I found Mikey pulling heaps of clothes from the hamper.

"Look, Kadee! I almost got them all!"

"You sure did." I forced a smile and poked him in his Play-Doh stomach. "Thanks a lot . . . you sure are a lifesaver!"

Mikey smiled back with a wide, knowing smile. "What flavor?"

"Hmmm . . ." I pretended to smell his neck but instead blew a loud raspberry there. He laughed so hard I could see all the way down to his tonsils. So I did it again, just for the pleasure of hearing him laugh his head off, then set him on his feet and answered, "Cherry, my favorite, of course!"

He pressed a hug into me, and I deep breathed in his sweet innocence. "Yep. Definitely cherry-flavored."

He beamed—cherry was his favorite.

"Go on out to the kitchen," I said. "I'll finish grabbing the laundry . . . looks like the hard part's already been done for me!" As he ran out the door, I patted him on his cushy-tushy. Then puffed out my cheeks and began sorting through the mess of clothes strung across the floor, pulling out the whites and stuffing the rest back in the hamper. Grabbing the basket, I trudged past the table heading to Daddy's bathroom and saw that Andrew was still engrossed in his book, but at least he was chewing on the end of his celery stalk without complaining.

Mikey grinned up at me from a piece of buttered toast. "Mmmmm! This is my favwit supper ever, Kadee! You are the best cooker in the world!"

"Why thank you," I said with a little bow. "And you are the best helper in the world. I'm already almost done. One more stop and then I'm gonna come back and swipe the rest of that toast!"

"Nuh-uh!" He laughed and pulled the plate of toast to him.

My lips were still curled into a smile when I wandered into Daddy's room, where my mood instantly dimmed with the lighting. The curtains were drawn, but you could still see Daddy's prized possession hanging—silent and malevolent—on the wall. How he could sleep (and peacefully I might add) with a gun hanging over his head was beyond me.

Hastily, I moved it to his bathroom and started loading Daddy's yellow-pitted T-shirts and tighty-whities into the basket, trying not to dwell on what created those stains. An immediate hand washing was in order, so I went to the sink. *Dang it!* Of course there was no soap in the dispenser.

I huffed out some aggravation before kneeling down to rifle through the various toiletries, toothpaste boxes, and extra toilet paper occupying the space. *Women's work really was never done*, I thought right as my hand touched on something cold and hard. *What the?* Curious, I pulled out the unexpected slick container and raised it to the light. Almost dropped it when I realized what it was—alcohol, and not the rubbing kind. My eyes widened. I scanned the label being unfamiliar with adult beverages. Scotch. And from the look of the bottle, *good* scotch. I pulled out the cork to investigate further. It let out a satisfying, squeaky pop, emitting pleasant fumes. I sniffed the amber liquid inside. *Mmmm.* It actually smelled really good—kind of smoky and woodsy and expensive all at the same time. Curiosity satisfied I placed the cork and bottle back, deciding *not* to refill the soap dispenser after all.

What's Daddy doing with scotch under the bathroom sink? To my knowledge, he didn't even drink alcohol. And if he was a closet drinker . . . for how long? What else did I not know about my father? *Where* he was at the moment, for one thing.

"Almost done with your toast, Kadee!" Mikey teased from the dining room.

"Comin', buddy."

Answers. That's what I needed. I tromped back to the compact closet off the side of the kitchen to get the load of wash started. I still had to hang it out to dry, which meant I would be doing it in the dark after I got the boys to bed. Another question was just added to the heap I'd already amassed so far: *How come a man so cheap he insisted on saving money by (me) hanging our clothes on the line, would then turn around and buy a gentleman's bottle of scotch?*

He wouldn't. So that meant someone gave it to him. *A gift?* That feeling crawled up my spine. *A bribe.* A few more pieces of the puzzle clicked together—it was that dang academy again. They were bribing Daddy and using Pete to "woo" me. What other tricks did they have up their sleeve? I slammed down the lid and punched start before going to see if I could pry some answers from my star-struck brother.

While slicing up some dodgy-looking bananas and dividing the few remaining whole vanilla wafers between the two boys, I tried to think of a good way to broach the subject without Andrew getting his back up. But like everything else lately—I was having no luck.

Nose still glued to his book, Andrew picked up a stale cookie. "No pudding?"

"Not unless you wanna pour tap water on your cereal for breakfast."

Mike giggled. "Ew, gross!"

"You need to go to the store," Andrew declared, crunching on a bite.

"I need to do a lotta things," I said. "Speakin' of which, I was thinkin', Drews"—I pushed down his book—"of maybe havin' Daddy pick you up from tutorin', so I could have more time to manage things better around here." He immediately looked like his cookie tasted bad. ". . . If Daddy does the honor, then I could grocery shop *and* get a jump start on our chores."

"Uh-uh! No way, Jose!" Andrew dropped his cookie on the plate forgotten. "He'll ruin everything, like he always does, and totally embarrass me in front of Pete!" He pleaded with me, "Please, Katie-Kat. Can't you still do it?"

I sighed. "Fine. I guess I could pack a cooler for the groceries." I had a feeling if I ruined this for Andrew, he'd never forgive me.

"Or . . ." Andrew's face lit up, "you could let Pete drive me home."

"No way, Jose!" I said, gathering dishes.

"Come on! Why not? He offered."

"Because it's way too far out of his way."

"He said he really wanted to." Andrew helped me by handing his plate over.

"He was just being polite, Drews." I added it to my stack and tightrope-walked to the sink, turning the faucet on high.

"Well, that's more than I can say for you!" Andrew followed me in. "Come on, Katie! He offered us *all* a ride in his Hummer. He's bein' so nice, and you're not at all!" Emotion colored his face.

I let the remarks about me being rude slide. How could I argue? "Maybe some other time." I said.

"That's what you *always* say! . . .You *never* let us have any fun!"

My own face flushed the color of mad. "Oh, I'm sorry, Andrew. That's too bad for you. I guess I should just spend all my spare free time makin' sure you have some"—I dropped the plate I was scraping to finger quote—"'fun' instead of say . . . spendin' it tryin' to make some extra money to put food on our table and clothes on your back!"

We were all on the verge of tears, and since we never fought, it didn't feel good at all, sorta like your favorite sweatshirt got shrunk in the wash and no longer fit right.

"You know what?" Andrew's voice elevated so fast it cracked. "I'm *not* gonna act less smart than I am anymore. And you know what else? . . . I *want* to go to that school!" He followed that bold statement up by kicking his chair over, and proving himself already to be at that boy age where anger was the only acceptable emotion to show.

"Oh, yes you are!" I thundered, grabbing him by his shoulders. I wanted to give him a good shake. "I'm your sister, and you promised me!"

"Oh, no I'm not!" He ripped away from my grip. "And just cause you're my sister, doesn't mean you can make me . . .'Sides, you promised we could take a ride in Pete's truck, so now we're even-Steven!"

"Andrew," I breathed, kneeling down. He wouldn't look me in the eye; I suspected there was some moisture there. "You don't know what you're sayin' about that school. You *don't* wanna go there."

"You don't know what *you're* sayin'—I do! Pete told me all about it, and it sounds awesome. Way more awesome than just workin' all the time and goin' to church!"

"Drews," I said, a quiet reprimand. "You don't mean that. Besides, it's too far away—we would miss you too much."

"Pete said they have designated visiting days—I might could even come back for Christmas."

The restrictive scheduling of family time caused my chest to tighten. I couldn't believe Andrew was okay with this. Apparently neither could Mikey, because he looked up from licking peanut butter from a celery stalk. "You don't weally wanna go to that school away from me and Kadee, do you Drewy?" Tears glistened, turning his eyes into twin ponds.

Andrew's silence was louder than words. That sinking-sand feeling in my gut began weighing me down, so I sank to the floor, pulling Andrew down with me. "Drews, please—I'm sorry about the no fun. I'm gonna work on that." He shot me a scathing look. "I will," I assured him. "You're right . . . I did say you could ride in Pete's Hummer, and I'll let y'all tomorrow." My other arm nabbed Mikey, corralling him into the fold. "I promise. Just please promise me that you will continue *not* gettin' everything right on the tests. That's real important . . . and don't act like everything's so easy for you either." I pleaded with a set face. "*Please* Drewy . . . for me. Okay?" I forced a hug out of him. "You have to trust me—I only have *your* best interests at heart."

Andrew pulled away. "So does Pete! He goes to that school, and he's awesome and cool and, and just like me. You just don't like him for some reason."

"That's not true."

"Is too! I can tell."

I sighed. "Look, it's complicated okay. I do like Pete . . . maybe a little bit too much," I admitted. "I just don't want us to get caught up in all the excitement surrounding Pete, so that it clouds our judgment about the school. That academy is *not* the right place for you, Drews. And Pete is *not* the same as the school. And don't forget he'll be graduatin' this year, so you probably won't even see him again."

I immediately saw this was the wrong thing to say. The tears that Andrew had been withholding began spilling over.

"That's not true!" He shoved the felled chair, so that it skidded over and thunked into the table leg. I mentally rearranged furniture, rotating sides to see if I could prevent Daddy from seeing the latest dent.

"See!" he raged. "You don't know anything about it! Pete said if I was accepted, he'd teach me how to dive off the high-dive. How could he do that if he's not plannin' on bein' there?"

A flash of anger at Pete darted through me for making empty promises to a young boy starving for adventure and male-bonding. Mikey stared at us wide-eyed, fat tears sliding over his roly-poly cheeks. He was way too young for this. Taking his hand and plate of cookies, I steered him toward the couch.

"Mikey, go eat your dessert in the livin' room."

"But why?"

"Because I said so," I said, stealing my father's line. "And you can also turn on the TV."

"But Daddy says no eatin' in the livin' room and no TV when he's not home to monitor us."

"Well Daddy's not here, is he?"

Mikey looked from me to Andrew and huffed out some outrage. "Fine!" He snatched his cookies and tromped away. About midway to where the juice stain ringed the couch like a socked-eye, he whirled back around. "But no more fightin'!" he yelled so hard veins popped out on his face, and wafers scattered from his plate like they were scared.

All the anger drained from my body like someone had pulled a plug. Andrew also seemed to soften, yielding against me into a hug.

"I'm really sorry, Drews," I said.

"Me too, Katie . . . I just really like Pete and wish you didn't hate him so much."

I took a deep breath, debating how much to divulge to an eight-year-old. "I don't hate Pete. As a matter of fact, I probably like him as much as you."

Andrew pulled a face. "You don't act like it. You're totally mean to him for no reason at all. Like you said—he's *not* the same as the school. And he really, really likes you. I can tell."

A wave of warmth washed over me. It seemed like my mind was constantly fighting with my body these days. I was only human—any girl would feel like they were lying on a beach under sunny skies if they found out a guy like Pete Davenport liked them.

"I told you . . . it's complicated."

He folded his arms, his head cocking to the side. "Complicated how?" When I didn't immediately respond he said, "And anyway, I *like* complicated things."

I saw my opening. "Maybe you can help me figure something out."

"Like what?"

"Like how Pete knows so much about me," I probed and watched as Andrew's eyes hit floor. "You wouldn't know anything about that, would you?"

Andrew looked a little sheepish. "Okay, fine—Pete told me he was gonna take you on a picnic, so he asked me what kinds of food you like."

A small sliver of light infiltrated my dark mood. "Really?"

"Yeah . . . so I told him. That's okay, right?"

"Sure. That's fine. Just don't let on that you're throwin' some of the test results."

"So you *do* like Pete?" His deflection didn't go unnoticed.

"I said I did." I rose to my feet now, doing my own deflection with some cleaning detail.

"Do you like him like a friend, or . . . like a *boyfriend*?" Andrew peeked up at me through his lashes, turning pink around the ears.

"Just a friend for now," I hedged. " We've only just met, remember?"

"But *could* you see yourself likin' him as a boyfriend?" he persisted.

I felt my own ears burn. "Well, aren't you the little fact finder."

"I like to deal with facts and probabilities," he informed me, sounding more like a statistician than a third-grader.

"Oh yeah?"

"Yeah. Since it's now a fact that you like him—and he likes you—then the probability that he'll be around more often increases exponentially!"

I huffed out a chuckle. "Wow! I gotta say it, Drews: you're quite the whiz kid."

He beamed like the star he was. "Now will you think about lettin' me go to The Academy?"

"I don't know . . . we gotta find out a *lot* more about the school besides the fact that Cadet Davenport goes there."

He threw his hands up. "What else is there to know?"

I sighed, picked up the toppled-over chair, sat down. "Listen," I said taking his hand as if needing contact to convey the force of my convictions.

"I know better than anybody how easy it is to get caught up in Pete's easy charm. However, I also met another . . ."—I grimaced at the memory—"IEA cadet."

"You did? When?"

"That's not important right now. It's already past bedtime, so really listen." My eyes bored into his. "The best thing I can say about Pete's friend is he's *not* as nice as Pete."

"What's that got to do with anything?" He broke from my grasp again. "There's good guys and bad guys everywhere—probably even church."

"You know how I get strong feelin's about things?" Andrew's open face was beginning to close, so I explained, "Mama called it my sixth sense, remember?"

"You mean like how sharks have an extra sense that allows them to feel electricity emitted from other animals from far away?"

"Yes, exactly like that," I agreed. "Only I sense certain things about people—whether they're tellin' the truth for example, or if they have good or bad intentions. And I've been gettin' a bad feelin' about this academy from the very beginnin'."

I could almost see the levers and pulleys of his mind working together to process this new information. "But I thought you only got feelings about *people*, not *places*," he said, finding the hole in my argument.

"Well, it's sometimes a feelin' about things. Like it can be as simple as a test question. I'm not as smart as you, Drews, but I'm a *really* good test taker. And I think it has to do with my ability. Somehow . . . I can just *intuit* the right answer, even if I can't figure it out."

"So you're like cheating."

I exhaled the last of my patience. "Andrew, I think you're missin' the point here. I have a sort of . . . ability that sometimes gives me very powerful feelin's. And I'm gettin' a powerful one that's tellin' me Pete's academy is bad."

"That's it," he scoffed. "A strong feeling? That's not dealin' with facts and probabilities—that's pure conjecture."

"I know it sounds like a lot of hocus-pocus, but sometimes there are things that even science can't explain." My brainiac brother still looked unconvinced, so I explained using evidence I knew he needed. "Remember when Mama first got sick?" Andrew allowed a cursory nod. "Well, I *knew*. *Right* away."

"Knew what?"

I was a dark quiet, remembering. "That . . . she wasn't gonna get better."

"She had *cancer*, Katie . . . It's kinda hard to get better from *cancer* when you don't even go to the hospital!" Andrew's words flew from his mouth like trapped crows from a cage.

I gripped his hands tightly, locking eyes again. "*Right* away, Andrew. I knew the *very* second she told us she was sick that she was gonna die. Remember how I ran out of the house cryin'?"

"Yeah. Mama sent me to go find you."

"Do you remember what you said to me when you found me? You were only about five, so you might not remember. You said *I* was the one that looked sick. You weren't worried, because Mama didn't even look sick at all. Then you noticed that I *smelled* sick, too. That's because the feelin' was so strong, it literally made me sick to my stomach. I ran outside and threw up—and that's the way I feel *now* about that academy."

It was a few beats before he spoke. "Do you get a bad feelin' about Pete?"

I waited another beat then said, "That's where it gets complicated for me."

"How? Either you get a bad feelin' about him or you don't."

I was still mulling over how I could convey my absolute convictions about Pete's academy, and my less-than absolute convictions about Pete, without losing credibility. Andrew could be too smart for his own good. And depending solely upon facts as scientific types tend to, could lead him down a wrong path. *How did I feel?* That Pete was essentially *good*, but involved neck-deep in *bad*.

Andrew filled up the pause. "Cause if you get the feelin' that Pete's bad . . . then I don't believe you anymore," he said levelly. "Cause I *know* he's not."

I nodded noncommittally. Even though Andrew confirmed Pete had been asking questions about me, there was still something off about it. My gut was telling me Pete was lying—I just couldn't put my finger on *what* he was lying about.

"Did Pete ask you what my middle name is?"

"That doesn't mean he's bad just cause he asked a bunch of questions about you! He only wants to get to know you better. He even told me that."

"Just answer the question, Drew."

"No," he admitted, looking like he'd just tattled on the cool kid.

"Well he knew what it was, and I didn't tell him."

"It was probably Daddy," he reasoned. "They had a big meetin' you know. He filled out a lot of paperwork about our family history. It was probably just one of the questions."

I nodded. I'd already thought of that, but the way Pete casually dropped it, suggested more than a cursory glance at paperwork.

"Aren't you satisfied now that you know he *was* askin' questions about you?" Somehow, I felt more pensive than relieved and it must've shown because he said, "Gosh! You act more like he's a secret agent and not just a super-cool guy that likes you."

"Is that fact or conjecture?" I teased.

"That's a fact."

"Okay fine . . . you've convinced me with your facts for now."

"So you've changed your mind about Pete?"

"For the time bein'," I ceded, pulling him into a hug. "But I want you to know I still *know* that academy is not the right place for you."

Andrew looked up, exasperated. "Is that a fact?"

I laughed, feeling a truce in the air. "Yes, that's a fact . . . *Any* school that takes you away from us is not the right one."

18

BACK ON

My alarm went off before the dawn cracked. This so I could head back out to pasture to set the water to trickling into the tank before heading back home to wake the boys. Daddy never made it home last night—at least not before the witching hour. I knew this because that's about the time I gave up on him. So I'd had to reset the alarm to go do the deed for him this morning. After factoring in the amount of stewing I did all night about the cluster of problems that threatened to choke me daily, I'd say I got about a solid, oh . . . four-five hours of shut-eye last night.

I yawned so hard through a red light, my jaw almost popped out of joint. Then I almost caved and pulled over to Clovis' one and only coffee house to help myself to some fancy three-dollar coffee. Unfortunately, I was running short on both time and money so resisted the urge for caffeine and sugar my body so desperately craved. So I rolled up to school bleary-eyed, confused, and weary of fighting off all the demons knocking at my door these days. And late. When I fell out of my car, Pete was leaning against his truck a few spaces away. I almost walked right past him (which was a testament to how tired I really was because the guy literally made me weak in the knees every time I saw him).

"Cutting it kind of close today, aren't you, Connelly?" He fell into step beside me.

I kind of growled out a half-ass acknowledgement.

"Don't tell me . . ."—one side of his cheek lifted—"you're not talking to me today?"

"Not really talkin' 'tall," I mumbled.

"Well good. Since you're not talking today, I'll be glad to do all the talking for you." I spared him a side-glance, and he flashed his teeth at me. "See, every time you talk, it's to accuse me of lying or spying . . . or *something* scandalous. I have to say—I'm a little flattered you see me in such a glamorous light."

I managed to arch an eyebrow at him.

"Here, let me take that," he said, relieving me of my backpack. "Pardon me saying so, Kate, but you look kind of dead on your feet this morning."

"Hmmph." I couldn't even summon enough energy to be offended.

"Didn't get much sleep last night?"

"Wow. Good-lookin', a gentleman, and intuitive . . . you really are quite the triple-threat, Cadet Davenport."

He threw his head back and laughed, and I couldn't help noticing how the morning light haloed his hair. He looked like a photo-shopped ad for shampoo. *Gah*! He really was impossible to resist. I felt myself melting already.

"Now there's the Kate I know and love . . . What happened to mute girl?"

"What can I say?—you know how to push my buttons."

His eyes lit up. "I'll take that as a compliment."

My insides were about the same consistency as room-temperature butter as we loitered on the front steps of the school, staring at each other. The sidewalks were pretty clear because the warning bell had already rung, which meant we'd both be tardy for first-hour. Hard to tell which one of us cared less.

His eyes started doing that smoldering thing again. I closed my eyes and fought the urge to lean against him and just breathe. It would, I thought, be a little like heaven on earth. I must've started to sway, because Pete caught me by my shoulders.

"Hey. You okay?"

"Um . . . yes?"

As if from some mental guidance from me, he dropped our backpacks and reached for me. For once, I didn't hesitate. I wanted to lean on somebody stronger than me. I wanted him to infuse me with strength, to fill in all the holes that riddled me with doubt and zapped my confidence, as crazy as that sounded. I'd never bought into the idea that having a guy makes you complete. But that's exactly how I felt in that moment—complete.

So instead of fighting my body's urges, as was so long the norm for me, I yielded to them. And to him. It was like two pieces of a jigsaw puzzle fitting together exactly right—his arms wrapped around my waist, my head tucked under his chin, his chin on my head. The steady rhythm of his heart was soothing to my frazzled nerves. I breathed in the heady masculine scent emanating from his black T-shirt. Like a smoker taking the first hit of nicotine of the day, I inhaled him all the way down into the farthest recesses of my lungs. I just hoped he wouldn't prove to be toxic.

He seemed the opposite of harmful to me this morning. More like a shield from the harm that threatened me as he embraced me in his capable arms. We stayed fused together like that for a few moments—right in front of the main entrance of my high school, in full view of the principal's office, gawking latecomers, God, and everybody. And it felt good in a way that was dangerous to the health of my heart.

He's here to tear my family apart I reminded myself again and again, even as we swayed together as one. Finally, self-preservation kicked in. I stiffened, and he immediately loosened his hold on me. With a little throat clear, I stepped away.

"Sorry . . . I don't know what that was about," I mumbled, fingering my bottom lip.

Pete's eyes darkened as he watched my nervous habit, but he kept his tone light. "Are you apologizing for needing a hug?"

"Yeah." I laughed, more than a little embarrassed. "I guess I am."

"You have nothing to apologize for—everyone needs a hug every now and again. And it just so happens I'm a hugger by nature. And . . ." he leaned in and whispered, "I needed one, too,"

I gave him a grateful smile. "I, um . . . we better get to class." I turned to go, but he caught my arm. *Gah!* Every little touch sent tingles like little electric shocks of pleasure.

"Meet me for lunch today . . ."

One step up from him, we were almost eye-to-eye. I couldn't tell if it was a command or a question. The hypnotic pull I felt toward him was almost impossible to resist. I wanted to believe in him so bad it was an ache . . . almost as bad as I wanted to lean in and kiss him. Not trusting myself to speak, I simply nodded my head and scurried to the library before I could get sucked in any further.

After re-shelving the books, I was able to shoot off an overdue email to Reese. She informed me my horoscope said I'd meet a mysterious, new love interest this year. Even though I had a feeling this was a made-up fun-fact, I just went with it, telling her about Pete but leaving out the weird way we met and the un-fun fact that he was not to be trusted. I couldn't very well tell her my suspicions about my brother's mentor being here on a secret, sinister mission, or else she would think I was certifiably crazy. . . . *Maybe I am?*

Her insights were sweet and thoughtful, but more than a little bit off the mark since she didn't have all the facts about what was really going on. She quickly suggested the elite boarding school would definitely be a good place for my brother, and immediately found the best perk: when I visited him, I'd be able to see the good-looking (I'd opted out of using the word *hot*) cadet at the same time. She also pointed out that with Andrew away to a great school, I'd have more free time to cut loose and enjoy my high school experience.

I didn't have the heart to tell her that was never going to happen—I had about as much in common with my high school friends as atheists do with Quakers. And after spending time with Pete Davenport, I was completely ruined for regular boys. It was like going back to burgers after dining on the finest steak in the world; you found your palette to be suddenly and irrevocably altered. Once you've had a taste of the best, it *really* was kind of hard to go back to the rest.

I heaved a sigh and trudged along to my next class, too preoccupied with scenarios of how things might play out to notice much of anything else. Miguel sidled up to me. Unsure if he was mad at me or not, I decided to greet him normally. "Hey, Miguel."

"Hey, Katie. Whazzup?" Standard greeting, but his face lacked animation.

We walked into class together and sat down in our regular seats—a good sign. My head immediately sought its desk pillow, but I was sure I would be drooling within five seconds if I didn't instantly yank it back up. So I did, yawning and unzipping my backpack at the same time. All the while, Miguel quietly studied me.

"*What?*" I threw my hands out.

It was hard to tell, but it looked like he might be blushing because his brown skin was slowly turning mahogany. "Katie, what's goin' on with you and that cadet guy?"

I did the head-shake-I-don't-wanna-talk-about-it thing. "Nothin' . . . really."

"Doesn't look like nothin' from where I'm sittin'."

Now it was my turn to blush. Several ears in close proximity suddenly tilted our way, so I just sort of rolled my shoulders, hoping he'd get the hint.

"You wait on the guy one time and now all of a sudden, you're hangin' out and havin' lunch together?" he prompted.

I decided to tell him a truthful mini-version of the story. It'd all come out anyway. Clovis was a lot like living in a fish bowl—sans water. "Actually, that was the first time we met, but I didn't know who he was at the time."

Miguel made a sinusy grunt. "And *who* is he exactly?" His face looked un-cute distorted with anger.

I puffed out some pent-up air, somehow not really wanting to say the words. "He's Andrew's new 'mentor'," I air quoted, not quite keeping the acid out of my voice.

"Mentor?"

"Yeah. 'Mentor,'" I air quoted again for good measure.

Miguel's anger came down a notch directly in proportion to how mine went up when I talked about it. "You mean he's only here to mentor Andrew and then he's leavin' again?" The relief in his voice was unmistakable.

"Yup. Pretty much . . . oh, and to see if Drew's a good fit for his '*elite*' school." More angry air quoting from me.

"So you don't really even like the guy?" His face brightened a little at this prospect.

"It's more like I don't like his school program," I said, picking around my words. "If Andrew's accepted, he'll leave the beginning of January."

"So you mean Davenport's here *all* semester?"

I gave Miguel an impatient look. "I think you're missin' the point, Miguel—Andrew, my eight-year-old brother, might be leaving for *boarding* school, in California, at the end of the semester!"

"Right. Wow. Sorry to hear that, Katie. I guess that kind of blows." Whatever he was going to say was cut short when the bell rang and Mrs. Jenkins started to take roll.

All during class, Miguel shot sympathetic sidelong glances while Ashley-Leigh shot daggers at me. It didn't really matter because neither one was really penetrating my sleep-deprived haze. Even the omnipresent butterflies that floated around my stomach every time Pete Davenport so much as flitted across my brain were subdued today. I could barely keep my eyes open. Lack of sleep and the strain of trying to keep my family together with nothing more than bubble gum and duct tape, while the enemy was trying to destroy us with army tanks and nuclear bombs, well, let's just say: It was beginning to take a toll.

Thankfully, Mrs. Jenkins never called on me, and the bell rang just as my head began to droop again. I remained seated, packing up slowly, hoping Miguel and Ashley-Leigh would head on to lunch. *Yeah right.* Miguel started up our previous conversation as if he'd been on pause and the bell signified the start button. He didn't get very far though, because Ashley-Leigh came storming up, waving her outraged grievances at me like purple pom-poms.

"Katie, I'm, like, so pissed at you right now!" she informed me. Like I was too obtuse to read her over-the-top social cues. I remained mute, packing up my books. "Why haven't you called me back yet?"

"Because I wasn't aware that you'd called," I snapped. It felt good to vent some frustration on someone so deserving.

"Well, I did," she sniffed, toning it down. "Like five or six times . . . and I left messages."

"Look, I'm sorry Ash, I've just been busy and there were no messages on the answerin' machine when I got in yesterday afternoon. Daddy must've erased them and didn't bother to leave a note."

"Well, if you'd just get a cell phone, like . . . oh, the rest of America, you wouldn't have that problem," she said, ever the problem solver.

"Great idea. Why didn't I think of that?" I yanked the zipper on my backpack. "I'll get right on it—right after I get my hair highlighted and my nails done." I threw my backpack over my shoulder and headed out with Miguel following and Ashley-Leigh bringing up the rear.

"*Uh!* Whadoya mean by that?" she asked, playing dumb.

Miguel and I exchanged eye-rolls in the doorway. "What do you want, Ashley?"

"I wanted to see if we could grab lunch today," she said, about as obvious as a room key presented at prom.

Miguel's girlfriend was standing around the hall waiting for him, so he slid past with a "We'll talk later, 'kay?"

I nodded and smiled and waved at his girlfriend. And then I saw him striding my way, making the dingy floors of our hallway look like a runway in Paris. As usual, everyone was openly staring at him. That meant that in about two seconds, everyone would be staring at me. I felt a wave of warmth wash over my face followed by a swell of giddiness inside at the thought that *he* was here for *me*.

Ashley-Leigh saw where my eyes had strayed to, and her face looked as if she'd just swallowed bleach. "Guess I have my answer."

"I'm sorry, Ash. Maybe tomorrow?" I said as insincere as her lunch invitation. But I had a feeling my voice fell on deaf, hula-hooped ears, because her focus shifted, along with her whole demeanor. She beamed at Pete with so much wattage I thought she might inadvertently shock him to death.

"Hey, Pete! . . . Right on time," Ashley-Leigh greeted. "We were just discussin' what we were gonna do for lunch today!" She smashed our faces together. "Right, Katie-girl?"

Pete raised his eyebrows at me, and I gave him a helpless look. "Is that right?" he said, bending to kiss my cheek. The wattage in her smile dimmed a bit, but I knew Ashley—she considered herself down but not out. Like a pro, she plastered the smile back on and went for it. It was kinda fascinating to watch, like a car crash you see coming, but the passenger in the car in front of you is too busy putting on lipstick in the mirror to notice.

"That's right." She nailed him in the chest with her finger. "We feel like it's unfair of Katie to keep you all to herself . . . and, like, visa versa I guess." She giggled like she'd just made a funny, but it fell flat without her backup laughers.

I had trouble following her one-sided conversation the second a possessive arm draped around my shoulder. Pete didn't seem to be paying attention at all. "Ready?" He looked down at me; I nodded up at him.

In tandem, we began walking through the hall with Ashley-Leigh trailing us like a high-heeled shoe attached to the newlywed's getaway car. She was gibbering on and on about how we used to be known as the "two Lees" and how we were more like sisters than friends growing up. I have to say: I kinda started feeling bad for her. She was trying so hard, and Pete wasn't trying at all. This would be pretty tough to take—things usually worked out for her in pretty much the way she planned. If Pete kept this up, she was liable to get frostbite.

We reached the exit, and he finally acknowledged her presence by holding the door open for her. "Why thank you!" she trilled up at him as if she were a southern belle twirling an umbrella instead of a prima donna wearing a hoochie day-glow tee.

"Looks like this is where we part ways," Pete spoke directly to her for the first time, then grabbed my hand and led me in the opposite direction of the parking lot.

Ashley-Leigh was left standing there with a hangdog expression, which she rapid-recovered from. "Okay, you two have fun! . . . Don't do nothin' I wouldn't do!" she called out for the benefit of anyone standing around to witness her dismissal.

Pete didn't acknowledge her in any way, so I threw a "We'll see you in Spanish" over my shoulder as we walked away. "Wow. Remind me to never get on your bad side."

"Why?" He gave me a wicked grin. "You plannin' on gettin' on my bad side?"

"You never know," I murmured, squirming under the heat of his stare.

We'd already arrived at his Hummer, on account of it being parked brazenly in front of the school, in the zone reserved for loading buses. I shook my head at him, laughing as he opened up the passenger door and helped me inside.

"What?" he innocently dropped, a playful smile tugging at his lips. "No one was using it, so I slipped in and took it—couldn't let a prime spot like this go to waste because everyone around here is too scared or stupid to go for it." His eyes twinkled. "It's just not in my nature."

"Maybe nobody took it cause it's against the rules," I volleyed back.

He laughed and shut the door, came around and returned with: "Well, you know what they say about rules . . ." then arched a brow poignantly at me before throwing his aviators on. Game over, he clicked in the key and fired up the engine. In no time, we were headed out west again while everyone else was going east. This time when he cut the engine, I was unsurprised by our lunch locale.

"Is this going to be a regular thing now?" I said, then immediately regretted the presumptuous statement.

No need because Pete immediately said, "I hope so. As much as I've enjoyed fighting with you, Kate, I sure would like to know what it's like to do…"—his eyes fluttered my way—"*other* things."

My face caught fire in a nanosecond. Thankfully, he hopped out to come around and get me before I could spontaneously combust in his leather seat. "I'm guessing you spoke with your brother yesterday?" he confirmed.

"I did."

"So—we good?"

"We're alright," I allowed.

"Oh, I think we can manage an upgrade from that." He gave me another smoldering look, and weird sensations migrated south of my belly. I felt distinctly tongue-tied as he helped me down and kept ahold of my hand. Pete, however, seemed unaffected by anything, whistling as we made our way to the same shady spot I was beginning to think of as "ours." In no hurry to force a conversation, he allowed me time to find my voice.

"You know, I'm startin' to feel like I'm not really contributin' much here," I finally said, swiping the blanket from him and spreading it out on the ground.

He stopped whistling and shook his head, eyes roving over my face appreciatively. "I beg to differ."

Man-oh-man is he turnin' it on today! My insipid blush was back, and I lowered my eyes, suddenly anxious to help unpack the food. Pete reached out and captured my busy hands in his. "I don't like it when you do that," he said, releasing them to rub his thumb across my jawline.

"D-do what?" My skin started tingling. I hoped water was in that thermos today, because it felt like I was catching fire.

He slipped off my glasses, then just stared at me until I got lost in his eyes. I fumbled around gracelessly for my confiscated disguise, feeling as exposed as if I were lying in this park buck-naked. But Pete wasn't having it—he tossed them out of reach before returning his hands to my face.

I swallowed. "W-what are you doin?"

His look was as hypnotizing as his touch. I was a deer in headlights. Unable to move. Completely at his mercy. He trailed his thumbs along the circles beneath my eyes. "You're working too hard, Kate . . . not getting enough rest."

"More like workin' my brain too hard," I said, closing my eyes and swaying under his spell. It just felt so dang good—being in this quiet, shady spot on a warm afternoon, feeling the breeze stir the air, the intoxicating feel of his hands stroking my face. Heaven. I felt a magnetic pull toward him from parts of my body that weren't even touching him . . . but wanted to with a force that was almost uncontrollable.

"That too," he said. "Mental stress is the worst kind. You're putting yourself through things that haven't even happened yet."

"Am okay." I fought a yawn. "Just need sleep."

"Here . . ." He repositioned us to a more comfortable position: his back resting against the tree, my back resting against his chest, his arms wrapped around me. I could have stayed like that forever; my problems seemed to vanish right along with my senses. "Better?"

Vague nodding and a deep breath in were my only replies. We rested like this a couple of minutes, listening to the chirping birds and the leaves rustling together in the trees. The feel of his heart beating rhythmically into my back, and his hands leisurely caressing my arms were soul soothing.

"You down for the count?" he asked, catching a tickling strand of hair blowing across my face and smoothing it back into place.

"Almost." I smiled a bit, eyes still closed. "I think I *could* quite possibly fall asleep right here."

"Why don't you?"

I huffed out a tired little laugh and sat up. "Uh . . . because we have class in half an hour."

"So?"

"So we have to get back."

"Why?"

I twisted around to read his expression. "Cause that's what we're supposed to do."

"Says who?" he challenged.

"The people in charge."

"Do you always do what the people in charge tell you to do?"

"Yes," I automatically answered but realized it wasn't true anymore. I'd been doing the exact *opposite* of what the people in charge were telling me: hiding paperwork, interfering with the mentoring, going to lunch with the mentor I was instructed to stay away from, throwing out the window almost every promise I'd made to Mama . . . except for the most important one: protecting my brothers.

"Well, most of the time anyway," I amended.

"Why?" He seemed genuinely interested in my answer.

"Cause I guess that's what I was taught to do—obey your mother and father, respect your elders and all that. Why? Don't you?"

"What if you knew your parents were wrong or your elders are not exactly . . . respectable, would you then *still* obey them?" It seemed like a loaded question.

I shrugged my shoulders. "I dunno."

"That's a cop-out, Kate, and you know it." His tone was really tense now, like his body, and his eyes had hardened, towards whom or what I wasn't sure.

A vision of Ranger popped in my head. I remembered the obvious animosity between the two cadets. At the time, I chalked it up to male competition—both guys trying to be the lion. Now that I thought about it, maybe Ranger was his superior? And Pete didn't much feel like his inferior or like getting bossed by him. After all, didn't Ranger say he couldn't make the "mission" too easy for him?

A ripple of understanding energized me because I felt like I'd instinctually hit on why I didn't feel as threatened by Pete, even though he was an ambassador for the enemy, as I did Ranger and his academy in general. Pete was here under duress and direct orders. I was sure of it. And I got the feeling now that he didn't much like the orders he was taking from them, but was forced to obey. Like I was forced to obey my father's crazy rules . . . We were both at the mercy of those in charge, and the ones in charge weren't ones we respected. It was a maddening position to be in, which would explain the anger I felt emanating from him now.

"Fine," I re-answered. "Then in that case, you should *not* obey orders you know in your heart is wrong."

"What if doing so negatively affects, not only yourself, but everyone around you?"

"Then do what I always do," I said. "Go with your gut."

Pete stared into my eyes, searching, before looking off into the distance. I suddenly knew just how he felt about keeping my eyes from him.

There were some squabbling birds in the trees above us, debating about whether or not we had any food to offer, and a couple of weary moms had brought their kids to the playground. Their animated voices rang out sharp and free, harmonious with the breezy afternoon. We were quiet now, separated by our individual worries and internal struggles.

His gaze returned, open with a dash of mirth. "Just go with your gut, huh?"

I felt like the Cadet Davenport mask was going to slip back into place any moment so decided to throw caution to the wind before both our guards were back up. Leaning up, I cradled his head in my hands. "Pete," I said in the voice I reserved for my loved-ones, "I'm gonna tell you somethin' my mother used to tell me when I wasn't sure what to do . . ."

He slow-blinked his eyes, which were curious and speculating.

I continued with an intensity that allowed no false pretenses between us. "Never let your sense of duty get in the way of doin' what you know is right"—I placed a palm over his heart—"in here."

Pete closed his eyes against me and dropped his head back against the tree. A crease formed between his brows that I longed to smooth away. It reminded me of how he looked that day at the diner—resigned. When his eyes clicked back open, mine were waiting, shining back with sympathy and understanding. I stared until flinty eyes softened back into the warm pools I was accustomed to seeing reflected back at me. Then, giving in to the urge, my fingers fluttered to his face. I traced the blue-fading-to-violet patch over his left eye (which was either the exact *wrong* or *right* thing to do, depending on which way you wanted to look at it).

I was aware of his decision before he even moved. As if in tacit understanding of my knees giving way, he reached for me. My breath caught. Eyes never leaving mine, he slid his hand beneath my head to lay me out before him on the blanket. Dozing butterflies in my stomach just woke up. Pete stared down on me for an immeasurable moment—still debating.

Unable to take the intensity another second, I closed my eyes, my lips parting expectantly. But, once again, he deprived me. I huffed out some frustration and opened my eyes . . . to witness the slow curving of his lips. Something about that knowing smile uncurled something within me. Whatever it was had the elite cadet breaking rank, because he advanced forward. His lips feather-brushed mine before trailing up to my ear, where he slowly exhaled out his sweet scent. I shivered and wound my arms around his neck to draw him closer. I did this as naturally as if I'd been doing it every day of the week instead of for the very first time in my life.

His journey—mapping my skin with his lips—continued south, bypassing my lips again to slide over the sensitive region of my neck. There he discovered the cross, nestled in the hollow of my throat, and paused to lift his lips in an ironic smile. He traced the sacred shape with his fingertip before moving along the line of the chain. My breaths became heavy, my arms pulling him down impatiently. He stopped me short to just hover over me.

"Kate," he breathed, a husky whisper. "What am I going to do with you?"

I was kind of wondering the same thing, but my body seemed to be the one with all the answers. It was still trying to close the fraction of distance still left between us, impatient for the fusing of our lips and our hips. This was something I'd never experienced in real life before, but felt as familiar to me as breathing—that need to push myself against him, to feel the contours of his muscular body meld into the feminine softness of mine.

Pete was still propped up on his elbows, keeping his weight off me, but I could feel his breath quicken, see his eyes transform into molten lava as he regarded me. It was suddenly more than I could take—this need, the anticipation, the chemistry cooking between us on a slow burn. Things didn't seem to be heating up as rapidly as my body wanted, so I made an involuntary impatient sound in the back of my throat, sure that if he didn't kiss me in that instant I'd start to cry. Telltale moisture gathered in my eyes.

Finally, *finally!* he released me from my purgatory. Closing his eyes in surrender—at long last—he brought his lips to mine. God in heaven, I'd never felt such a powerful force on earth as I did in that moment. His warm lips molded into mine in a lingering lip lock before parting them, firm and insistent. And it was like I'd never been kissed before. *This is heaven.* Yet I still wanted more. Grasping him frantically across his back, I yanked him to me, and oh—*yes!*—he finally collapsed his weight on me. I moaned in pure ecstasy.

His apparent expertise and my relative noviceness were irrelevant, because a better match was unimaginable. It was pure bliss for the senses: his taste, his smell, his feel. My hands ran along the muscles of his back, pressing him farther into me, like I could make one thing out of two. His hands were also busy: one pushing into the thickness of my hair, the other sliding along the contours of my waist. Our mouths melted together, moving in an enticing synchronicity that made me greedy for more, more, more! I moaned again, and his answering groan was music to my ears. My hands wound through his hair, clutching him to me. That's about the point he withdrew his lips to breathe out my name.

Why's he stopping?

"No," I whimpered.

He half-heartedly tried to get up, but I held him down in a vice-like grip, desperate for more of this smooth, sensuous feeling. We began passionately kissing again, his wandering mouth quickly forgotten and forgiven. My hips arched up, urging him on. I didn't even stop to think about stopping. I felt like I was beginning to be lifted off the earth. A warm, melty feeling starting in places I'd only imagined at. I literally felt like I was on drugs—high on Pete Davenport and drifting away on a cloud of pure bliss.

Finally, Pete was able to snap out of it. He wrenched his lips from mine. I immediately protested again, trying to pull him back. But he held my head firmly between his palms, leaning off me now. "Kate . . . look at me," he commanded in a low growl.

"No," I protested, not wanting to be brought back down to earth with a crash. *No, no, no, no, no!* I wanted to cry like a baby. Aggravation heaved from my throat. Then, resigned, I slowly opened my eyes like a good girl. I could see Pete's glorious face was also flushed, his breathing ragged, and he was sweaty . . . in a good way.

I reached up to wipe a bead of perspiration from his temple, brushing back his hair from his forehead. His eyes flamed into two smoldering embers of desire. He barked out a short, humorless laugh, and my own mouth quirked up. He closed his eyes, getting control over himself I presumed, because when he reopened them, the fires were put out.

"Sweet Jesus!" He rolled off me and sat up, drawing up his knees and in a deep breath.

I frowned at that, hating to think of him taking the Lord's name in vain. But in this instance, I could see how it was fitting. *A feeling this rapturous had to come straight from God, right?* I brushed back another lock of his hair, smiling lazily up at him feeling punch-drunk and starry-eyed.

"Would you please, Kate, in the name of God, please quit looking at me like that?" he said, rather unkindly, too, I thought under the circumstances. He slid farther away from me.

"Like what?" I asked, trying and failing to keep the hurt from my voice.

"Like you want me to ravage your body."

I huffed out a single chuckle. "Well, I hate to say . . . but that might be pretty accurate." I shrugged carelessly.

He snorted. "I swear you can actually *smell* the pheromones in the air."

I smiled at that—our chemistry was undeniable.

Pete seemed really preoccupied, and my body was still trying to come down from its high, so we sat like that for a bit, faces flushed and chests heaving. When I looked at him, I expected camaraderie, but instead, I saw his face harden in a way that made me feel brittle.

Could he be mad?

Unthinking, I placed a hand on his back. To my utter horror, he flinched back like I'd scorched him with a curling iron. I snatched my hand back.

"Kate, really. I mean it . . . just don't," he said in the clipped tone usually reserved for Ashley-Leigh.

What have I done to make him look like that? I searched his face for answers, found nothing but rigid anger. I fingered my lip to keep it from trembling, and he scowled at me. Winding around to face the playground, I tried to get control of my emotions, which had also just done a swift one-eighty.

I heard him swear under his breath. "Not right," he murmured, but I heard him loud and clear. Felt like my tender heart just got trampled on; it actually ached in my chest. How could kissing him be "not right" in his book when it was a blockbuster New York Times bestseller to me? How could I be so far off the mark here when he was talking about pheromones in the air? I thought about it a bit more while he was busy *not* talking to me.

Was he talking about me and my pheromones? Like I was so obviously hot for him he could smell it coming off me? Could this be a one-sided deal, and he only kissed me because I practically begged him too? *Again.* He did try to stop, but I forced him to continue on.

Oh my God!—I was the aggressor here. Suddenly, I had the urge to crawl under a rock. Was busy feeling like the country floozy Ranger took me for when Pete finally spoke: "Kate?" His voice sounded better, but I wasn't about to turn around, sure I was covered head-to-toe in a stinky layer of humiliation.

He put a hand on my shoulder, which I hastened to shrug off. *How dare he touch me now!*

"Kate, please. I'm sorry. Look"—he took my arm to turn me around—"let me explain."

Tears, I didn't want him to see, were pooling in my eyes. "Don't touch me!"

He chuckled a little, trying his hand at levity. "*That's* what you should've said two minutes ago."

It was the wrong move, making light of this. A hand, that I angrily smacked away, tried to turn me again. "Stop! Gah! What's wrong with you?"

Pete sighed deeply, running a hand through his hair. In a low, reasonable voice he said, "If you'll turn around, I'll tell you."

Everything was ruined now . . . *shoulda known heaven-on-earth wouldn't happen for me.* Liquid outrage began burning trails down my face.

"Kate," Pete said tenderly, "are you crying?"

"No." I furiously swiped them away.

He swore a low oath then forcefully picked me up to face him, holding me in place by my arms.

"*What?*" I glared through tears.

Pete sighed again, his eyes the dark pools of chocolate that always seem to melt my heart. "I don't know what to say . . . I'm sorry." He wiped a couple of drops away with his thumb.

"Sorry? Sorry for what?"

"Sorry that I hurt your feelings for one—that's the last thing I wanted to do." He wiped another hot drop from the other side now.

I sniffed a little, staring at him with wounded eyes. He did look like he felt sorry . . . sorry *for* me. He took my face and kissed me on the cheek, like a father does a child that's fallen down and gotten a boo-boo. Somehow, this hurt my feelings all over again. Did he just *not* see me in *that* way at all? *Duh. Obviously, Kate—he's majorly out of my league. Gah! How could I have been so stupid?* I was swallow-me-up-mortified and could not have this conversation now. Or ever.

I scrambled away from him and got to my feet, not wanting to be where I wasn't wanted. "You know what? It's fine," I said, brushing imaginary debris from my jeans. "I-I don't know what got into me. I'm really tired . . . and under a *lot* of stress." I glared down at him, so he'd exactly know *where* that stress was coming from. "So let's just pretend it never happened."

A strange assortment of emotions flitted across Pete's face before finally settling on his old standby. "Still friends?" he grinned.

Stiff nod from me.

He stood up, too, putting a hand out. "Well alrighty then, buddy . . . shake on it?" I was loathe to shake his hand at the moment but wanted to attempt to be mature so shoved my hand into his, barely meeting his eyes. He grasped it and pulled me into him, catching me by surprise and off balance, so that I fell into his hug. "Hey, I'm a hugger remember?"

He may as well have been hugging a statue for all the effort I put into it. He looked down at me frowning, though wisely remained silent. I stepped away from him the second he released me.

"Let's eat, shall we?" he said, a little too brightly.

Eating in front of him was the last thing I wanted to do now. While he unpacked food I wasn't gonna eat, I bent down to retrieve my glasses. *Dang it!* They had gotten broken, somehow, in our mishap of a make-out. That was the second pair in a week *because of him*. Pete must've felt the heat from my glare burning a hole through his T-shirt, because he looked up to see them dangling from my fingers like a wiry spider.

"Oops," he said cheerfully. "No big deal, right? They can be replaced."

His flippant attitude ruffled my feathers even more. "Right," I bit out. "No big deal . . . if you have twenty-twenty vision." It really wasn't a big deal because I could see just fine. But for all he knew, I actually *needed* those glasses to see with.

Pete's hands stopped arranging a gourmet's selection of snack items. He cocked his head sideways, reminding me of a golden retriever trying to make sense of what his master said. "Uh . . . right. I guess you do need those for class," he said in an odd-sounding voice, then quickly brightened again. "It looks like we'll be running a little late anyway, so we may as well run by an optometrist—give us a solid excuse for that tardy."

"I don't have my checkbook with me, and I don't have enough cash to pay for new glasses *and* buy groceries," I pointed out, which was a big mistake because I immediately knew what he was going to say next. And grit my teeth against it.

"Kate, of course I'll pay for them—no big deal."

"No big deal," I said cuttingly, suddenly wanting him to feel as bad as me. "Everything's 'no big deal' to you, isn't it?" He looked at me patiently, like I was a toddler pitching a fit over a dropped lollipop. "But what if it *is* a big deal? Because I *need* those glasses . . . and I'm *not* takin' your money!"

"I don't see why not," he responded reasonably (which really chapped my hide). "After all—it's my fault they're broken."

"Because I'm not, that's why!"

I furiously pushed his hand away when he tried to hand me some fancy trail mix. Somehow, that really got under another layer of my skin—the nerve of him feeding me his dang *gourmet* foods, driving me around in his over-the-top vehicle, giving me $*100* dollar tips. *Really, who does he think I am—freakin' Cinderella?* I didn't need or want his charity . . . in any form. Kissing me because he felt *sorry* for me. *How dare he!*

Pete sighed and rubbed at the back of his head. "Why are you being so unreasonable?" He glanced at my untouched lunch selections. "And why aren't you eating?"

"I'm *not* bein' unreasonable." I leaned back on my hands and crossed my ankles. ". . . And I'm not *hungry*."

A storm cloud darkened Pete's face. He took a moment and a deep breath. I thought, with grim satisfaction, how much I enjoyed seeing him struggle for calm. I would love to see him lose it completely. Be a dadgum *normal,* feeling human being for once instead of so controlled all the time.

So I tried my hand at pushing him over the edge—by pushing the plate of delicious looking cheese, fruit, and assorted crackers back at him.

He pushed it back. "You need to eat something."

"I'll eat somethin' later on." I turned my nose away.

He expelled some aggravation. "Listen, Kate, I wasn't going to say anything, but I don't think you're taking very good care of yourself. You have a lot of weight on your shoulders. You need more sleep. And you need to *eat* to keep up your strength."

I shot him a withering look. "I can take care of myself just fine, thank you very much for your concern." *Who was he now—my mentor? And what did he know about it anyway?* My foot started shaking furiously.

He rubbed at his jaw for a moment.

Gah! Why does he have to be so friggin' gorgeous? . . . It was like trying to piss off an angel. But I resolutely held on to my righteous indignation, refusing to meet his eye.

"Goddammit, Kate! . . . I said I was sorry, and I *am*. Okay?"

I flinched at his anger, yet kept my voice cool. "Would you *please* refrain from using the Lord's name in vain around me?"

Pete huffed out some more air, ran another hand through his already ruffled hair. "Sorry. But I thought you said you were fine."

"I am," I replied in a tone that indicated the opposite. "However, what I am *not* is hungry." I shoved the plate away so that the crackers spread out like a deck of cards, and cubes of cheese tumbled across his lap like thrown dice.

A murderous look crossed his face, causing a sliver of fear to ice my spine. *Have I pushed it too far?*

Pete got himself under control with great difficulty. "I thought we were friends again, remember? . . . We even shook on it." He tried infusing his voice with humor, but it didn't quite make it there.

I sorta snuffled out a little outrage, averting my eyes to the spiny foliage decorating the entrance.

"Okay fine—have it your way." His patience came crashing to an end, along with our cozy picnic. I looked over to see him rapid-packing up uneaten food then chunking the containers back into the cooler.

"What are you doin'?" I asked, slightly worried he would shatter the glass from the force of his throws.

"Packing."

"I can see that. But why? You haven't had anything to eat yet." *And why is my voice so small?*

He stopped to look me in the eye, arched a brow. "If you're not eating, then neither am I." He clamped the last lid on, effectively ending the conversation.

I watched him for a second, outraged he was turning the tables on me. Harrumphed. "Your obvious attempt at reverse psychology won't work on me."

One sharp, angry zip and the nylon cooler was closed. He stood up, looking down on me with what could only be described as disappointment. "I'm not playing games here, Kate. If you're bound and determined to make me pay for hurting your feelings by going on a hunger strike, then you leave me no choice but to join you. I refuse to sit by and watch you carelessly abuse your beautiful body to one up me."

I gulped, feeling the stinging truth of his words.

"You're already on the verge of collapse," he finished, continuing to stare me down while I felt myself shrinking in size by the second.

He was right: it was petty of me. I just felt so small and put in my place, I was unable to admit it—stubborn pride, plain and simple.

"You ready to go?" He didn't offer me a hand up this time, and I realized that I would rather *just* be friends with him than nothing at all. I also realized, with a sick hollow feeling in my stomach that I couldn't attribute to hunger, how much effort he put into packing things he knew I would eat. I assumed he was *not* also a vegetarian.

I jerked myself to my feet, two bright spots of shame coloring my cheeks in lieu of blush. Truth was: I probably *couldn't* choke down any food right now, no matter how delectable. I was teetering back on the edge of tears, sick with worry I'd ruined everything. Trying to do something helpful to make up for my misstep, I bent to retrieve the blanket, but it was snatched away before I could get my hands on it. I had no choice but to follow him empty handed, my head hung low.

We traveled in silence the short ride back. He didn't bother turning back on the rap compilation he'd downloaded for me. *Gah!* No wonder he felt "all wrong" about kissing me—I'd behaved like a child, and conversely, he was the most mature guy I'd ever met.

I braved a quick side-glance, saw only the rigid line of his jaw, and my stomach heaved. I realized I'd been taking all my fears and hatred of his school out on him, like it was his fault they were recruiting Andrew. Clearly, he was just following his superior's orders . . . cause that's what they do in military school. *Duh.* He'd been nothing but a slice-of-nice from the very beginning. He even went so far as to warn me about Ranger. And all I'd done to repay him was give him a hard time and a black eye. Now it was drops of remorse that started rolling down my cheeks. I faced out the passenger window for the duration of the drive.

We screeched to a halt in the parking lot, prompting me to hastily blot my eyes on my shirt. Only stragglers littered the sidewalks, which meant the bell had already rung. We would be tardy anyway, so I took a deep breath and turned to face the lion. He was still staring out the front window.

I cleared my throat. "Uh . . . thanks for a lovely time?" Got nothing for that one but crickets. My heart plummeted. "Pete, I'm sorry—you're right." My voice had an unapologetic edge of desperation. "I'm gonna eat between classes, okay? I think I have a crumbled-up granola bar in my bag somewhere."

I was just about to hop down when I heard him breathe in deeply through his nose. Turned in time to watch his nostrils flare. *Wow.* I'd thoroughly pissed him off, and I don't know if I'd ever felt sorrier for anything.

"Are you gonna park and come in?" It sounded like I was doing a Minnie Mouse impersonation.

He slowly expelled that pent-up air and faced me. After an agonizing moment of pinning me to my seat with his eyes, he extended his hand. But instead of reaching for me, he reached *past* me to open the glove compartment. Some kind of nutrition bar I'd never seen before came out in his hand. He tossed it to me, and I caught it to my chest. I thought he might say "nice catch" or something like that, but he didn't. He simply faced forward again. I took this as my cue to get out, so me and my sorry butt hopped out of his vehicle.

"If you really want to make it up to me, eat that instead." His voice came low and modulated.

I swallowed and nodded my head. "You're not comin'?"

Pete flicked his eyes at me. "Nah . . . you go on. I'm going with my gut on this one." I thought I saw his lips twitch a little before he said, "I still need to cool off."

He threw the truck into gear and sped out of the parking lot, leaving a trail of dusty gravel in his path . . . and an ache in my chest.

19

TRUCE

Sitting through Spanish without Pete's magnetic force field running interference with my brain function, should've enabled me to concentrate better. Not the case. I sat, shivering and miserable, with his desk lying cold and empty as a tomb behind me. Even the sweater I pulled from my backpack didn't help—I was bone cold.

Somehow Pete's mere presence in my world warmed me in parts of my body I didn't even realize were cold, like my heart. It had been like a dying battery inside my chest, slowly draining of life, until Pete jump-started it again. With every brilliant smile, he lit me up from within. It was a gift, his presence, in this small town, in my life. Every moment with him was like Christmas morning. But I'd pushed him away like yesterday's leftovers. Had I been so focused on hating Ranger, his organization, and my total lack of options in life that I'd been staring too hard at the gift horse in my life?

Mama said to trust my instincts because they'd never lead me wrong. But in this case, my gut was giving me mixed signals. I felt completely safe, cared for even, around Pete. The picnics were proven benign, as well as thoughtful, by my conversation with Andrew. And I sensed that he truly *did* like me and *didn't* want to see any harm come to my family.

Could it be he was in the dark about the sinister intentions of his own organization? Anything was possible, I decided. I sighed, feeling confused and frustrated by my lack of clarity. The bell did its thing, and I shuffled along after my classmates.

Ashley-Leigh came sidling up, chirping in my ear. "Hey! Where's Pete? . . . And where's your glasses?"

"He opted out of class this afternoon," I said, deflated, "and I broke them."

Immediate suspicion paused her. "*How?*"

My blush and pained look must've been answer enough because she said, "Lover's quarrel already?"

I just shrugged my shoulders, remaining tight-lipped.

"You *poor* thing." This was followed by one of her famous face-smashers. "You know you can talk about it with me, right?"

"Right." *Wrong!* No way was I gonna admit that I threw myself at him only to be rebuffed—she'd only gobble it up and ask for seconds.

"And I've always got your back, Katie-Kat."

"I know. Thanks." I smiled thinly at her bold overstatement of loyalty. I tried cutting her some slack because she probably at least halfway meant it in the moment.

"I mean it. You can tell me *anything* . . ."

"There's really nothing to tell." I scrounged for an exit. "Look, I gotta bolt. I'll see you in gym, okay?" I made a hard right at the next corner and left her behind. It's just, I was so bad at lying, and Ashley-Leigh was so good at weaseling her way into getting what she wanted.

I sleepwalked my way through Chemistry, dully writing notes and avoiding so much as a glance at Miguel's sulking face. As soon as the bell rang, I darted out the door, hustling to P.E. with my head down, wondering if it was my imagination, or if everyone was starting to look at me differently.

My question was soon answered because upon my appearance in the dressing room, everyone's heads whipped around like I was famous . . . or like I'd just been the topic of conversation. Sure enough, Ashley-Leigh decided to migrate to the Siberia side of the room to chat with her old buddy today. "Hey there. Feelin' any better?" Now I was the recipient of a weird back pat.

I mumbled something about being tired, then started changing from my discount-denim into my sale-shorts. She hovered around my personal space, watching me undress, hoping I'd drop some more gossip crumbs for her to gobble. I'm sure she was also sizing me up to see what a guy like Pete Davenport could possibly see in me. That's most likely why everyone was starting to stare now. My face grew pink as she ogled my figure, looking for flaws. She caught my awareness that she was checking me out so blinked her eyes away to focus on unstrapping her ridiculous wedge sneakers.

"You know . . . I think I like you better with glasses—they give character to your face," she said. Like her opinion was the last word.

"I'll keep that in mind," I replied as I knotted my sneakers. They of course reminded me of the one responsible for paying for them. I grunted to myself.

"So, why didn't you mention that Pete was Andrew's mentor?"

I smiled darkly, shook my head. I should've known that little secret would spread like wildfire. If Ashley-Leigh knew, that meant *everybody* knew. "How did you hear that? Did Miguel tell you?"

"No." She waved her hand airily. "You know how it is—Marie Walter's son is in class with Andrew. Drew told him, he told his mom, who told my mom. What can I say?" She shrugged her shoulders. "We barely have two degrees of separation in this town."

I huffed out a laugh. *True dat.*

"Why the big secret anyway? And why would you tell Miguel and not me?" She infused her voice with hurt but ended up sounding self-centered to my wizened ears.

I did the shrug thing. "He asked me in English today." Ashley-Leigh stuck out her gloppy lip like a two-year-old, so I added, "I would've told you, too. I just happened to talk to him first. And it's not a big secret . . . we just like to keep quiet about Andrew's giftedness."

While we wrapped our hair into practiced ponytails, I had a vivid flashback to when we were kids. So much had changed my life was almost unrecognizable. "And you know our family well enough to know Daddy wasn't exactly keen on the school sending his aptitude tests to all those boardin' schools."

"Why's he thinkin' about this one then?"

"Dunno," I admitted. "I guess cause it's supposed to be the best military academy in the world."

"Wow!" Ashley's eyes popped out of their sockets. "So does that mean Andrew might go to the same school as Pete?" She sounded as excited as if it were happening to her.

I slammed my locker, hoping to shut down this little convo, too. "Well presumably, if Pete graduates this year, he will no longer be there. But yes, it's the same school."

"*Dude*! I always knew your brother was, like, a baby genius or somethin', but I never thought it would lead to somethin' so . . . so glamorous!" she said, eyes shining.

"Right," I replied dryly. "Our life is very glamorous—us, the cows, and the trailer—we're just a ball gown and a brass band away from an award show over at the Connelly house."

She bapped my arm. "Oh you know what I mean."

"Not really."

"Think about it . . ."—she framed her hands to create a marquee—"*The World's Most Elite Military Academy*. That *is* so glamorous. I mean just look at Pete—can't you imagine him in a tux at some fancy party with, like, foreign diplomats or somethin'?"

"Uh, I actually think they wear blues and not tuxedos. It's a *military* academy . . . not Hollywood." I rolled my eyes at her, but I knew what she meant. There *was* something very sophisticated about him.

"Ooh! Even better! I just adore a man in uniform!" Ashley-Leigh declared, every bit the D-list actress she was destined to be. "If the other . . . what do they call 'em at military schools?"

"Cadets," I supplied.

She snapped her fingers, and I noticed a crystal was glued onto one of her nails today. *Honestly, where did she find the time?* "Cadets. If the other cadets at his school are even half as cute as Pete, then sign me up! You can ship me off tomorrow—UPS overnight, baby!"

I grimaced when she mentioned "other cadets," conjuring up a haughty face and hateful eyes.

"I know high-society and dressin' up and all that isn't really your thing," she said, misreading me, "but this is a chance for your brother to step it up in the world. Plus, you won't have to babysit all the time anymore."

People kept saying that. Did no one remember I had *two* little brothers? Maybe not living in big brother's very big, very bright shadow for a while might not be such a bad thing for Mikey. My stomach immediately lurched at the errant thought.

Was I already allowing that this academy might *not* be such a bad idea for Andrew? Were my defenses so easily chipped away, that I was already questioning my own judgment? It'd been like a domino effect ever since we received Andrew's first recruiting letter: first his principal and teachers, then Daddy, Andrew himself was next, and now Ashley-Leigh was on board? Even Reese had suggested this boarding school was the right choice for Andrew. *Am I the last man standing here?* No. I definitely had my shadow brother on my side.

. . . And what about the mentor cadet? Does he think his academy is a good place for my little brother? Does it matter?

The tardy bell rang, rousing me out of my reverie. Ashley-Leigh wasn't worried because the cheerleading sponsor always cut them some slack. Coach Sams wouldn't be so accommodating, so I had to get a move on. Plus, I was done with our chat. I was getting pretty steamed up at Ashley-Leigh's know-it-all attitude—you could write volumes about what she *didn't* know about me, and a haiku about what she actually *did*.

Coach Sams blew the whistle, and I made to line up when Ashley caught my arm to whisper a spur-of-the-moment plan in my ear. "If Drewy gets accepted, you can visit him all the time and hook up with all those rich, classy cadets. You gotta promise to take me along, okay? Remember—we're besties forevuh!" Cue face smasher. She ran off to her color-coordinated friends though Ashley-Leigh was about as transparent as glass.

I made it through another riveting round of Phys Ed, where I spent the entire time passing the ball between two lines fading into the yellow grass. I tried (without success) not to check the boys' side for Pete. When I didn't find him out there setting the field on fire, I heaved a huge sigh. I imagined my life the way it was before he showed up; it now seemed dull and repetitive as a day in jail.

No matter what the future held, Pete had awakened something in me that had lain dormant for years. (Not entirely sure that was a good thing.) It was the need for *more* in life. I'd tried so hard to suppress it, trying to be okay with my lot in life, get behind that notion to "Bloom Where You're Planted" like that stupid poster with wildflowers pushing up desert clay in the front office said. But it didn't work. Now the idea of going back to the way things were: chores-childcare-church repeat. Well, just the thought of living like that made my eye tick now. I'd have to think of some way around it before hopelessness became entrenched any further into my normal psyche.

The whistle blew, and I jogged off the field more sprightly than usual without my glasses bumping up and down on my nose. A hand gripped my elbow, and I gasped, my heart swelling like someone just pumped air into my chest. I whipped around to see Miguel, bulky in pads, standing there sweating with a scratched helmet tucked under his arm. Disappointment hit me like a two-hundred-pound linebacker. I tried to mask it with a friendly smile.

"Oh, hey Miguel . . . you startled me."

Must not have been my best performance because he said, "Expecting someone else?"

"No, not really." My pitch went off-key.

"Where's Davenport?"

"How would I know?"

"You two looked pretty cozy walking off to lunch together. But I noticed he didn't make the trip back." A tad bit jealous for someone who had a girlfriend.

"Oh. Well, uh . . ." I stumbled, "I think he had an appointment or somethin'."

"An appointment?" he sneered. "For what? More teeth whitening?"

"What's your problem, Miguel?"

"*I* don't got no problem, Katie." I shook my head and turned to go when I heard, "*You're* the one with the problem."

I whirled back around. "Whatd'ya mean by that exactly?"

"Nothin'." He stuffed his helmet back on. "Forget about it . . . none of my business anyway."

I stepped in front of him. "No, don't just walk away. You said it . . . now tell me what you meant by it."

Miguel faced me like we were opponents on the line of scrimmage. "That dude Davenport," he spat.

"What about him?" I already knew where this was going; I just didn't know where it was coming from.

"I—" he faltered, peering down at the scraggly grass and kicking up a tuff of the stuff with his cleat. It looked like he was red, but it was hard to tell in this heat. "I just don't like the guy."

"You don't even know him."

"I don't have to know him to know his type."

"His *type*?" I said, now using a note out of my range. "I didn't take you for a guy with a whole lotta prejudices, Miguel."

There was a trio of bored seniors standing around watching our little exchange, so in silent communication we toned it down. He placed a hand on my arm. "I just hate to see you make a fool of yourself, Katie."

"Well, thanks so much for your concern." I jerked my arm away. "It's real heart-warmin'." If there were daisies on the field, I would've trampled over them on my way back in.

Gah! What's with everyone today?

My hands were posed to hit gym doors when my head turned. It was that shimmery feeling up my spine that gave him away. Pete was leaning —casual and cool in loose navy shorts and fitted white tee—against the fence surrounded by a small crowd of admirers. But his face was anything but casual. His jaw was set, his arms folded in front of him. He seemed to hardly be paying attention to the lively banter going on around him. Instead, he was staring directly at me.

I froze, hands midair. He gave a little wave, and my heart gave a little leap. Then I colored, realizing that he'd probably been watching Miguel and I's little scene. I wondered what he made of it. In any case, he didn't look too happy at the moment. I hoped he wasn't still mad at me . . . *shoot*! I just remembered I hadn't gotten around to eating that nutrition bar he'd pushed on me. So I returned a little wave and ran into the building to follow up on that.

I'd taken a little longer than usual inside, so was unprepared to find him waiting for me when I pushed out the door into carefree sunshine and a duty-filled afternoon. He approached me, shades on, so I couldn't read his expression.

I tested the waters with "Hey."

Pete looked at me for a drawn-out moment. In a very contained voice he said, "What was that earlier on the field?"

"It was nothin'—just a misunderstandin'." I decided to switch rivers midstream. "What are you still doin' here? I thought you'd be with Drews by now."

"Aren't you glad to see me?"

"Yes. No . . . it's not that. Of course, I am. I just thought you had to be there at a set time everyday," I explained.

"I dropped off some aptitude tests for Mrs. Woodward to administer after school." He relieved me of my gym bag as we fell into step together to the parking lot. "I see you decided not to change today like you usually do," he said, apropos a nothing. "And I was wondering . . . why is that?"

I glanced down at my bare legs and bright sneakers, feeling inexplicably guilty. "I dunno . . . laziness I guess." I shrugged and tried not to notice Miguel, Ron, and another baller eyeing us as we walked.

"Kate, you are many things"—hand slipping around my shoulder, Pete squeezed me to him—"however, lazy is not one of them." He let it and me go to switch topics again. "I had a reason for going in a little later this afternoon—I wanted to talk to you in private."

"Oh." My voice and temperature rose at the same time. "I—" Cleared my throat. "Don't really wanna talk about it." The wound was still too raw and fresh to go poking at.

We'd reached my dusty car now and stood around awkwardly not talking, just kind of staring at the puffy clouds changing shapes then each other. A stray hair escaped my ponytail to float across my face. He reached out to tuck it behind my ear, bringing his sensual mouth in close proximity to mine. I was finding it hard to breathe all of a sudden.

Pete seemed to also be struggling for air because he deep-breathed in through his nose before letting it leak out slowly between his lips. Then he studied me like I was a newly discovered species he couldn't quite figure out. For someone who wanted to talk, he sure was being awfully quiet. I fervently wished he wasn't wearing lens that only mirrored back my own eyes.

After a few more moments of standing under his stare and jiggling my key chain, I went with: "I guess I better go pick up Mikey . . ."

He still hadn't moved his vocal cords, so I made to move forward with my plan, but the dadgum door was glued shut. He watched me struggle for a second before heaving another sigh and moving me aside to wrench it open for me.

"Thanks." I made a face. "It's, uh . . . kinda jammed."

He simply nodded.

Somehow, I didn't feel released from our odd encounter yet. So I stalled a moment longer, wondering if he'd actually start a real conversation but hoping he wouldn't if it involved more talk about our mishap of a make-out. He just stared some more until I saw myself flushing. *Something* was on his mind. I drummed my fingers on top of the car, standing half-in, half-out.

"Okay then . . . I guess I'll see you at 4:30." Spinning around to get in, I inadvertently whipped him with my ponytail.

"Hey!" He batted it out of his face.

I whirled back around. "Sorry!"

"It's fine." He gave a little laugh. "You know . . . you could probably classify that thing as a weapon."

"Uh . . . thanks?" I frowned at him.

"No, it's cute." He smiled and pushed the stray hair behind my ear again. "Except for the fact that it subtracts a few years from your age." There was that edge again.

"Well, I feel about *seventy-one* today," I said, right on the verge of yawning in his face.

He shook his head at me. "I told you—you gotta take better care of yourself." He said this in a teasing manner that didn't sting, and I could tell I was forgiven. It immediately felt like a weight had been lifted, and I was just sighing in relief when he said, "Kate, I know you don't want to talk about it, but I need to apologize again for today."

My chest swirled with emotion. "'Snothin' to apologize for," I mumbled, moving my eyes to my sneakers.

Pete chucked a hand under my chin. He removed his shades. "As much as I *enjoyed* kissing you, it was very wrong of me to do so. I'm Andrew's mentor, and it could be construed as a conflict of interest . . . especially in light of how opposed you seemed to be to the idea of him joining. Having that kind of relationship with you could cloud my judgment, and it's my duty as his mentor to give him his due diligence"—he batted my ponytail— "and not be swayed by ponytail-wielding vixens."

Is that why he's been sighing all afternoon? Does this mean we can no longer spend time together? Isn't that what I want? A reality check hit my gut. No, no it was *not*.

I must've looked stricken because he quickly said, "But there's nothing in the rules against us being friends. And I don't know about you, but I could sure use one right about now." He flashed me another of his brilliant smiles, and it literally took my breath away.

It wasn't what my body or my heart wanted to hear, but my head had to admit—it was a good idea. Because *he* was clouding *my* judgment. And wasn't I supposed to keep my friends close, and my enemies closer? . . . Pete just happened to fall into both categories.

Does that make him my frenemy?

He watched the play of emotions on my face. "Whadoyasay, Katie-Kat . . . friends for real?" He offered his hand, and I accepted it.

"Sure." This time, I was prepared as he pulled me into a hug. He really was a good hugger—none of those Ashley-Leigh face-smashers or one-armed things. He hugged with his whole body, but not in a lascivious way (unfortunately).

He threw his aviators back on and held up his palm. I slapped him five, and he held on to my hand, intertwining our fingers before letting go. "Okay . . . I'll see ya later then, buddy."

"After while, pal," I fired back.

He turned around and shot me with his finger triggers, and another spectacular smile, before climbing into his monster truck and driving off.

After Pete left to go do his "due diligence," I collapsed in my car awhile, using the steering wheel as a pillow. *Gah.* I was so tired. My body was tired, my brain was tired, my eyes were tired. I closed them for a second, thinking of everything. The problem was, I quite simply wanted to believe in a world where Pete Davenport was as good as he was good-looking, and more interested in me than procuring my gifted brother for his elite academy. I sighed. I sure needed some clarity. So I started up the car, determined to go on a fact-finding mission this afternoon.

I picked Mikey up from preschool, holding my breath that Mrs. Reyes wouldn't need to pull me aside again. She simply smiled and nodded to me from the playground. Nothing to report in regards to Michael Connelly was a good thing. I exhaled and squished his palm in mine, praising him lavishly. "Come on, baby bro, let's go shoppin'."

We skipped to the car with Mikey protesting indignantly at being referred to as a baby. Three stop signs, two stoplights, and a giant pothole later, and we were parked outside the always-busy Wal-Mart. I was in the middle of counting our money when Mikey broke my concentration.

"Hey Kadee, why aren't you wearwing your gwasses today?"

"Uh . . . I broke them today at the park, honey."

"Did you fall off the merry-go-round?" Mikey wondered.

I snorted. "You could say that."

"Huh?"

That's just what I was thinking. I recounted the money in my wallet. Weird . . . it had grown by twenty bucks. When you were as poor as us, you knew right down to the last nickel how much money you had on you at any given time.

"I wike you bettuh without your gwasses on anyway," Mikey declared. "You wook even pwettiuh."

I smiled and hustled us into the store. "Thanks, hon. But don't get too used to it—I'm buyin' another pair today."

Mikey relayed his objections as I pushed through the aisles, grabbing the staples we needed: bread, peanut butter, orange juice, all got tossed into the cart out of habit. But once we hit the cereal aisle, his argument switched from my glasses to a battle over brands. In the end, I caved to the cocoa-flavored puffs with the silly cartoon characters. After all . . . I had a few extra bucks today, so we could afford to splurge on an extra box with a prize inside. After adding tomato sauce and spaghetti noodles for Italian night, I headed to the optometry department to buy another pair of prescription-free glasses. I planned to carry on the charade Mama had insisted on "for my protection," realizing these past couple of weeks, she might not have died in a state of paranoia after all.

"No, no, no, Kadee!" Mikey started up again with his petition against glasses. "I don't weawly wike you as good with your gwasses on." He patted my face to take the sting out. "But I stiwl wuv you."

I sighed. "Fine. You win . . . *again.*" We were running short on time anyway, and I was starving. "Let's get outta here and grab some ice cream."

"Yay!" He threw his arms around my neck, and I smiled, accepting the loss with good grace. It seemed to take an inordinate amount of energy to go against young Mikey—energy I didn't have today.

Next to the checkout line was a display of end-of-season sunglasses on sale, among the miscellaneous nonessentials used to entice bored customers. I'd always been instructed to stick to my list, but today it seemed serendipitous for them to be right in front of my nose like candy when I had an extra twenty in my pocket. So I tried on a few, peering at myself in the miniscule mirror then checking back with Mr. Opinionated. After giggling together over the more outrageous ones, we finally narrowed it down. In the end, the cat-eye tortoise-shell we both liked knocked out the knock-off Ray-Bans.

Pretty soon me and my new sunglasses were rolling a full shopping cart and a chirpy four-year-old to the Hatchback, where I unloaded groceries under his supervision. On the way to pick up Andrew, we swung into a drive-in burger joint for some ice cream.

"We should buy one for Pete!" Mikey suggested.

"What a great idea," I said, wondering what it would feel like to *not* have to worry about money for a change, while I dug some of that out of the ashtray. "What kind do you think he'd like?" I thought over the foods I'd seen him eat. Somehow, I got the impression he would frown on imitation ice cream.

Mikey debated a moment. "Probly choc'late like me."

"Hmm. I was thinkin' vanilla," I teased.

"How 'bout a choc'late and banilla swirl?"

I laughed and ordered three chocolate and vanilla swirls, leaving myself out because I didn't have quite enough money for four. An overly friendly boy with splotchy skin brought out the cones in a tray. As soon as he handed them over, I backed out feeling bad because I'd cut him off—I never seemed to have enough time or money.

"Stop!" Mikey screamed in the panicked voice usually reserved for parents who accidently forgot to pick up their kid from school. "They forgot one!"

"No they didn't," I soothed. "I'm not really hungry today." A stomach growl at that precise moment contradicted me.

"Kadee, guess what?"

"You're crazy and I'm not?"

Mikey laughed his head off like that was the funniest joke ever told. "No!" He shook his head at me. "I've never *not* been hungwy for ice cweam before . . . *that's* cwazy!"

We rolled up laughing into the empty parking lot to see Pete and Andrew peering intently under the hood of the Hummer. I rolled my eyes. *Must be a Y-chromosome thing.* My theory was proven correct when Mikey let out a whoop of excitement like there was a pop-up circus camped out there.

"I wanna see! I wanna see!" He almost fell out the door in his hurry to scramble out.

I relieved Mikey of the decimated remains of his cone and began wiping off his sticky hands, but he was harder to hold on to than a greased pig. Finally, I just gave up and let him go. He went squealing straight to Pete, who didn't miss a beat—he scooped him up and tossed him in the air. After catching him, he held on to him to show him the fascinating engine. The infectious giggles I loved to hear spread quickly to Pete and Andrew like the laughing fairy had paid them a visit. Pete found my eyes, his smile turning into a grin.

Mine turned wistful. A sensation like a long-held wish—one that I didn't even realize I'd been harboring—was being fulfilled. It was a purely good feeling that seeped into every nook and cranny of my being. Seeing Pete and the boys like this: with easy, natural smiles on their faces. Like— *Poof!*—everything was exactly as it should be.

Pete looked over at me standing with dripping cones in my hands and set Mikey down to head my way. As he closed the distance between us, the feeling only intensified until it became a burning sensation in my chest. *This is it. Exactly what I want in life.* Laid out before me on this asphalt parking lot. Seeing it up-close-in-person made it so tangible I could almost taste it.

Like it would be as easy as reaching out to lick one of the creamy cones in my hands. I wanted it so much it hurt my soul. The want hardened into a need. I was afraid to so much as blink in case I disturbed the sensation.

Pete looked at me quizzically. "Need a hand?"

I was pretty sure my inappropriate feelings were written all over my face so was grateful to my new sunglasses for shading the windows to my soul. "Um," I snapped out of it to hand him a cone, "this is for you." I smiled ruefully. "At least pretend—Mikey insisted."

Pete grinned before taking a long lick of melting ice cream. "Mmmm. Chocolate and vanilla mixed is my favorite!" he said loudly enough to catch the ears of Mikey, who beamed as proudly as if he'd scooped it himself.

"I tole you, Kadee!" he crowed. "It was *my* idea Pete! . . . But Kadee paid for it," he confessed.

"Well, that was really nice of both of you," Pete said. We strolled together to the Hummer, where I handed Andrew the last cone.

"No sittin' inside until you're all finished, okay?"

"Duh," Andrew retorted.

"Hey!" I grabbed his arm. "Lose the 'tude, dude."

"OK. *Okay?*" He snatched his arm away.

My forehead and mouth formed parallel lines. Andrew had always been a bit precocious, but lately that was bordering on disrespect, and my feelings were hurt. *Doesn't he appreciate how hard I've been fighting for him?*

"Hey, man," Pete intervened pleasantly. "That was pretty cool of your sister and brother to bring you ice cream, don't you think?"

Andrew's ears pinkened. "Yeah."

"Yeah's not going to cut it at The Academy, Andy," Pete reprimanded lightly. "I know you've been taught good manners because I've spent time with you. It's part of what sets you apart—in a good way. And I expect more than just common courtesy for your sister. Do you understand?" Pete looked down on Andrew with a little more intensity now.

Andrew's Adam's apple bobbed. "Yes, sir," he croaked then his eyes found mine. "I'm sorry, Katie. Thanks for the ice cream."

I smiled warmly and gave him a hug, despite the fact I could tell he didn't want me to. "That's okay, Drews—it's already forgotten."

"Hey!" Andrew simultaneously broke from the awkwardness and my grasp. "Can we please take a ride in the Hummer today? You said we could, remember?"

"It's okay with me," I agreed, "but you have to ask the owner of the Hummer first."

Andrew's face brightened. "Can we, Pete? I mean may we please take a ride in your Hummer?"

"Yeah, I mean yes, sir. Can we pwease take a ride in the Hummer?" seconded Mikey, who was in the midst of his rendition of an irresistible face.

Pete laughed and reached down to hoist Mikey back up. "You can save the hard sell for another time, bud. I said I would. And we'll do it—just as soon as your sister helps me finish my ice cream." His smile scorched me, and I felt warm in places I oughtn't to feel warm in the presence of my brothers.

"Nice lens, by the way," Pete commented, throwing his free arm over my shoulder. We leaned against his truck trading licks of creamy sweetness. And I swear: I got the strongest sensation he was as happy in that moment as I was.

20

GOOD FEELING GONE

The ride around the parking lot, turned into a ride around the block, which turned into a ride around the town. By the time we circled back, it was way past time to go home. So we skedaddled back, driving through a fiery sun melting into the endless highway. A pleasant hum escaped my lips as I replayed the—ahem—*pleasant* afternoon I'd spent with Pete. I did this while simultaneously listening to the boys' rendition of their afternoon. The instant replay and laughter indicated the extent to which everyone had a good time.

Felt really good to have a good time, yunno? I couldn't remember the last time I'd felt . . . dare I say it—*happy*.

I stopped off at Mrs. Hildebrand's for milk and then at the mailbox, still halfway dreaming about the very dreamy Peter Davenport. While sorting through the mail, my fingers came across a familiar envelope. My humming ceased like someone clamped a hand over my mouth.

Good feeling gone.

I easily extracted it from the rest of the junk mail, because it stood out like Cadet Davenport did from the rest of the high school students—glossy and of much higher quality. The parcel even managed to arrive from two states away to land in this dilapidated mailbox without a smudge, dent, or crease. It positively reeked of money and prestige. I hated it immediately.

Was it simply the green-eyed monster in me creating these ill feelings?

I immediately dismissed the idea. No, it ran much deeper than that. It was an evil feeling that overcame me every time I thought of that academy.

The visceral feeling only intensified the closer I was in proximity to the paperwork. *Why is that?*

I'd been on autopilot, so completely forgot about the fact that Daddy wanted me to let him get the mail from now on. *But do I want to let him get his hands on it?* I debated how much trouble I would be in. Heaps.

Andrew leaned forward. "Is that The Academy paperwork?"

"Yup," I replied, shuffling it back in with the other mail.

"Awesome! Pete's been askin' me if we received it yet. He said if not, then he could just print him a copy or have Daddy sign right on his computer and shoot it back to The Academy right away."

"How helpful of him." I noticed he referred to that . . . *place* using the same language as Pete now.

"That's his *job*, Kate," Andrew pointed out.

"Right." And to keep me out of the loop. I thought back to our encounters and realized that he'd mostly avoided talking about his academy with me at all. *Impressive Cadet Davenport.* I mentally kicked myself for my lost opportunity this afternoon. What had happened to my fact-finding mission? I'd been too busy having fun to bother asking questions.

How remiss of me. Or how clever of him.

I hissed out some self-loathing. I was letting Mama down. This was the exact scenario she was afraid of. And I was doing nothing more than sitting back and watching it unfold right before my very eyes. Too wrapped up in a romantic interlude with one of their cadets to actually fight against them taking over my family like a nest of hornets feasting on honeycomb.

"Can I see it?" Andrew asked with the reverence one used for a rare artifact.

I thought of those metal detectors and that bogus excuse of using them for Indian arrowheads. They thought I was stupid. I thought of Pete saying the mission would be like "taking candy from a baby." They thought I was easy. A burn started in my stomach. I thought of my wanton behavior in the park . . . They thought I was a country bimbo. The burn worked its way up to my chest.

I didn't hesitate further. "Here ya go, Drews." I tossed the envelope behind me. "Knock yourself out."

"Yeah!" He actually fist-pumped before tearing into it like a birthday present.

Daddy would be furious he opened it without his permission, but Andrew would most likely not be punished as severely as me for disobeying his orders. I decided it was worth the risk to see what was inside. Knowledge was power, and I got the distinct feeling I was being left in the Dark Ages.

"Anything interestin' in there?" I asked.

"Ah . . . yeah." Andrew was already perusing the materials inside, oblivious to all else.

"Wemember, you gotta say yes, sir," Mikey corrected.

Nobody responded to that, and we drove the rest of the way in silence. As soon as I cut the engine, Blue jumped on my window, his barks and whines as impatient as my curiosity. I was about eaten up with it, so I turned around to stare at my brother's face as he silently read. The mental wheels were turning feverishly in his mind.

"*Well?*"

"Um." Andrew's eyes found mine. "What's a stipend?"

My heart speeded up. "Why do you ask?"

"Because we're gettin' one in the sum of . . ."—he unfolded a blue check that dropped from the envelope—"two thousand dollars." Andrew's brows knitted together. "Why are they giving *us* money? Shouldn't it be the other way around?"

Mikey whooped, thrashing his feet against the seat. "Two thousand dollars! We're wich!"

I snatched the check from Andrew's hand. "Lemme see that!" My eyes quickly scanned down. Under *for*: endowment was written in elegant script. *Endowment?* Well I guess they couldn't exactly put down bribe. I dropped the dang thing like it was hot. Seemed like it was messengered straight from hell. *What could this possibly mean for our family?* And then the burning question came: *Had Pete, our IEA ambassador, put them up to it?*

I felt an unpleasant jolt. It made sense. He knew things were tight for us, and that I was less than enthusiastic about the prospect of my brother joining their ranks. *Does he think greasing the wheels would get us moving faster to the finish line?* After all, I distinctly remember him saying that if Ranger hadn't of ruined everything then he would've been out of here in a week or two—tops.

I ground my teeth together. If he did, that was a huge miscalculation on his part. The only silver lining was that Daddy absolutely loathed rich people throwing money around to get their way. Hopefully, their plan to buy us off would backfire. This could be just the thing I needed to swing the pendulum back my way.

"Kadee? What's wong?" Mikey wondered. "You wook mad."

Andrew grunted and smacked the backseat with the back of his head. "Of course, she's mad—something good's happenin' to me, and she can't stand it!" He finally vented out the way I already suspected he felt.

But still. His words hit me like a whap from a tree branch you'd always counted on to provide you shade. Tears sprang to my eyes. "Is that really what you think, Drews?" Andrew shrugged his shoulders, refusing to meet my eyes. The brimming tears spilled over.

"No he doesn't!" Mikey yelled at me, and then his brother as if the force of his words could force a change of heart. "No you don't!"

Blue was clawing at the driver's door now, adding scratches to the already pockmarked door. I sighed and shouldered my way out to greet our neglected pet. After letting him lick the salt from my face, I opened the door for Mikey and caught him right in the middle of commanding big brother to tell me it wasn't true. I stared long and hard at Andrew.

"I'm sorry, Katie. I didn't really mean it," Andrew said with zero conviction.

"I toldja he didn't mean it!" Mikey repeated.

My gut disagreed, but I gave Andrew a ghost of a smile.

"It's just . . . you're so negative about everything Academy. All the time," Andrew said, slamming the door. "You haven't even given it a chance."

I unnecessarily lifted Mikey out of his car seat just for an excuse to extract some comfort from him. A kiss to his sweaty forehead and I set him down with his Spidey backpack, ignoring Andrew's comment. "Okay boys . . . y'all go change clothes while I haul in the groceries." I headed in with three giant plastic bracelets looped on one arm and my gym bag and backpack on the other.

"Here, I'll take one." Andrew relieved me of one of the bags, evening me out.

That was a first—him offering to help. Must be his idea of an apology. I decided to take it and even managed to lift my lips. Andrew grinned back at me. "Last one in is a rotten egg!" he hollered, before taking off with his shadow and me close at his heels. We arrived at the porch, laden with bags and leaning together laughing. I unlocked the double-bolted door. Then the trio of Connelly kids walked into our empty trailer together.

I suddenly wondered: *How many more times would we get to do that?*

We finished our chores in record time, and the boys were busy hammering out their homework while demolishing a bowl of popcorn. I'd come to the conclusion that Daddy would definitely punish us both for "meddling in his business." Technically, he was right—the envelope *was* addressed solely to him. But Mama made him swear on heaven and earth to let me be involved in all major decisions regarding the boys.

I'd taken it to heart so had been signing permission slips and going to parent-teacher conferences ever since Mama died. Daddy was only too happy to leave the heavy lifting to me, even deferring to my judgment in matters of health and discipline. It appeared Daddy had a recent change of heart. Since it was against his direct orders to retrieve the mail, and since it contained a loaded check in his name, some quick damage control was in order.

I picked up the two halves of the torn envelope—beyond repair. Switching envelopes with the one stashed in the cupboard was the way to go. So I boiled some water, hauled the step stool over, and fished around inside the flour jar. As soon as I pulled it out, an overpowering, ominous feeling closed my throat. I almost lost my balance and definitely lost my equilibrium. *What the heck is going on?* I'd gotten bad feelings about things before, but the only time it was ever this bad was when Mama first told us she was sick.

I drew in a deep, shaky breath. I didn't want to go through this alone. *But who could I tell?* Not Daddy. Zero tolerance. *And what would I say after all? I have a bad feeling this elite organization is evil.* I'd sound like I just escaped from Arkham Asylum. *Where was my evidence?*

Sides, the only person I really wanted to unburden myself to just so happened to be the messenger of the nefarious object in hand. No choice—I had to go at it alone. *Ugh!* My stomach roiled. The contents of this envelope gave me a feeling most dreadful, like nails-on-a-coffin. Whatever it was . . . was something that needed to be seen about.

Before I could change my mind, I held the envelope over the steamy vapor to loosen the gummy seal. After a couple of minutes of my poor-man's-facial, I turned off the burner and retrieved our sharpest knife from the drawer. Sliding the blade under the seal, I slowly worked the edge of the envelope up, removed the neatly folded contents, and replaced it with the check and letter we received today. Then rifled through the junk drawer for an old glue stick to reseal it.

After letting the boys know I was pulling the ole switcheroo, I left, feeling slightly like the bad influence Daddy accused me of for modeling deceitful behavior. While heading back home, through a foggy trail of my own dust, I debated about whether or not my gut was still a reliable source. *Maybe Pete's animal magnetism was running roughshod over my sixth sense?* It's just—he felt so good, and smelled so good, and looked so kill-me-good. When I was with him, I felt like a million bucks. I thought of the two-thousand dollar check, and the memory of his convo with Ranger pierced my brain. . . . *Acted* good—he was faking.

After sputtering to a stop, I drew in a measured breath then unfolded the original, pilfered flour-pot paperwork to reveal an embossed seal bearing the omnipresent roaring lion's head. The sick feeling overtook me again. *Here goes nothing . . .* With shaking hands, I read the standard formal greeting, skimmed over their bull-hockey mission statement, turned the page . . .

Hmmmm. Evidently, this was the second attempt to get a signature from Daddy regarding a . . . I continued speed-reading, hyper-focused and hardly believing my eyes. This document required a guardian signature to *relinquish parental responsibilities for the duration of your dependent's enrollment at the International Elite Academy.* It was referred to as an RPA form—*Relinquishing of Parental Authority.* In exchange, that entitled said "dependent" to be the beneficiary of the enormous tuition being paid in full, free room and board, school uniforms, food, and "any and all expenditures for the duration of his or her time at The Academy."

What?!

The letter went on in some detail that included a bunch of legal jargon and instructions for beginning the process. I didn't need to go on. *Relinquish parental authority? Who would do such a thing?* Could not believe Daddy was even entertaining the idea. *Is he?* At least he hadn't signed anything yet. That offered some small measure of relief. Not enough. I had to talk to him about this—talk him out of it! But how could I without revealing I'd been meddling? He'd hit the roof and shut me down even further. Turning your child over to strangers? That was just plain crazy! Mama would be rolling around her grave in agony.

Maybe that feeling is her scraping at her coffin? I shivered.

And to think, I'd been cavorting around with one of them. Willingly. *God help me!*

I clutched the gold cross hanging from my throat—a gift from Mama before she died. My talisman. I needed help to defend us against the relentless invaders that sought to destroy our family.

Things were slowly clicking into place in my mind. I was concentrated, my mind condensing facts and squeezing out inconsequentials—like how incredibly appealing I found Cadet Davenport.

Fact 1: They were after my gifted brother and wanted to do with him what they wanted, without interference from his family.

Fact 2: They were bribing Daddy with enticements—everything from free tuition and expensive scotch to cleverly worded bribery checks

Fact 3: They sent Pete Davenport here not just to "mentor" my brother, but also to razzle-dazzle us into signing his life away.

Fact 4: Their plan was no longer working on me.

21

WOLF IN CASHMERE CLOTHING

The next morning I woke up exhausted, with a pounding headache, and in desperate need of some proof this *elite* academy was up to no good. My first instinct was to throw caution to the wind and inform Daddy about what I knew. But I'd seen the pleased look on his face when he opened the envelope to discover a fat check inside. He'd looked around furtively before slipping it into his wallet. Obviously intended to cash the dang thing. I was shocked, but I knew that confronting him with the fact that I knew what was warming in his back pocket would only backfire, leaving me with even less power points than I already had. Could never thwart his authority without payback.

One time, Daddy got really serious by threatening to send Mikey away to "juvy hall" when he came of age. Then, just to prove his point, he had proceeded to buzz Mikey's hair bald. Now every single time Daddy put clippers to his head, was a reminder of what was in store for him "if he got out of line."

If Daddy was seriously considering selling out his favorite son, then who knew what more he was capable of for the children he cared for less.

I reevaluated the risks of everything I was doing now that was against his rules: wearing jeans to school and hanging out with the mentor I wasn't supposed to be speaking to. Since I was better off keeping my enemies close (and my father never seemed to be around to check up on me), I decided that was worth the risk. So as much as I wanted to punch Cadet Davenport right in his perfect face, I had no choice but to pretend everything was still peachy between us, like the besotted girl still falling for his charms.

Trying to keep a hard heart toward someone whose presence warmed you to the core, and whose smile took your breath away, was a lot easier said than done. For as soon as Pete's radiant presence showed up in the library this morning, I already started to doubt my theory that he was a wolf in sheep's clothing.

He sauntered in, with his tousled hair and come-hither smile, and I wanted nothing more than to run—not walk—to him and bask in his golden presence. Then wile away the day in conversation to discover every little detail about him—from where he was born to what kind of shampoo he used—instead of finding out whether or not he knew about the RPA letter, and if he was here to pull the cashmere wool over my eyes.

He gave me the once over and a wicked grin, like we were about to run off and play hooky together. I returned with a coy little finger wave. I'd be darned if I was gonna slobber all over him like the other girls. *But Gah!* It was like fighting off a mad urge to scratch: nearly impossible unless you knew scratching would do more harm than good, like spreading poison ivy all over your body.

It made it worse that he was completely oblivious that I was onto him, so he thought we were taking up right where we left off in the parking lot.

"Well, well, well . . . if it isn't little Miss Librarian," he drawled, leaning one shoulder against the lacquered bookshelves. His flirting should have seemed like a misstep to me—not the case.

I was standing on another stepstool in another pair of generic jeans, re-shelving books, and feeling exactly opposite from yesterday in my kitchen with the IEA paperwork in my hands. Like a ray of sunshine, warmth seemed to radiate from him towards me. I actually had to fight the urge to lean over and inhale him. Maddening!

Pete's eyes held their devilish gleam. "You know . . . you might single-handedly be responsible for reversing the stodgy reputation of librarians everywhere." He spoke out one side of his mouth in that charming way he had that drove me crazy. "Seeing you in your element might even make me start missing your glasses a smidge."

"Well I hate to disappoint you," I replied tartly, "but they might not make a return appearance."

"My offer to replace them still stands. After all . . ."—he peered up at me, one eye closed—"it was my fault."

A couple of different kinds of heat flooded through me at the reminder. "No thank you." I met his eyes. And stared a beat too long. "I don't really need them to see clearly now."

The flirtatious smile remained, but levity was no longer at the forefront of his tone. "All of a sudden you don't need glasses anymore?" Finger snap. "Just like that." He said this in the way that prosecutors do when they know their witness is lying on the witness stand . . . and are about to go in for the kill.

I was already exhausted and stressed, not to mention ticked at myself for having fallen into his pretty trap. So I did my own kind of snap: "Not that it's *any* of your business, but my eyesight doesn't happen to be that bad . . . 'sides, I was thinkin' of gettin' contacts anyway."

Pete tilted his head, gave me a cock-eyed grin. "I see someone woke up on the wrong side of the bed this morning. Didn't get enough sleep again last night?" He reached over to touch my face.

"Do you mind?" I batted his hand away. "I'm tryin' to work here."

"Don't mind at all," he drawled, brazenly staring at my butt, which was all up in his face.

I stumbled down the stepstool, foregoing the hand offer. I saw a flicker of hurt? irritation? in his eyes before he quickly manufactured more humor. "Did you know that your accent gets more pronounced the madder you get?"

"Did you know *your* accent gets more pronounced the more *arrogant* you get?" I clapped back.

"But my accent isn't as cute as yours," he said, and I glared at him. He began chuckling. "You're doing your little teapot impression again." He was referring to the hand I just set on my hip.

Who am I kidding? I would never make it as an actress. The smart play was to continue playing dumb. But I'd grown weary of it . . . and everything else. "Pete, what are you doin' here?"

Something flickered in his eyes again but didn't stay long enough to register. "Can't a pal come visit his buddy without needing a reason?" He tried again with the banter, but it splatted against my stone face.

I narrowed my eyes at him, waiting. I swear I saw the same levers and pulleys turning over in his mind as in Andrew's. The thought did nothing to improve my mood.

Pete let out a sigh. "Okay, fine. Since the pleasure part of our interlude is clearly over, I guess it's down to business—I came to let you know your father's going to pick up Andy today."

How did he know this, and I did not?

"Hey, don't shoot the messenger." Pete threw a hand up to block my death rays. "I figured this was bad news for everyone all around."

"No," I corrected. "What are you doin' standin' here in this library? In Clovis, New Mexico? And don't say the words mentorin' program because I don't buy it. Andrew was accepted to many boardin' schools, and nary a one came with a mentorin' program attached. You and I both know that a rich school like yours could've easily just flown Andrew out to administer all these tests in California. Or y'all could've used an independent testin' firm like all the rest."

"We're not like all the rest," he countered.

"Maybe that's what scares me so bad."

Irritation momentarily pursed his lips. After a deep breath in, he tried again. "Kate, there *is* an Academy Mentoring Program. It even has an acronym—AMP." I snorted at that one. "That *is* why I'm here. As cadets we can be pretty isolated at The Academy, so during senior year, the organization annually sends graduating cadets out to live amongst civilians and mentor a prospective cadet. It's been part of our tradition for many years."

I feigned a yawn to let him know I was bored. And to piss him off. The deepening hue across his cheekbones let me know it was working.

"The reason you haven't heard about us is because we're a *very* private, *very* exclusive organization," Pete droned on as though nothing were amiss while I continued to give him the glaze eyes. "Therefore, only share info on a need-to-know basis. Since your brother is being considered, you are one of the few in the know. Most of America—and the world—will never even hear the words International Elite Academy."

He was telling the truth, but I knew buried beneath that were stinky factoid nuggets about them he didn't want me to nose out. "Why do I always get the feelin' that you're hidin' somethin'?"

"Because you're paranoid."

I shot him a look darker than the navy of his tee.

"Look," he sighed, "you've been through a lot lately, and I'm not just talking about this past week. I really only have the best intentions." As if on command, his face softened, then his voice. "I know you're having a hard time coming to terms with your brother leaving."

"I'm not having a hard time comin' to terms with it . . . because *he's not leavin'!*" The volume of my voice rose in direct proportion to his decrease. "And I *know* there's more to it—I can just *feel* it!"

"Well I'm sorry to disappoint you, Kate, but you're wrong."

"*You're* wrong!" I threw back at him.

Pete puffed out some aggravation, swiped a hand over his mouth. "Look, I did actually come here for a purpose, and it wasn't to argue with you."

"You've already lobbed your little grenade, so you can march along now, Cadet Davenport."

"There's more bad news I'm afraid . . ."

"Is there any other kind?"

Pete gave me a strange, sad smile.

"Just tell me," I sighed.

"Your father informed me I wasn't supposed to share test scores with you. Or to discuss the mentoring sessions . . . or anything to do with The Academy in general." His words came as soft as his eyes now, but the impact hit like exploding shrapnel. "He wants to be the only one privy to Andy's info. That's why your father is picking him up this afternoon—we have the preliminary test results ready to go over. I'm sorry . . . I know this comes as a shock to you."

My face fell, right along with the last of my power points—right on the industrial carpet. Mortally wounded, I plunked down on the stepstool and buried my face in my hands.

"I'm really sorry, Kate—"

I felt a hand on my shoulder and quit feeling sorry for myself long enough to shrug it off.

"—I didn't want to mention it before, knowing it was a touchy subject, but your father told me about your mother. How she died in a state of paranoia. It all makes sense now . . . this-this obsession with The Academy being some kind of ruthless organization out to get you. That's just ridiculous. It's considered by every outside authority to be the most prestigious academic and military institution in the world."

Pete stooped down and softly touched my arm. "Your mother put that in your head," he whispered. "But she was sick, Kate . . . your father told me. You're a smart girl. I know you'll come to your senses and realize that soon.

In the meantime, I agree with your father. It's probably best if you take a step back—allow Andy to take advantage of this golden opportunity being offered to him." He sounded like a freaking psychoanalyst one minute, and an IEA robot regurgitating bullet points from the brochure the next.

Who is he?

My head snapped up. "Andrew, or just Drew, if you must."

"What?"

My feet stomped floor, anger rising up through the shock. "He *hates* the name Andy, FYI." Of all the things I could say in that moment, I don't know why I chose that.

"He never told me that."

"Well, he does."

Pete expelled some air. "Kate, I can see this conversation is going nowhere good. I highly suggest you go home and rest. You're overwrought and not thinking clearly. Sleep deprivation makes even the sanest of people irrational—it's even been known to cause hallucinations."

"*Really?*" I said, a switch inside me flipping on. "Am I hallucinating *you*? . . . You have always *seemed* too good to be true. How about when you and Terminator popped up in the middle of the night—on a deserted street—to kidnap me? Did I hallucinate that, too?"

"You mean when we rescued you from a pit bull and a pedophile?" he countered. "We've already gone over that."

"Oh right." I curled angry finger-quotes. "'The big coincidence.'"

Pete cupped my shoulders, using the full force of his male magnetism. "Kate, you're understandably angry right now. I get that. But we can agree to disagree for the time being, can't we?" He began rubbing circles like he was trying to thaw me out (or to work his magic into my arms). But boy was I feeling both Arctic cold and immune to his charms at the moment.

"This in no way changes the status of our friendship—at least in my book." Pete must've taken my silence for assent, because he pulled me to him. (I took that for him being an arrogant ass.) "I'm afraid our afternoon of fun is spoiled for the time being though," he said, using the kind of voice one would when he had a deep, underlying assumption of always getting his own way.

"Where's Daddy pickin' Andrew up today?"

He seemed puzzled by my innocuous, out-of-left-field question, but also, like, relieved I wasn't pitching a fit. "From The Learning Center, why?"

The bell rang at the same time I said, "No reason."

He tightened me into a hug that I allowed. *One more time.* I gave myself exactly a second. One single second to relive the fantasy, to breathe him in, to bask in his glow, feel the male perfection of his body.

"You'll see . . . it'll all work out for the best." He smoothed down my hair as if the strands were frayed nerves curling up at the ends.

I broke free from his arms. And his charms.

"What d'yasay, Kate?—still BFFs?" He raised his palm up, so sure of himself. I could almost see his tantalizing smile, even though I was staring beyond his shoulder—at my future without him. Funny how things can turn on a dime. I learned that little lesson early on, the day Mama came and yanked me out of school.

Yesterday, I recalled being so desperate to keep him in in my life—even if it was *just* as friends—that I was willing to overlook the fact he was playing for the other team. Yesterday, I would've laughed and went ahead and slapped him five, allowed him to throw his arm around me, and razzle-dazzle me all the way to class. Yesterday, I was happy to pretend he wasn't pretending.

Today was a different day.

I looked at Pete with steely eyes. "With friends like you . . . who needs enemies?" That said, I walked away.

But I may have been the only girl in history to ever leave him hanging.

22

![decorative divider]

LIAR, LIAR, PANTS-ON-FIRE

I fled down the hallway, ignoring the rubbernecking stares aimed at my back. Ashley-Leigh stopped mid talk-n-walk to gape, then began frantically waving me over, but I just whipped on by her like *she* was a hallucination. So the Queen-B buzzed over to attack me outside Pre Cal.

"Ohmigod! Katie, what just *happened?*" Not even attempting to cover the thrill in her voice.

I spun around, eyes flashing from her bug-eyes to where Pete was being enthusiastically comforted by some senior girls down the hallway. "You know what, Ash? You want him? . . . He's all yours!"

"I don't really think he's yours to give away," she smirked.

Pushing past her into the classroom, I hurled down my backpack, slunk into my seat, and immediately thunked my head on my desk to block out the stares. I focused on hatching a Hail Mary plan to salvage my credibility with Andrew and bring some proof to Daddy—before I was shut out further. For all intents and purposes, I'd been Andrew's mother for the last couple of years. *Where has Daddy been? Nowhere that's where.* And there'd never been a Cadet Davenport before, nor would there be again after Andrew was signed. He would disappear from our lives like he really *was* a hallucination. *Did no one but me realize this?*

Inexplicably, I felt betrayed Pete was in cahoots with my father. My face burned with the memory of the kiss in the park, the easy afternoon with the boys trading licks of an ice cream. How silly of me to forget he was here on a "mission" to procure my gifted brother. I was simply a stumbling block along the way. Well, I was gonna morph into a friggin roadblock!—starting this afternoon. While they were busy poring over inconsequential test scores, I would have a little "chat" with Mrs. Woodward. In the meantime, I just had to avoid talking . . . to anyone.

Not exactly easy to do when the hungry patrons of CHS were trying to unearth juicy gossip. But I managed to dodge everyone's questions and even refused to speak to Miguel in English. He tossed me worried glances, but I pretended to be too absorbed in *Canterbury Tales* to catch them.

I was fairly sure Cadet Davenport wouldn't be stupid enough to be waiting for me today. Correctomundo. Could not *believe* the dull ache of letdown that constricted my chest. It was crazy how he could evoke such powerful feelings in me. Even though I knew he was playing me like a particularly accomplished violinist would a country fiddle. Guess the heart really *does want* what the heart wants, no matter how bad for it.

I knew I had to completely avoid him like the plague until my heart had sufficiently hardened, so I spent lunch in my fortress of solitude. There was a sweet, upbeat email from Reese waiting for me, asking about my "new crush." I hammered the computer keys, the words spilling out as I tried to make her understand why I had to fight for my brother. No matter how "golden" this opportunity seemed, I was taking a pass—on the school *and* the mentor. Then I went proactive in my efforts to distance myself from Pete by going to Spanish early to persuade Mr. Sanchez to switch my seat. My broken glasses were a great excuse, so after a two-minute chat, I found myself sitting up front near Miguel. As soon as he came in, he bumped me on the shoulder.

"Whuzzup, Katie-girl?"

I looked up, bleary-eyed from my ten-second nap. "'Sup."

He peered sideways at me. "What's wrong with you today? You've been actin' like somebody ran over your cat."

"Nope. Just my glasses."

"That's why you're so pissy?"

"You don't wanna know," I mumbled into my arm pillow.

"Try me."

"They're tryin' to buy Andrew." I didn't quite make it without my voice cracking.

Miguel leaned over and put an arm around me. "Oh man. That's so messed up. I'm sorry."

I sniffed a little. "'S'kay. Hopefully, I can persuade him to *not* wanna go. But so far *Cadet Davenport*"—acid dripped from my tongue—"has him convinced everyday will be like Disney Land over there. "Who cares if they've got Olympic-sized pools and field trips to The Eiffel Tower? I *know* it's not the right place for him, Miguel!"

"Really?" he marveled. "The Eiffel Tower?"

"Yup," I sniffed. "It's in the brochure along with a picture of a bunch of *phony* cadets wearing berets."

That garnered a derisive snort from Miguel. "Told you that Davenport dude was no good."

I gave him a watery smile. "Hold on to the I-told-you-so's for right now. I don't think I can take it."

"I'll save it for a rainy day," he joked. "Anything I can do in the meantime?"

"No thanks . . . I'll find a way around it somehow." I just realized Miguel's arm was still around me and sat up. And didn't need to turn around to know that *he'd* walked in. His presence crept up my spine a beat before Miguel threw him the ole stink-eye on my behalf.

Then a grating voice called out like she was the town crier: "Looks like Katie switched seats to be next to Miguel. Maybe I could sit here today?"

Without waiting for his response, Ashley-Leigh flounced up to Mr. Sanchez to work her magic. He made short work of shooting her down, sending her straight to her regular seat, where she proceeded to sulk like a two-year-old. For the duration of class, I was the poster girl for front-row-student, keeping my pencil moving and my eyes glued to Mr. Sanchez. The bell rang, and I lingered about my desk to give our newest student ample time to make his exit, but needn't have bothered because when I turned around, he was long gone.

Well good.

Miguel and I lumbered together out the door from Spanish and then again after Chemistry, where we parted ways with a brief hug. I noticed his girlfriend's wave back to me was a little half-hearted and realized I wasn't the only one thinking Miguel's affection for me was a little overboard.

I was half-dreading, half-looking forward to P.E., and a hundred percent disappointed in myself for still having half a mind about Pete. I quickly dressed out, deflecting knowing looks and personal questions left and right.

P.E. was over with almost as soon as it began. This was probably because my body was on autopilot while my mind worked overtime, twisting and turning, frantically searching for a way to prove my theory.

I was very proud of myself for not casting a single glance at the boys' side the entire duration . . . until about ten minutes before class let out. That's when I noticed a tall, solitary figure exit the field early. His lithe, athletic body and sure, easy stride held my gaze captive before I caught myself and ducked my head back to my neon feet. That's when I let out a hard kick that knocked the ball plumb into the goal post. The whistle blew.

"Well done, Katie!" yelled an approving Coach Sams. "Only wait till it's your turn next time."

I "yes ma'amed" her, then continued playing subpar soccer for the remainder of class. Afterwards, I hippety-hopped back to the locker room to grab my gym bag and backpack, not bothering to change clothes. Even though I didn't want to have a serious meeting with Mrs. Woodward in a sweaty top and cut-off bottoms, I was in a big hurry, I really was. Fear and helplessness—two feelings I loathed—were fueling me on. I bypassed incoming athletes on my way out, practically sprinting to my car.

The Hummer was conspicuously missing from the lot, and I started to get an uneasy feeling. Yanking the door open, I threw my bags in, slid the key into ignition, turned it—nothing. *Aw, heck fire! Did not need this today!* My hand slammed against the steering wheel before trying again. It gave the smallest of clicks. That's it though, the engine never turned over. I was stranded—another thing I hated (especially in light of recent events).

An idea was taking shape in my mind. And it took the form of a certain cadet. *Hmmm.* Cadet Davenport leaves class early and suddenly my car doesn't start? Maybe I *really* was starting to get paranoid. I mean he couldn't *know* what I was up to. *Right?* And my car had been giving me trouble for a while. Only made sense that it would break down eventually. Despite these plausible arguments, I still had a *very* strong suspicion that *he* had something to do with it. *A simple coincidence?* I thought of him saying them seeing me that night was a coincidence. Then I thought of Mama telling me there *was* no such a thing.

But she was a paranoid, right? Wrong.

That switch in me flipped again, shedding light on his shady deeds. *How dare he play so dirty!* I flung the door open and sprinted back across the parking lot to find Miguel. After hurriedly filling him in on my situation, he handed me the keys to his pickup without hesitation. Two minutes later, I was heading back out of the parking lot—now stuck behind a train of cars all trying to exit at once. *Arg*! My face flamed. Thank Goodness Miguel's truck had A.C.

Five excruciating minutes of waiting with the air turned on full blast, and I screeched into the street only to crawl through the school-zone. Then I booked it down the side roads, leaving tread marks leading straight to church. I picked up Mikey (by literally picking him up) and flung him into the truck before speeding away, driving way too fast for a low-rider I noted.

"Wow! I get to wide up fwunt . . . and without a boostuh!" Mikey was too enthralled to notice my mood.

We crawled through another school zone to Andrew's school, where I pulled a shrewdy by bypassing the carpool lane to turn into the faculty parking lot.

"Hey Kadee, Pete said to pick up Drewy from The Learwning Center today—you forgotted!" he accused.

"No, I didn't. Daddy's gonna pick him up today instead, so I decided to talk to Mrs. Woodward about . . . somethin' important."

Mikey shook his head. "Oh no! Drewy's gonna be so mad!"

His own fault for playing for the wrong team.

I hoisted a backpack-strapped Mikey out and ran up the steps to stab the buzzer. "Katherine Connelly to see Mrs. Woodward," I announced, trying to sound official and unwinded at the same time.

"Do you have an appointment?" The by-the-books voice asked.

"Uh . . . yes? . . . She's expectin' me," I added, lying better.

A long pause ensued. "Mrs. Woodward is presently busy, dear. You'll have to schedule an appointment for next week; she has bus duty this week . . . unless it's an emergency," she added doubtfully.

Dagnabbit! Should I wait her out? I looked over to where the buses were loading and couldn't see Mrs. Woodward directing traffic. A dour-looking teacher, with a hat so outdated you could only call it a bonnet, was standing around in the heat doing the job. So that meant Mrs. Woodward was still in her room. But refused to see me. Now how could I get in there without attracting the drama that typically comes with claiming an emergency? An emergency of a different kind.

I stabbed the buzzer again. "Excuse me, it's Katie Connelly again." I tried for more casual. "Would it be alright if my little brother uses the bathroom? It's kind of an emergency—he's still in preschool." I winked at Mikey's indignant face.

A resigned voice said to come in, followed by the loud pop of the lock being released.

"Just go with it, okay?" I whispered as we hustled to the counter. Mrs. Jackson, the guardian of the front office, peered down at us suspiciously from behind thick glasses. Her eyes appeared owl-like and wizened, and I wondered if that's how I looked all the time.

"'Scuse me, ma'am," Mikey hit his mark perfectly, "where's the bathroom?"

"Down the hall and to the right." She pointed us in the right direction before getting back to the serious business of running the front office.

"Thank you!" we chorused before rushing out like we were both dying to go. We tore down the hall, heading left, before skidding to a stop outside Mrs. Woodward's room. I was slapping my little coconspirator five, when I heard the soothing tone of his voice. *Oh no.* High-pitched laughter reverberated through the door. *Oh yes* . . . He'd got to her first. Felt like ripping the door right off the hinges. Instead, I did the customary knock thing so hard my knuckles were bound to turn black and blue. My staccato rapping must've signaled both my arrival and the mood I'd arrived in, because the musical tinkle in the room instantly muted to low murmuring.

A put-upon Mrs. Woodward poked her head through the door. "Why Kate Connelly!" She conspicuously exchanged a backward glance with the unfazed cadet. "Your ears must be burnin' . . . we were just talkin' about you!"

I bet. "Good afternoon, Mrs. Woodward. I hope I'm not interruptin' anything," I said, hoping the opposite. No actual response was forthcoming, just a lot of hemming and hawing, so I continued: "I need to speak with you, if I may, for a few minutes." She turned as if to ask his permission while I prayed I could keep my hands glued to my sides.

"It's fine, Mrs. Woodward," he said.

"Peggy, please—I insist."

He chuckled a little. *Big fat faker.* "Okay—Peggy. I was just leaving anyway. Duty calls."

"Oh." Her face drooped disappointment. "I guess come in then." This was directed at me like I was an IRS agent.

I remained resolutely polite. "Thank you."

"Pete!" Mikey hurled himself at him.

I grit my teeth as the cadet—formerly-known-as-Pete—swooped him up in his arms like nothing untoward had happened. *Now I wanted to rip his arms right off and beat him with them! How dare he hug us from the front while stabbing us in the back!*

Mrs. Woodward clasped her hands together. "Well, it certainly looks like y'all are still gettin' along!"

"Like a house on a fire," I said, manufacturing a cardboard smile.

His lips twitched, but I had nothing on my face but malice for him. The shady cadet shifted his eyes back to Mikey before setting him down. "I really should be going. Andy and Mr. Connelly will be waiting for me." He said this like he wasn't referencing two people directly related to me.

Steam must've been coming out my ears by now.

Mikey tugged on my arm. "Can we go to The Learwning Center today, too?"

"'fraid not, buddy."

"Nobody wants to take *me* anywhere," Mikey said dejectedly.

"That's not true!" The cadet and I chorused together.

I glared at him so hard a lesser man would've melted. "We'll go next week, hon. Right now, I need you to wait out in the hall while I speak to Andrew's teacher." I retrieved a Batman book from my backpack and cut off Mikey's protest with a meaningful look. "It's important."

Mikey snatched the book from my hand, still looking mutinous, until the cadet offered his hand to escort him out. I heard Mikey trying to work him over as they walked to the door. And then I heard the cadet say, "It's more than okay with *me*, bud, but you have to get your *sister's* permission, remember?"

Why do I always end up looking like the bad guy . . . when it's really him? Like a crawfish in the pot, I was really boiling now. Cadet Davenport shot me a look of concern, which only succeeded in shooting flames up my face. I clenched my jaw against the urge to scream at him.

He paused at the door. "Goodbye, er . . . Peggy. It was a pleasure talking to you as always." He acknowledged me with a curt nod. "Kate." Then he left with a smile that left Mrs. Woodward beaming at the open door.

I felt all the energy from my amped up anger fizzle. This meeting was likely pointless now. *Score another one for Team IEA.* But I had to try.

Mrs. Woodward faced me, a good portion of her glow fading along with her eager attitude. "What can I do for you, Katie?" She actually had the nerve to pull out a stack of graded papers and begin entering them into the computer.

"I, uh . . . wanted to ask a few questions about the tests Cadet Davenport has been givin' to Andrew after school."

"I'm sorry, dear. I've been instructed that you are no longer to be involved in meetings involving Andrew—academic or otherwise."

"Did *he* tell you that?" I practically snarled.

Mrs. Woodward sighed and stopped typing to face me from her rolly chair. I was still standing, because she hadn't bothered with the courtesy of offering me a seat. I'd now been relegated to the status of mere sibling, a meddling one at that.

"Listen, Katie. I do feel sympathetic. However, I've been informed you strongly oppose Andrew joining The International Elite Academy." She said this as though I opposed the Clean Air Act. "You are too young and immature to understand the long-lasting impact this will have on your brother's life."

Are you friggin' kidding me? It felt like someone just thrust a red-hot branding iron at my face, and I had to just take the heat without flinching.

"This is a once-in-a-lifetime chance for Andrew. The Academy will pave the way for a golden future for him the likes of which your family could only dream of." *Peggy* sounded like she'd drunk the Kool-Aid. "I understand you have been workin' against the greater good . . . for your own reasons. We believe these reasons are selfish in nature and are hinder—"

"*Selfish!*" I advanced forward. "*Who* said that?" Mrs. Woodward's hand flew to her chest in fright. I *did* probably look like someone who was about to stab her with her own scarlet grading-pen. "Who is *we?*"

"Cadet Davenport, your father, and I," she said in the tone reserved for putting one in their place.

Who are they?—the Holy Trinity of Andrew's life all of a sudden? None of them really cared about him like I did. To them, my brother was just another feather in their cap.

"Since when?" I demanded.

"Since now," Mrs. Woodward stated flatly. "Pete informed me of your father's decision this afternoon." Seeing the animosity come to life on my face, she took up for him at once. "Actually, he was really quite gracious about it, not wanting to get involved in a family quarrel. He also seemed sympathetic to you but also felt it was in Andrew's best interests if you remain out of it."

My face crumpled, and I collapsed in a mini chair.

Her face softened so that her better nature shone through for a moment. "I know this must be hard for you, Katie. You *have* done a good job with Andrew up until now. However, a prodigy needs more guidance in life than a teenage sister and an . . . absent father. Andrew has so much untapped potential. You don't want it to go to waste. That would be a travesty for him, for them . . . for the world!" she added dramatically. "You don't want to be the one to hold him back from the life he deserves."

She was waiting for me to see the light, or drink the Kool-Aid, or whatever. So far, I had refrained. Maybe it was time to take a sip? See how it tasted . . . at least outwardly. I fabricated a smile, took a breath, and tried out my acting chops. "Well then, I guess I should be thankin' you for hookin' Andrew up with such a prestigious and generous school," I said.

Mrs. Woodward stuttered and turned pink. "Good gracious! I wish I could accept the honor. To tell you the truth, we thought for a long time it was your *father* who did it. Come to his senses about Andrew needin' a special school. Then he came thunderin' up here that day." She actually shuddered from the memory. "Created quite a scene about it, sayin' he was completely against sendin' his son away to *any* boarding school and that we should mind our own business. A few months later, he came back in singin' a different tune. He informed us he'd had a change of heart and even had forms for us to fill out."

The disgust on my face must've registered because she quickly explained, "Feeling it was in Andrew's best interests, we immediately complied. Though we were quite sorry to think of him leaving us—he's been such a bright presence here at our school," she digressed, beaming like a proud mother hen.

Oh please. Like she had anything to do with it. I continued the effort of my Miss America smile. Amazing how much this woman wanted to talk all of a sudden.

"It was only later on when your father thanked us for helpin' his son find The International Elite Academy that we knew it wasn't him. We assumed one of the other boarding schools turned his application over to them. It was bound to stand out—a youngster with scores like that. To this day, it's *still* a mystery how Andrew ended up on their radar."

The look on my face changed to one of horror.

"Don't worry, dear," she hastened to reassure me. "We all care for Andrew as if he were our own. We would never have filled out the paperwork without doing our due diligence. We spent a couple of days researching what we could find about the school. And found out, it was, indeed, the 'World's Most Elite Military Academy.'" A lot of pride went into her smile.

I wanted to hurl.

"When we were completely satisfied of the legitimacy of the institution, we reached out to them to identify ourselves and our purpose, and we were put right through. They were super cooperative from the start. Sendin' us their very impressive brochures and their . . . even more impressive representatives." Mrs. Woodward colored at the memory, her garish blush turning an alarming shade of salmon. "We've been more than a little honored we have an IEA candidate right here in our hometown! Were you aware they only accept the top *one* percent of the top *one* percent *in the world*?" She said this as though it were tantamount to earning a golden ticket to heaven from Saint Peter himself. And then as if to prove my point she said, "A gift from an angel is what it is. This whole experience!"

All my self-control seemed to be leaching from my pores; I mopped some from my forehead with the back of my hand.

"A gift from your mother to take care of her gifted son properly," she went on, placing a hand on mine.

I wanted to slap the earnestness right off her face. It was a true testament to how much I didn't want them to get their claws into my brother that I didn't move a muscle in that moment. I reached for sincere gratitude. "I hadn't ever thought of it that way, Mrs. Woodward. I can see better what's really going on now . . . thank you."

She patted my hand. "No thanks necessary, dear. I'm just glad you're beginnin' to understand the importance of not standin' in the way of something so wonderful happenin' to your brother."

I removed her hand like I did one of the creepy crawlies the boys put in my palm. "Well, thank you anyway for sharin' your insight with me and for bein' such a great teacher to Andrew." I finished with a smile so fake I shoulda taken home the crown.

Now that she was convinced she had convinced me to see the light, she got up to come hug me. "You're so very welcome, Katie. He's lucky to have a sister like you; I want you to know that. It's simply time to hand the reins over to someone with more experience in dealing with his level of giftedness."

"Maybe you're right . . . thanks again for the talk. I better go and get started on my homework. I'll see you later, Mrs. Woodward."

As I was making my way back to the door, I noticed it was cracked open a fraction—a peephole for a peep-eye. Mikey was staring over at Mrs. Woodward like it was his mission not to break eye contact. When I approached, he hung his head like a naughty puppy. I smiled down at him, rubbing my palm across his bristle. How could I be mad when I would've done the same thing? I helped Mikey up, thinking, *she'd helped me see the light all right.* Unfortunately, I still didn't have any proof—yet. I whirled around.

"Oh, one more thing . . ." Mrs. Woodward looked up from her desk warily. "Did Cadet Davenport ever ask any questions about . . . " I faltered and turned red, "me? I-I mean our family, in general?"

She gave me a condescending smile. "No, dear. I'm afraid not. Just tutoring stuff—strictly professional. Cadet Davenport really is so good with him, a natural . . . it's been an absolute pleasure to watch!" The pink glow was back.

I'm sure it was a pleasure to watch. "Well, thanks again for everything," I called, practically running out the door with my little brother in tow.

I sped back to school, my mind twisting and spinning like a Tilt-a-Whirl. After dropping off Miguel's truck, I had the maddening task of borrowing the office phone to call Daddy. His cell just rang and rang as I ground and ground my molars together. Of course, he wouldn't break up his precious meeting with Cadet Davenport to pick up the *dadgum* phone for his stranded daughter and four-year-old son! I punched in the number for The Learning Center like I was jabbing eyes out of sockets. At last someone obligingly tracked down my father (only after I insisted it was, indeed, an emergency). About ninety-nine minutes (while the secretary pointedly looked at the clock) later, he finally came on the line.

"Katie, what on God's green earth could be so pressin' that you had to in'errupt my very important meetin' with Cadet Davenport?"

Instead of snapping back at him, I found myself with two uneven pieces of chewed-up pencil in my hands. "Sorry, Daddy, but my car wouldn't start this afternoon, so Mikey and I are stranded in the high school parkin' lot."

"If yer car wouldn't start, then how'd you come by Mikey?"

"Because I borrowed Miguel's truck to pick him up."

"Can't he just give you a ride home then? We're pretty busy right now with IEA business," he said importantly.

I gripped the phone so tightly those blue knuckles turned white. While inhaling some germ-infected phone-receiver air, I heard a smooth voice in the background say, "It's fine, Mr. Connelly . . . we're almost finished here."

I actually had to clamp a hand over my mouth to keep from screaming. I'm sure he thought he really *was* almost finished here . . . and would be headed back to Cali any day now. Triumphantly. With my gifted brother. Like a knight presenting a head on a platter before his king.

"He *can't* drive me home," I hissed. "He's at football practice. So can you *please* come and get us?" *Really? I had to beg?*

Daddy acquiesced, with poor humor, seeing as how he had no other option. In the meantime, I ran to the bathroom to put on my bell skirt. Then Mikey and I slurped some water from the fountain and headed out the door, splitting a bag of chips I'd bought from a vending machine.

After about twenty minutes of sweltering out in the sun and regretting my salty snack choice, my father pulled in. With an entourage. Following behind him, in a cloud of heavy exhaust, was none other than Cadet Davenport. I noticed there was now a respectable enough amount of dust coating his truck to peg him as a local . . . and that my little brother was riding shotgun. I wondered how often he'd had to visit the car wash to keep the dang thing looking so shiny then mentally kicked myself for wondering.

"Look, Kadee! It's Pete," Mikey pointed out. "No fayer that Drewy gets to wide in the Hummer twice!"

I squeezed his shoulder as they arrived, pulling one mammoth truck on each side of my puny little hatchback. My father walked to the back to gather the licorice-colored jumper cables from his toolbox, without even coming over to greet his stranded children. Rejection stung the back of my throat. I'd had a hard day—it would be nice to think that *someone* cared.

"Hi, Pete! Hey, Drewy!" Mikey charged his brother, who was jumping from the Hummer with a shite-eating grin on his face. "This is excitin'!"

"Hey, shorty," Andrew greeted shortly. "Hey, Katie, look who we brought." He theatrically stepped aside, the unsaid "ta-da!" written in a cartoon bubble above his head.

"Hey, yourself . . . So I see," I acknowledged Cadet Davenport, who took one look at me and my sorry situation and went to his truck to pull out two familiar dark water bottles. Wordlessly, he opened one and gave it to Mikey, who looked intrigued at the steam fizzing out.

"Is this sody pop?" Mikey wondered.

"'fraid not, pal . . . just good old fashioned H2O."

"What's that?"

Andrew answered, "Water, you dope."

"Oh. Thanks, Pete!" Mikey beamed up at him, one eye squinting in the sun. "It sure is hot out here!"

"You're welcome." His smile faded as he turned his impenetrable aviators my way.

I declined the tempting bottle, wanting nothing to do with him or that institution. *I would not be drinking the Kool-Aid today, thank-you-very-much.* Had half a mind to snatch Mikey's away from him . . . and smack Cadet Davenport upside the head with it.

He sighed, shook his head, and left the bottle next to my feet to go over and speak with my father about mechanical things, I presumed. Meanwhile, I tried hard not to think about how hot and thirsty I was. Watching him expertly grab tools from my father's toolbox really needled me. I snorted. *Who does he think he is—freakin' Jason Bourne?* So galling. Especially in light of the fact that *he* was the one who had created this mechanical high-jinx. A crazy idea to sign up for shop next year popped into my mind. I made good use of my time, standing under the glaring sun, to do that very thing to him, every chance I got. If he noticed, he didn't show it.

After a few, Cadet Do-Gooder came over. "Kate, would you mind popping the hood?"

Imagining it to be a trigger, I pulled the lever. He propped up the hood like a professional grease monkey, thereby blocking the nasty curl to my lip. Then the quartet of males peered under there like a team of surgeons about to perform a lobotomy on my poor abused car. That is until Mikey offered a suggestion, and Daddy batted his head away. Mikey ran back to my arms while Team IEA decided to try jump-starting the battery first.

Cadet Davenport did the honors, hooking up the matching cables to the appropriate nodules on the battery while Daddy rearranged his Bronco in front of my car. I snorted and crossed my arms. *Shoot—I could do that.* Cadet Davenport gave him the thumbs up, and Daddy fired up the Bronco.

"Okay, Kate, try to start it up now," he commanded.

I rolled my eyes but complied. Sure enough . . . bupkis. Not the battery then. I *knew* it—he'd messed with my car! I vowed to lock my doors from now on then decided that would be a wasted effort . . . he could just as easily have slipped a nail under my tire. After a minute of conferring, he informed my father he knew a little bit about cars. Evidently, "The Academy" required two semesters of mechanics for all cadets.

"Well, now. How 'bout that? Bet you won't get that kinda schoolin' at Harvard!" my father said to an equally enthusiastic Andrew.

I rolled my eyes as he continued with his razzle-dazzle routine. I can tell you one thing: with each clever joke and every tinker and turn of the wrench he made, my father and brother were buying up whatever Cadet Davenport was selling like it was a hot stock tip from Bill Gates himself. As he worked, he threw in a lot of "yes sirs" and male banter disguised as shoptalk. They were eating out of his greased-stained palms by the time the engine turned over and sputtered to life a quick handful of minutes later. Apparently, Pete-the-Elite-Cadet had single-handedly resuscitated my car from the dead. *Shocker.*

A chorus of "yeahs!" from the boys, and a back slap and reciprocal handshake from Cadet Davenport, and we were all good to go. He glanced my way, and I reciprocated with a car slam. Daddy drifted over to pow-wow with him, so I started up the car and rolled up the window against the BS, but unfortunately, my wall of glass couldn't muffle it.

"No thanks necessary, sir. I'm glad I could put my skills to use. They get pretty rusty without practice. But you may *not* want to wait any longer on that transmission though. It's about ready to go any day now. Since it's an older model, you'll most likely have to order parts. Could take a couple of weeks to get here . . . I'm surprised it's lasted this long." He met my father's eyes directly seeing as how they were about the same height. "I know you don't want your daughter, four-year-old, and future cadet to be out stranded on a highway somewhere."

Was that an edge I heard creep in? I saw my father's face blister and found the silver lining of the day: Cadet Davenport might've just shamed my father into buying me a new transmission.

"Oh sure," Daddy spluttered. "I was just waitin' to see whether to keep her or trade her in. You know . . . this was Katie's mama's car, so she ain't in no hurry for a new one."

If there were any justice in the world, my father's nose would be a couple of inches longer right about now. Turned to check—nope, no justice.

Daddy quickly threw the heat of the spotlight back on me. "Katie girl!" he yelled so aggressively you'd think I was encased in a bomb shelter. "You gonna thank Cadet Davenport for fixin' yer car for ya?"

I fiercely rolled down the window. "Of course, Daddy!" I said, giving them a smile so saccharine you'd have to be a fool not to know it was fake. I removed my sunglasses and turned to the poser in navy. "Thank you *so* much, Cadet Davenport for *all* the mechanical things you did to my car today! The *many* hidden talents you've acquired up at that fancy boardin' school sure are impressive! I just feel so blessed"—my eyes blazed—"to have someone like you lookin' out for our best interests."

The upward tilt to his lips straightened. "I *was* looking out for you, Kate." He also removed his own sunglasses, presumably so I could see the sincerity in his eyes. But I wasn't so easily sold. Boy, he was good though, he really was. He should head straight out for Hollywood right after his little "mission" here was over.

Daddy looked from the plastered smile on my face to the cadet's intense focus on me and rearranged some phlegm. "Well that *was* mighty nice of you, Cadet Davenport."

He tore his eyes away from mine to shake my father's hand again. "Pete, please. I'd better get going so I can finish filling out the reports from our meeting. And since you agreed to the terms we discussed today, I'll go ahead and submit them."

I could tell Cadet Davenport was trying hard to duck the particularly lethal glare I was shooting him because he slipped his shades back on. "Don't forget Andy still needs a physical. You can use a local doctor if you prefer for the preliminary screening. However, The Academy will need a more thorough examination done on premises. You may, of course, be present for that. That is one of the items still missing from your checklist. The final date for that is September 29. It's highlighted in the paperwork."

"Sure-sure, Pete. I'll get right on it." My father was being Mister Congenial now. I was worried—my father was *never* Mr. Congenial.

After another round of farewells from my backseat, I was finally headed home for my afternoon of chores. I tried prying some insider info out of Andrew, but he was especially tight-lipped today being on the inside of the circle. "Good" was about the only adjective I was getting. *Not very creative coming from a genius.* I could almost see our cemented bond forming a crack right before my very eyes, and felt an equal one in my heart for it. I let it go for now. Any more arguments against that academy and its ambassador would only alienate Andrew further from me. I still needed proof they were up to no good. It would be next to impossible to prove that an organization so little was known about, and what *was* known was so impressive, was sinister.

So I would have to refocus on exposing their ambassador for the fraud that he was. If I had a chance of convincing a scientific person like Andrew, I would need to focus on the facts. And the fact was: Pete was a liar. I did receive *one* golden nugget today from the unwittingly helpful Mrs. Woodward. She'd confirmed my suspicion about the first meeting between Andrew and his mentor being all business. If she'd been present the whole time, then no way he would've pumped my brother for his big sister's culinary favorites. How very unprofessional. *Lie numero uno, Cadet Davenport—busted!*

I had to bide my time for the right moment to confront Andrew with the news. Right now, he was still riding high from the afternoon's secret meeting and rescue mission. But when the timing was right, I'd drop my newfound currency in the vault that was my brother's mind.

23

AN IDIOT'S IDIOMS

While I was out in the pasture waiting on the pump to fill the cow tank, I had a long time to cool down and really think things through. A big part of the reason I was going nowhere but backwards was on account of my temper. Like Cadet Davenport—it was still getting the best of me. I'd been using vinegar when I shoulda been using honey, or what Mama referred to as "my feminine charms." I just hated to stoop to that level; it reminded me of Ashley-Leigh and made me feel phony as those chicken cutlets she insisted we stuff into our training-bars in sixth-grade.

Mama used to say people were born with a strong sense of right and wrong. That you could teach ethical behavior but mostly it was an innate thing people either had or didn't have. She'd usually pull this little pearl of wisdom out when explaining why I either shouldn't be upset with Daddy or Ashley-Leigh.

I think in retrospect, she was also describing me—I really *couldn't* abide by any wrongdoing. It just went against the grain for me. Like when I was twelve and turned those high school boys in for playing baseball with a hapless frog they found on the field, or when Ronnie and his buddies put gum in that mentally handicapped boy's hair. I'd spent my whole lunch working it out with some ice.

And the plain truth was: I'd taken enough crap from Daddy in my short lifetime to fertilize every field within a twenty-mile radius. Being the constant recipient of wrongdoing had taken a toll on my affections for my father, and seeing it dished out to my undeserving little brother made it even worse.

The broken pump finally trickled enough water into the tank to sustain the cattle for the next couple of days. I set my chemistry notes aside (that I wasn't studying anyway). It's like my brain only had room for a finite amount of problems, and my quota was already filled. Falling out of the truck on heavy legs, I climbed up the railroad cross-tie—that doubled as a ladder—to shut off the switch. The only illumination on this dark night was from the sorry beam of light shining from the one working headlight. So I was standing on a precarious pole, with stakes driven into the side, in virtual darkness, while Daddy was kicked back at home "minding the boys."

Where was the justice?

A bubble of curse words reserved for boys' locker rooms erupted from my mouth because the last stake in the pole had just fallen out of the worn divot, causing me to lose both my footing and my temper. I fell the last few feet, landing roughly in cow-trampled muck. Then took an indulgent moment to holler and kick it around until Blue came trotting over warily to make sure I was still in one piece. I accepted his slobbery kisses, feeling plain grateful to him on this lonely night.

"Come on, boy." I chauffeured the door open for him. "Let's get home."

I got back filthy, exhausted, and with that feeling of dread that always accompanied having to confront my father. I had to remind him about the broken pump (for the fifth or sixth time), confront him about not being part of Andrew's meetings anymore, and try to strike while the iron was hot regarding my car's transmission. My righteous indignation would have to be put away for now, or else I would end up spewing a lifetime of pent-up vitriol all over him. And likely get nothing in return except for being shoved even further into the background . . . until I would be no more visible than our outdated floral wallpaper.

When I trudged in, the first thing I saw was socked feet. Propped up. In front of the TV. And a popcorn bowl balanced on a full belly. My hands started to shake at this cozy repose, but I held myself in check. Taking in a yoga-worthy breath, I said, "Daddy? Can we discuss a few things before I go to bed?"

After a few moments of noisy crunching, he sighed dramatically, set his popcorn aside, and actually clicked pause to face me. "First off Katie-girl, I wanted to talk to you about yer manners this afternoon."

Doh! When would I ever learn not to let my temper get the best of me?

"I wanted to commend you on yer nice thank-you to Cadet Davenport."
Say what?

"He really did us a favor. And he has alotta influence over yer brother's future. So I was glad to see you were extry nice. . . . I was afraid at first you was gonna act like an ungrateful brat seein' as how you're again' his Academy. But you didn't." Daddy gave me a sharp, approving nod. "I wanted to let you know I made note of that."

That was . . . weird. Like I said *only a fool.* I took this as a good sign and a good place to start, so went to sit on the couch next to his recliner. I tried an honest-to-God smile. "I wanted to start off apologizin' to you for my behavior these past couple of weeks," I began. "I've been pretty depressed at the thought of losin' Andrew. But I know you'd *never* sign your own flesh and blood away to some fancy boardin' school—even if it is military, so I decided not to worry so much about it anymore."

I gave Daddy the puppy-dog eyes that had served me well as a child and excused me from more than a few spankings then followed up with sweet words: "I also realize now that you're right about my job at the diner." The one-two punch had his face going slack at once. A smile was still spreading across his lips until I said, "I'll quit come January so we can start visitin' Andrew on the weekends."

Daddy's jaw went from slack to un-hinged.

"I really look forward to spendin' a *lot* more time with you from now on . . . Especially on all those road trips—you, me, Mikey—all singin' our way to California together. It'll be a real *bondin'* experience for us!" My final move was reaching across the divide to embrace his rigid frame. And that's about the time the recliner went down and Daddy stood up. Pretty spry for a crippled guy.

"Now hold up there a minute!" he spluttered. "That's kinda puttin' the cart before the horse ain't it? I mean nothin's set in stone yet. Quit countin' yer chickens before they're hatched!" Daddy's face had extra splotches, and three idioms in a row was a new record . . . totally had him on the ropes. I only wished Mikey were here, so we could tag team him with unwanted hugs.

"Why do you say that, Daddy?" Angelic smile. "Are you concerned about Andrew bein' accepted now? Is there somethin' botherin' you about that . . . *institution?*"

"No, no, nothin' like that . . . I think we both know our Andrew's a shoo-in." Daddy paused so I could share a conspirator's smile with him. "I just haven't quite determined that he has to go right this year. Been thinkin' back and forth about maybe . . ."—a spring of hope rose in my chest— "askin' them about waitin'. You know—not long. Oh, what's it called when you wait a year or two?"

"Deferrin'," I put in.

"That's it." He finger-gunned me. "Deferrin'. Maybe an extry year or two at the most. Think 'round a decade old seems 'bout right."

I knew enough not to jump up and do the happy dance yet. *Was that RPA letter what had finally slowed him down?* That's probably why they sent a fat check alongside it. *So it would go down easier.* A little sugar with the bitter pill parents had to swallow to give up their parental rights.

I nodded my head and said my father's favorite words in the whole wide world: "Whatever you think is best, Daddy."

He took a fortifying sip from his tumbler. "Yep. A lot to think on, Katie-girl."

After a moment of letting him think on things he *should* be thinking on, I added an extra layer of sugar on top. "I know that Drewy doesn't voice it a lot, but he's sure gonna miss his Daddy up there at that fancy boardin' school."

I uncrossed my fingers and decided to end the conversation right there, skip over the other two topics all together tonight. Nothing made Daddy madder than coming home to problems . . . except for having his playoff game interrupted by problems. So I did something I hadn't done in forever—I pressed my lips to his scruffy cheek.

He smiled and patted my shoulder. "Yer a good girl when you wanna be, Katie-girl."

Whoa! The fumes coming from his mouth coulda fueled our diesel tractor for a week. My smile tried hard not to turn into a grimace. "Thanks, Daddy. And thanks for comin' to rescue us this afternoon."

"Oh, sure, sure, honey." He patted on my shoulder again. "I guess it's kind of a good thing Cadet Davenport called this mornin' to have me pick up Andrew today."

I froze for a second while the wheels in my brain kept spinning. "*What?*"

Daddy looked at my strangled face and frowned. "I said it's a good thing I was called in to pick up Andrew this afternoon, because I had the tools to fix yer car and Cadet Davenport had the know-how. I sure am impressed they teach those kinds of—"

"What!" My feet stamped prints into the floor.

Daddy quit talking; the lines in his forehead looked like a plowed field. "Are you raisin' your voice at me, young lady?"

I quickly simmered down. "I mean . . . did-did you say that Cadet Davenport called *you* about pickin' up Andrew this afternoon?"

Daddy folded his arms across his chest. "I *am* his father. O' course he would call to inform me that *my* son's test scores were available."

"Sorry, Daddy. I didn't mean to take a tone with you. It's just . . . I'm confused. Did you ask P—Cadet Davenport and Mrs. Woodward not to include me in any more of Andrew's meetin's?" I held my breath.

Daddy cleared his throat. "Now, Katie, it ain't that simple see." He took another thoughtful sip from his tumbler. "I b'lieve Pete's the one who started the discussion by sayin' Andrew might be more excited about the prospect of bein' a future cadet if I was able to attend the meetin's where all his hard work was bein' acknowledged. I informed him that you usually like to be the one at Andrew's conferences and what not, and he said he thought it best for you to get used to the idear of lettin' go a little of the parental responsibilities."

My heart seized. *That rat!* "But Daddy, I promised Mama I would take care of him!"

"We thought it would be better off for you *and* Andrew in the long run—easier when the time comes to let go." Daddy looked, for him, apologetic. "I'm sorry Katie-girl, but I agree with him." He patted my hand. "Yer *much* too involved in Andrew's business. And since yer a very emotional young lady and are . . ." he switched tactics, "or have been so biased against The Elite Academy—I think cause your Mama put the fear o' God in you 'bout schools for gifted children—I agreed to take over. Yunno, whenever there was any major decisions to be made or paperwork to look over and what not."

"Did you tell that to Mrs. Woodward?" I pressed.

"Now honey," Daddy placated me with another hand pat, "I don't see no problem with you still goin' to those silly parent-teacher conferences in my stead . . . since it's so important to you. After all, we already *know* what she's gonna say—the same things *all* his teachers been sayin' since he started school." His broad smile fell into a frown when he saw the furnace that was my face.

"But, Daddy! Cadet Davenport told Mrs. Woodward that *you* said not to allow me in any of Andrew's meetin's anymore! And that *you* called *him* about pickin' Andrew up today. Don't you see? He's *lie-ing*!"

Daddy's face turned the same shade as mine. "That's plumb ridic'lous!" he immediately spat out like he'd just swallowed a fly. "Yer startin' to talk nonsense just like yer mama did when she got sick in her head. I ain't gonna stand for more o' that crazy talk in *my* house!"

"But Daddy, it's *true*! He came into the library this mornin' to tell me all this was *your* idea and he was just deliverin' the news." Daddy's face was unmoved, so I moved to begging. "Please! You gotta believe me!"

He looked, for half a second, into my desperate eyes. The muscles in his face loosened. "Why would he do that?"

"To cut me off!" I screeched.

"And why would he do that? . . . Are you makin' a nuisance of yerself?"

"Because he knows I'm *onto* him!" Flapping my arms, I started squawking about my bad feelings on the matter, when he cut me off by actually clamping a hand across my mouth.

"Now see here, missy. This is *exactly* what I was talkin' 'bout!" Daddy dang near thumped me in the chest with his finger. "Yer startin' to worry me with all this paranoid talk. I'll *not* live through that again with my daughter! I tol' you yer not to in'erfere in *any* way. Have you been meddlin'?"

Ignored that last one. "But, Daddy! He's *lie-ing!* Don't you see? I can prove it, if you'll—"

"*Enough!*" blasted from Daddy's lungs with enough hot air to singe my eyebrows. "That young man has been more'n nice and awfully helpful. Today is case-in-point. Not to mention the fact that he holds your brother's future in his hands."

I was *well* aware of that fact.

"If you talk like that again, yer gonna be in hot water with me. Do you understand?" He hit me with the Manson lamps.

I hung my head in defeat. Trying to reason with Daddy was like trying to climb Mount Everest with nothing but your fingernails for tools. "Yes sir."

"You best head off to bed, young lady. Mornin' comes early."

24

THERE SHE BLOWS!

I was up long before my alarm went off, long before the rooster roused himself to crow in the new day, and long before I'd found a solution to any of my problems. With a feral growl, I yanked back the covers. May as well get up. Stewing over everything wasn't helping anything. I needed to *do* something.

The only things I knew for sure—without the aid of my intuition—was that Pete was here on a mission to sign my brother and then get out, and that he had lied twice: It was *he* who initiated the phone call to my father, and he lied about quizzing my brother about me during the first mentoring meeting. Why I hadn't already realized this was beyond me. He'd covered his tracks by questioning my brother the *next* day at The Learning Center, knowing I'd never ask which day he'd actually asked the questions. He took a gamble that I'd be so relieved it was true that I would just drop it so I could bask in his golden presence. He'd been right, and right now I was creeped out.

How *did* he know those things about me?

I drew back the faded pink curtains, half expecting something to jump out at me. A chill tingled my spine. It was more than halfway through September and frost was now covering the ground in the mornings. His "mission" should've been over by now. I percolated a while as I watched the first rays of dawn finger their way across the wasteland that was our backyard. I hurriedly dressed, yanking on an old sweater the color of fresh cream. Feeling head heavy, I headed out to tend the animals all by myself. This would allow the boys to sleep in another half-hour and me to burn off the anxious energy tormenting my insides.

Upon my return, I woke them up without my usual rendition of *Good Morning to You* sung to the *Happy Birthday* tune. After pouring them each a bowl of granola, I sliced bananas over the top and ran to get ready for school. Ten minutes later, I was dressed in a long denim skirt and a boring white Oxford. I shoved my cowboy boots back on, and yanked the same wool sweater over my head.

There was a chill in my bones this morning that had nothing to do with the outside temperature. And nerves were eating my stomach lining alive. But I forced down some cereal and did a second shot of forbidden coffee, then speedily washed the breakfast dishes before heading back to the bathroom with my brothers to brush my teeth.

We kind of stared at our own reflections in silence as we brushed—a departure from our usual morning high-jinx. This was usually a comical time of making faces and jostling for position in front of the mirror while trying to stifle our laughter so we wouldn't wake up Daddy. This morning we were all unusually subdued. Andrew and Mikey were obviously feeding off my mood, glancing at each other and then at me warily.

I finally cracked a smile as we waited for Andrew to fix his hair. He always liked to brush it just so and end his morning ritual with a dab of unnecessary gel, added with a flourish. After which, he would smile back at his own reflection, admiring the effect, before heading out. Mikey didn't have enough hair to bother fixing, and I didn't care enough to bother. Today I would leave it a tangled mass of waves—kind of seemed befitting my mood.

I met Andrew's eyes in the mirror. His were apologetic; mine had a fire in them I couldn't quite extinguish. I gave him a tight-lipped smile, and placed an arm around each brother as if framing us for a picture. A lot was at stake here. Today, I would confront Cadet Davenport with the lies I knew he'd told. Today, I would get to school early to wait for *him*. Today, he would be unable to hide behind his glowing good looks and easy charm—he was busted, and we both knew it.

After whisking the boys away to school, I pulled into the near empty parking lot like I was on a stake out. Eventually the lot began to slowly fill, bringing in a cacophony of lively chatter intermingled with opposing music genres: rap, country, pop, all blurring and blaring from open windows of second-hand cars. Clumps of social groups posed for each other—those who knew they were being looked at, and those who were doing the looking. I felt so far removed from it all I may as well have been parked in the faculty lot.

A couple of chattering cheerleaders, who used to be my friends, caught my eye. *What do they really have to worry about? What color bloomers to wear under their skirts Friday night? Who they're going to homecoming with? Child's play.*

As the morning sun slowly warmed the car, I realized I'd arrived too early and with too many layers on. The waiting began to wear on my nerves and my confidence, so I mentally listed their transgressions. The slow burn of injustice started to boil my blood when I thought about how outmatched I was, the enticements they were using: money, alcohol . . . Pete. I thought back to all the encounters where he'd been a phony. Felt like I might need to unstick my jaw just to talk.

Miguel was right: What a little fool I'd been.

Feeling like The Hulk, I ripped off my sweater and looked up just in time to see a trio of curvy girls with straight hair elbow each other expectantly. He was here. I rammed out of the car and rushed over to where he was parking before anyone else could accost him. I had him in my sights—Pete was the bulls-eye, and I the arrow. When I was within target range, he looked up at me briefly before dropping his head to his chest. He let out a mighty sigh and grabbed his backpack but remained in the protected confines of the Hummer, I guess debating the merits of whether to hide or face the music.

Coward, I thought as I stood, obviously waiting him out.

I watched as he rubbed the heel of his hand in one eye as though the mere sight of me gave him a headache. And with a great shake of his golden head, he pushed the door open and stepped out slowly, as if putting off a particularly unpleasant chore. Backpack slung over his shoulder, he slammed the door behind him, walked a few steps forward, stopped to click the button that locked his precious Hummer. (I was really beginning to hate that obnoxious chirping sound.) Finally, he lifted his chin to face me squarely.

We stood about thirty paces from each other, looking as if we were about to engage in a western-style shootout. I was armed, cocked, and ready to go. But what he didn't know was: I was also loaded.

Pete must've found our little standoff humorous, because his mouth quirked up at the corner. Another time I would've found it funny, too. Today, I just found it to be very *apropos*—I'd been fighting off the villains for what seemed like a very long time. At last the battle had come to a head, in the middle of the town square as it were.

Unsure how to begin, I chewed on my lip a little. Pete made the first move by ambling forward to greet me. He was wearing his aviators, and I now thought they made him look more like an automaton than a movie star—robotic-like in his perfection without the warming presence of his eyes sparking up in humor.

"Good morning, Kate," he greeted in a neutral tone. "To what do I owe the honor?"

"I-I'd like to speak with you about a few things." *Dang it!—my voice quivered.*

"Now?" He said this like I was a crazy person for suggesting a deep conversation first thing in the morning, with a crowd of bystanders as witnesses.

"*Right* now."

Pete exhaled deeply, looked heavenward as if for guidance. I snorted, and he snapped his head back down, staring at me long and hard. *So I'm gettin' on his elite nerves, am I? Well, that's just fine cause Elite Pete is gettin' on mine!*

"What is it, Kate?" he said briskly.

I drew in a deep breath and just went for it. "I wanna know why you took it upon yourself to call my father yesterday, then lie about it bein' my *father's* idea to ban me from the meetings, when he informed me last night . . . it was *yours!*"

Not a single muscle twitch.

"Then I wanna know why you're trying to cut me out of my *own* brother's life!" I hissed, the rage monster in me making this a must-see scene immediately. Our curious audience crept closer.

Pete was sea breeze cool under the heat of my vicious glare and the open ogling of the crowd. "That's easy enough to explain," he said in a reasonable voice. "I did it because you've been sabotaging your *own* brother's academic achievements, putting his full-ride scholarship to the best military academy in the world in jeopardy in the process."

Someone in the crowd jeered, followed by a couple of "oohs."

"I—" faltered, unaware he was onto us. "That's ridiculous." I wasn't expecting to be put on the defensive.

"Is it?" He arched a brow, a move I used to find so charming but now just seemed arrogant. "Then explain to me, why is it, that your brother just happens to miss exactly five percent of the questions on every single test—usually right in a row, either vertically or horizontally on the page. A couple of times he got more creative by going diagonally. Sometimes, he appears to get bored so skips every other question until he hits the target number of questions missed. But any which way he slices it—it's always the exact same pattern of missing five percent on the dot. Do you have an explanation for that?"

Oh crap. Of course, Drews would do that; he was both creative and a perfectionist. And obviously wanted to create a not-so-secret code to let Pete know what was going on, without outright defying his sister's wishes. *Ingenious.*

While I stewed in guilty silence, he went on, "I guessed, of course, that you'd put him up to it. You haven't exactly hidden your negative feelings about The Academy—the one your little brother desperately wants to be accepted to. It's the *right* place for him, Kate. And everyone knows it, but *you.*"

Murmuring from the bystanders was going on as they weighed in with their opinions. I was up . . .

"Like you know anything about *my* family or what's best for *my* brother . . . or even care!" My voice cracked as though on a sour note—it still hurt that he'd been faking this whole time. "You're such a phony and a liar! All you *really* care about is gettin' results. And that equates to acquirin' more innocent, gifted kids to pack into your stupid *elite* academy."

Pete's eyes hardened, although his body remained casually loose. I was rigid as a cane.

"It doesn't matter to you who you've ripped them away from or how immature the child is," I raged. "Andrew's *eight*-years-old for God's sake! Much too young to know what he wants or what's good for him!"

The burgeoning crowd closed in around us, but I was focused on the cadet in front of me who was trying not to flinch at my words.

Backed into a corner, Pete came out swinging. "You are much too young and immature to know what's good for him. A boy's *father* is a better source of guidance than you, big *sister*. . . . Especially in this case—you've been biased against The Academy from the beginning."

I huffed an incredulous snort. "Have you *met* my father?"

"I have. Several times. And found him to be both supportive and accommodating."

"I just bet he's been supportive and accommodatin' . . . especially with a little palm greasin' from your dirty organization!"

A swell of buzzing followed that one. Pete straightened his shoulders, but otherwise ignored the hit. "He's doing what's in *Andrew's* best interests, not *yours*," he finished.

"How dare you question my intentions!" I lunged forward, trigger finger pointed. "How dare you minimize my role in my brother's life! And then *Jerry-rig* my car yesterday, so you could beat me to Mrs. Woodward!" I threw my arm out like it was exhibit A. "That was a new low by the way."

Pete openly scoffed, rolling his eyes to a couple of his fans like my accusation was ludicrous. Our audience was following along with rapt attention.

I didn't care. And didn't slow my roll. "It's *you* who doesn't care about Andrew's well-bein'; all you really care about is signin' him up and then gettin' the heck out of Dodge. Honestly, Cadet Davenport . . ."—my eyes lashed him—"how do you live with yourself?"

I could see up close that my words *were* affecting him: the marble smoothness of his face was cracking, his body now rigid as mine. But when he spoke, it was in a level voice.

"You know what, Katherine Connelly? I've had just about enough of your baseless accusations. I've been tolerant of your little tirades up until now because your father has apprised me of your situation . . ."

"Oh, yeah? And what situation would that be?" I sneered, thinking he would allude to our social-economic status.

Pete sighed and removed his glasses. "Your emotional imbalance," he let drop as though it pained him. I felt like punching him in his pretty mouth, but that would only prove his point. "I know it's not your fault. I realize you lost your mother a couple of years ago . . . and for that, I'm truly sorry."

I flushed blood at his intimation. My jaw creaked from the force of my clench. His followers were lapping up his words like dogs did kibble.

Allowing a brief moment of emotion to wash over them, he continued in a soothing voice. "What I'm also sorry for is *not* addressing your wild accusations about The Academy sooner. I felt sorry for you and let those feelings color my judgment. That was my mistake."

I physically cringed. He felt *sorry* for me?

"You have been downright *delusional* in your accusations," he shot and wounded me with his words, "and they've been proven false every time. If you persist in accusing me of shady conduct like rigging your car"—he guffawed and backed away from me—"then you'd better bring proof. Otherwise, I'm going to be forced to inform your father of your irrational behavior and false claims, and of the fact that you've been trying to sabotage Andrew's testing. Because what I'm *not* sorry for, is offering your brother a golden opportunity to better his life." His voice positively rang with sincerity.

"Prove it," I challenged.

"I think the proof from his testing is pretty definitive . . . not to mention your *own* brother's confession."

I swallowed thickly, shocked Andrew had turned over so easily. The crowd was high on drama; probably taking bets on when I would finally crack. Not long—I was seconds from tears.

Cadet Cutthroat went for the jugular now. "I believe, if I'm not mistaken, you've been forbidden by your father to interfere in *any* way with the mentoring process. He's already informed me how emotional and irrational you've been lately—almost paranoid—like your mother," he said, planting a seed.

How dare he! Threatening to tell on me for Andrew's sake. Making me sound like I needed to be put away for my sake. And then bringing my *dead mama* into it! That was below the belt (which was exactly where I wanted to kick him).

"You *would* rat me out to my father," I said bitterly.

He shook his head, holding a hand out to me like I was a jumper on The Brooklyn Bridge. "That's not what I want, Kate. All I want is for you to stop interfering with the process . . . and *trust me*," he said so softly only I could hear.

I laughed in his face. "I don't trust liars and con artists."

Pete's face went bone hard. "Kate, you need to stop interfering."

"Over my dead body."

Something scary flashed in his eyes. I took a step back from *him*. He shook his head and the scary fell away.

"Since you're being so unreasonable, you leave me no choice but to inform your father," he threatened.

I glared through the slit in my eyes. "Well I guess you gotta do what you gotta do, Cadet Davenport." It's like I had a big stick and couldn't help rattling it against the fence—even though I knew he could bite my head off at any moment.

"You sure that's the way you want it?"

Emboldened by the fact that I had a couple of arrows in my quiver now, I said, "If you take me down, I'm takin' you with me!" I punctuated this with a finger poke to his chest.

My little threat elicited the requisite *"oooh"* from our gawkers. We stood there for a moment engaged in a glare-off. The bell rang, and I immediately took off for my corner. Pete caught up with me a few strides later and grabbed my arm.

"Kate, please—don't do this. For *your* sake" he pleaded, dark eyes boring into mine. *A threat? Or warning?* It seemed like both, but it was so hard to tell. That's what made this so much harder—I was getting mixed signals.

"I know." I closed my eyes, not looking at him lest I get confused. "Cadet Davenport, the jig is up."

"Where's *your* proof, Kate?"

We were standing so close we'd become a crowd of two.

"Your little stunt with my car yesterday—"

"Ridiculous here-say," he cut in.

"—*almost* foiled my plans to get information from Mrs. Woodward. It was a nice touch actin' like you were simply the sorry messenger of unglad tidings." His face remained carefully neutral. "Anyway, your plan worked until I decided I would allow Mrs. Woodward to show me the light. And when she was sure I was beginin' to see it, she let loose a couple of gems I wasn't aware of before…"

A flicker of irritation blinked his eyes. "Do share, Kate. I would be very interested to know what you think you have."

My lip lifted in triumph; it was nice to finally have something in my arsenal. "I *know* you're lyin' about questionin' Andrew about me during that first mentorin' session. Mrs. Woodward was in the room the *whole time*. She said you introduced one another, chatted a little bit about The Academy, and then Andrew took the preliminary test." I counted off on my fingers. "So where in that short meet-and-greet session was there room for twenty-one questions about *me*?"

He rolled his eyes. "Not this again."

"I asked her outright, just to be sure."

"That's it? *That's* your proof?" His tone was so scathing it would've discredited me to all but my closest alliances. "I *told* you to ask him about it, and I thought you *did* and we were over and done with it. You keep bringing up the same old incidences like a broken record . . . or like a crazy person."

I swear—I almost spit on him then.

"I *did* ask your brother about you, although why I bothered . . ."

"Right. The day *after* we'd already had our picnic," I steamed. "Nice try coverin' your tracks, *elite* cadet . . . but you're busted!" A new kind of cold entered his eyes; it sent shivers of icy fear down my spine. But I didn't crack. "And if you tell on *me*, I'm tellin' on *you*—how y'all followed me that night, kidnapped me, held me against my will. How I had to escape out the side door of that pharmacy to get away from you. Think that little bit of intel— I've been keepin' to myself—might be mighty interestin' to my father . . . Maybe we should report it to the authorities?"

A pulse in his temple began a slow throb. Somehow, this fascinated me. I *wanted* to see him lose it—that glossy veneer of confidence that shone from him like painted-on glaze. I wanted it to crack, so he would be exposed for the imposter that he was.

"What'suhmatter, amb-*ass*-ador?" I taunted. "Afraid that shiny reputation of yours will get tarnished?"

He had to unclench his jaw to speak. "It's funny how you forgot to mention how we *saved* your sorry ass from *actually* being abducted. And I hate to break it to you, but you have no proof. I'd be careful if I were you, or you might come off sounding delusional . . . no one even saw us together that night."

"The *video cameras* at the pharmacy saw us together that night," I smirked.

"No, they didn't."

"Uh, *yeah* they did," I insisted. "And I bet we can still get the surveillance tape."

He smiled coldly. "*What* surveillance tape?"

I blanched, a new kind of fear enveloping me like a ghostly hug. "Who are you?" Before he could answer, my hand flew up. "If you think I'm gonna let my brother get snatched up by your evil organization, you're insane!"

"What's insane is your *head*," Pete announced loudly enough for the farthest recesses of the crowd to hear. He took a step back from me now like I was covered in crazy drool. "I see your father's right—you *are* absolutely delusional. Everyone knows that mental illness runs in families . . . and it looks like you inherited your *mother's* genes."

The words zinged through the air and hit me with the blunt force of a slap. So I did the only thing I could to retaliate—I slapped him back.

With the full force of my rage. It was loud. Our onlookers collectively gasped. But I could only focus on the imprint of my hand staining his perfect face. I was stunned. He was stunned. Everyone was stunned. Our eyes met, communicating the same thing—regret.

How could we have let it get so ugly?

I heard a tittering mixture of approval and outrage from the reinvigorated audience. The headliners were frozen, staring wordlessly at each other. My eyes teared up about the same time he slid me a reptilian smile.

"Feel better?" he said.

Shock, lack of sleep, constant fear, and being the center of a spectacle, which climaxed with me performing an act of violence, was suddenly too much. I stumbled back a few paces, my hand stifling a sob. It looked like his face melted, but it could've just been my blurry eyesight.

"Kate . . ."

Reeling, I turned and fled with the sound of my name still on his lips. I couldn't face him now—the ugliness between us—I wasn't equipped to deal with it. I made it back to the relative safety of my car and tried wrenching the door open, but the dang thing refused to budge. *Just like my life*—it was getting worse. After a couple of more failed attempts, I stalled out and collapsed over the top of my car, weeping.

Am I delusional? Am I paranoid like my mother and suffering from mental illness? I honestly didn't know anymore. All I knew was that I was flat-out, to-the-marrow exhausted.

Pete was behind me now. I couldn't even look at him, afraid of what I might see. I heard him swear under his breath. "Kate . . ." He hesitated before placing a hand on my shoulder. "I'm sorry. I lost my temper. I didn't mean for—"

"Just l-leave me a-alone!" I couldn't listen to his sorries right now. He'd humiliated and discredited me and talked bad about my *dead mama*.

He tried to pull me to him. I half-heartedly shrugged him off. Half of me *wanted* him to hug me. The half I hated right now.

"Kate, listen to me, please."

"I mean it, Pete . . . just l-leave me a-alone." I already felt alone. And helpless. A JV player transplanted into the Big Leagues against my will. Who was I kidding? I couldn't win. Sobs started heaving from my body.

"I'm not leaving until I know you're okay."

"P-p-please just go!" I begged.

He went to grab my arm again when something pulled him back. "You heard her. She wants you to leave her alone."

Miguel. Oh God! Did *not* need more of an audience to witness my nervous breakdown.

"You need to mind your own business," Pete said, a threat audible in there.

"Katie's more *my* business than yours." Miguel wise-guy laughed. "Dude, need I remind you?—you just got here yesterday . . . and nobody will miss seein' you when you leave tomorrow."

Loud, raucous laughter erupted from Miguel's running buddies. My stomach dropped. Emotionally charged crowds usually came with violence attached. I had to do something. But Pete had already turned his back on me to confront my well-meaning friend.

"Well, *dude*," Pete spoke down, as one only could, who was both taller and socially superior. "This has nothing to do with you. So I suggest you back up out of my personal space . . . while you still can."

"You gonna make me?" Instant encouragement spewed like sparks from Miguel's fired-up friends.

Oh Lord! This was escalating fast. I spun around, too alarmed to care what a mess my face was. "Guys, stop! *Please!*" I spread my arms out, imploring. "I just wanna go home."

I saw Miguel, Ron, and several helmet heads, along with a large crowd of hanger-oners willing to sacrifice a tardy for a good fight. I had a very bad feeling about this—they all had a blood thirsty look in their eyes that had very little to do with defending my honor, and a lot to do with trying to get even with Pete Davenport for . . . existing.

Fear for all parties clenched my gut, but a small part of me was *glad* that Pete must be feeling the way I'd been feeling for a long time: outmatched and outnumbered. However, my better nature quickly took over. "Please! You guys—just go to class. I-I'm okay."

Nobody moved an inch. It's like I was yelling behind a thick wall of Plexiglass. Pete seemed unfazed by it all, as usual. His face and his hands were still relaxed, unlike Miguel's, which were already clenched into fists.

Pete spoke up in an authoritative way. "Look, I don't want any trouble here."

"Oh, so *now* he don't want no trouble," someone jeered from Miguel's entourage.

Pete ignored them and spoke directly to Miguel. "I'm sure Kate appreciates your concern, but I only want to speak to her alone to apologize. And neither one of us wants an audience right now, so I'd appreciate it if you would do us the courtesy of giving us some privacy."

Miguel took a moment to smirk over his shoulder. "You sure do talk fancy for a military dude. Maybe that's all they do at that rich boarding school of yours—teach you how to run your mouth. Seems to me like you already done too much talkin' already today." Miguel nodded at me, and an onslaught of obliging eyes followed to my tear-streaked face. "You got our home-girl, Katie in tears. She's been through enough already without havin' some big talkin', *phony* cadet dredge up the past and bully her."

I noticed how he used my word *phony*. I also knew how that would set Pete off.

Miguel stepped forward as though over an invisible line. His girlfriend took this opportunity to shoulder her way to the front. Obviously, she'd heard through the wide-band grapevine what was going on. I watched as panic transformed her pretty face into a mask of fear. My mouth went dry. I knew the feeling.

"So, you gonna do somethin' sides talk, fancy cadet?"

A weary kind of sigh escaped Pete. He shook his head as though he were a parent at the end of his rope. After dealing with an unruly child. Who'd gotten too big for his britches. "I told you—I don't want to fight."

A round of jeers and boos emanated from the bloodthirsty crowd, followed by encouragement from a posse of girls who most likely didn't want to see their eye-candy smashed to pieces. *Where are the teachers? Probably cluelessly wondering where half their first-hour class is.*

Pete waited for the crowd to settle before continuing. "But if you throw the first punch . . . you leave me no choice." He shrugged, sounding so smug I almost wanted to punch him. Again.

Instead, I stepped forward to pull him back. "Pete . . . no!"

Pete must've been poised for attack, because he reflexively jerked me back so that I sort of crashed back into my car. It didn't hurt a lick, but I guess that was the catalyst needed to get this little rumble started. The next thing I knew, Miguel was on the ground and Ron and a beefed-up buddy were all over Pete. I started to scream but, when I opened my mouth, only a croak came out. And my feet were so paralyzed they couldn't seem to run for help. The amped up fighters and crowd were a blur. Everything happened so fast.

Ron came at Pete, Pete tripped Ron, Ron stumbled forward. Pete used the momentum, and a hard shove to the back, and Ron crashed to my feet, a slayed dragon. Then, lightning-quick, Pete ducked under bulky arms trying to choke him. He used a twisting motion on one of those arms, and the howling jerk dropped his beef real quick. Pete followed up with a jab-jab to his midsection and a deliberate kick to the kidney . . . and that guy went down (looking like he might not ever get back up).

Pete ended up facing me.

My mouth, like everyone else's, caved open. Our eyes locked. I don't know what he saw there, but he closed his eyes, looking pained. This little time-out cost him; it allowed Miguel his play. It was a dirty one: He came up from behind and sucker-punched Pete—*Bam!*—right on the side of his face. The sick sound of flesh pounding flesh was my undoing. I finally screamed as only hysterical females can. Pete retaliated with a sharp retracted elbow to Miguel's gut and a fist-whip to his face. And, after a kick-trip-push, Miguel face planted into the pavement . . . for the second time.

Miguel's girlfriend screamed the same way I just did. Now two more burly ballers stepped forward. A screaming wave hit the female spectators— panic and overwrought nerves needing an outlet. Pete crouched in defensive position. Ready. Burly guys didn't look so sure, each waiting for the other to go first. Finally, the frantic girls persuaded a couple of senior guys to pull back the remaining contenders still pretending to be brave enough to face Cadet Davenport. It wasn't a hard sell.

Then several more things happened at once: (I only caught peripheral flashes of each because my eyes were on the golden gladiator, who looked defeated even though he'd just won.) "Dude, did you *see* that guy?" a voice cut through the buzz as the not-so-innocent bystanders melted away the same time two coaches came running from gym hollering. Only the central characters remained. Miguel groaned and spat out a wad of blood. His girlfriend hustled over to help him up, but he brushed her off to stand on his own—unsteadily. Lastly, Ron scrambled back to his feet, looking bewildered. He said in a voice-no-one-but-him believed, "Dude, this ain't over!"

All of this and more I couldn't process was happening, yet I couldn't seem to tear my eyes away from Pete's face—and the swelling going on over his *other* eye now. I was half a second from going to him when Ashley-Leigh beat me to the punch. (Pardon the pun.)

"Pete!" She ran and threw herself into him, hysterically crying like her steady boyfriend had just emerged alive from a bad car crash. He staggered sideways before righting himself. Violet talons cradled his head. "Are you *alright*? . . . I can't believe those assholes jumped you like that!"

Our eyes met one more time before his crowd of admirers completely swarmed him, blocking my view. I ducked back into the melting crowd and did what I always do—tried to blend in. And avoid the avalanche of attention threatening to smother me as I scurried to the gym bathroom. I hid out in a stall until the hoopla died down enough for me to escape for the day.

I had saved up enough sick days in my lifetime . . . it was time to finally call one in.

25

~

GOING BACK TO CALI

Finding myself back in the sumptuous confines of Academy Headquarters should have been a relief after living in a luxury drought. I did have a new appreciation for the fragrant greenery and manicured lawns. The eye-popping arrangements of flowers, discreet koi ponds, and babbling waterfalls all titillated the senses.

The dry, flat plains of Eastern New Mexico were among the most barren and dismal places I'd ever seen. Not that I'd spent a lot of time in the middle of nowhere, amongst the economically challenged. I'd been living a privileged, closed-off life for so long I felt like a blind man whose sight had been restored. I wondered how tough things were for people when they couldn't even bother to fix a broken-down fence or replace a petered-out AC unit in the heat of summer.

Like Ranger, I should've been eager to leave the tedious, small town whose epicenter vacillated between a super-store and the high school football stadium. I distinctly remembered feeling so irritated at him for messing with my mission by scaring off Kate that I'd been ready to go toe-to-toe with a superior.

But I wasn't mad now.

This alarmed me even more. I glanced at the clock ticking down the time above the security door. The Connelly-Mission Meeting would begin in about two minutes, two seconds, if we were to begin on time. Which I'd bet the Connelly ranch we would. The Academy was a precision timepiece—the mysterious whirs and ticks of the machine moving in perfect synchronicity, despite any vibrating disturbances from the outside world.

The feeling I'd been fighting for the last couple of weeks was one I wasn't accustomed to here—warmth, that's what it was. I wasn't able to fully articulate what it was until I'd registered its absence. I thought of Kate, Civilian Connelly, as I would refer to her in the meeting. Her luscious face came to mind, as it so often did now. A smile tempted my lips when I thought of the fascinating blush that always seemed to be coming or going whenever she was around me. Then chastised myself for the hundredth time in two weeks—I couldn't afford to get attached. It wouldn't be healthy for her; it wouldn't be healthy for me.

I should just try harder to give the damn Academy what they wanted. It's not like the boy wasn't an eager recruit. I grimaced when I thought of Kate's lashing words. Andrew *was* too young to know what he was getting himself into, and The Academy liked to keep it that way.

I contemplated further on our last terrible encounter, replaying the action sequence as it was reflected on her lively face: the stubborn set of her jaw as she waited for me, defiance shooting from her eyes as she confronted me with her suspicions, the crimson flush creeping up her neckline and settling on her face as I verbally assaulted her. Finally, I felt a sick twist in my gut, as I recalled her wet, miserable eyes and crumpled face drained of color.

Causing an innocent girl to cry was bad enough, but seeing the defeat etched into her fresh face was something I couldn't live with. I hoped I'd only bridled her and not broken her spirit. I'd never be able to live with myself if I did. She was strong, but The Academy was stronger. Bitter coated the back of my throat.

The ring of high heels striking marble shattered the silence of the waiting room. I looked up to see the welcoming face of The Academy, wearing a serene smile that didn't animate her face. Another image of Kate flashed in my mind, and a hollow coldness stole across my body at her lack of presence in my life. *Better get used to it.* I rose to greet Weston's puppet with a smile.

"Cadet Davenport, they're ready to see you now," she announced.

"Right on time," I said in way of greeting.

She eyed my swollen eye, speculating, though she didn't comment.

"Occupational hazard," I supplied then gestured for her to proceed. "After you, Miss Rackliffe." My flirtatious tone fell flat, lacking the spark needed to come off the right way.

She smiled at me nonetheless. "Glad to see you dressed appropriately today."

I glanced down at my blues, made a face. "Well, I guess if I'm gonna play the game, I better look the part."

She nodded as if that made perfect sense then led me through the same unmarked door, and down the same narrow corridor, I'd walked three weeks ago. The same claustrophobic feeling hit me as before, but this time, I didn't fight it by slouching or stalling. Game face on, I marched right after her.

Another flash: the trio of Connelly kids. A lot was at stake here; I'd have to play it just right.

Blair did the honors for me, rapping lightly on the door then waiting a beat before poking her head in to announce my presence. I recognized the deep-throated growl of Weston along with the sure bassy tone of Commander Davies, Head of Missions. The General stopped speaking in his congenial manner. "Send him in."

"Good luck," she mouthed.

A facsimile of a smile appeared and disappeared from my mouth the second she turned to go. Drawing a deep breath, I prayed to a God I wasn't sure I believed in and pushed through the hearty door. Four pairs of eyes watched my progression in. I stopped just shy of the rectangular table.

"Cadet Davenport reporting for duty, sir." I snapped a salute.

General Weston squinted at me through a haze of curling smoke. After stubbing out his stogey in an ashtray (that doubled as an art piece), he slowly rose to offer his hand. "Welcome back, Cadet Davenport."

I shook his hand firmly. "Thank you, sir." I returned to attention. "It's good to be back."

"At ease, son," Weston lightly corrected and then: "Is it?"

"Excuse me, sir?"

"Is it *really* good to be back? I was under the impression, from our last meeting, that you were having second thoughts about a career in Missions." Before I could respond, Weston continued: "It's amazing what a little real-world experience can do to make one appreciate just how extraordinarily blessed our life here at The Academy is. This life is a gift—a privileged one—that ought not to be taken for granted. Am I right, Cadet Davenport?"

I played along like a Boy Scout looking to sell to a big donor. "You sure are, sir."

"Looks like you brought back a little souvenir." Weston indicated my eye, and I gave him a sheepish smile.

"Yes, sir." I said.

Weston and his A-Team at the table chuckled at my expense, providing me the opportunity to glance over the usual suspects. Ranger was there with his dark presence and omnipresent smirk, Commander Davies with his open file and closed face, and a strained-looking Reese. She caught my eye and gave an encouraging smile. A lot was written on that face in the split second before she resumed her professional mask.

This was a trickier situation than I thought—she still had feelings for me.

Weston clapped me on the back. "Come. Sit down. This is an informal meeting as you may have surmised." He gestured to the seat fillers and they all visibly relaxed on cue.

Playing parts. We were all playing parts for the puppeteer. *Don't they ever get tired of acting?* Maybe they were all so accustomed to doing what they were told, it became a way of life until their free will was completely stripped from them like discarded doll clothes. *Robotic Barbies.* I thought again of Kate and her fiery resolve. She never simply fell in line when it went against her principals. My mind crashed back to reality and the repercussions I would face if I failed to get them what they wanted.

Scraping back the empty chair, I sat to the right of Weston across from Commander Davies. The slim, neat, brown-haired man weighed down by a lot of chest candy nodded at me, and I followed suit. Then I rewarded Reese with her long-awaited-for smile and felt a dollop of tenderness for my former girlfriend. If *girlfriend* was what she was. Cadets didn't date in the formal sense of the word. No hearts and flowers. Ours was more an intimate relationship between two consenting cadets wedged between endless rounds of tactical training, tech skills, and class instruction.

These rendezvous were openly encouraged, as inbreeding was your only option here. Purity was paramount—The Academy had spent decades and billions of dollars assembling the best gene pool humankind had to offer. We were all biologically enhanced lab rats whose ancestors had been bred for specific genetic traits. Desirable traits like high IQ and tall genes. Then bred again and again until all undesirable traits like male-pattern baldness and degenerative diseases were virtually eradicated. We were the property of the organization that created us. Our lives—even our love lives—were not our own.

Sexual intercourse with a civilian was, in our world, tantamount to hiring a hooker. Although it was a well-known fact Academy cadets enjoyed dipping their beaks into the murky waters of the civilian pond on occasion (during those weekend passes). You'd just better be extremely careful. We were screened for illness and disease every month like clockwork. So the younger and more "pure" a civilian girl, the more desirable she was amongst male cadets—for entertainment purposes only. No sort of long-standing relationship or mating would be permitted.

There were a thousand-and-one Academy jokes about how easy it was to get a civilian girl in the sack. They were as common as blonde jokes around these parts. According to Ranger, it was as easy as "shooting fish in a barrel." I glanced over at his smug mug with an open look of distaste.

Ranger winked at me across the table. "So . . . she was a wild one, was she?"

I tried not to notice the discomfit that sprang to Reese's face, and to tune Ranger out. But that was easier said than done when his smirk was spreading like a stain across his filthy mouth. It was the same one he wore two weeks ago when he was imparting last words of wisdom. They were real gems: "Have fun but use condom sense," he'd said before tossing something at my head and slamming out the door. I reflexively caught the small item of insignificant weight then immediately flung it into the trash. How juvenile and lame—how *Ranger*.

I recalled how hard he fought to be the operative on this mission. How I wished at the time they would've just let him. I was still surprised he hadn't been able to persuade Weston. He had more field experience and was also scientifically tested to be a good match. A sick feeling wormed in my gut at the thought of Ranger trying to shoot for Kate like she was another fish. That, coupled with the way he was regaling Reese with inaccurate tales about Kate's "psychotic behavior," had me clamping my jaw shut to keep in the thoughts that were trying to form into words.

Had to play it cool, not show a weak spot for her. But I felt twin spots of heat flare along my cheekbones, despite my best efforts at reining it in. Reese noticed and something passed across her lovely Nordic features before she caught herself. I concentrated on slowing down my breathing, like I'd been trained to do since starting the program at the tender age of two.

Like a menacing maestro, Weston raised a hand for silence. Ranger about-faced, and Reese zipped her lips so quick you'd think a gun had gone off.

"Cadet Davenport, I've obviously been briefed on the preliminary results of The Connelly Mission, and must say—I'm disappointed. I thought you'd have this one all sewed up by now." Weston gave me one of his looks aimed at withering self-confidence. "Unless you're hiding the signed documents under your uniform as I speak . . ." He paused long enough to allow me to dutifully shake my head.

"Then I need to know what the hell is taking so long," he demanded. "This should've been a one to two-week mission, tops. The longer it takes for a family to sign the paperwork becomes exponentially that much harder for them to make the decision at all. It's not easy to get them to go through with our unorthodox terms and actually sign on the dotted line. So you have to strike while the iron is hot, while the thrill and the honor of our prestigious organization knocking on their plywood door is still running rampant in their wee small-town hearts." Weston's exaggerated gestures and speech came to an abrupt halt.

My turn. "I'm getting closer sir, but I've recently had a setback . . ."

Weston gavel-banged solid oak with his fist. It was a testament to years of self-control training that no one flinched. "Closer doesn't amount to a hill-of-beans in this game. I want that PGC signed up and ready to ship out in a week's time. Setback or no setback!"

"Honestly, it may take more than a week now, sir," I said.

"What exactly is the hold up? *Honestly*."

"It's the Connelly girl, sir. I've recently had to contain her, and she's pretty upset with me at the moment."

"She has proven resistant," Weston acknowledged. "But we knew going in she would be our greatest challenge. Isn't that precisely what *you're* for?" He indicated me with an expansive hand.

Ranger's smirk morphed into a sneer.

I shifted in my seat. "Civilian Connelly doesn't follow the normal pattern of behavior for civilian girls. She's . . . stubborn and highly resistant to the idea of her beloved eight-year-old brother being sent away."

"And so the irresistible Peter Davenport has proven resistible after all." Somehow Weston came off sounding amused by this bit of news.

Ranger lifted half a lip.

"She's smarter than we gave her credit for," I allowed.

"So she's a clever girl. Are you not a hundred times cleverer? If not, then we'll have to reassess our whole program." Weston chuckled, turning to his panel for support before swinging back my way. "You admire her?"

I lifted a shoulder. "Not really."

"It's no use denying it. It comes off in your tone when you talk about her. When you say stubborn, you may as well have said sublime."

Reese's hand fluttered to smooth back an imaginary hair that strayed from her chignon.

Damn. "I guess Civilian Connelly has moral standards I admire," I admitted to a lesser charge.

Ranger loudly guffawed. Reese shifted in her seat. Davies remained impassive. Weston made a growling noise as if I were speaking nonsense.

"*Morals?*" he spat out like a dirty word. "Let me tell you something about civilians' morals, my dear boy—they are like those plastic rulers they give to schoolchildren—easily bent to the point of breaking if need be. And civilian girls are shallower than a puddle of piss. You have the looks, the car, the smarts, the breeding," he counted off, seeming to run out of adjectives before fingers. "Don't tell me this civilian girl is impervious to *all* your assets?" He raised caterpillar brows. "Maybe you need a booster shot?"

Ranger risked a chortle at that one.

I didn't even deign a glance. "Civilian Connelly's moral code is more important to her than external trappings. She is unlike most teenagers in that sense. Therefore, I need to take it slowly or else risk scaring her away completely."

Weston turned his outrage on Reese like this was partially her fault that he hadn't received his shiny new toy yet. "I see from your reports, Cadet Caruthers, that the girl *does* indeed fancy your own Cadet Davenport," he goaded out of frustration. "What do you think is the hold up from a *female's* perspective?"

Reese cleared her throat lightly like one does before giving a long, rehearsed speech. "Civilian Connelly has led a sheltered life, and is therefore, naturally cautious around outsiders. It took much longer for Ryan and me to win her over than anticipated." She paused to emphasize her point: it wasn't *only* Cadet Davenport having trouble making Civilian Connelly cooperate with their agenda. "She also has deeply entrenched religious beliefs, and would be reluctant to shed those beliefs in the course of two weeks. I agree with Cadet Davenport's gradual approach in regards to her courtship . . ."

Ranger snorted rudely. "Of course, *she* would."

Weston held up a palm, and Reese continued: "Coming at her with too much too soon would likely result in her dismissing Cadet Davenport altogether as too worldly and amoral for her to bond with sufficiently. I-I think that was partly where Ryan went wrong," she added in an aside. "In addition, the strong bond she has with her brothers would take longer than a couple of weeks to weaken. As you can see from my report, she's not interested in being free of the burden of raising her brothers. It has actually become the most important thing in her life since the passing of her mother. I also agree with Cadet Davenport's assessment that she doesn't follow what is considered to be normal civilian behaviors."

Ranger interrupted again. "I respectfully *disagree* with Cadets Caruthers and Davenport. I've met the girl, and she struck me on both occasions as . . . I'll use layman's terms here—a clueless country bimbo. You should've seen the way she was dressed and out prancing around on the night we picked her up. In a trashy neighborhood no less."

My chest burned at the way he was spinning this. And I still couldn't make sense of the way he became irate every time he talked about her.

Realizing, or reading my mind, Ranger's eyes cut to mine before composing himself. "And just for the record, *I've* never met a civilian girl I couldn't nail in a week. Morals or no morals—I've hooked up with plenty of church-going girls on Saturday night who just turn right around and wake up a little extra early for church on Sunday morning."

"May I interject, sir?" I asked.

"By all means, son . . . shed the light upon us," Weston said with no small amount of irony—religion had no place in this scientific institution.

"Officer Nealson jumped to conclusions on the night he is referring. Civilian Connelly was most likely coerced into wearing something . . . out of the ordinary for the special occasion of her birthday. I've never seen her in anything other than demure skirts and jeans, except for that one exception."

Ranger huffed out an incredulous throat noise to convey how his opinion differed from mine.

"I can corroborate Cadet Davenport's intel," Reese joined in. "At the camp, she was the only one not wearing shorts, despite the heat. Knowing her socioeconomic status and wanting to bond with her over clothes, I suggested she could borrow some of mine. She declined, citing her father as the reason. Apparently, he adheres to very strict, old-fashioned ideas of what is appropriate attire and behavior for young ladies."

"Pish-posh!" Ranger slapped the table. "What is this?—a ladies' tea party? Are we here to ascertain the exact measure of length of that skank's skirt or whether or not her brother is really a gifted civilian?"

Commander Davies spoke up for the first time: "Ranger is right here—this is all irrelevant information."

Ranger leaned back, his arms folding across his chest. Reese colored slightly. I continued to look impassive though I wanted to reach across the table and choke fathead until he deflated.

"Do you have anything *new* to add in regards to the Potentially Gifted Civilian in question that is *not* currently in the report?" Weston chided.

I loosened my jaw (and fist under the table) to answer Weston. "The Connelly boy is very advanced academically as is indicated by the preliminary test results highlighted in the report. He's also physically superior—both in appearance and athletically—in relation to his peers."

"How did he score on that stress test again?"

"He scored a 74.25," I supplied, then paused to let Weston mull this over. Civilians were required to score in the ninety-ninth percentile across the board to be considered. Unless they were gifted.

Weston stared out the window at a cloud formation, drifting across his California sun.

"Unfortunately," I continued, "I've yet to see any definitive evidence that points to giftedness above and beyond the indicators I've mentioned."

"That's for *our* team to decide," Weston growled. "It's *your* job to deliver him to us. Sometimes these gifts are hidden, or the subjects themselves are even unaware of their unique capabilities. Being born that way, it simply becomes their norm. Or they may even try to suppress their specialness to fit in. You mentioned the boy was deliberately missing test questions; he may also be hiding other aspects of his talents."

I nodded, allowing this.

"Have they committed to sending the boy to headquarters for the physical?"

"It's in the works."

"It'd better be." Weston eyeballed me straight. "Or I may have to send in reinforcements—I have high hopes for this particular boy."

"The father has proven to be almost as hard to pin down as his daughter," I emphasized, trying to move some heat off Kate. "I believe he's more unwilling to part with his trophy kid than initially thought. I just received a verbal commitment from him two days ago regarding the physical. He was willing to agree to it . . . provided that he be present during the screening."

Weston looked aggravated by this bit of news. "You let us handle the father—you concentrate on the daughter."

"Yes, sir."

"We need her too preoccupied with Prince Charming to have the time, or the inclination, to whisper in Daddy's ear about sending little brother away."

"She's very upset with me at the moment—"

"If you can't handle this girl, Davenport, maybe it's time to step down and allow Nealson to resume control!" Weston warned.

Ranger lifted his brows, his palms rubbing together greedily. He followed up with his signature one-side-up lip curl.

My stomach clenched. Could *not* have that. "With all due respect to Officer Nealson's proven record, I believe that would work *against* The Academy's objectives in this case."

"Why is that exactly? I was under the impression Mr. Connelly is a big fan."

"I believe his daughter has a different opinion . . . and it's a strong one."

Weston looked aggravated again. "What makes you say that?"

I shifted in my seat, slanting a look at Ranger before ratting him out. "I didn't mention it in the report earlier, believing I could easily get around it, but Officer Nealson was most unprofessional in our initial encounters with Civilian Connelly."

Ranger's face burst into the shade of someone about to commit murder. He lunged across the table, a finger-stab aimed at my face. "*You're* the one being unprofessional by allowing a seventeen-year-old *girl* to get one over on The Academy!—kind of like the tail wagging the dog, don't you think?" My face remained placid as bathwater. Attempt to turn tables on me was a fail, so he redirected to Weston: "I guarantee the results you want within a week, or . . . you can demote me!"

"That might be hard to accomplish when Kate absolutely loathes you, and Andy loves me," I replied serenely.

"Oh, so now it's *Kate* and *Andy*, is it?" Ranger's voice got all nasally. "Now who's being unprofessional? You're allowing your *personal* feelings to get in the way of your mission!"

"Loathes?" Weston latched on to the word as though it were an impossibility for a product of The Academy. He shot Ranger a dark look before twisting his head back my way. "How could the girl possibly loath someone she's barely met?"

"It's just another thing in which Officer Nealson seems to excel at exceedingly well," I answered, not even trying to keep a straight face. Reese bit back her smile, and even Commander Davies looked amused. Weston looked the opposite of amused.

Ranger's complexion darkened further. When he spoke, it was through clenched teeth. "In my opinion, we've been too easy on this family already. If that girl won't turn, and the father won't sign, then maybe it's time we *make* them see the light. Resistance has never stopped us from claiming a Potentially Gifted Civilian before."

"Strong arming and scare tactics would only succeed in the Connellys digging their heels in further," I interjected. "These are not weak-willed individuals we're dealing with. And it would shed the public spotlight on our very private organization. The whole town is well aware of the prestigious honor being offered to the Connelly boy . . . and is paying attention to the outcome."

Weston pursed his lips, contemplating. "Davenport's right—"

Ranger sulked immediately.

"—claiming a PGC without parental consent is a sticky situation, even when we're dealing with a different country, much less in our own back yard. We don't want to end up on the evening news."

"We have enough sources in high places to squash a story before it gets out," Ranger countered.

"Calling in favors results in a redistribution of power and a deterioration of our funds," Weston fired back. "Not to mention a story can survive on social media alone these days. Even with our best tech guys on it, a story can snowball out of control in a matter of hours."

Commander Davies spoke up again: "If we're unable to get Connelly to willingly sign the paperwork, Plan B is to get him denounced as an unfit father, giving us the opportunity to swoop in and save the young man from his neglectful, alcoholic father," he reminded Weston. "How is our contingency plan going?"

"Plan B is underway and Mr. Connelly is playing right along. . . . . He just happens to be neglectful at best and abusive at worse," I said with obvious disdain.

"You are, of course, documenting everything?" Weston confirmed.

"Yes, sir."

"From my understanding, we have the school administration's support, the Connelly boy is chomping at the bit, the father is almost on board, and the Connelly girl is contained. Would that be an accurate assessment of the current condition of your mission, Cadet Davenport?" Commander Davies summed.

"Yes, sir."

Davies fixed his steady brown gaze on me. "Do you think another check at this point would grease the skids further?"

I breathed in, deliberating. "I'm not sure."

Ranger snorted and shook his head. "You're not sure of *anything*, rookie. I've *never* seen a civilian balk at free money. They all have 'big principals'," he air-quoted, "until you offer them a fat check. That's what always tips them over the edge and actually gets the pen on paper. They're all whores at the end of the day—just variations between streetwalkers and high-class call girls." Nobody stopped him to argue. "We paid them like a dime-store hooker, maybe they think they're worth more? It's probably worth it to us to save time and just cut the guy a check for fifty-thou and be done with it . . . once we *know* the Connelly boy is gifted."

I thought over what Ranger said; it actually made a lot of sense. I'd wondered for a while why The Academy was trying so hard to sign Andrew. Didn't even appear he was gifted. I felt there was something more—some vital piece of information I was missing or wasn't privy to.

"Another check could help at this point, or hinder, because this particular family has some pride about accepting charity," I ventured. "The father cashed the check, but only because we framed it in just the right manner and just the right amount so as *not* to be considered either a bribe or charity."

"I agree with Cadet Davenport," Reese said.

"Surprise, surprise," Ranger addressed the ceiling, then me: "If only you had this much influence over Miss Connelly."

Like a public fart, I continued to ignore Ranger. Reese shot him a withering look before continuing: "She is already suspicious of our organization to begin with and is now aware of the check and *already* considers it to be a bribe. She will most likely cite this as evidence to her father and brother that The Academy has ulterior motives and is trying to bribe them."

I inwardly winced. So Kate had already mentioned that in one of her little emails to Reese. I was surprised she was so forthcoming—she was usually very self-contained for a civilian. She must be feeling pretty desperate, and now the target on her back was even bigger.

Weston whipped his head back to me. "Were you aware that the Connelly girl knew about the check and considered it a bribe?"

I stuck with the truth. No telling how closely they were monitoring my performance. "Yes, sir. She just confronted me with that fact yesterday."

"I can't believe you let that crazy bitch give you *another* black eye!" Ranger jeered.

"This came compliments of one of her suitors, who needed an excuse to vent his petty jealousies."

"Even worse—I suppose you can't hit a civilian girl, but I can't believe you let some high school punk get his shot in!"

Weston and Davies looked like they agreed with Ranger, so I decided to paint the right mental picture for them before they considered me weak. "Actually, it was half the football team. And this I got by being jumped from behind when I was . . . preoccupied with other matters." I recalled Kate's horrified face and felt a tightening in my chest.

Ranger grunted. "Still. A shiner from a civilian twice in three weeks is a very poor showing. I've had plenty of jealous civilians try and jump me . . . and not one was left standing."

"Beating her high school friends to a pulp seemed counter productive to our goal," I put in mildly.

"He's right again, Nealson," Weston agreed, somewhat reluctantly. "I can see you are indeed the right man for the job after all, Davenport. Sometimes a *lighter* hand is what's called for in these situations . . . instead of a sledgehammer." He spared a glance at Ranger. "You get the chicken by hatching the egg, not by smashing it."

Weston turned back to me in the hotseat. "You mentioned in your first report the Connelly girl is uncommonly astute. I've seen her scores and they are altogether average—above average to be sure, for civilians—but nowhere near Academy standards. However, now I'm suddenly more curious about her . . ."

My pulse spiked like I had sudden onset fever.

". . . The girl seems to have good instincts. Do you feel there's something more to her astuteness than meets the eye?" Weston's eyes bored into mine to get a good, solid read.

I straightened my shoulders and commandeered my face (and sweat glands) into stillness. "I've considered that already, knowing siblings often have similar abilities. However, I do *not* believe that to be the case here. The Connelly girl is only above average in intelligence and there is nothing to her that even hints at giftedness, unless one considers the art of surviving to be a gift. I now attribute her good instincts to her morals and unwillingness to break up her family . . . and nothing more, unfortunately," I answered dispassionately.

"Would you agree with that assessment Cadets Nealson and Caruthers?" Weston faced Ranger first.

His mouth twisted around before opening to say, "That would be the *only* thing Cadet Davenport has said all morning I *do* agree with."

All eyes moved to Reese. She paused for a moment, pulling her lips into line formation. Her pale green eyes flickered to mine. "I concur," came out in a low voice, almost a whisper.

I exhaled. Weston stared me down again before leaning back in his chair, pensive. After a nail-biting moment, he rifled through the navy folder, drawing out two photographs: one, a surveillance photo of Kate in the fields with her brothers, open-faced and smiling, the other, a closed-mouth yearbook photo of her with glasses. He set them side-by-side, staring at them a few seconds too long.

"I'm curious Davenport . . . you only spoke to the Connelly girl's intelligence as being slightly above average. How would you rate her physical attractiveness?"

A pregnant pause ensued where both Reese and Ranger froze, and my hotseat turned hotter.

"Above average," I hedged, in a careful voice.

Weston hemmed and peered down at the photos another moment before pointing himself at Ranger. "Nealson?"

Ranger gave a derisive half snort. "I concur," he agreed grudgingly, "but only *slightly*."

Weston *harrmmphed* and nodded his head a few times, amusement playing on his lips. He rifled through the paperwork again, taking a moment to skim a report sheet.

"I believe your predecessor had a differing opinion of his mark . . . I'll read Ryan's succinct final summation before his dismissal." He cleared his throat dramatically. "'Apple-cheeked and apple-bottomed, everybody likes her. " Weston tossed that my way before withdrawing another report. He faced Reese's pinkening one. "And this one is an excerpt from one of yours, big sister, written after the recon camp mission: 'Don't let the accent fool you—she's not stupid.'"

Weston's sharp eyes cut to mine. "Can you tell me what Cadets Caruthers are seeing"—he swiveled to include Ranger—"that you two are not?"

"Not much," I dismissed. "We've allowed she's not stupid and that she's not unattractive." *Cue understatement police.* "But nowhere near Academy standards."

"For once, I couldn't have said it better myself," Ranger pitched in. *To help me?* I was suspicious at once.

Weston did one last stare down on each of us while we did our mutual Queen's Guard routines. He relented with a grunt. "Okay then . . . the Connelly girl will only be considered an obstacle to remove so we may procure her gifted brother. Does anyone have anything more to add before we adjourn? Ladies first."

Reese hit it: "Civilian Connelly is especially strong-willed and clever more than book smart. I *wouldn't* underestimate her ability to sway her father and brother from signing with us. However, she seems to have two particularly obvious weaknesses to exploit: one is her temper . . ."

Ranger's hand shot up. "I concur."

". . . and the other is her attraction to Cadet Davenport. I suggest we continue to allow him to chip away at her defenses. She is extremely loyal, so once she finally puts her trust in him . . ."—her eyes met mine—"she'll be putty in his hands."

My eyes dropped to my guilty mug, reflecting back from polished oak.

Weston nodded as if satisfied. "Nealson?"

"I think . . ." Ranger started, then drew in a deep breath before blowing it out in a long stream, "we are going to a *lot* of trouble and expense for a civilian boy who may *not* even be gifted. The Academy's focus on this particularly small sector of cadets is short sighted, not to mention fiscally taxing. We've already shelled out millions for the gifted program—"

"I will thank you to keep your opinions regarding Academy policy to yourself and focus on the mission at hand!" Weston boomed "The one *you're* in charge of Nealson—you've not sufficiently moved up the ranks to warrant putting your two cents in."

"Do not act as though you have arrived when you've just been invited to join the party," added Commander Davies, in a warning tone.

I thought it satisfying to finally see Ranger put in his place; he'd been an Academy favorite for years. Reese and I shared a brief, conspiratorial smile.

Ranger scowled but quickly apologized and rephrased: "The way I see it, we need to move the boy on premises pronto to conduct more tests. Maybe his only superpower is being super-smart. If that's the case, well . . . I suppose we'll *still* want to use his superior brain power for the greater good of The Academy," he said with an edge in there I found interesting. "So we still need to force a signature. Just let me know when you're tired of pussyfooting around and allow the sledgehammer to step in." He flashed his teeth and fisted his hand.

I took a measured breath. "Civilian Connelly is currently contained," I began, then paused to let that linger in their ears. "Even if she cannot be won over to our side, I have successfully discredited her to both her father and brother. I think the Connelly boy's excitement and willingness to leave home is a key point here. His wants and needs are of the upmost importance to the father, second only to his own.

"And I think we should allow Mr. Connelly the time it takes to blow through his allowance before offering up another check of the same value. Anymore and her point about it being a bribe will seem more valid. And I don't believe a bribe, in-and-of-and-by-itself, will be enough to get Mr. Connelly to hand over his prized possession to us anyway. Appealing to his ego—that he was able to manufacture such a gifted progeny—and emphasizing the military training portion of our organization, in addition to a little kickback, is our best bet." I stopped there, allowing Weston and Davies to assimilate my words.

Davies dropped his pen and closed his folder. "I concur."

Weston finger-brushed his mustache, contemplating. "I also tend to agree with you, Davenport. Anything else you want to add?"

I shot Reese an apologetic look. "I respectfully disagree with Cadet Caruther's assessment of Miss Connelly's ability to manipulate either her father or her brother at this point. I've discredited her to the point she's out of power points among her own family, and is quickly losing credibility within the community. This is a recent occurrence, and therefore, is not in the reports."

"You're sure she's contained?" Weston reitereated.

"Yes, sir. Quite. This is the reason I've lost communication with her at the present time."

"A lover's quarrel already?" mocked Ranger.

I cleared my throat and placed a slick palm on the table. "Therefore, I respectfully ask permission to withdraw from pursuing Miss Connelly further—in a romantic capacity."

"Why would you do that when that is *precisely* the reason you were chosen for this job in the first place? . . . You weren't exactly my first pick," Weston reminded me, "and we have no way of knowing how long the tenacious Miss Connelly will continue to be contained."

"She's underage," I argued.

"According to what law?" Weston recanted. "Not one that governs our organization. No, I'm afraid that's quite impossible—much like snatching back a new toy from a toddler. She's already quite attached, just angry at the moment. And I want her so dizzy with love that she's desperate to come visit her Romeo at The Academy. If you do your job right, she'll be willing to sign her own brother away to do so."

I looked across to Davies in appeal. "The girl is barely seventeen and has led a very sheltered life, as was mentioned by Cadet Caruthers. I believe her to be innocent to the point of being pure . . . I don't feel comfortable seducing a seventeen-year-old virgin!"

Ranger guffawed and leaned forward as if forcing the point. "The girl works at a truckstop diner and wears Daisy Dukes and cowboy boots to the local watering hole. She's no virgin—she's playing you, rookie!"

"My dear boy, what you feel comfortable with is entirely irrelevant. However, I would like to point out that this is *not* a mission to steal some poor country girl's virtue, but to procure her gifted brother," Weston reminded me mildly. "The point of you seducing Miss Connelly is to have her so besotted with love that the bond she has with her brother is weakened and the one she has with you, her first love, is strengthened. Quite harmless— and romantic—in my opinion."

"Well, in my opinion," I countered, a tad too audaciously, "a flirtatious friendship would be just as effective in creating a bond . . . without pushing the boundaries of decorum."

Weston narrowed his eyes at me. "I understand your concern and even admire your ethics . . . to a degree. However, you have to look beyond one single civilian girl to the bigger picture we're creating here. Consider her collateral damage, if you must consider her at all."

Collateral damage. I clenched my jaw so hard you could actually hear it snap shut. Reese darted me a soft look; I returned one—this couldn't be easy for her. Ranger was glowering, while Commander Davies appeared to be more bored than anything else.

Weston dispassionately went on: "Most civilians not only pollute themselves, but the very world we live in with their lack of self-control and instant self-gratification. We have only to look to global warming and the impact that is having on our planet because of sheer laziness and lack of innovation on their part. Fortunately, The Academy is changing all that. That is why we must obtain greatness—when and where we find it—to harness and nurture for the betterment of all mankind, instead of allowing it to go to waste," Weston finished as though giving a speech to prospective donors.

"And, Officer Nealson seems to have a differing opinion on Civilian Connelly's experience." He held up a preemptive palm. "Furthermore, the young lady is no longer a child. It wasn't so very long ago a seventeen-year-old female was considered mature enough to marry off, run a household, even bear children. And, according to a report you wrote yourself, this particular young lady falls into that category. I'm paraphrasing here: 'Miss Connelly is mature beyond her years.'"

"Only in certain aspects of her life," I argued. "She's had to take on the responsibilities of a mother at a young age, but in other ways—"

"And *you* have responsibilities to this organization!" Weston bolted up, ghosting his chair backwards. "You can't allow *one girl* to get in the way of your duty. Therefore, you *will* pursue her again, make amends, and seduce her to the point that she forgets her own name much less that of her brother's. It's basic biology—a female cannot focus on anything but her paramour while her brain is being addled with the rush of love-induced hormones.

"More potent than any drug, Davenport. Therefore, I think a *Booster-T* is warranted in this case. We're not taking *any* chances with this PGC . . . I have high hopes for him," he added again, absentmindedly picking up a picture of Andrew.

"Yes, sir," I acquiesced with poor grace.

"Because if this girl gets in the way of our goal one more time . . ."—he looked pointedly at Ranger, who grinned manically as if on cue—"I'll have to send in backup. Since you obviously have such a soft spot for the young lady, I'm sure you can appreciate how your lighter touch on her life would be infinitely better for her than The Sledgehammer."

The twin spots of heat were back on the ridge of my cheekbones.

"We understand each other?" Weston's eyes were twin nuclear beams of threat.

Too angry to speak, I jerked my head up and down.

"Good. And if it makes you feel any better, I believe the age of consent in most states is, in fact, seventeen." After I gave a single incline to my head, he continued: "I'll give you two more weeks to reach your goal of signing young Andrew Connelly. I can see how this setback would affect her trust in you, and coupled with her obstinate nature, would take a little longer than anticipated." He flashed me the peace sign, managing to make it look ominous. "But just *two* more—I'm more than anxious to get this boy on premises to see what particular assets he has for us to use." So much greed dripped from his mouth someone should've offered him a napkin.

Plucking a fresh cigar from inside his suit pocket, he waved it around with a pleased expression. "You are dismissed." Everyone rose to leave. "Caruthers, type up a summary of this meeting for the files and submit it to Davies by the end of the day."

"Yes, sir," Reese replied, gazing longingly at me as I made to leave.

Weston clapped a hand on my shoulder, arresting my flight. I erased the disdain from my face and turned around.

"May I suggest using good old-fashioned jealousy as a means of entrée back into Miss Connelly's life? In my day, it seemed to do the trick when I was dealing with a particularly willful filly."

I nodded noncommittally.

"Cadet Caruthers," Weston called to Reese, who was hovering unobtrusively by the door. "What is the name of the Connelly girl's friend, my dear?"

"Ashley-Leigh Montgomery," she supplied.

"Ah." Weston slithered a smile my way. "I would try courting the lovely Miss Ashley to get . . . Kate is it?" I nodded curtly, hating the sound of her name in his mouth. "Kate's attention again. Stoke the fires of jealousy, m'boy . . . gets the young ladies' loins heated in a hurry. . . . That and a testosterone-shot," he said, grinning broadly.

"Yes, sir." I felt sick to my core with revulsion for this man—this organization. It had already gone too far, my first mission. If this was what it would be like—plucking innocents from their families, destroying lives—I knew I wouldn't last a year. But the threat to my parents, Reese, and now Kate wasn't an idle one. I just didn't see a way out . . . yet.

"Oh, Davenport . . . one more small thing."

I about-faced reluctantly; it felt like I couldn't breathe until I got out of that room. "Sir?"

"How about the youngest Connelly child? We haven't really given him much thought. Do you think there's anything there?"

"There's not much to think on, unfortunately," I replied dispassionately. "He's just a typical four-year-old attending a subpar, church-based preschool. The family and teachers caught onto Andrew's giftedness early on. Not the case here, I'm afraid. There is no indication that he's even above average academically. He is slow and clumsy, and his speech even seems underdeveloped . . . no gold to mine there."

Weston stared me down again before clapping a heavy hand on my shoulder, lightly massaging it. "I know it goes without saying . . . everything that goes on in a Mission Meeting is strictly confidential. Even with the clearance your parents have acquired, sometimes missions are strictly off-limits to *anyone* not directly involved. *This* is one of those times."

I worked to mask my surprise. "Yes, sir." That was weird. My mother used to be the lead scientist in the Gifted Program, and my father was one of the on-staff doctors who performed the physicals on all PGCs. They were privy to *everything* Academy, as far as I knew. It had always been *them* keeping secrets from *me*. It was discombobulating to be the other way around.

"Alrighty then. I'll let you go say hi to your parents, maybe spend a little R&R with Cadet Caruthers, hey?" Weston lightly jabbed at me like we were old buddies.

I tried infusing my voice with enthusiasm. "That sounds great, sir."

"And don't feel too bad about the Connelly girl. Those civilian girls never make it to the altar intact . . . better you then some hick with a can of chewing tobacco in his back pocket. Am I right?"

"I couldn't agree more," I said, actually meaning it.

Weston clapped me on the shoulder again. "You're a good man, Davenport. You're doing the right thing. The Connelly boy deserves better in life than the neglectful home environment he has now. You can feel good about helping him find his rightful place—living with us, among the elite."

I was quiet. Not the response he was hoping for. "Am I right?" he prompted with another hardier than necessary clap on the back.

"I couldn't agree more" got coughed up. Weston at last seemed satisfied enough to let me leave.

What I'd really wanted to say was: I couldn't *disagree* more. Because the way I saw it, Andrew Connelly was already living among the elite—especially when you accounted for the fact that his father was almost never home.

26

GRUDGE MATCH

It had been more than a week since we'd so much as acknowledged each other's presence. Oh, he'd tried a couple of times to get back into my good graces. His overtures had been in vain. Since my last rebuff, he was sub-zero cold whenever he so much as glanced in my direction.

People had taken sides. We were like two boxing opponents set to participate in a grudge match—with the sudden uncanny ability to polarize most of the student body. The divide was an almost even split between the sexes. Every line on my dance card was suddenly filled with knights-in-shining-armor, offering to carry my backpack or take me to lunch.

The girls flocked around Pete like a pack of hungry dogs chasing down raw meat. And the claws were coming out now that he was finally showing a modicum of interest. He was nothing short of a phenom in our small town, creating pandemonium wherever he went. Several near breakdowns had occurred in classrooms, parking lots, and bathrooms around campus all week. A couple of girls were even sent home due to hysteria.

I rolled my eyes at their total lack of self-respect. But a part of me could totally identify with falling apart from the littlest thing going awry in his presence—a hardening of his eyes, a dismissive turn of the head, for instance. It was a cold, cold world after living in his bright spotlight.

As it was, I felt like I was barely holding it together using bailing wire, steely pride, and a prayer. If it weren't for my total conviction that their organization was evil and the indisputable proof that Pete had lied to me, then I would have had a hard time not throwing myself at his mercy, along with the rest of the pack.

It had been a narcotic-like pleasure being in his company. I was still suffering from withdrawals. Too bad I had neither the time nor the money for rehab. Weaning myself from him was almost killing me. Going cold turkey was the only way I'd make it, so I'd been having Daddy pick up Andrew in my stead. And I'd been walking a different route to class lately, hoping to avoid him. And Ron Tillman. I grimaced. He'd been dropping hints about homecoming all week. I figured avoid, avoid, avoid was the best way to deal with him and everybody else these days.

I was walking back from lunch, from the unpopular west side of the gym, when a compact but loud gathering caught my eye—unusual activity over here. It was his Hummer, practically straddling the sidewalk. Hip-hop thumped from open doors, and a gaggle of scantily clad females were vying for his attention. It was more like a scene from a flashy music video than real life. I tried not to look, but really had no choice—it was either keep on walking, or else turn tail and run like a dog with its tail between its legs.

Guess I was walking right by then.

Surprisey!—Ashley-Leigh was there, brightly standing in the driver's side door, hanging halfway out of the truck . . . and her shirt, I noted with a stab of pain. I couldn't help but watch furtively behind my sunglasses. The tilt of my head must've given me away because he looked right at me. *Busted!* I flushed, but raised my chin a fraction.

Slummin' much?

Ashley's eyes followed to where his had wandered. Suddenly, a wild, gushy scream erupted from her throat followed by her literally pouncing on him from her predator's perch. He caught her easily, if somewhat stiffly, as she wrapped her filthy paws around him, shrieking with laughter while her blown-out hair spilled over his face in a daisy-yellow curtain. He clutched her waist with his hands, and bile rose to my throat. It apparently was to remove her from his body. But *still*. I clenched my jaw to keep my face from shattering as I whisked past them.

Anger flared up and ignited inside me. I hated her. I hated him. I hated me. And mostly . . . I hated my whole dang life! I stomped off to class trying to smother the flames before they engulfed me and everyone in my path. Of all the girls in school! *Really?* And here I thought *I* was the immature one.

First in class (last in life), I hurled down my backpack and slumped into my seat, the very picture of misery. *So that's the way he's gonna play it?* Well, fine—two could play that game.

Miguel came trucking in after me. We were partners again now that I'd moved seats and moved on from Pete Davenport. He took one look at my face and said, "What's wrong?"

I just shook my head, smoldering in my seat.

He sighed and dropped his backpack. "Well, somethin's wrong cause you were walking faster than most people run." A long beat of silence. "*Davenport* again?" His mouth crunched on his name like glass.

"No."

"Liar, liar, pants-on-fire . . ."

"I don't wanna talk about it." And I didn't. *Where was the future anyway?*

As if reading my mind Miguel said, "He's not worth it, Katie . . . 'sides, isn't he leaving, like, any day now?"

I sighed, not believing I could be even more miserable than I was before. "I dunno. Maybe. I think it depends on if Daddy signs the paperwork or not. And Drew has some kind of big physical he has to pass first in San Francisco. I think it's scheduled for the end of September."

Miguel perked up immediately. "That's only a week away."

"I know." Misery drooped my mouth.

He gave me a sidelong glance. "You know what you need?"

A new life. "What?"

"A manly-man who's gonna stick around for a while, not some pretty-boy preppy cadet."

I snorted. "Oh, really. You know any of those?"

"Just so happens . . . I do." I arched an eyebrow at him. "And he's a pretty good student—not as smart as you, but damn close, *es muy guapo*," he said, brushing invisible lint off his shoulder, "and can cook up a mean batch of cheese enchiladas."

I laughed despite myself, partly because I was amused, and partly because I wanted him to know I considered it to be a joke. "Well, it's too dang bad nobody that fits that description happens to be available at this time," I said pointedly.

He held my smile a beat too long. "Yeah . . . too dang bad."

My gaze shifted right in time to see Pete staring me down from the doorway with Ashley-Leigh, looking too much like a yapping Maltese at his heels, not to laugh. His face remained stony, so I quickly faced forward before I could absorb any more of his-and-hers cold stares.

Miguel looked to see what I laughed at, nodded his head backward. "Well, well, well . . . look what just dragged in the cat."

"I already knew."

"I'm sorry, Katie. I don't know how he could go from *you* to *her*—it's like escaping from Fiji to go spend a weekend at Padre Island."

I snorted. Then giggled. Then laughed together with Miguel until we took off into outright hysterics. The good kind of tears leaked from the corners of my eyes. Miguel was funny and a good friend. He was also loyal, and not a liar and con artist. Why couldn't it *be* him?

"Thanks, Miguel. I needed a laugh." Impulsively, I poked a finger at the crease in his cheek.

He caught my hand and held on to it. "Anytime . . ."

Feeling stares pounding the back of my head, I withdrew my hand as quickly as possible without hurting his feelings. I felt bad because it didn't take someone with a sixth sense to figure out how Miguel felt about me, and I didn't want to lead him on.

Class rolled on, and by the time the bell rang for fifth-hour, I had a gigantic crick in my neck from holding my head at a twelve o'clock position for fifty-five minutes. Miguel and I packed up with him chatting me up with renewed energy all the way to Chemistry. After class we normally parted, so he could escort his girlfriend to her next class. Today he stayed glued by my side. I hoped he wasn't getting his hopes up, and hoped his girlfriend wouldn't notice the slight.

As we filed out together—with half the school—for the ever-popular gymnasium, I got a steady eyeful of Ashley-Leigh sashaying along next to Pete. I noticed most of the energy was coming from her, though he did turn to reward her with a smile. She beamed back at him like she was lit from within. I had to bite my cheek the whole walk over, fighting a ridiculous urge to run over and tackle her. I'm telling you, I was so amped up I could've taken on the whole offensive line all by myself.

Pounding into the dressing room, the first thing I saw was Ashley-Leigh self-reflecting on all her glory in front of the mirror. This only mounted my anger higher, and it gathered force with every millimeter the self-congratulatory smile spread across her face. She caught me staring and her smile turned into a smirk. Then, rubbing salt in the wound, she proceeded to indulge in louder than was strictly necessary bragging rights. A blanket of tittering magpies quickly covered her so that I no longer saw her smug face in my line of vision, but I could still see her legs wrapped around Pete, his arms around her waist. It was an image burned into my brain. The burning moved to my chest, and now my stomach churned with a surge of tumultuous emotions. It was like a lifetime of frustrations and hurt was boiling over in my body, demanding an outlet for justice.

I remembered Mama always telling me to be the bigger person, to let her petty transgressions go. Allow her to have the spotlight she craved. And I obliged—no problem and no complaints. I mean, why should I care if she always got to go first on the swings? Or if she took credit for class projects? Or if she won class president in seventh grade, even though I was nominated too? (I had declined to run, opting instead to be her campaign manager—at her insistence.)

I mean, who really cared about any of that? Not me. It was easy to let her have her way, let her win, let her be the best at everything. But the truth was: she wasn't. Not even by half. And we both knew it. It was an unspoken thing between us, like a dark family secret that went without saying—you never mentioned it. That's why we could never truly be friends. She couldn't stand knowing I was smarter, prettier, more athletic . . . and liked. So I'd been throwing my game so long to appease her and Mama and everybody else, it'd become like second nature to me.

Then Mama plucked me right out of school in the middle of seventh grade. I was no longer even allowed to play sports because she said I was drawing too much attention. That's it. Game over. No more competition for Ashley-Leigh. She'd won. I mean . . . who really cared about *any* of that anyway when your mama was sick and dying? I no longer cared about anything since then, except for taking care of my brothers.

But I did now.

I slammed my locker shut, making a mousy junior named Shelby jump next to me. "You okay, Katie?"

I rattled the bench with my shoe, furiously whipping my laces into shape. "Fine. Why wouldn't I be?"

"I-I heard about Ashley-Leigh hooking up with that cadet," she said hesitantly. "I'm real sorry."

"No biggy." I said this a little too flippantly to be believable.

The whistle blew, and we lined up. Ashley-Leigh smirked at me on her way out. Holding on to her triumphant gaze, I narrowed my eyes at her until her smile deflated into something that resembled a helium balloon two hours after the party ended. I could swear there was a hint of panic flickering in those baby blues before she flounced over to whisper into Madison's ear. They both laughed in my face, but I didn't so much as blink. It had the opposite of their desired effect—fueling my anger. I was burning now, but not with embarrassment. I didn't feel an ounce of embarrassment—there wasn't room for any emotion but anger. I carried it with me like a weapon, all the way outside and onto the soccer field. I wasn't exactly sure how I was going to unleash it yet, but I was certain it was going to be soon or I would combust.

Well they say the Lord works in mysterious ways. And I fully believe that now, because it just so happened that Coach Sams and Coach Hampton were lining the boys' and girls' P.E. classes up together. Apparently, a game of coed soccer was on the docket today. Counting us off in teams of One and Two, the intent was to get an even assortment of bad and not-as-bad players on each team. I saw Coach Hampton point to Pete and say "One." I fervently prayed that I would be Two.

My prayers were soon answered because Coach Sams set a hand on my shoulder and said, "Two." Then she blew the whistle, calling all Twos together for a quick huddle. During the briefing, I eyed my fellow teammates somewhat dispiritedly. The sum of all our parts didn't equal one Pete Davenport. That was okay . . . I had rage on my side.

I was only halfway paying attention to what Coach Sams was saying, so intent was I on staring down a bored-looking Pete and Ashley-Leigh, who was busy lining up with the other cheerleaders on Team One's side to practice their cheers by cheering on Pete. *Well good* I thought. I *wanted* an audience today. You could practically hear the *Rocky* theme song playing in my head as I scraped my hair into a ponytail. Mentally crossing myself, I lifted my cross to my lips. Then, in an incongruent move to the one I just performed, I folded down the waistband of my shorts, which had the dual purpose of making them shorter and exposing a slim expanse of belly—a little trick I could thank Ashley-Leigh for. I smug-smiled, bouncing up and down on the balls of my feet in anticipation.

The whistle blew, but before I could spring into action, Coach Sams caught my arm. "Take charge out there today, Katie . . . no holding back."

Steely determination reflected from my eyes. "You can count on me, Coach Sams."

She smiled widely back at me before blasting the whistle. "Okay, play ball!"

Our team, it was decided, would kick off first due to the fact that we didn't have Pete Davenport, and therefore, the obvious underdogs. A stoner by the name of Jake (who might could've been athletic at one point in life) took the lead. He kicked it out in one predicable line towards another guy on our team. Pete easily intercepted the ball, dribbling it around players—trucking to their field positions—like they were standing still. He would be halfway to the goal before anyone could catch him. So I held back from the throng going for the ball, hiding out behind lagging players, ready to make my move.

I didn't have to wait long because Pete dribbled it back my way, around a knot of inadequate defenders. While his focus was momentarily distracted by a junior boy, who vainly attempted to steal it, I sprang forward like a panther, coming up as he kicked it left to intercept it right out from under him. It was a split-second sneak attack that caused him to crash into me so that I toppled over and fell. It wasn't pretty, but it got the job done. The ball went sailing back to our side, where it shot straight out to an unprepared team member . . . to roll out of bounds. The whistle blew.

It was an opportunity lost by Team Two, but a big opportunity to stick it to one Pete Davenport by Kate Connelly.

His head whipped around to see who'd finally gotten the better of him on the soccer field. When Pete saw me sprawled on the grass with a triumphant smirk on my face, he looked absolutely dumbfounded for a split second. Then he threw his head back and laughed. It was so mesmerizing I momentarily forgot to be mad. A hand was quickly offered, which I accepted, and he hoisted me up. I immediately withdrew from his grasp but couldn't find it in me to move yet—it was the first time I'd seen humor transform his glorious face in a fortnight.

I couldn't help the curve of my lips. We stared at each other—all animosity momentarily forgotten—until awareness that I was already getting sucked back into his vortex nudged me. Wordlessly, I turned and trotted off towards my team. I heard him jog up behind me, and then watched as he blew past in a swirl of colors before slowing to a backwards jog.

"Somehow . . ." he said, eyes dancing, "I don't think that was a lucky shot." I just smirked back at him, and he flashed me a grin before turning himself around to join his team.

The ball was put in play again, and I was determined to stick to my game plan: focus on the *ball* and not the *man*. Because if I didn't implement that strategy, I'd definitely lose my concentration on the field. And I had to work twice as hard as Pete, being the fairer sex and naturally not as fast or muscular. So I'd have to outwit him, if I could.

It was frustrating, hard work, playing defense against the master. I held him off better than anyone else from getting a clean shot at the goal. But that only lasted for as long as it took me to realize he was laughing, deep in his throat, as he took me back and forth across the field. Soon, it became an itch I just had to scratch. Infuriated, I shot him a dirty look. He took advantage of my lapse in concentration to bypass me, then sent the ball hurtling toward the goal before I could so much as blink. I didn't even have to turn around to know it hit the net.

The whistle blew, the cheerleaders jumped, I ground my teeth in frustration.

Pete took one look at my face and busted into a grin. "That's for cutting me off," he said.

And I knew he was referring to more than just cutting him off on the soccer field. A guy like Pete was used to getting his way in life. Everything was probably gift-wrapped and handed over to him on a silver platter. But I'd proven more difficult than he'd anticipated. Most likely even getting him in trouble with his organization, I realized with a small pang. So he was mad at me, and using my former best friend to punish me. It just dawned on me that he probably didn't even *like* her. *How could he?* I glanced over at her blowing kisses at him. *Puh-lease. I* didn't even like her . . . and she used to be my best friend.

It occurred to me that the best revenge would be to simply sit back and let him *be* with her. That was punishment enough—just allowing him to marinate in her high-fructose life until he rotted from all the sugar. I barked out a laugh.

His head tilted my way, a smile already forming. "What's so funny?"

"Your girlfriend."

He obliged by looking over to where Ashley-Leigh was busy tying up her shirt with the assistance of one of her minions. Never one to miss an opportunity, she smiled and blew him a kiss, just in case he missed the first three. He turned back to me for a laugh, but I was already gone.

Coach Sams called for a timeout, and we huddled up, most of the misfits already wheezing. "Jake, I want you to fake right to Diego, but get the ball to Connelly instead. He can't man the field all by himself, so let's take advantage of the sleepers out there. "Okay Team Two . . . let's break!" Team Two couldn't even manage to clap our hands in unison; I shook my head in dismay.

I also knew my own limitations on the soccer field so grabbed Shelby-from-the-locker-room and whispered in her ear while I watched Pete idly bouncing the soccer ball from knee-to-knee then foot-to-foot, as was his custom. Unable to help myself, I trotted over.

"Showin' off again, Cadet Davenport?"

He laughed and caught the ball. "Trying to impress a girl."

"Anyone special?"

"Oh, she's *special* alright." Pete stared into my eyes, all traces of humor gone.

The way he said this made my stomach feel funny. I swallowed, feeling guilty even though I didn't quite know why. And I didn't have time to dwell on it, because we were up to kickoff. Jake was the kicker again, and he made an obvious eye-intent to Diego that anyone with half a brain would realize was a fake out. Sure enough, Pete pointed two fingers at his eyes and then at me—he was watching me.

I rolled mine and feigned looking off into the distance, trying to keep the smile I was feeling inside from creeping on to my face. Jake did his best imitation of a fake-out then kicked the ball to me. But instead of immediately intercepting, Pete allowed me to safely get the ball before getting in the game. He was throwing his game, which was so galling because I was bringing my best.

Dodging in front of me, arms hanging loosely by his sides, he said, "Okay, Connelly, let's see what you got."

I narrowed my eyes at him, trying not to focus on how exasperating he was. And hot. *Gah! That* word just popped right in my head. I made an effort to refocus and set forth my very best effort of moving the ball forward without him taking it away. As I had foreseen, he easily stayed with me, so I was unable to move it more than a few feet. Time to implement my plan: tapping a toe on the ball, I halted it then kicked it backwards to a (hopefully) waiting Shelby. She was back there, but immediately botched the play because of nerves and general lack of know-how, kicking it directly out of bounds. Honestly, it was like playing with fourth-graders, but I didn't care—I'd managed to hold my own with Cadet Davenport.

Pete's face lit up at my little maneuver. "Lady's got moves," he said, twisting his baseball cap around and leaning, hands on his knees, so that we were eye-to-eye. ". . . Looks like I'm gonna have to bring my A game today."

I laughed but felt more like crying. Of course, I realized with a dispirited pang, Pete had *not* been playing his "A" game this whole time. We were doomed. But at least I was alive out there on the field. I hadn't laid down for him and everybody else to run over me. And I wouldn't anymore.

No more throwing my game.

A new flare of determination rose in my chest, so that I was burning up the soccer field. I managed to intercept a pass meant for Jake and shoot a long, hard kick at the goal before Pete had a chance to come along and steal the ball away. It missed by a couple of feet, but it was a nice attempt. Some of the spectators must've thought so, too, because half the football team started cheering. I even heard a shout-out from Steph Aguilar, before Ashley-Leigh smacked her on the arm for her lapse. The whistle blew, and Team One and Team Two huddled up again. It was 2-0 in favor of Pete Davenport, because he may as well have been the sole player on his team, everyone else being mere props for his dazzling performance.

I was getting pretty winded but tried to act otherwise, desperately wanting to stay in. Coach Sams and I were on the same wavelength today— she obviously wanted to beat the notorious, misogynist Coach Hampton at his own game as much as I wanted to beat Pete. I glanced over to their huddle to see that Coach Hampton appeared to be disgruntled, and that Pete was walking off the field. He sat on the bench, squirting water into his mouth, looking for all-the-world like a commercial for some kind of manly product. It could be anything: soap, sport drink . . . jock-itch cream. No matter—females would've gone out in droves to buy it.

Realizing I was staring, I snapped out of it and ran back to the field determined to take advantage of Pete's absence. The whistle blew, and I was off. And to use his own expression: It was as easy as taking candy from a baby without him in the picture. I accepted the first pass and easily drove the ball all the way to the goal, sidestepping two defenders to fake left, but kicked right . . . and the ball nailed the goal with a rewarding *thwang* that reverberated off the goal post and into my soul.

Team Two just scored one goal. The round of applause coming from my team and the football field was nice, but I only had eyes for the one, who rose from the bench, to cheer with everyone else.

That reminded me of something about Pete I had suppressed due to my anger at his betrayal—he was nice. As I stood there watching him cheer, I remembered how Mama always reminded me to never underestimate the power of being nice. Pete Davenport wasn't just nice . . . he was kind. And, now that I thought about it, I realized it was actually his most dominant trait. Forget about the looks and athleticism, the smarts, the prestige that dripped off him like sweet sweat, he was just a great guy plain and simple. I felt this in my core, the same way I felt his academy was bad. That's why his betrayal cut me particularly deep. I also realized that he'd *asked* Coach Hampton for a break, in order to give me mine. He did it in a way that he hoped I wouldn't notice. But I did notice, as I did all things Pete Davenport.

The whistle blew and both teams huddled back up for the second half. Coach Sams ended up playing me the whole time. It felt good to finally flex my athletic muscles after years of atrophy. And more than once, after a particularly swift kick or steal, Pete would shake his head and chuckle to himself like it was the funniest thing he'd ever seen.

The game ended with a whistle blow and groans of disappointment from the crowd. Our little soccer match seemed as fascinating to the spectators as The World Cup. The final score: 4-2 in favor of Pete Davenport. But I was pleased with my performance. Apparently, so were my team, Coach Sams, and an exuberant Miguel and Ron, who came bounding over from the football field. I found myself encircled by a small crowd of well-wishers. Ron even hoisted me up, so I was able to see Pete's own fan club congratulating him on another victory. Ashley-Leigh was hugging on him, but his eyes searched to find mine. We grinned over at each other, two sweaty gladiators showing mutual respect for a well-fought match. An intrusive pat on my behind brought a frown to my face at the same time Pete's grin slid from his. That was the last thing I saw before being twirled around and set back on my feet. I felt dizzy and euphoric and shy all at the same time.

As we headed back to the locker room, everyone settled back down to a more normal temperature. I was still way too sweaty to put my street clothes back on so just grabbed my gym bag and backpack and ducked out the door, heaving a sigh of relief. It had long been ingrained in me not to seek attention, so I had my fill quickly, much like when I had cotton candy at the county fair—savoring the first few bites before the beginning of a stomachache set in.

I'd just made my escape when Coach Sams came trotting over, her whistle bobbing up and down the same way my glasses used to.

"Katie!" she called, "wait up."

"Hey, Coach Sams," I greeted her with a wary smile.

"Katie," she huffed with exertion, resting a hand on my shoulder, "I want to talk to you about your performance this afternoon."

"Okay."

"How do you think you played?"

"Um . . ." I hesitated over the adverb, years of inbred modesty causing me to remember why I'd felt guilty. I thought of Mama claiming I made a spectacle of myself when I out-performed my friends. "Well, I guess," I answered with a shrug.

"*Well?* Yes, well, I'd consider that to be an understatement. I always knew you had loads of untapped potential, but really . . . I had no idea what an athlete you really are!" Her face was the kind of bright that accompanies discovering gold. "Your performance today could rival Mia Hamm on her best day!"

Uh-oh. I got a sinking feeling my temper had caused me to make an error in judgment today. "Um, thanks," I said, "but I think that might be an overstatement—I probably just got lucky."

"Luck has nothing to do with a performance like that." She eyed me speculatively. "Not only did you perform like a pro, but you looked like you were sure having a lot of fun out there."

I smiled and shrugged again, scuffing the toe of my sneaker on a piece of gravel. After an awkward pause, she finally got to the crux of why we were standing outside gym having a conversation.

"Katie, is there *any* way at all you could join athletics?" She saw my face freeze and quickly added, "You could certainly earn a scholarship that way."

I shook my head sadly, my throat feeling full. "I'm sorry, Coach Sams. I really can't. I have to take care of my brothers after school and help with the ranch."

"Maybe I could talk to your father, work something out?"

"I'm sorry . . . it's impossible. But thanks for thinkin' of me."

She sighed, clearly disappointed, but let me go. "If you change your mind, my door's always open."

"Thanks, Coach Sams." I smiled over my shoulder. "I really do appreciate it."

The wind in my sails abruptly subsided under these sunny skies. Hunch-shouldered, I wove my way through the parking lot. Life was unfair. *What's the point of being good at something you can't do? Or falling for a guy playing for the wrong team?* It all seemed senseless as a crossword puzzle in Chinese.

I slipped on my shades, averting my gaze in the opposite direction of someone calling my name, already slipping back into my bubble of solitude. But someone was able to penetrate the protective surface of my bubble.

My head automatically pulled to where Pete stood, rubbing at his jaw while staring at me with an inscrutable look on his face. My feet stopped in their tracks. His hand dropped to his side. Ashley-Leigh was standing right next to him, one hand attached to him like a barnacle. But she was relegated to the size of an ant in my mind, so I paid her no matter mind.

I thought, for half a sec, that he was going to head my way. I felt the intent. But he simply mouthed a quick goodbye to her then opened his door and climbed in. After one last look at me, he fired up the engine and roared out of the parking lot, kicking up a deluge of gravel in his wake.

Ashley-Leigh and I were left standing with our shadows. She attempted to engage me in another staring contest, but I looked right through her like she wasn't even there. She'd disappeared altogether now . . . even less than an ant.

27

MY DAY IS A WORKOUT

"Hey, champ!" A voice, I was overly attuned to, called out to me as I struggled to crack open my door. "Wanna come with us to the gym?"

Didn't we just come from gym?

I spared him a glance, and he nodded towards a truckload of my peers amped up on rap music and Red Bull. Pete had accumulated an odd assortment of friends during his short duration of stay with us. I noticed Jake, the burnout from our P.E. class, intermingling with the senior class president. He gave me a cheery wave, and I waved back cordially. Conspicuously absent was Ashley-Leigh. I suppose she'd already used up her quota of tardies to cheerleading.

"No thanks," I tossed over my shoulder, still sticking to my avoidance game plan.

Before I could take off, Pete jogged over. "Aw, come on, Kate!—live a little."

I snorted derisively. "I can think of many more things I'd rather do with my time than go to the gym and work out . . . and that includes stayin' home to wash my hair." I busied myself digging in my backpack for the key.

"Come on . . . come work out with me." He bit his lip, nodding his chin back in an enticing way (which only succeeded in making me weak in the knees, but not in changing my mind).

It took me a second to find my voice. "Can't. I still have to pick up my brothers—it might be *your* day off, but it's not *mine*." To leak some bitter out,

I made a stab at a joke. "'Sides, I'd like to think of my *day* as a workout." I said this as airily as possible before closing the door on his absurdly attractive face.

I was still trying to feel proud of my powers of resistance, when I heard the Hummer roar to life and the squeal of tires peeling off pavement. A dispirited sigh exited my body the same time his vehicle exited the parking lot. My forehead banged steering wheel. A moment later, I was startled from my misery by the passenger door popping open. And then my eyes popped open to see Pete standing there in shorts, a sleeveless athletic shirt, and a smile. My heart did an instantaneous flip-flop.

"In that case, country girl, I'm going to your house to work out." Pete eyed me appreciatively. "Whatever your method is . . . it seems to be working for you." That said, he hoisted himself into my passenger seat and closed the door.

"Uh!" I huffed out, both secretly pleased and miffed he'd taken it upon himself to join me without asking. "I don't recall givin' you an invitation."

"It got lost in the mail," he replied, eyes sparkling.

Gah! The way he was looking at me—it felt like I needed a daily inoculation against his charms. Heat crept up my neck as I allowed myself a full two seconds to drink him in. If I wasn't careful, I'd start falling for the enemy again.

"Listen. As much fun as this . . . little after-school playdate sounds"—I glanced out the windshield to gather myself—"I have actual *real* work to do this afternoon. And I need to get started so . . ." My mouth didn't seem to want to form the words "get out" because every fiber of my being wanted him to stay.

"What? You just gonna leave me stranded?"

I *harrumphed.* "First off, that's somethin' *you* might do, but *I* would never do that to someone—your buddy Ranger bein' the exception to the rule. And I'm pretty sure that you *do* actually own a cell phone in workin' order." I arched an eyebrow at him. "So, just call up one of your cronies, and I'm sure they'd be happy to turn your monster truck right around to pick you up."

Pete smiled wryly. "Just for the record, I never left anyone stranded that didn't wander off on me."

I folded my arms.

"Come on . . . *please?*" He put his hands together à la Mikey, amping up the wattage of his glittering eyes. "I really, *really* wanna see the famous Connelly ranch."

"You'll only ask for a refund."

"I doubt it." He smiled winningly at me.

With a turn of the key, the hatchback sputtered to life, and I threw caution to the wind. Before we even left the parking lot, Pete started fiddling with the knobs on the dashboard.

"Do you mind?"

"Sorry," he said, not sounding the least bit contrite. "It's a tad warm in here . . . blame it on the hot driver."

I bit back a smile. "You can turn it on, but I can't guarantee the air will be cool."

"Why not? If you need more coolant we can pull over, and I can put some in for you."

"Ah." I nodded sagely. "Those mechanical skills sure do come in handy in regards to my car."

Pete shot me a sidelong glance but didn't make a retort. During the quiet, I remembered all the things he *had* done for me, like warning me about Ranger and leaving a hundred-dollar tip when I sure did need the money. Gratitude swelled my throat. I'd never thanked him for either one, knowing, somehow, not to bring it up.

I cleared my throat. "That's, um, very nice of you, but unnecessary. The whole unit's been busted since about . . . oh, the globe started warming or so."

He looked at me funny for a second. I cringed, thinking he was going to start a pity party for me, but he just smiled ruefully and rolled down the window. "Well, I guess that sucks for you!"

I laughed a little at that bold understatement. "Yes, it does."

"Well then, you better put the pedal to the metal, sister and get us to The Ponderosa *pronto.*" He stuck his head out the window then peered back in at me. "Come on!—let's see what this little baby can do!" he howled out the window like a maniac, forcing a laugh out of me, despite myself.

The warm afternoon beeze ruffled through his golden hair. Wonderstruck, I stared at him. Never in my wildest dream-guy could I have ever conjured up a Pete Davenport. *Lucky air . . .* I'd been dying to do that with my fingers for ages.

After picking up two very surprised and exuberant boys and some fresh milk from Mrs. Hildebrand, we bumped and chugged our way along the winding road with more amusement than a carnival ride. About fifty yards from our house, an impatiently waiting Blue came bounding from the shade of a yucca to greet us. I stopped to load our latest exuberant passenger, and he proceeded to jump all over Pete, welcoming him with slobbery kisses. *Lucky dog* . . . I'd been dying to do that for ages.

"Blue! Stop that!" I laughed while half-heartedly trying to pull him off.

"'sall good." Pete rubbed his chin on his shoulder and Blue affectionately behind his ears. "I always wanted a dog."

"Yeah, but probably not all his slobber," I said, parking the car in its usual spot—the end of the dirt trail.

Pete helped unload our bags and backpacks and even held the still-warm jug of milk for me while I helped Mikey out. He peered doubtfully into the open container at the creamy, frothing liquid inside.

"Now that's what I call fresh squeezed," he deadpanned. "Goat milk?"

I laughed at the expression on his face. "Nope. Just good old-fashioned Jersey cow."

"Ah," he said with a queasy mile.

But I was too busy looking at our shabby lodgings, as though for the first time, and trying not to cringe at the thought of Pete seeing it through his eyes to make a response. I took a deep breath. "Come on." I nodded him forward. And our little band of brothers walked together to the saggy front porch.

"Why don't you just milk your own cows?" Pete inquired while waiting for me to work on a convoluted series of locks.

"Um . . ."—I jiggled the last one open—"we actually have what could be considered more of a ranch than a dairy, I suppose."

He nodded at me, staring. I blushed and bent over to straighten a pair of sneakers sprawled haphazardly on the porch, more to give my nervous hands something to do than the urge to straighten.

"Pete," Mikey piped up, "you gotta take off youwer shoes before you come in the house."

"That's just for us, you dope!" Andrew contradicted quickly.

Poor Mikey immediately hung his head. Pete laughed and rubbed his hand against the grain of his buzz in the same way I did. "Thanks for the heads-up, buddy." Mikey beamed up at Pete, the adoration plain as the nose on his face; he wasn't used to such fair treatment.

I had to clear another lump from my throat. "Michael Connelly," I reprimanded gently, "thanks for bein' so informative, but we don't require that of our guests." I turned to Pete. "We don't get many out here."

"I don't mind . . . I'm in for the whole Connelly-after-school-experience," he said, spreading his hands wide before gamely pulling off his sneakers.

"Hasn't anyone ever told you to be careful for what you wish for?"

Pete smiled into my eyes. "Oh, I always do."

Before he could read the secrets of my soul, my eyes scrabbled away to the bit of scrub still bravely greening up our deserted wasteland.

"Where do these go, buddy?" He held up two aerodynamic, navy sneakers.

Mikey's face brightened. "Wight over hewer, Pete." Grabbing Pete's hand, he led him to a rusty metal tray staining our porch. *Lucky Mikey.*

After finally managing to get up the nerve to turn the door handle, we all stepped into our stuffy, neat-as-a-pin trailer. I immediately turned on the ceiling fan, despite the fact it wouldn't do much more than stir the air. As if instantly on vacay-mode from the mere presence of Pete in our house, my brothers tumbled into the living room to watch some forbidden TV. I headed to the kitchen to make snacks.

"Don't get too comfy boys," I called over my shoulder, instantly feeling like a party-pooper. "We have hungry calves to feed."

Pete trailed me into the kitchen and sat on one of our abused barstools, then set about the business of watching me work. I tried hard not to feel self-conscious about anything. Easier said than done, because the way he was looking at me was akin to the way Blue did when I prepared pot roast. And I was very sure that Cadet Davenport had never even laid eyes on the outside of a trailer house before, much less the *inside*. And I was hyper aware of every crack in the floor and chip in the dishes I set out.

But you'd never know it by looking at him. As usual, Pete was completely at ease and comfortable in his own skin, aside from the evidence of hyperthermia he continually swiped from his brow. I grimaced and edged over to the dining room, where a window was stuffed with the dinosaur that coughed and wheezed out cool air. *What's one more infraction?* I thought as I punched in the button for our—ahem—*hot* guest.

Meanwhile, our forbidden guest continued chatting me up like there wasn't a mechanical nightmare in the corner groaning in pain. And like he'd never tried to undermine me. Or that we'd never had a fight that had gone viral overnight. He was all rather blasé about being here, with me, in our dumpty trailer. Guess it was all water under the bridge for him.

I wasn't so forgiving.

However, it was hard not to feel the pull of his potent magnetism. He had swiveled to see where I'd got off to, still going on in that entertaining way he had that had us all so mesmerized. So upon my return, I was rewarded with an eyeful of perfect profile. It was an odd juxtaposition—this immaculate specimen, sitting on that worn-out stool, in this cheap kitchen, with its outdated wallpaper. *Talk about shabby chic.* I wondered what it must be like to be so shiny and felt instantly shabby as our furnishings next to him.

Usually, I wasn't embarrassed about being poor; there were lots of folks here that didn't have much more than we did. I remembered once complaining to Mama because we couldn't afford to buy matching necklaces with Ashley-Leigh. They were those fourteen-carat gold, heart-shaped, BFF novelties she thought we should buy each other for Christmas one year when we were about nine. She'd had it in her mind to show them off at school after the break.

Mama made me tell her we couldn't afford it. I remembered it being one of the few times I had outright defied her. I'd really told Ashley-Leigh I didn't want to buy the necklaces because they were dumb. So of course she went off crying to her mom, and then her mom called mine. Well, Mama set the record straight right away. I was mortified. And angry. I'd felt the childhood sting of life not being as fair as it ought to.

Later, Mama had found me out crying behind the chicken coop when I'd taken too long to fetch the eggs. She'd hugged me to her then proceeded to set the record straight about how lucky I was to have the gifts God gave me. She'd said that I didn't need shiny things to show off in order to make myself feel good, because I already had everything . . . and then some. "In fact," she'd gone on to say, "you're *so special* I should lock you up, like a princess in a castle." I remembered her exact words because of the way they tingled my spine. And I'd never heard them before or again. Afterwards, she'd squeezed me to her, telling me that people see you the way you see yourself. And that being poor wasn't so bad to bear if you owned up to it. It was the *pretending* not to be poor that was so hard.

I never forgot that lesson and tried to keep it in mind while this paragon of privilege and beauty watched me throw together some peanut butter crackers and lemonade. In honor of my mother's memory (and our esteemed guest), I decided to use real lemons and sugar. There wasn't time to boil down the sugar, so it'd have to be a little grainy this afternoon. Anyhow, the boys wouldn't mind.

"Can I do anything to help?" Pete's voice rose, automatically adjusting to the ebb and flow of the noise pollution. "I kind of hate to ask because I'm kind of enjoying watching you get your Susie Homemaker on."

I arched a brow at him and handed him the instrument we referred to as the "lemon-squeezer," a paring knife, and a wide-lipped glass that used to have a jelly label on it.

"Although, I must say"—he dropped one side of his mouth and lowered his volume again—"I'm a little disappointed there's no pink, frilly apron."

Ignoring his flirty banter, I swiped peanut butter onto salty squares. "Hope you weren't expectin' anything fancy this afternoon."

"Only caviar and a bottle of your finest champagne."

"Well, you'll have to settle for crackers and lemonade instead." I clattered a plate in front of him.

"My favorite!" he cheered loud enough to catch the boys' ears.

Mikey twisted his head over his shoulder. "It's my favewit too, Pete!"

"Katie-Kat, can we eat in here today?" Andrew called from his belly position in front of the TV.

"Why not?" I said, stacking plates on my arm and scooping up two slopped-together fresh-squeezed lemonades to bring out to the living room. I was becoming quite the rule breaker these days. Pete followed suit, carrying his plates in one hand and the other two lemonades in the other, like me.

"Wow. I gotta say Pete: I'm impressed . . . if all else fails, you could make it as a waiter."

"It's good to know I have some options in life," he said wryly.

"Uh-oh. Looks like you forgot *my* plate though." I wagged a finger at him. "That's gonna cost you a dollar."

Pete laughed appreciatively, lassoing me around the waist as I walked by to retrieve it. "It wasn't a mistake—I thought it would be more fun to *share*." This last part was imparted into my ear.

I froze, the smile sliding from my face. He was doing it again—trying (and succeeding) at winning me over. He let me go to plop himself down in the middle of our sunken couch.

"Come on Kate . . ."—he whapped the seat next to him—"take a load off."

The feeling of warmth I always felt around him overcame me again. He was almost irresistible. *Almost.* I had to constantly remind myself: he's only here to snatch my gifted brother from us. Then getting the lead out. So I sat down . . . at the farthest recesses of our couch.

Pete looked over at me and groaned. "Kaaaaaate!—you're so far away. I ambushed you today because I missed you!" He removed the plate from between us and sidled up next to me, proffering a cracker. "Peace offering?"

"No thanks." I stared straight ahead, trying to concentrate on *Tom & Jerry*'s escapades.

"Please don't be mad anymore; tell me what I can do. How about if I peel some grapes and feed them to you?" he breathed into my ear.

"Sorry—all out." I folded my arms, hoping he wouldn't notice the goose bumps he'd just raised on them, making me look like a freshly plucked chicken.

"Kate?" He hijacked my hand to rub his thumb along the pulse line.

A feeling of pleasure so keen it was painful rushed through me. I removed my hand and leaned forward so that I was no longer mixed up in his personal space. "Hey guys . . . we gotta get to work right after this cartoon," I reminded.

The boys habitually complained but otherwise didn't argue, fully engrossed in the colorful animation on the screen. I leaned back, feeling the weight of Pete's eyes on me, so I focused on him focusing on signing my brother's life away.

"Kate," he tried again, "I'd like to call a truce."

"I'd like to call BS."

"I want to be friends."

I want to be more. Arg! I shot him a filthy look, ignoring his searching eyes. Drawing a deep breath in through my nostrils, I closed my eyes and tried to picture him with devil horns and a tail. Didn't work, because I just inhaled a lungful of his stimulating scent, so that he became devilishly tempting *and* beautiful as an angel. I let out a snarl, then stood up and snatched a cracker and lemonade off the coffee table.

"Where are you going?" Pete rose to his feet to follow me.

"Away from you," I announced before stalking to the kitchen.

He instantly looked wounded. *Don't care* I told myself as he tried to melt me with the heat of his stare. I stared back, willfully. Then had the wonderful idea of stuffing the whole cracker into my mouth. So I did, and re-answered his question. "To work," I said, spewing out little bits of cracker.

Pete arched a brow, a smile playing on his lips. "Didn't work—you still look ravishing."

I rolled my eyes while I chewed and swallowed. Then, holding up my lemonade in a mock salute, I tipped it back, downed it in five loud gulps, and clunked the empty glass down on the counter to face him squarely. A trickle of lemonade had dribbled down my chin in the process, so I swiped it off with the back of my hand.

He shook his head, a wide smile crinkling the corners of his eyes. "Uh-uh. Sorry—that was just plain sexy."

I scowled at him. He was impossible. And now his eyes began doing that smoldering thing again. "Except you missed some," he said in a low voice I felt in weird places.

Before I could think to move, he took my face in his hands. I sucked in a breath, half-panicked, half-expectant. Closing his eyes, he slowly drew me forward. My heart started galloping wildly as I helplessly waited for his next move. He surprised me by licking off the remaining traces of sticky sweet from my chin. Stopping just shy of my lips, he opened his eyes to peek at me beneath impossibly long lashes.

"There . . . all better," he murmured before stepping away, leaving me breathless and wanting for more.

My hand gripped counter. He was something else all right; I'd give him that. He was a friggin *weapon* was what he was. One he definitely knew how to use. That wasn't playing fair, because I didn't seem to have the same effect on him at all.

He casually called from the living room, "Hey! *Bugs Bunny*! My favorite!"

"Can we watch one mower, Kadee, pwease?" Mikey begged.

"Please, please, please!" Pete joined in with the boys.

Immobilized by current events, I fingered the blazing trail his warm tongue had left on my face. "Fine," I snapped more harshly than I intended. "But right after this one, get your work clothes on and meet me out back." Needing some time to gather myself, I stomped to my room to change into jeans and boots.

When I emerged a couple of minutes later, Pete was waiting for me with a fat grin. "All's missing to complete my fantasy is a cowboy hat."

I just huffed right past him, trying to hold on to my righteous indignation. "Now where are you going?" he asked.

"To mix up the calf bottles." I banged out the door.

A short moment later the door banged again. "I'll help you," he said. I tried not to feel thrilled by his choice.

He trailed behind me at a leisurely pace, whistling cheerfully as I led the way to the tin shed where we stored our feed. In no mood for his good mood, I grumbled to myself as I scooped the powdered milk into the dino-sized plastic bottles. Wasn't fair of him to tease me this way. We were naturally falling back into old patterns: the ones where he was fun, nice, and charming . . . and I fell for it hook, line, and sinker.

I sighed, weary of fighting off Pete's good vibes and his academy's bad ones. While I began filling the bottles halfway up with hot water, he retrieved the scoop and finished filling the remaining bottles. *Maybe if my life wasn't quite so pathetic, he could actually like me for real?* His acting was so good I actually *believed* that he really liked me. No warning bells. No queasy stomach. Just a bunch of strummin' cherubs floatin' around, stirring up feelings of—I banged a metal bucket down and started scooping grain. *What's he so dang cheerful about?*

"Can you *please* stop all that dadgum whistlin'?"

He immediately stopped to peer at me, one eye half-closed. "Aren't you supposed to whistle while you work?"

"Ha-ha. Very funny." I switched the faucet to cold and filled the bottles the rest of the way up, then grabbed the rubber nipples from the bucket they were soaking in and started snapping them on. I looked expectantly at the back door for my no-show brothers. This was a three-man job—feeding fourteen hungry calves at the same time.

"I'd better go see what's takin' them so long," I said.

"You go on. I got this," he assured me, then started whistling again. I whipped around to glare at him. "Sorry—I didn't realize it bothered you so much."

"I didn't realize you whistled so much."

He looked up from his work, beaming as brightly as the North Star on a lonely night. "I only whistle when I'm happy."

Arg! I stomped back to the house to fetch my brothers and the truck keys. *Gah! Why did he have to be so dadgum irresistible?* It was like trying to refrain from reposing in a tropical oasis, after a long, scorching journey through The Sahara Desert—sure, you could decline the invitation to join, but why would you?

A few minutes later, found me backing the old work truck up to the shed. Those crates were pretty heavy, and I had to admit: it was nice to have Pete here to do the heavy lifting for us. (Not to mention how nice it was to see him do it.) I watched as his muscles flexed in his sleeveless shirt, noticing the way the fabric clung here and there along his torso during his movements. It literally made my mouth hang open a spell before I caught myself. He'd insisted on hoisting them up himself, along with the fifty-pound bag of feed and the three bales of hay, claiming this was all part of the "workout portion of the program." I had to swallow another lump down and remind myself— it was all part of the act.

We jostled together over the tire tracks worn into the pasture, with the boys laughing like mad every time Pete pretended to pop up when we hit a pothole. "Whoa! Crazy driver at the wheel," he shouted. "Look out!" Mikey was very nearly in hysterics. His infectious laugh even infected me, and I found myself laughing along with the antics.

We arrived at our destination—a large parcel of fenced-in pasture reserved for the calves. These particular ones were bought for a bargain at auction because they were so sick and weak, they were half expected to die. I'd spent all summer long nursing them back to health and was proud as a mother hen of my herd. They all came trotting over like over-grown, hooved puppies, frolicking and kicking up dust, each one butting the other to try to get ahead.

"Hey, babies!" I cooed, getting out to greet them through the barbed-wire fence.

Their dry sandpaper tongues began licking my hands, arms, shirt. I bent over to rub them down while Pete went to retrieve the crates with the boys nipping closely at his heels. On the way back, he paused by the front fender, holding on to the crate handles and just staring at me. I felt silly and self-conscious in my worn jeans, in the middle of a huddle of overgrown babies, licking at me all over. Must've been quite a culture shock for Pete because he was still staring.

"Need a hand?" I called out.

"Nope. Just taking a moment to enjoy the scenery."

I felt myself flush and turned to fight off a particularly effusive lick from a spotted calf, pushing him back a little before rubbing at his pink muzzle. "They like the attention," I explained.

"Lucky calves," he said, ambling forward with the first crate of bottles.

I shook my head, fighting a secret smile. "Set it right here." I indicated a worn spot near the fence. "We have to feed them all at the same time or else they try to trample one another."

"How do you manage that?" he wondered as we walked back together to grab another crate. Each crate held six bottles, so he took the full one, which left me the one holding two.

"I'll show you." I smiled.

By the time we returned with the bottles, the jostling and butting were no longer fun and games. The calves were all business now, automatically lining up across the fence line impatient for their dinner. I grabbed two bottles, turned to my two regular helpers. "Okay boys, let's show'm how it's done," I said before shoving each bottle into a make-shift slot in the fence that Andrew and I had engineered for precisely this purpose.

"Clever. I didn't even notice that," Pete said.

"Thanks." I smiled proudly. "It's somethin' Drew and I came up with this summer . . . with Mikey's help, of course," I added quickly.

"Simple and creative," Pete approved. He grabbed two more bottles and followed suit. Soon we had fourteen hungry calves greedily sucking down milk. Pete grinned over at me feeding a black and white Holstein I'd named Buttercup by hand. "You'll spoil him."

I laughed out loud, patting Buttercup's head as she nudged for more. "Shows how much you know, city boy—Buttercup's a girl."

He threw his head back and laughed. "I guess I am looking at the wrong end. In my defense, from this end, *she* looks like a *he*."

Stuffing the bottle between my knees, I covered her ears. "Don't listen to him Buttercup!" I scolded Pete: "You'll give her a complex."

He gave a throaty chuckle, but his eyes turned serious. "I gotta say Kate . . . you're quite the little mama."

"Um . . . thanks." Unable to withstand his constant scrutiny, I decided now was a good time to check their water supply, so I hopped over the fence. A string of calves trotted after me. Pete followed, agilely climbing over to join me like he crossed barbed-wire fences every day. A few of the calves eyed him suspiciously before finally deciding he was okay to also nudge and rub up against. I sighed . . . *lucky calves.*

"Hey!" He yelped a laugh. "Can you call off your brood? I think I'm being attacked."

My brothers chorus laughed before climbing the fence and jumping off like mini superheroes to the rescue. Pretty soon all three boys had different calves chasing after them. Everyone was laughing and having a really good time—myself included. *This is dangerous. Very dangerous.*

"Hey, Kate . . ."

"Yeah?"

"Why are these calves not with their mothers in the pasture?" Pete asked, patting a particularly sweet-natured black Angus.

"Because most of them never even got a chance to meet their mother when they were born before they were snatched away." Disgust huskied my voice.

"Why not?"

"Because these calves were born on veal farms, and, well . . . you don't want me to go into it. Suffice it to say, they started off life with a pretty raw deal."

His eyes turned soft. "Thanks to you, they seem to be doing pretty well now."

"Yeah, I guess. We lost three of 'em though . . . too far gone when we got them—starved to death, actually." My voice cracked at the memory.

He came over to brush my hair with his hand. "Yeah, but think about how many you were able to save."

"That's nice of you to say. A lot of our success comes from buying colostrum from Mrs. Hildebrand. That's the mother's first milk, and it has all this protein and antibodies in it the calves need to survive illness. It's pretty gross though, because it looks a lot like drinkin' bloody milk." I realized I was babbling on. "Sorry. I'm sure that was TMI."

"No," he contradicted. "It's fascinating actually. This is the one thing they don't really cover at The Academy."

"Not a lot of FFA members there, I take?"

"You see," he said around a smile, "you say that like I know what it means." I laughed and briefly explained Future Farmers of America to him. "No, I'd dare say nary a one," he laughed, rubbing the white star on the little heifer's head. "I have to say I'm glad I've never eaten veal now."

"Good. Because if you said it was your favorite food, I'd have to turn my brood on you in a Texas-sized stampede! I'm glad but curious. Why not? It seems like something they *would* serve over at that fancy boardin' school of yours . . . that and bunny soufflé."

He pulled a face but let that one pass. "They don't serve it because it's on the 'forbidden foods list,'" he quoted.

"Because of moral reasons?"

"Because it's unhealthy for us," he corrected. "All the antibiotics they shoot them up with."

"I guess that's *something* about your academy not to hate," I conceded.

"*What?*" Pete dramatically covered his heart with his hand. "I'm hurt, Kate. Can you not even think of *one* good thing to associate with it?"

I lightly punched his arm. "Don't push your luck, buddy." We began heading back to the fence, leap-frogging over newly plopped cowpatties steaming on the ground. "I'm curious now. What else is on the 'forbidden foods' list?"

"Oh, you know," he said, "the usual suspects."

"No, I don't know!" I burst out with impatience. "*Please* enlighten me." I hoped he wasn't going to clam up on me again, or worse—start quoting from the brochure.

He slid me a sidelong glance. "Fine. Uhhh, let's see . . . there's hydrogenated oils of course, anything with artificial flavors, colors, or preservatives is banned, the popular MSGs, candy, soda—all junk food."

My eyebrows shot up. That was a pretty long list and must be difficult to maintain. I was quiet for a moment, processing. "What *can* you eat?"

"Basically unadulterated, organic fruits and vegetables, whole grains, free-range poultry and meats, wild-caught fish, a lot of raw foods . . . except for sushi. Yunno—all the non-fun stuff." He shrugged.

"Wow." I looked at him incredulously. "I didn't think it was possible to actually feel *sorry* for you, Cadet Davenport. But I gotta say—I kinda do."

He tossed his head back, his sharp, pleasant laughter filling the empty pasture, and my empty heart up with joyous vibrations.

"So . . . " I stuck my hands between the coiled barbs on the wire, poised to hoist myself over. "You've like *never* eaten a donut before?"

"I never say never," Pete said, stepping behind me. His hands circled my waist with the confidence of ownership before lifting me high into the air. After I'd safely landed, he hopped over after me, lickety-split, and grabbed my hand. "And I'm *not* above breaking the rules from time to time," he finished with one of those looks that made me squirm.

I wish I could say I was strong enough to snatch my hand back before I could start feeling attached again. But the sad truth was—I was more like holding on for dear life.

After unloading the feed, Pete reloaded the truck with wriggling boys, who cheerfully ganged up on me about my driving so he could take over. While the boys and Blue bounced around in the back like bottles of soda ready to pop, Pete took advantage of their absence by slipping an arm around my shoulder. He was still going on about "woman drivers," and I was trying hard not to laugh at his jokes. After a particularly un-PC punchline, I elbowed him in the ribcage, and he gave me a boyish grin. Again, I had the strongest feeling that he was having as much fun as me.

When we got back, we were running a little behind because of all the extra horsing around, but it was worth it to see the shiny happy reflected on our faces. I sent the boys in to wash up and get started on their homework. Pete stayed behind to help wash out the bottles and put them back in their crates to dry and sanitize in the baking sun.

We'd just finished the job, when he said, "That was a lot of fun. Thanks for letting me ride along to help."

"Thanks for actually *bein'* of help—the boys can sometimes be more trouble than they're worth," I said with no small amount of affection.

"You're something else, Kate Connelly." His gaze on my face was so soft it felt like a lover's caress.

Something stirred in my chest. "It's funny . . . I was just thinkin' the same thing about you earlier on."

He arched a brow. "Do tell."

My little confession had turned my face pig-snout pink, so I busied myself scooping gold nuggets of grain with a cut-off plastic milk jug. He countered by placing a hand on the sway of my back, drawing me to him.

"I guess great minds think alike," he murmured into my hair, causing my spine to do a little shimmy.

"Um . . . I gotta get back to work." I began backing away from his force field.

"You mean there's more?"

"Uh—yeah." I swiped a hand through my hair. "So I better drive you home now, so I can get back and finish before dark." I started to go when he caught my hand.

"Hey, I said I wanted to help you work this afternoon, so I'll stay until it's finished."

I eyed our clasped hands. "I believe you only mentioned somethin' about workin' out, which you've accomplished. And I have to get you back in case my father surprises us with an early return and catches me here with a . . ." Boy wouldn't work, and guy seemed too generic for him. I struggled to find the correct word. "*Male* friend," I finished, making us sound salacious.

"Maybe we can finish before he gets back?" he suggested. I shook my head, an unconscious sigh escaping. Pete looked at me sharply. "Kate?" He squeezed my hand when I didn't answer.

"Hmmm?" I was absentminded with worry about the prospect of Daddy arriving any moment so I didn't pick up on his mood change right away.

He made sure to make eye contact with me. "How much more do you have to do?"

"Just, um, yunno, get dinner on the table, kids in bed, cleanin' up." Suddenly seeing where this was going, I puffed out some air. "A few more chores . . ."

"*More* chores?" He searched my face while I looked off in the distance. "Kate, I swear to God!"

"I wish you wouldn't."

"Then tell me! *All* of it. And I mean *everything*," he said, shaking me a little out of my silence.

"Just a few more things. It's no big deal—all part of the package when you have a ranch. Usually Daddy helps out a little with hay bales and pasture stuff but lately he's, um, been . . ." I kind of petered out when I saw Pete's face go rigid. I shrugged my shoulders. *What could I say?*

"When do you get your homework done?"

"I used to do it after the boys were in bed. Now I do it while the water tank fills. The uh . . . tank is broken. Actually, there's somethin' stuck inside, I think, so it's been tricklin' out real slow." I quit jabbering, realizing I'd said too much.

"Does your father have a job outside the home I don't know about?" I shook my head, watching his face change colors. "Then why the hell isn't *he* out here helping out?" he exploded.

"Um—he sorta has a bum leg," I explained.

He snorted. "Bum is about right."

"Hey, listen." I grabbed his arm. "I prefer him *not* to be around most of the time, anyway."

Pete ignored my last statement to grill me. "Where's he supposed to be?"

"Buyin' feed?" I tried.

"Buying feed," he repeated. "All this time? That's his excuse?"

"Well, usually it's . . ."—I lowered my voice to my father's decibel—"'I'm busy runnin' a household.'"

"Right. Tell that one to the cows . . . I think we all know who's running this household," he muttered before averting his face to stare out at the fiery horizon. I watched as the sun framed his silhouette in its lazy glow.

"Well, I guess now you can see what I meant when I said 'my day is a workout,'" I joked.

"Kate, please . . . don't make light of this." Pete seized me by the shoulders, his eyes pleading with mine. "I didn't know"—he gestured around—"any of this . . . I was never apprised of your situation."

I thought the way he said that sounded funny. *Why would he be?*

He released me to pace around like a caged lion. "I mean I knew you had chores to do—dinner, housework, laundry that included a washer *and* a drier. You know . . . inside lady stuff." I slanted him a look at that last remark. "But I never realized that a teenage *girl* was doing the back-breaking labor of running a ranch inside and out, with the aid of an eight and four-year-old!"

I just stood there red-faced and tight-lipped, feeling exposed and regretful that I'd aired our dirty laundry. And stung by the way he referred to me.

"And then to top it all off, you head out to waitress on the weekends!" He threw this out, with his arms, before whirling around as though unable to face me and my sorry situation another second. It was kinda fascinating to watch him unravel over something as trivial as my pathetic life.

"Pete, it's alright." I tugged his arm loose from his side and tried to shake out his tension. "It's not that bad—really. The boys help me, and we get to hang out together. I usually don't have much to do with the cattle in the pasture. It's only been lately that Daddy's been so-so . . ." I sighed, not knowing how to phrase it without it sounding bad, "MIA," I finished.

Pete looked pained, his eyes slipping away from mine. He smeared his hands over his face and through his hair. Made a snarling noise. "Please don't make excuses for him—I really don't think I could take it."

"It's really not such a bad life." I tried to turn both him and the situation around. "At least we get to eat donuts every once-in-a-while." I nudged him in the side, trying to force a smile.

Pete shook his head, gazing down on me with the soulful eyes of someone trying to communicate something of vital importance. A hug came crashing into me, and we stood like that, absorbing each other's comfort and strength. Somehow, our relationship seemed to be symbiotic—he inexplicably seemed to need me as much as I needed him. I peered up at him with newfound appreciation.

"What's that look for?" he wondered.

I just smiled enigmatically until he bent and kissed me—one swift, bruising kiss on the lips. After which, he visibly brightened.

"You know what, Country Kate? Your life is about to change . . . for the better!" he declared before snatching Daddy's old Stetson off a hook in the shed and plopping it on my head.

"Oh really?" I snorted. "Don't tell me you and Drews figured out the winnin' lottery numbers durin' all those mentorin' sessions?"

"Nope," he popped at me playfully. "Nothing that dramatic. But you just wait and see—I have a few tricks up my sleeve."

I forced a laugh and removed the dusty hat from my head, feeling miffed by where this was going. I was already trying hard not to feel like a rescue puppy when he reached out and ruffled my hair.

"We're gonna make some changes 'round here." His sincere words were all drawled out in humor, so I didn't have the heart to tell him he was overstepping his boundaries.

"Fine. You get right on that. Meanwhile, I've got a ranch to run, so I have to drive you back now, cowboy." I set the Stetson on his head and stepped back to admire the effect. *Sigh.* Of course, he looked hotter than a Ralph Lauren model, a country superstar, and the Marlboro Man all put together.

I turned to go when he caught my hand and held it over his heart. I could feel it beating there under my hand, steady and sure.

"I mean it, Kate—I want to help you. Nobody should have to bear the burdens you do at seventeen."

Words that had me feeling more like a charity case than a girlfriend. Was he here because he felt *sorry* for me? He'd said that, not once, but twice before. *Am I so pathetic that pity is the only emotion I can elicit from him?* My stomach twisted. I didn't want his charity. Or his pity. I yanked back my hand.

"If you *really* wanna help me, don't try and take my ranch hand away!" I snarled then spun around to stalk off.

"Kate, listen to me, you stubborn girl." He grabbed my arm. "You need help. Your family—"

I whirled back around. "Was doin' fine before you got here! So just stay out of our lives! Go back to where you came from . . . and we'll be just fine when you leave." My voice hitched at the end, giving me away.

Pete withdrew his hands from my shoulders, stuffed them into his pockets. A long moment passed where he scrutinized my face, and I set my jaw against him. He started to say something, then stopped to remove the Stetson from his head. Running his hands along the rim, he looked me in the eye.

"You *really* want me to leave you alone? Just disappear like I've never been here, so you can go back to the way things were?"

Big shaky breath in, I nodded my head. I couldn't speak around the lump lodged in my throat.

He barked out a humorless laugh. "Because I gotta tell you the truth, Kate—things didn't look like they were really working out too well for you before."

I raised my chin a fraction higher. "I was fine."

"Don't kid yourself—you were right on the verge of drowning when I showed up."

My eyes glistened with unshed tears. I had that *déjà vu* feeling, like we were back in the western, engaged in a duel—Pete with his Stetson, me with my boots, our weapons, once again, angry words lashing out to hit the other where it hurt most.

"What are you my lifeguard now?" I sneered.

"You need help, Kate. Admit it . . . if not for yourself, then for your brothers."

"Oh, so now it's about helping *my brothers* is it? You really had me goin' there for a while Pete, the-Elite-Cadet, our whole family's savior." My arms flapped wildly about. "Fix all our woes by snatchin' up my little brother and leavin' behind a big ole fat check to assuage your guilty conscious. You almost had me convinced you *really* cared."

Hurt instantly muddled the shine in his eyes. "I *do* care and think you should let me help you."

"That's rich!" I cackled. "Pardon the pun. *You* helping *me*?—you can't even help yourself!" I lifted my palm. "Look at you! Your life is so golden, is it?—with your pedigree, gourmet foods, shiny Hummer." I used my most mocking tone. "If your life is so great then why are you always stalking me? *Huh*? Don't you have *better* things to do than hang around with a *seventeen-year-old girl*?" I flung his words back at him, because he was always bringing up my age like he was my big brother or something. ". . . Don't tell me—it's lonely at the top after all?"

Pete was frozen, like in shock that I'd turned on him. Didn't care; I wanted to hurt him as much as he'd hurt me.

"No," I shook my head, "I don't think it's *nearly* as great as you make it out to be. As a matter of fact," I bludgeoned on, sensing the truth as I said it, "I think you're more than just a little bit lonely and desperate. So desperate for somethin' real—maybe for a *real* brother of your own—that you're willin' to steal mine!"

I saw that my zinger hit the bulls-eye, because he actually staggered backward, as if from a blow. I felt bad right away, like the arrow had pierced me instead, oozing out crimson anger instead of blood. But it was too late—his eyes had already gone flinty on me.

"Well, I'm sorry that's how you feel, Kate," he said coldly. "But I'm here to do a job . . . and that's exactly what I'm going to do from now on."

A few tears escaped to run down my face, but there was no softness left in his eyes when he looked at me.

"Think it's time to leave the Ponderosa now." He flung the Stetson back into the shed, where it landed on some Tillman Mills feedbags. He turned to go.

I made a desperate grab. "Pete, I—"

He shrugged me off roughly, sending shock waves of despair all the way to the soles of my boots. I never wanted to feel that powerful anger towards me again, but here it was, scorching in its intensity. I forgot how mercurial he could be—going from Death Valley to Absolute Zero in two seconds flat.

Pete was beating a hasty retreat, kicking up little arcs of dirt, when he did an abrupt about-face. I looked up expectantly for a truce, was quickly disappointed. "I can do *one* thing for you, Kate . . ." His voice was rigid as his face. "I will no longer *stalk* or hang around with you."

"That's *two* things!" I screeched, with the requisite number of fingers.

I didn't *ask* him to come home with me today! Didn't ask him to try and save me—as if I needed *his* help! He was trying to turn the tables on me by playing the victim, but I remembered how he'd lied and manipulated me, how he was *still* doing it.

"Why don't you add, *talk* to me while you're at it!" I flung at his retreating back.

He spun back around like I'd pegged him with a dirt clod. "Be careful what you wish for, Kate." He repeated my earlier words.

"Oh . . . I always do." I did the same.

Pete searched my eyes one last time for the hidden truth I kept buried. "Fine . . . have it your way—I'm out." He sounded and looked defeated. "You're on your own." Turning his back on me, he slammed through the door.

Aren't I always?

28

BROKEN SILENCE

Be careful what you wish for, cause you just might get it. These words echoed in my mind as I trudged along to gym with the other sanguine pedestrians on a Thursday afternoon. Pete had stayed true to his word—he didn't even so much as glance my way the few times I saw him across campus. Or entering and exiting Spanish. Or out on the athletic field.

I saw him now, strolling along the sidewalk like the Pied Piper, with a string of followers in his wake, hanging on his every word. His jovial mood seemed out of place with the one going on with me. I'm not sure what I thought: We were two halves of a whole? If I was miserable then he should be miserable in equal proportion like disjoined twins? Well, obviously, that was *not* the case here.

My mouth twisted bitterly as I tried to pay attention to whatever inane, one-sided conversation Miguel was having with me: something, something football, something, something homecoming. I couldn't be bothered to keep up, although I tried to be unobvious about it, smiling and bobbing my head like a dummy at appropriate times. And I seemed to be so tired lately, not really falling asleep until well into the morning.

P.E. wasn't an improvement. Pete continued to withhold his gaze from me—even when we were within striking distance from one another, even when we were on the same team, and even after a particularly hard-fought goal was made by me. The hollow sound of ball hitting net resonated with the hollow feeling in my stomach when I realized he wasn't going to slap me five. Or shock me with a dazzling grin. Or throw his head back and laugh like my prowess on the soccer field was the punchline to a hilarious joke that only he got.

I'd unconsciously turned his way—already knowing his exact geographical location on the field like I had a GPS tracker on him. It's like something didn't really happen to me until I shared it with him. In the short span of time he'd been here, he'd become my person. But I just witnessed my person stare right through me before turning to stalk in the opposite direction.

I tried not to feel hurt; it would be easier to unboil an egg. Lifting my lips, I accepted praise from Coach Sams and palm slaps from my supportive teammates. But the smile didn't reach my eyes or lift my mood. I tried rationalizing. After all, my person was a known liar and con artist, whose sole purpose here was to get us to sign my little brother's life away. I reminded myself of this over and over. But it was hard work to be at war with your own body . . . and everybody else.

I felt like a beat-down, bloodied warrior the battle switching from one combat zone to another these days. I was at it again with Andrew, because he'd overheard me yelling, then witnessed Pete bang out the door to go catch his ride. He accused me of chasing his favorite cadet away. I said it was a good thing to chase the bad guy away. Of course, Andrew didn't believe that—which I was sick to death of—so I just let it all out on him, my eight-year-old, star-struck brother. I pulled out my facts and reason and whapped him over the head with it. Apprised him about eavesdropping on Pete's little convo, that we were a mark to him and nothing more. I revealed how Pete had quizzed him about me the day *after* we'd already had our picnic, how he'd said that he was just a kid and probably got his days mixed up.

Andrew saw the light all right. And I saw the light go right out of his eyes. It seemed he finally believed, which I thought would be a good thing. But he'd wanted to believe with his whole heart—like I did—that his mentor was one of the good guys. It was like I'd told him Batman was really the devil in disguise. He was disbelieving, then disappointed, disillusioned, and finally disgusted—mostly at me, the bearer of bad news, for telling him and blowing his perfect image of his hero. Not only was he mad at me, but he was more discontented with his life than ever, and willing to overlook everything anyway for a chance to go to "The Academy." Pete or no Pete.

Full disclosure was a wrong move. I thought maybe the truth would realign us back together. Instead it set us further apart. I realized now it was a selfish decision. Really, I'd just wanted *someone* to unburden myself to and had hurt my brother in the process.

My chest felt tight. Trying to catch breath, I stopped loping after the herd. Looked up to seek guidance from the blazing sun, and a wave of dizziness overcame me. I heaved some carbon dioxide from my lungs. *Man!* I was flat out exhausted. Exhausted from lack of sleep. Exhausted from fighting. *Why am I even fighting so hard?* All I wanted to do was close my eyes and go to sleep. I swear—I could've dropped on this very spot, in this itchy grass, even if it was located smack dab in the middle of a minefield. *Maybe I'm getting sick?* Overwhelmed, I leaned over, deep breathing in ozone and dust.

Coach Sams noticed and jogged over. "Katie, you all right?"

"I, um . . . feel kinda dizzy, actually," I admitted.

"Can you walk?"

I inhaled a deep breath through my nose, willing myself to hold it together. "Yes, ma'am. . . . I think so. I'm sorry."

"No need to apologize. Here, let me get someone to assist you back to the gym." Before I could think to stop her, Coach Sams called out, "Davenport, can I get some help over here?"

I looked up, horrified, to where Pete was standing on the sidelines, yucking it up with good ole Ashley-Leigh and her purple posse. She rolled her eyes exaggeratedly and mouthed a snarky comment—no doubt about this being some lame ploy to get his attention. I saw him squint in our direction, creating a hand-visor so he could see better. The lively expression fled his face when he saw me crouched over with Coach Sam's arm around my shoulders. A couple of teammates drifted over to see if I was all right. I tried to assure everyone I was fine, but my voice had no volume. I was actually mortified by the thought of an icy-cold Pete having to help me hobble to the gym like a little old lady.

He came jogging over, a grim look on his face. *Oh Gah! Not more sympathy.* That was worse. I didn't think I could take one more ounce of his pity. If I was feeling sick before, I was feeling positively faint with humiliation now. A few more players trailed after him to investigate. *Oh Lord!* I propped myself up as best I could, even as my head swam. I *needed* to lie down.

"You know what, Coach Sams . . . I'm feelin' much better," I lied unconvincingly. "I-I think it was just a cramp in my side." She looked doubtfully at my blanched face. "Really. I'm fine. I don't need any help . . ." was just coming out of my mouth when Pete arrived.

He immediately snorted at my feeble words. "Why am I not surprised you would say that?"

I tried to look indignant, but it was hard work when I was on the verge of collapse. My ears were ringing, and my face was fish-belly white, I'm sure.

"Okay, everybody back away," he said like he was king of the universe. Why was I not surprised when everyone instantly complied? And then, like a stick of gum, he bent me over and stuck my head between my legs. "Just deep breathe, in and out, Kate."

God almighty! Maybe I should try to pass out? It was a testament to how sick I was that I couldn't conjure up a single twinge of color anywhere on my face. I wanted to argue but knew if I opened my mouth at that moment, I would throw up all over the cheerfully bright sneakers he'd paid for.

"Someone toss me a water bottle, quick," he commanded again. About five seconds later, I felt the cooling rush of water pouring over the back of my neck. It dribbled onto my face, helping wash the sheen of sick off. I instantly felt a wee bit better and attempted to rise, but he didn't allow it.

"Keep breathing in and out slowly for a few more seconds." Pete used the calm, neutral voice of a trained paramedic at the scene of an accident.

I complied, too weak to do anything else. And was only grateful for his commanding presence when he made everyone leave. Despite the fact I felt like he despised me, I gradually started to feel better, at least like I wouldn't faint in the upright position.

"I think I'm okay now," I murmured, trying to stand up again.

"Come up nice and slow, Kate," he said, rubbing my back gently.

I nodded my head, feeling mortification catch up to, and surpass, sickness as I slowly unfolded myself. I kept my eyes closed, preferring the colored spots behind my eyelids to the cool distance in his eyes or worse—pity. Finally, I opened them to see Shelby and Jake staring at me like they were on a deathwatch. A few scattered claps began like I'd just emerged from the bottom of a particularly brutal football heap. *Man was I ready to exit stage right!*

I was still too pale for the heated flush of embarrassment to take hold and still couldn't meet his eyes, but felt like I ought to say something. "I-um . . . guess I should say thank you." I hated so much that he'd been the one to have to help me. Right after I'd told him I didn't need his help.

Pete gave a snorty laugh. "Don't over exert yourself—you already look like you could go down any second."

I moved to glare at him, but it didn't have any force of energy behind it. "I'm fine."

"You are far from fine, Kate," he said, the ice in his tone thawing slightly.

"I'm just a little tired."

"Yeah, I guess carrying the weight of the world on your shoulders would get a little tiring."

"I wouldn't have the weight of the world if you weren't tryin' to bust up my family!"

Just then, Coach Sams came trotting back over. "Feelin' better, Katie?"

"Yes, ma'am," I answered, dodging her eyes.

She set a hand on each of our shoulders. "Pete, would you mind escorting Katie back to the gym now?"

He nodded at her; she nodded back. Before I could argue, she'd taken back off to get the game going again. So Pete and I set off, silently, back to the gym. About halfway there, he took my arm to make me stop and rest.

"I'm fine now. *Really.* I can take it from here." A pretty unbelievable statement when I was winded just from the telling of it.

He shook his head and unset his mouth to say, "I'm trying to be patient here, I really am. . . . Did you even eat lunch today?"

I finally felt blood seep into my face. "Not that it's *any* of your business . . . but yes, I did." I thought of the protein bar I had in the library while I emailed Reese and typed up my English paper.

"Are you getting sick? You don't look well," he informed me as my face changed colors again.

"Of course, I'm not well!" I vented. "I'm practically worryin' myself to death thanks to you and your shady organization!"

"Right. And working yourself to the bone has nothing to do with this little episode."

"As a matter-of-fact, it doesn't. I . . . just had a panic attack, if you must know. That's it. Like I said—*fine*." I thumped myself like a moron.

"A panic attack? That's how you're going to spin this?"

"Yup. But I'm over it . . . and you," I announced, then watched as his nostrils flared in and out with each breath he took. *Better than icy indifference.* "So you can run on back to dazzlin' everybody out there, cause your performance is wearin' thin on me."

I thought that might make him turn around, but he simply screwed up his mouth and glanced heavenward. Then he gripped my arm and practically hauled me the rest of the way in, pausing only to open the gym door for me. We marched past staring volleyball players to the girls' locker room, where he deposited me.

"I'll be waiting for you," he warned.

Well that got my ire up. I stomped in to retrieve my gym bag and backpack and abruptly ran out of energy so I sprawled out on the bench to compose myself before trudging out. True to his word, he was waiting. I sighed. *This* wasn't healthy—I might get used to it.

"You can go now," I said in my most acid tone while he relieved me of my bags. "Please, Pete." My voice cracked. "I've got it." I reached for my bag.

"We can do this the easy way or the hard way, but I'm escorting you to your car, then seeing that you get home safely." He eyed the set of my jaw and let out a long sigh. "For once in your life, Kate, take the easy way . . . I'm sure you're already embarrassed enough without everyone watching me carry you across the parking lot."

"Fine!" I hissed, then did my best imitation of stalking past; it felt like I was wading through water.

We stopped to pick up Mikey, who requested a Hummer ride. I was way too tired to protest, and thought it wasn't a bad idea anyway—just in case. But I made it back home without further incident, even managing to shove out of my car without the jaws-of-life prying me out.

Pete stared at me leaning against my car, and his forehead creased. Feigning disinterest, I watched as he withdrew the first-aid kit from the backseat and shuffled through it looking for something. I had a funny feeling it was something for *me*. Sure enough, he glanced over at me again, looking miffed when he came up short. Then he rummaged around in the glove box before coming up both empty-handed and aggravated-looking. But he didn't come away completely empty-handed—an exuberant four-year-old stuck his hand in there, yapping in his ear the whole walk over.

"Okay bud, it's the end of the road today." Pete fist-bumped Mikey. "I gotta get back to your brother. You take care of your sister, okay?"

"Okay, Pete, I will," Mikey returned solemnly.

"Go on into the house and turn on the air conditioner for her, so it'll be nice and cool while she rests on the couch."

"Yes, sir!" Mikey hugged his leg and then ran to do his bidding.

The boss-of-the-universe leveled me with a look. "Kate, you need to rest . . . and I'm not just talking about the present moment. You're probably slightly anemic on top of exhausted. Since you don't eat meat, you should take iron supplements for a while."

I snorted. "Don't tell me—you also have an MD I don't know about. I told you, I'm fine. Just tired and *stressed*."

He ignored my excuses (which were as tired as me). "I'll be taking Andrew home every day now." I started a protest he cut off. "It'll be better this way. Better for you. Better for me." Words that hammered the fragile shell that was my chest. ". . . Easier all the way around. Don't bother arguing, because I'm going to set it up with your father."

I folded my arms across my chest, mostly in an unconscious gesture to quell my breaking heart. "Who died and made you boss?"

Bait not taken, he took another moment to stare at me with an expression I'd describe as the opposite of distant. "Take care of yourself, Kate."

I didn't do anything but stare wordlessly as Pete walked away from me . . . again.

29

BEST LAID PLANS

The growl of the Hummer's engine, and the flash of its shiny black metal, were novel additions to our tedious, rural landscape. Pete came idling to a stop, waiting for Andrew to jump out. I heard the animated rise of my brother's voice being carried away by the wind followed by the heavy thud of a well-built door shutting off music.

Again, true to his word, Pete had arranged with Daddy, much to the delight of Andrew, to drop him off every day after tutoring or mentoring . . . or whatever else they were calling it these days (*brainwashing* came to my mind). I wondered how much this had to do with him not wanting to see me, and how much it had to do with him wanting to help lighten my load. It did give me a jumpstart on my chores, so I was no longer up half the night finishing everything.

I held my breath for the driver's door to open, ears straining, chest swelling with anticipation. I kept hoping Pete would come in, so we could kiss and make up. Stubborn pride prevented me from making the first move. The familiar band closed around my chest when the Hummer zoomed off, exiting at a faster pace than arriving. *Who could blame him?* I looked at our dismal little spread through his privileged eyes. All the things that were supposed to be colored were slowly turning gray: our house, pasture, fence posts. Even the twittering birds, pecking uselessly on the ground were a burnt-out ash.

I bet Pete couldn't wait to get back to his old life. He'd probably wash the dusty film off his Hummer—and his hands of us—the minute he walked away. I remembered him complaining to Ranger, because he'd made his job more difficult. Pete had made it clear he was aiming to wrap it up in one week, two tops. It had been the amount of time it takes for summer to meld into fall. And for me to warm to him, and for him to chill to me.

I harbored grim satisfaction in the way I'd thwarted their plans for us. *Easy mission, my rear* I thought, yanking a rope of wet clothes from t he washer. So far, so good. We were holding steady, our little team. Andrew held up his end of the bargain—reluctantly. Daddy *still* hadn't signed t he paperwork, not liking the fine print once I pointed it out to him. Mikey . . . well Mikey was still shadowing Daddy every chance he got, insisting he *not* send Drewy away. I think that's why Daddy was staying away so much—he couldn't take the heat so was getting out of the kitchen.

I watched, through the framed picture of our front window, my brother's daily glow fade the minute he faced our house, and felt a sharp pang for it. I was forcing him to bridle his gifts. He balked every day, hating to dumb himself down. Like putting a chain around the hoof of a racehorse, it went against nature. Even though Andrew understood the situation better, he still blamed me and wore his resentment like one of his new "Academy" T-shirts. I couldn't blame him. I'd felt the same way towards Mama when she made me throw my game. It was a terrible way to feel towards someone you loved—a double whammy because you felt guilt on top of resentment.

I was busy taking out the very thing I'd just been thinking of: a sharp navy tee with a gold lion emblazoned on the front. I handled it like I'd just pulled it from the cesspool instead of the washing machine. Felt like mixing it in would taint the whole wash like a red sock in a load of whites.

Just like those mentoring sessions—even a little bit of that a cademy seemed to be tainting my little brother. He was suddenly privy to all he was missing in life. How good things could be. Would be . . . if he'd just sign on the dotted line. I think ignorance would've been preferable for us. Not bliss, but easier. I mean now that we'd had a taste of Pete Davenport's world, how could we possibly go back to our old existence and have a hope of being satisfied? It seemed as bland as a bowl of oatmeal after a vacation filled with elaborate breakfast buffets.

"Hey, Drews!" I called from the kitchen, dropping my basket to come in for a hug. "How'd it go today?"

"Fine."

"Just fine?" He shrugged his shoulders, and I decided not to press the sore point. "Are you hungry?"

"Nope."

"Not even for homemade chocolate-chip cookies?" I used my most tempting tone.

"*Especially* not for chocolate-chip cookies."

"Since when do you not like chocolate-chip cookies?"

"Since I learned cancer cells feed off sugar," Andrew replied with more emotion than he'd shown in a long while.

I was quiet a beat, thinking of how to turn the conversation away from the dark side. "Well, I guess it's a good thing you don't have cancer then." This was met with a scathing look, like I just didn't get it. (I'd been on the receiving end of that look for quite a while.)

"Can I have his share?" Mikey came up behind big brother to unabashedly hug on him. Andrew managed to turn it into a headlock. I waited for him to let go until Mikey's face started to turn the same color as boiled hot dogs.

"Stop that!" I yanked on Andrew's arm. "You know I don't like it when you do that to your little brother, who has been waitin' all afternoon for you to get home," I said pointedly.

"Aw, Come on!—I'm just showin' him some of me new moves." After which, Andrew tripped and flipped Mikey over his leg, so that he came crashing to the floor like a feedsack.

"Andrew!" I scolded as I peeled his shadow from the floor. "What's gotten into you?"

"It's okay, Kadee. I'm not hurted." Mikey spun around for my inspection. I grabbed my littlest brother and wrapped my arms around him. I couldn't help notice the divide between us. *Intolerable.*

"I know what would make this better," I said, reaching over to nab Andrew. "A Drewy sandwich!" I pulled him into a squishing hug between a squealing Mikey and me, squeezing him like the force of my hug could push out the old Andrew, from before all this Academy malarkey started. The best I got was a giggle that finally pushed its way through his sealed lips to burst out into an open laugh. Satisfied with that, I let him go but not before ruffling his hair.

"So, what's this about not wantin' my homemade cookies made especially for you? I even added my secret ingredient—the one sure to combat cancer." Mikey grinned. Andrew rolled his eyes, but there was a hint of a smile on his lips. "Can anyone guess what it is?" I teased.

"I can! I can!" Mikey's feet left floor the same time his hand hit air. "Wuv!" he blurted out triumphantly, unable to refrain from revealing the punchline to our long-running family joke. Plus, it had the added appeal of being the only answer he could come up with faster than big brother.

"That's right," I said, taking his doughy hand, and one whose fingers were already almost as long as mine. "Love."

Andrew looked up at me with his wide, intelligent eyes; it was my vulnerable little brother standing before me now. "But Mama got cancer and she *always* used love as her secret ingredient."

"Oh, Drews." I pressed his face to my chest, hoping he could feel my love beating into him.

We were just sitting down to dinner when the thud of heavy work boots (which was a misnomer if I'd ever heard one) outside the door crashed our party-of-three. Blue jumped up from under our feet, growling a moment too late to be a proper watchdog. We watched as he skidded over to greet his prodigal master, tail wagging, never one to hold a grudge.

The rest of us weren't so forgiving. It'd been a few days since we'd seen Daddy, and that was for about the span of two commercials—long enough to hand down a bunch of orders and instruct us about what we were doing wrong, then let us know he didn't want to be bothered while he watched the game.

"Uh-oh. Looks like The Sarge is home," Andrew announced the obvious.

Our eyes cast around for something we had done wrong, some object left out or muddy shoes left on. I wondered why we hadn't heard the unmistakable, unmuffled noise pollution of his Bronco pulling in. And then realized: he must've planned a covert sneak attack to bust his wayward kids on some kind of infraction we were getting up to in his absence.

I felt the familiar contempt creep over me. Not much he could say though—we didn't even so much as have the TV on tonight. When Daddy barged through the door, you could practically here the *dunt-dunt-dunt!* His eyes zeroed in on me occupying the space at the head of the table.

"Katie, what's that dog doin' in the house?"

"Sorry, Daddy." I rose from his seat to let a whining Blue out; he left a bundle of sad dismay.

"If a commander can't trust his troops to hold down the fort in his absence, then how can I trust you to follow my rules when you're called to duty?"

Daddy said, forming some kind of analytical logic I was too tired to grasp. He looked down on me like he was waiting for more contrition than I was willing to offer up. When none was forthcoming, he began a preacher's pace across the length of the dining room table.

I breathed in through my nose, deciding on a preemptive strike against his sermon. "I'm sorry, Daddy. I was seein' to his sore paw with the salve you use for the calves, and then forgot he was in the house when I started dinner. It won't happen again." I went with a half-truth.

His hard look hadn't softened one iota. What was I missing? *Earnestness.* I blinked up at him, my eyes trying to conjure crocodile tears. "I'm really sorry, Daddy."

A few seconds of listening to the clock tick with three kids sitting at a table still as stones happened before Daddy relented. "Is them cookies I smell?"

"Yes, sir." I immediately hupped to it. "Would you like some supper, Daddy? I have your plate warmin' in the oven." I'd found the missing ingredient at last—solicitousness.

"That sounds good, Katie-girl." He was mostly angry we hadn't all jumped for joy that he was rewarding us with his presence. He plopped down, in the chair I'd just warmed for him, satisfied in the knowledge he was still king of his castle. "How's them lessons goin', boy?" He cuffed Andrew on the back of his neck—the closest thing to affection Daddy willingly gave.

"Good," Andrew replied, digging into his cooling meatloaf.

"The Davenport cadet treatin' you all right?"

A couple of chews and a swallow happened. "Yes, sir. He's been great."

"Good. Really apply yerself and get a lot outta these lessons, son. After all . . . they're free."

"Yes, sir."

With hot-padded hands, I brought out Daddy's dinner and switched out my cooling plate of mashed potatoes and vegetables, then went and sat on the other side of Mikey. "Hey Daddy," he piped up before I could think to stop him. "Didjaknow that Pete took us for a wide in his Hummer?"

I sighed, feeling like he coulda talked all day without saying that.

The fork going into Daddy's mouth halted mid-air. Andrew and I exchanged looks. *Shoot.* We forgot to tell Mikey not to tell. It happened over two weeks ago, but there was no statue of limitation on Daddy's consequences. His fork went down, and his anger went up. Mikey was on the receiving end of one of Daddy's filthiest looks.

"Now why would he do that?"

"Because I asked him to!" Mikey boasted.

"Excuse me, Daddy," I quickly intervened because Daddy's face was starting to change colors, "it was very early on and Andrew had finished testin' for the day. We had a few extra minutes, so he took us for a ride around the parkin' lot."

"I do not want Andrew's mentorin' time wasted on joy rides anymore. Do you three understand me?"

"Yes, sir," we chorused.

"We got more work to do around here than I can shake a stick at. And it continues to go undone, because *you*"—Daddy air-stabbed me with his fork—"claim there's not enough time in the day to do it . . . We got fences to mend, pens to muck, fertilizer to spread, need I go on?"

"No, sir."

"I've said it once, I've said it twice, I'll say it a thousand times: idle hands is the devil's workshop. You kids need to keep yer time occupied with fruitful activities like learnin' and workin' this ranch—teaches invaluable life skills." Daddy turned an approving eye on Andrew. "You see how my discipline plan is pannin' out for Andrew here. He's not only top of his class, but he's at the top of all eighth-grade kids across America, accordin' to the reports I've been gettin' from Cadet Davenport."

Now it was my turn to put down my fork. Nobody told me anything anymore. I wondered if Andrew knew and turned appraising eyes on him. His expression was about the same as Mikey's Batman mask, which scared me.

"He'd be a shoo-in at West Point. Although I don't know why we'd wait or fool around with senators' nominations," Daddy said derisively, "when the best o' the best is already offerin' up such a good deal."

Alarmed, I leaned around Mikey. "But Daddy, you read the contract. It says you have to give up parental rights for the duration of his training. You're not seriously considerin' that, are you?"

"Well, I'll give you the short answer to that—maybe."

"*What?*"

"Now you listen here, Katherine Lee," Daddy said, his voice going to a place that led nowhere good, "I ain't just handin' my son over to just anybody. This here Elite Academy is the very best there is . . . in the world!"

"But Daddy!" I spluttered for the hundredth time in a month, "You promised Mama you wouldn't send any of us away to special schools!" Even to my own ears I sounded like an over-played sad song you'd grown accustomed to tuning out.

"I ain't sendin' *you* or *Shadow* anywhere. . . . Far as I can tell, Andrew's the only one bein' sought after here."

"He's only eight-years-old!" I reasoned, not taking the bait.

Daddy pointed the blunt end of his knife at me. "You forget yer place, missy. Andrew is *my* son, and I'll do with him as I see fit . . . as I will *all* you kids, for that matter. Now I talked over my concerns with Cadet Davenport, and he said ninety-nine percent of the cadets' parents sign the paperwork. It's just a formality, so that meddlin' parents won't in'erfere with the trainin' . . . and there are reg'lar visitin' days allowed."

"*Allowed?*" I said.

Mikey shifted in his seat. I knew he was about to say something, so I squeezed his thigh under the table. But a determined Mikey was a lot like a penned bull right after the chute opened. "Daddy . . ."

"You will speak when yer spoken to, young man!" Daddy interjected quickly, eyes wildly bouncing around the room, refusing to settle anywhere near his youngest child's face.

Mikey reared across the table. "Daddy, you'wer NOT sendin' Drewy away to that school!"

We watched as Daddy's face turned the same color as the baked-in ketchup coating his meatloaf. Andrew and I exchanged glances again. Mikey, relieved of his mind-load, shoveled a mound of mashed potatoes into his mouth.

Some of Daddy's firm resolve seemed to implode like a cake pulled out of the oven too soon. "I've still not made up my mind, that's fer sure. It's a big decision. I sure don't like the idear of not seein' him ever' day."

I inwardly bristled, thinking he *didn't* see him every day but didn't say anything, as this was a step in the right direction. He almost sounded like a real father for once. The result of all this reasonableness was me wanting to unburden myself to him. Explain my mystifyingly strong feelings about the school, let him know we'd been followed and spied on, divulge the proof I had that Pete lied, that we were being conned. I wanted help to make sense of it all. To lay it all out on a bulletin board like a complex unsolved mystery.

But I didn't. Daddy had had it up to his eyeballs with female intuition and conspiracy theories, having lived through Mama's vivid breakdowns. He'd made it very clear he wasn't going through that again. Proof. That's what I needed. Like a victim of a crime—with no witnesses—coming to the police to report it, there would need to be solid evidence before an indictment. Or else I would end up sounding deranged. It was pretty much my word against theirs. And frankly, they were more credible than my intuition. They had all the numbers and facts on their side that Daddy loved so much. Especially his favorite number in the world—one.

Unfortunately, the only proof I actually had was against Pete. If I convinced Daddy about his lies, he would most likely just demand another mentor. A picture of a dimpled-brute with a smirk-smile entered my mind. I shuttered to even think of it. And the catch twenty-two was: blowing the whistle on Pete would result in his dismissal from my life. Even though I knew he wasn't on the up-and-up, I still didn't want him to go. Not yet . . . not ever. I couldn't even fathom having him disappear from my life as though he never existed. It was like suddenly trying to live without the sun—I was already severely deficient in my vitamin D from my self-imposed sabbatical of the last couple of weeks. But I still had the same problem I'd had since the beginning: I loathed his organization and everything it stood for—preying on the weak, lying and cunning, evil intentions creeping out from all sides. But I felt the direct opposite of that about their ambassador.

It was an impossible position to be in—falling for the enemy.

The boys had gone off to bed, and I'd just finished packing lunches for school the next day and was headed off to my own bed, loaded down with a basket of clothes and a bushel of worries.

"Night, Daddy," I called over my shoulder.

"Hold on a minute, Katie-girl." Daddy clicked pause on the TV, and I froze in the hallway. "I wanna talk to ya."

Warily, I plodded over to his duct-taped recliner. Daddy stood up, a wall of denim-on-denim. My head tilted up, a little crease forming between my brows. He cleared his throat before pulling me next to him on the couch. It felt awkward and strange but not entirely bad. My heart rate was holding steady . . . I didn't think this was anything too bad.

"Katie, I—" he *harrumphed* again. "I just wanna say I understand how you feel 'bout keepin' Andrew home. I know it comes from a good place, you tryin' to keep this family together. And I want you to know that whichever way it goes, my decision will be based on *nothin'* but doin' right by my boy."

Yeah right. I could practically see the dollar signs in his eyes so I averted mine to the fake wood paneling.

"One of the worst things that can happen in life is to live with regret. I know all about wasted chances," he said, referring to the track scholarship he lost back when he still wore a mullet and didn't have metal pins holding his ankle together. "I don't want Andrew to look back and blame me for keepin' him from movin' up in the world. This ain't some high-falootin' prep school we're talkin' about here—it's the world's most elite military trainin' facility. Do you understand what that means?"

"Yes, sir." I wondered if he did.

Daddy shifted on the couch, a peculiar look taking hold now. *Uh-oh.* Whatever was forthcoming, was the *real* reason we were sitting here having this little father-daughter chat.

"And that brings me to the next thing I wanted to say." He straightened up and gave me the kind of toothy smile usually reserved for game-show hosts. "I was over at Tillman Mills this afternoon gettin' feed. Ronald Tillman Junior was there and made a special point in comin' over to talk to me." He paused, waiting for my excitement to catch up to his.

"Uh-huh."

"Well, I think I must have quite a reputation in this town," he added like it was a compliment, "because that varsity football player was more nervous than a whore in church."

"Uh-huh."

"Well, the truth is Katie—you're growin' up and bein' seventeen and all—I can't hide you forever, much as yer mama wanted to. So I went ahead and gave my permission for Ronald Tillman to take you to homecomin' next Friday!" Daddy blurted out the same way Mikey did when he was chosen star student-of-the-week.

"*What?*" I rocketed up. Me avoiding him all week had been for not.

Daddy frowned at my tone, getting his first whiff of my feelings on the matter.

"What did you say?"

"I said you'd love to go!"

I dropped back down, clapping my hands over my face.

"I know, honey . . . it's excitin' news," he said, choosing to misunderstand my horror for excitement. "Now you know why I was upset to see you breakin' house rules when I was gone. I gotta be able to trust you to do the right thing when I'm not around . . . like when yer out on a date." Daddy's cheeks were two red apples, reminding me of where I got my easy blush. An awkward pause, and more throat-clearing ensued. "Did . . . did yer mama have a chance to talk with you about boys and maintainin' your virtue till marriage?"

OMG! I'd rather go muck those pens than endure a sex talk from my father. *So* completely bypassed that last question like a landmine. "But, Daddy, I don't even *like* Ron Tillman!"

"Why not? He's a handsome enough young man . . . and plays football," he added as though it were a check in the "pro" column.

"Because I don't like him *that* way," I reasoned, sounding like a sixth-grade version of myself.

I could tell, for him, he was trying to be patient. "That don't matter much, honey. You'll learn to . . . he's a good match for you."

"What do you mean by that?"

"It means that Ron Tillman is the eldest son of Ronald Tillman Senior, owner of Tillman Mills, and therefore, will inherit his father's business when he passes away."

"So?"

"So he will most likely stay right here in Clovis and marry a local girl."

"What does that have to do with me?" I said.

He sighed impatiently. "You could *be* that local girl."

Are you friggin' kiddin'? He was talking as if he were arranging a marriage instead of a date. Did he know what country we were living in? What century? I found myself back on my feet. "Daddy, I ain't gonna marry Ron Tillman!—I'd rather die!" I added dramatically.

Daddy lifted himself up to his full height, in the same manner he did before reaching for the paddle. "Now you listen up, young lady. This here is a good opp'rtunity—that family has all kinds of money. And this is your chance to put yer God-given assets to good use. . . . A girl in your position could do a *lot* worse for herself than marry Ronald Tillman Junior."

I could think of nothing worse—not even drowning myself in the cesspool.

"Now I do not want you to squander this opp'rtunity with yer mule-ish notions of what you ought to be doin'. Do I make myself clear?"

"Daddy, I think you're puttin' the cart before the mule here," I said, calming down. "One date does not a marriage make."

"Yes, well, Mr. Tillman has told me, on more'n one occasion, that his son speaks highly of you. It's up to you to parlay this into a relationship . . . you ain't likely to do better for yerself in life than to marry well."

Did a college degree and a career never occur to him for his daughter? I snorted but kept my mouth shut. After all, Ron Tillman would likely blow me off the second I didn't let him get to first base, so this whole convo was a waste of oxygen. And time. I decided to try a different tactic.

"Well, by homecomin', I'm sure you realize that a *dance* is involved."

"I'm well aware of that," he said. "As far as I can see, I'd rather my daughter be at a chaperoned dance than—out who knows where doin' who knows what at night. Anything bad usually happens after eleven anyway, so I let him know up front that that would be yer curfew. Yer to go to the game and to the dance and back home. With no stops in between."

I guffawed at that one. "And he *still* wanted to take me?"

"He sure did. Said he understood perfectly, and that he respected that."

I pictured Ronnie's dopey face leaning in to kiss me and felt nauseated immediately. "Daddy, I don't have a fancy enough dress to wear to a homecomin' dance and no money saved up to buy one." I'd never been so happy to be broke.

"I already thought of that." The proud papa fished around in his back pocket for his wallet, then counted off some bills with great ceremony. But I refused to accept them, knowing both where they came from and what they would be used for.

"That's a hun'erd dollars, young lady," Daddy said, impressing upon me the seriousness of the matter while pressing the money into my hand. "Now that's a lotta money. I expect to see some receipts and a purty, but modest dress . . . not too modest, I don't wantja tuh look dowdy, but not revealin' neither. Don't want the boy gettin' the wrong idear about you—you are the marryin' type, not the carousin' type." He leveled me with another look.

I growled in my throat. "Is goin' to homecomin' with Ron Tillman a direct order?"

"You know what? I'm *tryin'* to do somethin' nice for my daughter and gettin' spit in the eye for my trouble." Daddy glowered down at my defiant face a moment before snatching back the cash. "Suit yerself . . . you can work yerself to the poor house down there at Norma's for all I care. If yer too stupid to take advantage of a golden opportunity like this, then I've raised up a fool of a daughter . . . and you'll reap what you sow."

And so will you I wanted to spit, but kept my mouth firmly clamped as Daddy stuffed the cash back in his wallet, tossed it onto the coffee table, and sank down onto his reclining thrown. He released the bar to kick his feet back up. "Get to bed," he dismissed, clicking the TV back on. "Mornin' comes early."

I stomped off to my room in an even fouler mood than before. *Ronnie Tillman? Really?* The best he thought I could do for myself in life was to marry a beefy, spoiled, small-town rich kid whose muscles would surely turn to fat the moment he quit playing football.

Storming around the room, alternately flinging clothes into drawers and my closet, I wondered if he was right. *Is becoming Mrs. Ronnie Tillman my best option?* My stomach turned over every time I pictured the blank canvass that was my future: living in the trailer with my brothers and Daddy's tyranny, starting on the basics at junior college, then driving thirty miles to Portales to get my four-year degree from ENMU. I imagined myself going to classes during the day and working nights at the diner. Shuddered at the very bleak picture.

A glint of navy caught my eye. It was the jacket Pete gave me the night they'd been following me. It was juxtaposed in the closet next to a beat-up, old denim one. I thought of Pete and his glossy world. I thought of my dreary life waiting tables and taking English 101 at the JUCO in a couple of years.

Ugh! It wasn't that I thought I was too good for that life. I didn't think I was better than anybody else, except for that Ranger character, I thought scathingly. But if you really wanna know the truth—deep down, I always felt more like a Thoroughbred than a workhorse. I understood Andrew's frustration and resentment. He *did* belong in the world of the elite. Just *not* that Elite Academy. Come hell or high water, I was still determined to prevent him from going.

Maybe I needed to rethink my strategy? So far, I was getting shoddy results and punishing myself in the process. Daddy was half a wink away from signing up, and Pete was barely acknowledging my presence anymore. Perhaps I should go back to the old adage: Keep your friends close and your enemies closer. Instead of pushing Pete away this whole time, maybe I should've been trying to draw him in closer, see if I could get him to reveal his secrets. This new plan would certainly be a whole lot *funner* anyway.

Using feminine wiles seemed to have worked for Mama with Daddy, and it seemed to be working in Ashley-Leigh's favor. I mean it had gotten her pretty far so far. (A pang pierced my heart when I thought of her going the distance.) Maybe I should give it a go, too?

Thinking along these lines, I reevaluated tomorrow's ensemble like I was arming myself for war. Since the fallout with Pete, I'd gone back to my regular, drab clothes because it fit my mood. I reopened my jean drawer and peered inside. Only three pairs, and that included my old work jeans. I pulled them back out for consideration. They were faded and even had a couple of tiny tears in the leg where the fabric had worn thin. I only wore them around the ranch because they were so tight Daddy would never let me out the door in them. I understood why a little more now after remembering Pete's gaze lingering on me in the pasture . . . He seemed to approve of the country look on me.

Technically, I was forbidden to wear jeans to school at all. Since I was breaking house rules anyway, I decided to go for broke. So I set them out, along with one of my button-downs. I could do nothing about the boxy shape except maybe tie it into a knot around my waist. Last out I pulled a pair of clean socks to wear with my trusty-dusty boots. I headed to the shower whistling, the smile of a Cheshire cat spreading my lips.

Vigorously, is how I shampooed and conditioned my hair. My legs were meticulously shaved then oiled up with lotion as though they were due for inspection. Usually I just went to bed with wet hair and brushed it out in the morning, too tired to bother trying to style it. But tonight, I took the time to blow dry it ruler-straight. It was time for me to bring *my* "A" game. So on the agenda for tomorrow afternoon, was a little side trip to Walmart; it was time for some overdue shopping.

I went to bed dreaming of what I could've bought with that hundred dollars Daddy handed me.

30

CATCHING FLIES

Homecoming was exactly one week away. Reminders, in the royal color, littered the halls, and announcements from perky cheerleaders made the morning announcements. Everyone was buzzing with up-to-the-minute reports of who was going with whom. It was first hour, so all the hubbub was on mute for me.

I'd arrived early to avoid Ron and to zip out a quick email to Reese. She kept asking what was going on with Andrew and his cute mentor, as if she were really intrigued. I'd mentioned before that Pete had lied to me, explaining the situation as best I could without divulging my strong intuition that his academy was really some secret organization trying to snatch my little brother up for . . . God-only-knew what purpose.

I didn't want her to think I was weird. Or a witch, or anything like that. I always went for *normal*. I'd simply stated their ambassador was too good to be true, and leaving town soon anyway, so wasn't worth the effort. She immediately responded back with a: Maybe it was just a misunderstanding? And said I should definitely give him a second chance, because he was probably just trying to impress me. I snorted. *As if.* It was kinda hard to describe Pete on paper. He was like a miracle—you'd need to see to believe. Calling him cute was like calling the devil bad.

Reese also suggested *again* that a nice boarding school with a good reputation would be a good place for Andrew, and I should consider giving him my blessing if he wanted to go. That niggled me for some reason, though I didn't dwell on it too much. I mean . . . she was in the dark. Actually, it was sweet of her to care. I knew she couldn't get it—her life was probably the demon-free kind.

The thought of losing Andrew was enough to put me into a tailspin. My brothers were all that I had in life. All that mattered . . . until Pete crashed into my life. I bit my lip. My desire for him hadn't waned one bit with the knowledge he was a con artist. It felt like I was suffering from a sickness, and it seemed to have spread like wildfire through the entire student body, turning friend into foe and even brother against sister. I fervently prayed that Andrew would change his mind and wait for Ivy League.

The latest gossip hadn't caught up with me until I reached third-hour English. I could tell something was up right away, because a smug-looking Ashley-Leigh and Madison were jawing away in the area around my desk. I started to automatically tune them out, taking out my notes to unnecessarily go over before the quiz.

"Pete's been droppin' hints all week about *special* plans this Friday," Ashley-Leigh said so loudly she may as well have shouted it in my ear.

I had to admit—she got my attention. If not, her skirt would've. *Didn't know they sold spandex in fuchsia.*

"OhmiGod!" Madison squealed. "Do you think he's gonna ask you to homecoming?"

Ashley gave a high-pitched giggle. "I dunno cause the bell rang, and he had to get to class. But he said he'd tell me after school today." She paused to let that sink in. "Sounded mysterious . . . that's just like him you know."

Couldn't help myself, I snorted.

She looked down sharply. "Bitter much?"

"Sounds like a straight up blow off to me," I shot back, then ignored her to focus my attention on what plans Pete might be referring to. I couldn't fathom him going to our ridiculous homecoming at all, much less with the even more ridiculous Ashley-Leigh as his date.

Miguel slipped in after the bell, and we shared an eye-roll at Ashley-Leigh's expense. He leaned across the aisle. "Hey, I wanted to ask you, are you actually going to homecoming with the Ron Man? Cuz that's the word on the street."

I saw Ashley's back stiffen and couldn't resist a dig. "He asked my father's permission to take me, but I'm workin' Friday night," I said, giving Ron an out.

"Oh." Miguel's face relaxed. "That's good. Cuz I might've had to go along as your chaperone."

"Don't you mean you and *Jenn* might've had to go along as my chaperones? I think that's what they refer to as a double date." I smiled to take the sting out.

Miguel smiled sheepishly. "Right."

Class passed swiftly. I was in an especially good mood because I didn't purposefully miss any answers on the quiz today. It felt good. More than good—it felt right. I headed out the door with Miguel, who was chatting a mile a minute about the subject of the week. He promised to stop by the diner to cheer me up after the game, since I was stuck working. A pretend smile lifted my lips, but I wasn't too thrilled about a pack of crazed classmates, wearing ill-fitting suits and dresses with enormous mums pinned to them, sitting in my station feeling sorry for me. Not exactly a cheerer-upper, but I didn't say so.

"I'm lovin' the boots, by the way!" He smiled at me a little too long before disappearing into the crowd. The smile slowly faded from my face. I really liked Miguel but would have to do something about him. Sooner rather than later.

After a quiet lunch of hiding out and finishing my Pre Cal homework, I left the confines of the library and stepped outside for the first time since morning. The sky was a wide expanse of periwinkle blue, with a few wispy clouds dispersing into thin streaks with the blinding sun. As if on a whim, the wind picked up, vigorously blowing the new season up my tied shirt. I shivered and threw my arms around my waist.

I decided I'd tried about a day and a half too late for this look and wished fervently for one of my shapeless sweaters as I leaned into the wind. A group of senior guys, lounging over the hood of their Tundra, began cat calling. I waved back shyly but continued forward with wolf-whistles following my trail. I smug-smiled to myself—looked like my jeans were doing their job.

Predictably, I was the first one in class so I marched right up to Mr. Sanchez to plead my case. And I only felt a twinge of guilt telling him I got contacts. *After all, hadn't I been lying about needing glasses all along?* He easily agreed to move me back to my original seat. I beamed and headed for the door with a cheerful, "Thanks, Mr. Sanchez!"

"*De nada.*" Mr. Sanchez's smile was a little too enthusiastic for a teacher.

Oh Gah! I scurried out the door, cringing at the thought of my teacher checking out my assets. I still wasn't accustomed to wearing pants to school, much less butt-hugging jeans that clung to my legs like second skin.

Apparently, more than just Pete liked the "country Kate look." This morning one of the most popular senior boys said something that made me roll my eyes and blush at the same time: *I hate seeing you go . . . but I love watching you leave.* Really—so cheesy. Still, it brought a smile to my face, because it had been as easy as walking by. Who knew catching boys' attention could be so easy? But I wasn't fishing for just any ole big fish in our small pond. I was hoping to attract an angelfish . . . from somewhere beyond the sea.

Firmly holed up in the bathroom till class, I made use of my time smoothing down my hair with my slick palms. I took another minute to self-evaluate and decided to add some lip gloss and mascara to my shopping list this afternoon to add more oomph to my look. I still eschewed makeup as a whole; couldn't stand the clogging feel of it on my skin. When Ashley-Leigh used to use me as her life-sized Barbie, I would run to wash off all her efforts the second she let me go. Mama always referred to these sessions as "gilding the lily." I sighed, thinking: *como cambio el mundo*—how times change. I wished we could still be friends because I really missed her mom and female camaraderie.

But I was on a whole different wavelength now.

The warning bell rang. So with a final swipe of vanilla lip balm, I headed out, not wanting to be tardy, just late enough that Molly Donaldson already had a chance to move seats. I saw her sitting up front and center in my newly vacated seat. It was hard to tell who was scowling more: her, Miguel, or Ashley. *Definitely* Ashley-Leigh. I stifled a smirk because Miguel turned around to give me a disapproving grimace. A helpless shrug was my only stab at commiseration before slipping into my seat in front of Pete. I gave him my Mona Lisa, not exactly sure where we stood with each other. He instantly shot back with the kind of primal smile that should be tamed before it turned indecent. Blood swarmed to my face, shot down my neckline . . . and headed south.

Gah! Try to at least act cool, Kate.

I forced my body into stillness, but it took roll call and the bell-ringer just to get my heartbeat regulated. The expectation was killing me. Heaving a sigh, I flipped back some hair along my neckline and attempted to focus on the Spanish film we were watching today. A beat later, soft movement rippled down the length of my hair—Pete's finger parting the curtain and trailing along the back of my neck. A pleasurable, almost unbearable chill swept down my spine. I whipped around, my eyes flashing to his dark ones.

Slowly, one cheek lifted in that way it did when he was aroused to humor. "Sorry," he whispered, "I was just removing a hay seed from your hair."

I narrowed my eyes, trying but epically failing, to keep a smile off my face. "Ha-ha, very funny. Aren't you supposed to *not* be speakin' to me?" I followed that bit of maturity up by turning around and grinning like an idiot.

"Fine. I won't talk then," he mouthed into my ear, then proceeded to flick my hair with his pencil every few seconds, presumably just to annoy me (although it was having the opposite effect).

Playing hard to get, I refused to turn around. A minute later something crackly poked my back. I sighed exaggeratedly, waited a beat, then opened the note with Ashley-Leigh shooting sidelong daggers at me.

Does this mean you're talking to me now?

I scribbled back a brief *sí*, and tossed it back over my shoulder. Warm air stirred the back of my hair as he chuckled quietly. I noticed we were on the receiving end of several curious glances—guess it was pretty hard not to attract attention with a mile-wide smile on your lips. I was pretending to take notes when I felt paper brush the forbidden half-inch of exposed skin on my waist. My eyes cut to Mr. Sanchez, who had paused the TV to point out the vosotros form was used in Spain but not in Mexico. Apparently, we were visiting Barcelona today, but I had no idea because I was over the moon. Feigning impatience, I unfolded the note.

You're wearing my favorite outfit . . . and look particularly ravishing today.

Another grin threatened to split my face. So, he'd taken the bait. I scribbled back: *Flattery will get you nowhere* in my fanciest scrawl, then tossed it back over my shoulder with nobody noticing but Ashley-Leigh, who looked like she'd just popped a *Sour Patch* candy in her mouth. Pete coughed out a laugh before quickly stifling it with a cleared throat. Once again, I marveled at how much difference a day makes.

The bell rang, and we stood up, grinning at each other like a couple of goons . . . until I felt the pressure of Miguel's eyes on my back. I turned to see him savagely stuffing books into his backpack. My easy smile faded, and when I turned back around, it was to find Pete zipping his backpack around his notebook while waiting *for me*. Miguel almost tripped over my backpack in his rush out the door. Pete continued to quietly observe me as I finished packing up. I had a sudden, sure feeling that he'd missed me almost as much as I'd missed him. My stomach took a plunge at that heady thought.

About that time Ashley-Leigh decided to make her exit, flouncing past us with a look-what-you're-missing smile aimed at Pete. He returned a semblance of a smile before maneuvering me—hand to the small of my back—through the jam-packed hallway. Together, we exited out the door and into a blast of crisp autumnal air. As if in mutual appreciation of the moment, we paused to watch the flags snap and billow in the breeze. Then my backpack was confiscated from me, and we began ambling our way up the sidewalk behind the stragglers stringing behind the pack.

"You know . . . those jeans ought to be outlawed." Pete's icebreaker was followed by a lazy, lop-sided grin.

"It's funny you say that. They're on my father's," I paused to air quote, "'forbidden list.'"

He barked out a laugh. "In this particular case, I can't say that I blame him."

"Well, maybe you two outta get together and go bowlin'—you do seem to have a lot in common," I said way sharper than I intended.

"No offense, but I sincerely hope not."

"Military background, dead-set on sendin' my little brother away for strangers to raise, antiquated notions about what constitutes suitable attire for females," I listed out for him, and then immediately regretted my momentary lapse; I hadn't planned on busting up the good vibe so soon.

Pete pursed his lips. "Nah," he disagreed lightly, "just antiquated notions about what constitutes suitable attire for *one* particular female." He nudged my shoulder. "Sides . . . I'd rather go bowling with his daughter."

Happiness surged through me. *God, how I missed him!* His gorgeous, heart-stopping smile, the flirty banter, the just plain ole basking in his golden presence.

"Well I hate to break it to you, but as far as I can tell from the conversation I had with my father last night, I'm already spoken for by another"—I cleared my throat—"and I used the term loosely here—man."

Pete snort-laughed. "What's one more hurdle?" I didn't have time to decipher the edge in there because he said, "So . . . who's the lucky guy?" He leaned over and put his mouth to my ear. "You'll have to point him out, so I can kick his ass."

"I think you can already check that off your to-do list," I said with a grin.

He threw his head back and laughed. "Good to know—you're way too good for any of these guys anyway."

Almost to gym now, we paused before going our separate ways. A portion of his entourage was waiting for him inside, fiending for their allotted time with their hero. The dismal little P.E. class had been basking in Pete's refracted popularity; their self-esteem suddenly bolstered by the esteem in which Pete was held. Most likely their whole day revolved around the glory of sharing a gym class with him. I hated to tell them their days with him were numbered . . . as were mine.

Pete acknowledged his fans with a chin lift, and we shared a conspiratorial smile over his instant, overwhelming popularity. I laughed out loud. I loved him being a good sport.

"Think I'm ready for my fifteen minutes to be up," he said with a grimace.

An immediate jolt shook my system, my smile kind of imploding on me. I shifted my eyes to the flow of multi-colored hoodies ahead of us, bottlenecking to get in. Pete would soon need to go left while I went right—seemed like a metaphor for our life.

"What's wrong?" he asked.

"Nothin'." I shook my head. The truthfulness of his statement stung like an insult. He was *ready* for his time here to be over. He *wanted* to get back to his real life—the privileged one he belonged to. Who could blame him? There was nothing remotely interesting in this small town to keep a guy like him interested. A heaviness seeped into my chest, dragging me back down to earth.

"Kate, did I say something to upset you?"

Oh Gah. I was doing it again—bringing him down, the mood down.

"I-I was just thinkin' about that awful fight you got into on account of me," I said, making something up on the spur of the moment.

"It wasn't your fault—I was being an ass."

I pulled a face. "No disagreement there, but you still didn't deserve to be ganged up on like that."

"It worked out okay. But I gotta say: two shiners in two weeks is a record for me . . . one I definitely don't want to break anytime soon!"

"Right." I forced a laugh. "I never apologized . . . sorry about that."

"Sorry for not apologizing or sorry for the shiner?"

I laughed more naturally. "Both. . . . That reminds me of something Ashley said about you the first day of school."

"Ashley Squared?" I nodded, and he rolled his eyes. "This outta be good."

"Actually, it *was* good."

He arched a brow. "Do tell."

"She, uh, said—" I broke off, blushing. "You know what? Never mind. It's not important." I was heading off to the locker room, when a tug on my backpack snapped me back.

"Oh, no you don't!" Pete scolded. "You don't get to just laugh and say I remember what someone said about you and then just sally away like that . . . It's just plain rude."

"Is it?"

"It is," he insisted.

I looked up at his face all lit up with humor, noticing how it softened the chiseled perfection. I must've been staring too long, because he cleared his throat.

"I'm waiting . . . "

"Right. Um, she said that you looked like you'd be more of a . . . uh . . ."—I did my own *hmmm-hmmm*, mentally kicking myself for bringing it up—"lover than a fighter."

His lips twitched. "And do you agree with her assessment?"

A sly smile spread my lips. "I *would* tell you . . . but then I'd have to kill you."

My borrowed funny was followed by a burst of pleasant laughter. "Well, I agree with Ashley-Squared for once"—he brushed his thumb across my lips—"I'm *definitely* more of a lover."

I swallowed and failed at speech.

The tardy bell did its thing, and I didn't linger further, running to go change into my shortest shorts and tightest shirt. This I did in record time while Shelby relayed her hopes to me that Jake would ask her to homecoming. I smiled warmly and told her they'd look cute together. She beamed then hesitantly asked me about Pete. I gave her an abbreviated update. Couldn't deny we were *something;* the intensity of our relationship was fairly obvious.

Thankfully the whistle blew, and we filed outside to our half of the practice field. Coach Sams counted us off again, only this time, Pete and I ended up on the same team. I hoped *this* was the symbolism our future held. We worked together really well, passing the ball back and forth with little (on my part) to no (his part) interception. The coaches had put Jake, Diego, Shelby, and anybody with any athletic ability at all on the opposing team, yet we were still up four to zip at halftime. Coach Sams must've taken pity on the other team, because she benched Pete and me for the duration of the game, reorganizing the teams to allow other players a chance to play.

In companionable silence we sat together on the bench, dispassionately watching the disaster unfolding on the soccer field. I noticed he was drinking from the same dark bottle he always seemed to have on hand. He twisted off the cap, and a wisp of vapor evaporated into the air.

"What kind of water is that exactly?" I asked. "I don't think I've ever seen it before . . . not that I'm a bottled water expert." I took a sip from my metal canteen. "All I drink is good old-fashioned Clovis well water."

"You drink *well* water?" He said this like I'd just said I went out back to use the outhouse.

"Yup." I took another defiant sip.

Pete looked funny for a second, then swung the bottle between his legs, staring intently at our kicker as he attempted a long-range field goal.

Awkward.

"Forget I asked." I leaned my elbows on my knees, and my chin in my hands, and watched as the ball just grazed through the posts.

"It's purified, oxygenated water, provided by the Academy," he finally answered, as though the field goal had earned me three little facts.

"Oh." *Weird.* Did they ship it to him because Clovis water was polluted? Was the plethora of regular bottled water you could purchase at any convenience store still not good enough? I was trying to lure in an elusive, exotic creature, so didn't want to make any big, sudden movements. So I just let it go for now—he obviously didn't want to discuss his life at The Academy in any kind of personal way.

The wind whipped up again, rushing stinging bumps down my arms. I shivered. Weather this time of year could be volatile, dropping twenty to thirty degrees in the blink of an eye.

"Are you cold?" he asked.

I shrugged. "I'm okay."

He pulled off his long-sleeved navy T-shirt and handed it to me. Underneath, he had on another tee, only this one was worn and tighter so that it clung to his chest. I took a moment to admire his physique. Pete had the kind of musculature that manifested itself in a natural way—say from playing lacrosse all day rather than pumping iron.

"Thanks." My smile faded when I noticed the gold motif on the left side of his shirt. It was hard to make out at first because the letters were peeling off like chipped paint, but the roaring lion head was unmistakable.

After a moment of me holding on to his warm shirt, he slid a smile my way. "You gonna put that on or continue to wound my chivalrous pride?"

I glanced down at the plush cotton I longed to wrap around me and inhale. I slipped it over my head, and it seemed to swallow me whole. An immediate smirk formed on his lips.

"What?" I began rolling up the sleeves.

"I've been wanting to do that all day," he replied.

"What do you mean?"

"It means I don't particularly care for the way some of these guys are starting to look at you."

I shook my head at him. "Not this again."

"Hey," he laughed, "just tellin' you like it is."

I couldn't wipe the smile off my face. My heart—my whole body— suddenly felt much, much warmer. I turned so that I faced the practicing football players instead of the wicked gleam in his eye. Leaning against him seemed like the natural thing to do, but I resisted, leaning over instead to hug my knees and surreptitiously breathe in his shirt. It smelled lightly of expensive cologne, good health, and something else all his own—essence of Pete, and it was an electric combination that I could never get my fill of.

"So which one is it?"

I peeked over my shoulder at him.

"The guy . . . the stud you made mention of earlier. I'm assuming he's one of those purple jerseys out there."

I chortled and rocked back on the bench. "I'm not interested, so what does it matter?"

"Is it Miguel?" he persisted.

"Nope." He looked like he didn't believe me, so I said, "He has a girlfriend."

"Don't you mean a girl who's a friend, but he'd like it to be more?"

I laughed at his convoluted language. "It's not like that."

"Hm-hmm."

We watched as a helmet-head nudged another helmet-head and nodded our way. He shouted something to Ron, who looked over from his squatting position on the field. My face burned knowing I was the object of much speculation and gossip since Pete's arrival. I usually liked to just fly under the radar.

"Is it that guy?" Pete jerked his head over to indicate Ron. "The big one who put his hands on your ass?"

Not wanting to stir the pot, I kept mum but had to suppress a smile. It's funny how he didn't recall that was the same "big one" who'd put his hands on him during the fight.

"Come on, Kate," he wheedled. "Which number?"

"Why does it matter?"

A broody expression crossed his face. "I don't know. It just does. Come on!—*tell* me. I promise I won't kick his ass . . . unless you want me to."

"You know what?—no!" I said, exasperated. "You don't tell me *anything* I wanna know."

"What? How can you say that? I'm an open book."

"You mean an open brochure."

"Okay fine . . . If I answer one of your questions, will you answer mine?"

Yes! Finally! "Deal," I said, offering up my hand. After we shook on it, I swiveled around to stare deeply into his eyes, like a weirdo.

Pete laughed at my serious expression and squared up his shoulders. "Okay, take your best shot."

"Is Andrew gettin' accepted to your academy?"

He sighed wearily like I'd missed my mark. *What did he think I was going to ask? Whether or not he believed aliens really landed in Roswell?* "That's confidential information," he chided. "*I* don't even know yet. I simply submit his test scores and my observations to the committee, and they decide."

I stared him down for a few seconds. His answer felt right, so I accepted it. "Fine . . . I'll ask a different one." And I knew just the one to ask. It started right at the center of my core, vibrating out until it spilled from my mouth in a rush. "Do you think your academy is a good organization?"

Lightening-quick, an invisible shutter closed over his eyes. "Absolutely," he said, trying at real conviction. "The Academy is not only an elite military academy, it's also an organization that caters to gifted children just like Andrew. Its goal is the self-actualization of every cadet. It also promotes innovation in science and technology; our groundbreaking discoveries are enhancing lives every day. And philanthropy is also a big part of our program. We've given millions away to help worthy children from around the world, who ordinarily wouldn't have a chance to fulfill their potential. Andrew is one of the select few to receive an invitation. I think he would thrive in such an environment and is extremely lucky to have this opportunity." Pete took in my neutral expression and broadened his smile.

I blinked. He'd lost me at "absolutely." His face hadn't changed from the open, earnest expression, and he didn't shift his eyes, but I knew he was lying. I felt it instantly like someone had dumped a cooler of melted ice over my head. I shot up from the bench. Guess there was no symbolism to us being placed on the same team today. We would always be playing for different teams as long as he was associated with his academy.

Pete stood up, too, warming my shoulder with his hand. "I'm sorry, Kate. I wish I could tell you more about whether Andrew will be accepted or not, but it's honestly not up to me." The only sincere words on the topic.

I folded my arms across my chest, deep breathing in the intoxicating scent of his shirt. I knew I should take it off and give it back to him, but all I really wanted to do was take it home and use it as a pillowcase. I moved a couple of steps away from him.

He gave a throaty chuckle. "You may want to tuck that shirt in . . . it looks like you're standing around in nothing but a very short dress." He was trying to smooth things over with his signature blend of humor and flirtation. This only reminded me of that night when the same thing happened with his jacket, and Ranger said I looked like a flasher. Shortly after, I'd overheard their little convo about his mission here being as easy as taking candy from a baby.

I started to simmer.

The shrill of the whistle signaled the end of P.E. and our useless conversation. Wordlessly, I watched all the players come rolling in from the field.

"You never got around to telling me what number," he said, closing the distance to murmur along my exposed neckline. "Come on . . . a deal's a deal."

Suddenly, I couldn't take anymore contrived flirting, wanting him to *finally* get real with me. Wrenching off his shirt, I threw it at him. "Number twenty-three," I said, picking a random number I'd just noticed wasn't out there.

I watched his eyes widen and his hands close around the shirt as it bounced off his chest, then I jogged off to help gather balls and neon orange cones for Coach Sams. I left him standing there to figure out that I'd just lied, too. Didn't have to wait long, because he accosted me as soon as I pushed through the gym doors.

"What was that about? And why did you lie to me? There is no number twenty-three." Pete stepped into pace with me as I bustled to the comfort of my little hatchback warming in the sun. "Kate?"

Picking up the pace, I tried turning myself into a blur.

He swore. "Great. So now we're not talking again. This must be some kind of record for you finding reasons to get mad at me."

"I never have to look far."

"What the hell did I do? I have no idea."

I wound myself around parked cars at breakneck speed, with him easily keeping up. "If you really don't know, then you have sorely misjudged my BS detector."

Ashley-Leigh stopped tapping up-to-the-minute fake updates about her and Pete to motion to him that she was waiting by his Hummer. Like he couldn't see her standing right there. She still acted as if she had a snowball's chance in hell with him. On some level, I had to admire her tenacity.

"Looks like your homecomin' date's waitin' on you." I couldn't resist a jab.

He snorted. "I don't have enough fingers to count the ways that's wrong."

"Well accordin' to her, you were gonna reveal some big, mysterious plans this afternoon." I nodded over at her, and she waved cheerily like we weren't in the middle of a battle. Which I guess we weren't, because I'd completely stepped out of the war. "So . . . you'd better get after it." I stepped into my car and closed the door in his face, then immediately reached over the backseat for one of Andrew's hoodies and slipped it on even though it was too short and too tight. That reminded me—I was going shopping.

The loud creak of the door being wrenched open preceded Pete plunking himself down in the passenger seat. He slammed the door behind him with a little too much force. My car's windows rattled.

"You break it, you bought it," I quipped.

He snorted then threw his head back and laughed, but it sounded all off—more like he'd finally had it with me than he actually found me funny. I huffed out a long sigh and turned to face him, worrying about that very thing. I'd lost my temper . . . again. It's like I had emotional Tourette's or something.

Pete also sighed heavily, his head lolling back on the headrest. He closed his eyes, raked his hands through his hair, made an aggravated throat noise. Then was quiet except for some weird chuckles that escaped at odd intervals. I watched him struggle, thinking it always looked like he was a couple of weeks shy of a haircut for a military cadet. My fingers longed to reach out and smooth back his hair. I hated being mad at him. I hated him being mad at me. I hated being on opposite teams. The whole dang thing was frustrating as all get out.

After a much-needed moment, he found my eyes. "So . . . here we are again." Humor clung to his defeated tone.

"Here we are again," I confirmed sadly.

He shook his head. "What am I gonna do with you, Connelly?"

"Dip me in tar, roll me in feathers, and string me up by my toes?"

A flash of something—that sent a chill through me—darted in and out of his eyes before it could crystallize. He laughed harshly. "That's one I've never heard before. I'm going to miss those kinds of colloquialisms."

I laughed too, a little nervously. *Did I imagine that?*

"Yeah, I guess you don't hear that every day round your neck of the woods," I said, pulling the conversation back to the problem at hand.

Pete drew in some air and released it, momentarily fogging the window. "You're one tough nut to crack, Katherine Connelly," he stated flatly; it didn't sound like a compliment. "But I gotta say," his eyes returned to mine, "I'm going to miss you when I'm gone."

A shadow crossed over my heart. That was twice now he alluded to leaving. It felt like the airbag just burst from the steering wheel, caving my chest in. My shoulders actually hunched forward. There was no way to keep the despair out of my voice, so I didn't even try.

"So . . . you're leavin'?"

He sighed, fiddled with the air vent. "Tomorrow."

I swallowed the lump that jumped to my throat. "Your big, mysterious plans." It somehow irked me even more that Ashley-Leigh knew before me.

"My big, mysterious plans," he confirmed. His eyes seemed as sad as mine, somehow wet-looking though he wasn't crying.

"Does Andrew know?"

"I'm going to tell him today after tutoring. I won't be here tomorrow afternoon, so plan on picking him up from school."

I did the nod thing, unable to formulate my next question. Maybe not wanting to know the answer. I stared out the windshield at things I couldn't see. "Are you comin' back?"

"I think so but I'm not really sure. They may have enough information to make a decision. I'm uh . . . being summoned back for another meeting."

I wasn't aware there had been a first meeting. "Why?"

A humorless huff. "I'm not doing a very good job," he confessed.

"Whadaya mean?" I came to his rescue immediately. "Andrew adores you, I don't remember a time he's been so happy since Mama died, Daddy's proud as a PTA mom, braggin' to everyone that'll listen about Andrew goin' to the 'World's Most Elite Military Academy.'"

Pete gave me a wry smile. "I still don't have your father's signature of agreement. We can't continue spending money on a dead end. I'm the ambassador for the school. If I can't get the family to sign up for the program, then I'm not doing a very good job representing our organization. If it looks like the family, in this case your father, won't sign, then they pull the plug on the mission." (I noticed this was the first time he'd actually used that word.)

"Is that what this meetin's about?"

"I think so. It's taking longer"—he gave me another wry smile—"than we thought."

"Isn't Andrew exactly what y'all are lookin' for?" I argued.

"Yes, Andrew is a very desirable candidate. However, he's not the only one in the world. They'll move on to another potential cadet soon, one in New Guinea or New Zealand, for example. Or—" he broke off, looking tense.

"Or what?" He shook his head, and I attached myself to his arm. "Tell me, Pete! I have a right to know. This is my brother we're talkin' about!"

He expelled some pent-up air. "They might replace me with another cadet—a superior with more experience most likely."

Oh God. "Ranger?"

One sharp confirmation nod. Our eyes met, communicating the same thing —alarm.

"Noooooo!" dropped from my mouth. "They can't do that!" Pete's silence spoke volumes. "We won't allow it!" He smiled, a little sadly at me. "*I* won't allow it. I would *never* work with him!" I insisted staunchly.

"I wasn't aware you'd been working with me," he said with a little ironic smile. "And let's just hope it doesn't come to that." He moved to get out when something possessed my hand to clamp onto his arm again.

"Pete, will you get into trouble? You know . . . if Daddy doesn't sign?"

He shifted his eyes to the milling crowd doing their mass exit. When he looked back, it was with the warmest eyes; it made me feel like my bones were melting. "I'm touched, Kate . . . I didn't think you cared." He moved to get out again, but I held him in a death-grip.

"Will you?" I had a feeling this was as bad for Pete as it was for us. That put a whole different spin on things.

"Don't worry about it," he dismissed. "I'm not." Then he removed himself from my car and quite possibly from my life.

I watched him go, unable to tear my eyes away from his departing back. If you can believe it, Ashley-Leigh was still waiting around for him, gleefully running over and throwing her arms around his neck to dangle like a human garland. *She has some balls.* I hoped she'd get a handful of demerits for being late to practice.

Maybe her effort was worth the wait, because I saw him give her a quick side hug and mouth something to her. Whatever it was, it made her laugh and glow pinker than her lip gloss. That was it though. He quickly slid into his truck and drove off with a courtesy wave out the window. I guess it was enough for her because she walked away grinning as triumphantly as if she'd just been crowned homecoming queen.

Pete had that effect on you.

31

BAKING AMENDS

So I went ahead with my shopping spree even though my heart was no longer in it. I mean, who cared if I looked cute if the person I wanted to look cute for wasn't around? But I'd already mentioned it to Mikey. And Walmart was a place that boy loved with his whole heart, so no way could I ship out straight for home and chores without hitting the super-center first.

I randomly picked out some jeans and a plaid flannel shirt, the changing weather outside and the imminent demise of my crush most likely affecting my choices. Not even bothering to try them on, I headed off to the toy aisle. Mikey fist-pumped my decision. As I absentmindedly watched him wreck the display toys, pushing buttons and pulling levers with wild abandon, I mulled over what Pete had revealed. He'd called me "one tough nut to crack." That was the closest he'd come to admitting outright that I was some kind of mark to be won over, so we'd all feel just peachy about signing Andrew's life away. But I'd proven tougher than expected.

This was obviously why they sent charming ambassadors with chiseled faces—to lure prospective families in, like scouts trying to sway sports stars into playing for their teams. And if the families still felt reluctant to give their children away, they moved on to bribes. Any way you wanted to look at it, it was a nasty business—cherry-picking the world's brightest kids out from under their parents. I didn't care how much legal paperwork was involved; it was akin to kidnapping in my book.

How could Pete be involved in such a sinister organization? I harbored the suspicion he didn't even like the academy he was trumpeting, even though he was trying hard not to show it.

"Kadee . . ." Mikey stuck a plastic replica of a Hummer between me and his rubber cheeks. "Can I have this?"

"I don't know, sweetie . . . how much is it?" I dug in my wallet even though I was sure we didn't have enough. *Maybe if I put back the jeans?*

"It's twenty-four, ninety-nine dollars," he matter-of-factly read the numbers on the tag.

I chuckled. "Wow. That's a lotta money."

Mikey's shoulders immediately sagged. "I know . . . but it's just wike Pete's."

I deliberated. I'd planned to buy the boys a couple of long-sleeved shirts, always having to be practical. I thought of Daddy covertly spending that IEA money on who-knows-what?—not groceries or new coats for us kids, that's for sure. Really perusing the contents of my wallet now, I recounted the money mentally subtracting what all I had to buy. *Hmmm.* I could swear there was an extra twenty that wasn't there earlier. Again.

A funny feeling came over me.

"You know what, Mike?" The lift in my voice turned his hopeful face gleeful. "It's yours."

"Yay!" Trophy Hummer held over his head, Mikey ran and dumped it into the cart before hurling himself into my arms.

"You deserve it," I said, squeezing him to me. "You're such a good boy."

He tilted his head back, grinning to the gum line. "I know . . . I haven't made anybody do nothin' in cwass for a wong time!"

I laughed at his funny wording, leading him away from the toy-traps. "That's good to know. How about doin' somethin' for me instead?"

"What, Kadee?" He looked up at me, earnestness personified. ". . . I'd do *anything* for you."

"Even help me pick out which color lip gloss looks the prettiest on me?"

Mikey giggled as embarrassed as if I'd asked him to put on a frilly dress and skip around the store with me.

I bent the top of his ear. "How about if we try to find the exact same shade of pink as your ear?"

He laughed and shook his head. "Oh, Kadee! I don't know 'bout that!"

We spent the next five minutes discovering the make-up aisle together. Since it was my first visit, I felt a little overwhelmed by the choices. *Should I go for volume or length for mascara? Black noir or brownish black?* In the end, I randomly grabbed a black tube from a line that was having a weekly sale, and picked a neutral gloss from the same brand. I added them to the cart before heading to the grocery side of the store, idling wondering if Pete had ever done the one-stop shopping thing in his life. Highly doubtful. Just like it was highly doubtful I would ever shop for my wardrobe in a store that only sold clothes.

An image of a classic blonde in crisp outfits came to mind. Reese Caruthers—that was the kind of girl who belonged with Pete. Polished, pristine, yet so personable every single member of camp fell in love with her, including me. Just like Pete. When you were with them, you felt like you were at the center of the universe, no matter where you were. Clovis, New Mexico had never been so desirable. Now it seemed exciting as New York City and glamorous as Paris, France. My desire to flee had fled me ever since he'd set foot in town limits.

The thought that Pete was leaving tomorrow—maybe for good—was enough to make me sick with longing. *Why had I wasted two whole weeks avoiding him?* Oh yeah . . . because he'd lied and tried to sabotage me with my family, and was only here to snatch Andrew out from under us for his evil academy. Idiotically, I didn't care about that little bit of relevance at the moment. He hadn't succeeded so far, and couldn't help whom he was working for, I reasoned. All I focused on right now was the side of Pete I sensed was good and not out to hurt us, the one who did find me attractive and enjoyed spending time with me.

A desperation to extract every last drop of time from him as possible overcame me. It was the same intense feeling I'd had right before Mama died. Everything seemed to have been heading in the right direction until I'd lost my temper. Maybe I could still salvage things? I quickly jerked the cart back out, remembering another feminine wile my mother used on my father.

"Hey!" Mikey protested. "What are ya doin?—we were next in line!"

"I'm suddenly in the mood to bake," I announced with a huge grin.

My coconspirator fist-pumped my decision again. "Yay! . . . This is the bestest day evuh!"

I morphed my grocery cart into a go-cart, careening back around the food aisles, hoping the way to a man's heart really was through his stomach. We made it back in record time, half-running half-stumbling into the house, loaded down as pack mules. Blue's excited yelps and jumps could no longer be ignored, so I dropped the bags, and a kiss on his whiskery face, and tossed him a refrigerated ham bone. Then ran around like a cyclone, slamming cans into cupboards and cramming produce into bins.

"Mikey!" I overly yelled while whipping together butter and sugar. "I need you to scoop one and a half cups of powder into each of the calf bottles while I get the cookies started."

He appeared, defiantly hugging his Hummer to his chest.

"Please. You said you'd do *anything* for me, remember? Then we'll have your favorite cookies—oatmeal, butterscotch-chip. But you gotta help, okay? . . . I'm gonna invite Pete to join us for snack today."

"Pete's comin'?" Mikey clarified, and I nodded my head. "Okay, Kadee. I'll do it." He spirited his prized possession away and ran whooping out the door to the shed. Looked like Pete was the magic word.

I sighed, reaching over to preheat the oven. I realized Pete's exit from our lives would affect us all. *Maybe this was a bad idea?* It felt slightly irresponsible, like bringing home the most irresistible puppy in the world, only to give it back after a couple of weeks because you were allergic to it. It was so much harder letting go once you'd already fallen in love.

Too late for me . . . I'd already fallen.

I didn't have time to ruminate further because I was in business mode. When the first batch of cookies was baking, I grabbed the slop bucket and ran to the shed to check on Mikey.

"Great job, buddy!" I acknowledged his hard work. Mikey beamed at me from the last bottle. "Now feed and water the chickens, then you're all done for now."

After a quick reward hug, we set off down our respective paths, weighed down but light-hearted at the prospect of a Pete-filled afternoon. The wind picked up, whipping my hair into a frenzy and flying bits of grit into my eyes. In the distance, dried brush waved back and forth, and the earthy smell of sunburnt pasture reminded me: time was marching forward.

I dumped the water and slop, then ran back to the house with two plastic buckets clanging around my ankles, making it back just in time to pull out the first batch of cookies. I set them out on the counter to cool and fragrance up the place. A quick glance at the ticking clock, and I skedaddled to the bathroom to freshen up.

After splashing water on my face, I yanked off my shirt and flung it into the hamper before pulling on a pink-hearted fresh one. Then released my hair from its bondage to brush it so that it spilled down my back in an obedient line—an exercise in futility, for the moment I walked outside, it would simply knot itself back into a mass of tangles. However, my girly urges could not be denied, so I finished with a couple of sweeps of my new mascara, immediately feeling like a cuter version of myself. I was skipping back to the kitchen like the Easter bunny with my basket of dirty clothes when Mikey banged in from the outside.

"Mmmmm! It smells good in hewer!" It was hard to say who was salivating over the cookies more: Blue or Mikey. From the puddle of drool at his feet, I'd have to give it to Bluesy.

I beamed at him, sailing past to Daddy's room. Looked like my feminine wiles were working on those two males, but they were an easy audience. After hastily sorting through Daddy's dirty clothes, I went to the sink to wash my hands. And peek at his scotch stash. Sure enough it was still there, only almost completely full now. *A new bottle? Watered down?* Whatever the case, it looked like the teetotaler was still imbibing. I shoved it back under the sink and headed back to the kitchen, where the sweet butterscotch and vanilla smell embraced me like a hug from heaven. *Mmmmmm.* I inhaled, feeling a pang touch my heart—making Mama's favorite cookies always had a bittersweet effect on me.

The unmistakable rumble of the Hummer, prowling over the uneven terrain, caused my stomach to do its own rumble, and the dormant butterflies to stir. I hightailed it to the oven to remove the next batch. They were already here, so I didn't have time to gloss my lips without running the risk of him taking off on me. It just now occurred to me: I didn't have a way to get in touch with Pete outside of school. I didn't even know where he was staying for that matter. It was an odd sensation—feeling so drawn to someone I knew so little about. Almost like falling off a steep cliff. I just hoped there was a net somewhere at the bottom, waiting to catch me.

Determined to remedy that situation right now, I burst out the door to greet them, fully prepared to throw myself in front of his two-ton truck if need be. Bounding down the steps a little too enthusiastically, I realized I probably looked like a dork so forced myself to a more dignified pace. I obviously caught Pete off guard because a brief look of surprise crossed his face before he shoved the gear into park, a grin already forming.

The window whirred down. "Missed me already?"

I settled my restless hands on the window frame, my chest swelling with hopeful expectation. Before I could say anything, Mikey came bounding down the same steps, whooping and hollering like his pants were on fire. "Yay! Pete and Drewy are here!" The second Andrew's foot hit dirt Mikey attacked him with love pats and whaps. "We're gonna have cookies with Pete today, Drewy!" he announced, managing to turn his hug into a power lift.

Feet still dangling from the ground Andrew grinned, his eyes finding mine for confirmation.

Pete had been watching Mikey's antics, and now his eyes also found mine. "Cookies?" he said.

"I, ummm . . ." My cheeks tingled, but I determinedly pushed through. "We wanted to invite you in to have some cookies with us this afternoon." I moved my eyes from his sensual mouth back to his captivating eyes. "You know . . . kinda like a good-bye party."

He was quiet a moment, staring down on me with what could only be described as tenderness until a gleam of humor sparked in them. "Are they homemade?"

I smiled broadly, bobbing my head like an idiot. "Uh-huh. From scratch. Oatmeal and butterscotch chip. It's, ah . . . my mother's recipe." I swallowed, suddenly feeling vulnerable.

"Come on, Pete! "Andrew chimed in. "Join us."

"Yeah, Pete, join us!" Mikey clawed at the door handle, determined to drag him out if he had to.

"You don't have to ask me twice!" Pete killed the engine and pushed a button. The window whirred back up to separate us. But not for long, because as soon as he stepped down, he grabbed my hand like it was something we did every day. "Lead on!" he grinned.

A swift surge of pleasure shocked me with joy. I felt as much like jumping up and down as Mikey, but tried to play it cool. I led him into our trailer, memorizing the dry, rough texture of his palm, just in case I never got to feel it again. Andrew's eyes bugged out when he saw us, but Mikey beamed and scampered over to take possession of Pete's other hand.

"Come on, Drewy!" Mikey beckoned to his brother. "Let's pway fowow the leaduh. Kadee's the leaduh!"

"I'll follow her wherever she goes," Pete said, winking.

"That's for babies," scoffed Andrew, though I could tell he wanted to join the fun.

"No, it's not! Pete's doing it . . . and he's a *grown-up*," Mikey pointed out.

My eyes flew to Pete's.

"What can I say," he shrugged around a grin, "I drive a manly truck."

"They're not playing follow the leader, you idiot—they're holdin' hands." Following this announcement, Andrew's face turned the same shade as mine.

"Oh." Mikey looked up at Pete with new eyes as we crowded into our entryway. Pete dropped my hand the moment we stepped inside. I'd still been holding on like an idiot. *Gah.* This whole boyfriend-girlfriend thing . . . or whatever we were, was confusing. I didn't know the rules because I'd never played the game. As if sensing my discomfort, Pete pulled me into his chest, his chin resting on my head.

"Smells delicious," he murmured. "My mouth is watering already."

I was just thinking the same thing about him. "Mikey and I have been hard at work. Right?"

"Why am I not surprised?"

I chose to ignore that, moving to the kitchen to set out plates and cups. "Okay boys, wash up for snack."

"Pete, come with us," invited Mikey.

"Guess I am one of the boys," he said. "Lead on . . ."

"Yay! Now *I'm* the leaduh!" Mikey grabbed Pete's hand again and dragged him down the hall.

"I'll show you our room, Pete," Andrew said, squeezing ahead of them to take the lead. "I have some cool quartz and Indian arrowheads."

"And I have Spiduhman sheets, and Kadee bought me a Hummuh, just wike youwers!" Mikey bragged, almost beside himself with pride.

"Is it parked out back?" Pete teased.

Andrew laughed while Mikey set the record straight. "No, it's in my woom . . . it's not a *weal* one."

I couldn't erase the smile on my face as I worked and listened to their boy banter. A visceral sensation—I hadn't dared hoped for since Mama died—overcame me again. That everything-is-exactly-as-it-should-be feeling. It felt like a soothing balm on the parched skin of my soul. Tears shimmered in my eyes as I set about pouring milk and slicing bananas. Setting a sunny plate of warm, gooey cookies on the center of the table, I called for the boys. They all elephant-trumped back in, smiles of anticipation brightening their faces.

Pete's eyes found mine. "Where should I sit?"

"How 'bout here?" Mikey pulled out the chair at the head of the table.

"You sure?" Pete hedged. "I feel like I'm taking someone's seat."

"Sure I'm sure . . . that's Daddy's chair, and he's *nevuh* home," declared an ever informative Mikey.

I didn't dare glance at Pete as he lowered himself onto the padded chair, instead, placing napkins on each place mat during the second awkward pause of the afternoon so far. I plastered a smile. "Dig in."

"Don't mind if I do," Pete said, grabbing a cookie off the top.

We Connellys used our manners and waited for our guest. I realized we were all staring at him with baited breath, adding weight to the inconsequential moment. He held the cookie midair, his lips appearing to be too occupied with suppressing a smile to take a proper bite. I had to laugh because the impatient, frozen anticipation on our faces as we waited for Pete to take his first bite was something right out of Mikey's *Green Eggs and Ham* book. Finally, before the suspense threatened to kill Mikey, he took a slow, giant bite.

"Mmmmm! Oh man!" Pete exaggeratedly worked his jaw, humming noises of pleasure and banging on the table, acting as if it were so good, he was rendered speechless. After a hard swallow, he said, "Wow!—that might be the best thing I've ever tasted!" My brothers' faces illuminated like light bulbs. Then in an aside to me: "Well . . . maybe the second best." He winked, and I whacked him with a dishtowel, blushing all the way to the tips of my toes.

"Ow!" Pete rubbed at his arm. "What was that for?" I just shook my head. "Our girl has a hard time accepting compliments," he informed the boys. They merely smiled and nodded at him, too busy chewing on their own cookies to add their two cents.

"Do not," I disagreed.

"Do too," he insisted.

I poked my tongue out at him, then went around to sit next to Andrew, partly because I hadn't seen him all day and partly because Mikey was all over Pete, regaling him with a litany of knock-knock jokes. After inhaling a couple of bites of my hard work, I raised my milk glass to Andrew.

"Cheers, big ears," I said, clunking our mismatched glasses together.

"Cheewers with *me*, Kadee," demanded Mikey.

"Why don't we all cheer?" Pete raised his glass toward the middle of the table. He cleared his throat dramatically. "I propose a toast: To our favorite girl . . . and the most delicious cookies I've ever had the pleasure of tasting."

There were a couple of enthusiastic, loud clunks each, and predictably some of Mikey's milk splashed out. Pete quickly caught it with the dishtowel before it spilled onto the floor. A split second later, I returned from the kitchen with a fresh towel that Pete immediately whipped from my hands with magician-like panache.

"Thanks," I said.

"What for?"

"For cleanin' up the mess, the sweet toast, stayin' for cookies, for . . ."—I lowered my eyes to the floor—"bein' so nice to us."

Pete chucked up my chin with his finger. "I'm the one who should be thanking you . . . *Nobody's* ever made me cookies before."

"I know you don't usually eat this sort of thing, so thanks for goin' along with it."

"It was entirely my pleasure," he said, sounding like he really meant it. "But I have to confess something . . ."—my eyes shot wide—"I would've come in anyway, even if the cookies *weren't* homemade."

I laughed and bapped him with another dishtowel. "Just so you know . . . these aren't nearly as bad as say, a donut. I used my mother's recipe, which is really just a bunch of oats and some dates to sweeten it. The butterscotch chips are a recent addition," I admitted. "They're not exactly healthy, but they sure taste good."

"Well, like I mentioned earlier, I'm not above cheating from time to time. Plus, we all deserve a little something sweet in life," he said, staring straight into my eyes.

About three cartoons and twenty-one knock-knock jokes later, the boys finally had their fill of cookies and Pete, running off to their room to change clothes and play with the Hummer. It was a little past time to feed the calves, but I found myself stalling, stretching the time out as long as possible, not sure when I would see him again.

I was unaccountably nervous without the boys there as a buffer, so decided to prep dinner to keep my hands busy. As I got to work pulling out ingredients for spaghetti and meatballs, I felt Pete's eyes on me, although he didn't say anything. Taking up the slack this time, it was I who jabbered away as I worked. But my progress soon stalled out by an unsuccessful wrestling match with a jar of pasta sauce. I went to the sink to run hot water over it and bang on the bottom. In the midst of this endeavor, Pete came up behind me and removed the jar from my hands. After drying it off with a dishtowel, he popped it open with a simple twist and handed it back to me with a long look.

I cleared my throat. "Thanks. One of the good things about the boys gettin' bigger than me is they'll be able to do that."

"Where's your father?—off buying more feed at Tillman Mills?"

I pried a glob of cookie dough from the counter with my thumbnail, wondering the same thing. "That's a good question. He might be back any minute, so . . ." Again, I couldn't say the words to make him leave.

Pete gave a derisive snort. "I highly doubt it; looks to me like he's got his timing just about right."

I tried a smile. "You're probably right. But I do have to go feed the calves."

"Can I help?"

"You don't have to help," I demurred, setting a pot in the sink to fill with water.

"I know I don't have to." He turned off the faucet I just turned on to gaze directly into my eyes. "I want to."

And I wanted him to, but I had a strong feeling Daddy was going to make an earlier appearance tonight. How could I explain that *without* sounding crazy? "Um," I tapped at my lips, thinking, "It's just . . . we took longer than usual for our snack, so his, ah . . . timing, will be a little off today. And if you're still here when he comes home . . ."

"I could simply say I came in to give him an update on Andrew," he pointed out.

"I just don't want you here when he gets home, okay?" I touched his arm to soften my words. This clash of worlds would remind me too much of the *real* reason he was here. And I wanted to pretend a little longer, to live in denial for just a while—a gift to myself before he left.

He sighed. "Fine. But before I go, will you do something for me?"

I searched his unfathomable eyes for a clue. "Sure?"

"Show me your room."

"*W-what?*" I spluttered. "Why?"

"I want to see where you sleep." His mouth didn't trip over the bold words I didn't have the courage to say. I felt the telling heat that always stained my cheeks, and he smiled down on me wistfully. "I'm going to miss this thing of beauty," he said, cupping my cheek with his palm.

My heart instantly ached in my chest. I didn't want to be reminded of his imminent departure just yet. I already felt bereft just thinking about it, and hoped he meant for the weekend and not for good. I debated for a moment, mentally making sure I hadn't left anything embarrassing out like underwear. For once, I was only grateful for my father's militant rules.

"Fine," I caved. "I have to throw on some sweats anyway." He followed me back, pausing in the hall to inspect the hodge-podge of framed pics displayed there. I called through the boys' open door, "Five more minutes!"

"Kadee, we're goin' outside to dwive my Hummer in the dirt," Mikey informed me right as Andrew plucked it from his hands and took off. "Hey!" Mikey immediately stampeded after it, his towel cape flapping behind him down the hall. As soon as the back door slammed, Pete sauntered into my cubby of a room, his large frame managing to make it look like a playhouse.

"So . . . this is it," I said, gesturing. Then watched, mortified, as he took in my old-timey wagon-wheel bed, with the pink and yellow quilt I'd had since I slept with a night-light, the bulbous dresser with mismatched knobs, and the faded wingback chair in the corner that matched nothing.

A quick inventory, and he turned back around. "No teddy bears?"

"Sorry to disappoint."

He ran the back of his hand across his forehead. "Whew!"

I laughed a little self-consciously, and stood there, hot-faced and squirming, studying him studying my room. I wondered what insight about me my room revealed and reassessed my meager décor. Much like my wardrobe, I had kept it stupid simple, figuring less was more when you didn't have the time or the money to find the right pieces.

On the wall opposite my bed, were three pictures framed in light pinewood. One was of the Eiffel Tower blazing up the night sky, the floodlit metal enhanced and glowing like a fairytale. The one in the middle was a vintage Oscar de la Renta sketch. The caricature of the red-lipped model in her striking LBD had appealed to me for no good reason when I'd run across it at a garage sale last summer. I'd bought it on a whim for two dollars then added black matting to bring out the charcoal lines. The third was a Leonard Afrenov painting aptly name *Lovers* that I'd copied from an art book in the library and blown up. Something about the vivid colors and romantic silhouette had drawn me in.

After thoughtfully studying my prints, Pete ambled over to my bed and sat down, lightly bouncing on the springs. Seeing him here—in the personal sanctuary of my room, on my childhood bed, looking impossibly handsome—made him seem even more like a fantasy somehow. Like one of my framed pictures had come to life, a prince from once-upon-a-time.

"You know . . . you've seen my room, and I don't even know where you're stayin' while you're here, or your number, or even somethin' as inconsequential as your favorite color or favorite food," I blurted out.

He appeared quietly amused by my unprompted outburst, taking the moment he should have answered to smile lazily up at me. I was right on the verge of retreating when he finally spoke: "I'm staying at The Caprock Inn at Cannon Air Force Base, my number is 415-220-5559, my favorite color right now is the exact blue-green shade of your eyes, and my favorite food . . ."—his lips twitched—"happens to have recently changed to oatmeal, butterscotch-chip cookies with dates instead of raisins." That said, he laced his fingers behind his head and leaned back on my pillow. "What else you wanna know?"

I was pleased a literal pink and placated for the time being. "I guess that'll do for now," I mumbled. There were only about a million and one things. However, I could *not* say that without sounding like a stalker.

His amused eyes left my face to roam to my nightstand. He leaned forward, his face changing forms. "Is this your mother?" He indicated the single portrait keeping vigil over me as I slept. I nodded my head. "May I?"

I raised a shoulder, trying for nonchalance.

Carefully, he lifted the gilded frame, and after a few seconds of quiet study, his eyes found mine. "She was beautiful."

My throat got that full feeling. I blinked back tears. Put a scattered hand up to my face. "Thanks."

He studied me for a hot, heavy moment. "Come here," he said in a low voice.

The weight of these simple words leadened my feet, and I hesitated before crossing the threshold to stand before him. He placed his hands on the tops of my arms, one on each side, sliding them down to encircle my wrists. An immediate trail of goose bumps followed his movements.

"Sit down." His voice was huskier than it was a moment ago. And if it was possible, his eyes were even darker—shiny black orbs staring up at me as though mesmerized, like me.

I swallowed and obediently sank down, my knees folding beneath the pressure of his gaze. His body heat immediately penetrated my bare legs, stifling whatever slight chill was left. Stomach swimming with expectation, I stared straight ahead, feeling unspeakably vulnerable. He reached over and filled his hand with my hair, caressessing the strands between his fingers before brushing them aside to expose my neck, a newly recognized erogenous zone. He pressed his lips against the pulse of my throat as though reading the race of it.

"Mmmmm," he breathed me in. "You smell like vanilla."

My heart accelerated. "I-I do?"

A low chuckle from his throat. "Um-hmm," he murmured in my ear, zinging pleasure straight down my spine. Despite my rapidly rising temperature, I shivered. "And sugar and spice and all things nice." He nuzzled a sensitive spot behind my ear that I was entirely unaware of until that moment.

I breathed out, unconsciously tilting my head back to allow easier access to the teasing sensations invading my body via my neck. A small smile curved his lips as he cradled the back of my head, laying me down on the pillow. My eyes felt heavy lidded at once. He leaned over me, and I breathed in the heat coming off his skin, the musky scent as intoxicating to me as if Aphrodite herself mixed it up just to drive me crazy. It was like I was high on some kind of drug—the rapid-fire responses in my body were quite beyond my control. It was as alarming as it was arousing.

Pete watched me color and squirm beneath him, and I longed to feel his hard masculinity pressed into me again. I felt impatient with it. Once again, my body naturally began urging his down using little enticing movements I was barely aware of: arms reaching, hips arching, lips parting. Things I'd never done before I'd met him. Things that were old as time. As natural as breathing. It seemed inevitable as two magnets, the coming together of our bodies. I felt it at the center of my being. The certainty of it. The rightness.

He ran a long, teasing finger along the length of my leg, bringing back the pleasure-bumps. Dipping just under the hemline of my shorts, he paused to stare down on me. My breath caught, my stomach lurching in the most pleasing way possible, like that second's pause at the top of a roller coaster before the drop. But there was no forthcoming drop—he just left me hanging.

I gave a little strangled throat noise and closed my eyes against him. *Why's he doing this to me?* It was half-torture, half-teasing. I didn't understand it. If you can believe it, I just now considered that he most likely had a girlfriend back home. In Elitesville.

Feelings of inadequacy clogged my throat. I huffed out some frustration and hurt and pushed my hands against the wall of his chest. (I would've paid a year's wages at Norma's to do the opposite.) Anyhow, this was neither the time nor the place—the cheerful voices of my brothers penetrated my flimsy walls.

His restraint was totally vexing. But it probably did me a favor in the long run, although I felt a letdown so deep, you'd need a coal miner to get it out of me. Pete heaved a sigh and sat up, hanging his head between his legs to stare down at my bland carpet. He raked both hands through his hair.

Aggravation? Anger?

I felt both. And feverish. And trembley. I was still sprawled across the calico quilt like a wanton woman, and couldn't help but cringe at what Daddy would think if he saw us this way—on my bed, Pete's hair disheveled, his breathing heavy, mine too shallow, my body too languid to move. It didn't take a genius to figure out what we were . . . *almost* up to.

Pete turned around to penetrate me with a look that was borderline disgust. "You better go put those sweats on now."

Stung, I got off the bed, awkwardly, making sure not to touch him. Then Frankenstein-lurched to my dresser to pull out a pair of sweatpants. Walk-of-shame, is how best to describe my trek across the hall to the bathroom. The reflection that greeted me was telling: two bright spots rouged my cheeks, my eyes were glassy, and my neck looked like a rash had recently sprouted. I hurriedly twisted my hair into a ponytail and threw on my sweats. When I yanked the door open, it was to find Pete filling the doorframe of my bedroom, hands hanging from the door jamb like he'd just performed a slam-dunk. He looked so tousled-sexy I almost bolted over to tackle him back onto my bed. Just managed to hold on to my dignity.

"Hey," I muttered, focusing on a spot over his shoulder.

"Hey, yourself."

I dared a peek at his face and found him smirking down at me. "Sorry about that," he said as though he'd accidentally bumped into me in the hall.

I didn't know how to respond. *That's okay* seemed inappropriate and insincere. "I, uh . . . better get off to chores. I think it's easy enough to find the way out." I swished past him down the hall—*Bang!*—right out the door. "Boys!" I hollered, "Go time!" I began hoofing it when an arm snaked around my waist. I whirled around. "*What?* What is it, Pete? I have to go now!" I masked my hurt and confusion with a double dose of anger.

"I—" He paused to rub at his jaw. "I'm sorry."

"So you've already said." I turned to flee, but he nabbed my hand. Expecting more apologies or humorous flirting, I was unprepared for what I got.

"Kate . . ." Pete looked down on me with a serious enough expression my heart arrested in my chest. "You should prepare yourself for the idea that Andrew will most likely be going to The Academy come January."

"Why? Did you find somethin' out?"

He shook his head. "I just don't want you to be crushed . . . if things end up not going your way."

"I'm very accustomed to things *not* goin' my way." I yanked my hand back. "However, this will *not* be one of those times."

"How can you be so sure?"

"Just am." I could hardly explain my intuition.

"I want you to prepare yourself—just in case."

His pity face flared my skin into further irritation. "I ain't gonna stand by and watch while your thievin' superiors snatch my brother away!"

"Kate . . ." he started, then screwed his mouth shut for a moment. "You need to stay out of it—for your sake. And Mikey's."

A sinking feeling, like my stomach just got coated in cast iron, nearly took me down, but I put steely resolve in my voice. "I think you should prepare yourself: I'll take the boys and run if I have to."

"You need to give up, Kate." He took hold of my hand again and squeezed. "*Please.*"

"If you think I'm just gonna give up, then you don't know me at all, Pete Davenport!" Sadness, madness, and fear were all clashing up against each other producing tears—a weakness I didn't want him to see. I averted my gaze.

He grasped my jaw, lifting my face to his. "That's where you're dead wrong, Kate Connelly—I know you're strong-willed but sweet natured, fiercely loyal, and one of the best mothers I've ever met. I also know that you're smarter than is for your own good, appreciate Impressionist art, and play soccer better than half the girls' Olympic team." A few tears escaped, but he didn't let me go. "And I know for a double-throw-down fact, that you're way, *way* too good for Ronald Tillman!"

My mouth flew open. "I—" was speechless. And no longer able to work up the energy to be mad at him after his little speech. To tell you the truth, I was more than a little touched but couldn't afford to get mired up in sentimentality. "Well then, you should know that I'm not givin' up! I'm sorry if you're gonna get in trouble over it . . . more than you know. But I just *can't* let them get their claws on my brother!"

Pete sighed and dropped my hand. "I actually think—knowing everything I do—that the best-case scenario, for everyone involved, would be if Andrew *does* go to The Academy next year." I gasped and retreated back a couple of paces. "You have to trust me on that one, Kate . . . and I don't give a damn about *me* getting into trouble." He gave me a meaningful look.

A sliver of fear paused me. *Is he trying to scare me?* That was one tactic they hadn't explored much. But what might've been more worrisome was that I felt like he was just strictly worrying about me.

"I think I'm beginnin' to understand the ruthless lengths y'all will go to get what you want, Pete. But since bribery didn't work, what makes you think scare tactics will?"

Pete didn't get a chance to respond because Daddy's Bronco came roaring up the road like some kind of smoke monster, billowing up clouds of dust. "Looks like the only thing worse than his parenting skills is his timing," he said, reluctantly stepping away from me to go greet my father.

I knew he'd be early today.

32

PETE WHAT'S-HIS-NAME?

We both missed homecoming. Pete didn't return all week. Nor did he make an appearance the following Monday, Tuesday, Wednesday, or Thursday. It had been more than a full week now without a word, other than the registered letter, delivering two first-class tickets to San Francisco—for my father and his prodigy.

Finally, *finally* everyone at school stopped pestering me with questions about his whereabouts, finally believing me when I said I didn't know anything. It seemed Pete had disappeared as quickly and mysteriously as he'd arrived. And after the hysterical mourning abated, everyone went back to normal. Almost. Ashley-Leigh and the no-longer-bolstered-motley-crew-P.E.-class being the most obvious exceptions. I didn't count, because I knew I'd never go back to normal (not that I ever was).

It was a benign Friday morning, and I was slumped over in Pre-Cal, trying and failing to look alive, when a knock on the door caused me to bolt upright. Almost as if someone had called my name. *Hmmmm.* Why was I so fascinated by the office-aid handing over a note? *Boredom.* I was getting ready to settle back into my slump when my name was called.

My heart gave a jolt. My feet found floor. And then I was standing in front of the class with my hand out. I almost tripped over a couple of backpacks in my rush back to tear into the note. It said: Your father called. You don't need to pick up Andrew from school this afternoon. *That's it? He couldn't've said anything else?* The lack of information was galling.

Better not get my hopes up. Most likely Daddy was going to take Andrew clothes shopping after school for the big bad trip to San Francisco on Monday. But I couldn't help feel a niggle of hope nudge into my chest . . . only to be crushed each time Pete's golden presence failed to manifest throughout the day. I kept visualizing him, as though I could will him into the empty desk behind me in Spanish, or on the dismal-feeling soccer field. By the end of the day, I'd given up, dejectedly picking up Mikey from preschool before heading straight home for a predictable round of chores. Or so I thought . . .

The last thing I remembered, as we headed into lonely pasture, was thinking I hadn't seen Pete's glistening eyes for more than a week. But they were the first thing I saw when my eyes fluttered open . . . some time later. I found myself being brought round from blissful, cave-like oblivion by sure hands methodically probing my body. I closed my eyes, groaning against the blinding light.

"Andrew, get my first-aid kit from the truck," a familiar voice ordered in an urgent, clipped tone.

Ow. I wanted to protest the probing going on around my head, but only a groan came out, until he found the cartoon-like knot protruding from the back of my skull. And then I gasped in agony. So that's why my neck was turned at such an odd angle. *Oh, please, please don't do that again!* I heard the heavy clunk of metal being dumped on the ground. Urgent rummaging was going on, along with some kind of wailing noise that made me want to cry.

"Kadeeee!" crested over the sound of sobs. "I didn't m-m-make her m-move!" More sobs followed this bizarre announcement that nobody replied to.

Maybe I'm hallucinating? Ow. Something tight and unyielding clamped around my throat. *Is he going to strangle me?* That's okay—I sought the darkness now, not fighting it. It closed over me again, blissfully catching my fall with waiting, tar-like wings.

"Kate?" Tense arm stroking. "Can you hear me?"

Quit screaming in my ear, so I can go back to sleep.

"Andrew, go back to the truck and get my phone . . . I better call 911."

911? No! He can't do that! I groaned again, trying to fight my way out of sticky tar to find the words that were sloshing around my brain. *Pete.* Thought I formed sound, but it seemed like no one could hear me through the wailing. *Mikey.* Those cries were coming from Mikey. *Why is nobody comforting him? Oh. Because of me . . . How hurt am I?* I couldn't move my head; it felt bowling ball heavy on my neck. I tried moving my mouth instead.

"Pete!" I cried so forcefully I almost fell back to the dark side.

"*Kate*! God, Kate! Can you hear me?"

"No," I said, realizing vaguely I made no sense because I just answered him back—I was referring to the 911 call.

"Bring my jacket out of the back while you're at it," he called out.

I remembered where I was now. The cold was a reminder. And the wet. The water tank. I'd finally fixed the problem. Apparently, a rat had crawled into the pump rod, blocking the flow of water. I distinctly remembered seeing the windmill in the distance, churning like a giant mechanical sunflower. I remembered attaching a wire hanger to a fishing line, then dropping it into the pipe again and again, until it finally caught on something fleshy. And pulling with all of my might until —*Thock!*—a rat spit out. Then realizing, a second too late, the release of pressure would gush the water out. And it did, like a fireman's wrench discharging a line. I wasn't prepared for the sheer force of the surge. It knocked me over in an instant. And it didn't feel like a feather, I can tell you that.

That's all I remembered: a torrent of water hurtling into me, filling my nose, mouth, and throat. I couldn't breathe. When I came up for air, all I could think was . . .

"Mikey!" I cried out again, struggling to sit up. I was panicked that he had gotten hurt or drowned because he was standing right next to me.

"Kadeeee!" he cried in return.

"Careful, buddy. Don't bump into her."

"I won't." I felt Mikey's warming presence, kneeling beside me, stroking my arm.

"Shhhh, Kate," Pete soothed. "He's okay. Not a scratch on him . . . can't say the same for you though. You don't appear to have any broken bones, but I'm concerned about your neck and head."

"I got it!" The swishing of dry pasture could be heard as Andrew ran. And panic, the same trembling timbre to his voice as when Mama died.

"She's awake now, but I'm still calling 911."

"No!" I insisted more fervently now.

"Lie still, Kate. Your neck."

"Doesn't hurt. Just my head." I focused hard on prying my eyes open. "Please don't call an ambulance . . . we don't have any insurance," I pleaded, finding Pete's eyes just long enough to see him purse his lips—the pain and the light were blinding in their intensity.

"Hand me the jacket," Pete said, then I felt him burrito-wrap me up and instantly felt a little better. I recalled him pouring cool water on the back of my neck when I was faint, how I'd also felt instantly better then, too.

Why's he always being so nice to me? I didn't deserve it. I'd only been surly and ungrateful to him. *Oh right—because he's the enemy.* But I didn't *want* him to be. And then I started crying for some inexplicable reason and felt more than one pair of concerned hands stroking my limbs.

"Kadee, I'm sowry. I didn't make you move, and you got hurted!"

"It's okay, buddy. Nobody blames you," Pete assured him.

I could've kissed him for it, except now I felt like throwing up. The crying hurt my head even more. Like tiny jackhammers drilling the inside of my skull to get out. And there was a distinct ringing in my ears, but I didn't complain in case Pete decided to make that call. I screwed my eyes shut, willing the peaceful blackness back.

"Kate . . ." Pete stroked my face. I pried my eyes back open and was rewarded with dark angel eyes looking down on me in a way that stirred my chest. "Honey, I at least have to drive you to the hospital. I'm not sure how long you were out. You definitely have a concussion. You could have a skull fracture, bleeding in your brain . . . a broken neck. You need a CAT scan to tell for sure."

Does he have an MD? Somehow nothing seemed impossible where Pete was concerned. He was like the gift that kept on giving, a boundless well of surprises.

"I'm fine, Pete. Just a King-Kong sized headache."

"Kate, I'm afraid you lack the clear judgment needed to make an informed decision right now . . . not that you make clear judgments and informed decisions anyway," he muttered under his breath.

"I heard that," I mumbled, snuggling into his warm body. My teeth were beginning to chatter.

I felt as much as heard him chuckle. "And you may be going into shock."

I couldn't focus on answering; I was going back to sleep now.

"Come on, baby . . . I need you to try and stay awake for me."

"Hmmm?" *Where am I again?* I was so tired I couldn't remember.

Next thing I knew, I felt the ground leave my body as Pete scooped me up, cradling me against his chest as he carried me. I must've drifted off again because the next time I came to, I found myself in a mechanized vehicle. Moving rapidly over rugged terrain and jostling around too much for my delicate state. I groaned in protest.

"I'm sorry, Kate. I know it hurts. We're almost to the road . . . just hang on."

Oh God. A wave of sick overcame me—the momentum of the powerful machine, the bumping around, the pain. "Pete!" I breathed sharply through my nose. "Pull over!"

He must've been prepared for the possibility I might hurl all over his plush leather seats, because his emptied backpack was handed over in the nick of time. The pressure in my head, the throbbing, the sickness—I was in too much pain to even feel embarrassed.

"Oh God!" I wailed when I was able to speak. I buried my face in my hands, groaning.

"Don't worry about it."

I wasn't. I wasn't worrying about *anything* except the possibility of the pain getting worse. My eyes closed again, despite Pete urging me to keep them open. I heard him toss something in the back.

"I guess you better call your father," he said, allowing the disrespectful edge.

Oh Gah! Just when I didn't think I could feel any worse! I groaned again.

"I know," he commiserated. "I'm sorry. We have to—technically you're still a minor. There will be forms to fill out."

"He'll be furious," I whispered.

"He won't be the only one."

I faded out. The next thing I knew, I was being carried through emergency doors and into a waiting room with lights so bright they should be illegal.

"She has a concussion." I heard him say. "Blunt force trauma to the right parietal."

"Are you her boyfriend?" An unfamiliar voice.

"Friend of the family."

"How did this happen?" The voice turned suspicious.

"I'm not exactly sure. I found her lying on the ground in the pasture, soaking wet, with her brother crying nearby."

I kept my eyes resolutely shut, but felt like I should speak up. "Cows couldn't get water. Thought somethin' stuck in pipe . . . used fishin' wire . . . worked—pulled dead rat out—except water knocked me back. Hit tank . . . 'sall I 'member." I felt like I jumbled it all up even though I was trying to speak clearly.

"Alrighty then," the mystery medical lady said as if this made perfect sense. Only in a farming community would this scenario be plausible I thought. And then wished I didn't, because it hurt to even think of my own name, which was exactly the next question on the line-up.

"Kadee Connelly," a desperate boy pitched in from below.

"The nurse is asking *her*, you *idiot*," hissed an anxious-ridden Andrew.

"You must be the little brother."

"Yes, ma'am," Mikey responded with a colossal attempt not to cry that about tore my heart out. The nurse asked the boys to wait out in the waiting room. "Is my sistuh gonna be alwight?" Mikey uttered in a voice even smaller than his age. I reached down to squeeze his hand; couldn't find it in me to speak.

"She's gonna be back to bossin' you around in no time," declared the nurse in a voice that instilled confidence.

Now I wanted to kiss her. I pried my lids up to see a wide smile and kind eyes set in a dark, no-nonsense face.

"Howdy. My name is Gloria."

I felt rude, unable to partake in pleasantries right now. She shined a tiny flashlight into my pupils. Frowned.

"Her pupils always appear dilated," Pete disclosed before stepping away, so I could focus my eyes on the line of her finger.

"Okay, Miss Connelly, can you tell me the name of the young man standin' beside you right now?"

Couldn't help it—a stupid smile spread my lips despite the throbbing of my head, and the wretched nausea roiling my stomach, and the annoying ringing in my ears. I would've known who was standing next to me in a pitch-black cave, after being blindfolded and spun around.

"Pete." The word was loaded with meaning. He grinned at me, and I did my best to imitate the movement.

"Hmm-hmmm," Nurse Gloria said, clearly not satisfied with my answer. *What else did she need?* Standing there, looking down at me with the brightest dark eyes I'd ever seen, he was purely Pete—nothing else to know.

"Okay, let's try again using his first *and* last name."

Seemed silly. Piece of cake. I knew exactly who he was. "Pete . . ." I floundered for a second. Of course, I knew this. Just couldn't seem to conjure it up straight away. *Frustrating.* I looked up for reassurance from the one I knew so well. He smiled down at me encouragingly, and my heart surged with pure joy and, and . . . *love.* "What was the question?"

His face fell a little before he rearranged it. He glanced over at Nurse Gloria. *Nervous.* Even if I couldn't remember his last name, I could still read him like a book. He was nervous and wanted reassurance from the nurse. That touched me, it really did. I frowned, not being able to give him what he wanted.

"That's okay, sweetheart. It'll come to you in a minute," said the kindly nurse, writing something down in her chart again. She wrapped my arm with a Velcro cuff and started pumping what looked like a small black balloon. The pressure built up tighter and tighter before releasing in a whoosh of air. I hadn't minded the squeezing sensation of the device, because it momentarily took my mind away from the squeezing in my head.

It was fascinating to be here. I'd only visited the doctor once before, for a physical in sixth grade. I recalled enjoying the same sensation of pressure building up before the relief of release, and the annoying mini hammer knocking into my knee, and peeing into a plastic cup while giggling hysterically with Ashley-Leigh as we switched pee cups for no good reason but to laugh. And most of all: the pleasure feeling of feeling like a *normal* twelve-year-old.

Nurse Gloria made more notations in her chart. I tried to read what she wrote, but couldn't turn my head. "Excuse me? Can I take this . . . thing off my neck now?"

"Your boyfriend was kind enough to put it on there for you, so I b'lieve we should just let it sit a while longer till the good doctor gets a gander at that CT and gives the okay to remove it."

I kinda stopped following her after the *B*-word. "Boyfriend," I said it aloud, trying it out in relation to Pete, who was still smiling at me, like, since that was the only thing he could do, he was bound and determined to do a bang-up job of it.

"That's right. You heard me—*boyfriend.* Cuz the way you two youngsters is lookin' at each another, don't fool me a bit . . . Friend of the family, my foot," she declared as definitively as she'd said I'd be back to bossing my brothers in no time. I liked her, I really did.

After a series of tests, seemingly designed just to drive me crazy, the doctor finally came in, looking sturdy and capable as a doctor should. He shook hands with Pete and introduced himself. (I'm ashamed to say I couldn't remember his name two seconds afterward.) Then he commenced to probing around my head till I was swimming through stars and felt compelled to puke—again—right over the railing. It splattered onto the floor before ricocheting in a sickly-green arc, adding a charming backsplash to the curtain partition behind where Pete was standing.

The word *mortified* suddenly sprang to mind.

"Sorry!" I gasp-groaned.

"That's quite alright, darlin'," Nurse Gloria said. She held up a plastic boomerang-shaped bowl hanging out beside me on the bed. "That's what this is for . . . just in case it happens again."

Oh God. Didn't think it was possible to be *more* mortified. And didn't dare look up at Pete as I profusely apologized again. I had no idea *what* that thing was to tell you the truth.

"No worries. We had to get you outta those wet, dirty clothes anyhow and into a dressin' gown."

"Dr. Shaw," Pete interrupted, "is there any way we can get her started on some pain meds?"

"I think we might be able to do that, Cadet Davenport," he said jovial enough to be at a picnic in the park. His tone didn't have much of a chance to rankle my nerves because the moment he ordered up some pain meds from good ole Gloria, I wanted to kiss him, although he vaguely looked like Santa Clause's slimmer, better-looking cousin. (And not mentioning the fact that *nobody* wanted me to kiss them right now.)

"And some water please," I croaked, feeling parched even though I'd almost drowned earlier.

Nurse Gloria and the good doctor left the room.

"Thanks, Pete . . . Davenport." My grin turned into a grimace. I just noticed the antiseptic hospital smell was quickly being swallowed up by my vomit.

"You remembered!" Pete beamed at me.

"No, I cheated," I confessed with a frown. "Heard Dr. What's-His-Name call you Cadet Davenport."

He chuckled. "I'm a little hurt, Kate—I thought I was unforgettable."

"You are," I sighed. "That's the problem: even a big knock on my head can't make me forget you."

Pete brooded for a moment, and I took the moment to decide it was a good look on him. "You *want* to forget me?"

"Yes. No. . . . I dunno. I'm all mixed up and my head hurts." He made a face. "Pete. The smell. It's so bad. I'm really sorry . . . and your poor Hummer."

"So you can remember the name of my truck, but not my last name?"

"Yeah. You know me. I'm real-real . . ." I struggled for the word to make the joke work.

"Materialistic," he supplied, reading my fuzzy mind.

"Right." I smiled up at him until another waft of throw-up brought to my attention the fact that he was most likely standing in it. "Pete, why don't you wait out in the waitin' room?"

"Not a chance, Kate."

As if on cue, a bustling Gloria came back in with a mop-wielding orderly, a pale-blue dressing gown, a scary-looking syringe, and a Big-gulp medical cup that she plopped onto an overbed tray—just like on TV. "We're gonna get this mess cleaned up, get the pretty lady into some clean duds, and then get her into X-ray," Gloira directed.

Pete stepped around to my other side, brushing his hand from my shoulder to my fingertips. All kinds of tingling sensations momentarily confused my pain.

"But first," Gloria bent the accordian straw my way, "let's do somethin' about that headache and thirst."

When I gratefully leaned forward to gulp it down, Pete snatched it away before I could do much more than swallow a sip. Feeling gypped, I looked up for answers.

"Boyfriend's got trainin'," Nurse Gloria approved, thumping the side of the syringe. I scowled. "Sorry sweetheart . . . don't want you throwin' up again, do we?" I grimaced. "Here." She slipped me a package of Saltines. "Nibble on these—should help with the nausea. Okay, looks like Mr. Jameson here is all finished workin' his magic. Boyfriend, you gots to leave, so I can get Girlfriend feelin' better."

Boy, were they efficient. Everything was back to antiseptic hospital smell, only times a thousand. While I was busy nibbling on a cracker, Pete pressed his lips to my temple and then withdrew from me.

"Pete!" Panic seized me. "Don't leave!" I was afraid he was going to disappear on me again.

"I'm only stepping into the hall while you change and get your . . . er, happy shot." He grinned his way out the door.

What's a happy shot?

Two minutes later, I found out. When Pete came back in, I was feelin' no pain. "Heeeey!" I chirped as though he'd been gone on a tour of duty.

"Hey, yourself." Pete gave a conspiratorial smile to Gloria. "Looks like someone's feeling better."

"I got a shot in the butt," I explained with a loopy grin.

"Fo sho . . . Girlfriend ain't feelin' no pain now," Gloria added. While they chuckled together, I focused hard on wiping the smile off my face. "Okay, Miss Connelly, it's time to wheel you down to X-ray . . . see how hard that head of your is."

"They don't come no harder," Pete quipped, and the two of them laughed it up again.

"Hey!" I protested, yet couldn't seem to work up any real feelings of irritation. *Weird. And wonderful.* Despite the lump on my head, a perma-grin seemed to be fixed to my face like the Joker. I rose to my feet—with the aid of Boyfriend—realizing, a moment too late, my assets were bared for the world. I knew I should be embarrassed, but, like irritation, the feeling was mysteriously absent.

A giggle tickled my throat as Pete set me carefully into the wheelchair. "I can walk yunno . . . my legs aren't broken."

"No, you can't!" Pete and Nurse Gloria chorused.

I scowled up at them as best I could, but was simply feeling so good my heart just wasn't in it. "Can he come with us?" I asked plaintively.

"Only if you can tell me who *he* is," she challenged.

"Why that's easy!" I smiled smugly. "Pete Davenport."

"Very good." Nurse Gloria nodded her approval, making me feel like the star patient. "Guess Boyfriend's comin' with."

"Yay!" I threw my hands in the air like I was doing the wave.

Pete gave me his trademark crooked grin, knowing full well I'd cheated. "I think I like you better this way."

"Me too!" I emphatically seconded.

A few minutes later, I was being wheeled out—sans neck collar—by Boyfriend while Nurse Gloria gave me post care instructions that included a bunch of stuff that wasn't likely going to happen, like taking it easy for the next couple of days. Apparently, I was to have no physical or mental activities, which included screen time (the only thing on the list that would happen), no school, no chores, no anything except for bed rest.

"But the doctor says he thinks I just have a *simple* concussion," I argued. "I should be fine after a couple of days."

"Right," she agreed, "*if* you follow doctor's orders, and *if* there are no complications."

"What if I'm feelin' better tomorrow?"

"Kate . . ." Pete stopped wheeling to walk around and kneel to my level. He stared me straight. "There's *no* such thing as a simple concussion. You hit your head pretty good. There's swelling, and the levels of brain chemicals are altered. It takes about a week for those to stabilize again." He waited for my sluggish brain to process this before going on. "Your normal level of activity is *not* conducive to healing your body. You simply *have* to stay in bed for the next forty-eight hours minimum. And then you can slowly add activities back, but only on a limited basis. You cannot afford to get another brain injury that could cause long-term damage." He looked serious as a heart attack now.

The smile finally left my face. *Boy is he a buzz kill.*

"Your brain is who you are," he continued. "I *like* who you are—the outside is just a pretty package you happen to come wrapped in."

I tried scowling at him even though I was very much touched. Unfortunately, I had a house to run. "Who's gonna look after the boys and the animals?"

"I see what you mean by the hard head," Nurse Gloria said to Pete.

"Someone besides you." I started to protest, when he cut me off. "The world will not stop revolving because you lay low for a couple of days." I started to argue when he said something funny: "Your father can take over for the next few days." I actually laughed. ". . . Or I will."

"Aw, Pete." I gazed at him with love-shining eyes. "You've already done enough for us already."

"Looks like Boyfriend's a keeper," Nurse Gloria said to me.

"If only that were possible." I sighed, feeling the first stirrings of reality set in. Pete looked at me, and if my intuition was correct, he was feeling the exact same way.

After Pete had me tucked back into my triage bed in the curtained off partition he said, "I better go check on the boys. They'll want to know you're all right."

A few pleasant moments of resting later, and my brothers came creeping in, stopping just shy of touching me. I smiled lovingly down on them—one light, one dark—marveling at their little-boy beauty as though seeing them for the first time.

"You can come closer." I beckoned. "I won't break."

Andrew spoke up, because a forlorn Mikey looked like he might never speak again. "Pete warned us that you're fragile right now. He said we had to treat you like a porcelain doll for the next week or two, so your brain won't swell again." I almost didn't recognize his voice because it lacked its usual trumpet of self-confidence.

"I bet a hug is permitted." I reached out.

Mikey backed away crying. "No! I don't wanna bweak you, Kadee! I alweady letted you get huwrt today, and Pete said we can't let you get huwrted again!"

"Hey-hey! Come here, sweetie. I'm okay. Just a bump on the back of my head . . . it's *not* your fault. I don't know why on earth you think it would be."

They were still resolutely standing a couple of inches out of arms reach. "Come on," I coaxed, and Andrew came up to hug me around the middle. I brushed my hand from the top of his head to the nape of his neck. "I love you, Drews," I said, getting choked up.

"Me too, Katie . . . I love you, too."

I looked over to an almost comically miserable-looking Mikey. "Okay— your turn." I threw my arms wide, and he came forward with his need for me warring with his need not to break me. At last, after he was sure I really wouldn't break, he gingerly laid his head on my lap. Then started sobbing.

"Shhhh . . . I'm fine. Everything's okay," I crooned to him while stroking his back.

Nurse Gloria came in a few minutes later with Pete, who had quietly slipped out of the room. "Hey-hey. None of that cryin' now," she commanded sternly. "What'd I tell you? She's fine. Just needs a little TLC for the next few days. You can help with that, right?" Serious head nods followed by "yes ma'ams" and shimmers of tears all around.

"Okay, Miss Connelly, you are officially discharged. Your father's waitin' for you in the waitin' room. Here is the instructions." She handed me what looked like a master's thesis amount of paperwork. "Make sure he reads it—not you—and does everything he's supposed to do tonight and tomorrow especially. As much as I've enjoyed your visit . . . we *don't* wanna see you back in here."

"Yes, ma'am." I smiled. "Thank you."

"You're welcome. Now I have to wheel you on out now—rules is rules. But it don't say nothin' 'bout helpers." She eyed my brothers. "Which one of you strappin' young men would like to help push?"

Two hands shot up. "Me! Me!"

Nurse Gloria chuckled. "That's about what I thought. Come on . . . I guess we'll do one on each side."

I was wheeled—slowly and carefully—out the swinging double doors and into the waiting room. That reminded me: I'd have to let Norma know I couldn't work this weekend. A smile lit up my face at the thought of a whole week taking it easy. That smile lasted as long as it took my eyes to register Daddy, the lone stander in the waiting room. Arms folded, he glowered down at me like he'd been called in to pick me up from the principal's office.

"Hi, Daddy," I squeaked.

He nodded at me, cleared his throat. "You alright, Katie-girl?"

I nodded my head. (The first time I'd voluntarily moved it since the accident.) "Just a concussion."

"Well that's somethin' good I 'spose." Daddy's lips pulled into line formation. One, two, three beats: "Do you have *any* idea how much this little stunt's gonna cost me?" Unable to keep it in for all the tea in Texas.

I drew in a shaky breath, aware of awareness from others of our situation. "I was only tryin' to help" came out the same time Pete came striding through the double doors. He was carrying a plastic bag most likely containing my soiled clothes and a handful of paperwork.

"Nothing," he said, his timing so impeccable I had to wonder if he was hiding out behind the door eavesdropping. "It will cost you nothing, because it's already been taken care of—compliments of The Academy."

"Oh, hey, Pete . . ." Daddy faltered. "I didn't know you was still here." He thrust a hand out for Pete to shake. It looked to me like Pete would rather shake hands with that dead rat I yanked from the tank, but he rallied quickly enough, coming forward to shake hands cordially, if stiffly.

"I gotta say thanks, Cadet Davenport. You saved the day once again."

"Don't mention it," Pete said.

An awkward pause ensued that Daddy filled with some cringe-worthy babbling. "Boy!—kids." He shook his head. "You gotta watch 'em all the time, or they get into trouble ever' minute." This as though I'd been off breaking windows with stones in my spare time.

A thundercloud appeared on Pete's face that he couldn't quite seem to manage to stave off. Meanwhile, Daddy was going on, quite oblivious to the fact that not only was he singing off key, but he was singing to the wrong choir entirely.

"I told her I'd take care of the tank problem." Daddy spared a glance at his injured daughter. "But you know young ladies . . . impetuous as the day is long."

"Hey!" Mikey interjected hotly. "That's not twue!" I immediately grabbed his arm, but he simply stepped out of my grasp.

Daddy turned the color of summer beets, smiling like a criminal before a jury. "Young man, where are yer manners? You do not in'errupt grown-ups when they're speakin'." He looked at Pete as though for support, but Pete's face remained unmoved as the Statue of David.

"Anyhow," Daddy went on, clearing his throat and switching gears. "As much as we appreciate the offer . . . we don't need no charity from yer academy. We take care of our own bills. Always have . . . always will." He clamped a hard hand on my shoulder, making me aware that I had an ache back there. "Katie will pay it back from the money she earns waitressin'. Right, Katie-girl?"

"Yes, sir." I nodded my head earnestly up at Pete. "That's what I was plannin' on doin' anyhow."

"You see?" Daddy beamed at me proudly like I'd finally hit my mark. "That's the way I raise up my children—to be real responsible. I bet she won't be so careless next time," he crowed.

I saw the thundercloud shadowing Pete's face again, and worried, like lightening, he was about to strike. His jaw worked back and forth until he got it together enough to release the tension so he could speak.

"Well, we can get the *trivial* matter of the bill settled later. For now, the important thing is your daughter's recovery." He looked, I thought, a bit too sternly at Daddy. "She will need full bed rest for forty-eight hours minimum. After that, if there are no complications, she can gradually add light activities back—no calf feeding, no heavy lifting—only light housework. I'll let her teachers know of her condition." He addressed Nurse Gloria: "Would you be so kind as to get a note from Dr. Shaw?"

"Yessir, boss man." Nurse Gloria graced Pete with her gap-toothed smile. "I see you got this."

"Thank you." Pete turned back to Daddy. "In the meantime, go ahead and get her home. I'll pick up her prescriptions."

"I don't really think that's necessary. You done enough already, Pete. Anyhow, I think we got a coupl'uh Advils rollin' around somewhere in the back of the medicine cabinet . . . does the job just fine when my leg's actin' up."

"No Ibuprofen," Pete swiftly countered. "It could cause bleeding. Acetaminophen is okay, but a prescription strength pain reliever is best. She'll most likely wake up to the biggest headache of her life in a couple of hours when the morphine wears off."

"Huh?" My father seemed perplexed by this onslaught of information. "You sure do seem to know a lot about it. Are you studyin' to be a doc or somethin'?"

"No, sir. My father is one of the physicians at The Academy, so I've picked up tidbits here and there over the years. Plus, all cadets are required to take a six-month course in medical training."

"Is that right?"

"Yes, sir."

"Huh," my father said the same time I thought it. I filed that little snippet about his father away for now. I would take it out later to inspect further. But right now, I was tired, I really was.

"Why don't you get Kate home and into bed." It was said as a command. "No noise, no TV, no anything but rest." Pete looked severely down at me.

I smiled, nodding my head up and down. Usually I hated being bossed around. And feeling helpless. Right now . . . not so much. *Huh.* Must be the "happy shot." I closed my eyes and must've drifted off because the next thing I knew, I was home, and two vigilant little brothers were helping me walk in, one on each side. I looked down, horrified, to see I was still in my hospital gown.

The only thing keeping it from gaping open was Pete's navy IEA jacket, zipped up over it.

33

SLEEPING WITH THE ENEMY

rap-tap-tap roused me later. I wasn't sure how much later because it was dark outside. A presence—too polite to be my father—began asserting itself behind the door again. Didn't feel polite though, reverberating from inside my noggin. *Ow.* Pain. Coming on stronger every second. I heard voices.

"Pete, you might wanna just let 'er sleep it off." This said as though I were merely hungover. "She'll be alright—my Katie's one tough cookie."

"Yes, well, sleeping it off is something she *can't* do uninterrupted tonight. Did you read the patient information sheet? . . . I highlighted it in yellow."

"Uh, well . . . not quite there yet, Pete. Just got the boys off to bed and was sittin' down a spell to watch the game. Why don'tja come on in an' join me?"

"I better check on Kate. She'll be wanting these pain pills soon . . . maybe something to eat first. I brought her some—"

"Well now. That sure is awfully kind of you. Above and beyond the call of duty really." Daddy sounded almost as disapproving as Pete. "I'll be sure to let yer Academy know what a swell job yer doin' with my *daughter*, as well as my future cadet." My Daddy may be uneducated, but he wasn't stupid.

"Thank you, sir . . . though unnecessary. It's a cadet's duty to help out the host family in any way possible for the duration of our stay. I'll just drop off her prescriptions and food and then be on my way," Pete said smoothly.

Dang it.

Another *rap-tap-tap*.

"Come in," I croaked, sitting up in bed and immediately wincing from the spotlight Daddy just turned on. Pete informed my father that bright lights were a no-no and turned it back off, then came in and snapped on my tulip lamp instead. A disgruntled Daddy followed, coming up from behind to loom over us like a giant buzz kill.

"Hey." Pete stared at my face with a soft, inscrutable look until I couldn't take it—my lashes fanned my cheeks.

"Hey." I pulled the slippery hospital gown back over my shoulder.

"How you feeling?"

I shrugged a little, tried a smile. "Head hurts."

Pete smiled back. "I'm not surprised. I felt the size of that goose egg."

"Goose egg?" I said incredulously. "Feels more like an ostrich egg to me!"

Pete chuckled lightly. We were both hyper aware we were being scrutinized by my father. "You must be hungry." He looked at me for confirmation.

"A little, I guess. It's hard to concentrate on anything but my throbbin' head."

"Well, you can't take the pain meds on an empty stomach without risking another vomiting episode."

"Oh man . . . don't remind me." My face heated instantly. "Sorry 'bout that again, by the way."

"Don't apologize for being sick," Pete reprimanded lightly.

I merely nodded, feeling extremely awkward with Daddy hovering. Pete began unpacking what appeared to be a child's paper bag lunch.

My father coughed into his hand. "Is there anything I can do tuh help?"

"A spoon would be great," Pete said, unpeeling the foil from a yogurt cup.

"One spoon comin' up!" Daddy announced before tromping out the door. Pete and I shared a couple of long looks and secret smiles before he came back in, brandishing the proper utensil proudly. "Here ya go, Katie-girl!"

I winced a little at his volume. "Thank you, Daddy."

"Yer welcome!" Daddy beamed at me and kind of stood around shifting his feet and snapping his fingers.

"You can go on back and watch the game, Daddy," I suggested. "I'm just gonna eat a little sandwhich and take my pills, then go on to sleep."

"That's a good idea," Pete seconded. "She's not supposed to have a whole lot of stimulation tonight. I'm just going to go over some last minute instructions. . . . I'll be back to check on her in the morning and help out with chores, if that's okay with you, sir."

"Well, now." Daddy knocked knuckles against my dresser with a cheerful nod. "That's mighty nice of you." After a little back and forth about the way tomorrow should go, and after Pete agreed to catch the last half of the game with him, Daddy finally left us alone—after swinging the door wide. We both visibly relaxed as soon as he was gone.

"Ready for some meds?" Pete asked when he saw me rubbing the back of my neck, which was pretty sore, too.

I nodded but not too enthusiastically—the throbbing was getting worse.

He cracked open the RX bottle and shook out two oval-shaped pills. Then pulled out one of his famous dark water bottles and twisted it open to some zippy steam. I quickly swallowed them down, ready to feel some relief.

"Anything you want to do bathroom wise, you better do it now," he advised. "These are going to knock you out pretty good."

"Would you mind handin' me the alarm first?"

Pete narrowed his eyes. "You're not really planning on getting up tomorrow morning?"

"No," I said, miffed he didn't think I was capable of following directions. "I'm settin' it for three hours, so I'll make sure to wake myself up through the night."

A certain look I was starting to recognize softened Pete's features. "You can't rely on your father." He stated the obvious.

My eyebrows slanted down. "Have you met my father?"

He chuckled and patted my leg. This confused me: *Was that a love tap, or a brotherly pat?*

"That's a good idea, but unnecessary . . . I'm already one step ahead." I looked up to find eyes that were twinkling, and a mouth with a distinct smirk upon it. "Trust me," he said.

I took in a breath, deciding not to ask questions—just trust him. It felt *good* to rely on someone else. Besides, I couldn't remember ever being so tired. And that was saying something. All I wanted to do was fall blissfully back to sleep. But first, I urgently needed to use the bathroom.

"Um, would you mind leavin' while I cross to the bathroom?" I didn't want to get up with my hospital gown flapping open like a backwards flasher.

"Okay, but don't lock the door. And I know it goes without saying not to wash your hair. Also, don't stand up in the shower." The look Pete gave me was medical-grade stern. "You can't afford another fall right now. And don't take more than ten minutes . . . or I'm coming in after you."

"Got it," I said, kinda wanting to give him a sardonic salute. But honestly, I didn't have the energy to spare.

Approximately ten minutes later, I'd sufficiently showered and brushed my teeth and was back in bed. My eyelids were beginning to droop when Pete showed up to crown my head with a frozen bag of peas.

"You're quite the Boy Scout, Cadet Davenport," I murmured, losing the battle with consciousness.

He chuckled. "Comes with the territory."

"Seriously." I gazed up at him, all the emotions in my heart shining through now that my defenses were down (not to mention my inhibitions due to the two magic pills I'd just swallowed). "Thanks . . . for everything."

"You're seriously welcome." He gave me a strange smile before drifting to the window to peer out.

"Not much of a view, I'm afraid," I said around a yawn. "Why I hung the pictures on the wall . . . dream about Paris . . ."

He clicked off the lamp and leaned over to brush his hand over my hair. "See you soon . . ." I thought I heard him say before I was out like a light.

> *Little boy soldiers in plumed hats were lined up in arrow-straight rows. Raising their swords in a Hitler-like salute to a navy and gold flag with a roaring lion head on it. Everything was pristine and sparkling under the sun. Even the horses were decked out with gold buckles and ribbons, their tails swaying in the wind the only movement. The pageantry of the moment seemed out of place with the flag, which slowly dripped blood—from the lion's open mouth. Nobody seemed bothered by this except me. I was desperately searching a sea of blank faces for Andrew. Couldn't find him anywhere.*
>
> *I noticed a boy up front. Smaller than the rest. Something about the block shape of his head looked familiar to me. I could see he was the only one with real features on his face. Fighting my way through lines of robotic boys, I frantically ran to him and grabbed his shoulder. When he turned around, it wasn't Andrew . . . it was Mikey.*

I cried out, and a low voice soothed me. Sure hands stroked my arm in rhythmic caresses that melted my fear. *Must be dreaming. This dream is better.* I drifted off again.

I was awoken, not by the nerve-jangling sound of the alarm going off, but by the same soothing voice from my dreams murmuring words of encouragement. I was at the bottom of a deep well. With a wall of concrete pressed against my chest. I couldn't push it off. It was ten times—a hundred times—heavier than me. I wanted to cry for help but felt like it would be muffled and not worth the effort.

Warm hands stroked my back. Strong, capable hands helping me. Calmer now, I was still in deep though not alone. "Kate, you need to open your eyes for me," that same velvet voice exhorted me.

I felt like I *might* could do it. With his help. A dim light went on. A pinprick really, from the bottom of the hole, but it was something to focus on besides the darkness. I wasn't so lost now.

"Kate, wake up." *Ow.* A slight stinging sensation on my face. "Kate!" The voice was no longer velvet but insistent now. I groaned. Coming up was hard work. I needed a minute. "Open your eyes." The voice thought I was being lazy. I would try harder. As I drifted up to the surface, little flickers of involuntary reflexes were going on.

"Hmmm." There. That was good. I needed praise for that.

"Come on, honey . . . open your eyes."

Awareness slowly settled in. The pain helped, a reminder. The flickers I could control with some regularity now—my fingers, then my eyelids. At last, I pried my eyes open to see bottomless black pools staring down on me. Relieved.

"Welcome back . . . again," Pete said.

I felt warm just from his smile. Now that I saw him sitting here, on my bed, I was sure I was out cold again. Or in a drug-induced hallucination. No matter. I wanted to fall back to the darkness and bring him with me. My eyes drifted closed again.

"Oh, no you don't!" He patted my face again.

How could he do that to me? He was a gentleman—nothing gentle about that. I halfway tried to cover my face with my hand, but it was too much effort. "Stop," I pleaded.

"I'll stop if you open your eyes again."

"Deal." I drew in a deep, drugged-up breath and willed my eyes open.

Flashy teeth greeted me in the darkness. "Remind me to only give you *one* of those pills next time."

I gave him a loose, groggy smile. Now that I was awake, I wanted to talk all night. Settled for staring at the moment.

Pete blew out some air. "Whew—you had me worried there for a minute, Katie-Kat."

My smile gained momentum. I liked the way my nickname sounded coming from his mouth. *Oh God! That mouth.* I focused solely on it. Sexiest mouth I'd ever seen. My hand fluttered up, but Pete caught it midair, shaking it a little, as though a reprimand. This wounded me more than my wound.

"Thirsty?" He held up a dark bottle with one of those bendy straws.

I took a couple of sips, surprising myself by not dribbling it down the front of my shirt. During this exchange, I had a chance to inhale him and almost swooned in ecstasy. If he wanted to wake me up, he should've just leaned over—woulda worked better than smelling salts in bringing me round. *That scent could raise me from the dead.*

"What's that smile for?" His eyes warm and teasing.

I shrugged a shoulder. "You smell nice." I finally spoke, and it was to say the biggest understatement of the year. Maybe second only to: you look nice.

"She speaks!" Pete broke into a grin. "And even better—to give me a compliment."

I huffed out an embarrassed chuckle. "What are you doin' here?" I mumbled, thick tongued. "If my father catches you in here, he might send you packin' back to California with his shotgun pointed at your back."

Those lips I was staring at quirked up. "Your father is passed out on his recliner, and won't be getting up too much before . . . oh, say noonish tomorrow."

I raised brows at this bit of news, but made no comment.

"How are you feeling?" he asked.

I took a breath, assessing. Ecstatic he was here, for one. Kept that bit of intel to myself. "A little sore and a lot of achy," I answered.

"Imagine how you'd feel without the meds."

"Don't wanna." I sat up and winced from the effort of moving my head. "When did you get here?"

"I never really left," he revealed. "Just sat on the couch watching sports with your father until he passed out. Then came in here."

"Oh." I was sure there was more to the story; better not to ask questions. "How long have I been out?"

"About three hours. It was time to see if you could wake up. How's your stomach?"

"Holdin' steady," I said, giving it a little reward pat.

"Good, I'm glad."

"Me too." We seemed to run out of words, so relegated ourselves to staring until I remembered my dream. My forehead creased. "Pete, how did it go with your meetin'? Are you in trouble? I saw the tickets for Daddy and Andrew. They're supposed to leave on Monday . . . but I guess they're not goin' now on account of my injury."

Pete looked at me with a guarded expression. "I'm not in any trouble, Kate. Whatever gave you that silly idea? The Academy isn't a punitive place. We only hope to gain a gifted boy like Andrew because we sincerely believe it's the right place for him. . . . You'll soon see all this worry was for nothing," he finished with a smile that didn't crinkle his eyes.

Even in my half-drugged daze, the false ring to his tone was unmistakable as a ten-carat cubic zirconia presented at a backyard wedding. My eyes widened. *Who was talking just now?* A mouthpiece for The Academy? He didn't sound like Pete . . . at least *my* Pete. I leaned away from him, repelled as if an alien just inhabited his body.

"In regards to the tickets," he went on with his ambassador impersonation, "I'm sure we can postpone Andrew's visit, if you need more time to heal."

After a moment of soaking up my accusatory stare, Pete rubbed at his forehead as though *he* had the headache. "How's the goose egg?" He made to change the mood, picking up the wilted pea bag to inspect my head. "Down to a regulation-size chicken egg now," he said, smiling winningly at me. "We're making progress."

I arched a brow. "Are we?"

"We are," he affirmed, his eyes conveying a strong telepathic message— one I chose to believe. So I lay back on the pillow, too tired to argue for once.

When I awoke next, it felt like my head was in a vice. And that vice was slowly and steadily tightening. Tortuous. I groaned, feeling the urge to hurl again. "Pete!" He was there immediately, handing me a pill. I needed the help; the pain was awful. Apparently, the painkillers had left the building, and a gang of angry squatters had moved in with their hammers, tearing the membrane of my skull down from the inside. I swallowed it down, wincing from the movement.

"How bad is it?" he asked. "Scale of one to ten?"

I whimpered and threw all my digits at him, tears leaking from the corners of my eyes. He handed me another pill. I took it without question. The state I was in, I was thinking the more pills the better.

"I'm sorry, honey—I didn't wake you up when your meds wore off because I had so much trouble waking you up before. I had to see if you could wake up on your own."

I had nothing but groans to say to that. My nauseous stomach was battling it out with my brain for dominance over my body. While waiting for the pills to take effect, Pete methodically rubbed my back. I knew I was beginning to feel better when the sensations coming from my back were more pronounced than the throbbing of my head, and when the circles began to feel more sensual than soothing. I drew in a deep, shuttering breath.

"Better?" He brushed some hair back from my temple.

I nodded my head—a good sign. The wonderful, smooth feeling was coming back, the pills sanding down all of life's rough edges for the moment. I looked up at his spectacular face and noticed he looked like a photocopied version of himself.

"You look tired," I said, copy-catting him to brush the errant lock from his forehead. My fingers itched to touch his mouth. Instead, I continued reciprocating the good vibes by stroking my hand down the length of his arm.

Pete immediately froze. "What are you doing?"

"The same thing you were doin' two seconds ago," I replied.

He removed his arm from my hand. "I don't think that's a good idea."

I faced him with a face with no shame. "Why ever not?"

He stood up. Abruptly. "Because I don't."

His clipped tone wasn't much of a deterrent to me in my current state. "Name one good reason why."

He rattled the pills at me. "You're on narcotics for one."

I pouted, feeling bereft with him gone from my bed. Had to get him back.

"Don't leave!" I pleaded as he stepped away. He drew in a breath, debating. "Please . . . I'll be good. I-I just don't wanna be alone. *Please.*" I threw the puppy-dog eyes at him.

Pete's eyes were unreadable in the dim light, but I heard him sigh and lower himself back down on the edge of my bed, warily, as though he might have to spring up at any moment. My body's cravings weren't satisfied.

Hmmm. What could I do? I scooched over and threw back the covers—an invitation . . . that backfired. He sprang back to his feet.

"No!" I lurched for him. "Please don't go . . . I'm about two seconds from fallin' asleep, and I can't bear the thought of you sittin' up in that cold chair all night starin' at me sleep."

Pete was undecided, peering down on me as though a scorpion were wrapped in the pink sheets.

"*Please*, Pete?" I used my best little girl voice. "What's the harm in that?"

"What's the harm indeed?" he muttered but he seemed to be caving. After releasing a sharp gust of air, he snapped off the light and crawled into bed . . . *Yes!*—with his back to me—*No!*

I was lying on my side (the only way I could with a newly formed speed bump on the back of my head), facing him and thinking: *So this is spooning?* Satisfied, nope. I wriggled closer.

"What are you up to, young lady?" Pete demanded, in his best grown-up voice.

"Nothin' . . . just breathin'," I amended, breathing in his heavenly scent. His body heat radiated out to me, making me aware—I was half naked. *So close . . . yet not close enough.* Some pent-up frustration streamed from my lungs.

"Goodnight, Kate," he said sternly.

I was drifting along the lines of sleep and wakefulness and contentment and mutiny for a few more moments. "Pete . . ." I breathed into his back.

"Go to sleep, Kate."

"Almost there," I chirped. For some reason, his curtness didn't bother me. "Just wanna ask you somethin'."

"What is it?" he grumbled.

"Turn around."

"Not a good idea."

"I jus' wanna see your face," I said, a little slurry at the edges.

Pete made a big show of sighing before turning around to face me. Our eyes met in the witching light peering through the lace curtains. And as I stargazed into his fathomless eyes, the muscles in his face began to loosen.

"You had a question?" He was trying for annoyed but didn't quite make it there.

My lips curved. I nodded, my eyes moving to his mouth.

He stiffened and threw back the covers. I countered by yanking him to me. "You're playing a dangerous game, Kate," he warned, but he allowed me to pull him back down.

"Not playin' games," I said around a loopy smile.

"You have three seconds to ask your question, or I'm leaving." A heaping dose of resolve was packed into that threat.

"Okay, fine." I'd finally worked up to his level of annoyance—beginners. He was only *acting* annoyed. I leaned in closer, staring directly into his eyes. "How old are you, *really?*"

Caught off guard, Pete froze, eyes going wide with surprise tinged with something else that should've frightened me. All this happened in a nanosecond before he closed the shutters to his soul. "Old enough to know better," he said.

After this pearl of wisdom and a sigh, he remained facing me, eyes closed, lips parted. I took this as a green light to do the thing I'd been wanting to do for a long, long time. The most natural thing in the world—pressing my lips against his to test their firm fullness.

"Kate . . ." He gently tugged me backwards. "You're not in your right mind."

I sighed and resigned my head back to the cold pillow. "'m *never* in my right mind when I'm 'round you."

He chuckled, put his mouth to my ear. "I know the feeling." His warm breath tingled all the way to the base of my spine. I squirmed closer, slung an arm around his back, and pressed into him. *Mmmm. Nice.* "You're testing my self-control," he said, but he didn't move.

"Good." I pecked him on the lips. "You have too much of it already." My fingers began to explore the planes of his face, and were just moving to trace the sharp angle of his jaw, when he snorted and took my hand.

"Not where you're concerned," he said.

"Coulda fooled me." I ran my free hand through his hair, feeling the texture that waved its way through the softness. I took a breath. "I guess I'm plain terrible at this seducin' stuff—not really sure how," I admitted lamely, dropping my hand with a voluminous sigh.

"Coulda fooled me," he whispered, then gave in to run one hand along the curving shape of my body, pausing on the hill to grasp the jut of my hip.

My breath hitched. Our eyes locked. I tugged at his shoulder, my lips already parting. But Pete closed his eyes against me and dropped his hand. He let out a throaty growl and rolled onto his back, one hand splayed above his head as if in half surrender. I almost growled back. Instead, I took advantage of his belly-up position by leaning over his exposed neck to do my own deep breathing. Sighed with deep satisfaction. I kissed the side of his throat, feeling slightly silly. *Was that okay?* I was so sure and unsure at the same time.

"Kate . . ." he growled.

"Hmmm?" Suddenly, I had a very strong notion our bodies should be horizontally attached, so tried to attempt that very thing. *That wasn't so bad . . . was it?*

"What are you up to now?"

"Umm, layin' on you. No wait . . ." I changed my mind. That sounded stupid. "Huggin' you?"

Pete chuckled deep in his throat. I could feel the vibrations hum their cheerful way into my heart as I managed to straddle myself across the controlled cadet without any more protest. I had him pinned now, as we faced each other in the dark.

"What am I gonna do with you?" he breathed up at me.

Leaning over boldly, I offered up a challenge: "That's what I'd like to know."

Pete deliberated a heartbeat. As though of its own volition, the hand above his head moved to my face. And in the same manner, my face moved to fit the contours of his palm. Using the pad of his thumb, he traced my lower lip. My breath caught while I waited for his next move—carefully sliding his hand behind my neck, he drew me to him. He was done with the resisting. His intent was clear. Like magnets closing the distance, our hungry lips met. A few skipped heartbeats happened where our mouths sunk together in a long, sumptuous kiss that left me reeling and breathless for more.

I only felt sensation, wasn't thinking with my brain at all. It was turned off. Closed for the night while my body took over. I pressed into him, longing to feel the architecture of his body, his hard against my soft. I wanted to absorb his heat, the essence of him. And like our bodies, our minds were in sync because his well-behaved hand strayed under my hemline the same time my hand raked up his shirt. Strong arms fastened around me, so that our bodies melded together as we made out like bandits on top of my wagon-wheel bed.

The pleasant humming in my throat turned up to a moan. I heard his answering groan as he cupped me to him. I felt his careful restraint waning, his body's responses heating up despite his best efforts. *So euphoric!*—my last thought, right as an overdue surge of dulling depressant coursed through my bloodstream from my quickened pulse. The lights started to go out in my body now, way before I was ready.

Oh no! . . . Not now!

"Kate?" stirred my hair as I drooped over him. "Did I hurt you?" I pressed lazy lips to his hot throat before snuggling up on my favorite place on earth—his chest.

"Kate?" I felt more than heard him sigh in frustration.

"Hmm? Sorry . . . so sleepy," I slurred.

He chuckled softly, tickling my ear. "You're hurting my ego here—I'm pretty sure I've never put anyone to sleep before."

"Mmmm . . ." I was almost gone.

"Guess it's for the best," he murmured, slowing the stroking on my back to a more leisurely pace.

I wanted to argue, but I was down for the count.

34

~~~~~~~~

CAUGHT RED-HANDED

I awoke to the pneumatic drillers in my head again. Opened a peep-eye to find him still sleeping, as though posed by Walt Disney himself: on his back, mouth closed, errant forelock falling over his forehead, managing to make him look both mischievous and sexy. My heart studded to a stop with the force of emotion I felt for this boy—this man, I automatically corrected myself.

Ugh! How could I be in so much bliss and so much pain at the same time? They seemed to be completely incongruent feelings, but here they were comingling. Like us.

Apparently, I'd been zonked out half on him with my face smooshed into his chest, his arms wrapped around me, the beating of his heart in my ear. *This* was even better than spooning. I inhaled deeply, then couldn't take it anymore, the dull throbbing of my head forcing my hand. *Dang it!* I had to get some meds in me before it got worse and became debilitating.

OMG!—Daddy! I sucked in a rush of panic until I remembered what Pete had said last night about him sleeping till noon. I sure hoped he was right. Not the boys though. It was Saturday, so they would sleep in a little, but not much. Sigh. I looked out the yellowing window. Time for the rooster to crow.

And time to get up and scrounge for some meds. With Pete here, I didn't want to be so out of it today. I wanted to enjoy every minute, every second I could. But hating to move so much as an inch, I decided I could withstand just one teensy minute more of pain, just so I could indulgently stare at him. So I did, noticing a new smattering of scruff running along his chiseled jaw.

I'd never seen that before; it felt like I'd just discovered gold buried beneath my front porch. I longed to rub my fingertips against the grain to test its texture, but I was afraid of waking him—afraid to burst the bubble. Having him here was a dream, one I didn't want to wake from.

I frowned, wondering again how his meeting went, why he was talking so weirdly last night, how much longer he would be here. Not long. I could feel it, like a change in the atmosphere before a storm. Even though I still had a thousand questions, I would try to temporarily tamp them down so as not to fight. Despite the differences that manifested our separate destinies, I still felt completely drawn to him in a way that was both frightening and natural. But I still couldn't trust him. No matter how much I wanted to—I still had my doubts.

Slowly, I inched my way out from under him. He stirred once, sighing when I moved his arm, but he didn't wake up. Up on my feet now, I stared down at him. His chest continued to rise and fall in an even rhythm. I had a mad urge to take a picture. Settled for a mental one instead, then crossed the hall to use the bathroom. The reflection in the mirror conjured a grimace, but not a hairbrush—I still couldn't bring myself to run bristles through my hair just yet. My head felt like it was thrust into an angry beehive, and I didn't wanna stir 'em up.

After scavaging under the sink, I gulped down a couple of generic Tylenols with tepid tapwater straight from the sink. It was still faucet-dripping quiet in the house, so I snuck back to my room with the sleeping angel-like creature, finding it strange that I didn't find him sleeping in my bed the least bit strange.

Tip-toeing to my dresser to pull on some sweats, Pete's wallet nodded good morning to me from its post on top of the nightstand. *Hmmm.* I paused to finger it speculatively. Looked down guiltily at the innocently unaware owner of the wallet for even having the thought cross my mind. But now that it did, I couldn't quite get it out. Nor could I seem to talk myself out of doing it, despite the fact that I knew it was wrong. But it wasn't *that* invasive, right?

What's the harm in peeking?

While the angel and devil on my shoulders held a debate, I dared another peek at the sleeping cadet. I should back out now but knew I wouldn't. I was absolutely compelled to do it, almost as if it were calling my name. Diving in, I quickly rummaged past the slick plastic credit cards until I found what

I was looking for—his driver's license. My greedy fingers plucked it out for inspection even as I was being eaten alive by guilt.

Gah. Even his boring, old driver's license picture looked like a model's headshot. The only difference in his appearance was his hair was a bit shorter in the picture. I sighed. Wasn't fair, all his gifts. But I already knew that. Quickly scanning down, I found his birthdate: November 10. *Huh . . . a Scorpio.* Filed that snippet away, too. Then I fingered the date, noticing it was slightly raised. *Hmmm.* Sure enough, that would make him eighteen in about a month.

But as I studied the state-issued California driver's license, I knew it was a fake. Oh, not the driver's license itself—it came complete with the state seal and perforated outline of the California brown bear. I was sure it would pass any government inspection. No, the date of his birth year was wrong.

I just *knew* it.

I felt such a powerful surge of emotion holding the official document and knowing it was a fake that I didn't even notice that Prince Charming had awoken . . . and was staring at me staring at his driver's license. A deliberate throat clearing had me jumping out of my skin. The card dropped hot from my hand, landing on the floor between us. Like a bloody knife. After stabbing him in the back.

"Find anything interesting in there?"

His wallet, still in my hand, was now clutched to my chest. I stammered and blushed scarlet, my face heating so fast you could practically fry an egg on it. "P-Pete! You're awake!" I made it sound like an accusation.

"It would seem so." He sounded more amused than mad, but it was hard to tell because he was keeping a straight face. "You didn't answer my question."

"I, umm . . ." *What could I say?*

"If you needed some funds, all you had to do was ask."

I spluttered and gasped. *Stealing?* He thought I was *stealing* from him! I was so mortified I could've died on the spot. Hot tears sprang to my eyes right away. "I wasn't stealin' money from you!" Was desperate for him to know that. "I would *never* do that!"

"Then what *were* you doing?"

I thought I saw Pete's lips twitch. Did he think this was *funny*?

"I was . . . I was just . . ." I swallowed, deciding to just be truthful—it was less mortifying than being called a thief. "Your age. I was checkin' to see how old you really are."

"And?" he prompted, a distinct smile playing on his lips.

I looked away. *Harrumphed.* "It *saaaays* you're seventeen," I said in the same resigned voice a child uses to repeat back to a parent something they've been told over and over.

Laughter busted out of him.

"'snot funny!" I raged, hurling his wallet at him. "I would *never* steal money from you!" I repeated again for good measure, disgusted he would even think that.

"So, you're saying it's not okay to *steal* from me, but it's perfectly okay to *spy* on me?"

"I—" He got me. "That's exactly what I'm sayin'."

Pete leaned back on my headboard, stuffing my fuzzy, pink pillow behind him. "So . . . did you find anything interesting, Nancy Drew?"

I set a hand on my hip. "Yeah . . . I didn't take you for an organ donor."

He chuckled again, clearly more amused than angry. Almost as if he'd set a trap for me, and was delighted I'd fallen into it. *Surely not. Right?*

"Well, I'm glad you've enjoyed your mornin's entertainment." I huffed over to the dresser to yank out some sweats. I hadn't accounted on him spending the night, so was still standing around yapping in nothing but Mama's tree hugger T-shirt and cotton underwear. This seemed to only add to his amusement.

"Lucky trees," he smirked.

"Ha-ha. Very funny."

"I'm serious." His eyes twinkled. "I don't know why you can't take a compliment."

Not quite knowing how to respond to that, I said, "The boys will be up soon . . . so you'd better think about gettin' goin'." A sigh escaped at the end.

He rearranged the pillow. "Why?"

"So they don't wake up to find a boy sleepin' in my bed!"

Pete grinned at me. "Oh, so now that you've *confirmed* I'm seventeen, I'm suddenly relegated back to being a boy?"

"I didn't say I *believed* you were seventeen," I shot back before stepping into the bathroom to change. When I emerged, I found Pete clogging up the hall with his good mood and shave kit. I made to move past him when I bounced off a well-defined arm.

"Where do you think you're going?" he demanded.

"To the kitchen. I'm actually famished and need to get breakfast started."

The earlier amusement left his face. "Are you forgetting you're not supposed to do anything but bed rest for the next forty-eight hours?"

"I figured I'd already used up a good portion of my vacation time last night. And since my father is apparently indisposed . . ." I arched an eyebrow.

"You're going back to bed, young lady." I stood in protest, debating the merits of arguing. "Now!" he practically yelled in my face.

While I slunk off to my room, Pete stepped into the bathroom, emerging a few minutes later to poke his head into my room. Looked like he'd gotten *his* beauty sleep.

"I'm making breakfast this morning," he declared.

I crossed my arms. "This outta be interestin'."

His mouth quirked up before he left me to my foul mood. In my defense, my head *was* still hurting something fierce, and I was still smarting that he'd caught me at such an inopportune time. I just didn't want to admit to either one. The boys were up now; I could hear their bright voices wafting through the walls along with the smells that accompanied breakfast. My salivary glands began to produce water. Even a vegetarian could still appreciate the enticing smell of bacon and eggs.

Pete strolled in a few minutes later with a smorgasbord that included more yogurt, granola with stuff in it I couldn't identify, an assortment of fruit, and some very strong-smelling coffee. *Yum.* I muscled myself into upright position, wincing again as my sore neck battled it out with the back of my head for precedence in my mind. But they both lost out to the dapper cadet, spreading out the breakfast fare on a plastic serving dish with some smiley bananas painted on it by my eight-year-old self.

"The best I could do on short notice," he said.

"Impressive."

He shrug-smiled. "You're pretty easy to cook for."

"Still. Just knowing your way around the kitchen is a pretty spectacular feat for someone of the male persuasion in my household. And no burnt toast smell to go with the bacon and eggs. I gotta say, Cadet Davenport . . . you got mad skills, yo." I forked a piece of strawberry in my mouth.

"Kitchen detail," he explained with a good-natured grimace.

I laughed, wanting to know the back-story there, but not wanting to pry open that can of worms in case it spoiled breakfast. "This is great, Pete. Really. I'm so hungry I could eat a horse." I dug into the granola now using the big spoon.

"So that's why I didn't see any out there."

I choked on my bite, laughing. "That is so wrong. Actually . . . we used to have a little Paint horse named Pinto that I used to ride bareback all around the ranch."

"Bareback huh?"

Despite the wicked grin that put a gleam in his eye and hot spots on my cheeks, I managed to say, "Most of the time, I just jumped right on him in the pasture and galloped away."

"I would've loved to have seen that—I bet you looked like a wild little Indian."

My smile turned wistful. "That's what Mama used to say. She called us her wild little Indians." It took a while for me to swallow. "We're actually part Cherokee. Mama was half."

"It's an interesting and beautiful mix," Pete remarked, taking a thoughtful sip of his coffee.

"Yeah, she was really beautiful, but like mostly on the *inside,* if you can believe it. She was the best person I've ever known—so nice to everyone. She volunteered at the church when she could, which wasn't very often cause she was the one who ran the ranch and tended the vegetable garden. And everything seemed to thrive under her care. . . . I'm not doin' so hot at it," I confessed with a rueful headshake.

The sudden slant of Pete's eyebrow indicated a difference of opinion, but he remained quiet so I went on, my mouth seeming to want to gush out the stored words. "And she was super-smart, too. She did all the bankin' and tax stuff and she even home-schooled us kids for a good part of our education. She just seemed to know so much about everything—random stuff like what the Latin sayin's on the back of a dollar bill mean and how to tie, like, twenty different kinds of knots."

I stopped there, getting the feeling I was revealing too much. The awkward silence I filled with a sip of coffee. It was just the way I liked it—extra strong with cream and a pinch of sugar. I looked up at him.

Had I mentioned that?

Pete's body seemed to have tensed during my little spiel, but his face was impassive as always. "She sounds like an amazing woman," he finally said.

"She was." I took another contemplative sip of my coffee and watched him do the same.

"What happened to Pinto? Did you outgrow him?"

I shook my head. "Daddy sold him right after Mama died." I quoted my father: "'Horses eat money.'"

"I guess there goes my fantasy of riding off into the sunset with you."

I chortled at that one. "I can't picture you on a horse, city-slicker."

"Oh, really?" Pete challenged indignantly. "It just so happens I have a little horse experience . . . looks like you didn't read all the brochure."

"Stopped at the fine print."

He ignored that to finish: "The Academy keeps a well-stocked stable. And even has been known to throw polo matches on occasion for expedition games and fundraisers."

"You play polo?" I snorted a laugh. "Why am I *not* surprised? . . . You sure have crammed a whole lot of livin' into seventeen years, Cadet Davenport."

"What can I say?—it's the IEA way. And I didn't say I played *well*. I never made the team," he admitted.

I dropped my jaw. "I'm shocked. Could it be I've finally found the one thing you're *not* good at?"

"Looks who's talking."

"Hardly," I said, spooning in more yogurt.

Pete shook his head disapprovingly but remained silent, watching me chow down while sipping his coffee.

"I feel guilty eatin' in front of you. Why don't you go eat with the boys? I'll be fine." I was actually feeling self-conscious with him staring at me but didn't want to admit it.

"Already ate—toast and farm fresh eggs." He broke into another dazzler. "Maybe I'm missing my calling . . . farm life doesn't seem half bad."

"Easy for you to say when you get to escape tomorrow. For good," I said, not really thinking about my words until they popped out of my mouth. Then it hit me—this was probably true. I had trouble swallowing again.

"What makes you think I'm leaving tomorrow?"

Did his voice just go up an octave? I searched Pete's face for answers, saw the twinkle leave his eyes. "Dunno," I shrugged "just a feelin' I have, I guess. Anyhow, it's gonna be sooner rather than later, isn't it?" I tossed my spoon aside and looked up at him with sad-sack eyes.

Pete regarded me a long moment while I watched the dust motes swirl in the halo of light above his head. "Honestly," he said, "I don't know if there's much more I can do here with Andrew. We have all the information we need to make a decision. All that's left is the results of the physical coming up on Monday."

"Aren't you supposed to *not* be talkin' about it with me?"

He lifted a shoulder. "I'm not sure it makes much difference now—either he'll pass the physical or he won't. We'll see. If he does . . . then he'll most likely enter into the admissions process, which basically boils down to your father signing the paperwork."

"That ain't gonna happen," I stated flatly.

Pete looked aggravated, no longer lounging against the wall haphazardly. "It's the right place for him, Kate."

"Is not." I would keep saying it till the cows came home.

"It's a great campus—all the bells and whistles. You did hear about the stable, right?" He didn't give me a chance to respond. "Well, I better get off to chores now . . . hi-ho, hi-ho and all that." He shrugged off the wall with his half-full cup of coffee to come over and gather the dishes. It seemed like he was in a rush to leave all of a sudden.

Good mood gone.

"Okay," I said, smiling a little too brightly, afraid I'd spooked him off. "Have fun. And thanks—I haven't been treated to breakfast in bed in ages."

Pete smiled back with the real deal now, piercing my heart with sadness, which was just a pinprick compared to the devastating hole he would leave when he left. For good.

"Well you deserve it. Now get some rest." He turned to go.

"Why didn't you call the whole time you were gone?" I blurted out, feeling like a desperate girl with a crush (which was exactly what I was). He didn't immediately answer, and I couldn't bear the void where his reassuring words should've been, so I spluttered on: "I-we didn't know when or *if* you were comin' back."

His eyes shifted to the tray in his hands, where his fingers rearranged my spoon so that it nestled on top of the fork. Then he picked them both up and dumped them into his coffee cup with a sigh.

"I wanted to, but, well . . . we kind of left on a sour note. And technically, it's still a conflict of interest." Pete chin-nodded at me on the bed. "I've seen your powers-of-persuasion at work." His grin gained momentum according to my growing blush. "And *you* could've called *me*."

I huffed out a laugh. "I've never called a boy in my life! That's much too forward—you mighta got the wrong idear about me. Plus, I don't recall you leavin' me your number."

"What?" He mimed getting struck in the chest. "How can you say that? I gave it to you right before I left. It's not *my* fault you didn't write it down."

"Well, if someone wouldn't have swiped my favorite pen, I may have just done that," I joshed, overjoyed Pete seemed back to his old self.

He laughed unrepentantly.

"And besides," I went on, deciding to let him in on a little secret, "I didn't need to write it down." I tapped the side of my head. "It's all up here. I happen to have a Herculean memory—not even a Texas-sized bump on the head could knock it outta me!" Then I repeated, verbatim, the number he'd spouted off the other day.

I was laughing it up until I realized—I was the only one. *What did I say?* I thought back but couldn't think of anything inflammatory that would cause that look of alarm on his face. Unless . . . unless he was afraid I might *really* call him. *Duh. Of course, he has a girlfriend back home.* My light-hearted laugh petered out completely while I watched him put his face back together. And his posture wasn't right—no longer loose and easy, but all stiffened up like a police dog on alert.

My forehead crinkled. "Pete, did I—?"

"Okay. Enough kidding around for now. I'm heading out to wrangle some over-grown calves, feed some chickens, slop some pigs . . . or whatever it is you do with them," he drawled out, but I noticed the smile he put back on was forced.

"Well go on then . . . get your country on," I half-heartedly quipped.

He came over and buzzed the top of my head with his lips. "Get some rest, Katie-Kat," he urged before heading out my door, and then out the back door. With a bang.

What was all that about? I tried to recall what I'd said that upset him, ruminating on it as I brushed my teeth. I crawled back into bed still not knowing. I thought about how he left: with a peck on my head. *Maybe he thought of me as a kid sister?* But that was definitely not a chaste kiss last night. *Oh man!*—it was *me* trying to seduce *him*. Again.

Was I mistaking his niceness for something more? It felt like he really *did* care for me . . . just obviously not in the same way I cared for him. The squeezing pain in my heart far surpassed the one in my head.

What did I expect? Thoroughbreds don't really get together with Paint horses—they always breed them with other Thoroughbreds. I fell asleep wondering what kind of horse I really was.

35

BULLCRAP

Sometime later I awoke to the jarring sound of my father telling off poor Mikey, for some minor indiscretion, I'm sure. My chest felt heavy immediately. Back to reality. Why couldn't I have lived a little longer in the cocoon of smooth, good-feeling I had achieved with Pete last night? The pleasurable moments in life seemed to be fleeting as a butterfly fluttering nearby, and then flitting away before I could focus on its beautiful colors. Or even really be sure of what I'd seen.

I pushed out of bed and made my way over to the window to let in some fresh air. There was some Tylenol left for me on my nightstand, along with a note: *Be back tonight*.

Not very loquacious. Hungry for more, I flipped it over, but it was blank. Nevertheless, I knew I'd keep that note forever.

It was all coming to an end that was for sure. I felt sick to my stomach that Daddy might really sign Andrew up on Monday, and heart sick that Pete Davenport would disappear from my life on the same day.

How could I go on either way?

Despondently, I dragged out to greet the boys. Even though Andrew was his favorite person in the whole world, Mikey would be needing me by now. I was the only mother he could remember. And now his brother might be leaving soon. For good. It seemed like a sin to bust up that kind of love.

Another dose of anger at Daddy, and hatred for that school, coursed through me. It momentarily brushed my consciousness how easily I disassociated Pete with his academy now, compartmentalizing my personal time with him as having nothing to do with his mission to sign Andrew.

Like they were entirely mutually exclusive—wishful (and foolish) thinking on my part.

"Kadee!" Mikey forgot himself and came barreling into to me.

"Hey, buddy—careful. Porcelain doll, remember?" I smacked the top of his head with my lips.

"Hey, Katie-Kat." Andrew went in for a quick hug and a faster release. "Didja know that Pete's comin' back this afternoon to help with chores again? And he's bringin' dinner. And he's stayin' with us—even though *I* don't need a babysitter." Andrew paused to scoff before continuing on with an increasing upwards lilt to his voice. "He's gonna hang out with us tonight, so Daddy can get some business taken care of before—" He stopped short, cutting his eyes to his brother, who was looking sideways at him.

"*Really?*" I said unable to keep my voice neutral. I looked to my father for confirmation. I wondered what kind of business had to be taken care of that couldn't wait till tomorrow.

"Yep," Daddy confirmed, wobbling the toothpick between his lips. "Cadet Davenport agreed to watch the boys while I get ever'thing all squared away . . . for that thing I gotta do." He removed the half-shredded stick from his mouth and shot a hard point at me. "Now I wantja in yer bed at eight sharp. Door closed. Lights out. Do you understand me, young lady?"

"Yes, sir."

"If yer so bad off to warrant gettin' out of chores and church then you need to be in yer sick bed." This for the transgression of being unable to fulfill my quota of responsibilities.

Unable to speak, I bobbed my head.

"If you woulda used that noggin' for somethin' other than knockin' a hole in my water tank, you woulda realized that water woulda come blowin' outta there fasterna freight train. And you will always lose in a battle with water. It's a force that can't be fought with. Trust me . . . I've seen some things in my time!"

I was in too weak a state to argue my case, even though it was a strong one. To tell the truth, I just wanted him gone—when you're already feeling low, you don't want someone handing you stones.

"Yer a smart girl like yer mama," Daddy bulldozed on, "but you lack her good old-fashioned common sense. Maybe the back of that tank knocked some sense back into yer head."

I considered that to be salt in the wound. Tears pricked my eyes. Daddy was generally authoritarian to the extreme, but he was hardly ever downright mean. To me. I could tell he was stressed out about his upcoming IEA meeting on Monday, and the idea of signing Andrew and his parental rights away. It must be weighing pretty heavily on him. Guess he was shifting some of that weight onto me. I also suspected he knew he'd made himself look bad in front of Pete, so was punishing me for being the catalyst to revealing his true self in front of someone he held in high esteem.

Mikey openly glowered up at Daddy, and even Andrew stepped back into me as though offering his support with his nearness. One or both of them was about to say something. I didn't want anything to upset the balance of Daddy skedaddling out of here, so I placed a hand on each of their shoulders, shaking my head in wordless communication.

Daddy's fleshy lips drew together at the sight of us walling up on him. He yanked me out of my position and marched me into my room, where he instructed me to pack a suitcase for Andrew. I was to pack his nicest church clothes, and under no circumstances tell Mikey that he and Andrew were leaving for San Francisco.

Something fishy was going on, but I had too much of a headache to concentrate on it at the moment. I also wondered how stupid he thought Mikey was while he continued doling out stuff for me to do when I was supposed to be taking it easy. Daddy informed me he was taking Andrew into town to get a fresh haircut and a new suit for their all-important visit to "The Academy." Then, without so much as a backward glance, he slammed out the door with an eager Andrew in tow. I pondered, again, what the heck kind of physical was so important that Andrew had to go all the way to California for it and decided to brave asking Pete about it tonight.

After a late lunch of nuked frozen burritos, Mikey and I leisured away the afternoon playing *Chutes and Latters*, the only game not likely to boggle my brain at the moment. Afterwards, I sent him in to watch TV while I showered and packed a suitcase for Andrew. I popped two more real Tylenol that Pete had kindly left for me, keeping my headaches at bay with clocklike precision of pill taking. I didn't want to chance the severe headache coming back tonight with Pete here, determined to enjoy every moment, knowing it could be our last. I sighed, leaning over to stare at my reflection in the mirror, noticing I still had faint circles under my eyes, despite the good amount of sleeping I'd been doing. There was also a large purple bruise over my right shoulder, and my neck was still sore.

Aggravated by my unkempt looks, I blamed it all on the strain of worry and sleeplessness catching up with me. I wondered if a little mascara would help improve my appearance (and if it would be noticed by either Daddy or Pete). In the end, I compromised with one sooty layer that had the instant result of making my lashes feel decadent. After blowing out my hair, I brushed it where it didn't hurt until it shone. Then, slipping out of my baggy sweats and into a pair of snuggly gray leggings, I topped it off with one of my handy-dandy five-dollar tees, this one in pink.

What could I do? Dress up for my date with my bed? Daddy would be suspicious if I was wearing anything that looked too good, and I desperately wanted him to leave. To keep my eyes off the clock, I couldn't help straightening the bit of clutter that had accumulated over my sick leave. I was busy swiping some creamy vanilla onto my lips when Mikey wandered into my room, looking glum as only a kid can.

"Kadee, is Drewy comin' back from his trip with Daddy to Pete's school?"

"How'd you know about that?"

"I heard them talkin' 'bout it when they didn't know I was listenin'."

Apparently, I had a never-ending supply of sighs because another one leaked out of me, long and weary. I took his hand and sat on the bed. "I'm sorry you had to hear about it that way. Daddy wanted to keep it a secret . . . you know how he is. I was gonna tell you about it but didn't wanna worry you unnecessarily."

"Is he comin' back?" Mikey pleaded.

I nodded my head, feeling confident in my answer. "Yeah, honey. He's comin' back soon. They're just lookin' around at Pete's school, and he's gonna see a doctor for some tests, and then they're turnin' right around and comin' back home."

Mikey plucked at my clean shirt with grubby hands. "Is he sick like our mama was?"

"No, of course not! It's only a well-check, I promise." I collected Mikey's doubtful face between my palms, stared into his muddy-green eyes. "I want you to know, I'm not worried anymore. I have one of those strong feelin's I sometimes get that Andrew's not goin' anywhere any time soon," I said, trying to reassure us both.

Mikey nodded up at me. "I know. It's cause I've been tellin' Daddy ever chance I get not to sign him up for that bored school. . . . But I can't stop him if I'm not there!"

"Nobody expects you to, honey. I don't want you to worry—everything's gonna be alright." I bolstered this flimsy declaration with a tight hug.

"I don't want Drewy to go away!" Mikey wailed, the gathering tears beginning to disperse into the thin fabric of my shirt.

"Shhh." I rocked him back and forth. "Hey, remember? . . . The good guys always win—just like in Batman and Spider-Man."

"Is Daddy a good guy?"

"Drewy's a good guy," I evaded. "One of the best. So everything's gonna work out okay for him. Don't you worry," I soothed, thumbing away the salty streams rolling over cheek-hills.

"How do you know that?"

"I just do."

Unable to deal another second, I snapped off the light and crawled into bed, dragging Mikey with me. Curling around him like a question mark, I whispered in his ear "Everything's gonna be okay" over and over until we both fell asleep.

I awoke by an irritating light reflecting the back of my eyelids at me. This was followed by equally irritating laughter. Recognizing the low rumble right away, my eyes popped open.

"Looks like you have no shortage of dashing young men to share your bed." Pete stood there with his casual hotness, prettying up the room.

"You're back!" An insta-smile sprang to my mouth. "Mikey, Pete's here," I announced, shaking him out of his sleep.

"I hate to break it up, but if I let you two sleep any later, you'll be up all night."

Mikey pried his eyes open. "Hi, Pete." He yawned hugely. "Is Drewy back yet?"

"As a matter of fact, he's crashed on the couch, watching Youtube on my phone. We just got finished feeding the animals—Buttercup says to say hello," he said, just when I didn't think my smile could grow any bigger. He smiled back, and my heart did its backflip thing. "I'm fixin' to rustle up some vittles right now."

"I know what vittles is," Mikey informed Pete before cannonballing off the bed into his arms. "It's weally just a fancy word for food."

"That's right—you sure are a smart little guy, just like big brother." Pete tossed him up and almost knocked my dang ceiling fan down (which would've been an improvement seeing as how it was both oversized and outdated).

Mikey grinned ear-to-ear, planting his hands on either side of Pete's face. "How come you didn't wait for me to do chores with you and Drewy?"

"You guys looked like two comfy peas-in-a-pod, so I didn't have the heart to wake you," Pete answered, poking Mikey in the stomach before flipping him upside down so that he landed on his feet.

"Whoa!" Mikey giggled, staggering sideways before running to catch up with his brother. The sound of his squeal interrupted Pete and I's stare fest. "Whoa!—you gotta short cut, almost wike mine!"

My starter-smile morphed into a yawn. I really felt like I should be better rested. "Thanks again for helpin' out," I said, hoisting myself up. "That's awfully nice of you."

Pete nodded thoughtfully, staring at me until my face warmed. "You look pretty warn out."

"Words every girl dreams of hearin'." I resisted the urge to smooth down my hair.

His lips didn't even twitch. "You have to take better care of yourself, Kate. Slow down a bit. Don't work all the time—try to enjoy yourself every once-in-a-while." He recommended this as if the ideas had never crossed my mind.

"I'll get right on bookin' a spa retreat to Cabo right after my mani-pedi on Monday," I said, pushing the covers off a little too airily.

I was trying not to be combative but felt piqued. *Does he think I enjoy living like this? Like it's a lifestyle choice?* I tried not to be mad. He probably couldn't fathom how hard things were in my world, having had the good fortune of being born with a silver spoon in his mouth. I looked over at his polished perfection—make that *golden* spoon. I yanked the covers back up, hastily making my bed.

"You see what I mean?" He held out his palm. "Just leave it for goodness sake."

I wheeled around. "Some of us don't happen to have a merry maid to magically come along and pick up after us when we leave!"

Pete sighed, running a hand through his hair. "I'm not trying to criticize. All I'm saying is—try to cut corners a little. Take some time out to have fun. You have too much responsibility on your young shoulders."

"Says the seventeen-year-old boy," I shot back, then punched my pink, fuzzy pillow and tossed it on top of my bed.

He ignored the hit. "Why didn't you go to homecoming?"

"Because the guy I wanted to ask me happened to be out of town," I mumbled, finding the need to straighten the picture frames on my nightstand.

Pete came up behind me and pulled my hair to one side. He kissed my shoulder, grazing the tender bruise with his lips. "I would've loved to have taken you to homecoming," he breathed down my neck.

I shivered, in an entirely pleasant way, then huffed out a chuckle. I had a hard time picturing him at our cheesy homecoming dance. It seemed so juvenile and . . . lowbrow for him, and I told him so.

"I can picture it," he disagreed. "And your spectacular body in a little black dress. Would've been a kick—I've never been to a homecoming. It's actually been a little fun for me taking a hiatus from The Academy to experience regular high school. Feels . . . normal."

Ah. My word.

"Well, I hate to break it to you, but there's nothing *normal* about you." My eyebrows remained suspended at this revelation. I'm not sure why because it really did seem like he was enjoying himself, almost like he was on a vacation. I recalled us kicking back that afternoon, trading licks on an ice cream cone. How happy and content I felt him to be. But I still wondered: How much of it was real, and how much was part of the mission to win me over? I really hoped he wasn't faking—that would kill me; it really would.

I forced an upbeat tone. "And I think that ship has already sailed."

"There's always prom," he said.

Spinning around in his arms, I tilted my face up. "Yeah right—prom. I won't hold my breath for that." I tried for jovial but ended up with wistful.

He wrapped his arms around my waist. I wound my arms around his neck, and we kind of just swayed together until he stopped to grimace. "Just promise me you won't go with Ron Tillman."

I forced a laugh. "I can virtually guarantee that."

It seemed like we were starting to say our goodbyes already, and I wasn't ready for that, so I led him by hand into the dining room, where the smell of

French fries was calling my name. After a thoughtful dinner of veggie burger for me, and regular burgers for them, we played a few hilarious rounds of *Bullshit,* or "*I Doubt It*", as it was called in my house. Pete had to intervene on that one, so we settled for "*Bullcrap*" to the delight of the boys, who thought they were getting away with something.

Mikey and I won of course, because I *always* knew when Pete was lying. And called him out on it *every* time. He seemed to grow exponentially quieter the more rounds he lost, until every spec of good humor was gone from his face. Finally, he threw down his thick stack of cards and groaned that it would take till midnight to get rid of them all. But his humorous tone seemed forced.

Could it be he was a sore loser? Life's winners were often the worst losers. Maybe I should've cut him a break, like I did everyone else? But I was really enjoying sticking it to him for playing for the wrong team.

We sent the boys off to get ready for bed and began clearing the dining room table. As he slid past me with a plate of stumpy fries bloodied from their ketchup-drowning, I poked him in the ribs. "Don't tell me you're feelin' sore cause I finally found somethin' I can beat you at?" I teased.

Pete looked directly at me for the first time since I last blasted him with *Bullcrap!* Half a lip lifted. "You should quit waitressing to become a card shark."

I laughed a little too heartily. "Don't think I haven't thought of that. But alas, gamblin's a sin, so Daddy'd never go for it."

He laughed, a little less heartily. "Probably for the best. Why don't you go ahead and get ready for bed while I finish cleaning up?"

I dropped my dishrag into his palm. "Don't have to ask me twice."

A quick goodnight to the boys, and I was in the bathroom brushing my teeth. It was about at the end of this endeavor when my brain started to feel two sizes too big for my skull, so I decided to pop a couple of more Tylenols. But before I could get 'em down the hatch, Pete came up behind me and replaced them with two Vicodin. I looked askance at the intervention.

"Acetaminophen's workin' just fine. Plus, those happy pills tend to really knock me out." I politely declined the offer—*so* wanted to stay awake right now. Gulping down my pain reliever with some coffee had even crossed my mind.

"You could use the extra sleep," he said gently. "And I kind of like seeing you when you're a little . . . *less* inhibited." This little revelation preceded those lips, I'd been admiring all night, nuzzling my neck; I practically swooned right there on the bathroom floor. But before I could melt into a puddle of pink ooze, he popped a pill between my lips. "Bottoms up," he commanded with the kind of smile that dropped panties.

I wasn't sure, so Pete gave me a reassuring squeeze, running his hands over my shoulders and down my arms. Then, biting his lips, he gave me the eyes and an accompanying head toss. *Gah!—so sexy.* I was able to witness this contrived move, and the corresponding bloom manifesting upon my cheeks, from our reflection. But before I could reflect further, he pushed the pill into my mouth. I automatically swallowed it down with the water he tipped to my lips, and a sweet kiss was swiftly bestowed upon my cheek.

Pete reversed his fingertips to trail up the insides of my arms, dredging the pleasure bumps back up. Then a second pill pressed against my lips. I hesitated, feeling funny—I didn't take him for a pill-pusher. He countered with another panty-dropper and got back to work on my neck. I c ould barely breathe, much less think straight. My eyes found his in the mirror. Something flashed there . . . until a small shape coming up behind us moved our eyes to a wide-eyed four-year-old.

"Pete, will you—hey! Are you a vampire?"

Pete threw back his head and howled at that one. After which, Mikey immediately persuaded him into leaving, but not before he did the sexy-lip-biting-head-toss thing again. I gave him my Mona Lisa and popped the pill into my mouth. A dazzling smile was my instant reward for good behavior, but the second he walked out the door I poofed it out into my palm. I'd save part deux for later—I could handle a little headache as long as it came with a side of Pete.

Being stuck in the confines of a matchbox all day had me feeling way too stir-crazy to go straight to bed, so I went out on the front steps to get some air. It was a beautiful night for stargazing; the air was crisp, the sky a black velvet. I sat there, absentmindedly petting Blue and reflecting on everything. The creaking of loose floorboards—and the thrilling chill along my spine— alerted me to Pete's presence.

"Whew! I don't know how you do that every day," he said. "I'm bushed!"

"It's definitely a labor of love." I smiled and leaned against the splintered wood column holding up our porch while he stared up at my part of the sky.

"Have you ever played poker?" he asked apropos of nothing.

I laughed. "Why? Are you challengin' me to a game of strip poker?"

He waggled his eyebrows at me. "Maybe."

My smile faded. "Actually, yeah. My mother taught me when I had the flu. Turns out—I really have a knack for cards. She made me solemnly vow to never play anyone for money, sayin' I was too good at it for my own good."

"I bet she said that a lot."

I shrugged. "What can I say?—a mama's love."

Pete worked his mouth around before coming up with another one of his smiles. I could read him like the cards now—this one was fake. "Remind me to never play strip poker with you then—I'm afraid I'd come out on the losing end of that gig. Defeat the whole purpose!" he said, ending with the real deal.

"Yeah, you would." I laughed along, my eyes sparking with a flash of suppressed anger. "It'd be as easy as takin' candy from a baby."

Pete started laughing at the same time I quit—to stare meaningfully at him, for as long as it took. Not long. The boy was a gosh dang *elite* cadet after all.

I saw it happen—that thing that passed between us—the tacit understanding, a realigning of all that we thought we knew, with what we now knew. Waves of different emotions came rolling across his face with neuron-rapid speed: surprise, denial, anger . . . humor. He threw his head back and barked out a harsh laugh, then walked forward and planted his hands across the twin beams of rotting wood straining beneath their weight. After taking a long moment to stare up at the heavens, intermittently chuckling and acting thunder struck, he finally spoke. "Of course . . . I should've known."

Arms wrapped around my knees, I rocked back and forth, smirking up at him. Pete was still processing, so I decided to fill the silence: "Of course, you know . . . the only problem with takin' candy away from a baby is they howl and cry and point fingers, makin' a big ole ruckus," I warned. He looked down at me sharply. "And then they never, *ever* fully trust the one who took it from them. No matter how much they might want to, or how nice the person is—they *never* forget who stole their precious candy . . . and will *never* forgive them."

Pete took in my face and the kind of deep breath that only yogis do. After expelling it out in a long stream, he looked down on me with a tender cross between respect and aggravation. He held out his palm. *Peace offering?* I accepted it, and he hauled me to my feet. We padded a few yards from the house, gazing up at the same night sky that suddenly looked a whole lot different. A full moon, like a Chinese lantern, shone out from a blanket of shimmering stars. It seemed to be a portent of some kind — a reckoning was coming — a change, and not just of the seasons, was in the air. I shivered.

We obviously couldn't go on like this—feigning ignorance on both ends. Not now. Not after the cat just got dumped out of the bag by my happy pill. Pete was struggling, his thoughts running unchecked as first graders at recess across his face. He let out another gusty sigh, raked both hands through his hair. Twice. I just indulged in my favorite pastime—staring at his face. A few moments of windy silence, and Blue whined. I shivered patiently in my T-shirt. The evenings were cold now that we were digging out the last dregs of September.

He barked out a couple of laughs that sounded arrogant when the notes weren't warmed with humor. I recalled how I saw him that first time in the restaurant—rude, arrogant, privileged—and tried to reconcile the Pete from the past with the one I now knew. I'd have to take well-spoken off the list because the ambassador was rendered speechless.

A wind blew, seeking something in this forlorn land to push up against. It chose me, making me sway like a corn sapling. "Whatever you gotta say, Cadet Davenport, you better spit it out, because the sergeant will be makin' his way home soon."

Pete guttered a laugh, one I was glad I wasn't on the receiving end of. "I doubt it. Daddy Dearest is down at the local watering hole, imposing penance upon himself by drinking himself into oblivion . . . for selling out." He finally spoke, and it was a doozy.

Now I was speechless. "Ahhh," I finally said. "That explains a lot."

A glimmer of a smile when he looked at me. "I could say the same." He scrubbed a hand up the back of his neck, stalked away from me, swung back around. "I guess I should apologize for being an asshole," he said. "My only excuse is it comes with the territory."

"That's real comfortin' seein' as how my precious brother is on his way to the territory Monday mornin' bright and early."

Pete growled out some aggravation. Looked on the verge of saying something. Instead, he bent over to rub at his face again and again while I dispassionately watched him. When he righted himself, he came up with a face deeper in color—a shade I'd call shame.

"I'm sorry, Kate. I really am. I don't know what to tell you. I *can't* tell you anything *but* that, okay?"

"No," I said, my throat aching. "It's *not* okay! I deserve better than that. My *brother* deserves better than that—he looks up to you with god-like devotion. You should feel ashamed of yourself!"

Pete fast-paced forward, throwing his arms out, like for mercy, as if there were a jury out there in the pasture. "I do! Alright?" he yelled, losing his voice to a break. He dropped a sigh, his arms. His voice came next. "Look, I'll recommend Andrew *not* be admitted to the program. . . . Honestly, I don't even think that's in everyone's best interest, nor do I believe it will do much good, but there it is—the best I can do for now."

I stared into his eyes; he was telling the truth. That was something at least. "How bad is it, Pete? Are y'all like devil worshippers or somethin'? Why don't you just quit?"

He laughed mirthlessly. "Religion—in any form—isn't exactly a factor at The Academy, so I wouldn't worry about that," he said, answering only one of my pointed questions.

I shiver-swayed with the wind again. "Pete, can we go back in? I'm freezin' and startin' to get a little woozy."

He pursed his lips at me. "Hold on a second. It's a beautiful night. I'm going to miss all these stars. One good thing about living out on the flat plains of nowhere is I've never seen such beautiful skies . . . or girls," he added, with a brief, bruising kiss before sprinting to the Hummer. He grabbed something out of his console and tucked it into his back pocket. Then walked around to the back to grab the infamous blue jacket. I was beginning to feel like it was *my* jacket now, and shuddered from the thought (or from the cold I wasn't sure which).

"You know," I began when he jogged back to grab me, "I can think of a great deal many things I'd rather wear than this thing . . . and that includes one of Tillman Mill's feed sacks."

He chuckled and held out the jacket for me to slip my arms into. "Humor me, one more time," he said, zipping me up. This made me feel a little like a child being attended to, and I frowned at the thought that he saw me that way.

By this point I could hardly stand up. Unfortunately, there was nothing for us to sit down on because we were standing on what would normally be considered a front yard, but in our case consisted of dried brush with the odd cactus thrown in for unpleasant surprises. Pete held me steady in his arms while I snuggled up, deep breathing him in.

"Kate . . ." It sounded like the beginning of a goodbye.

My spine stiffened immediately. "Don't say it yet," I pleaded, feeling heartsick even as my stomach dropped. I clutched his arms as if I could hold him hostage here—to this spot a long ways away from his world—just a little longer.

A few more moments of me trying real hard not to cry later, and he tried again. "Kate . . ." I looked up to face my bleak future. "I only came back to pack and escort your father and brother back to San Francisco. I have to go back, be the ambassador, show them around campus, facilitate the paperwork. The mission is essentially over, honey."

I didn't think my heart could sink any further in my chest.

". . . At least if all goes as expected. They're planning on having attorneys present Monday to sign the official documents."

"But-but we don't even have an attorney!"

"The Academy has provided one for your father."

"Right," I snorted. "Very helpful that."

"Kate, I-I just want you to be prepared . . . this could be the end. I don't want you to do anything rash that could get you into trouble. I'm doing the best I can to help you, but you're not making it very easy for me."

So little time, so many questions. "Pete!" It just dawned on me he was leaving. Forever. "But there's just one more day! What is that physical even about? Should I be worried? Is it even safe?" I gushed out questions. "I have to find out everything I can to help my brother! Pete!" My face crumpled. "*Please!* I love him so much! I don't wanna lose him, too. I'm so scared!"

Pete looked down on me with pity but firm resolve. "I've told you everything I can."

"Which is exactly nothin' that's not in the brochure. Or why you lied to me! Or why y'all feel the need for parents to *give up their rights* in order for their kids to attend!"

He sighed. "You didn't take that second Vicodin, did you?"

"Why? Are you waitin' for me to pass out, so you can run off with my brother?" I realized his bag was already packed. By me.

Pete looked pained while my ears strained for a denial. "I didn't want to end this way with you—again. It seems like we can never have a good ending. Maybe . . . there isn't one for us." His voice sounded raw.

"Because you're still masqueradin' as a cadet. Still not bein' forthright with me." I pounded on his shoulders, hating his dispassionate face. "What *am* I even to you?" My disjointed thoughts actually came out sounding exactly right.

His eyes shifted in the moonlight. "I don't know exactly." I waited him out for a better answer. He shook his head, looking up, searching. "Something . . . *real* I need to protect for one."

"That's real poetic comin' from the guy who set out to win me over with lies and deceit."

Pete's face fell, and when he spoke next, his voice sounded thick. "I can understand how you could feel that way, knowing what you know now. But I've always had your best interests at heart, Kate . . . you have to trust me."

"I wish I could—there's just too many unanswered questions. And until you answer them . . . I can't."

"And I can't really say anything more," he said, wrapping up.

"So this is it? We exchange email addresses and follow each other on *Instagram?*"

He let out a hollow laugh. "I guess so," he said, but we both knew it was a lie.

I felt like crying. It was going so fast. Time: it was the force that couldn't be stopped. Not water. Water could be quelled, dammed, bottled up. Not time. It couldn't be manipulated. It was a constant, propelling us forward into the black void of our futures . . . whether we were ready or not.

"Aren't you comin' back tomorrow?" Desperate, even to my own ears.

Now Pete's face crumpled a little. "Only to pick up your father and Andrew at the crack of dawn."

"*What?*" I distinctly felt like I'd got my wires crossed. My concussion, sleep-starved body, and pill weren't helping matters. "I thought they weren't leavin' till Monday mornin'!"

"That's what your father wanted to let you and Mikey think."

"So y'all *tricked* us!" I tried to break free, but he wouldn't allow it.

"I'm sorry, Kate." Pete sighed again, shaking his head. "He thought you might . . . or Mikey might . . . I don't know exactly—sabotage the trip or something. I have to tell you the truth: I went along with it because it sounded like something you *would* do." Betrayal snapped from my eyes, so he said, "I'm just trying to keep you out of trouble."

"So you keep sayin'." At least he told me now I consoled myself. Maybe I could still think of something to do. I was still lost in my thoughts when Pete glanced at his watch.

"It's getting late," he said. "I better get you in the house."

"So this is really goodbye?" My heart felt like it was a victim of our lemon squeezer.

"I'm afraid so. I'll maybe see you very briefly in the morning when I come for your father and Andrew. But we'll be in a hurry. I've got to turn in the Humvee before heading to the Lubbock airport. Everything else is being shipped out."

My mind was reeling. It was hard to process everything; it felt like my in-box was jammed. And the happy pill I'd taken wasn't really living up to its name. It had only succeeded in dulling my senses some, which I supposed was a good thing on one hand, but my brain was functioning in slow gear.

I looked up at his face, horrified to think it would be for the last time. It just didn't seem real. He'd become the center of our universe. Now he was going to leave a black hole right in the middle of our lives . . . and right in the middle of my chest. I stared at him, uncomprehending that this was the end of the road for us.

"Pete!" I cried, begging for a different scenario.

"I know, Kate—I'm sick about it! That's the way these missions are. They never last more than a couple of months."

"Why didn't you tell me?"

"I didn't want to mention it before because you got hurt. And then I just didn't want it hanging over us like a dark cloud, ruining our time together."

Time . . . the last sands were slipping through the hourglass. My mind scrambled for ways to plug it.

"Will you stay with me till I fall asleep?" I asked in a small voice, hatching a plan to stay awake all night.

"Of course I will . . . until your father comes home." My face fell. "He won't be passed out tonight since he knows he has to get up early tomorrow for our trip," Pete explained.

"But I have a lotta questions for you . . . "

Before I could start on them, he seized my shoulders, staring intently at me. "Kate, listen . . . I want you to follow your mother's rules for a while."

"Huh? What do you mean?" I was confused and tired and apparently crying now.

"Look at me!" His hands gripped my face into obedience. "This is important!" I must've looked blank, because he explained, "I mean no more Alex Morgan on the soccer field, no more bragging about your photographic memory, or talking about your strong feelings about things."

"Who? What?" *When did I do that?*

"And promise me you'll take care of yourself—no more sacrificing your safety for some cows! Leave that to your father."

"I didn't—" I started to argue, but he shook me a little.

"I don't want to have to see another hospital bill because you're out trying to do a man's job!"

"I'll pay you back the money . . . just tell me where to send it."

Pete's hands bit into my shoulders, so that I felt it this time. "Don't mention that damned bill to me one more time!" he blasted at my face. "You're concentrating on the wrong things!"

I started bawling in earnest now. He was scaring me with his sudden intensity, the shifting into high-gear, last bits of advice. So final. I thought we had the morning, but it felt like this was it. I suddenly couldn't take another word or thought about it—the departure of my brother in the morning with the one I was falling in love with faster than a cow can say moo. I couldn't focus on anything but the overwhelming feelings of loss cutting me to the bone. I hadn't felt this much pain since Mama died.

"Y-you're really l-l-leavin' and t-t-takin' Drewy with you, and I'm n-n-never g-gonna see you again!" The words hiccupped out of me. "And I m-might n-not even get m-my b-b-brother back?" It was too much to bear. I started sobbing.

Pete looked alarmed. I was always putting on a big brave face, but clearly I was just a scared little girl.

"He's coming back! He signs up for next semester by October first, but he won't leave until January second . . . if he goes at all," he threw in at the end to appease me, I'm sure. He was hugging me to him now, holding me together really.

"P-Pete!" I sobbed. "I-I'm g-gonna m-miss you so m-much!" I was shaking, blubbering like a baby. It was like snatching the sun away—I instantly felt cold.

He kissed my temple, wiped some tears away. "You're strong, Kate. You'll get over this. This . . . this is just your first crush."

I started wailing at that one. *Did he not understand the way I felt about him at all?* I always knew he wasn't from my world. That he was going to leave and go back to his privileged one. I was crying not only for the loss of him, but for all that he'd brought back to my life: hope, laughter . . . love. He'd brought me back to life only to wish I were still half dead. Now it would be so much worse for me—the knowing what I was missing.

I already knew Pete didn't feel the same way about me, but calling me out for having a crush on him was just brutal. *How many ways could I be hurt?* I felt stupid and minimized. And inconsolable. He tried shushing me, rocking me, murmuring in my ear, but I couldn't stop weeping. I could barely breathe. Somewhere in the recesses of my mind, I processed the fact that the mascara I had carefully applied tonight (for his benefit) was most likely smeared across my face.

"Kate, get a hold of yourself!" he ordered, a bit too sternly I thought under the circumstances. "Your father will be back any time now. I can't take you into the house like this—you'll frighten your brothers to death. You have to pull yourself together . . . if not for yourself, then for Mikey."

I couldn't catch a breath to answer him. I was heaving and sobbing, blubbering and soaking the front of his jacket, ruining the glossy sheen, I'm sure. I couldn't trust him, but there was no one I wanted to trust more. Nothing made sense. My world was turned upside down.

Pete cursed under his breath, then pulled out the thing he had squirreled away in the back pocket of his jeans. My jacket was lifted up, the fabric clinging to my backside pulled down. I felt a shaft of cold air hit me a split second before he plunged something into my upper right hip. I gasped at the unexpected pain. My head fell back. I stared up at him in shocked surprise.

"I'm sorry, Kate."

Pete's determined face was the last thing I saw before my eyes rolled back into my head.

36

~

INTERIM

I awoke to more crying. But it wasn't coming from me this time. Mikey. Was crying like . . . well, like his big brother and best friend in the world was instantly gone from his life and unlikely to return for the duration of his childhood. My head still ached a little, but I realized my body felt better—as though it'd been hooked up to an electrical charge all night, zapping back all my energy. My body felt renewed, but my heart felt tired as Grandma Moses.

Last night was hazy. I struggled to recollect the wisps of real memories that got tangled up with my dreams. I knew Pete had left. *For good.* A wave of despair knocked me over. Literally. I could not get back up even to comfort my little brother in his time of need, my own need being greater than the power of my will to get up.

What I almost hated more than not seeing his eyes spark up with humor, or his mouth turn down in a lop-sided smile, was the fact that absolutely *nothing* had been resolved. I still didn't know why I had such a terrible, visceral feeling about them. I still didn't know anything about Pete Davenport, other than the fact he was a Scorpio and had mad life skills. Not even if he was one of the good guys or not. And my little brother was *still* going through the admissions process, even as I was sitting here crying for the one that put him there.

What had I really accomplished these past couple of months besides getting my heart broken?

I finally roused myself enough to trudge into the boys' room to check on Mikey. Pete was right—I had to stay strong for my brother. From what I could gather from the words slipping through the hiccupping sobs (I cringed, remembering that's exactly how I sounded last night), Mikey was so upset because nobody had bothered to wake him up to say goodbye.

I knew just how he felt. Nobody had bothered to wake me up either, and I'm guessing that was no accident. I glanced at the nightstand shoved between their twin beds; Spiderman's eyes glowed 10:02. I calculated they were mid-air, in route somewhere between Arizona and California. I pictured them, kicked back in first class, drinking celebratory mimosas. Pete, I was sure, was very relieved to finally be leaving the Ponderosa for good.

Holy cow!—the calves needed their breakfast . . . and so did we for that matter. I hug-walked Mikey to the living room and plopped him down in front of the TV, then went to the kitchen to get breakfast going. Life's needs must be met even in the direst of circumstances. Mama's death taught me that grumbling hunger could worm its way into a young boy's stomach, even during the darkest hour of mourning.

While I was getting some fortification for our systems, the blinking light of the answering machine caught my eye. Despite the fact it was probably just Mrs. Hildebrand wondering why we hadn't come by for fresh milk the last couple of days, I felt compelled to listen to it—right away. I pushed play, slipped some bread into the toaster, then froze when the message came on. It was Pete's voice, crystal clear even through the scratchy recording and staticky background of what I surmised to be the Lubbock airport.

Kate . . . I asked your father to leave a note for you but wanted to follow up, just in case. The animals are already taken care of and will be until Friday, with the exception of Blue. A hired-hand of the Hildebrand's is coming, so do not do any outside chores or heavy lifting—not even a laundry basket for the duration of the week.

If you don't have any further complications like blackouts or severe headaches, then you can gradually resume physical activities next Monday. Make sure you read the information pamphlet Dr. Shaw sent home regarding concussions. Follow the instructions and guidelines exactly. Do not blow it off! Returning to your normal physical activities too soon could result in permanent damage. So don't do it!

Hopefully, you're feeling better this morning. I gave you a Vitamin B cocktail last night to help jumpstart your system. I . . . A few seconds of static ensued where I could hear a boarding call in the background. *I'm sorry I didn't get a chance to say goodbye to you this morning. We left while it was still dark outside so decided not to wake you. Please tell Mikey I said goodbye and give him a high-five from me. Kate* . . . Another long pause. *Take care of yourself.*

Tears sprouted from my eyes like a faucet turning on. I instantly replayed the message just to hear his crisp, commanding voice again. *Why did I have to feel this way?* A burning desire for someone I couldn't have was torturous, not to mention impractical . . . and I was nothing if not pragmatic.

Wasn't fair. He'd come and stirred up all these dormant feelings I had, like desire and the possibility for something more than my own life had to offer. Then disappeared, leaving me reeling and unable to cope with the whirlpool of feelings left churning around inside of me.

Mikey and I spent the whole day crying it out together in front of the TV. After binge-watching mind-numbing cartoons and replaying Pete's message eighty-eight times, I finally deleted the message and snapped off the TV to fix us some supper. I found, upon closer inspection, that someone had thoughtfully restocked the fridge and pantry. My throat felt full again.

Monday and Tuesday came and went in much the same fashion. I made phone calls to the schools and Norma to inform them of my situation; everyone was real understanding. The calls I made to Daddy's cell phone, however, went unanswered. The fourth consecutive time it went to voice mail, I started chewing on my thumbnail. Normally this wouldn't faze me, because Daddy often neglected to pick up the phone when I called, or even call me back. But since they were presently in the confines of that academy, being strong-armed into signing their souls to the devil, I was fraught with worry.

Tuesday evening, after putting Mikey to bed, I tried again and got the recording again. Drumming my fingers on the kitchen counter, I recalled there was a number in the brochure. But it was after hours so the office would be closed. I huffed out some pent-up air and began pacing up and down with Blue at my heels, looking woefully up at me for answers. *I could call Pete's number.* An instant giddiness bubbled up inside me at the thought of hearing his voice live.

Something told me he didn't *want* me to call. For one, he didn't once say, "Call me." But he never said *not* to either. Before I could change my mind, I grabbed the phone and dialed the number he'd rattled off to me that afternoon. My palms were the sweaty of a girl calling a boy for the first time, only multiplied by a thousand on account of what kind of boy I was calling and the reason I was calling. On the third ring someone picked up, and my chest swelled with expectation.

"Hello?"

My lungs deflated. I sank to the floor like a grounded kite. "Um, Can I..."—throat clear—"Is this Pete Davenport's phone number?" That feeling I tried to ignore was mocking me.

"I'm sorry," the man on the line said. "You must have the wrong number."

"Oh." I was already near tears again when I heard *click*. "Sorry," I whispered to the dial tone.

I just held on to the phone, staring into space, until that obnoxious noise that lets you know the phone is off the hook molested my ears. *Another* lie—I knew I didn't get the number wrong. I wondered, yet again, if the cadet I'd given my heart to was one of the good guys . . . or a wolf in sheep's clothing.

Daddy finally called Wednesday morning to let us know they were coming home Wednesday night. That's all he would say though. So in our boredom and hiatus from school, we made a huge Welcome Home! banner. While Mikey colored it, I fried some chicken for supper. We welcomed them back home with much fanfare. I gleaned the visit went well by the way they rushed-talked over each another in their haste to tell us everything. The campus, the state-of-the-art facilities, the cadets, even the "amazing" drive over the Golden Gate Bridge was relived in vivid detail.

What I really wanted to know about was the meeting. I had to be patient for that bit of news. At last, I got my answer. Not the one I was looking for, although it was the one I was expecting. Yes, as a matter-of-fact, Daddy did go ahead and sign the paperwork. Andrew was officially in the International Elite Academy admissions process. Now we were all just waiting for their official acceptance in the form of a letter or phone call, or trumpeting foot soldiers . . . somehow they weren't exactly sure.

Job well done, Cadet Davenport, I thought acidly as my stomach boiled. Did he put me to sleep so I wouldn't intervene? I considered what I could have done anyway. Sugar in the gas tank, the best I could come up with. I comforted myself with the knowledge that it would've only bought a couple of days at the most. Did he really even recommend that Andrew not be admitted? Or was it just another lie my lie-detector didn't detect because my heart was running roughshod?

Over the next couple of days every time the phone rang, Andrew or Daddy would jump up to answer it only to frown and grumble into the phone. Mikey and I were delighted in equal proportion to Daddy and Andrew's disappointment. When almost a whole week went by and we hadn't heard anything back from them, I began to get my hopes up that the feeling I had that Andrew wouldn't be seeing the inside of "The Academy" again was accurate.

The following Monday found me back in school and on my regular schedule, except for P.E. I was allowed to sit out for the duration of the semester, in case someone hit me in the head with a ball. Probably for the best—I didn't think I'd have the heart to play soccer. Ever again.

I tried to resume my life as normally as possible, but my lifelessness was commented on by more than one person. It was hard pretending okay when the whole world was drained of color. Overnight, it was back to the same muted sepia tone from before Pete's arrival. Soon, I feared, it would digress further into nothing but black and white. And then even further . . . into gray.

Late afternoon, nine days after Pete left, I was picking up the mail when impatiently expectant hands snatched the tidy package right out from under me before I even had a chance to realize there was something to snatch.

"Aw, man!" Dejection radiated from the backseat. "It's for you." Andrew immediately tossed it back over.

"Hey! I'm sorry there's no news, Drews, but you still can't throw things at my head right now." I was lying—as far as I was concerned no news *was* good news.

"No-news-Drews! No-news-Drews!" Mikey began gleefully chanting.

"Shut-up!" Andrew blasted at Mikey. Then to me: "Sorry . . . it's only a stupid box."

I eyed the unmarked box. I certainly hadn't ordered anything. *Hmmm.* I picked it up and felt a zinging jolt radiate up my spine. A second later my foot stomped gas petal, spewing gravel behind us as we careened back to our house. I abandoned the boys in the smoking hatchback while I sprinted to the kitchen to wrench open the knife drawer. Then proceeded to butcher through the cardboard in my haste to pry it open for the prize inside.

I felt like a girl about to pull out a little black velvet box. Instead, I found myself holding a plastic case with a pair of tortoise-shell glasses inside. Hands trembling, I put them on. Sure enough—they were prescription free. So Pete hadn't been fooled after all. I wondered what he made of me walking around wearing glasses every day when I could see just fine. I was about to find out. There was a folded note inside.

Kate,

Here are the glasses I owe you. Sorry they are so late coming, but I didn't have a chance to get them to you before because I left rather unexpectedly and had too many other loose ends to tie up. Wear them in good health. I agree with you . . . your mother was an exceptionally smart lady.

-Pete

Right the next day, we got another bit of gold delivered to us in our tin metal mailbox (although I considered this one to be fool's gold). It was Andrew's long-awaited-for acceptance letter to the International Elite Academy, delivered with zero fanfare. I read it over twice through my clear frames. Weirdly, I didn't get worked up over it. I chalked it up to just being numb—I wasn't feeling much of anything these days.

And that was the last we heard from Pete Davenport, or his academy, for quite some time.

37

KISS OF DEATH

Octuber blew away, along with the flurry of snowflakes that dusted the ground in ghostly white. November emerged cold and desolate as the horizon of my future. Teeth brushed and barely showered, I was heading off to bed when a faint knock at the door stalled my feet. *Huh*? I hadn't heard Daddy's Bronco or any other vehicle for that matter. Blue started barking and wagging his tail at the same time. *Some guard dog.* I debated about going to fetch Daddy's shotgun, but Blue began whining and scratching at the door, looking up expectantly like I should know what his canine senses had already picked up.

And then — *Shezam!* — like a bolt of lightning, it hit me. My heart stopped beating and everything. I flew to the door.

"You always open the door late at night when you're home alone?"

"Pete!" I gasped.

He looked, for him, like hell—disheveled and like he hadn't slept in two nights. But it was more than that, like he was weighed down by the weight of the world. Like the rest of us mere mortals. It was disconcerting to see him this way—the way a child feels the first time he sees a parent break down in front of him. Like your rock just cracked beneath your feet. I'd never seen Pete anything less than commanding and in charge. He honestly looked on the verge of collapse.

I was momentarily rooted to the spot . . . until he reached out to me, stumbling over the crowbar habitually placed at our doorstep at night. And then I snapped out of it to catch him as he half fell into me for a hard hug. I was too alarmed to even appreciate it.

"Pete! What is it? What's wrong?"

Pete shrugged off his navy coat and let it drop before slinging a heavy arm over my shoulder. We trudged together over to the couch, where he sank heavily into the sunken cushions. He made a face at my face, closing his eyes against me as though I were too much to bear.

"*Pete!*" I shook his shoulder.

He lolled his head back, his eyes popping open to stare at me. An encyclopedia's amount of emotions flitted across his face before landing on his old stand-by—humor.

"I have some good news and some bad news. Which one do you want first?" He spoke so softly I had to bend over to catch it.

"The good news!" I cried, straightening up. I was desperate for some good news, especially when he looked like this.

He reached up, in slow-mo, to pull me back down. "The Academy is no longer as interested in Andrew," he whispered so softly I wasn't even sure of what I'd heard.

"What's the bad news?" *And why are we whispering?*

"The Academy is no longer as interested in Andrew."

I caught a whiff of alcohol on his breath. *Is he drunk?* That would certainly explain the odd behavior. I, for one, thought this was good news all around so didn't understand why he looked like someone just stole a kidney. I was about to form this question when he pulled me closer. *Did. Not. Mind.*

"Kate . . ." he began.

"What is it, Pete?" My eyes flicked back and forth across his face before homing in on his eyes; they appeared flat and black as his shirt.

"Will you do something for me?"

"Yeah, sure. *Anything!*" I cried. "Whatd'ya want me to do?"

A coil of something terrible rolled around his eyes. He laughed harshly. Ran a hand through his hair, which was shorter and stood on end after he did that now. Like the hairs on my arms. I'd already noticed his haircut of course: it was neat and uniform and diametrically opposed to his present state.

Eyes half-closed, he smiled sloppily up at me. "Kiss me," he said, changing tactics mid-play.

"*What?*" Isn't that the exact thing he'd been trying to get me *not* to do since we'd met?

Pete gave a devil-may-care grin, yet his eyes didn't sparkle like his teeth. "Kiss me. I don't care if there are a million reasons why it's wrong. Just—"

My lips fused to his, fervently kissing him as though the force of my kiss could eradicate the demons tormenting him. I caught him by surprise, but it only took a second for him to catch up. He gripped the back of my head, holding me to him (*as if I would leave*) then used his other arm to pull me into his lap.

His lips lit me up; it felt like I was sparkling with electricity. He'd never allowed himself to kiss me with such wild abandon. I was alarmed by his passion—alarmed and thrilled! I also allowed my passion to flow through my veins unchecked, a torrent of lovesick emotions. We were intertwined and kissing as though the end of the world was outside our doors.

I was lost in his arms, in our kiss. Lost in time and space. On a whole different planet. Every fiber of my being was pulled toward him. We were a tangle of limbs—one of his hands gripped my waist, the other digging into my hair, one of mine splayed across his back, my other clasped around his neck. Hooking one leg sinuously around me, he flipped me over. And the unbearably delicious weight of his body released a pleasure sigh from my chest.

He wrenched his lips from mine, staring into my eyes with eyes clouded with desire. He whispered something idly down at me, "Mmmm . . . best part of the job" was what I thought he said before molding his lips back to mine. And then I couldn't process anything further, reveling in the feel and thrill of him. It was all encompassing, the sensations washing over me—the roaring in my ears, the thundering in my chest, the swirling in my stomach.

He unfastened his lips to go exploring. I started a protest, then quickly changed my tune as his warm mouth cupped my neck, blazing a trail into unchartered territory. Approval hummed from my throat. His clever hand wandered over to my stomach, where lazy fingertips trailed beneath my shirt till I was quivering beneath him. He stopped nuzzling my neck to stare at my flushed face and passion-drugged eyes. I could barely focus, was completely gone . . . as drunk as he was. High on pheromones. Over the edge of reason. A sweet smile of satisfaction on his lips, he teased mine back open to kiss me within an inch of my life.

Oh. My. God! I dug insistent fingers into his back, pleading. For what? . . . I wasn't sure. I was writhing and panting. *Wanting.* As he gripped me to him in a delicious grind, my mind reeled with possibilities, new erotic sensations, and conflicting emotions. The intensity was suddenly too much for me.

"Pete—" I cried, a little unsure edge to my voice.

A glance to my face, and he shifted off me. I immediately clamored for him back, but he simply brushed his lips back and forth across mine, teasing now. I squirmed beneath him, impatiently urging him on in a vain attempt at . . . something. Something I always thought I wanted to wait for marriage for, and was suddenly having a hard time remembering why.

"Kate," he whispered my name, which was a good thing because I could barely remember what it was. He grasped my face between his hands, kissing me so deeply I was thrumming with desire. "Mmmm . . . Kate," he moaned as if *he* couldn't get enough of *me*.

When I heard my name escape his lips again in passion, a feeling of pure bliss bubbled up inside of me. "Pete . . ." I broke off the kiss to let the words I'd been holding in for weeks spill out.

He growled at me from deep within his throat before continuing south for his onslaught of pleasure.

"Pete." I lifted his head, needing eye contact for this. He reluctantly wrenched his mouth from the valley between my breasts. I just realized two buttons were undone . . . and couldn't recall how that was done.

"What?" he breathed, a kiss of sweet whisky on his breath. I mentally thanked the fire-whisky gods for precipitating his loss of control tonight. *This right now . . . this was heaven on earth.*

"I . . ." Instantly felt shy and exposed as an open diary but I was determined to let him know where I stood.

He filled the pause by kissing the hollow of my throat, trailing his lips past the point of my cross. And I almost couldn't stop him from continuing his slow torture on my love-starved body. But some kind of insistent voice persisted. I needed to say this before we went any further. I needed to know he felt the same way. If we were in love (which I firmly believed we were), then surely, *surely* this couldn't be wrong. *Right?* Needing reassurance, I palmed his southbound face back up to mine.

He growled his protest but obliged, peeking at me from beneath lazy lashes. He looked befuddled and love-drunk; a sloppy smile adorably split his face that caused my heart do a summersault. Skimming his nose down the side of mine, he said, "What's on your mind, Kate? . . . 'sides drivin' me crazy."

He stared at me, indulging me in my moment to slow down in the midst of this madness we had created together. And his patience made my heart burst at the seams with the force of my feelings. Looking deeply into his eyes, I swallowed then just put it out there.

"Pete . . . I love you."

I felt his reaction before it registered on his face. It was a slight stiffening of his body. Followed by a slipping of the sloppy smile. Then the soft, dewy eyes staring into mine closed.

Oh God. The emotion misting my eyes suddenly turned into a lid full of tears as realization crashed over me. Like a tidal wave of melted ice. *He doesn't feel the same way.*

Realization, that realization had registered on me, registered on him. "Kate. God. I'm sorry. I—"

I didn't wait for him to finish before I was shoving him off me. "It's fine." My voice was brittle as Popsicle sticks left in the sun. "It's good to know where you stand." I hastily did that very thing now, yanking my shirt back down. Could not believe what I was about to let happen. What I had *already* let happen . . . and with a known liar and con artist. An enemy. I was shaking. My fingers could barely redo the buttons.

Of course, he doesn't love you! You little fool! I mentally cursed.

Pete's curse was out loud. "Kate—" He grabbed my arm, but I jerked away from him.

"Tell me somethin', Pete . . ." It was hard to speak; my throat felt swollen and hurt as if I'd just swallowed something I was deathly allergic to. "Why?" I croaked. "I mean if you were only after a piece of ass"—he flinched at my words—"you could've had any number of girls at your disposal."

My brain had finally unfogged enough to process what he'd said minutes ago: "Best part of the job." *I was nothin' but a J-O-B.* My stomach twisted. "But no. You *wooed* me," I spat his words back at him. "*Courted* me. Why? You knew no matter how I felt about you,"—an angry flush at the admission—"I'd never stop fightin' for Andrew. So what was the point of hurtin' me?"

Pete looked weary again, defeated even. The pull I always felt for him started again. I longed to smooth that miserable furrow from his brow even as my heart was breaking into a thousand pieces. Shoulders hunched he leaned forward, hanging his guilty head between his legs. Both hands clasped the back of his head. His eyes were open, staring as though mesmerized by the pattern of brown rectangles on the floor.

After a full minute of dead quiet, his head jerked back up. "Kate, do you really love me?" Pride didn't let me answer, so I merely shrugged, my eyes glistening with the sting of unrequited love. His face melted. "Do something for me."

I stared dumbly at him, sniffling quietly. *He has some nerve.*

He abruptly stood, placing a finger to his lips in the universal sign of *be quiet.* "Come with me." He beckoned. "It's a beautiful night . . . I want to make love to you beneath the stars."

What? The delivery of this soap opera line lacked its usual panache, and a chill, not a thrill, ran up my spine. And I was so shell-shocked I didn't even protest when he jerked me to him. His eyes were intense, and I was mesmerized as he drew my face forward as though for a kiss. But I stalled out on him, so he bent over and put his mouth to my ear.

"I need to speak to you outside," he whispered. "It's urgent."

Subsequently, I was led into the kitchen where he left me leaning against the counter to go dig in the utensil drawer. Trance-like, I stared at him as he pulled out our sharpest knife from its exact location, next to the serving spoon. *What's he gonna do with our paring knife? Stab me for not cooperating? Maybe that's why he's acting so weird—they're making him kill me cause they know I'm gonna raise hell when they come for my brother. And the only way to shut me up . . . is by murdering me.*

Hysteria bubbled up inside of me. Made sense—he obviously didn't want to do it. That made sense, too—Pete *was* a nice guy. But that didn't necessarily make him a *good* guy.

A hand grab, and he wordlessly led me through the gloomy living room, where he paused to slip on his coat and out the front door. I followed him like a little lamb being led to slaughter. Stark night air washed over me, waking me from my reverie. The crunching of our feet over frozen pasture and the howling wind were the only sounds.

"Pete, where are you takin' me?" My voice seemed loud, sharply bouncing into nothingness as he took us off trail. I tripped along, looking at his grim face in the moonlight, puffing out steam as he pulled me along. He still looked absurdly hot, but somewhere close to the edge of madness. Panic started to creep in. My feet stalled.

"Not here." He tugged on my arm. "A little farther." His tone was cold now, detached almost.

I dug my heels in. "Pete!"

He countered with a yank. "Come on, Kate . . . now that I've decided to go through with it, I really just wanna get it over with as fast as possible."

Surely not. Right? Surely I was just letting my imagination run rampant. Pete stopped frog-marching me forward to reach into his coat for a flask. Come to think of it, he hadn't offered me his coat, or even asked me to get mine. Almost as if he knew—I wouldn't need it. My blood ran cold.

He took a serious swig from the flask, then offered me some. But I declined, wanting to keep my wits about me. As I watched him take another fortifying swallow, a siren went off in my head. He was obviously drinking away his dread. Numbing himself. Bolstering his courage for what he was about to do. He stared me down in the dark, and I felt the intent manifest itself.

There would be bloodshed tonight.

I whimpered a little. Wanted to run, but my legs felt like two limp noodles attached to a wood block.

"Come on, Kate," he coaxed.

"Daddy will be back any minute," I threw out.

He snorted out more steam. "No he won't. He's at Cannon with some old military buddies, bragging about his son's bright future with the 'world's most elite military academy.' And, unfortunately, he has a flat tire to see about tonight."

Of course—car-rigging, his specialty. My heart studded to a halt along with my feet, suddenly stubborn as a mule's.

"Pete! You don't have to do this!" I tried wrenching my hand away, but he used his other hand to redouble his grip on me.

He sighed heavily, shook back his golden head. The combo of steamy air and steely eyes made him seem almost possessed. "I do, Kate. They've left me no choice."

I gulped, panic stealing the breath from me. This was it. He was losing his patience. Abruptly, my legs gave way. He swore, clamped the knife between his teeth, and bent down to scoop me up, carrying me like a child a few more yards to the old elm tree I had leaned against this summer to read romance novels. I wondered what different steps I could've taken to prevent the path I was on . . . the one leading to bloodshed.

Pete set me down. I immediately dropped to my knees, a beggar. "You ready?" he asked. Words wouldn't come, so I shook my head vehemently. "Here," he handed me the flask, "it'll help take the edge off."

Very sporting of him I thought, accepting the flask with palsied hands. I took a tentative sip, choking as the fiery liquid burned its way down my throat. I thought of my two little brothers, sleeping innocently in their beds. Tears streamed down my face. Now I was only grateful we were away, so they wouldn't hear or see anything.

He regarded me, and his face softened. He spoke encouragingly, "Trust me—this'll be a lot harder on me than you."

Trust me: the two words that had brought me down in the first place. Instantly, I was more mad than scared. Maybe it was that, coupled with the alcohol fumes, but a fire just ignited inside my belly. *Easy mark my ass!* I knew Pete was a highly trained fighter, but I would try one last time to beat him at his own game. Even if I failed, at least I went down fighting. Mama would be proud. My brothers were safe. . . . That's all that mattered.

Nodding my head, I acted resigned to my fate. He nodded back, took another glug from his flask, and after drawing in a deep breath, he poured most of the remaining liquid over the knife, presumably to sanitize it. *For what purpose?* Surely, he couldn't be worried about a little bit of bacteria? That would be inconsequential to a corpse. My whole body shivered like someone just stepped over my grave.

"Did you never care for me at all?" The same question niggled me to the very end.

His face came undone. Warm palms cupped my tear-stained cheeks. He stared into my eyes like he could see all the way into my soul. "Of course, I did! That's what makes this so hard—the thought that I won't see you again after tonight."

I stared into the black of his eyes and saw the truth: He *did* care for me. Fear slithered around my heart like a cold snake. *What kind of organization had such power over its underlings that they'd be willing to kill—even someone innocent, someone they cared for—just because they got in the way?*

I couldn't allow them to get their claws into Andrew. I would have to do the thing Pete was dreading. The unthinkable. *Murder.* Someone I had just professed my love to. Someone I'd almost just made love to. Someone standing in *my* way of saving my brother. Then I would run. Living off grid, hiding from the world, suddenly . . . it made a whole lot of sense to me.

Pete closed one eye to peer down at me. I was pretty sure he was drunk as a skunk, which was the only advantage I had tonight. "It's time, Katie-Kat," he said softly, eyes hard.

The near-empty flask was beside me. Sloppy of him. He must be even more out of it than I thought, which made me think I really had a shot now. Eyes trained on his, I felt around on the ground for the flask. "Are you sure this is the only way, Pete?"

He nodded. "Believe me . . . I've tried to find another way."

My heart sank—I *did* believe him.

"Now no more talking," he said. "Let's just get this over with." Gripping the knife in his right hand, he pulled me up with his left. *Gallant to the very end.* I offered him my own left hand, keeping my right one—with the fisted-flask—behind my back. As soon as he helped me up, he let me go to start unbuckling his belt.

What the?!

I didn't dwell on it. Instead, I used the opportunity to crack him over the head with the flask. Pete must've felt the violent intent of my movement, because at the very last second, his forearm instinctively deflected some of the blow so that only a portion of metal hit. But it was enough to send him reeling.

He roared, falling onto one knee, a shocked hand feeling for the wound. "What the *hell* are you doing?!"

I wasn't gonna tell him; I was gonna show him—my foot swung back to finish him off. But I was too slow, or untrained, because Pete dropped the knife to catch my obvious foot, then threw me back in the dirt. I went down hard, my tailbone splintering pain, air exploding from my lungs. I barely felt it before scrambling back up with a handful of icy dirt.

"Kate! Goshdammit! What the hell's *wrong* with you? I'm—"

I hurled it in his face. He quickly spun, so that the majority of it rained on his back.

"Alright, you little hellcat! You asked for . . ."

I whipped around, running for the house like my back was on fire. But instead of a cold shower, I was running for the shotgun. I fervently prayed it was loaded. And that I could beat him to the house. I had a pretty good head start on him, and his head had to be ringing pretty good. And, inexplicably, I'd completely caught him off guard.

Did he not know me at all?

Crushing steps and heaving breaths were coming after me now, a freight train of anger-fueled adrenaline and superior strength propelling him faster than my legs could go. Pete didn't bother calling my name—he knew I wouldn't stop. *Smart.* He shifted into high gear now, right on my tail. Then stumbled. Over something—a clump of grass, a frozen chicken, it didn't matter.

All that mattered was . . . I was home free now.

38

RECKONING

I don't remember going up the steps, opening the door, reaching for the gun. Next thing I knew, I was pointing the barrel of Daddy's prized Winchester. At the one I was in love with. *How could I have been so wrong?* I'd never been more wrong about anything in my life. I could never love someone who was willing to commit murder for a sinister cause. And just like that—BAM!—my heart crusted over like frozen tundra. I knew I could do the unthinkable. To save my family.

Pete must've seen the stone-cold look on my face, because he froze immediately. Not another step forward. Hands up, face pleading. "Kate!" he cried, "Youdon'twannadothis! I can explain—you're making a big mistake!"

I saw his head oozing red, his sun-kissed hair gingered by the blood. He staggered slightly, whether from blood loss, or loss of coordination caused by alcohol consumption (or acting), I couldn't be sure. Nor did I care I told myself, even as a stab of remorse pierced my gut. *My gut!—that betrayer.* It had led me wrong this whole time.

Mama was wrong—I didn't have special intuition. My gut flip-flopped on me all the time. Even now, as I stood pointing a gun at my hot hitman, even after the obvious botched attempt at my murder, it was telling me: he wouldn't hurt me. I'd blamed everything on his academy, wanting so badly to believe in him because I was falling in love. My heart must've been sending stronger signals than my gut this whole time. It had led me down this wayward path. I'd been a colossal fool—*a fool for love.* But no more. I wouldn't listen to his mouth, dripping honeyed lies.

I firmed up my resolve, and my hands on the shotgun. . . . *Trying to help me, my rear.* One eye closed, I cocked the hammer and aimed right over his heart.

Pete bent over. "God almighty! How many friggin' times am I gonna be hit on the head because of you?" The porch's naked light bulb spotlighted his face. *Now* he looked murderous. I'd never seen this level of fury coming at me before, not even right before he was going to stab me. It was disconcerting to the core.

He rounded on me with an incredulous look upon his face, like your favorite pet had suddenly turned rabid on you. "You aiming to give me the next concussion?"

"I was thinkin' of doin' somethin' a little more permanent than a knot on your head," I replied.

Pete's face was a Greek tragedy mask, like he wasn't sure if he wanted to laugh or cry. He settled on laughing. Hysterically. "You're the only girl I know who could go from professing her love one minute to pointing the barrel of a shotgun at you the next."

"You provoked me."

"Put the damn gun down, Kate. You know you're not going to shoot me."

"You don't know me as well as you think you do, Cadet Davenport."

After focusing on my determined face for a moment, his mouth relaxed into something dangerously resembling a smile. "I know you wouldn't shoot me in the back." That said, he turned his back on me and marched down the steps.

Well okay then, I'd take the bait. I didn't want the boys waking up from a sound sleep by a gun going off. And then walk out to find their favorite cadet lying in a pool of his own blood. With me holding the smoking gun.

I marched after him, my feet stumbling only after he whirled around with the paring knife in his hand. *What? Is he gonna fling it at me tomahawk style?* I flashed back to when he'd used it to slice lemons for our lemonade and how much fun we'd had that afternoon, doing chores of all things. My hands started shaking now, my trigger finger turning numb. This was serious. *In the leg. I could get him in the leg.*

"I'm sure it goes without sayin', but a gun trumps a knife in a duel." I trembled my way through the bizarre live enactment of this old maxim.

"Kate, Kate . . ." He said it so wearily, like a particularly disappointed parent does when a wayward child has finally gone too far. "When are you *ever* going to learn to trust me?"

"Says the elite cadet wielding a knife."

Pete took in a monster breath and blew out a hiss of steam. "I guess I should've explained myself first, but to tell you the truth . . . I'm a little out of sorts tonight. And couldn't say anything in the house anyway."

"The boys are sound asleep and Daddy's not home. But you already knew that—which is why you chose now to come do your dirty deed."

Another sigh fogged the air. Then he said, "There are bugs in the house."

Huh? At first I was insulted, my mind conjuring up images of black-winged creatures and spindly green things with antennae. All sorts of creepy crawlies I loathed and successfully kept at bay with rigorous housekeeping. *What's he talking about? Why can't we go in the house because—oh.*

I lowered my gun an inch. "*Bugs?*"

He nodded his head. "I was taking you out of the house so I could *finally* tell you everything. You see, you might not trust *me*, but I do trust *you*. You may be the only person in the world I do trust . . . and you whack me upside the head the first chance you get! . . . When I came back to warn you." He shook his head then winced, holding it in his hand. "I'm beginning to regret my decision to come here tonight—first you almost knock me out then you point a gun at my heart. Think part one of our reunion went a whole lot better," he finished wryly.

In no mood for his flirtatious humor, I narrowed my eyes. "Then explain to me why it is you felt the need for a knife before our little chat?"

Pete looked me dead-on. "Because I need you to cut out the microchip I have imbedded in the back of my neck."

My jaw dropped. The gun drooped a little more. Out of all the words in the world, that particular combination did not once cross my mind. "Now those aren't words you hear every day," I said.

He snuffled out a humorless laugh. "Neither is 'I love you' from a girl you're about to make hate you."

"You-you weren't gonna kill me?" I edged around his other statement for now.

"Do I strike you as the type of guy who would use a kitchen knife to stab an innocent girl to death? One whom I was just considering making love to two minutes before? *Really?*" He hit me between the eyes.

I stared at him, unblinking afraid I might be falling for another trick. Tears blurred my vision.

"Would I really be so careless as to leave my fingerprints all over the place?" he continued. "Not to mention the amount of blood a stab wound produces, and the amount of time it would take to cover up such a vicious crime. And my DNA is all over you from our brief . . . interlude." He looked at me like he was mortally wounded. "Think back, Kate, to all the times we've spent together. Use your *God-given* intuition." His serene voice went up a pitchy octave. "Do I really appear to hate you or be capable of such malicious violence?"

Pete was either really hurt, or else he was the best actor in the world. It did scare me, because he was so *good* at everything. My arms were shaking, being both cold and tired. The gun dropped to the point of about his kneecap now. I didn't want to kill him—even if he was here to murder me.

"If I were really going to kill you, I would've shot you up with an overdose of codeine, left the empty bottle of Vicodin on your bedside table, then typed up a suicide note. Everyone knows how crazy you've been over losing your brother to The Academy . . . how depressed you've been over me leaving. That's the route I would've taken, had I *really* come here with the intent of killing you." Pete leveled me with a look. "And you never would've seen me coming, nor would you have felt a thing."

I sank the gun all the way to the ground, crying. My gut was telling me he was telling the truth. *My gut better be right.*

He swore and tore the hem from his shirt, holding it to the gash in his head.

"You want me to cut a microchip out of your neck, using a *paring* knife?" I repeated it out loud, just to make sure I got it right.

He nodded at me woefully. I dropped the gun altogether, and my hands, now lightened of their load, were trembling from the enormity of what almost happened. We both stared at them. It was really cold out here, but I was shaking from shock. The wind had picked up, howling mournfully and swaying dead-limbed trees and skeletal bushes around eerily. We stared at each other for a long moment, the bonds of trust quickly regenerating.

"How old are you, *really*?" I demanded.

A little huff. "I guess that's as good a place to start as any."

Pete walked back a few paces to where we'd just tussled in the dirt and slumped down heavily against the elm tree. I followed behind with the gun and set it down before lowering myself, in the same cautious manner, next to him, in case he flinched back or yelled at me. I had hit him pretty hard—a sharp pang of remorse hit me back. But I wouldn't apologize just yet. There was still that little matter of him saying I would hate him to attend to first. So I waited, teeth chattering in the pale moonlight. He unzipped himself out of his coat and draped it around us both, so I had no choice but to snuggle in.

"Twenty-three this month," he admitted.

I processed this quietly, doing some swift mental math. Six years older. *Not a catastrophe.* Not exactly legal either. Honestly, I was a little relieved; he seemed even older than that to me. But I already hated to think of our relationship—precious to my heart—as being illicit.

He had quietly settled into the tree, still as a statue, so I prompted him. "Why were you really sent here? Is there even really a mentoring program?"

"I *was* sent here to vet your brother for The Academy," he began, "and there is a mentoring program. But it's only for a highly specialized sector—PGCs, which your brother was thought to be . . ."—he spared me a sidelong glance—"but no longer is."

"PGC?"

"Potentially Gifted Civilian."

"What do you mean by *gifted* exactly?"

"I mean gifts above and beyond the physical and mental ones that Andrew has," he said.

"You mean like *super-natural* stuff?" I was no longer thinking about the cold.

Pete looked at me. He nodded gingerly, one hand holding the dampening rag to his head. I swallowed, my mind reeling with frantic thoughts and questions.

"Like *what*?"

"Like being able to tell when someone is lying, just by looking them in the eye. Or having really strong feelings about things that *usually* . . . "—he shot me an exasperated look—"sway your actions in the right direction."

"You mean like havin' intuition about stuff? But everybody has that," I dismissed.

"Your intuition, Kate, is a mite sharper than the average Joe's."

I set that bit of information on the back burner for now. I already knew that about myself, although I never considered it to be supernatural. "Is that why your academy is no longer interested in Andrew . . . because bein' super-smart and super-talented isn't enough to earn you a one-way ticket to Elitesville?"

"Pretty much," he confirmed. "That used to be enough, but more recently, The Academy is after people like you, kids preferably, because it's easier to indoctrinate and manipulate them." The disgust in Pete's voice was unmistakable. "And The Academy *is* still interested in your brother . . . just not as much. Andrew's tests for giftedness were negative. He's just a regular, straight-up golden boy with no extra-special gifts, apart from the obvious intelligence and athleticism."

We were quiet a moment. The cold came back to me—from the inside. "But what if k-kids," I stumbled over the word, hyper-aware of our age difference now, "like me don't wanna sign up for the gifted program?"

He stared into my eyes and said, "They have no choice in the matter."

"So-so . . . y'all just *take* them? Snatch them from their beds in the middle of the night?"

"Something like that. If we can't get them to sign with us—which is highly unusual but does happen from time to time—then we have to go the, er . . . extra mile. As you see, we're very persuasive. Running into holdouts like you and your father is rare."

"Isn't that a little suspicious?—snatching kids from their families. Don't the parents . . . I dunno . . . alert the police, call the FBI or something? Don't y'all ever get caught?"

Pete sighed as though I still weren't getting the gist of it. "Kate, The Academy is a very old and very secretive government institution. It's also one of the most powerful. If there ever was a whisper of something negative directed our way, it would quickly be squashed."

"Friends in high places and all that," I said, trying to grasp the magnitude of what he was saying.

"The Academy pretty much stocks the high places with former cadets."

A quake of fear shook me again; the confirmation of my suspicions rocked my world. "So, what's next for the Connelly family?"

"I'm not sure," he answered truthfully, then paused. "Nothing I hope . . . although they still have a lot of surveillance in the house." He studied my face to see how I was taking the news. Apparently, I looked like I was holding it together, because he proceeded. "And they asked me to procure your standardized tests—see if I can find a pattern similar to the one I found with Andrew."

I tried to picture unknown people, clinical CIA types, sipping burnt coffee and listening in on our mundane domestic life. What exactly had they gleaned from our conversations?

"*Where* are they exactly?" I tried real hard now not to freak out.

"There's one in the living room and dining room, one in the boys' room, and I just added one more recently—to your room." He said this as if he were listing the number of phone jacks instead of *really* invasive spying devices.

Something twisted inside me. "When you asked to see my bedroom . . . ?"

Pete nodded. That one hurt. It must've shown because he took my hand, as one does when delivering bad news. Which kept on coming. "And the phone is tapped."

"Is that why you didn't call?" I asked.

"Precisely why."

While I slowly started to process, Pete examined the blood-drenched rag. He wasn't kidding around when he said he was going to explain everything. I wondered what else there was to find out and shuddered at the thought that, like the *Titanic*, we'd only hit the tip of the iceberg. I decided to put that on the other back burner to focus on what else he'd just said.

"Wait. You said they wanted to look for a testing pattern with me, similar to the one you found with Andrew—you *told* them about that?" I withdrew my hand so fast my elbow hit tree, jangling my funny bone.

He breathed in deeply as one does before an admission of guilt, but no apology came out with his exhalation. Instead, he said, "If I didn't cooperate with them . . . at least to a certain degree, then they were going to make things very unpleasant for me, my parents . . . Reese. Then send Ranger— who is lead officer in charge of this mission, by the way—to finish the job."

The thought of him and his hatred coming for me made me shudder again.

"It's been a tough balancing act for me—giving them enough accurate, new information so as to appear that I'm doing my job well, and hiding the other truths I've discovered along the way."

"What truths?" I asked.

"Don't pretend you don't know, Kate. I thought we were done pretending." Pete looked me in the eye.

Oh that. It was hard to think of myself as gifted per se. It was really just a lot of strong feelings about things I usually tried to tune out. "Does-does this mean they know about me?"

He sighed, propped his arms on his bent knees, looked up at the crescent moon as if it had all the answers. "I have a hunch they do. . . . As a matter of fact, I think part of this mission was to access whether I could recognize giftedness when I see it. I suspect the powers-that-be already knew going in that Andrew wasn't the only gifted Connelly kid—even though he blatantly embodied all the usual markers." He gave me a strange, sad smile. "You did a much better job of hiding your gifts."

Pete continued on with things that continued to chill me, one vertebrate at a time. "They still had me monitoring you even after we found out conclusively that Andrew isn't gifted. You see, The Academy's filled to the brim with kids like him—myself and Ranger being two examples. Like I said, they've turned more towards flushing out these other enhanced abilities like yours . . . like—"

"Wait!" I flung off the coat. "*You* were listenin' in?"

He put his hand on my thigh as though to keep me in place. "It was part of my job, Kate. But they have access to the surveillance tapes—no telling how long until they listen in on you talking about your strong feelings."

"Speakin' of strong feelin's . . . why does Ranger hate me so much?" I wasn't sure why this was such a burning question. But it was.

Pete puffed out some air. "That's a really good question," he said. "I've been wondering the same thing." He was quiet a moment, lost in his own thoughts.

"I mean . . . if y'all were so keen on signing us—Andrew and you say possibly me—then why was he so hateful to me? Wouldn't that go against the mission?"

"Don't take it personally. Ranger's an asshole . . . even amongst cadets, and we already despise each other. So naturally, he wanted to give me a hard time on my first mission. Plus, he disdains all civilians in general. He sees them as being inferior and not worthy of his time. I don't think he's even aware of your potential for giftedness. Like I said, you were pretty good at hiding your light under a bushel. We looked at your school records during preliminary meetings—you keep your average at a solid A-minus, making sure you never make higher than a 92 or lower than a 90. I suspect that's no accident."

Pete stared at me until I gave in with a little shrug. "I suspected as much," he said. "But that's nowhere near good enough to be considered for The Academy, so he most likely quickly dismissed you . . . and I think we can only be grateful for that." He sighed. "But The Academy will most likely see that as the pattern it is before too long. I'm afraid it's only a matter of time before they're onto you. Didn't take me very long to figure it out." He frowned and drew me back into the shelter of his arm. ". . . And when they do, they'll most likely send Ranger in to access you. He's been chomping at the bit since day one."

I shook my head. "I can't fathom him being here this whole time instead of you."

Pete gave a little huff, then looked at me with a peculiar expression. "He almost was, but he failed the first test . . . the one I passed with flying colors."

"The first test?" I asked and watched as his mouth quirked, his face telling of some inside joke I wasn't privy to. "Pete? What was the first test?"

"To see which cadet you would be most attracted to," he finished with a smirk-smile.

"What? You mean at Norma's when y'all came in that afternoon? Ranger was being a world-class ass! I can't believe he'd think *anyone* would find that attractive."

Pete shook his head then winced, reminding me he was in pain. And it was my fault—again. "No before then." My face was a blank slate, so he prompted, "Remember the church camp you attended over the summer?"

I nodded, realization slowly dawning on me. "You mentioned earlier . . . you mentioned the name Reese. That wouldn't happen to be . . ."

He looked into my eyes, and killed me with the answer. I was too thunderstruck to speak, staring at him while he worked over the bloody rag in his hand. This was by far the most surprising news. I guess because I'd already guessed at most of the rest. But this . . . *this* I'd had no idea about.

He was about to go on when I finger-halted him, needing another moment to process. "Wait. Doesn't that mitigate the idea that I have super-natural intuition?" I was thinking aloud. "But I did think she was always askin' me a lot of personal questions . . . and I mostly answered because I thought she genuinely—" An incredulous laugh cut off the humiliating thought. "I can't believe how much I revealed to that phony!"

I had full burners of damning information boiling in pots, and was starting to feel pretty steamed.

Pete squeezed my thigh. "Don't be so hard on yourself. Honestly, these gifts are often hit or miss, especially when you're as unaware of it as you seem to be. They always need to be worked on to develop properly, much like building a muscle or getting good at a particular sport . . . you can have natural ability, but you still have to practice to be really great."

Hot tears burned my eyes. "I can't believe it!"

He slipped his arm around my waist. "She really did like you. And didn't mean you any harm . . . unless you got in the way of the mission, so you wouldn't have gotten any bad vibes from her."

Despite the warming presence of his palm against my ribcage, another chill crept farther up my spinal column. "Wouldn't have harmed me *unless* I got in the way," I repeated.

"Reese is a hardcore cadet," he explained. "Lives and breathes Academy. Believes it's her life's mission to fulfill theirs. And she thinks a boy like Andrew would be better off in 'The Academy's superior care', rather than"—he gave me an apologetic look—"'living out in the country, in a trailer house, being raised by his teenage sister'—no offense," he finished, lifting his hand to deflect my glare. "Hey. Don't shoot the messenger . . . you know *I* don't feel that way."

My shoulders slumped. He was right. I just felt so betrayed and duped. But now that I knew Reese was one of them, I couldn't believe it hadn't occurred to me before. She fit the prototype exactly: beautiful, intelligent, sophisticated. So, so far above everyone else at that camp except for . . .`

Oh my God—Ryan! I'd completely forgotten about him since . . . well, since Pete walked through the door. Obviously, he'd been a set up, too. I cringed, feeling so manipulated. Reese had practically pushed the two of us together from the moment we met. Did Pete know about that? He watched the play of emotions on my face, waiting for my speech to catch up with my thoughts.

"Where does Ryan fit into all this?"

Pete made a little face. "He was first in line for the mission, hand-picked by the powers-that-be."

"Why? Because he's my type?" I thought back to Ryan's poster-boy good looks. Didn't do it for me. It was more me being flattered a guy like that was interested in me than me being interested in him. Plus, he got all sneery about Bible class, rolling his eyes at every camp activity that didn't involve sports. I hadn't really liked his attitude but was willing to overlook it because he was very solicitous towards me . . . I guess I knew why now.

The slow burn heated up.

Pete gave a little grunt. "I guess so, partly anyway. The Academy is really arrogant, always surmising a civilian will fall for any cadet."

I hated to admit they were probably right about that.

". . . So that was the assumption going in. Ryan's also a couple of years younger, so they probably thought he could play the part better. And Reese was already signed up for the mission . . . just seemed like a natural fit to use him. But as the days went on, it was clear you didn't immediately have the chemistry with him The Academy was counting on. So they had to . . . improvise." Pete's mouth had the audacity to quirk up again.

"Improvise?"

"Do you remember Reese instigating a little game with all the girls from your cabin?"

I stared into the space that was my past, feeling slow and stupid, my mind literally boggled as if I'd been cavorting around with aliens this whole time.

"She was always leading the charge for something: shaving cream fights, underwear up the flagpole, truth-or-dare," I said, visibly seething at her for getting one over on me so completely.

"The T-shirt game," he prompted.

I thought back a second and froze. I knew what he was referring to now. Reese had invented a "super-fun" game where she confiscated shirts from "all the cute boys in the senior cabin." Then she blindfolded the girls and had us pass them around to smell, noting which ones we liked best and rating them in order from best smelling to worst.

I remembered all the hilarity surrounding this game as we tried matching shirt to owner. Of course, she declared *my* favorite belonged to her brother, Ryan, then squealed and hug-jumped up and down with me like we were the winners of the game. She even went so far as to say we were going to be like sisters. I thought back, with a putrid burn in my stomach, to how flattered I was.

What a little faker. Were all cadets such good actors?

I just realized the real reason behind that little high-jinx was to see which *cadet's* smell I would be most attracted to. And then get *him* to do the mission. My eyes flew to Pete's.

He flashed his teeth at me in the dark. *"I* was the proud owner of the winning T-shirt."

I flushed *Hot Tamale* red. Clapped my hands over my face. "Oh. My. God!" I groaned, *not* using The Lord's name in vain.

"I know," he simply said, relocating his hand to my shoulder.

I drew in a deep breath and looked at Pete with new eyes. "So, this-this *thing*," I struggled for words, "this mission was a setup from the beginning . . . Y'all *were* spyin' on us—I thought I was crazy!" I listed aloud all the things as they occurred to me: "My books disappearin', that four-wheeler out in our pasture, you comin' here—our relationship . . ." My voice broke after finally giving voice to my fears. "My emails back and forth to Reese, talking about *you*. You bein' in my Spanish and P.E. class, the *whole* thing was a mission just to sign Andrew up, because he was thought to be a-a . . . *PGC?*"

He nodded. "Now you know the lengths they will go to procure the gifted."

"What . . ." I swallowed, almost too scared to ask. "What do they do with them?"

"Whatever they want," he stated flatly.

That feeling was right on my neck now, making the hairs stand on edge like prickly little icicles. "And you said *Ranger* wanted to do this mission? To be the one to vet my brother?"

Pete's face turned grim as the reaper. "Yes. Next to Ryan, he was the favorite. He was pretty disappointed he was passed over." He said this in a way that let me know it was an understatement. "Ranger knows it's the wave of the future for The Academy. They're sinking millions into the GAP program, and he wants a piece of the action. Procuring a legitimate gifted would be yet another notch in his belt."

"I don't understand why they would've considered him. I mean if you were the um . . . best man for the job."

"Because I wasn't *anyone's* favorite for this mission"—tight smile—"except for yours," he added, his expression softening. "As a matter of fact, I was probably Weston's last pick. Fortunately, the T-shirt contest changed all that."

"It was really down to a T-shirt contest?" It sounded more like a spring break game for frat guys than something an elite military academy would participate in.

"They wanted someone who would appeal to both you and Andrew," he explained. "Ranger argued his case all the way up the ranks to Weston himself that he could and *should* do it because—" Pete stopped short, shook his head, and looked off into the black wasteland

"Because . . . "

He hit me with a look then hit me with: "Because he was T-shirt number two."

"No!" My hands flew to my mouth, where they stayed a while.

No way!—The Terminator?

"That's right." Pete barked out a humorless laugh. "Ranger came in second place. And nothing makes him madder than that . . . except for losing to me."

My hands fell to my lap, causing my mouth to cave open. But no words came out.

"That's likely another reason he hated on you," Pete said. "I told you, don't take it personally. Ranger should've just chalked it up to pheromones. But I'm sure on some level he blames you for not choosing him—he's an egotist and a sore loser. And he's going to do everything in his power to make you pay if he loses. That's just who he is. That's probably why he gave you such a hard time at the diner . . . and to give me a harder time on my mission."

My face contorted. "Well, I would *never* have fallen for him!"

Pete had nothing to say to that bold declaration. His eyes penetrated mine as if searching . . . Something flickered there for an instant. *Doubt?*

"*Never!*"

"That's something my mother would refer to as 'famous last words,'" he remarked in a way that sounded like a warning.

"Not if he was the last man on earth!" I added dramatically.

He pursed his lips. "Well, it's a specious argument anyway."

"And nobody would've believed he was in high school," I added an addendum before switching to a less touchy topic. "I still don't quite understand why y'all went to such great lengths for me if nobody but you knows about my, er . . . gifts."

"Prior to the camp set-up, we approached your father about signing Andrew. He turned us down flat, citing you as the reason. Said his daughter would never allow it, seeing as how you had your mind set on raising the boys. I believe his exact words were . . ." Pete looked up, as though to scroll through his brain, "'you'd promised your mother, before she was made an angel, and that you'd fight like the devil to see it through'," he finished with a fond smile.

I was also taken aback by this bit of news. Not the meeting Daddy never mentioned, the turning them down flat part. Thought he was Team IEA all the way.

Pete continued: "We were unsurprised by this, already privy to the fact your father had turned down several exclusive schools that offered scholarships. So we set about sweetening the deal. We felt your father would cave with bribes, some ego-stroking, and by emphasizing the military portion of The Academy. But we knew you had the most influence over your brother.

"This made you our target. You and Andrew. Andy, it turned out, was the easy target." Pete said this in a way that made me want to slap him. "He was smitten with the whole idea from day one. You—not so much."

"The easy target," I repeated in a wooden voice.

Pete's eyes slanted down at the corners. "I'm sorry. I don't mean to sound calloused. I really like Andrew; he's a great kid. I'm just trying to be as forthright as possible."

I slowly nodded. "Go on."

"So they followed you, finding very little from their surveillance because all you do is work, go to church, and take care of the boys. Then wake up and do it all over again," he summed up my life, and I cringed at how accurately and succinctly he did that. "Finally, they got a break: you were going to that church camp for a week. The Mission Team thought you needed to be thrown into the midst of a teen romance."

I shook my head in disbelief; it felt like evil gamers were playing with my life.

After my disgruntled growl, Pete continued: "So they sent Reese and Ryan on a field trip to Oklahoma. She was to friend you, gather new intel, get you warmed up. Then Ryan was supposed to swoop in and—as you so aptly put it—'razzle-dazzle' you. Didn't quite work out that way. It was pretty obvious you were only going through the motions, so they initiated the T-shirt contest to see if they could get you more motivated. And . . . voila!" He indicated himself. "I found myself recruited for a mission I was never slated for."

I felt myself go iron-bar cold. *A set up the whole time.*

"The mission was to loosen the maternal bonds with your brother by making you fall—" My face began to crumple, so he deftly rephrased, "For me. To win you over . . . you and your family."

Fresh tears stung my eyes. *No better.* Any way you wanted to look at it, it was sickening. I felt violated and humiliated. Pete looked distraught, pained, chagrined—all the things he *should* be feeling. He tried to hug me, but I scrabbled away. I should've been less mad since he *was* being so forthright, but I wasn't. My female pride and tender heart were taking a beating.

"Kate, honey. I'm sorry. I've been so torn up about it."

There he went again being a good guy. But you know what? I didn't care whether he was good or bad, or purple with pink spots. I was way too mad to see anything but red.

"A con," I spat. "Everything was a dadgum con!" We didn't have anything real. He'd been faking—*acting* like he liked me, *pretending* to find me pretty. My intuition was spotty as the rainfall round here.

I was the kind of sick that twisted intestines. I wanted to retch in the brushy bushes. Wished I would've thrown-up *on* him in the hospital—big, fat faker he was! The smoldering eyes and heart-breaking smiles, the concern, going the extra mile . . . all for the friggin' mission.

"Well congratulations, Cadet Davenport . . . job well done!" I heaved myself away from him, into the bitter cold. "Really—they should give you an armload of Oscars for your performance!" I declared, using my own arms as a tourniquet to hold myself together. I couldn't stop myself from crying, quite like the baby I was, I guess.

But really, how much could one girl take?

"I told you you would hate me," he said, sounding almost as miserable as he should.

"You were right," I sniffled out, trying hard not to fall apart over something I'd suspected the whole time. However, it was hard being reasonable about matters of the heart. He reached for me, and I recoiled back as violently as a girl who'd just had buckets of pig's blood dumped on her by all the cool kids. Waving away his second attempt at contact, I choked out, "I sh-shoulda h-hit you h-h-harder!"

It was just . . . after being so elated to see him again, sharing that wildly-passionate "interlude," and *then* having it confirmed, it made my stomach burn with shame as much as my heart break.

"Kate, listen to me. You have it wrong. It's not entirely like that."

"Yes, Pete. It's *exactly* like that . . . you just *confirmed* it." I swiped hard at my tears. "Anyhow, I guess I should be thankin' you for tellin' me the truth."

He heaved a sigh, looking down at me through those lashes. "I *do* love spending time with you . . . when we're not fighting, someone's not fighting me, and you're not bashing my head in."

"So that's to say exactly five minutes of our time together," I said.

He huffed out a chuckle. "Something like that." He pried my hand from my side to draw me back to him. I let him. I felt so weary all of a sudden. And strange. Like I was spiraling through space, hurtling towards my death, yet couldn't even get worked up enough to pull the string on my parachute. My chin dropped to my chest. He put his arm around me and rubbed at my arm as though trying to bring feeling back, but I was emotionally numb, in a near-catatonic state.

After an indeterminate amount of time, I straightened up. "I don't believe in the power of my intuition—you had me fooled, Reese and Ryan had me fooled, you all had me fooled. God! How y'all must've laughed at me!"

"Don't do this to yourself." He took my hand and squeezed. "It's *not* just you. Can't you see? I *do* have feelings for you—*inappropriate* feelings. Wrong on so many levels." He sighed and dropped my hand, staring up through the emaciated limbs of the elder tree. "I already have a hard enough time living with myself for being part of this whole sordid mess. If I took advantage of you, I'd never be able to live with myself."

I let silence speak for me.

"Kate, listen—your intuition *was* working, because I *wasn't* faking with you. I love spending time with you! *Nothing* was a lie there. You pretty much busted me on every single lie I've told since I met you . . . and they all had to do with Academy business."

I was listening.

"And the chemistry is also working both ways," he whispered, looking at me in a way that made my thigh yearn for the warmth of his palm again. "Trust me. It was the best and worst part of the job. The best—for obvious reasons. And the worst . . . because it was almost impossible to stop myself when I was around you."

I gave him a watery smile and leaned into him now, reabsorbing his warmth.

"You're just so young and inexperienced," he explained. "It would've been a crime to take that away from you."

I was silent awhile longer, cuddled up in the nook of his arm, thawing out my body and my heart. I stared out at the black bleakness, thwarted by a million stars and wondered what they had in store for us.

"Do you still hate me?" His voice sounded thick.

How could I? He was risking his neck to warn me, to tell me the truth. Inhaling as deeply as I could through a stuffed nose, I shook my head. "Nope. But I don't think I love you anymore either."

Pete tried a smile that didn't take hold. "Good." He squeezed me to him. "I don't deserve your love anyway."

"So, my first crush ended up crushing me in the end."

"God, Kate. Don't say that . . . our timing's off is all. You're everything a guy could want and more: loving, passionate, loyal, not to mention beautiful . . . but more, like, on the inside, if you can believe it," he said, using my words about my mother. (I think my face was out glowing the moon by this point.) "I could go on all night, but unfortunately, I don't think I'm gonna last much longer."

I was busy swallowing the lump in my throat when he said, "I know I've hit you with a lot of heavy stuff, but there's one more thing I need to tell you."

I searched his face in the moonlight and watched as his eyes turned sober on me. *Oh God.* I felt so fragile—like I'd shatter into a million pieces at the slightest provocation.

"Is there anything left in the flask?" It felt like I was barely able to get my mouth to move.

He gave me a watchful look before handing over the offending thing. "Just for God's sake don't hit me with it again!"

I tried forming both a smile and an apology, and couldn't quite make either one happen. Instead, I gracelessly sputtered my way through the last dregs of alcohol. "Okay, so where were we?" At this moment of suspension, dread was my most dominant emotion.

"This concerns your mother."

My heart quit pumping. "My mother?"

"I think she was an ex-cadet," he said, not mincing words.

"*What?*"

"I think she escaped and hid out here in the middle of nowhere, hiding her gifted children from the world because she was afraid The Academy would find you and snatch you back for themselves."

Even as my eyes bugged out of my head, I instantly knew he was right. Images from my childhood began whirring through my mind, things clicking into place, stacking evidence in favor of this new theory. It sure explained a lot—the paranoia about special schools, her lack of family outside our core unit, never allowing outsiders in, always reminding me to miss a few test questions. Then, when Andrew attracted so much attention in kindergarten, just giving up to home-school us. And she certainly fit the profile, I thought, seeing her natural beauty in a whole new light.

I was quiet so long Pete squeezed my leg. "Kate, think about it—it makes sense. I had my suspicions before, but when your father informed me you were so paranoid about The Academy because your mother had poisoned you against schools for gifted children, that's when I knew for sure."

I stared out into the minefield of my past so shell-shocked I couldn't even appreciate how intimately his fingers were gripping my inner thigh.

"There's other evidence too: organic farming, raising your own livestock, and I had the well water checked for impurities—it's clean. That's Academy all the way," Pete continued on as though having to convince me. I was only half tuned-in, reevaluating the whole of my existence.

"Kate . . . are you listening?" I dummy-nodded. "Good because there's more."

"More?" I whispered even as I knew what he was going to say. I thought back to how Mama always knew the right thing to do, her uncanny way with people, how she always got Daddy to do her bidding—he was like a whole different person since she died. I no longer thought it was just grief that made the immediate difference.

"Not only do I think she was an ex-cadet," he said, "but I also think she was gifted."

My head bobbled around for a while before I found my voice again. "She was."

"You knew?"

"Just found out ten seconds ago."

Pete studied my face. "One more thing . . ."

I huffed out an incredulous laugh. "Hit me with it."

"My mother is a neurobiologist and at one time headed up the Gifted Program. One of the markers of the gifted is . . ."—his eyes locked onto mine—"enlarged pupils." We stared into each other's eyes until I blinked.

"So that's why Mama always made me wear those stupid glasses in public

". . . so my large pupils could be explained by the lens magnifying them?" I wondered aloud.

"Sounds reasonable," he agreed. "That and to help hide your beauty—not that it did much good."

"Is that why you told me not to look Ranger directly in the eyes?"

He nodded. "His father was a biopsychologist who did research with my mother in the GAP program, so he would've also been familiar with that marker."

"Neurobiologist? biopsychologist?" I repeated. "You say that like I know what it means."

He smiled without feeling at his recycled words. "Let's just hope you never find out."

So Pete *had* been trying to help me. From the very beginning. I thought of all he had done for me, and just like that, the love feeling was back on—only times the power of ten.

"Think back, Kate," Pete interrupted my thoughts. "Did your mother have a scar on the back of her neck?"

I sifted back to the exact day I laid eyes on it, the visceral memory still fresh as a newly dug grave. I was still just a spindly girl with dirty knees, Andrew a wobbly toddler. We were out in the pasture on a hot summer day, the kind that melts technology left on dashboards. I remembered watching my mother lift her dark hair to allow for a breeze. She had hidden beneath that velvet curtain, a jagged, ugly scar running the length of her neck that was so incompatible with her smooth skin it made me want to cry.

"Mama!" I'd screamed, running over almost hysterical at once. "There's something real bad on the back of your neck!" I'd had an immediate visceral feeling about it that squeezed my throat and made me sick to my stomach . . . the same immediate feeling I'd gotten about The Academy.

Mama turned around to look at me, in that funny way she did when I got sudden, strong feelings about things. "This old thing? It's just a childhood battle scar, Katie-Kat, same as the one on your left knee when you fell off that swing in kindergarten."

She'd lied to me that day, but I let it go because Daddy was nearby, and I knew instinctively this wasn't a discussion to have with him around. So I waited until that night when she was tucking me into bed. She said sometimes an ugly truth is best covered up with a pretty lie . . . I would just have to trust her on that.

I looked up at Pete in awe. So many pieces of the jigsaw puzzle of my life he'd been carrying around in his pocket, only to hand over to me tonight. I thought of the brother who shared my genetic mutation, and the one who didn't. Now that I knew more of what the final picture of my life looked like, I wasn't sure I wanted to fully complete it.

"Holy shit...ake mushrooms!" I cried.

"You took the words right outta my mouth," he said, like I'd finally given him the reaction he was looking for.

"So-so she escaped, cut out her microchip," I crunched on those words like they were icy pebbles, "married my father, and moved all the way out here just so she wouldn't have to be in your academy anymore! Is it that evil? What do they do to you?"

He leveled me with another look and recycled his words: "Whatever they want."

"Why don'tja just quit?"

Pete took in another breath, cradling the side of his head in his hand. "You can't . . . so I've been trying to get kicked out for years."

"How's that workin' out?"

"Not so good," he said. "My parents keep saving my sorry ass." He grunted, shifting into a more comfortable position; it looked like he was having a hard time even sitting up now. "I think botching this mission—which I must say I've done an admiral job of—would've finally done the trick." He mangled a smile.

I was still in data processing mode when Pete slumped, finally rousing me from my self-absorption. Looking closely at him now, I saw that he looked truly terrible. His head had stopped bleeding, but clumps of blood matted his hair, his face was ashen, and shadows that had nothing to do with the darkness hollowed his eyes. He looked like he was in dire need of that shot he'd given me a few weeks ago. So preoccupied with the onslaught of mind-bending information, I'd totally overlooked the fact that Pete was in the midst of his own crisis.

"Pete! God! Sorry! I forgot you're still hurt and . . . messed up," I said for lack of a better word. But it was more than a little apt, and I felt terrible f or adding to his pain. I just realized all he was giving up: his parents, security, the whole of his life as he knew it. I'd seen the fear on his face when he appeared on my doorstep. I thought of all the stress he was under now because of the risk he took to warn me and was beyond grateful for his help. And it was beyond time for me to start helping him back. A strong, compulsive urge to hug him overcame me, so I did.

"We can talk about this later. Right now, let's get you inside and fixed up." Stiff-jointed, I struggled to my feet first, then helped Pete do the same.

"Told you," he said, swaying a bit. "We can't talk in there."

"Yeah, but it's a much better place to perform surgery than the cold, hard ground . . . with a dirty knife."

"That's what the alcohol was for."

"Well I hate to tell you," I said, "but I just drank the last bit of sanitizer." Pete leaned pretty heavily on me now, a sacked quarterback. "Come on." I urged him on, and he objected, but in a pro forma way that led me to believe he was very nearly on the verge of collapse.

Together we trudged back to the house, the glowing lights from our tatty trailer a welcoming beacon from the cold darkness and grim news.

39

HACKJOB

"We can do the deed in the bathroom and then you can sleep in my bed," I declared, helping him up the porch. My thoughts—and my body—immediately warmed at this idea. "Daddy's always the last one up in the morning, so I can sneak you out early." I craned my neck around. "Where's the Hummer?"

"I came on a motorcycle; it's parked in the shed," Pete answered, then hesitated in the doorway. "Listen, Kate . . . there may be more bugs in the house than I know of. We'll have to be extremely careful in case they're listening in."

After I nodded my understanding, we stumbled our way into my bedroom, where Pete immediately face-planted across my wagon-wheel bed. Relieved of my load, I stepped back and took a moment to soak him in. He was in pretty bad shape, like one button-snap away from coming undone. My own nerves were jangling wildly about. *Gah!* I hit him pretty good and hoped he didn't have a concussion. *Maybe he just had too much to drink?* I tried to convince myself.

I leaned over his inert form. "Wait here while I get some supplies," I said unnecessarily, because he wasn't likely going anywhere anytime soon. He half groaned an acknowledgement.

I pushed back everything I'd learned tonight to the back of my brain so I could concentrate. I was good in an emergency—steady. The kind of person you'd want in your foxhole . . . or so I'd always prided myself on. He deserved me at my best after all he'd done for me. I'd only repaid him with anger, violence, and a hard time. I wouldn't let him down now. In his hour of need.

He was obviously falling apart on me. It wasn't like him to be so unprepared and unsure of himself. I thought of him pouring alcohol, from a flask he was guzzling from, over a paring knife, confiscated from my kitchen. For me to cut his—I mentally cringed—*microchip* out. Sloppy and haphazard: two words I'd never associated with Pete Davenport.

I scurried to the medicine cabinet and wrenched it open. *Doh!* We were running low on bandages and didn't have near the size we needed. Growling, I grabbed alcohol and the last web of gauze before adding tweezers, surgical tape, and clean washcloths from the linen closet to my stockpile. I set them all out on the bathroom counter, then stood, tapping my fingers. *Oh yeah.* Digging back into the medicine cabinet, I came away with a sticky tube of antibiotic cream and my bottle of "happy pills," just in case. Then I hustled to the kitchen and rummaged around some more for our handy-dandy role of duct tape and a Sharpie before heading off to Daddy's bathroom to nab a razorblade from under his sink. While slipping it out of the cartridge, I noticed, on a side note, that his scotch stash was almost depleted.

Back in the bathroom, I dumped the remainder of the supplies and swiped down the whole area with alcohol. The sharp chemical smell dizzied me, so that I was well on my way to hyperventilating myself into passing out. I went into the hall to get some air and calm down, pacing and prayer chanting: *Please God, let me get this right!* over and over until my hands stopped shaking. And it was with a calm demeanor that I went in to rouse my patient for surgery.

"Pete." I shook his shoulder.

"Hmmph?"

"It's time."

His obsidian eyes opened, and I saw the whites of his eyes, usually so brilliant against the dark iris and black pupil, were veined with red—stress and lack of sleep—I knew the look well.

I drew his hand to my chest. "Pete, are you sure?" Eyes tightening with determination, he nodded. "Okay," I said, "come on."

Pete hoisted himself up only to slide to the floor, reaching around under my bed for a second before coming up with a small metal disk. Like the boys with their creepy acquisitions, he held it in his palm for my inspection, this thing more revolting than any insect. I shook my head at him. He grimaced back at me and hung his head. I exhaled some sharp air and helped him back up (he almost helped me down), and we made it to the bathroom, where he immediately flushed the dang thing down the toilet. Then he stood, unconsciously stooping a little beneath the low ceiling, his eyes roving over the array of crude surgical instruments lined up on the counter. He picked up the black marker.

"A Sharpie? Duct tape?" Humor infused his tone.

I nodded sagely. "Never underestimate the power of duct tape."

Pete lifted half a lip. "I'll keep that in mind." Suddenly, he yanked me forward. "Kate," he searched my face, "are you *sure* you wanna do this?"

I nodded. We were leaned in whispering, in case of waking sleeping boys or bugs without antennae. "Don't worry," I assured him. "It'll be quick and I have my leftover pain pills to give you. . . . I know you're not supposed to take them when you've been drinkin' alcohol, but I think maybe you should take just one before we begin."

He looked at me intently for a long moment. "No. I mean take the boys and run away with me—it's the only way I know you'll be safe, and we can be together."

My eyes widened a split second before I jerked my head up and down. I'd never been more sure about anything. Pete rewarded me with a sloppy smile and fastened his hand behind my neck, bringing our mouths so close together I almost forgot why we were standing there. We stared, forehead-to-forehead and pupil-to-pupil, until all I could see was my own reflection.

"Okay, Nurse Kate—let's do this thing."

I smiled as if lit from within, ridiculously happy despite the morbid circumstances. "Don't you mean *Dr.* Connelly?"

He huffed out an amused chuckle. "Right. I'm all yours, Dr. Connelly."

"Okay," I said, shifting into business mode again. "First, take this." I handed him one of my happy pills and Mikey's Spidey cup filled with tap water.

"Bottoms up," he said before downing it like a good boy.

"Sit down." I indicated the stepstool. He obliged immediately, and I drew his head forward, cradling it to my stomach. Brushing aside the soft fringe at the nape of his neck, I fingered along the edge of the thin, precise scar. Sure enough, there was a small sliver of a foreign object. Really *really* hard, is how I tried not to freak out while I marked it with the Sharpie.

Pausing there to breathe, I detected, right beneath Pete's euphorically sweet smell, a sharp whiff of sweat coming off him—the odor of anxiety. And my heart squeezed for all the trouble he'd gone to to save us Connelly kids from the same fate. I squeezed him to me, taking a moment to knead the worry knots from his back. After his muscles began to relax, I very gently felt along the side of his head for the small lump. When I bumped up against it, he immediately flinched.

"Look at me," I commanded, staring deeply into his eyes again. I knew these eyes—had been examining them for the better part of two months. Except for being clouded with fear and pain, they still looked the same—no concussion.

"Okay, take off your shirt," I ordered.

Pete tilted his head, looking up at me with one eye closed. Grinned. "Yes ma'am" slid out the corner of his mouth before he reached for the bottom of his torn shirt and yanked it over his head.

Oh man! I paused to swallow. He nearly knocked *me* out. I had to focus, and staring at his bare chest was *not* the way to do that. After a little throat clearing, I said, "Okay, kneel down and hold your head over the sink."

He obliged, his neck exposed as one before a guillotine. I picked up the intimidating, straight-edged blade and made to make my first incision.

"Kate, wait!"

Swear to God, my head almost crashed through the ceiling I jumped so high. "Pete! Dagnabbit! Don't ever do that again!" I hissed. "You almost made me slice your dang neck off!" One hand flew to my chest like it could regulate my heartbeat.

"Sorry. It's just . . . I can't guarantee I won't make any noise." Pete rose to his feet again, unbuckling his belt before unlooping it from his jeans. I couldn't help notice how they slipped down an inch or so lower on his hips, revealing an extraordinary V-shape I was suddenly very interested in. I swallowed again. He placed a strip of belt in his mouth, biting down to test the pliability of the leather. He nodded at me.

"Right. Of course," I hastily said as though I were perfectly in control. *So that's what he was doing outside earlier.* Remorse hit me, like a slap in the face. "Ready?" I wasn't sure if I was talking to him or me.

He nodded his head again, and leaned back over. I swabbed the back of his neck, my hand, and the edge of the razorblade with alcohol. After a deep breath and a quick finger cross, I proceeded to slice open the beautiful, smooth flesh of his neck. Bright blood bloomed along the incision line, making it impossible to see my marked line immediately. He sucked in a sharp pocket of air but otherwise remained quiet while the blade parted the thin layers of dermis like I was skinning a chicken. (But with the added burden of my subject being alive and bleeding.) His muscles alternately clenched and spasmed, but he held his head steady as was humanly possible with someone slicing into you with a razorblade. Finished with my incision, I put down the blade to lift up the flap of skin and probe for the chip.

My heart sank—the incision wasn't deep enough.

I would have to recut deeper, down to the bony segments of cervical vertebrae. My stomach lurched at the thought of butchering the one depending on me to get it right. As I relayed what more I had to do, I tried to keep my voice steady, even as my entire being trembled. Pete just nodded his head, gasping and straining to hold still as I sank the razor deeper into his skin. The blade hit upon the object I was searching for, and his head jerked up with a mangled groan. His jaw muscles clenched together. Blood dripped down both sides of his neck, hitting the sink in violent splotches before running down the drain in a river of gore.

"Sorry, Pete! I found it. Hold on just a second longer while I dig it out . . . It's really small," I added unnecessarily.

I put down the bloody instrument-of-torture to pick up my pre-sanitized, pharmacy-grade tweezers. And with a firm grip on the chip, I tugged. But it just pulled at the skin, appearing to be bonded with the tissue. I would literally have to hack it away from his moist, bloody tissue. Feeling that dread would only add to his misery, I decided not to inform him of anything else.

How do you do the thing you don't want to do?

You just do it. So I did, slicing it out of there as close to the oblong cylinder as possible while leaving the tissue behind. This I did while Pete banged into the plywood cabinet with his knee.

It was a hackjob to be sure, but the dadgum thing was out.

"Got it," I announced in his ear before dumping a whole bunch of alcohol on the gaping hole left by my inexpert excavation.

An ugly guttural noise escaped his throat, but I didn't bother blowing on the wound before mopping up the excess bloody alcohol from his neck with a sun-stiffened washcloth. Instead, I quickly cut strips of surgical tape, mentally chastising myself for not doing this chore pre-op. Then, squeezing the flapping-gap closed with one hand, I applied surgical tape with the other, praying it would hold the incision closed for the night. I smeared a thick layer of antibiotic cream on top, added the thin layer of gauze over that, and then watched, horrified, as it immediately seeped blood. *Dang it*! Using the last-resort-clean-washcloth, I secured it mightily over the soaked gauze using a double dosing of duct tape. Done.

I sagged over him. "It's over, Pete . . . You can get up now," I whispered while hands—the color of murder—covered my face. I breathed in and out the rusting-metal smell of his blood until I was able to stand long enough to wash it from my hands. Pete remained down a little longer, alternately groaning and cursing under his breath.

My hand trembled to his arm. "Pete?"

He rose to stare at my ashen face. "Well that was no fun."

The understatement made me giggle like a loon for a hysterical moment. "Oh God, Pete! I'm sorry! I know that was awful!" I half-wailed, half-whispered.

"Good Lord, Kate! What were you doin' back there? Diggin' for gold?"

"I'm so sorry!" I snuffled into his chest, having to lean on him for support. He immediately fell back onto the stepstool, and my head immediately dropped onto his shoulder. I felt like I'd butchered him up for good. Tears amassed in my eyes.

He graciously put his arms around me and sighed, slack-mouthed. "Bioglass is designed to bond with the surrounding tissue . . . 'snot your fault."

I quit my indulgent sniffling. He was beginning to slur. If he passed out, no way I could pry him off the floor without a forklift. "Come on," I urged, "let's get you to bed." As soon as Pete stood back up, he swayed, so I hug-walked him to my bed, where he sprawled out on his side facing me. His eyes closed so firmly I was half afraid if I lifted the lids, I'd be facing X's.

Kneeling before him, I brushed the damp hair from his forehead. "Can I get you anything else?"

His eyes rolled open. "My souvenir."

I nodded and turned the ceiling fan on for him before returning a moment later with the miniscule glass vial. I held it up for his inspection. He surprised me with the valor of his grin.

"Well done, Dr. Connelly!" he praised me, slipping it into the front pocket of his jeans.

A wobbly smile was all I could give him until I thought to run to the kitchen for a frozen bag of peas. After gently crowning him with it, I headed to the bathroom and hurriedly cleaned it up before the boys woke up to discover their bathroom looked like a crime scene.

It was rounding about midnight now, and I couldn't believe Daddy had stayed away this whole time. I didn't ruminate about it though, because Pete occupied all of my attention. I stared down at my patient, marveling at the role-reversal, as I prepared to stay up all night to watch over him.

A rousing growl from his throat. "Katie-Kat . . . come to bed." He beckoned to me, half-in, half-out.

Didn't have to ask me twice. After locking the door, I paused then hid behind my nightstand to slip out of my jeans and into my tree-hugger shirt. With an amused lip twitch, Pete scooched over, and I dove in, snuggling into his bare torso. He threw a heavy arm around me, tucking me in closer so that we fit as exactly as two Russian nesting dolls. The heat from his chest warmed my skin through my T-shirt, and the beating of his heart felt steady and sure against my back. He squeezed me tight, breathed in deeply, then exhaled as one does after a long ordeal is finally over.

"That's better," he murmured.

"Pete," I whispered, another unanswered question just occurring to me. "Hmmph?"

"What were those metal detectors *really* for?"

A heavy sigh stirred my hair. "A chip was found a few miles from your ranch. We were headed out to look for it that night. Tol' you . . . *was* a coincidence we saw you walkin' that night . . . good thing." He squeezed me again, snuggling into me.

And that was the last thing I heard from him until the very soft snoring in my ear that I intended to tease him about in the morning.

40

SHARK IN A FISH TANK

I was sleeping, cocooned in the comfort of Pete's arms, when something like an echo roused me into awareness. Not an echo exactly, more like whatever comes before an echo—a flicker of a synapse, a whisper of danger. *Something. Daddy?* Had he returned home to find his daughter sleeping in the arms of the cadet he trusted? I'd locked the door, but he could've picked the lock. It was as easy as poking one of his toothpicks through the miniscule aperture until the lock popped. No, if Daddy were aware of last night's sleeping arrangements, I'd know it by the bellowing.

Instead of feeling relieved, I was alarmed. I knew, instinctively, to keep my eyes shut a little longer. Feigning sleep, I surreptitiously ran a hand under the covers along the ridges of Pete's stomach. This elicited a pleasurable little groan and a slight tightening of his arms—not the reaction I was looking for this morning. I hated to pinch him, I really did, but my instinct was telling me it was time for the sleeping cadet to wake up.

I would've given anything not to open my eyes and face the music, or the buzz kill, or *whatever* was out there that needed my attention. After drawing in a last deep breath of intoxicating contentment, I gave Pete's thigh a warning squeeze. Then flicked my eyes open. The sight that awaited me was so bizarre that I insta-closed them again, dismissing it as being way too preposterous to be real. Must be a dream. Scratch that—a nightmare. But just to be sure, I reopened my eyes . . .

. . . to Ranger. Kicked back in the armchair in the corner, legs splayed out and crossed at the ankles. Staring at us. Or I guess *me* since it was my eyes that were open. A huge comical grin split his face. That was weird enough. But what was weirder, the preposterous part—he was wearing my tortious-shell glasses.

"Good mornin', Glasses!" he greeted in the same kind of voice one usually says *Cheerio, top of the morin' to ya!*

I shifted into panic mode at the speed of light. For one: the grin on his mouth didn't match the furor in his eyes. For two: he wasn't even remotely trying to be quiet. For three: *Ranger* was in my bedroom!

This is bad. Very bad. My heart seized.

"I'n't that sweet?" he sneered. "Katie and Petey sittin' in a tree, k-i-s-s-i-n-g," he sing-songed, then leaning forward, he squared up his knees. "But aren't you kinda sleeping with the enemy? That is . . . unless Cadet Davenport has switched sides on me. To tell you the truth, I'm not sure *what's* going on. All I know is—I turn around, and my underling's gone *AWOL.*"

I made my first move to sit up at the same time Pete's body stiffened. I was pretty sure he was only pretending to be asleep now, although the rise and fall of his chest hadn't changed rhythm. I would try to stall Ranger as long as possible while Pete hopefully thought of some kind of James Bond move to get us out of this situation.

Meanwhile, Ranger removed the glasses—Pete had gifted me—from his face to inspect the lens. And then, in a move that sent chills down my spine, he snapped the delicate frame in two—a vile sound akin to a rib breaking.

"Congratulations, Miss Connelly on being the very first civilian girl who isn't exactly what she appears to be." He froze any move I was about to make with his words. ". . . Guess I'm gonna have to get a new nickname for you."

"What are you doin' here?" It wasn't the cleverest comeback, but it got the ball rolling.

Ranger chuckled. "Why to divest you of your gifted brother, of course."

The unmistakable edge of sarcasm jarred me further. "Isn't that what Pete's here for?" Playing dumb, I remained sprawled against Pete's inert form, not exactly sure whether I should move away; it felt like shielding him was the right thing to do—violence radiated off Ranger.

He laughed without an ounce of humor. "Cut the bullshit, Annie Oakley. The jig is up. You two love birds are in a lot of—"

A whiz of something solid flew past my head, landing with a shattering crash against the wall behind Ranger's ear. Apparently, Pete had grabbed a picture off my nightstand and hurled it at the intruder in the corner mouthing off. Ranger narrowly—I mean *narrowly*—missed getting hit in the head with the corner of the gold frame that housed my mother's picture. He must've been expecting it, or else he never would have been able to duck in time. I instantly thought how sad Mama would've been that it missed the mark.

A half-second later and both cadets were facing off in ready position— almost laughable in the cubbyhole confines of my room. Having Ranger in our trailer instantly felt like someone just stuck a shark in a fish tank.

"Don't you think you should've removed the chip *before* you came to get the girl," Ranger taunted.

"Wasn't thinking that far in advance," Pete retorted calmly.

"Not very smart, Davenport. But I always knew you had shit for brains."

"I have been told I don't quite have the right character for espionage."

Ranger barked out a harsh laugh. Hatred crackled the air between them. A few more seconds and they would tear at each other's throats with their twitchy hands. I had to do something fast, but felt myself slow to catch up to where they already were.

My feet, still tangled in pink gingham, found mattress. "Stop!" I screamed, throwing my arms out like a referee. Not even a single hair on either cadet stirred. I tried again. "My father's in the next room, and he's likely gonna be in here with his shotgun in two seconds . . . so I'd leave if I were you!" I threw out the empty threat, for if my father were available, he would've already come crashing through that door wielding his shotgun. And we all knew it.

Ranger spared me a quick, smirky glance that managed to convey a lot.

"I mean it," I said in a voice less weighty than a potato chip. Obviously, Daddy was . . . indisposed. Two sleeping angels in superhero sheets flashed in my mind. "Where are my brothers?" I demanded, refocusing.

Ranger did the maniacal laughing thing.

"*Where* are my brothers?" I repeated in a deadly voice.

"Which one? The gifted one or the ungifted one?" he inquired pleasantly.

"Both." I picked up the next frame.

Ranger smiled like my move was cute. "They're a little tied up at the moment."

I'm ashamed to say the frame fell from my hand the same time I tigress-leaped off my bed. Landing by the door, I had one hand on the handle poised to dart out, when my flight was stalled by a pair of waiting catcher's mitts grabbing me around the waist. Ranger crushed me to him as I fought to leave, calling loudly for my brothers.

Why isn't Pete helping?

Batting away to no avail, I tried my ole standby—head butt to the face, but he twisted my head around in a move my brothers refer to as a headlock. "Lemme go you—" Whatever I was going to say was choked off. Couldn't move. Couldn't breathe. I was no better off than a bunny in a wolf's jaws.

"Let her go, Ranger!" Pete ordered. ". . . It's me you want."

"I'm not so sure, Pete. You're not exactly my type. She's not either, for that matter. However, she *is* a little prettier . . . though not by much."

The witty one began doling out one cruel squeeze for each useless whap, claw, or kick I landed.

"You know . . ." he started, unfazed by the girl gargling for mercy beneath him. "I'm sure you were probably wondering this whole mission why the hell The Academy is spending so much time and money on young Andrew Connelly. He does of course look the part and *almost* has all the qualities we're looking for in young recruits . . . except for the *one* thing Weston wants most"—he tweaked my nose—"giftedness. I'd already figured it out, of course, a long time ago."

Ranger twisted my head up so that I was staring into his cold blue eyes. "You see, it's a classic case of bait and switch: golden-boy Andrew was the bait. Unfortunately for him, he's not the Connelly The Academy's looking for . . . so I'll be making the switch today." He smiled snake-like at me.

Pete stepped forward. Ranger retaliated by squeezing my head in a boa-constrictor grip that had me seeing stars.

"Careful, Ranger!" Pete quickly warned. "You don't want to spoil the merchandise. Don't forget she suffered a concussion a few weeks ago. Think how pissed Weston would be if you brought her back damaged goods."

"That's probably just more bullshit you wrote in your reports to throw us off the trail," countered Ranger, but he loosened his hold. "So tell me, Davenport . . . what's your exit strategy?"

"Working on one as we speak," Pete reported mildly.

Ranger huffed out another mirthless chuckle. "You always did go off half-cocked. Speaking of which . . ." He removed the arm clamp from around my head long enough to remove a gun from behind his back.

So that's why Pete hadn't made a move.

During this impressive display of showmanship, Ranger's other arm had remained fastened around my neck, steadfastly tightening. I was dizzy with panic and lack of oxygen. *Think!* I couldn't let a monster like Ranger win. I had to do *something*, so I did *nothing*. Playing possum, I quit fighting and slumped over. With every ounce of weight I had. It took a couple of moments before Ranger swore and loosened his grip . . . just enough I could gasp for air. Gulping once, I tucked down my chin, and bit into his forearm.

"Fu—aaaagh!" he howled, shaking me off while Pete kicked the gun out of his hand. Ranger dropped me like a hot branding iron so the real battle could ensue. He retaliated with a fast fist to Pete's face. Pete went sprawling backwards onto my dresser. A split second later, Ranger went back for the gun. I dove for it—just beating him—and tossed it out of his reach. A kick to my soft innards was my reward for that endeavor. I cried out, clutching my gut and rolling around on the floor in agony. What little breath I'd purchased was just knocked out of me.

Pete rallied with my alarm clock, hurling it like a grenade at Ranger's head. Ranger deflected it with his hand, causing it to ricochet into the wall with a clang. He swore and shook out his hand.

"Playing dirty, Davenport? I didn't think that was your style."

Please don't take the bait, I thought right as Pete dropped the jagged piece of tulip lamp in his hand. My heart dropped anchor to my gut. I wanted to protest but felt myself sucking air through straw (and that straw had leaks).

They circled each other like furious lions. From my insect view, I saw the duct tape was holding steady. But I couldn't hold on to a second of relief because the elite cadets began exchanging blows, fighting in weird jabs and darts, swift kicks, and more thrown objects. A wooden hanger hurtled at Pete, only to be caught and hurled right back. I wasn't aware my bedroom stored so many weapons. Now Ranger used his mass advantage to bulldoze Pete back into my dresser. Pete slammed two fists down, hard and fast, into Ranger's ears. Ranger roared in pain and fury. Somehow the dresser got dumped over in all the chaos, and they started wrestling around on the contents of my wardrobe.

I saw that things could go either way. And I wasn't the kind to cower behind some upended furniture, peeping out every-once-in-a-while to scream while the villain beat up on the hero until the hero was able to rally. For one thing, my hero was working at a disadvantage this morning being both injured and hungover. Plus, Ranger ambushed us while we were sleeping, and I considered that cheating. Not to mention that he was the type of guy who looked like he chewed up HGH for breakfast every morning. Oh, and there was the little matter of him bringing a gun.

The gun! Where was it? It was lost under a blanket of covers, clothes, and combat objects. I scrounged for it until my hard-backed bible went soaring past my head, and then I duck-dove out of the way of Ranger's foot as it went through dry wall. They were going to break down my walls if they didn't break each other first. Finally, I rallied to crawl to the door, where I stood, a shocked survivor from the battlefield. Ignoring the pain radiating from my midsection, I half-lurched, half-limped into my father's room to get his gun down for the second time in eight hours. I was dismayed to find my father splayed across his bed like a felled grizzly across the hood of a Chevy, snoring away peacefully while World War III broke out in his house. Drugged no doubt.

God he was worthless.

Crap! The gun was missing—still outside by the elm tree! Adrenaline pumped my legs out the door to go fetch it, despite my achy gut. When I picked it up, it felt satisfyingly heavy in my hands. I lope-limped back into the chaos. Crashes, smashes, and grunts greeted me at the door. I needed to get back to the frontlines, but some instinct steered my body towards my brothers' room instead. Slamming through the door, I found them lying on top of their beds. Bound and gagged. The whites of their eyes flashed terror, tears streaming over wind-chapped cheeks. I howled with fury. Spinning back to the bathroom, I dug the razorblade from the bottom of the trashcan. And, still working on instinct, I ran it back to Mikey and sawed through his ropes.

"Untie your brother and run!" I screamed as though my mouth weren't right next to his ear. Then me and my shotgun crashed into the now ominously silent bedroom. I came upon Ranger, dangling the same piece of broken lamp that Pete had dropped earlier. Over Pete's face.

"Guess good guys really do finish last" was just coming from a sweating, heaving, bleeding Ranger. Even in the midst of the crisis, he sounded like he was reading from the villain's role of a bad western.

On cue, I delivered my own line: "Not today they don't." Theatrically, I cocked back the hammer of the shotgun.

Ranger guttered a laugh. His hands reluctantly went up as the jagged glass went down. "I was wondering where that shotgun had run off to."

"Right now, it's pointed at your back." I nudged him with the barrel to prove my point.

He started laughing again—at me, Pete, the situation, I wasn't sure. "You're quite the little Tom cat, Miss Connelly. Maybe that'll be my new nickname for you at The Academy . . . Katie-Kat seems a little too tame for you."

"Stand up." I punctuated this command with a hard kidney poke.

Ranger slowly rose, the grin on his face made more malevolent looking by the blood dripping from his mouth. I peeped around the architecture of man, standing between me and Pete, who didn't look so good. He was also bleeding. Profusely. And I wondered, with a shot of fear, if the blood smeared all over Ranger was actually Pete's. I saw the washcloth had finally come off—ripped off most likely. I didn't see how it could've *fallen* off. Hot anger oozed from me. I leveled Ranger with a decimating glare.

"Come on, Connelly," Ranger cajoled. "You know you're not going to shoot me . . . I believe that's Commandment numero uno in the Good Book: Thou shalt not kill."

"Number six," I corrected.

"Huh," he said, using his shoulder to wipe some blood from his lip. "Could've sworn that was the first one. . . . What is number one, then?" He seemed genuinely interested.

"Thou shalt not have any Gods before me."

"Well, I guess it's true—you *do* learn something new every day."

"But it don't say nothin' 'bout shootin' off a foot," I warned as he made to move. He appeared to kick at something—most likely the pistol. I stalled him with my aim.

"Well it ought to . . . doesn't seem very Christian-like," Ranger put out there, along with an arched black brow.

I could hear Pete start to rally a little. "Pete, are you okay?"

He kind of groaned from the floor, holding his head in one hand and giving the thumbs up with the other.

"You know what I can't believe?" Ranger inquired pleasantly, despite the fact he was still dripping blood all over my carpet. Neither one of us answered him, so he continued on. "Well, quite a few things really . . . like how you could prefer slummin' it out here, at the warty, bare-ass end of civilization with trailer-trash, to your privileged life at The Academy for one." He used the same conversational tone members of the church did when socializing at potluck dinners.

Ranger went to go on with his monologue, but Pete had to protest this. Grunting, he muscled himself into upright position. "You don't deserve to lick the dust off her boots, you piece of shit asshole," he said, managing to rise unsteadily to his feet.

Ranger looked at my face in mock horror, yet seemed utterly delighted by this. "Now that don't seem Christian-like at all. Am I right, Kate? . . . Doesn't seem like you've been a very good influence on him."

"Don't even say her name," Pete warned, grabbing the discarded, busted lamp globe that seemed to be a key player in this battle (and it was pink no less). He pointed it at Ranger.

"Wow. You got it bad, man. I almost feel sorry for you. But I've digressed too far already regarding your poor choice in women—oops!—*girls,* I should say." Ranger seemed so smug, like someone who was sure they were holding the ace of spades, and not like someone who was outnumbered and on the receiving end of a long-barrel shotgun. "Know what else I can't believe?" He cleared his throat. "I said . . . know what else I can't believe?"

"What?" I felt safe enough to take the bait now that I had a gun. I raised it up a fraction, but had a sinking feeling.

". . . That no one bothered to check to see if there were actually any bullets in that old thing." With a vicious laugh Ranger lunged forward, yanking the barrel to him. I countered by pulling the trigger to what I knew would be a very disappointing—*click.*

"I can't believe you did that!" preceded a whap of a slap that left my ears ringing. Ranger followed up by wrestling me into another headlock. *Honestly, did he have no other moves?* When I could focus, it was to see that Pete now had Ranger's pistol in his hand. *Halleluiah! . . .* I was wondering where he'd got off to during that whole exchange.

"It's over Davenport. Drop the gun, or I'm snapping your girlfriend's neck, just like her glasses." Ranger wasn't kidding around. I was already blacking out—for real this time. I tried shaking my head no. Wanted to yell: *Take the boys and run!* But the only noise I was making was a very scary gurgling in the back of my throat.

For the second time, I wished Pete wasn't such a good guy because— *clunk!*—of course, he dropped the dadgum thing. Ranger immediately released a little of the pressure. Still, I couldn't see, the blurry spots now blacking out my carpet. I fought to stay awake, not liking the direction things were going. The bad guy was currently winning. Winning and kneeling down—taking my head with him—while he snatched up the gun. He stood us back up, pointed it at Pete, cackled: "You lose Davenport. I got the gun. I got the girl . . . Game over!"

I was just thinking: *too bad he doesn't have a handle bar mustache to pull,* when out of nowhere a little ball of fury came hurtling in, charging at the giant. Ranger simply knocked him to the ground, where he landed on a pile of clothes.

"Mikey!" I screamed. "Get outta here!" Mikey just hauled himself up to face off with Ranger, in a David-and-Goliath-like manner.

"You got a slingshot in your back pocket, shorty?" Ranger asked, like, amused despite himself. I couldn't believe we were thinking along the same lines . . . spooked me a little.

"You let Kadee go wight now!" Mikey shrieked up at the cadet so hard he looked possessed.

Inexplicably, Ranger immediately complied. I fell to my knees, gasping for breath. Mikey flew over to save me and knocked me over. By the time I scrambled to my feet, Ranger's face was looking about the same as Mikey's from a moment ago—possessed.

Pete spoke next in a sure, commanding voice: "Mikey, tell him to drop the gun."

Ranger bellowed now, all sense of superior calm depleted from his voice. "Slater, back up!"

What's going on? That was a strange thing Pete just said. And then it dawned on me—who the gifted brother really was. Of course! Mikey also had the enlarged pupils. I wrapped my arms around my littlest brother, who was busy staring down the giant. "Tell him to drop the gun again," I whispered in his ear.

"Slater! Get your ass in here!" Ranger yelled so loudly, I wondered if he knew the bedroom bug was swimming around the cesspool.

"Hurry, Mikey!" I exhorted.

Eyes trained on Ranger, Mikey patted my face. "Dwop the gun," he said, voice trembling.

Ranger's muscles strained, his face going the color of boys in P.E. during a pull-up. His hand began to shake from the effort of holding on to the gun, so he brought the other one up to steady it.

I could tell it wouldn't be long now. Slater (whoever that was) was on his way. They were better prepared than us. After all, it had been an ambush. No wonder Ranger had been so smug this whole time—he hadn't come alone. They would win. We would lose. I felt it clearly now — in that peculiar way I had — the way this would all pan out.

I knew what must be done. They weren't going to hurt us—we Connelly kids. But they *would* the bleeding renegade who had turned on them to warn me. Very soon, I wasn't sure how long, Pete would be dragged from here. Maybe never to return. I had to save him.

While Ranger was preoccupied with controlling his gun-holding hand, I turned my conviction on to Pete, grabbing hold of his arm. He tore his eyes away from Ranger. It seemed like we hadn't so much as glanced at each other since this whole mess started. Seemed like forever, but was probably only the span of a handful of minutes.

"Pete," I breathed, "you have to run! They're not gonna hurt us. But you . . . God, Pete! You have to go!"

"Not happening."

"Pete, please. You have to trust me. Run! Now!"

"I'm not leaving you guys behind."

A *bang*! like the back door just got blown off its hinges, interrupted us. Ranger was still hanging on to the gun. Barely. He was sweating and shaking, and obviously in so much pain, he looked like a man who needed to be put down.

Mikey kept repeating: "Dwop the gun."

I thought his voice was too quiet, like he was just saying the words. "Harder Mikey. Yell it like you mean it!"

"Dwop the *guuuuuuunnnn!*" Mikey bellowed.

Heavy boots could be heard tromping efficiently through the house. I slammed the door and locked it. Ranger was now bent over at an odd angle, his face contorting into a grotesque grimace, like Bell's Palsy had suddenly struck. The pistol finally shook from his hand, dropping—right into Pete's hot hands.

Why am I not relieved?

"Run, Pete! *Please!* . . . It's your only chance."

His only move was to turn the gun back on Ranger, who was on the floor gasping for breath. A loud *Crack*! from combat boot splintering hollow wood rattled us. I would've laughed under normal circumstances—all he had to do was use an insignificant toothpick to do the job. But I was so scared my knees were actually knocking together.

Then several things happened at once: The foot attached to that boot bludgeoned through the door, creating a manhole right in the middle of the flimsy thing; Ranger yelled, "Dart the littlest boy!" and I paid him back with a swift kick to *his* gut; he groaned and rolled over. A calm voice behind the door said, "Drop the gun. We have the boy and your father, and we won't hesitate to shoot unless you toss the gun through the hole in three seconds."

Why's Andrew still here?

Pete spoke up, using the same level tone. "The boy is gifted, and the mission has been to get him for months—you can't harm him unless you want Weston up your ass."

This was getting more complicated by the minute. I could barely keep up . . . and I was right in the thick of things.

"No, he's not! The gifted one's in here, and he needs a tag, ASAP!" Ranger hollered back while quickly rolling away from my attempts to thank him for clearing things up. He grabbed my foot out from under me, and I went down on my backside, landing like a breech birth in the messy aftermath of our war.

"You weave my sistuh awone!" Mikey screamed, kicking him in the foot.

"Stayawayfromhim!" jetted from my throat in a hysterical mangle, like he was one step away from the devil. I grab-carried my brother to the window with the intent of dropping him outside.

Debating was going on outside of that door. Someone had ungagged Andrew because he was shrieking my name. Felt like my ears would bleed from the sheer terror in it. I clutched Mikey to me like a teddybear, unsure what to do next. Pete stepped up to the mound, hurling the last picture frame at Ranger. This time it hit the mark—the middle of his back—cutting off more orders.

"You open your mouth again, and the next time you walk, it'll be with a peg leg," Pete said. Statement, no threat.

I was thinking we were at a stalemate, so wrenched open the window feeling like we *did* need an exit strategy. A couple of quiet minutes later, and they made the next move. It was a good one. *Bastards!* My blood froze at the sight before my eyes: Andrew's head, stuffed through the manhole, with a noose fasted around his neck.

"Katie!" he screamed, his face almost unrecognizable in his terror.

Pete and I exchanged dark looks. *God help us!* I was shaking like our washer in the spin cylce. "Mikey!" I shrilled. "Tell them to let Andrew go!"

"You let my bruthuh go!"

Nothing happened . . . except someone on the other side pulled the rope tighter. Andrew's face turned the color of Red Death.

"Again, Mikey!" I panted, panic constricting my lungs.

"Let my bwuthuh *goooooooo!*" he bellowed with all his might, tender vocal cords cracking under pressure.

This only succeeded in Andrew's tethers tightening further. Veins popped out on his forehead like uprooted trees, his eyes bulged from their sockets, noiseless gasping jerked his head. It was the most gruesome and sickening sight of my life . . . and I'd watched my mama die.

I looked over at Pete, horrified to find a matching expression on his face.

"We're going to give you one last chance to save your brother's life," the voice on the other side said, loosening the noose so that Andrew could suck a lungful of air.

I was a pillar of fear and indecision. "Why isn't it *workin*?" I screeched at Pete as if he had all the answers.

"I-think-he-has-to-have-eye-contact," Pete replied, rapid fire. "I'm shooting Ranger's leg in two seconds if you don't remove the noose," he informed calmly. "One . . ."

Ranger made a move (another good one)—dive-snatching Mikey right out from under me. *What the?!* I retaliated with a punch to his face when I shoulda moved out of the way so that Pete could follow up on his threat. I came to my senses quick. Dodging left, I shrieked, "Shoot him!" Ranger plunked Mikey down as a human shield.

"In the chest!" I directed because his torso was still exposed.

Pete shook his head. "Too risky. . . . And he's wearing a vest."

"The head then!" I pointed like a madwoman, not caring I was ordering someone to commit murder.

Ranger quickly crouched behind Mikey, holding him firmly. "Proceed with the plan, Slater!" he ordered. "Quick!"

The noose tightened again. Andrew's face transformed into a bloated tomato. A solitary spit bubble fluttered from his guppied mouth. Wretched, writhing movements twitched his head. I screamed in horror, careening over to physically wrench off the noose—gnaw it off with my teeth if I had to.

Pete quickly yelled, "We surrender! Let the boy go!"

Immediately the pressure was off. Andrew gasped for breath.

"Toss the gun to Ranger, or I yank and it's all over," the hateful voice behind the door informed us.

Ranger advanced forward with his Mikey shield to snatch it from Pete's hand, then unlocked the door. The owner of the boots stepped in. Predictable Academy material: he was tall, he was dark, he was handsome. Another brute. Well muscled with a no-nonsense look about him. Some kind of race mix that created skin the color of coffee with a hint of cream. His eyes were the same khaki-green of his fatigues, and he came in packing two extra guns.

How many guns and cadets could fit in here?

"Good God Slater, took you long enough!" Ranger looked whatever was two days beyond pissed.

"I thought you said you had this one, man. '*Piece of cake*' I think were your exact words," he reminded him.

"It *would've* been a piece of cake if this kid hadn't interfered." Ranger indicated Mikey, who had sadly peed his pants. "You got the tag?"

"Yup."

"Do it."

"*Whataretheydoin*?" I screeched to anyone and no one as the one called Slater pulled out another frightening pistol. "Stooooooooop!" I screeched my throat bloody, diving for him right as he pressed it into Mikey's neck. And pulled the trigger.

He yelped, "Kadee!" before slumping over.

"Mikey!" I screamed, but only ragged hoarse sounds came out. My voice didn't work, but my arms did. I immediately used them to batter at the arms, chest, impassive face of the latest cadet. He flung me backwards as if I were a flimsy thing, not worthy of his time.

"Was that really necessary?" Pete demanded, stepping forward to catch me before I could fall ass-over-elbow again. "He's four-years-old for God's sake!"

Ranger turned to address his foe. "Uh . . . did you just witness the same thing I did?" Then to Slater: "Could you hear what was going on?"

"Nothing came through. But when I came in, I quickly ascertained that you were having your ass handed to you by Davenport and some kids," replied Slater with an attitude I was beginning to associate with The Academy.

Ranger pulled a face. "Davenport must've squashed the bug." He pointed the butt of his gun at Mikey.

I broke free from Pete to go cradle him in my arms. He was dead-feeling when I picked him up, his head lolling back like it was broken. I buried my face in his chest, sobbing.

"That kid's the one we're after. Screw the other one," Ranger said, referring to Andrew. "He's nothing but a pretty face . . . we don't need him anymore. We'll leave him with his Daddy—a consolation prize for taking the other two," he added heartlessly. He pointed at an unconscious Mikey, lying lifeless in my arms. I glared at him like the force of my hate could knock him out.

"*This* little guy single-handedly took me down. Whatever he told me to do, I just did it, like I was his slave and he was my master. It was some freaky shit, man!—I couldn't *not* do what he told me to do! No matter how hard I tried. Weston's gonna cream his pants over this one! We'll take him and the girl." Ranger acted like I was a done deal; he underestimated me.

"What about Davenport?" Slater nodded to Pete, and all eyes followed to his ashen, beaten face.

"I'm going to take care of him *personally*," Ranger said, using a tone meant to induce fear.

Pete had no comeback. He was injured, weary, bleeding. Most of all, he just looked resigned. Had I mistaken his calm for resignation? God I hoped not.

"Dude, we've got to get him back. He's still an elite cadet, and his parents will want him to have a fair trial," argued Slater

"Fair trial, my ass!" Ranger exploded. "They'll let him off with a slap on the wrist, like they always do, because of who his parents are. No, not this time . . . this time he has to pay. He's been pissing all over The Academy for years. He almost ruined this whole damned mission by running off with the goods." Ranger jerked his thumb to his chest, flashing a gold insignia patch on his shoulder—nearly subdued by the stain of Pete's blood. "Think what that would've done to my career! He doesn't give a shit about anyone but himself and this"—he waved the gun at me—"country bimbo."

I took my cue again: "Just let him go! I'll voluntarily go with you! *Please*. It's enough to appease The Academy. Just please let my brothers and Pete go, and-and . . . I'll do anything you want!"

Ranger stared into my pleading eyes, his lips nursing a smirk. And after taking in my bare legs and torn shirt, he cocked an eyebrow. "Anything?"

"*Anything*," I ground out.

A flicker of something unexpected flashed in Ranger's eyes—softness maybe, but I couldn't tell because it came and went in an instant.

"Well I hate to break it to you, sweetheart, but I can do *anything* I want with you anyway. And you don't really have a say in the matter."

Pete spoke up again. I knew he would, but I fervently wished he wouldn't. I sensed anything he said would only make our plight worse. "Ranger, I swear to God, if you touch one hair on her head, I'll personally kill you."

Ranger roared with laughter, slapping his knees like he was at a Hootin Annie. "Oh Lordy! Did you hear that one, Slater?" He swiped at his eyes, then walked over to where I was sitting on the floor with Mikey, leaned over, and ceremoniously plucked a few hairs from my head.

Oh crap. I looked at Pete. He no longer looked impassive. I'd never seen him look so livid. I wished he'd take all that boiling anger and tae-kwon-do himself out the open window already. I stared very hard at him, trying to convey this very thing.

When Ranger spoke again it was to start barking orders to his sidekick. "Get the flex cuffs and secure the premises."

I scrunched up my eyes, rocking a limp Mikey, trying hard to decide what, if anything, we could do to save ourselves. The last instinctual thing I'd done was open the window. So far the only thing that accomplished was to let in a cool breeze. *Please.Please.Please, God!* And then inspiration hit.

"Run, Andrew! Ruuuuuun!" I hollered with as much conviction as this life and death moment warranted. "Run for help now! Ruuu—" My voice screeched to a halt.

Ranger looked like he wanted to slap me again. "What the . . . ?"

We heard little footsteps charging through the house—*Bang*!—out the front door.

"Dammit! Whatareyouwaitin'for? Go after the little bastard!" Ranger ordered.

I was prepared. Right as Slater lifted his boot, I latched onto it with both hands. He kind of stumbled around and tripped over me, and was just in the process of kicking me in the head, when both Ranger and Pete came to my defense simultaneously.

"Don't do it, Slater!" yelled Pete, lurching for him a split second before Ranger shoved Slater then Pete back. I knew it—they really did want me delivered as undamaged goods.

"Not in the head, asshole! She just had a concussion. You wanna give her brain damage?" And just when I thought there might be *some* good in Ranger, he followed that up with: "What good is she to us then?"

Pete had moved positions when Ranger was preoccupied. Ranger called him on it immediately, firming up his grip and repositioning the gun straight at his temple. "Give me a reason, Davenport."

Meanwhile, Slater had peeled me off as easily as a bandage and took off after the runner. But I wasn't worried: they'd also underestimated Andrew—not just a pretty face. He'd be so far ahead by now there was no way for anyone to catch him. I slammed the shattered slab of plywood, locking it again.

Ranger *tssked* me. "You're already on my bad side, Connelly. Why are you making it so much harder on yourself?"

"I wasn't aware you had a good side," Pete quipped, as though unable to help himself.

Ignoring Ranger, I walked straight to Pete and stood in front of him. I stared one last time into those shining, dark eyes I loved so much, willing him to understand. "Pete, leave right now out that window. If you care for me in any capacity, you'll go now before Slater gets back."

"Uh . . . 'scuse me." Ranger waved his arms around. "I hate to break up this Hallmark moment, but there's a big, scary man wielding a gun here."

I whirled around to face him. "Yeah, but you won't shoot me." I backed up to Pete, wrapping my arms around his waist as a human shield.

"Kate, don't do this," Pete urged. "It's not over."

I began backward-walking us towards the window. "Pete, you told me to trust my God-given instincts. So I'm goin' with my gut . . . it *hasn't* led me wrong. Trust *me* like you asked me to trust you."

Pete hesitated. "Kate . . ."

"That open window's for you—your escape to freedom. It's all over for you if you don't go right now!" I shoved him backwards, but he didn't move. "*Please!*" I begged. "If you don't go, they win . . . *everything.*" My voice cracked.

"Okay, cut the crap, Kitty-Kat . . . or whatever the hell your name is. Enough of the *Romeo and Juliet* drama. If you don't think I'll shoot you, you're sorely mistaken." Ranger waved me back with his gun. So sure of himself. Hubris—his Achilles heel.

I faced Ranger with a face devoid of fear. Pete's back was against the windowsill now. "Go now, Pete!" I pleaded, tears streaming down my face.

"Kate . . . " Pete whispered my name one more time, enveloping me in a survivor's embrace.

"*Please!*" My voice was gut-wrenching even to my own ears.

"If you don't think I'll shoot her, Davenport than you—"

I felt the briefest kiss brush the back of my head. And then Pete hopped out the window. "I'll come back for you," I thought he said, but it was hard to tell, because Ranger was screaming . . . and charging at me, like a bull.

"Gahdammit!—you bitch!"

But what Torro didn't know was that the guest star was making another appearance—Pete just handed me that jagged piece of lamp he'd squirreled away in his back pocket. I whipped it from behind my back just in time for it to do its job—Ranger screeched to a stop when he saw what my hand was wielding.

He yelled several expletives, pointed the gun at my foot. "You might be the first lame *PGC* ever accepted into The Academy."

"I doubt Weston will be too pleased to see you managed to mangle the merchandise after all," I said, wondering who in the world Weston was, but taking a shot in the dark.

A sick smile grudged its way onto half his mouth, winking a dimple at me. "You're gonna pay for this, little girl."

I just smirked back at him (which my gut told me not to do, but I ignored).

"You think you're pretty smart? . . ." Stalking over to the armchair, Ranger picked up the dart gun, aimed, and without further ado—shot. It emitted a loud *poofing* sound before piercing me, right over the heart. Stunned, I stared, slack jawed, at blazing-blue eyes before I quickly thought to remove it. Even so, I felt the effects immediately as tranquilizer-laced poison pushed into my bloodstream.

"How's that? You like that, Connelly?"

A rush of woozy inertia overcame me. I stumbled forward like a drunk. The jagged, pink weapon fell from my hand. I knew I was done in just a few more seconds, so I lurched over to lie with my brother. Unable to walk in a straight line, I teetered sideways and fell . . . right into the waiting arms of the cadet who shot me.

He brought me up to his chest to stare into my bleary eyes. "Welcome to The Academy, Katherine Connelly," he said, not in an unkind voice before slinging me over his shoulder like a fallen soldier. Then he reached down and hooked a limp Mikey up and hoisted him over his other shoulder, marching us from my busted-up bedroom, through the hallway of family pictures, past our shabby kitchen and living room, out the front door, and down the rickety steps.

I had a very strong feeling this would be the last time I ever saw our trailer so I tried focusing, but it was getting harder by the second. The deep rumble of Ranger's voice roused me round once more.

"Slater, stay here and clean up this mess. Cut the guy a check for two-hundred thou to keep his mouth shut, and convey to him the importance of *keeping* it shut if he wants to hang on to his last kid."

"Yessir."

"Oh, and thanks for your help, man. . . . This got a whole lot hairier than I anticipated."

"It always does. You outta here then?"

"Yep," Ranger confirmed, windmilling us back around. "I'll see you back at the fort."

I guess as far as endings go it wasn't so bad. For most parties involved. Only the Connelly kids continued to get screwed. Everybody else more or less getting what they wanted in the end: Daddy got to keep his pride and joy. Ranger—the biggest winner in all of this—got two acquisitions for the price of one, and two more notches on his belt. The International Elite Academy would be the beneficiary of more gifteds to mold, manipulate, and use . . . for God-only-knew-what purpose. And Pete . . . well, Cadet Davenport finally got his lifelong wish fulfilled—a life free of the organization he'd always loathed.

I could still hear the mechanized buzzing of the motorcycle fading into the distance as we tromped steadily forward. I hoped Pete was going far. Far away from this God-forsaken place to start a new life, as something he *wanted* to be.

Ranger stopped tromping to open the back of a black SUV. He laid us inside, side-by-side. I was almost gone. Not quite . . . hanging on out of sheer stubbornness. I could feel Ranger's hands on my body, carefully rearranging me to his satisfaction. And then the relief of hair being brushed off my face. My eyes fluttered back open. I expected more mouthing off liberally sprinkled by insults, but he didn't say anything at all. He just stared intently at me while I watched glacier eyes warm to ocean blue. Then he made a move I couldn't flinch for and didn't need to: He rubbed a thumb from my mouth to my hairline, right over the tender spot where he'd slapped me.

This was my final undoing. I closed my eyes at last, surrendering to the blank darkness coming for me. A light blanket was thrown over me. The door slammed shut. A moment later, the engine's vibration We drove back down the winding dirt road toward our destination . . . The organization simply known as **The Academy**.

Acknowledgments

I'd like to thank my husband, Jeff, for his support and for always helping me with the nuts and bolts of life; my boys, Dylan and Brandon, for being sparks of inspiration; my mother for gifting this book with its first words; my father for all the great "country-isms," and my little sister, Tiffany, for being my biggest fan.

I'd also like to give a big Texas thanks to Nicole Liebnick, Anastacia Sadeh, Tona Jebbia, Jenni Roy, Lane Crall, Stacy Hunt, Renee Alcala, and Amy Shoultz for being the best friends and beta readers any girl could ever ask for. Y'all are truly blessings, and I appreciate you more than you'll ever know.

ABOUT THE AUTHOR

C J Daly moved from New Mexico to Dallas, Texas to study English literature. After graduating cum laude, she taught English for a few years, then decided to stay home to raise her boys and pursue her passion—writing. *The Academy* is her debut novel and *The Academy, Cadet in Training* is the sequel.

Please visit CJ on her website at:
theacademysaga.com

Made in the USA
Coppell, TX
15 April 2021